P9-ECK-211

GEODESICA

GEODESICA

GEODESICA: ASCENT
GEODESICA: DESCENT

Sean Williams
with Shane Dix

Publication History: Ace paperback, February 2005

Publication History: Ace paperback, February 2006

First SFBC Fantasy Printing: February 2006

Published by arrangement with:
The Berkley Publishing Group
a division of Penguin Putnam Inc.
375 Hudson Street
New York, NY 10014

Visit The SFBC online at http://www.sfbc.com

ISBN 0-7394-6391-8

Printed in the United States of America.

Contents

GEODESICA
ASCENT

For K.

*With thanks to Simon Brown, Ginjer Buchanan,
Marcus Chown, Richard Curtis, Nydia Dix,
Mikolaj Habryn, Jeff Harris, Jeremy Nelson,
Garth Nix, Robin Potanin, Kim Selling,
Lilla Smee, and Stephanie Smith.*

+PRELUDE

Ten years before

The Palmer Cell *Jaintiapur* was a long way off its usual course. A regular on the Eliza and Whitewater Detours, it had struck out even farther from the Arc Circuit in response to a plea for help from one of humanity's most distant colonies. Eliza, that colony's nearest neighbor, was over ten light-years away, but weather had been favorable in the Local Bubble and the journey took less than a year.

Palmer Horsfall, chief officer of the *Jaintiapur,* didn't begrudge the long journey. It could have been worse. Humanity's exploration of the galaxy had advanced rapidly through regions with the least amount of matter between the stars. The frontier world of Scarecrow—recently annexed as Mei-Shun-Wah by the Exarchate, around a star identified as 59431 in the Hipparcos catalogue—was the present holder of the record for most distant. Not far behind were Hipparcos 59432 and the *Jaintiapur*'s destination, Hipparcos 66704. The former had been known as Severance before the Exarchate christened it Newbery-Vaas. The latter's new name, White-Elderton, would never stick. Ten years after the *Jaintiapur* docked, eighty-two long light-years from Sol, people would still call it Sublime.

The *Jaintiapur* came at speed in response to a request for scientific assistance from the colony's Exarch. Since that request had been lodged, the news had spread along the Arc Circuit: of a hitherto unknown type of ROTH artifact that had drifted from deep space into the colony's gravity well. People as far away as Little Red began to whisper about what that might mean. A working alien machine offered more than just interesting xenarcheological relics. All of the seven alien races known to have passed through the Local Bubble at various points in the previous million years had been more advanced than humanity.

Palmer Horsfall, chief officer of the *Jaintiapur,* didn't have orders to move the artifact or to take samples elsewhere. She simply brought instruments and personnel from the better-equipped Eliza colony to its frontier neighbor. Among those personnel was her sister, a vacuum physicist normally stationed in Alcor. Deva Horsfall wasn't a xenarcheologist, a fact not lost on the people aboard the Cell.

"Maybe it's a diversion," one of the crew suggested.

"For what?" Deva Horsfall was determinedly pragmatic. Probing the empty places of the universe soon leached the romance out of life.

"Something they've made, rather than something they've found."

"Invent a better VOID drive," quipped the ship's wit, "and they'll beat a path to your door."

"It's more likely to be the other way around," Deva said. "Would they wait for us this long if they didn't have to?"

"You get your kicks where you can, I guess, on a frontier world."

Palmer Horsfall didn't like to encourage speculation until she had the facts in front of her. In that respect, she was much like her sister. She thought it perfectly conceivable that a find could relate to her sister's field of expertise. The details could wait until they reached their destination.

Within twenty-eight hours of the arrival of the *Jaintiapur,* Deva Horsfall and the rest of the payload were delivered safely to the colony. The alien artifact, if such it was, had been carefully sequestered within a containment facility of Exarchate design. The Cell's sensors couldn't penetrate its outer shell. What lay within was a mystery to those outside. The discovery was being treated with great secrecy.

"I hope this doesn't turn out to be a waste of your time," Deva had said when leaving the *Jaintiapur*.

"We've been well paid," said the Palmer, meaning the words in more ways than one. The trip had been an opportunity for them to reacquaint themselves with each other. Long absences and light-speed delays had stretched a formerly close sibling relationship almost to irrelevance. "I have no regrets."

"I'm just trying not to get too excited." The feverishness in Deva's eyes belied her words. "This wouldn't be the first time people have gotten worked up over nothing.

"What's the worst that can happen? If you *do* find nothing—well, that's your specialty. It's a win-win situation."

"Either way, I'm about to find out."

They had embraced and said farewell.

Sublime's Exarch took the scientific payload and put it to immediate effect. The crew of the *Jaintiapur* watched from a distance as arcane sensors stirred and strange energies brewed. Deva Horsfall disappeared into the artifact's containment facility to conduct her investigation under the tightest of security, so what she and the Exarch did was never known precisely.

That they did *something,* however, was of little doubt. The footage of the colony's final moments soon became familiar to every citizen of the Exarchate. It was broadcast across the whole of colonized space, leaving a horrified, stunned silence in its wake.

As though a detonator had been tripped, the artifact suddenly and without warning disgorged devastation on a scale never before witnessed by humanity. A raging, luminous ball of plasma spread rapidly across the *Jaintiapur*'s forward sensors in a blaze of golden light, devouring everything in its path. The containment facility went first, then the colony's main base. Nothing stopped it. The more it consumed, the more it propagated, exploiting a terrible arithmetic progression to gain total dominance of the system. Within hours it had destroyed not just the colony, including Exarch Elderton and everyone under her care, but four of the system's inner worlds as well.

The *Jaintiapur* barely outran the fatal front, capturing images of the destruction as it fled. The expanding bubble of hostile alien replicators left a fine mist of vicious nanotech in its wake. As soon as it was safe to do so, Palmer Horsfall turned her Cell about to consider her options. Endlessly breeding and vigilant, the alien replicators devoured anything that strayed too close, and buried everything within its borders in a howl of electromagnetic noise. Palmer Horsfall sacrificed numerous Cell components in a vain attempt to penetrate the borders of the affected area. She pursued every possible means of communication. A dozen members of her crew lost their lives when the unpredictable ROTH tech took offense at the Cell's continued presence and swatted at it as a human might an irritating fly.

Eventually the chief officer of the *Jaintiapur* decided that nothing could be done for the people of Sublime, if any remained in the infected mess of the system at all—her sister included.

Despairing, the *Jaintiapur* turned tail and fled.

In the following years, other Cells attempted to breach the boiling borders of the alien-infested system. None were remotely successful. Overtures of communication continued to be rebuffed. The theory prevailed that the Exarch of the colony had inadvertently triggered a sophisticated defense mechanism that blindly destroyed everything within a certain radius of the artifact. The artifact made no other response to the civilization that had poked its doorbell and run away—and neither did the defense mechanism, except to strike out every now and again at the automated monitors stationed around the system, ready to sound the alarm should the contagion show signs of spreading.

The Palmer who had obediently delivered her sister to the maelstrom resigned from the *Jaintiapur* and took charge of Horsfall Station, in a deep elliptical orbit around Sublime's primary star. There she waited, maintaining a grim vigil for the many who had died in the budding colony, victims of unknown killers. She would find those responsible, she swore to herself. And she would make them pay.

No matter how long it took . . .

+1

According to the map the pipe was rated for humans, but Melilah Awad, one-eighty centimeters long, only just fit into it. Curved, cream-colored walls veined in yellow rushed by as she hurried to the next hub, pushing herself along with hands and feet in the negligible gee. Lights in visible spectra were few and far between, and she navigated by infrared when the darkness was complete.

An air current blew from along the pipe at roughly her velocity. She imagined a bubble of her exhalations accompanying her like an unseen shroud and quickly quashed the thought. It made her throat tighten as though she were actually suffocating.

She pushed on, conscious of time ticking away fast. Her watchmeter told her she still had work to do. Fourteen people were observing her from afar, locked on to her trace as she plumbed the innermost regions of the giant habitat. Seven of them she knew well: fellow gleaners, keeping tabs just in case she'd caught a whiff of some new, rich vein of overlooked information. Four were friends she'd asked to tag along for the ride, until the time was right. Two of the remaining three were unknown to her, possibly pseudonyms for the Exarch and, therefore, of some concern. And the last . . .

She checked the time. Thirty-two twenty. Another three hundred seconds.

"I told you, Gil: leave me alone." She spoke aloud. The echo from the pipe's smooth walls gave her words extra substance, if only to her ears.

"Now, don't be like that, 'Lilah."

She cringed at the use of the nickname. "Why do you go to so much trouble to track me when you're not even prepared to listen to what I've got to say?"

"And why do *you* resent my surveillance of you? Seems strange for one who expends so much energy on defending the openness of our society."

"It's not the surveillance I mind, Gil. It's *you*."

The distant man chuckled. "Could be worse," he said. "You could be so dull that nobody would *want* to watch you."

"Sounds like heaven."

"I know you're lying."

Gil Hurdowar was right, but that didn't make him any easier to tolerate. Melilah could picture him, a scrawny figure jacked directly into the Scale-Free Bedlam feed. His face was lined, and his hair possessed a disconcertingly piebald quality that spoke of badly maintained antisenescence treatments. She had learned from her one and only in-person confrontation that his cubicle smelled of burnt sugar, as though a saucepan of ruined toffee had been hidden in a cupboard and forgotten months ago.

She—elegantly youthful, in appearance at least, and meticulously clean—took offense at his interest in her, and she made no bones about showing it. That was how the system worked. He could watch her if he wanted to, but she didn't have to like it. Especially at moments such as these, when being observed was exactly what she didn't want.

One hundred fifty seconds. Her watchmeter was down to twelve. At the hub, she kicked right, then almost immediately right again. The new pipe was slightly wider along one axis, giving it a squashed feel. Although there was no real indication that this area of the habitat was experiencing undue structural load, Melilah was distinctly aware of how near the center she was getting. With thousands of kilometers of pipes all around her and unknown cubic hectares of chambers piled high above, it was no wonder that the heart of Bedlam had long ago collapsed into a solid core. What had once been perfectly habitable spaces were now flattened foundations for new architecture. That new architecture would, in turn, one day collapse on top of the layers beneath, if Bedlam kept growing at its current rate.

Melilah sincerely hoped she would be well away from these pipes when that day came.

"Looking for something in particular?" Hurdowar pressed, voicing the question that was undoubtedly on the minds of many of the others watching her movements. “Data cache? Hard-copy store?”

“Who says I’m looking for anything?”

“You only come down here when you are.”

“That’s not exactly true.” Bedlam’s basement was vast and, for the most part, empty. The habitat’s many citizens naturally tended to gravitate upward, resettling as fast as each new layer could come online. This constant migration left a labyrinthine vacancy in its wake. She wasn’t the only person looking for things left behind, and she knew for certain that she wasn’t the only one who used it as a repository for her own private data. The core of Bedlam was a graveyard for many things best left forgotten.

Melilah didn’t have to justify herself, but she wanted her cover on public record. “Since when has amateur archeology been a crime?”

Hurdowar snorted. “If that’s what you’re doing, then I’m your guardian angel.”

“The information laws are there to protect us all. I’m doing the community—and the Exarch—a service by upholding them.”

“And making a tidy profit while you’re at it. Hell, you don’t need to explain it to me. I’m just jealous. Why else would I be snooping at you every waking moment?”

“I thought that was because you’re an insensitive asshole.”

“Some would say that. Consider the rest a bonus, then.”

Twenty-five seconds. The pipe ended at a chamber large enough to have earned a warehouse rating, way back when. She took a moment to get her bearings. Five exits led from it, two deeper still. She took one of the latter, following her internal map.

“I’ll ask you again, Gil: will you *please* leave me alone for a while?” The irritation in her voice was real.

“When the show’s just getting interesting? I don’t think so, ’Lilah.”

Her internal timer hit zero. Far above the lowly tunnel, the system’s primary flared. Magnetic fields flexed and snapped like whips. Huge gouts of supercharged particles poured through interplanetary space, frying every unshielded object in their path. The poles of magnetically active worlds and moons flickered blue. With the uncanny promptness of a vast machine, the symptoms of Hipparcos 62512’s grumpy restlessness overtook the lumpy, half-made skin of Bedlam’s outermost layers—and would have rendered them and what lay beneath utterly sterile, but for the sudden opacity of PARASOL in orbit between the station and the sun.

Melilah's watchmeter noted the departure of her four friends, as planned. Five of the gleaners went with them, and both of the unnamed traces. That left just two gleaners and Hurdowar.

"Is it a big one?" she asked them, knowing what the answer would be. She'd checked the solar weather reports in advance.

"Huge," said Hurdowar. "Pretty, too."

One of the two remaining gleaners took the bait. Melilah slipped into a pipe too narrow for her to stand in and shot along it like a bullet down a barrel. *Close, now.* She stretched in her crawl-suit, enjoying the physicality of her quest.

"Not as pretty as what I see right now," Hurdowar added.

She swallowed revulsion. "Give me a break, will you?"

"No can do, 'Lilah. But please, feel free to watch me back if it makes you feel any better."

"Thanks, but I think I'd rather gouge my eyes out with a blunt spoon." The pipe constricted to the point where she had to put her arms at her sides and let her feet kick her along. "Listen, Gil: you may have your rights, but so do I. I'm not some animal in a zoo; I'm not your *property.* Try to corral me, and I'll take whatever means necessary to stop you."

"But I keep an eye out for you. I give you leads!"

"My gratitude has its limits. I can cope just fine without you."

"Really?" A sly tone entered the man's voice. "Did you realize that the *Nhulunbuy* requested permission to dock fifty minutes ago?"

At Bedlam? The words were almost past her lips before she could stop them. She hadn't known, and the news took her by surprise. "What business is that of mine?"

Hurdowar chuckled again. "You don't fool me, 'Lilah. You know as well as I do who's running the *Nhulunbuy* these days. And you know he wouldn't come here unless he had absolutely no choice."

"Damn you, Gil," she cursed. The last gleaner winked out, perhaps from embarrassment. "My relationship with Palmer Eogan is none of your business."

"Can't blame a guy for being curious—especially when you still call it a *relationship.*"

She brought herself to a sudden halt. *Here.*

Calling up a series of virtual displays, she scrolled rapidly through them and launched a package of countermeasures, prepared in advance against just such a contingency. If Gil Hurdowar wouldn't go away voluntarily, she would just have to make him.

There wasn't a hell deep or hot enough for someone like him—and to hell with penalties, too. The Exarch could cut her off completely for all she cared. At least she'd be alone.

"I'd love to continue this engaging conversation, Gil, but—"

Hurdowar's channel died with a squawk. Her watchmeter clicked to zero at last.

Zero. She focused her thoughts on the task at hand. No one was watching her. This was her chance—and it wouldn't last long. The Exarch would be onto her in moments for shutting Hurdowar up like that. In Bedlam, there were many crimes, but few were as fundamental as restricting a citizen's right to information. Loathe him though she might, Hurdowar was a citizen, and the Exarch imposed the laws protecting him with the same rigor he imposed those of the Gentry.

Damn them, too, she added to herself, but didn't dwell on it. The seconds were flying by. She had brought herself to a halt by a narrow niche that only appeared on the most detailed of maps. Most importantly, it was out of sight of the nearest CCTV feed. She'd checked it some years earlier and found it to be empty. A scan of the area since then showed no signs of anyone moving in. But just because no one had, didn't mean that she *shouldn't.*

Reaching into a pocket of her crawl-suit, she produced a flat packet as round as her palm. Colored to match the pipe's milky wall, it was designed to stick unobtrusively and remain out of sight forever. Should anyone trace her path to the niche, they would assume that she had already cleaned it out and might not bother taking a second look. Even if they did look, the camouflage would probably still fool them.

Melilah reached inside the niche to stick the disk in place, and was startled to find something already there.

What the hell? She pulled her hand away. The niche should have been empty; she was certain of it. Putting her disk back into its pocket, she leaned into the hole and examined what she'd found more closely. It was standard model data fiche, solid-state, unsecured. She pulled it loose and held it up warily in front of her. Some data caches—like hers—were booby-trapped, rigged with viruses or EMPs designed to take out both the idly curious and the deliberately invasive alike. She swept it while she had the chance, while Hurdowar was off-line and the others were busy with the flare.

The fiche was clean of traps. Accessing it, she brought up the contents in an internal window and scanned through them.

Old letters. Some pictures. Two faces recurred: a pair of women, one with brown hair and a square jaw, the other skinnier, shorter, a redhead. They had been lovers, had gone surveying together; there were maps of a tangled, convoluted space Melilah assumed was Bedlam. Most of the photos portrayed happy times, snapshots of contentment; they had holidayed at Sublime on at least one occasion, before the Catastrophe. But Melilah sensed sadness lurking behind the smiles. People didn't bury good memories without a good reason.

In this instance, it looked like someone had beaten her to it.

She tossed the fiche in her hand, momentarily indecisive. The data she had found was valueless on the open market. It was no business of hers, of anyone at all except the person who had put it there. She would be doing them a service by replacing it and moving on.

But that would leave her business unfinished. The simplest thing, she told herself, was to replace the fiche and do as she'd originally intended. She doubted the person who had placed it would ever come back—and if they did, they probably wouldn't notice hers, tucked away behind it. Most likely both of them would remain there, untouched, as this layer of Bedlam compacted around them. Both repositories would be buried physically as well as mentally.

So that was what she did. She replaced the fiche and stuck her disk nearby. Then she kicked herself away, pretending to be heading elsewhere just in case someone happened to glance at her at that moment and wonder what she was doing.

The flare had been roiling around Bedlam for two full minutes. Her surprise package had kept Hurdowar busy all that time, forcing him to untangle knotted data lines and unclog stodgy feeds before he could get out. She didn't care what he thought of her, what weird sort of kick he was getting, following her around as he did. But pretending it didn't affect her was the surest way of letting him know that it *did*.

The Nhulunbuy *requested permission to dock fifty minutes ago . . .*

She opened a link to Gil Hurdowar. It would look good for her if she made the first overture, made it appear as though the breakdown in comm was a genuine accident. Worth a try, anyway.

"You there, Gil?"

Silence. The link registered as being open, but nothing came along it.

"Gil?"

She tried another line, and another. More nothing. She dialed an acquaintance at random with the same result. Frustrated, she punched in the code for the Exarch himself, and only echoes of her frustration returned to her down the pipe.

"Is *anyone* out there?"

The feeling of claustrophobia returned as one by one all the lines she had opened shut down. For the first time in years, Melilah Awad was truly cut off.

+2

The alarm, once triggered, spread rapidly through the colony's infostructure. Exarch Isaac Deangelis normally skimmed the surface of temporal flow like a stone over water, experiencing individual days as though they were minutes, riding the ebb and flow of the economy, watching Palmer Cells come and go like darting pond creatures, embracing the sure vantage point of long time as was his birthright.

When the alarm reached the outer layers of his distributed consciousness, however, his entire self jerked abruptly to a temporal halt. It felt like a transport collision in slow motion. A single moment crystallized around him, spreading out in branched waves of supersaturated connectedness; what had once been liquid and smoothly flowing suddenly coalesced into an incredibly complicated snapshot of the colony as a whole, caught in the seed crystal moment of the alarm. As he changed gears from very long-term overview to minutely microfocused, he sought the source of the disturbance and critiqued his agents' autonomic reactions to it.

The first name he saw prompted a sigh of resignation. *Her again.* He didn't need to see the footage in detail to recognize Melilah Awad's elegantly angular features or her naturally grown hair, dyed brown and white in geometric streaks parallel to her fringe. Her tight-fitting semi–pressure suit accentuated her natural physicality with a brazenness that unnerved him only slightly more than her resentment of him. She seemed to be at the heart of every disturbance in his domain. When the Exarchate had annexed the colony, forty-odd years earlier, Awad had been Deputy Counselor, second only to the system's nominal head. Although the annexation had been conducted with the same swift efficiency as those in other habited systems, with very little loss of life or material assets, the aftereffects were pervasive and tenacious. Awad, left with no functional role to play in the system's new government, made a point of encouraging anti-Exarchate demonstrations whenever she could, and would, he was sure, foment active dissent were it not for the system's antiprivacy laws that would immediately finger her as the ringleader. Deangelis couldn't stop her from talking, not if he wanted to maintain the system's unique character, since imposing absolute rule would prompt even greater resentment than he already experienced. He tolerated the rumblings and was proud that, so far, the situation had never flared into open revolt as it had once or twice elsewhere.

Even if it had, the outcome would have been the same. The Exarchate was unassailable. That was the one, pure fact that Awad had never been able to digest.

She appeared to be on another prospecting mission, insinuating herself deep in the belly of the habitat. That, he assumed, was what had triggered the alarm. Foraging under cover of an attention-grabbing flare was a common tactic, as a great number of observers directed their attention toward the celestial event. Despite it being two hundred years since a similar flare had expunged all life from the system, this was still a significant event and worthy of close study. Deangelis scrolled back through Awad's movements to confirm that her behavior matched that of someone engaged in a secret-retrieving pursuit. There was no discrepancy. She had even launched a software guillotine to cut off the one remaining viewer watching her when the time came, so what she found would remain unseen by anyone but herself.

Ultimately her destination revealed her intent, and he would have been alarmed for that reason alone had he seen her coming in advance. Luckily for him the deeper layers of deception seemed to be holding. The fiche was back in its place, read but not recorded. At least one of the habitat's few secrets was still concealed from prying eyes.

He was about to reinforce the good judgment of his agents—rewarding them so their complex decision-making nets would respond similarly next time such a circumstance arose—when he realized that it wasn't Awad who had triggered the alarm at all. It was in fact a more complex juxtaposition of names and words. The object of Awad's software guillotine had dropped the names into their conversation with the clear intent of provoking her, and those names—innocently in one sense—combined with a comment from Awad had been enough to set alarm bells ringing.

A chill went down his many spines when he examined the data. The agents had made a spot decision based on weightings he had given them, and based on the conclusion they had come to, their response was—again—absolutely correct. If his secret had been sprung, if word of what was slouching to Lut-Deangelis got out, it would undo everything he had worked for. *Everything.*

He immediately set in motion an emergency shutdown of all of the habitat's communications networks. He couldn't let word spread any further than it already had. This was too inflammatory to hesitate over. Even with his relative time slowed to a near standstill, he worried at his tardiness. Awad was busy replacing his cache back in the niche; Hurdowar was still trying to untangle the software bomb. But who else knew? How many other lips were spreading the terrible truth? How fast had incriminating light sped along which optical fibers?

Silence spread like ice through the habitat. Conversations were cut off in midsentence. Data flows ceased without warning. A normally thriving semantic space devolved into a multitude of truncated termini, spasming futilely to reconnect.

Exarch Deangelis reassured himself that he was doing everything he could, that no one could blame him if it wasn't enough. Word was bound to get out eventually, and contingencies were in place to deal with it when it happened. He had his orders, just as his agents had their key words, *Nhulunbuy* and Palmer Eogan among them.

He examined the exact instances in which each trigger word had been used, dreading to see precisely how much damage had been done but knowing he had to in order to begin repairing the damage. Part of him was already drafting an explanation to send to Sol, detailing the instance in which the leak had occurred, the precise mechanisms—once he isolated them—by which the leak had been allowed to happen, and the many ways in which he was already beginning to heal the breach. If the ftl network was decoherence-free, he could have a response within minutes. The swiftness with which judgment could fall both appalled and relieved him. Abrogation of responsibility always came at a price. Sometimes the price was worse than the circumstance from which one was trying to escape.

Even as data flows staggered to a halt all through his domain, a second realization—that he had been wrong twice in as many microseconds—struck him a near-physical blow.

Try to corral me, Awad had said, replayed for his benefit by the software agents, *and I'll take whatever means necessary to stop you.*

He thought of the fabled king who, for the want of a pin, lost his kingdom. Would Isaac Forge Deangelis lose *his* kingdom, now, over an accidental *pun?*

No, he told himself, torn between relieved laughter and despair at the stupidity of the situation. The agents had misread a critical word on which he had placed, perhaps, too much weight. Erring on the side of caution was, he supposed, sensible, but on the basis of that error he had just shut down a habitat containing over forty thousand people, of whom many already resented his interference and all valued their connectivity. His crystalline moment had gone from bad to worse—then back to bad, with a side order of chaos.

He forced himself to view the situation philosophically. Mistakes happened, and in this instance this one could be corrected swiftly and simply. Problematic though it was, it was definitely better than if the truth had gotten out. In the case of such a leak, shutting down the habitat would have been only the beginning. The truth, as ever, was as volatile as a genie, and once released would not be easily recaptured.

Exarch Deangelis reprogrammed his agents to avoid a similar mistake in the future, and put into motion the lengthy process of reconnecting the many millions of severed lines. Even though the grunt work was usually performed by more specialized agents, this he oversaw personally, thereby ensuring that no further mistakes would be made. Indeed, if the reconnection went smoothly, many people might not even notice the sudden glitch. The task also gave him something to keep his mind off the disaster he had avoided through no quick thinking of his own.

He had been complacent, content to rule from the privileged position of Exarch, even though he knew the coming days to be critical. He understood now that he could no longer afford that luxury, that agents were insufficient to handle the minutiae of day-to-day governance in such critical times, that from now on he was going to be furiously, relentlessly busy—at least until the initial crisis was past. The truth remained buried under layers of deception, behind multiple falsehoods all resembling the truth. Balancing so many lies was a task worthy of a master juggler.

He was confident that, despite this bad start, he was more than up to the task. It was what he had been born to do. From his first conscious thought, the Archon had refined and fine-tuned his every capacity and instinct in order to create the perfect head of governance. He and the other Exarchs were the pinnacle of human evolution, the potent products of evolution both random and self-directed. No matter what the universe threw at him, he was certain he could handle it. In the long term, if not the short, the future was assured.

Still, part of his mind, no matter how furiously he occupied the rest, stayed firmly focused on the imminent arrival of the *Nhulunbuy.* The Palmer Cell and its contents descended upon him with all the deadliness of an axe. The next slipup might result in much worse than a slight inconvenience to the casual telecommuters of his domain.

+3

The *Nhulunbuy* hove to around Bedlam in a graceful arc, strung out like pearls in a necklace. Each of its seventy-eight components was spherical and perfectly reflective. Each reflected the solar storm's radiation—that which wasn't absorbed and put to nondestructive use—back into space, lending them a flickering, brilliant shine. Ranging in size from drones barely the size of a fist to bulky freight containers large enough to contain a small house, each of the Palmer Cell's components had the capacity to function as a completely independent starfaring vessel. Linked by protocols capable of withstanding the stresses of high-velocity space deformation, together they formed a single VOIDship under the command of one man.

Palmer Eogan crouched in the womb of the *Nhulunbuy*'s second largest component, N-2, and watched gloomily as Bedlam loomed large and silent in his instruments. It had been a long and stressful journey; normally he would have been glad to be coming out of the Dark and into port. This time, though, he felt far from glad. He would find no rest as long as he remained around Bedlam; of that he was completely certain.

While his thoughts should have been on the thing in N-1 and the wreckage they'd found around it, compacted and sealed in every available compartment throughout the Cell, instead his mind was on Melilah Awad.

I'm so sorry, he thought. *I didn't ask to come here like this. I didn't ask for any of it. If I could make it any other way, I would.*

He knew better than to call her. Forgiveness was not—and had never been—an option. But he wanted to anyway. Even after so long, he still missed her.

Fortunately, the communications blackout currently gripping the colony put paid to any suggestion of breaking his vow. The silence from the colony was as ominous as it was unexpected. Could something have gone wrong with PARASOL? Or was the cause more sinister? Reflexively, he tightened the distance between the Cell's components, drawing the *Nhulunbuy* close around him in case it needed to move suddenly.

The thing in N-1 resisted the change in momentum as it had throughout the entire trip. He felt as though he had a tiger by the tail—a very heavy tiger that might wake at any moment and bite the hand pulling so insistently at it.

With a snap of static, the lines were suddenly open again.

"This is Lut-Deangelis Traffic Control," said the smooth androgynous voice of a routing AI. "*Nhulunbuy,* your approach is noted and your vector has been approved. Stand by for further instructions."

Eogan confirmed receipt of the transmission by opening data channels. "What happened back there, LDTC? You went awfully quiet."

"Interference from the flare," supplied the AI. "An EMP took out a major communications hub. The problem has been rectified." Without changing tone, Traffic Control continued: "In accordance with Lut-Deangelis Information laws, you are required to open all memory and channels to public scrutiny. Please immediately supply access codes and encryption keys. Upon verification, you will be allotted temporary citizenship and allowed full access to local systems."

Palmer Eogan hesitated only momentarily before sending the requested codes. Once they were verified, anyone in Bedlam would have access to every piece of knowledge he and his crew had gathered on their journey from Mizar. Theoretically, he would be unable to keep secrets from anyone.

He had no choice but to accept the condition of entry into the system. Without doing so, he would be forced to go elsewhere, and that was simply not an option. Carefully, with no evidence of obvious deception, he had configured the data in the Cell's stores so it wouldn't point directly at the truth. Convenient and very plausible deceits stood in the way of anyone curious about what lay at the heart of N-1. Even the persistent would be hard-pressed to penetrate to its core.

"Codes and keys verified," said the AI. "Welcome to Lut-Deangelis System, Palmer Eogan."

He didn't respond. It would have been a lie to say that he was glad to be there. He felt exposed and vulnerable, and conscious of a large number of games tangled around him. The AI's explanation for the blackout was a little too pat. To take out the communication web enclosing not just Bedlam but the entire system would require more than just the destruction of a major hub. That would require hitting at least a quarter of the hubs at once, or shutting down the Exarch himself.

A flood of information swept over the Cell. His crew broke radio silence to inquire about friends and colleagues last visited many years before. It had been a long time since the *Nhulunbuy* had been this way.

"You have an unusual manifest," said a new voice over the comms. "How intriguing."

Eogan checked the ID before replying, even though he thought he recognized the warm, contralto tones. The ID confirmed his suspicion.

"That was quick, Luisa. Good to see you're still on the ball."

"Quick nothing. Every snoop in the system will have checked you out already. I'm just the only one who can get past your firewall and speak to you directly." He could hear the welcome in her voice, and couldn't help a slow smile in return. Luisa Pirelli had flown several legs around the Arc Circuit with him before settling down on Whitewater, years ago. It was good to hear her voice again, even if she was asking all the questions he wanted to avoid.

The features of her diamond face and the cast of her round eyes were deliberately neutral. He knew that look. "Want to tell me about 2358M1S willingly, or will I have to come up there and find out for myself?"

"There's nothing to find out," he said. "You have all the data we have."

"Yeah, right. It's big, whatever it is. Much bigger than anything else found on a sweeper run. Could it be a ROTH artifact?"

"Your guess is as good as mine, Lu. I'll leave the answers to the experts."

"No experts here, Eogan. We're just a bunch of amateurs—and starved of excitement, to boot. Expect to be thoroughly *probed* in the coming minutes." A thick edge lent her choice of words a prurient double meaning. "You should be used to that, working for the Gentry."

"How's James?" he asked, ignoring the jab. The Palmers were theoretically independent of the Exarchate empire, although in practice it was the only organization with the resources to pay for interstellar travel, and, therefore, wielded a great deal of influence over the guild of starfarers.

"The same," she said. "Still as crazy as coat hangers in free fall. But you know: he occasionally makes sense. The latest glitch will have him jumping."

"The blackout?"

"No. You." She was still smiling, but the comment wasn't entirely playful. "Will you be staying long?"

He hoped not. "I don't think so."

"Drop in, if you deign to come down to our level."

"I will, if you're offering dinner."

"You'd better believe it. I'll keep the vodka on ice. By the sound of your voice, you need it more than ever."

He didn't know how to respond to that. After so long plying the trade lanes, his social skills were rusty. He'd thought he was being perfectly affable to Luisa, and he *was* genuinely glad to hear from her.

"Just call her, Dominic," Luisa said into the conversational void.

"Call who?"

"You're not fooling anyone, you know."

The line shut with a click.

Eogan sighed and forced himself to concentrate on the Cell as it locked into orbit and assumed new symmetries reminiscent of an ancient model of a molecule. Independent fragments drew together; some of them touched, merged into one. He tapped into an external feed to admire the ballet, and was startled at how obvious it looked that the Cell was hiding something. He tweaked the distributed intelligence guiding the maneuver, moving N-1 out of the heart of the formation and putting it on the edge, as though it was nothing important. He downgraded the shields, now that the Cell was under the shelter of PARASOL, and they dimmed to a reflective brown-black. Instead of a collection of highly polished ball bearings, the Cell now resembled a clump of Christmas ornaments made of smoked glass. Angular, indistinct shapes lurked within.

"Palmer Eogan," said a third voice. Brisk and authoritative, this one radiated no welcome. There was no visual.

"Exarch Deangelis," he sent back, wondering if the chill was an act put on for those observing. He had expected the Exarch to call earlier. Now that the moment had come, he was more aware of being watched than ever before.

"You've posted some irregularities in your mission log," said the Exarch. "These will require explanation."

"I am aware of that." He fought the urge to add *sir.* "I'd like to discuss the details with you at your earliest convenience."

"That might be sooner than you were expecting. An envoy is on its way to you as we speak."

Eogan checked telemetry and noted a small vessel powering toward the *Nhulunbuy* from behind the giant habitat. Bedlam occupied the heart of the Trojan point trailing the system's largest gas giant, Ah Kong. PARASOL, the flare-shield, hung like an improbably large contact lens between Bedlam and the sun, assuming full opacity only when solar radiation was at a maximum. Numerous vessels and other structures huddled beneath its black shadow, jostling each other under the influence of Bedlam's weak gravitational pull. The flare painted the edges of PARASOL bright orange, casting a peculiar light over the assembly. Magnetic field lines, PARASOL's second line of defense, rippled and swayed like the tentacles of a luminous jellyfish, hundreds of kilometers long.

"I'll have my data ready for your inspection," Eogan said. Telemetry put the envoy's ETA at five minutes.

"Do. There are a number of issues that need to be clarified immediately. I trust the *occlusion* is adequately contained."

Eogan caught the slight emphasis. "Inasmuch as I can tell."

"Good. Let's keep it that way."

"I have no intentions of doing otherwise," he said, realizing only at the end of the sentence that he was talking to himself.

Damn him, Eogan thought, allowing himself no external display of anger. *Damn them* all *to hell.*

His gaze drifted to N-1, and he idly toyed with the idea of opening it to the vacuum and dumping its contents unceremoniously onto Bedlam. Or Lut-Deangelis, as the Exarch had insisted it be called since annexation. Let *them* deal with it, whatever came out of its hellish throat. Without that particular albatross around his neck, Eogan would be free to run again.

But even as he thought it, the question "Where to?" surfaced, as it always did. He could no more flee the Exarchate than he could his guilt. Both would always be there, until he confronted them head-on.

The comms bleeped, indicating that he had a personal message waiting for him. He took it with a sinking feeling, knowing who it was from before he opened it.

DE
Let's talk.
MA

A mixture of hot and cold rushed through him. The overture barely comprised a single sentence, but it was the first in one hundred and fifty years, and more than he'd dared hope for. It should have been a good thing.

So why did he feel so terrified? Why did he reach out to his peripherals and give the command to delete it? Why didn't the fact that he knew she was watching him do it give him any kind of satisfaction?

It wasn't about revenge or shame or fear or any such simple emotion. It was none of those and all of them. Until he was certain exactly what he was feeling, his history with Melilah Awad was one Pandora's box he preferred to leave shut.

One out of two, he thought, as the Exarchate's envoy accelerated steadily closer to the thing in N-1. That was the most he could hope for.

+4

An alarm rang, signaling that it was time for Melilah's exercises. Grateful for the break, she shut down her interface and her watchmeter. It didn't worry her if people observed her during this particular daily ritual, but it helped if she wasn't distracted by the knowledge that they were there—and so many of them at that moment, too. She dimmed the lights.

Thickening shadows fell across her collection of personal paraphernalia. Her quarters consisted of a double-lobed chamber—a peanut stretched thin in the middle. One lobe, slightly smaller, was her personal area, where she saw to the needs of her body; the other lobe, with its entrance to the outside world, was where she worked, socialized, took messages, and so on. There, she was surrounded by trinkets she had collected or been sent from a dozen worlds. Near free fall enabled her to utilize every surface to its full potential. Viewed from one angle, it revealed a collection of fine, earthy artworks originating on Eliza and New Eire. From another, gleaming novelties fashioned from intricate titanium wire peeked out around delicate Little Red bonsai. The room was a puzzle box with numerous solutions, and each solution was a slice of her life.

She floated in the middle of the room and activated the exercise program.

Immediately, a face appeared in the 3-D screen curving around one segment of the chamber. The man's features were both familiar and friendly. Generous lips curved in a smile; deep green eyes twinkled.

"Hello, Mel." The man's voice was warm and couldn't quite hide the accent of a Friday native. "It's been a while."

"It has indeed," she told the part recording, part simulation. "But I still remember you, Bernard Krassay. You were my doctorate supervisor. As far as I know, you're still alive and living on Altitude."

The image nodded and winked out. A second later, it was replaced by another, this time a woman with a long, narrow nose and a shaved head. Fine, gold lines within her skin traced fractal patterns across her temples and cheeks. A deep tingling in Melilah's occipital implant indicated the receipt of a neural packet.

Melilah hesitated before opening it, not remembering the woman at all. Was she friend or foe? Was the packet safe or loaded with neuron-scrambling signals? A decision either way, in real life, could make the difference between offending someone who had once been a dear friend or risking permanent insanity.

Two things she had learned from her political career were that society depended on interpersonal networks, and that everything could turn on a simple misidentification. In her fifties she had set about ensuring that her memory remained good in order to avoid the latter. Anthropologists had known since the twentieth century that people were born with a ceiling on their social groups. Once Melilah exceeded the Dunbar and Hill number of 150, and rapidly acquiring still more associates, it became progressively harder to keep track of everyone she had to know. As she passed her hundredth birthday, it became only worse. Some of her contemporaries opted for cortical grafts and other memory prosthetics. She, motivated by a gut-level—some would say "irrational"—desire to keep her body as free of technology as possible, opted for other means.

She had found that using a name once every two months was enough to keep the memory fresh. Any longer than that between reminders, and the associations faded, rendering recall unreliable. So she programmed a complete list of her occasional acquaintances and enemies into a database and programmed it to cycle through them every sixty days, shuffling the order each time.

A hundred years on, she was still in the habit of skimming fifty or so names a day, just to keep on the ball. By flicking through images, voice files, place names, and more abstruse clues, she felt confident of recognizing any of the several thousand people more or less likely to interact with her at any point in the near future. The list had grown and shrunk down the years, and many people had dropped off it entirely because of death or distance. Sometimes she had added names to the list only to be surprised that they had been on it once before, decades ago, and she had forgotten them completely. That only reinforced the need for the list and the effort to keep it fresh in her mind.

Some names, however, simply would not fall out of her head, no matter how she tried to ignore them.

"Szilvia Animaz," she said eventually. "I wouldn't open a packet from you if I had a knife at my throat."

The angularly beautiful woman with the gold-inlaid skin vanished. Another face took her place, followed quickly by another. And so it went.

Melilah stuck at it for an hour. It was penance, she told herself, for giving in to antisenescence treatments that reduced the need for physical workouts. Her body would remain fit and healthy for decades regardless of what she did to it; but maintenance, she thought, was an important part of any health regime. She needed to remind herself that existence needed to be worked at, or else it soured. She had seen too many people burn out within decades, despite being wired to the nines with technology intended to squeeze every drop out of life.

She didn't want to be a god, but she *did* want to be around for a very long time. If only to see the end of the Exarchate, as had to come sooner or later. Nothing was permanent; no empire lasted forever.

At the end of the hour, she'd had enough of her own company and headed to ben-Avraham's to get some breakfast. The restaurant was nearly full. More people arrived in a flood after her, and the maître d' soon began turning them away. As she ordered, a familiar voice rose up above the crowd, calling her name.

"Grandmother Mel! Over here!"

Melilah looked up and saw her four-daughter Yasu struggling to get into the restaurant. She called over the waiter and explained she would need another setting at the table.

Yasu looked flustered when she joined her. "It's crazy out there!" Yasu exclaimed, pushing a long, blue fringe out of her eyes. Natural flesh tones vied with postdermal patches that seemed to float a millimeter above her skin, moving around her body with apparently random but well-coordinated modesty. "You're the hit of the airwaves today. Did you know that?"

Melilah had forgotten to turn her watchmeter back on after her exercises. The reading had been high enough then to dispel any doubts planted by Gil Hurdowar that she was *uninteresting*.

She shrugged. "So?"

Yasu laughed with gusto. "Don't pretend you don't care! I know you better than that."

Indeed she did; of all Melilah's descendants, Yasu was the one she liked most. For a time, while Yasu's father had been stationed on Phad 4, Melilah had been her primary guardian, cementing a bond that had already been strong.

"Is that why you came here?" Melilah asked, throwing the accusation back at her. "To bask in the limelight?"

"That, and to find out what's going on. Who is this Palmer Eogan guy? Why have I never heard of him before?"

"He's old news." She buried a small pang. "You can't expect to know about everyone I've met."

"Only the important ones. And you dropped him a note, so he must mean *something*." Behind the ribbing, Yasu's expression was serious and sympathetic. "Is he my four-father?"

That stopped Melilah short for a moment. Why would Yasu guess that? What the hell were people *saying* about her?

"You have lots of four-fathers, my dear."

"Only one of them that no one talks about."

"When people do that sort of thing, there's usually good reason."

"But if it *is* him, and he's back . . ." Yasu took her great-great-grandmother's right hand in both of hers. "All the reason in the world won't make him go away."

Damn her. Melilah felt a surprising upwash of grief and affection, half-directed at Yasu. She didn't say anything for a long while, just squeezed the young woman's hands and wished she could take herself back almost two centuries and undo her mistakes. It probably wouldn't change a thing, though; she had done what she had done while in a perfectly clear state of mind, and that mind had not changed greatly down the years. But to experience it all afresh, firsthand . . . She was slightly appalled to realize that part of her wanted to go back *because* she would do it all again, not in order to change it.

Her fingers had typed the note to Eogan without apparent connection to her mind. All the justification in the world about pursuing a lead cut no ice when it came to the logic of her gut. She could have called him directly—if she'd been truly serious about it—but she wasn't nearly ready to see his face, to see what he had become.

She had made the first move; the rest was up to him. But she wasn't going to sit around waiting for him. The last thing she wanted was to be back *there* again.

"I'm hungry," she said, safe in the knowledge that only Yasu could read her expression accurately. She genuinely didn't care what the others watching her thought. Life in Bedlam wasn't for the faint of heart.

They ordered breakfast and talked about other things: Yasu's work in transspatial physics; her current partner, a coworker younger than she whose persistent flirting had finally paid off, although she confessed to being more intellectually stimulated by the AI assisting the project; and the flare, which had been officially designated the fifth-largest on record.

"Can you imagine what it must've been like for the First Wavers?" Yasu shook her head, echoing the very same sentiment she had expressed as a stricken four-year-old. "Without PARASOL, they wouldn't have lasted a second."

"They didn't." The current wave of colonists had inherited the habitat from predecessors who had sowed it into the rock of a nickel-iron asteroid over three centuries earlier. The name Bedlam suited the rambling, organic structure it had become in all those years, along with its similarly convoluted custodian AI that had spent much of its long life utterly alone. The First Wave colonists that had brought it into being hadn't stood a chance against the primary's fiery wrath.

"All fried up and turned into walls." The older Yasu looked around her, at the elegant furniture and iridescent drapes. Gone was the horror the thought had once evoked in her, twenty-five years earlier. Eyes as green as emeralds came back to focus pointedly on Melilah. "Like our memories."

Melilah raised a fruit smoothie in salute. "If you want to know what I was doing down below," she said, "just ask."

"Maybe I could come with you on your next expedition and find out for myself."

"I've offered plenty of times."

Yasu acknowledged the deflection with a roll of her eyes. "You know I'm never going to do it."

"Maybe. I still don't entirely understand why you're so certain of it, though."

"Ennui," her four-daughter said. "Information is only interesting if it's, well, *interesting*. What's the point of mucking about in the underbelly if all you find is someone's old tax statement? Without a guarantee of something at the end of it—and I know that's impossible—I'll stay right here, where I know the supply is reliable."

"There's interesting stuff to be found down there, believe me."

"Well, when you've found it, perhaps you can tell me about it." Yasu tipped a wink to someone behind Melilah. "I'm not a pioneer, like you."

The comment surprised her. "Is that really how you see me?"

"Kinda." Yasu looked embarrassed. "When you're not digging around in garbage, that is."

The young woman got up to lean over the table and kiss her four-mother on the lips. "I love you even if you won't tell me what's going on. Give 'em hell."

With a sweep of energy and life, she was gone.

Melilah finished her smoothie, paid, and left, checking her watchmeter as she did so. The numbers outside the restaurant had dwindled slightly, as had the number of onlookers. Her studied nonchalance had convinced some at least that there wasn't going to be a grand revelation anytime soon. That was good. She had work to do.

When she brought her apartment interface back online, it whistled politely to indicate that she had received a large number of messages. Most were junk, propagating rumors about the blackout. She had instructed her spam filters and data moles to retain anything even tangentially related to her current interests. There was nothing about the couple whose memories she had invaded, not a single recent rumor concerning Lost Levels. Even Gil Hurdowar was quiet, for a change.

She took matters into her own hands and began probing.

First up was to get her civil record cleared after her stunt with Hurdowar, so she *could* dig. Within minutes of her software bomb, she had been issued with a temporary civil rights suspension order. It wasn't the first time a suspension order had been issued against her. The AI responsible for delivering the news did so with a cautionary smugness that made her want to gag. Two more, it warned her, and she would risk permanent downgrade. Two more after that, and she would exceed the maximum allowable for one year. The Exarch could only be *so* lenient. If she persisted beyond that point, she would qualify for expulsion from the habitat.

Fuck that, she thought. *It's going to take more than some freakish hybrid to kick me out. This is my home.*

But right then wasn't the time to fight that battle. She apologized for the incident and went about her pretend business. She didn't ask about the blackout, although she was sorely tempted to. The communications rupture had healed over within moments of forming; to all intents and purposes, nothing had happened. Later, in front of the interface in her quarters, surrounded by the welcoming clutter of two centuries of life, she'd learned that the breakdown had been noted in some quarters but completely ignored in others. As usual, a raft of unlikely and/or paranoid theories abounded to explain the incident: that the colony had experienced a near-catastrophic infostructure failure, and the Exarch was denying the fact in order to hide the precariousness of his rule; that imperialists from Alioth had finally made their move, attacking by viruses, EMP, and other exotic means; that someone had stumbled across something momentous and the Exarch was trying to cover it up. Melilah browsed them all, but was satisfied by none. Except, perhaps, for the last. She couldn't shake the impression that the blackout was somehow related to her. Although the cache she had found contained nothing but personal data, the synchronicity of her finding it and the blackout was too unlikely to be unconnected.

As paranoids and skeptics alike acknowledged, only one person had both the authority and the ability to deliberately bring Bedlam to a halt. That person was the Exarch. But why, she asked herself, would he protect a file of lesbian love letters and some amateur treasure maps? Everyone who came to Bedlam dreamed of finding the Lost Level, a supposed vault of hidden riches long buried on the fringe of the core regions. Melilah had traveled enough kilometers down there to suspect that official maps were mostly accurate and that there were no new large finds to be made. The odds were remote to an extreme that the two women in the file had stumbled across anything new.

Still, when Palmer Eogan failed to respond to her note, she decided to take another look, just in case her cursory steganographic scan had missed information buried deeper than normal in the files. Negotiating with her parole AI for permission to go back down was galling, but she forced herself to be polite and reasonable. Yes, she had done wrong. Yes, she must be punished. No, the data in the disk she had accidentally left behind couldn't be accessed later. No, she couldn't just dredge up a copy. The whole point of burying stuff so deep was that it couldn't be easily accessed.

It let her go on the grounds that she posted the data on a public node so the Exarch could examine it. *Fine,* she thought. If the data belonged to the Exarch in the first place, she wouldn't be showing him anything he didn't already know—assuming, of course, that the data was still where she'd left it. Although she'd checked security scans of the area to make sure no one else had been there, that didn't mean the fiche hadn't been scrambled or destroyed by remote.

The niche, when she returned, was undisturbed. Cool confidence in the face of a near disaster? She couldn't tell. Just in case she had missed something blindingly obvious, she quickly took a copy and replaced the fiche, then proceeded upside to post the data publicly, as instructed.

"Not up to your usual standard, Melilah." The voice of Isaac Forge Deangelis was coolly patronizing. "I expect better of you."

"Count yourself lucky, then," she said. "You'd better hope I don't strike it rich next time."

The Exarch's laugh was mocking, and ended with a click before fully played out.

A deliberate slur, she told herself. The Gentry did nothing involuntarily. Every move was calculated, every word chosen for a particular effect. Even the tone of his voice had been contrived specifically to rile her.

It was working.

+5

Like an ancient mechanical model of the solar system, with planets and moons rotating around a central point in a precisely controlled ballet, Exarch Deangelis's mind was technically in many points at once. Part of him watched Melilah Awad as she followed her instincts back to the fiche. Another part monitored communications traffic along a dozen or so well-patronized networks, tracking public speculation and rumor about the *Nhulunbuy.* Numerous parts dedicated themselves to overseeing the intricate economic and social systems required to keep Lut-Deangelis stable.

Just one satellite mind interrogated Palmer Eogan—but that one was keenly aware that, for the moment, the orbits of all the others were centered on him. What was said and done in the next few hours would determine the course of the future. There was no *could* about it.

"I have examined your mission log, Palmer Eogan," the envoy said, knowing the information was irrelevant but following the protocols of conversation with the same rigor as he would handshake a modem.

"I'd just like to reinforce that we've made no attempt to hide the irregularities," said Eogan. The chief officer of the *Nhulunbuy* hadn't got up on the Exarch's arrival, but that was a result of necessity, not bad manners. The Palmer was still in the process of untangling himself from the Cell he commanded. His body, where it sat hunched in a podlike chair before the curving interior bulkhead of the container called N-2, seemed at first glance to be sprouting roots like an overripe potato. A more detailed examination revealed that some of the threads originated in the chair, not him. Either way, the roots were retracting, retreating millimeter by millimeter, leaving bare skin in their wake.

The process seemed ludicrously primitive to the Exarch. The Palmers, although significantly more cyborg-savvy than Naturals like Melilah Awad, were generations behind the Exarchate. It felt sometimes like talking to a tree.

"I will grant you that," he said. "But your openness does nothing to explain the irregularities. I and the citizens of Lut-Deangelis deserve a full account."

"You have my full agreement on that point."

Was that sarcasm? The Exarch couldn't tell. The Palmer's face was almost invisible behind a beardlike spray of fibers.

"Good. You can begin by describing the contents of the component you call N-1."

"If I could do that," the Palmer replied, "we wouldn't be having this conversation."

An apt comeback, one perfectly in line with the script they had prepared over ftl before the *Nhulunbuy* had docked. Exarch Deangelis nodded, as though deep in thought, and instructed the Palmer to begin at the beginning and to leave nothing out. The process wasn't for his benefit, but for the audience's. The soap opera was entirely for them.

The *Nhulunbuy* was one of several sweeper Cells plying the trade lanes of the Arc Circuit. Its usual routes were along the twenty-five-light-year sweep taking in Mizar, Alioth, and several other major systems in the area. Its function was simply to keep the lanes clear of the interstellar dust that downgraded average deform ratings, thereby causing voyages to be longer and less efficient. Occasionally, hard debris strayed across the lanes, forming serious occlusions that could cause catastrophic accidents. Such navigational hazards were difficult to clear, and the *Nhulunbuy* had a reputation for reliability and promptness in the face of such crises.

The report of a major occlusion on the lane between Mizar-Cazneaux and Lut-Deangelis had, therefore, led to the *Nhulunbuy*'s immediate dispatch to clear it. Apart from the occlusion, the lane had been relatively clear, so the *Nhulunbuy* had made impressive speed. Averaging a deform rating of just under 5.0 and a subjective velocity of 0.9 c, the *Nhulunbuy* had crossed the six light-years to the occlusion in a little under a year, local time.

Everything seemed normal to that point. It was when they arrived at the occlusion that the data took a turn for the screwy. The occlusion, it turned out, was no cometary fragment expelled from a nearby solar system. Neither was it a brown dwarf, an ejected planet, or a micro black hole.

"Describe what you found."

"You have my scientific data."

"Yes, but I don't have your firsthand experience. Tell me."

The Palmer took a deep breath. "From a distance it looked like a puff of dust, and I thought at first that it might be a holed Cell. But closer you could tell that it was something much stranger. The dust was old and cold, and wasn't rotating. There wasn't one solid core, as there would have been with a First Wave wreck. There were lots of solid bodies in there, and they were cold, too. They'd clumped together in no apparent order, but radar suggested that they were intact, not damaged. We saw smooth hulls, portals that could have been air locks and smaller companion craft that might have been shuttles, all docked."

"You're saying that these objects were space vessels."

"Yes." The Palmer didn't hesitate. "They were ships, all right. ROTH ships. I've never seen anything like them before."

Races Other Than Human. There had been several xenarcheological discoveries made in the last century, scattered across human space. All had been of ancient, dead cultures that had traveled and left detritus behind, much as humanity did. Nowhere had a home or colony world been found; if such existed—as surely it must—it was presently beyond the expanding bubble of the Exarchate's influence.

Exarch Deangelis was human enough to feel a tingle of excitement at the thought of what it must have been like to study those ghostly radar images and to realize that what one was seeing were the works of other hands, other minds, other lives . . .

How terrible, then, that the wonder had been so swiftly turned on its head.

"Is that what you have in N-1?" he asked the Palmer. "ROTH artifacts recovered from the occlusion?"

Palmer Eogan shifted slightly in the embrace of the Cell. "In a manner of speaking, yes."

"In *what* manner of speaking, exactly?"

"I'm sorry, Exarch Deangelis, but I hesitate to discuss this publicly."

"You are aware that the laws of Lut-Deangelis forbid you to hide information, especially when it is in the public's interest."

"Information, yes—but not speculation." The Palmer's eyes stared up at him unblinkingly from his mess of tree roots. "Forgive me if I seem intransigent. The *Nhulunbuy* isn't equipped to carry out the investigation required to do this thing justice. Until we have more data, I'd prefer not to make any judgment calls."

The Exarch imagined a ripple of excited whispers spreading out across the system at the revelation.

"I understand. But why bring it here? The ROTH Institute on Jamgotchian-McGraw is the best equipped on the Arc Circuit to examine such a find."

"I chose to bring it to Bedlam because you're closest," the Palmer explained, "and because your neutral political stance and open information policy would ensure that the information wasn't kept secret. This is an important discovery. People should know about it."

"We're honored you chose us." Exarch Deangelis wondered if the conversation sounded as prepared as it seemed to him. No matter. Most people would lap it up. "We'll take it off your hands and make sure it's studied properly. We have the rough specifications you've given us; I'm building a containment facility as we speak." This was true. A nanofacturing seed was already blossoming alongside the habitat, fueled in part by the energies of the recent solar flare gathered by PARASOL. Within hours it would be the size of a small asteroid and secure enough to handle such a discovery. "Your swift and prudent actions are greatly appreciated."

The Exarch intended the words as a dismissal. Once he handed over the occlusion, Eogan's work was done. There was no real role for the Palmer organization once the thing was out of their hands.

"My science officer has requested that she be part of the investigation," Eogan said. "I trust you won't have a problem with that."

Exarch Deangelis allowed no outward sign of annoyance at the departure from the script. "The examination of the object will take time. I wouldn't like to delay your departure any longer than be necessary, as committing an important member of your staff to such a procedure undoubtedly will."

"Thanks for your concern, but I believe the investigation to be more important than maintaining my schedule. My SO has first-hand experience with the object. That sort of information could be priceless."

The Exarch seethed. Was he being threatened with disclosure of the truth if he didn't submit to Eogan's request?

"Of course," he said aloud. "Palmer Vermeulen will be welcome to sit in on the analysis. I'll notify you of where she should report when the time comes." *And I'll make you pay for blackmailing the Exarchate over something like this,* he swore to himself. *This isn't the time for petty power games.*

"Thank you, Exarch Deangelis. I'll await your word." Eogan looked up innocently from his entangled seat. "No doubt you'd like to take a look at the object while you're here. I've authorized entry for your envoy into N-1. Is its body shielded?"

The question surprised him, as did the sudden depersonalization. "Yes, of course."

"Good. At a standard rating, it should last about five minutes. That'll give you time to become acquainted."

The Exarch just stared at the Palmer for a moment, unable to grasp what he was hearing. The envoy's body was rated to withstand the full force of Hipparcos 62512's solar flares indefinitely. A thousand years of exposure to cosmic rays would leave him functionally unharmed. *What the devil had Eogan brought him?*

Know your enemy, he told himself as he took his leave of the Palmer and entered the shuttle again. The loss of one body was a small price to pay for a closer look.

Half an hour later, standing on the lip of the monster and staring at the throat that lay open before him, he felt an exhilarating sense of despair. Space whipped and spun in Planck-sized whirlpools around him. He could feel their miniscule tides tearing at his hardened flesh, ripping it to pieces molecule by molecule. Cerenkov radiation flashed in the fluid of his eyes. Strange neuronal storms preceded massive cerebral shutdowns. He had almost immediately lost all feeling in his legs and torso, and that numbness crept steadily up his fingers to his elbows. As the nerve and chromosome damage mounted and his ability to communicate with the rest of his mind decreased, he wondered at the wisdom of belling this particular cat.

I'm dying, the envoy thought, alone at the end. *And what for?*

White-stained violet streaks flashed down the sides of the rotating cylinder in which he stood. It wasn't a solid object. The boundary ahead of him was utterly black. Wormhole black.

To be the first to die.

That was the doom-laden thought that accompanied him into the abyss.

The first of many.

+6

When the Exarch left him, Palmer Eogan was immediately bombarded with communications from Bedlam—mainly text, voice, and image but with the occasional more exotic protocol thrown in for good measure. Expecting such a reaction, he ignored them all. The notion of ROTH artifacts at such close proximity spread through the general populace like wildfire, exciting imaginations and encouraging all manner of speculation. Only later, as the ramifications sank in, would more sober concerns float to the surface.

None of the communications were from names he recognized.

"That's a dangerous game you're playing, Palmer Eogan."

He looked up. The voice came over the intra-Cell channels from one of the other components. With it came an image of a round-faced woman with gold eyes and silver hair.

"I'm aware of that, Palmer Vermeulen. We're a little short on options."

"You and me both." She didn't say as much in words, but he could see the reproach in her expression clearly enough. His science officer had requested no such attachment to the ROTH investigation. Vermeulen would probably be happier on the other side of the galaxy, given a choice.

But he needed someone at ground zero. And he owed Palmers Cobiac and Bray the attempt, at least, wherever they were. Without the Exarch's guarantees of assurance on that score, the Palmer guild could soon find itself cut out of the equation, as they had been on Sublime, and as he was sure the Exarch wanted them to be everywhere.

Until the Exarchate Expansion of forty years earlier, the

Palmers—so named after ancient pilgrims who returned from the Holy Land laden with gifts—had had a stranglehold on interstellar commerce. The only reliable means of getting from A to B anywhere in human space had been on the back of a Palmer Cell, following trade routes eked out—and vacuumed clean—by many years of constant travel. The VOID drive systems, with their algorithmically evolved nanotech, possessed advantages no existing competitor could match; within a century of leaving Sol, therefore, almost all human transport beyond the system had depended on the goodwill of the guild.

That situation was unsustainable, of course, and pressures within Sol had grown to remedy it. After the True Singularity, technological advancement hit a new upward slope, and whole new sciences evolved. Unbeknownst to the First Wave colonies and the Palmer Cells that helped found them, the Exarchate had devised its own, carefully guarded means of propagating through the Dark. The system, even forty years later, appeared to be too inefficient to permit true trade—from what little the Palmers had been able to deduce about it—but it had been sufficient to seed invasion fleets in every human-occupied system, and to allow the takeover of human territory within two years. The posthuman aftermath had seen incremental erosions of Palmer control, until the possibility that Cells might be supplanted altogether began to look frighteningly real, perhaps even imminent.

If the Exarchate was throwing him a bone to keep the Palmers happy, Eogan would take it with both hands. It indicated, if nothing else, that Exarchs were still willing to make deals. And it proved that Isaac Deangelis was still human enough to succumb to a little extortion.

His command couch vibrated beneath him, indicating that his separation from the Cell was now complete. Gingerly, relishing the newfound freedom, yet sad at the same time that the intimate, familiar connection had been severed, he stood up for the first time in almost a year.

"There are those famous legs," commented Vermeulen dryly. "Got yourself some shore leave, handsome?"

"Something like that." He stretched more out of habit than any real need. His body had left behind such inconveniences as stiffness, cramps, and pins and needles long ago. "I'll bring you back a souvenir."

"Some real food would be good."

"You can join me when you've finished with your new toy."

A slight tightness around her eyes betrayed a thought similar to: *If there's anything left of me.* But she was good; it stayed just a thought. He had briefed his Cellmates carefully on the long flight into Bedlam space.

"Trust me," she said instead. "This is one port where you really *should* find yourself a girl."

He smiled, simultaneously amused and unnerved by the bandwidth presently devoted to his history with Melilah Awad.

"I think the Exarch needs it more than me," he shot back.

The memory of Vermeulen's quick laugh accompanied him through N-2's air lock and out into the vacuum of space.

For a wonderful moment, he was an ant exploring a sack of marbles. Sunlight caught the Cell over the limb of Bedlam, daubing its manifold components with warm yellow light. Refracted and reflected a million incalculable ways, that light shivered around Eogan with an intensity he could almost feel. It was like floating through the heart of a quartz crystal. Nature, as his father had once said, was at its most beautiful when least expected.

Then a large, white shape hove into view, emitting bright flashes of blue light from reactionless thrusters as it adjusted its relative velocity. A giant triangle, not dissimilar to a folded paper plane, its lines were stark and lifeless, designed to intimidate.

The Exarch had come for his prize.

Eogan gave himself a nudge toward N-14, a midsized bauble dwarfed by the new arrival. Intelligent systems in the Cell negotiated docking maneuvers without the help of any of its crew; it didn't need to request authorization, either, as he had already told it to expect something like this. The *Nhulunbuy* knew what it was doing.

But part of him itched to take over anyway—to issue the commands, to chart the trajectories, to activate the thrusters—because what was the point of being chief officer of an interstellar vessel if you didn't actually get to *fly?* It had been a long time since he had piloted anything more complex than a hopper. He missed it.

That feeling, he knew full well, came from the loss of control he was experiencing in the current situation. He felt trapped and impotent under the Exarch's thumb, and to dream of flight was to yearn for escape. Again came the urge to dump N-1 and run, even stronger than before. No doubt Vermeulen would support such a decision, along with the rest of his hostage crew.

The glaring white triangle powered closer. N-2 swung up to meet it. There was no attempt to hide anything. It all happened out in the open, as it was supposed to.

The triangle folded gracefully, and with no small sense of menace, like an origami praying mantis. Triangle-tipped edges converged on the glassy sphere beneath it. Four slender tines impaled it, stretched it into a tetrahedron. More white walls folded down to enclose it. Eogan thought he detected a gamma-ray flash as the Cell containment failed, but he couldn't be sure.

"We'll be compensated for that, I hope," he broadcast into the white shape's flank as it closed shut over the *Nhulunbuy*'s sacrificed component.

"Your trading account has already been credited," the Exarch confirmed.

Eogan checked. It had been, at exactly the right amount.

"Well and good," he said. "I look forward to seeing what you make of it."

"In good time."

Eogan couldn't be sure, but the Exarch sounded distracted. Physically, Isaac Deangelis manifested in the form of a young, blond man with delicate, almost translucent features. Eogan didn't know if it was the Exarch's genuine appearance or designed for a particular effect. Either way, it unnerved him that someone so inexperienced-looking could have access to something of such destructive potential.

"You will be careful opening it, won't you?"

"Be sure of it." The origami-ship banked sharply and angled away from the *Nhulunbuy* like a robot swan.

Eogan thrust to a gentle halt next to N-14 and rapped on the hull. It peeled back, exposing a dozen hopper bays arranged inward in a circle. He picked one at random and folded himself into it. He could have flown on his own down to the surface of Bedlam, its gravity being barely that of a small moon. But Traffic Control imposed strict limits on nonvehicular traffic near the giant habitat, and he'd never got around to renewing his license.

He'd never thought the opportunity to use it would arise again.

The hopper slid out of its niche with a smooth hiss. Facedown on his belly, Eogan piloted the craft with his fingertips instead of direct linkage to the controls. *Surrogate wings,* he thought as he powered away from the collection of spheres that had for so long been his home.

"I still have the helm," he told his second officer, Palmer Flast.

"If I plan on going out of range, I'll let you know."

"Right you are, Palmer Eogan," came the calm, masculine tones in reply. "Properly speaking, of course, 'out of range' is not an option here."

"You never know," he replied, as Bedlam's pockmarked face ballooned in front of him. "I hesitate to take anything for granted at the moment."

"Good weather," Vermeulen wished him.

He didn't reply.

+7

By midnight, the object officially known as 2358M1S had been dubbed "the Mizar Occlusion." Network commentators speculated freely about its origins and nature, training instruments on the Exarch's new containment-and-observation facility. Much larger than the Palmer vessel that had ferried the Occlusion from deep space, the Occlusion observatory had grown in a series of concentric polygons around the white tug that had claimed it from the *Nhulunbuy.* Each layer, according to amateur reverse engineers devoted to probing the technological secrets of the Exarchate, offered different means of both inspection and protection for the thing at their heart. Melilah Awad wondered if whatever lay hidden inside it minded the game of pass-the-parcel being fought over it in the skies of Bedlam.

ROTH artifacts were the prize sought by every interstellar citizen. Very little of what the ancient aliens had left behind was on actual worlds. Most of it was space junk following ancient orbits around moons, worlds, and primaries. Some of it drifted through interstellar space. There were hulls of space vessels drilled through by high-velocity impacts, shells of habitats destroyed in accidents so severe that the wreckage was radioactive enough to kill an un-Natural, mysterious machine fragments suggesting technologies that ranged from the mundane to the bizarre—and much more. There were even bodies, every now and again. A jettisoned corpse had been found two decades earlier just off the main trade lane between Phad and Severance. Initial T-scans revealed a creature with two stalklike eyes protruding from a thick, curled shell at the center of ten jointed legs. Each leg was tipped with three opposable digits. Its thick exoskeleton suggested an insectile ancestry, but deeper analysis refuted that theory, revealing that the creature's outer layers were artificial, not natural. The alien, dubbed the Snailer, might have been a Natural of its own species, modified barely enough to survive in the hostile environment of space, or it could equally have been an extreme variant with only passing resemblance to its relatives' usual morphology. There was no way of knowing until they found another corpse or decipherable records.

The knowledge that a ROTH artifact had arrived at Bedlam was genuinely exciting. Melilah could understand the interest of her fellow citizens and the Exarch's desire to handle the investigation carefully. She could also understand why the *Nhulunbuy* had come to Bedlam rather than any of the other, more central colonies. The rivalry between Friday and Alioth would only spark friction, no matter who got their hands on it; New Eire was still rumbling after the attempted uprising ten years earlier; Altitude could have been a good choice, but it, too, fancied itself a player on the Arc Circuit, and couldn't be relied upon to do the research required with complete objectivity.

What Melilah didn't understand entirely was why Palmer Eogan had traveled physically to Bedlam and *still* not replied to her message.

"Feeling snubbed?" asked Gil Hurdowar, after her third check of the Palmer's movements. "It doesn't look like he's going to come your way anytime soon."

"You've got a fucking nerve," she said, shutting down the query window and hating the flush that wanted to rise to her cheeks.

"What I've got is *rights,* Melilah," he shot back.

"That's poor grammar, Gil," she offered lamely.

His tone was smug. "Why fight it? You know you need someone to keep an eye on you, to keep you out of trouble."

"If I did—which I don't—then it sure as hell wouldn't be you."

"But we have such a beautiful rapport."

"'Rapport' isn't the word I'd use."

He chuckled lightly. "You'll come around."

His conceit was really starting to irritate her. "Don't you have anything better to do, Gil?"

"It may surprise you to learn that I don't."

She took a quick peek at his log. "It's been a while since you cleaned out your junk file. And some of your auxiliary routines are looking a little frayed."

"Minor stuff compared to—"

She turned the volume down without waiting for him to finish. He could talk as much as he wanted, but she didn't have to listen.

Besides, it was time for her weekly Defiance meeting.

Once every eight days, in a small chamber off Bornholdt Chasm, an obscure suburb well away from the main pipe routes, a group of people dissatisfied with the Exarch's rule met to discuss what could be done about it. The meetings were conducted openly and with no attempt to hide their times or the identities of those attending. The inconvenient location had been chosen simply to weed out those who might attend to heckle or waste time. Melilah had no patience with either type. If they didn't mean business and couldn't be bothered going out of their way to be there, they weren't welcome.

The trouble was, she was beginning to lose patience with the people who *did* show up, and there was no easy way to say that without admitting that the cause itself was at fault.

"The Mizar Occlusion is just another example of what I'm talking about," one of the more strident voices was saying. Angela Chen-Pushkaric was a stocky food tech from Havlin, one of Bedlam's three industrial sectors. "We've lost our name, our independence, our governance—and now we're losing our science, too. The Gentry are bleeding us dry. How long until we're nothing but a nuisance, a pest to be eliminated entirely? What are we doing to stop that from happening?"

"The Exarch needs us," argued Werner Gard, a programmer whose skull had been elongated lengthwise to accommodate the Third Hemisphere interfaces required to keep up with specialist AIs. His face was pushed forward and seemed stuck in a permanent grimace. "There are things he can't do."

"Not yet."

"Not ever. He's just one point of view. The Exarchate knows it needs variance and dissent in order to survive."

"The Gentry *say* that, yes, but—"

"I'm not arguing with you over whether they're lying or not, Angela." Gard's long fingers splayed out in front of him like a net to catch her words. "I'm just saying that the Exarchate could have wiped us out or made overtures toward doing so long ago. It didn't, hasn't, and doesn't seem likely to in the near future. Spreading panic isn't going to do the cause any good at all."

"But what *is* the cause," asked white-haired Prof Virgo in her calm, reasoned voice, "if it's not to remove the Exarch from his position of absolute power? He might indeed need us, as you say, but the fact remains that what freedoms we still have exist solely at his whim."

"I don't see an easy way around that," said Kara Skirianos, another person, like Melilah, displaced by the Exarch when the local government had been decapitated. The blow might not have been literal, but it had definitely spelled the end of Bedlam's self-rule. What was the point of maintaining a bureaucracy when one person thought he could do so much better?

That that person was some sort of superhuman and could be in numerous places at once certainly added to the argument that he might be right.

"We can't openly attack the Exarch," Skirianos went on, the attention of the room on her, "because we're technologically outmatched. We can't actively subvert him, because our own laws—the laws he let us retain as a conciliatory gesture—will expose our intentions before we even get started. All we can do is appeal to his sense of reason. If we can convince him that we deserve the right to govern ourselves, and that we're capable of doing it, he may let the reins go."

Chen-Pushkaric snorted. "With all due respect, Speaker, the Exarch didn't invest so much energy into taking over this system just to hand it back to us when we *ask nicely*."

"We don't know that for certain." Skirianos's voice was thin and sad. Before the takeover, she had been Speaker for the habitat, the highest political officer in the system. It was she who had signed the peace accord with the Exarchate that many in the extreme wings of Defiance described as a betrayal of humanity. "Isaac Deangelis has consistently stated that the Exarchate has no intentions of ruling in the fashion of past empires. In other words, no mailed fist. He lets us speak against him when many despots wouldn't. We're free to do as we will."

"But we're still trapped," said Prof Virgo.

"Trapped by who we *are.* Perhaps the point of all this is not to subjugate us but to spur us on to bigger things. We know the Exarch doesn't like Naturals, for instance."

"So he wants to turn Bedlam into a happy little posthuman paradise, like Sol. Great." Chen-Pushkaric swung her wide face slowly from side to side, as though triangulating. "Giving him what he wants doesn't sound like victory to me. It sounds like defeat."

"It sounds like survival," said Gard, his long skull catching the light. "I can think of worse things."

Melilah could see where both points of view were coming from. Her position was simple. She resented the arrogance with which the Exarch's superiors had Gentrified Bedlam without once asking its inhabitants if they wanted it or not. She loathed the automatic assumption that Sol knew best, and that everyone else's opinion counted for shit. The technological superiority of Bedlam's new governor worried her, for she suspected that Chen-Pushkaric was right on one point: that the Exarchate would soon possess the ability to wipe out the rest of humanity. She didn't like the idea of living with a gun to her head, especially when the gun was wielded by someone whose mind she couldn't even begin to imagine.

She didn't hate Exarch Deangelis, nor did she want him dead. She just wanted her world back, one way or another, and her old life with it. The universe was big enough for free humans and the Exarchate to coexist peacefully. At some point, the Exarchate was sure to realize that, no matter how unreasonable a dream that sometimes seemed. She needed to feel as though she was working toward making that dream a reality, at least incrementally.

The Defiance group, on the other hand, seemed more and more to be a bunch of malcontents arguing among themselves, divided by details of their disgruntlement.

"What about you, Melilah?" asked Chen-Pushkaric. "You're being quiet today."

She glanced up from her introspection. "We're tying ourselves in knots," she said. "There are no conclusions we can come to about the Mizar Occlusion until we know what it is. Finding that out should be our first priority."

"If the Exarch doesn't tell us, we'll never know." Chen-Pushkaric glowered theatrically. "No data has been posted on the network."

"The new installation has only been there a few hours. Give him time." Melilah turned to Gard. "Is it even operational yet?"

"Hard to tell. Something's going on in there, but what exactly . . ." He shrugged. "Your guess is as good as mine."

"Wait another day, then start making assumptions," she suggested. "We can at least give him a chance to do the right thing."

I hope you're listening to this, she thought to the absent Exarch, who had the capacity to eavesdrop if he wanted to. *Hard though it is to believe, I'm actually sticking up for you.*

"A day could be too long," said Chen-Pushkaric. "Doesn't anyone remember Sublime?"

"Of course," said Melilah. "It's not the sort of thing we're likely to forget."

"Well, what if we're sitting on top of another one of those? What if it goes off because the Exarch mishandles it?"

The thought, Melilah was sure, had already occurred to everyone in the room. Perhaps everyone in the habitat.

"The odds are against it," said Gard. "There have been other ROTH objects recovered in the last ten years, and many more before that. None has been as dangerous as the one that destroyed Sublime. That was probably just bad luck: a piece of munitions left over after a war, or a cache booby-trapped against tampering. Mostly all we find is just junk."

"It doesn't look like the Exarch is taking any chances," said Skirianos. "The installation is very secure."

"They thought so in Sublime, too, remember?"

Melilah did remember. Everyone on the Arc Circuit did. Shock waves had rippled along the local trade routes, and beyond. All investigations into ROTH artifacts were put on indefinite hold, pending a closer examination of the Sublime Catastrophe, as it quickly became known. Humanity's grip on the stars had suddenly seemed decidedly precarious.

There had been political aftershocks, too. Palmer Horsfall had spared no effort in alerting the systems around her to the disaster that had befallen Sublime and her sister, thereby revealing the existence of an ftl communications link between all Palmer Cells and the Exarchate. How that link manifested was not known—the prevailing theory, that it relied on entanglement between elementary particles, fell apart in the face of the fact that signals decohered too fast to reach more than a light-year or two—but the sure knowledge of its existence rocked the relationship between subjugated colonies and the supposedly neutral traders that plied the lanes between them. The ability to communicate instantly with neighbors would have greatly assisted any effort to unite against the Exarchate. By not offering that ability to all, even for trade, the Palmers had passively assisted the Exarchate in their Expansion.

Tempers had been strained. Cells received unfriendly welcomes in some ports, accused of collaboration with the enemy. Palmers had denied the charge—and denied it still—but suspicion remained. Melilah herself had organized a habitatwide protest against the technological embargo enforced by Sol on other human-controlled worlds. What right did the distant home system have to keep potentially lifesaving technologies from those who needed it?

The fuss had died down eventually. More distant colonies had no choice but to embrace what means of connection with the rest of the Arc Circuit they could maintain, and the harsh reality was that the Palmers had such a stranglehold on interstellar colonies that to spurn them was to choose complete isolation. No matter what one thought of the Palmers *or* the Exarchate, in the minds of most people having them around was better than the alternative.

Despite the political wrangling, the thirteen thousand people who died in the Sublime Catastrophe were never forgotten. They had relatives and friends in many different colonies, on and off the Arc Circuit. Monuments and memorials were dedicated to them, the first known human victims of the ROTH. The lesson had been learned.

And she remembered the buried snapshots of her holidaying couple in the same system. She'd performed a search on the names recorded on the fiche and learned that both women had left Bedlam separately, more than a year ago. Their trail went cold from there.

"Again," she said, "we come up against the fact that the Exarch is in the best position to analyze this thing. Sure, if we had access to his knowledge and technology, we might be able to do better—but we don't, so we just can't. Instead of bitching about what we can't fix, why don't we try turning it to our advantage?"

"How do we do that, exactly?" asked Chen-Pushkaric, skepticism writ large across her broad features.

"Well, we're not worthless chattel. We do have some skills. Lets apply them to what we can lay our hands on and prove that we're worth collaborating with. Going off half-cocked will only ensure that we remain out of the loop forever."

"Collaborate, in other words."

"'Thinking long term' is how I'd rather put it," she said, cursing the food tech's blunt lack of sophistication. *Read between the lines, you idiot. I didn't say that the Exarch would give us the information* willingly . . .

Melilah gave them another half an hour before giving up. She had better things to do. Their hearts were in the right places, but their methodology was all screwed up. They were a fire burning without fuel, consuming itself and liable to do little more than that, no matter how hot its flames burned. She came away from the meeting feeling frustrated and angry, with no clear vent, apart from the Exarch. She felt like doing something bold and stupid—and that was dangerous for someone already on probation.

Instead she sealed herself in her quarters and set about digging. She didn't tackle the Exarch's defenses head-on. She took her time, nibbling around the edges of the problem like the experienced data-gleaner she was. In the day since the Mizar Occlusion had arrived at Bedlam, many people had crudely probed the core secret and gotten nowhere. She doubted that she could do any better. But there would be peripheral secrets hidden less successfully, and other gleaners whose data she could lift without having to duplicate their efforts. If there was one thing she knew about the Exarchate, it was that there were no easy solutions. Going at it like a battering ram wasn't going to get anyone anywhere.

Time passed. Leads came and went. A picture slowly began to take shape. Two people were missing from the *Nhulunbuy*'s crew register, without explanation. And something about the Occlusion observatory didn't look right to her. The two thoughts, seemingly unconnected, nagged at her as though potentially significant.

So immersed was she that she barely heard her door buzz. When she glanced at who it was, the floor seemed to lurch out from under her, a feeling utterly at odds with her low-gee conditioning. Her first instinct was to bury herself back in the problem—the lesser, it seemed, of two—and hide.

But she didn't.

"Hello, Melilah," said Palmer Eogan, when she opened the door. "I owe you an apology."

She just stared at him, and wondered where the last one hundred and fifty years had gone.

+8

Caught in the moment like a microbe in an ice crystal, the Exarch didn't even notice the reunion that had the habitat abuzz. His thoughts were dominated by much more important issues. Even at the slowest possible speed he could maintain, events were unfolding with disconcerting rapidity.

The Occlusion was safe for the moment, wrapped in a cocoon of instruments and shielding. Preliminary data were suggestive but inconclusive on a number of points. There could be no doubt, though, about what he had in his possession.

And the Occlusion wasn't all he had to worry about. Long-range tracking had picked up two unidentified blips on the borders of the system. They were without doubt vessels running silent, decelerating with drives filtered to resemble astronomical objects, like early airplanes swooping out of the sun. One of them was impersonating the spiral galaxy M97, the other the bright globular cluster 47 Tucanae, just a few degrees removed from the Small Magellanic Cloud. Close inspection revealed emission lines consistent with tanglers from out-system. Where precisely they were from, he couldn't tell—but he suspected that the first was from Kullervo-Hails system. The Exarch of that colony, Lazarus Hails, had a weakness for word games. M97 was also known as Bode's Nebula.

Bodes ill, either way, Exarch Deangelis thought to himself. He wouldn't have spotted the newcomers had he not been looking specifically for them. He wasn't sure if he should feel relieved that his paranoid notions had been confirmed—or worried that he wasn't being paranoid *enough.*

The tanglers must have left their systems barely moments after he had posted his report about the Mizar Occlusion to Sol, months ago. Even as the full explanation of what had happened in Sublime was arriving in his system, others were preparing their own response. He had no way to predict exactly what form that response would take. On the surface, communication with his neighboring Exarchs was as polite as always.

That wasn't all. Palmer traffic was up across the board. Four more Cells had hailed the habitat since the *Nhulunbuy*'s arrival: *Studenica* and *Umm-as-Shadid* from Alioth-Cochrane, *Inselmeer* and *Patrixbourne* from farther afield. He expected more in the coming week. Some were haring in with VOID drives blazing in furious deceleration, indicating the tremendous hurry with which they had left their home systems. He had no way of knowing who was spreading the word. All he could do was batten down the hatches and prepare for the worst.

There were consolations. With attention shifting to focus on Lut-Deangelis, the political landscape of the Arc Systems was drifting away from Friday in 78 Ursa Major and Alioth-Cochrane. That could only be a good thing, from Exarch Deangelis's perspective. Too long had those two neighboring systems dominated the region. The time was overdue for his independent, open alternative to rise to the fore.

Excited and terrified in equal measures, he composed a brief report for Sol—confirming the identity of the Mizar Occlusion and outlining the surreptitious incursions into the system—and sent it on its way.

The reply came almost immediately.

"Stand firm, Isaac. We're on our way."

He didn't know quite what to make of the last sentence until his own tangler reported a rapid influx of data. Ftl transmissions were a severe bottleneck when it came to information flows between inhabited systems. Bit rates rose only as a cube root of transmission power, so it took eight times as much energy to send twice as much data. The most he could manage without crippling the habitat was a few tens of kilobytes a second; Giorsal McGrath in 78 Ursa Major, the most industrialized system in the Arc Circuit, could do a megabyte a second at a stretch. During the Exarchate Expansion, Sol had converted whole asteroids to energy in order to power the transmissions that had beamed Deangelis and his peers to their respective systems, one bit at a time. It had taken weeks for him to upload into the tangler parked out of detection range of the Bedlam government, there to begin preparing in earnest for takeover. Now, the tangler was reporting a transmission rate in the order of terabytes per second. The burst was expected to last three days.

He didn't know who exactly was coming down the pipe at him—but they were big, whoever they were.

Rather than worry about that—too much—he threw himself into research. The Occlusion was an odd beast, hard to pin down. From a distance, it was much as Palmer Eogan had described it: a dimple in space that accumulated interstellar dust much as a navel attracted lint. But it didn't end there. Palmers like Eogan made their living scraping trade lanes clear of dust that might downgrade their VOID drive deform ratings, but that process didn't create a vacuum as pure as the one at the heart of the Occlusion. There was still the quantum foam, seething away at Planck levels: all manner of exotic particles popping into existence, then disappearing again before they could make a difference.

The Mizar Occlusion somehow punched a hole through that foam, leaving true emptiness in its wake. What that emptiness consisted of wasn't space-time as Exarch Deangelis knew it. It was another creature entirely.

After the destruction of his envoy and Eogan's own experiences in transit, the Exarch was reluctant to get too close to it in any of his personae just yet. Instead, the installation designed and made instruments to send into the Occlusion, while clearing it of dust and other debris. The alien vessels Eogan had retrieved went into a smaller inspection chamber for cursory analysis. They were twisted, spindly things, with oval compartments strung out like seedpods at odd attitudes. He had seen their type before in archival records. Similar to other wrecks left behind by a civilization dubbed Merchant B, they had already been scoured of all worthwhile data during the trip from their resting place. He arranged for them to be transferred to the habitat for scientists there to pore over at their leisure. A pacifier to appease a grizzling child.

One by one, as that was done, exploratory instruments disappeared into the Occlusion. Data trickled back in meager streams, confirming his expectations. The relative tranquillity of the hole punched in the quantum foam didn't last long. Nature abhorred a true vacuum: what it lost in one place was more than made up for in another. In the heart of the Occlusion, the underlying substrate of the universe twisted and flexed. Constants vanished in a hail of imaginary and impossible numbers. Equations adopted dozens of new dimensions, or collapsed down to just one or two. Strange new particles popped into existence, then disintegrated in showers of exotic energies.

But that region of discontinuity didn't last long, either. And what lay on the far side was even more remarkable.

Coral, he thought. It was an appropriate descriptor for something upon which his career—perhaps even his life—might founder, like a wooden-hulled boat on a submerged reef.

He opened a Most Secure ftl channel and, bucking the data flow coming in-system through his tangler, hailed a woman everyone assumed was dead.

"Isaac?" Jane Elderton's voice was distant and low-res. "I was wondering when you'd call me."

"You know, then."

"Of course."

"I wanted to ask you . . ." He hesitated, suddenly doubting the wisdom of the conversation.

"Did I go into it?" she finished for him.

"Yes."

"I understand what you're feeling, Isaac. The first glimpse is terrifying. We could never have built anything like that. It's as alien to us as we are to the Naturals—perhaps even more so. And the other side . . ." Elderton sighed. "Yes, I went into it. Who could resist? We're still human."

Exarch Deangelis had never felt more human in his life—in all the negative senses of the word.

"Were you punished?"

It was Elderton's turn to hesitate. "What do you think?" she eventually said. Her voice was sad and impossibly distant. "It's lonely here, Isaac. But I'm too scared to do anything about that. So much has already been lost."

He ignored a shiver of apprehension in his core body. "Someone came to you," he said. "From Sol."

"Yes."

"Who?"

"The Archon."

"Itself?"

"In full."

No wonder the data transmission was so enormous. “What for?”

“To oversee the operation,” she said. “To make sure nothing went wrong.”

“What *did* go wrong?”

She was silent for a long time, so long he wondered if they had been cut off.

“Jane?”

“They’ll be listening now, Isaac. You must know that. We have no secrets from them.”

“That thought doesn’t frighten me.”

“It frightens me,” she said. “This whole situation frightens me. I shouldn’t be talking to you. You have my data. That should be enough. I don’t want to contaminate you any more than you already have been.”

“I have your data, yes, but I need so much more than that. You’ve been through this and I haven’t. I need to know what to expect. I need your advice. I need to know—”

What I might lose.

“—what the Archon will expect of me.”

“I’m sorry, Isaac. I can’t give you anything. It’s all changed now. Nothing will ever be the same. I opened the door, and now no one can ever close it.”

“But—”

“I have to go.” Her transmission was graying. “Be careful, my friend. Don’t lose yourself like I did.”

The Exarch of White-Elderton colony—formerly known as Sublime—disappeared in a wash of white noise.

+9

On arrival in Bedlam, Eogan had immediately downloaded an up-to-date map in order to avoid getting lost. The surface of Bedlam was a morass of constant nanofacturing, as the indigenous replicators, much evolved from the original seed planted by colonists three centuries earlier, doggedly continued their work. The pitted, seething surface where the expanding boundary of replicators met the vacuum boasted numerous tapered spines that speared up through the steel gray morass. These doubled as instrument berths and docking towers, and looked like thorns on a cactus with acne.

An elevator took him from his arrival point along a wide pipe that spiraled as it descended into the habitat. The gravity was negligible, but more than he had experienced for over a year. It took him a moment to adjust. Few landmarks on the map struck Eogan as familiar. Numerous sections had succumbed to the relentless pressure as the habitat grew, with favorite haunts that had once been on the surface now squashed flat far below. The programming of the replicators was simple: to construct walls and spaces of varying sizes sufficient to house a growing human population. Like much of nature's produce, the end result was a scale-free network, with relatively few large chambers multiply connected throughout the habitat. This meant that routes through the habitat were rarely straight lines and frequently changed as new chambers were added. A map was essential, even for regular visitors. Some names remained the same, despite being housed in radically different locations.

Automated security systems scanned him inside out for various biological and artificial pathogens. Once cleared, he was allowed deeper into the station. The process was entirely unstaffed. Not until he reached a depth of forty meters or so did he see his first local. The woman, a surveyor of some kind, testing a length of pipe with her gloved fingers, looked up at him with vague interest but said nothing. It was clear that she knew who he was. That was only to be expected, he supposed, given the open information policy of the habitat and the circumstances of his arrival. He had been steeling himself against an agoraphobic reaction for days.

He took another elevator to the nearest hub, an enormous doughnut-shaped chamber named after Réka Albert. Throughout all of Bedlam's creeping layers of habitation, there had always been an Albert Hall. This one was as busy as the one he remembered, with numerous restaurants, shops, and entertainment facilities covering the floor, ceiling, and much of the curved walls. Pipes large and small led into the enormous space; slender, brightly colored transports whizzed by overhead with tiny margins for error; the air was rich with numerous fragrances and the sound of voices. Everywhere he looked he saw unfamiliar faces.

It made the blank walls of N-1 look decidedly drab. No matter that sensory addenda allowed any number of backdrops and interactive scenarios, driven by peripheral AIs with easily sufficient power to imitate any human interaction. He still *knew* he was sewn to a chair in interstellar space. There was no substitute for getting out of it and walking around, every now and again.

Stares met his with disconcerting frequency. Most people were curious; he could understand that. Some were hostile, and that, too, was not unexpected. It was the solicitous ones he was keen to avoid, wherever possible. He didn't want to get stuck in a conversation with someone who thought they knew all about him just because they had access to his public file.

He wandered at random, in no immediate hurry. A line of jewelry makers occupied one inner side of the Hall, and he stopped to admire the handiwork on display. Few people in Bedlam actually worked for a living. Nanotech and fusion power gave the habitat all the physical resources it needed to maintain itself. But there was always room for creativity and ingenuity. Craftspeople, poets, dancers, musicians, public speakers—and thieves, spies, con artists and charlatans—all thrived. Over three hundred years earlier, human society, especially those founded in space, had adapted to selling nothing but nonmaterial wares. Wherever money existed, people found new ways to spend and earn it.

"There's a field effect generator in the clasp. My own design."

He looked up from a silver broach so fine it was barely visible.

Glassy, artificial eyes stared back at him from the face of a spry, bald woman with fingers that tapered to wicked-looking points. To manipulate the materials she employed with greatest precision, he presumed.

"Remarkable," he said. "I wondered how it could possibly hold together. How much is it?"

"Four hundred Sols."

Sol Dollars, he thought, marveling at how quickly merchants adopted the victor's currency.

"I'll take it."

She shook her head. "Save your money," she said. "Mem Awad already has one."

"She—what?"

"Your friend, the one you're here to see. She bought one very much like this last year."

"I see." He stared at her, feeling like an idiot. "Thank you."

"You're welcome, Mus Eogan."

He walked away shaking his head, dimly acknowledging the artisan's thick Prime accent. She was a long way from home, having probably come to Bedlam by hitching rides on Cells bound along the Arc from end to end. The Arc Circuit had been a busy trade route for over a century, ever since the Sol-ward legs of the Great Bear Run had been severed in the double interests of profitability and self-determination.

Your friend, the artisan had said, *the one you're here to see.*

There was no privacy on Bedlam. People naturally gravitated to the source of greatest interest. At the moment, after the Mizar Occlusion, that was him and his connection with Melilah Awad.

Eogan had forgotten what it was truly like to be in the public eye, caught in a spotlight so bright it made him feel completely transparent. No amount of preparation could steel him against it.

Still, he told himself, the artisan had saved him from wasting money on something Melilah already owned.

"Five Sols say you wouldn't have bought it anyway," said Vermeulen from the *Nhulunbuy*.

He ignored the gibe and spoke to Palmer Flast instead. "How's the transfer coming along?"

"The new installation is sealed and operational," came back the voice of his second officer. "No word from Exarch Deangelis."

"The skulls?" *Skull* was Palmer shorthand for alien remains, wrecked ships in particular.

"On their way to the big house."

"Get me the name of the person assigned to them," Eogan said. "I'd like to assist in their examination."

"Roger. One moment."

Wheels turned fast in Bedlam. Routine decision-making was handled mainly by AIs, and the few humans involved actually *wanted* to be. Operational inefficiencies were therefore minimal. Eogan didn't think it would be long before the wrecks he had scavenged from the dust-heavy environs of the Mizar Occlusion were tucked safely away inside the habitat.

"Dr. Iona Attard is the person you want," said Flast.

"Set up an appointment for one hour from now. Tell her I might have someone with me, and that we'll need full access. There are some unique features I need to point out to her that aren't obvious from our report."

"I'll tell her that. Can she contact you directly if she has any questions?"

"I'd rather not be disturbed."

"Yes, sir."

Eogan closed the line, wondering what the hell he was going to do for an hour, but almost immediately coming up with several possibilities. Hailing a transport and jumping inside, he took a swooping, complicated journey to ben-Avraham's to see if the coffee was as good as he remembered.

It was—but the empty setting opposite him, placed in defiance of his request for a table for one, wouldn't let him relax. He drank the coffee before it had properly cooled, paid, and left.

The address was the same, 14A Jeong Crescent, although the actual suburb had changed. The air of Bonabeau Fold was fresh and smelled faintly of green things growing nearby. Subtle strip lights painted fuzzy geometric patterns on the curved pipe walls, shifting like underwater sunlight in slow motion. Angular, rhythmic music came from one apartment he passed; his heartbeat tried to match its brisk pace, and he felt light-headed as a result. Or was that nervousness?

He kicked himself along the pipe to a door not dissimilar to the one he remembered and soundly pressed the entry buzzer.

The habitat seemed to fall deathly silent. His breath curdled in his throat.

The door clicked and hissed open.

"Hello, Melilah," he said. "I owe you an apology."

She didn't move. Her face was unnaturally still, and her eyes didn't saccade. Her left hand anchored her body to the frame, and Eogan didn't doubt that it was within easy reach of the switch that would close the door in his face. He could feel her warring within herself over the impulse to do just that.

And *him* . . . He felt as though every muscle in his body had turned to inertia gel: perfectly fluid until shocked, then suddenly rigid. At any moment, he could freeze and shatter into a million pieces.

It was *her.*

"You took your time," she said eventually. Her voice was exactly as he remembered it, warm and rounded, with cultured vowels and an unhurried pace. She was as tall as he was, but slighter, more elegant. Her hair hung in alternating stripes of black and gold. Her skin was flawless. Her green eyes were fixed on him, waiting for him to respond.

"I'm sorry," he said. His body wanted to break out into a sweat, but he kept a tight lid on his autonomic reactions. It felt good to say it, at last. He'd been carrying it for so long. "I'm truly sorry, Melilah."

Her head moved slightly: the beginning of a shake, carefully contained. "It's old news, Palmer Eogan. We've both moved on."

"Yes."

"You're lucky I even remember you."

"I've never forgotten—not us, or what happened to us."

"I had to forget, or it was going to drive me insane." Her stare was accusatory. "If you'd apologized back then, it might have meant something."

"It wouldn't have made a difference, though."

"To you, maybe."

"There seemed no other way out." He looked at his feet brushing uselessly against the wall of the pipe. They longed to kick away, to run. Again. "I didn't think I had a choice."

"Is that all you came here for?" She retreated slightly, as though preparing to shut the door. "I'm not interested in hearing an explanation. Not after so long."

Eogan shook his head, reminding himself that there was a reason for coming to her. He wasn't just exorcising—or indulging—an old regret.

"I want to show you something," he said, meeting her challenge. "The skulls we found. The ROTH ships. I'd like you to see them."

She eyed him suspiciously. “Why?”

“I think you’ll be interested in them.”

“The data will be available soon enough.”

“Data is data. It’s not standing in the same room with them. It’s not touching something made by another race of intelligent beings. It’s not standing where aliens once stood, and wondering what they looked like, what they breathed, what they *felt.*” He chose his words with care, hoping to appeal to the deep streak of curiosity that was an integral part of her personality. The enthusiasm he felt was real. “You don’t have to take it as a peace offering,” he said. “Just look at it as an opportunity to do something you’ve never done before.”

“How do you know I’ve never done it?”

“I checked the public record when I arrived.”

She did a double take. “Of course.” He could see her thinking to herself, wondering what else he had checked for. Employment history? Public code violations? Lovers since him?

The truth was that he had looked for nothing more than her address and her experience with ROTH artifacts. Nothing else had concerned him.

She looked behind her, then back at him. “Okay. You’ve got my interest—but don’t expect anything more than that.”

“I don’t.”

“And you’d better deliver. Give me a second.”

The door hissed shut.

He endured a small eternity, feeling like a teenager waiting for his first date to turn up. She had changed. Physically she still looked young, but there was a palpable weight to her presence that spoke of fifteen decades of extra experience. It manifested in her stare and in her bearing.

Many years of VOID travel had slowed his ageing relative to hers, so he was in effect fifty years younger than she now—and he felt it. Maybe she *had* gotten over him. Maybe his apology was completely irrelevant to her.

She emerged from the room dressed in a businesslike black one-piece covered with pockets and straps—a work uniform and symbolic gesture both—and locked the door behind her.

“Lead the way, Palmer.”

He did so in silence, unwilling to force her into a conversation she probably didn’t want. He had what *he* wanted, for the moment. All he had to do was keep her with him until the time was right, and then they could deal with what was truly important.

+10

Melilah kicked alongside Eogan through the pipes of Bedlam with one thought stuck in her mind. *He looks the same.* Despite one hundred and fifty years of separation, of trying so hard to get over him and to put the hurt behind her, he turned up on her doorstep wanting to apologize, and he looked the fucking same! She couldn't let go of it. Had he done it deliberately, to wound her or—God help her—to woo her? Was he wearing that face to hide the ghastly reality beneath, so she wouldn't flinch at what he had become? Was he manipulating her or genuinely trying to be considerate?

He looks the same. Dark hair and friendly, square features. A stocky, strong body with broad chest and reliable hands. His teeth were white and straight, apart from one that had rotated slightly on his lower left jaw. There was a suspiciously smooth patch on his upper lip, as though he'd had corrective nanosurgery as a child.

All fake, she reminded himself. That body was him no more than her work garb was her—or his simple brown shipsuit was his actual skin. He was a ship-symbiont now, physically grafted to the Cell he commanded.

And, dammit, part of her was still jealous.

"Tell me something I don't know about the Mizar Occlusion," she said, trying to turn the situation to her advantage instead of letting it drag her down. "Unless that's what you're taking me to see."

He shook his head. "Everything I know is on public record."

"That's a cop-out," she said. "No one has the time to scour the entire public record. It's hard enough finding specific things, let alone every possible thing."

He kept his eyes forward. "I guess that was always going to be the problem with the Bedlam model."

Melilah responded automatically to the implied criticism. "We don't keep *everything*. Zero access records are deleted after a year, unless considered of particular value. More popular or relevant information lasts longer. AIs maintain the archives, making sure the information is accessible. But still, there are forty thousand people in Bedlam, and every one of them is laying down a minute's worth of data every minute—and that's too much data for even the most determined of peepers."

"But there are filters and search algorithms. It's not as if you can't follow a thread to its conclusion."

She glanced at him; he still wasn't looking at her. "I don't think you realize just how much of a fuss you've created, bringing that thing here. I'm good at finding details; people pay me to do that for them, when other methods fail. But you've got me stumped on this one. The truth is locked up supertight."

"Either that," he said, "or it's exactly what I've said it is."

"Whatever." She kicked ahead of him and into a medium-sized hub. A crowd of people looked up from a game to watch them fly by. Elbows nudged; hands went up to cover lips. Frowning, she hailed a chevron-shaped purple two-seater transport and climbed inside. The gesture was purely symbolic, but it helped.

"Why is someone called Gil Hurdowar hailing me?" Eogan asked as he climbed in after her.

"Ignore him," she said, "and give this thing a destination."

"Dr. Iona Attard," he said. A second later, as though he had just had a silent exchange with someone else, he added, "Four-oh-nine Barabási Straight, Pastor-Satorras."

The transport accelerated smoothly beneath them and left the gawpers behind. Eogan steadied himself with one hand as inertia pressed him into the seat next to her. Their thighs touched.

Dear Jesus, she thought in response to long-forgotten feeling. *He even* smells *the same.*

"Why are you really here?" she asked him, edging away and turning so she could face him. "You're obviously not going to spill any great secrets, your apology is a hundred and fifty years late, and we have nothing in common anymore. Is there a point to this, apart from some old ships I could probably see more clearly in VR?"

Finally, he looked at her. "I wanted to see you. Does it have to be more than that?"

She searched his eyes. Had he been an ordinary human, she would have thought he was telling the truth.

"It's been so long," she said. "You can't just stroll back into town and offer me a trinket, like I'm some Wild West hooker who'll pretend she's glad to see you."

He smiled at the analogy, but it had the look of a grimace. "That's a little harsh."

"Well, I don't owe you anything, Palmer Eogan. And to be perfectly frank, you don't owe me anything in return. There's a statute of limitations on crap like this." *Or if there isn't,* she added to herself, *there damn well ought to be.*

"I know what you're saying," he said softly. His gaze drifted away from her and settled on his hands. "But you can't erase the silence. That's not something you can get rid of, once it's there. You lay it down, and you're stuck with it forever."

"If you try to blame me for that—"

"I'm not. I know where it started. But I got tired of it, Melilah." He spoke her name carefully, as though afraid his tongue might trip over it. "It's quiet enough in space. The journeys are long, and there aren't many other people to talk to. Palmers are an insular bunch; we don't make close bonds easily, so the thought of leaving people behind for years at a time doesn't bother us, on the whole. Most passengers sleep out the long legs, but we don't have that option. We have to be on our toes, constantly. That gives us plenty of time to think. Plenty of silence in which to play back remembered conversations, and to wonder at conversations that never happened." He took a breath as though to gather himself. "Well, the silence is over now. No matter if you and I never say another word to each other after today, at least that stretch is finally behind us."

She stared at his broad, all-too-familiar face, surprised by the side of him he was showing her, and feeling herself relent a little. *This* was new. And she was an idiot for being thrown by that. She had changed in numerous and very significant ways since she had last seen him. She had to let herself believe that—maybe—he had changed, too.

He seemed to have run out of words for the moment, and so had she. The irony wasn't lost on her. Color and motion swept by as the transport carried them headlong toward their appointment with alien wreckage he had brought to Bedlam.

• • •

The skulls were much larger than Melilah expected, dwarfing the scientist and her team assigned to study them. Spindly, asymmetrical, and self-contained, they couldn't have been more different from Palmer Cells. Technicians swarmed over them like ants, scanning them with delicate instruments.

"I'm not sure what you expect to show us that we won't see on our own, Palmer Eogan." Dr. Attard was a slight, narrow-faced Natural wearing an all-encompassing white cleansuit. Melilah and Eogan had been sprayed on entry to the examination facility with a quick-setting nanofilm designed to keep contamination from the alien wrecks. The films didn't interfere with their respiration or senses, and would decay automatically as soon as they left the facility.

Eogan strode confidently around the base of the largest of the seven vessels, trailing Melilah and Dr. Attard in his wake. The alien hull of the vessel was pitted and scored like ancient basalt; Melilah couldn't tell if it was supposed to look like that or if its appearance resulted from long exposure to the interstellar medium.

"There are some things best observed *in situ,*" said Eogan. "You see the hatches? They're all open."

He pointed at various oval holes in the wreck's hull. To Melilah's eyes they looked more like structural flaws than doorways.

"We had noticed that," commented Attard dryly.

"They were like that when we recovered the ships. There were no bodies."

"We have never recovered the occupants of Merchant Bees, whole or in residue. They either decay without trace or are removed from the wrecks."

"Maybe they never had bodies as we know them," commented Melilah.

Eogan glanced at her and smiled. "It's possible. The ships are very old. Any information they contained has long since decayed into noise."

He stopped near a junction between two wide, knobbed "arms." Like a giant, ancient tree, the bulk of the ship stretched up and around them, bulging in odd places and narrowing in others. Even in the low gee, invisible fields were needed to stop the structure from slumping down on them.

"Here." Eogan indicated the oval entrance before them. "Take a closer look at what we've got here."

Attard *tsked* in annoyance. "We will be doing exactly that when you let us. What exactly is it you're trying to show me?"

"We know the Merchant B civilization used matter where we'd use fields. We know they grew doors open and closed where they needed them. We know what their air locks look like." He pointed at the inner lip of the entrance. The material came in layers, alternating porous and solid; it looked fearsomely resilient. "Does this look like an air lock to you?"

Attard leaned closer. "No. There's only one seal." She looked up at Eogan. Her eyebrows met. "What are you trying to tell me? That this is an atmospheric vehicle?"

"I'm not trying to tell you anything. I'm just pointing out an anomaly."

"But that doesn't make sense." Attard leaned back and put her hands on her hips. "What would an aircraft be doing in deep space?"

"It's your job to find that out, I guess."

She nodded, distracted by the problem. "If you don't mind, I think I'd like someone else to look at this."

She hurried off.

Eogan took Melilah's arm. "Come on," he whispered. "In here."

She resisted automatically as he tried to pull her through the oval entranceway. "Wait a second." She yanked herself free. "I don't think this is a good idea."

"It's okay. We won't damage anything."

There was an urgency to his gaze that was totally at odds with his light, almost playful manner. "What are you up to?"

"Nothing. Trust me, Melilah. This is your big chance."

To do what? she almost responded. She thought of her probation and wondered what a scientific violation might cost her. Was it worth it just to step inside a ship of unknown age built by unknown hands?

But a small part of her whispered that maybe this wasn't what Eogan meant.

She nodded, and he waved her ahead of him. Apprehensive, she kicked herself up a tube wide enough for two people that kinked and contorted like an ossified intestine. Unlike Bedlam's pipes, the walls were rough under her hands; if she misjudged a push, she'd suffer a nasty scrape. The ambience darkened around her as the entrance fell behind them.

He pulled her to a halt in the crook of a right-angle turn. There was another entrance ahead, but it hadn't quite come into view. "Here will do."

"I don't see anything special about it," she started to say, but he put a hand on her shoulder and leaned in close to her ear. His voice was hurried and emphatic, all sense of play utterly gone.

"Listen carefully: there's something about the Occlusion you need to know. I can't tell you in public because the Exarch will hear. I brought you here because the wrecks aren't tapped yet. It's the only place where we can speak in private."

She checked her watchmeter. It said zero.

Her heart beat a little faster. "Okay. Tell me."

His words were hot in her ear. "I will. But you have to be careful. I can understand Deangelis wanting to keep this secret. People might panic if word gets out."

"Is this something to do with your missing crew members?"

"Yes. I have it all on fiche. We—"

He looked up at a slight sound from the entrance above them. She couldn't see anything, but that meant nothing. Airborne drones were tiny. The Exarch could take control of one and fly it into the ship as easily as thinking about it.

She glanced at her watchmeter. It said *one.* If Eogan gave her a fiche now, the Exarch would see him do it. And there would go her only chance to know what was going on.

She grabbed the front of his shipsuit and pulled him hard against her. He resisted for a bare microsecond, then their mouths met. She felt his left hand, shielded by their bodies, slip in and out of his pocket and into one of hers. Then it was pulling her closer to him still, and she knew she should have been pushing him away. Her lips parted automatically, relishing the taste of him . . .

A shrill voice calling their names from below lifted the spell. "What are you doing? Come down from there at once!"

They separated, faces burning. Melilah could feel the heat steaming off him—and her, too. She hadn't been kissed like that for one hundred and fifty years.

Damned pheromones, she swore to herself. *They haven't changed, either.*

"We're on our way!" Eogan called down to Dr. Attard. He glanced back at her, and his flush had become one of embarrassment and apology. "That wasn't what I wanted—or expected—to happen."

She smoothed herself down. For the benefit of the camera watching them, she said, "The cliché upsets me more than anything else, although I hate to admit it."

When they reached the bottom of the shaft, Dr. Attard was waiting for them with a stern expression on her face. Members of her team clustered behind her, clutching scientific instruments as though they were weapons.

"You were gone too long," Eogan explained smoothly, "and we got bored. Melilah has never been inside a Merchant B before. There's no substitute for firsthand experience."

"If you've contaminated the sample—"

"You've still got six more." Eogan didn't feign annoyance at her attitude. "*Contamination's* the least of your worries," he muttered.

"We're sorry if we've caused you any inconvenience," said Melilah, still thinking of her probation. "Thanks for your time. We'll get out of your hair now."

"That's an excellent idea."

Attard escorted them to the door and coldly sealed it behind them. Melilah resisted the urge to make a face at it, like a rebellious teenager.

"Do you have time to grab something to eat?" Eogan asked her, as they kicked themselves along Barabási Straight toward less industrial regions. "It's been a year since I had any real food."

She surreptitiously touched the flexible plastic square that he had put in her pocket.

"I've got a few other things to chew over first."

His nod was steeped in disappointment. "I understand."

"Will you go back to the *Nhulunbuy*?"

"I don't have to. Not yet."

"Perhaps you should stick around for a bit, then." She felt tired, then, afraid that he would take her meaning the wrong way. She just wanted to talk about the contents of the fiche once she had read it.

"I understand," he said again, like a simple voice-response program. That impression—that he was an artificial, false thing, a machine—contrasted with the vividly remembered feel of his tongue touching hers, and she felt suddenly nauseous.

"I'm going this way," she said, kicking into the nearest pipe and propelling herself as fast as she could along it, away from him.

He took the hint and didn't follow. When she dared to look behind her, he was gone.

+II

Tanglers, holes in the quantum foam, a dire warning from someone who had once been a dear friend . . .

The intricate mechanism that was Exarch Deangelis's extended mind had lost some of its clockwork momentum. He felt isolated and beset upon at the same time. All he needed was for word to get out, so he would have a riot to deal with as well.

Only then, as he checked on the whereabouts of Palmer Eogan, did he realize that his greatest domestic security risk had gone missing. He wasn't on the *Nhulunbuy,* having flown to the habitat some hours earlier. Standard surveillance had tracked him on his arrival and followed him through his wanderings. His location should have been instantly accessible.

But it wasn't. A sweep of the entire habitat revealed no trace of his whereabouts. And it wasn't just him. Melilah Awad was missing as well.

Deep in the forgotten folds that had once been known as Milgram's Crossing, Exarch Deangelis broke into a cold sweat. He called up every available record of their movements, and within microseconds had traced Eogan and Awad to the Merchant B artifact examination facility hastily cobbled together off Barabási Straight. There were numerous surveillance cameras and other sensors in the chamber and adjoining areas. None of them contained the missing pair.

Inside the artifacts. He scanned through the recordings to pinpoint their probable location with greater accuracy. Sensitive vibration sensors caught the sound of voices from within one of the alien ships, but the hulls were too dense to penetrate with the resources available. In the time it took for Iona Attard to take one step, Exarch Deangelis commandeered a remote probe from its human operator and sent it arcing at full velocity into the nearest hull opening.

They were exactly where he expected them to be. And they looked guilty, like illicit lovers caught in the middle of a hurried embrace. He was about to transmit a warning when he realized that that was *exactly* what they were.

He wasn't a slave to hormones as less evolved humans were, but he understood their operation. During his training, he had been deliberately subjected to the emotional storms such primal chemicals could cause, the better to understand the people who would ultimately be under his care. Emotions were, like senses and the intellect, a means of understanding and interacting with the world. And just like Natural human senses and intellect, they were imperfect. Sometimes they overrode the *actual* signals one was supposed to be paying attention to.

Was this what Palmer Eogan and Melilah Awad were experiencing: an emotional storm ignited from century-cooled ashes? He knew their history, and what it must mean to both of them to be reunited after so long. The senses available to him registered temperature and respiration rises in accord with that theory. But he couldn't let himself believe that this was the entire story.

Even when they kissed, and the signs of biological arousal reached new heights, he refused to accept that he could relax.

Exarch Deangelis stayed silent, transfixed by their embrace. He who was not a slave to biology could not begin to imagine what an exchange of complementary chemicals must feel like. He could only stand outside it and watch from afar, a stranger staring out of the bushes at the heat of a campfire and the people warming their hands around it.

He had seen people kiss before. He had watched them court each other, dance around each other with all the grace and blind determination of animals convinced that what they were doing was unique and special. He had seen them make love, have sex, fuck to utter satiation; he had heard the words they used and comprehended with clinical intimacy the processes involved.

He had never experienced *longing* before.

"Hello, Isaac," said a voice he hadn't heard over light-speed channels since the heady days before the Exarchate Expansion. "I'd like a berth, if you'd be so kind."

He wrenched his attention away from the two lovers, already

pulling apart at the outraged cry from the scientist below. Every part of him was focused on that moment, transfixed. Only with difficulty did he realize that he wasn't alone.

"Lazarus?" He hurriedly shook himself together. Lazarus Hails of Kullervo-Hails system, last seen impersonating Bode's Nebula, had arrived. "You've caught me at an awkward time, I'm afraid. My facilities here are—"

"Perfectly sufficient for one small hopper, surely."

Exarch Deangelis scanned the skies for Hails's vessel. Unexpected though it was, Exarch Hails did appear to have arrived in the tiniest of single-passenger craft. His tangler was still stationed far out of the system, carefully camouflaged to all but Deangelis's most perceptive eye.

"You're not an invasion fleet, then," he said.

"Don't sound so relieved, my boy. I'm here purely in an advisory capacity—and already I can tell I'm needed." Hails's hopper curved in toward the habitat with no high-tech displays of deceleration. "Don't give me any special treatment. I'll be just one of the puppets, as far as anyone's concerned."

Exarch Deangelis instructed Traffic Control to allocate the incoming hopper a vacant berth, and took the moment to think the new development through. Lazarus Hails hadn't made the seven-plus-light-year trip from his system just to talk. There had to be more to it than that.

He scanned the hopper as it came in to dock. Lazarus Hails's body contained no obvious threats, overt or covert. It was a standard shell through which Exarch Hails's expanded intelligence could operate. Outwardly it looked perfectly human, taking the appearance of a large man with profuse white hair and strong chin. The only difference to the standard design lay in expanded memory and processing capacities. Hails had packed as much of his extended mind as possible into the shell before committing it to the front line.

Hails's patriarchal physical appearance was designed to trigger subconscious feelings of submission in his charges, thereby decreasing the likelihood of rebellion. Exarch Deangelis had gone down the opposite path, choosing the likeness of a young, slightly sexless male. There was room for such divergent philosophies in the Exarchate, which ruled many hundreds of human colonies, scattered across the bubble of human space, each of which had different needs.

"Everything's under control," he told the new arrival, using secure channels unknown to the people in his charge. "I can manage without your help."

"You think so, now," said Hails as he climbed out of the hopper and flexed his long limbs. "I assure you that will change."

Exarch Deangelis bristled at his words. "Are you threatening me?"

"Hardly, my boy. But there are plenty of others who will. As soon as word got about what you had coming your way, no one's wasted any time."

"How *did* word get out?"

"One can only wonder. Someone's either made an intelligent guess or taken advantage of a leak back home."

"Who did you hear it from?"

"I received word from your friend and mine: Lan Cochrane."

Cochrane was the Exarch of the system formerly called Alioth by ancient Earth astronomers—and the closest to Lut-Deangelis by a hair. She and her compatriot Giorsal McGrath in neighboring 78 Ursa Major had ruled the Arc Circuit ever since the Expansion. Neither of them took kindly to any suggestion that *his* system would be a more sensible choice for regional capital.

Cochrane might well have alerted other systems in order to goad them into action rather than taking direct steps herself. The tricky questions were: who else had taken the bait, and in what fashion?

"You haven't actually told me what you've got," said Hails. "Am I safe in assuming that what I've heard is correct?"

"That depends on what you've heard." Exarch Deangelis repressed a sigh of weariness. "Come on in, and we'll talk properly. I'll give you a false ID to cover you while you're here and show you the data I've recovered so far. If nothing else, I could use a second opinion on that."

"Excellent. A tour of the object in question would be welcome at some point, if I could take one without arousing suspicions."

"Not at the moment, I'm afraid."

Hails cocked an eyebrow. "Natives restless, are they? We'll see what we can do about that, too."

You'll keep your damned hands off my habitat, Exarch Deangelis thought to himself.

But he said nothing.

In response to that silence, Hails laughed and walked grandly among Exarch Deangelis's subjects.

+12

"So what happened in the skull?"

Palmer Eogan looked up from his meal into the knowing smile of Luisa Pirelli. He couldn't meet her stare.

"You didn't see?"

"Oh, no. It was a complete blackout while you were in there." She put her chin in one hand and narrowed her blue eyes. "You're not going to tell me that was an accident, are you?"

He shook his head. Luisa's partner, James, returned from the kitchen with another bottle of wine and he thought he might be spared the interrogation. The hope was short-lived.

"We may like living in the dark ages, Lu and I," James said, tugging at an imitation cork with a manual opener, "but we're not idiots. And we know *you,* friend. You can't pull anything remotely fleecy over our eyes."

As fragrant Shiraz gushed into his glass, Eogan leaned back in his chair and told himself that they meant well. Despite his late notice, the evening had been perfect. The two of them had prepared a roast that had all the texture and nutritional properties of the real thing—along with the taste, which was exquisite. The act of savoring every mouthful left little opportunity for talk, but he managed in about half an hour to bring them up to date on the years since they'd last dined together.

They waited for him to answer with the patience of ages. Compact, dark-haired Luisa was an archeologist specializing in First Wave colonization. James was taller and long-faced, and a pre–Space Age historian. Both were determinedly anachronistic.

Not only did they refer to themselves as husband and wife, but they both also wore corrective glasses and sported various degrees of biological imperfections. Their apartment was a fair imitation of a twenty-first-century Western abode, complete with up-down orientation and latched doorways. There were some things they couldn't replicate: the wine for one had to be squeezed out of a plastic bottle and would have floated away had not field effects kept it in the glass. James's tie kept rising up to his chin. But the pretense was an admirable one, and Eogan was grateful for the effort they had made.

He owed them, he supposed. Within reason.

"I just wanted to talk to Melilah," he said, "without a thousand eyes watching."

"Only a thousand?" Luisa looked at James and raised her eyebrows. "Is that all it rated?"

"I think he's being metaphorical." James used a fork to scoop a gravy-soaked segment of roasted carrot into his mouth. Slightly muffled, he continued, "And his point is not invalid."

"Most people would be proud of such a moment," she said to her husband. "When I think of all those soap operas and reality TV shows we had to sit through for your thesis . . ." She grimaced. "If they'd dared cut a climax like that, the viewers would've sued!"

"My life isn't a television show," Eogan protested.

"It is if you come to Bedlam," Luisa corrected him.

He couldn't argue with her on that point. He had known the laws before setting course. There were no exceptions—except, maybe, for the Exarch, and no one had yet found certain signs of that. Any odd blank spots inevitably attracted attention.

He wondered if that was why Melilah had seemed angry when they'd parted. It couldn't have been the kiss, since it was she who made the first move. Nor could it have been the offer of information. Was it that he had robbed her public record of a dramatic moment many people would have longed for?

The theory wasn't unlikely to be true, but it didn't accord with what he knew of her. He would have to wait to see what she did next, after she had read the fiche.

"Okay," he said, resigned to telling at least part of the truth. "I was afraid of looking like a fool. You know how long it's been since we last saw each other. I had no idea how either of us was going to react. I didn't want to screw things up with the entire colony watching."

"And *did* you screw it up?" James asked, eyes alight.

"You both looked a bit flustered when you came back into view," said Luisa.

"I don't know," he confessed. "It's too early to tell."

"Yes, probably." Luisa diverted her gaze from him at last. She looked satisfied by his answer, as though she had expected nothing more. He was briefly tempted to shock her by revealing that he had in fact kissed Melilah, but the impulse quickly passed. He still didn't quite believe that it had happened himself.

"Don't eat too much," she said, helping herself to another spoonful of peas. "There's dessert to come."

Eogan went for seconds, safe in the knowledge that he could eat as much—or as little—as he wanted.

"We'll ease off on the Melilah front," James said, washing down his food with more wine, "if you tell us what you found between here and Mizar."

Eogan feigned exasperation. "Don't you people *ever* let up?"

"Not when one of our best friends lies to us," said Luisa, poking him in the side with one purple-polished nail. "You said you didn't know if it was a ROTH artifact—then there were skulls practically dropping from the skies."

"It seemed prudent to keep the truth under wraps," he said, knowing the excuse wouldn't cut plasma. "Think of it as a reflex action. I'm sorry."

"Forgiven—if you tell us what *else* you brought." She raised her chin in challenge. "What's in that observatory up there, Palmer Eogan?"

He shook his head. "I really don't know for sure, Luisa. Honestly this time."

"But you have an opinion," she said. "Why not share it with us?"

And the rest of the colony? He wondered what would happen if he tried. The Exarch could kill him before he finished the sentence, if he so desired.

"I'll pass for the moment."

"There are a number of theories in circulation," said James, wiping his lips on a cloth napkin. "One is that you found a whole new class of vessel—maybe even a working Merchant Beehive. With crew still in hibernation, waiting to be woken up."

"Now that would be a find," Eogan said.

"There are numerous variations ranging from operable superweapon platforms to research stations containing the original exogenesis germ line."

"James accepts that all of them *might* be true," said Luisa, fondly patting her husband's knee.

"There's always a chance, no matter how remote."

"Your mind's as open as ever, then," said Eogan. "That's good to hear."

"Well, there's the lunatic fringe," James went on. "Those who think you've found the Grail, the Ark, a generation ship stocked with Yeti, whatever fantasy's triggered them off this month."

Eogan laughed easily. "I can solemnly swear that there are no Grays within a light-year of this habitat."

"Most people just assume it's got something to do with the Sublime Catastrophe," James concluded. "And I can understand that. It's the one big setback we've had with the ROTH, and it happened only ten years ago. Putting it together with this thing—which seems to have both you and the Exarch completely on edge—is an obvious if not entirely logical operation."

Eogan did his best to maintain the smile. It had died inside the moment James mentioned Sublime. "I guess we'll see. The Exarch has to tell us what he's found eventually."

"Deangelis doesn't have to tell us a damned thing if he doesn't want to. And neither do any of the Gentry. They're as bad as you are." James took the sting off the comment by raising his glass. "And here you are, my friend. Whatever brought you here, wherever it takes us, it's nice to see you again. Here's to happier times."

Eogan toasted with his friends, although the taste of the wine had turned bitter on his tongue, and all appetite for the feast had vanished.

What are you doing right now, Melilah? he wondered. *We gorge ourselves on the brink of destruction. We take our fill while, unknown to us, death may already be spreading its dark wings over this fine, strange world you have made. Is there anything I would say to you now, if this was the only moment I had left?*

Eogan's depressive mood swing did not go unnoticed. His friends let him go when he protested weariness, even though they knew as well as he did that physical tiredness was another complaint from which he need never willingly suffer. Taking a transport, he instructed it to fly at random through Bedlam's many tangled ways, wherever its miniscule AI whim took it. He turned down numerous offers of accommodation from the generous and the mercantile both. A room didn't interest him. The last thing he wanted was to be shut up alone again.

Read the fiche, Melilah, he wanted to tell her. *Read it, and find us a way out of this god-awful mess.*

+13

Melilah floated in the center of her pitch-black apartment. To the casual observer, she would have appeared asleep, but she was very much awake. She had gone back to her apartment as soon as she'd left Eogan, but hadn't immediately accessed the fiche. That would have drawn too much attention. Instead she memory-exercised for an hour, then joined Yasu for a quick meal. Her four-daughter had been full of questions and speculations about Eogan again, and to avoid them would also have looked suspicious. She had to go about her life as though nothing more urgent than usual was pressing.

She said nothing about what had actually happened in the alien wreck, but Yasu knew her well enough to guess that a secret was being withheld from her. Her sly almond eyes gleamed.

The fiche Eogan had given her weighed in her pocket like an anvil.

There's something about the Occlusion you need to know.

She shrugged off Yasu as soon as politely possible and headed back to her quarters.

But you have to be careful.

She went through her usual preparations for sleep, getting into silken purple pajamas that tied at wrists and ankles, setting an alarm for three hours hence, and turning down the lights.

I can understand Deangelis wanting to keep this secret.

The fiche was in her left hand, palmed as she had undressed. She sank into low gee and brought it up to her face, half-opening her fingers as she did.

People might panic if word gets out.

And well they might, thought Melilah, if there was any connection between what had happened in Sublime and what had come to Bedlam—as Angela Chen-Pushkaric of her Defiance meetings suspected. The Exarch might fear political and economic instability more than the sheer loss of life should the Catastrophe be repeated, but she knew squarely where her priorities lay. If either Eogan or the Exarch had willingly put her home and her friends at risk, she wouldn't rest until she saw them both take a long walk out an air lock.

For a moment, though, she hesitated. What if it wasn't an ordinary data fiche at all? What if it contained dreadful Palmer programs that would get into her system and corrupt her, change her, *dehumanize* her? She didn't want to be like Eogan. She didn't want to be Alice foolishly swigging at the bottle just because it said, "Drink me."

Trust me, Melilah. This is your big chance.

Her lips tingled as she raised the fiche and pressed it close to her chest, where her skin could read it. She opened the fiche and browsed its contents, keeping her hand carefully over it so no one would suspect its existence. It contained an extremely large amount of data, many, many terabytes mostly in the form of detailed reports and analyses, much of it in exotic formats she couldn't read. It had the air of something dumped unceremoniously and at great haste, when an opportunity presented itself. She would probably need Eogan himself to decipher half of it, or else would need access to more sophisticated decrypting tools to nut out the rest. For a good minute she cursed him for forgetting how much she disliked Palmer protocols.

But he *did* know that, she reminded herself. That had been the whole point of their breakup. And he had as good as told her that he had been obsessing over their final moments for one hundred and fifty years, so that wasn't the sort of thing he was likely to forget.

He wasn't stupid. If he wanted her to read it, he must have provided a way.

Melilah looked deeper, beyond the information itself to the way it was arranged on the fiche. Directory structures, file labels, sector assignment, fragmentation . . .

She found it. Buried in a cluster of recovery files was a string of labels that, when taken as a series in order of size, spelled out a message in old ASCII code. She unreeled the string one way, and read nothing but gibberish. Parsing a simple pattern recognition net over it took less than a second, and generated instant results.

The string had been garbled using an eight-digit modifier based on the date 04-03-2287: the day they had last seen one another.

You sentimental fool, she thought, touched despite the cynic inside of her who insisted he was trying just a little too hard to demonstrate just how much emotional baggage he had, where she was concerned.

Putting that aside, she turned over in the darkness and read his message.

Melilah, forgive me. By telling you this, I might well be putting your life at risk. But you need to understand that your life is *already* at risk, irrespective of what I might involve you in. You have a right to know the truth.

What we found between Mizar and Bedlam wasn't an artifact, at least not in the sense that you and I would probably use the word. It wasn't a ship like the Merchant Bees we brought back, although we did find them alongside it. I'm not entirely sure *what* it is—but I know what it looks like to me, and I think it's dangerous to suppress that possibility, for any reason.

A lot of the report is true. The Occlusion was drifting across the lane in the location specified. It looked from a distance like a haze of dust. The dust became a real navigational threat as we approached, even with our magnetic cowcatchers. We had to shut down the VOID drive half an AU out and use thrusters the rest of the way; otherwise, we would've been holed for sure. None of us had ever seen anything like it. No wonder it was screwing up deform ratings so badly.

But it was manageable. Dust is just dust, after all, and there wasn't *that* much of it, not compared to a brown dwarf or microsingularity. All we had to do was take some broad sweeps to mop up the bulk of it, then let robot cleaners do the rest. It'd be gone in a week. Even when we found the Bees clustered around the heart of it, we didn't think we'd have a problem. The skulls made the job *interesting*. They didn't make it difficult.

Only when we took a closer look did we realize we had something weird on our hands. The dust cloud and the wrecks were just symptoms. The real occlusion was in the center, where our probes couldn't get any sensible data. We noticed it first because it was interfering with the signals between the *Nhulunbuy's* components. We got lags where there should have been none, and odd reflections off things that couldn't possibly exist. When we'd isolated our hardware and determined that they weren't causing the problem, we took a closer look at the environment in front of us. There was a patch of space that didn't measure up—and I mean that quite literally. When we tried to pin it down, we got readings ranging from millimeters to light-seconds across. The best we could do was measure the edges, where it *didn't* screw up our signals. We placed it at around five meters across. A perfect sphere, right at the center of the dust cloud. A sphere of something very odd indeed.

We cleared it off as best we could. I don't understand the science too well; it's not my field. Palmer Vermeulen, my SO, described it to me as a "tightly bound region of distressed space-time." We found nothing visibly maintaining it; it didn't seem to be spreading or shrinking, for all the weird measurements we took of it; it was just there. When we sent a probe into it—

that was when things got really strange. The probe disappeared from all our sensors, except for those trained into the sphere.

It's a hole, Melilah. A wormhole. *Not* a singularity; there's no warping outside the boundary; there's no event horizon as we understand them. But it's definitely a hole of some kind. The sphere at the center of the dust cloud is the outside of a kind of multidimensional throat. I don't know what kind of throat it is. Vermeulen couldn't get her head around that part. But it's hellish in there, to say the least. Our first probe was instantly fried, and so was the next one we sent in. The third managed to get back a few microseconds of data before it melted, too. The fourth hinted that there might be something on the other side of the throat, then it, too, burned out.

I don't mind telling you, Melilah, that this thing scares me. I've been traveling the lanes for a century and a half, and I've never seen anything like it: a hole in space you can float right through, if you come at it just the right way, but fry before you reach the far side. What sort of thing is that? Why would someone build it, then set it adrift? I dread to think what would've happened if a Cell had hit it at speed.

That's when I called the nearest colony. I was completely out of my depth, and I needed advice. I had a choice. I could've called Mizar, where we'd come from, but I chose Bedlam because it was closer. I described the thing we'd found, and sent what data we could. The bandwidth is terrible out deep, so I could only give Deangelis a vague description. I thought he'd just laugh at us, call us crazy, and tell us to stop wasting his time. But he didn't. He told us to bring it in immediately. He didn't seem thrown at all by what we'd found.

We were thrown instead. I replied saying that I didn't have the first idea how to shift the thing out of the lane, let alone haul it all the way to Bedlam. He came back straightaway, cool as anything, with detailed instructions of how to convert one of our cargo components into a magnetic cage. The cage would enable us to move the thing we'd found, just like any other piece of space junk. Vermeulen said it was never going to work. But at Deangelis's insistence we tried it, and it *did* work. He may have neglected to tell us how *heavy* it was going to be, drag-wise, but he was right about everything else. The cage took hold, and the thing was caught.

What the hell, I thought. The Exarchs are way ahead of us; they know all sorts of crazy shit. They probably concoct dozens of things twice as weird as this in Sol every day.

We delayed barely long enough to wipe the lane clean and pick up the skulls. The Occlusion itself was tucked up nice and tight, and Vermeulen was happy that we'd have some months yet to poke at it before we handed it over. At the time that didn't seem like such a bad thing. This was obviously the product of advanced ROTH tech, and the more we got from it, the better for us. We burned up several tons of mass on probes, algorithmically designing them so they'd withstand the strictures of the throat. What it's made of, we never found out, but Vermeulen kept talking about exotic matter and negative energies with the Cell AI. None of us could follow them when they started—and probes kept coming back with even stranger data.

After the throat, things level. It begins to look like almost plain sailing. Almost.

Vermeulen was becoming pretty good at keeping the probes alive, and the data they were sending back from the far side was amazing. Zero radiation; zero gravity; zero hazard. If this thing was a hole, we asked ourselves, then where does it lead? The pictures from the probes couldn't have been less interesting, only adding to our curiosity. A wormhole could take us anywhere in space *or* time. Even if this one opened in the heat-death of the universe, that would be something!

Vermeulen wanted to go through, but I wouldn't let her. Two volunteers went instead: Palmers Cobiac and Bray, two people I'd served with for thirty years. Vermeulen kitted them up like high-tech torpedoes, morphing their bodies back to the bare essentials and giving them everything they'd need to survive the passage through the throat. At that point in the journey, we were one month from Bedlam. Deangelis didn't know what we were doing. The ftl link doesn't work when the VOID drive is on, so there was no way to tell him, even if we'd wanted to. All of us were aware that we had a shrinking window in which to find out what was on the other side before the Gentry took over.

But even then I was having second thoughts. Deangelis's reply had been too quick, too assured. He *knew* something about this thing: what it was, or how it worked, at least. How had he pinned it down from our quick description? He or another member of the Exarchate must have seen something like it before. But where? There was nothing in the records that I had found. If the Sol labs have been building holes in space behind our backs, we've yet to see any sign of them. And the only other truly anomalous ROTH artifact we've ever come across, and about which we know next to nothing, caused the Sublime Catastrophe.

By the time the connection truly began to worry me, it was too late to cancel the expedition. Cobiac and Bray were ready to go. Vermeulen was acting like she expected me to pull the plug at any moment; maybe she was hoping I would, since she didn't have the guts herself. But with nothing but my own misgivings to go on, I didn't feel I could do anything, and let the mission go ahead as planned.

Cobiac and Bray went into the Occlusion, and they survived the throat intact. What they saw on the other side wasn't unexpected; we'd had pictures back from the probes, after all, and it wasn't interesting viewing. But the subjective experience, the knowledge that *one of us* had gone through something so strange and emerged unscathed, *was* amazing. It gave us a sense of subjectivity—of *reality*—that had previously been lacking.

Space is curved on the far side, wrapped around itself to form a tunnel that stretches into the distance in a perfectly straight line. The throat is at one end. We still don't know what's at the other. Cobiac and Bray took passive readings, but picked up nary a photon from more than twenty meters into the tunnel. They tried radar and got nothing back from that, either. The vacuum is as pure as our detectors had ever registered before—which is saying something; remember that the *Nhulunbuy* is a sweeper Cell—so that ruled out any sort of sonar. Seismic readings were nonexistent. Cobiac tried going a little farther up the tunnel and reported some odd spatial distortions. At five meters from the throat, he stopped, then came back to check the link. He measured his return journey at over seven meters.

I should've called them back then. My gut

was screaming that something was severely fucked up, that if we pushed our luck any further, it was all going to go wrong. But Vermeulen kept at me, and I knew we might not get a second chance. We *had* to know what was at the other end of the tunnel—and both Cobiac and Bray wanted to find out. If I'd been in their shoes, I would've wanted to go, too.

So I let them. I authorized an advance to fifty meters. They sent back a transmission from forty saying that everything was fine, that the way ahead was clear. And that was the last we heard of them. One minute they were there; the next they were gone. Telemetry completely lost them. We waited—hours at first, then days—but they never came back.

Vermeulen sent a probe after them. It disappeared, too. A closer examination of its final transmissions picked up further weird special effects. There were signal lags over the final few microseconds suggesting that its actual distance was far greater than forty meters from the throat. The last ping taken off the probe put its location at just under three hundred kilometers away—as though something had reached out of the depths of the tunnel and snatched it from us.

That was it. I wanted nothing more to do with it. I ordered N-1 sealed until we were in Bedlam. I locked what data I felt safe to give the Gentry into a deep-crypted file and briefed the crew on what they were and weren't to say when we arrived. I wanted Deangelis to think that we'd left the Occlusion alone—because that was the only way we were ever going to get a chance to warn someone about what might actually be going on.

The data is inconclusive, Melilah, but it

is suggestive. If this thing really is a wormhole, then there has to be another end to it. So where does it go? What's waiting for us at the other end?

There's no way of knowing the answer to those questions at the moment, not now the thing's in Deangelis's hands. All I know is that I've already lost two crew members, and I want to leave it at that. Bringing it to Bedlam was the worst thing I could have done. Either way, I lose. The best-case scenario is that everything I've guessed about this thing is wrong: I've lied to the Exarch, risked an interstellar incident, and forced my fears onto you with no sound provocation at all.

Or I'm right . . .

In my worst nightmares, the other end of the tunnel is in the heart of Sublime, and even as you read this file another Catastrophe is boiling our way.

+14

On the lip of hell, an arcane fire burned. In a distant, distracted way, it hurt. Deangelis tried not to notice it, because if he did, it might snare him as it had snared the others who had preceded him and burn him back to nothing. The effort wasn't entirely successful. Deep inside, unacknowledged, part of him was screaming.

"There's a storm coming."

The Exarch pulled himself out of the viewpoint of the fragment of him standing on the brink of the Occlusion. He had too many events happening at once to reply immediately to Lazarus Hails's comment. While the Exarch of Kullervo-Hails system strolled by the mundane temptations of Albert Hall, nodding pleasantly at people he passed and indulging in the occasional real-time conversation, Deangelis was monitoring no less than five significant situations unfolding in widely separated parts of the habitat and beyond. Some of his eyes were on the tangler still masquerading as the globular cluster 47 Tucanae. Hails's tangler in Bode's Nebula—if that was indeed who it belonged to—was quiet, but there were faint signs of activity on the other side of the system. Deangelis could do little more than guess at its nature, while at the same time battening down the hatches for whatever it augured. Habitat security, internal and external, had been surreptitiously increased on several fronts. It didn't appear that anyone had noticed yet, but he kept a close watch on that, too.

The influx of data from Sol continued to mount. His hourly reports were met with the most cursory of replies from home, assuring him that help was on its way. Although tempted to connect such blandishments with the mysterious tangler, he was wary of accepting such a comfortable assumption without further evidence. And without knowing what sort of help Sol was sending, exactly, it wasn't much of a comfort.

Defiance, the local and largely ineffectual resistance group, had met again, this time without Awad and some of the more reasonable voices to keep them in check. Their stridency warranted close observation, lest they provoke unrest at a critical juncture. The local crime rate was up, as were information infractions. With several Cells now on station around the habitat and more on the way, numerous destabilizing influences were entering the picture, one by one. The *Inselmeer* had come, its chief officer declared, to renegotiate the terms of its trading agreement with the colony, seeking to renege on a science and technology clause the Palmers had signed decades ago. The Arc Circuit's Negotiator Select, Palmer Christolphe, had made the long journey from Ansell-Aad to stick his nose into the situation, and had already hinted that he knew more than he had previously let on. A bluff, Deangelis assumed, but one he couldn't afford to ignore. A clane of identical bodyguards accompanied Christolphe everywhere he went. They were in the process of unloading the Negotiator's administrative paraphernalia and relocating it all in the habitat's business district.

At any other time, this development would have pleased him. To have Palmer Christolphe in-system was a boost to Lut-Deangelis's significance in the region. But with so much else going on—and the Occlusion that provoked it all still requiring constant study—he barely had a moment to consider the ramifications. He could only take it at face value and assume that Christolphe hadn't come for a social visit.

A storm was coming. Hails was absolutely right, in his bluntly provocative way. Deangelis could feel it in every part of his extended being—like a spider sensing vibrations in the web from which it hung. Crisis was inevitable, sooner rather than later. He just couldn't tell which direction it was coming *from.*

"Try the Pinot Noir at Ormerod's," he advised Hails, feigning disaffectedness. "You'll find it surprisingly pleasant."

Hails did, smiling charmingly at the maître d' and paying with a debit line put in place by Deangelis. He settled into the zero-gee bar like a debonair autocrat from the late twentieth century, ruby red wine in one hand and eyes that took in everything around him. Outwardly relaxed, he, too, was surfing the channels, dipping into the habitat and tasting its many flavors. Deangelis monitored his mental movements closely, wondering what conclusions the visiting Exarch was drawing.

"You're not fooling anyone, you know," Hails said. "This is too big for you."

"The situation is under control."

"There's no shame in admitting otherwise, Isaac. I'd have been outclassed, too, if the Mizar Occlusion had come to my system. You need help, and I'm here to offer it to you."

"Sol will provide."

"We're a long way from Sol, my friend. Their objectives are not necessarily ours."

Deangelis couldn't argue with that. The Exarchate had its rifts and tensions just like any human society. The Arc Circuit, although part of the Exarchate, regarded itself as semiautonomous, when it suited it, and the individual systems within the Arc Circuit did the same. Deangelis wasn't immune to the impulse, either, but he remained acutely aware that he was in power by the grace of the home system.

"That doesn't mean," he said coolly, "that Sol's objectives are wrong."

"They sit in their ivory towers and dictate to us, unaware of the harsh realities of colonial life."

"If they're not aware, it's because we have failed to *make* them aware. That's one of our primary functions."

"They're as removed from us as we are from the puppets. They've forgotten what it's like down in the trenches. No—they've never known. Sol might as well be in a different galaxy, sometimes. What holds there doesn't apply here."

Deangelis wondered what the Archon would think of such talk. "That's why they're sending someone here," he said, hearing the naïveté in his words even as he uttered them.

Hails laughed derisively. "They're coming to take over. At the first whiff of trouble, they dispel the illusion that we're even remotely autonomous and apply the iron heel. We would do that to *our* subjects; why wouldn't they do it to us?"

Deangelis's first instinct was to deny that he *would* do that to his subjects. Even with activists like Awad and Defiance wandering freely through the habitat, he had never had to apply force to maintain control. Authority was an emergent property; it couldn't be forced on a system. Not for long, anyway. After the initial Expansion, he had tried to insinuate himself into the life of the habitat so the thought of doing without him was inconceivable. In return for granting him that authority, he allowed the system its odd perks—open information laws and the like.

He felt that, for the most part, his method was working. Awad and Defiance were exceptions, not the rule. Most people in the habitat had become accustomed to his presence and, through him, that of the Exarchate. Undisturbed, he was certain he could guide his wards to the best possible future available to them.

Undisturbed . . . That, he supposed, was the problem.

Palmer Christolphe hailed him to schedule a meeting. The Defiance group decided that they should take action immediately, somehow. A fight broke out in a public reading room that left one woman with a broken nose and another hollering for security. Lazarus Hails sipped his Pinot Noir and cast a knowing, aloof eye across the people around him.

Deep in the heart of an impossible space, another fragment of Exarch Deangelis vanished from sight, perhaps never to be seen again.

He remembered:

On the morning of his birth, the sun was shining. He opened his eyes on a world of color. Wind blew across a field of green grass, making it ripple. Leaves rustled. Clouds scudded through the sky in slow motion, casting liquid shadows upon the world.

He knew where he was and *who* he was. Spring had come to the Clare Valley early, in a profusion of colors. He was leaning with his back against a rough-barked eucalyptus near the summit of a low hill, high enough to see that there had once been a settlement near a small creek below. Stubs of walls protruded from thick tufts of grass; straggly rosebushes clutched with skeletal hands at long-decayed water tanks; tilted, crumbling slabs of tarmac revealed where roads had once led.

Part of the one who had made him had lived there, once. A long time ago, when humans had walked the Earth.

The name *Isaac Forge Deangelis* had been chosen for him by his maker. The Archon wasn't his parent, and he wasn't the Archon's son, but intrinsic to their relationship—even at such an early stage—was the awareness that one had generated the other. The process was complicated, intuitive, and unpredictable. As with biological breeding, input was taken from many sources, and much was left to chance. Not even the Archon, with its godlike intelligence, could know what Isaac Forge Deangelis would be like when allowed to live in his own right.

And Isaac Deangelis *was* alive. There was no doubting the fact. He might not have been conceived of human parents or grown in a flesh-and-blood womb, but he felt life coursing through him just as vigorously. He wasn't a robot, or a homunculus, or a golem. Nor was he a puppet dancing at the Archon's will, with an illusion of self pasted over it to make it think it was alive.

The wind stroked his bare arms, and the sun bathed his face. The scent of a clean, free world made his nostrils tingle.

Then something very strange happened.

On the moon, another version of him was born. He, too, opened his eyes and embraced the world before him: the rolling gray regolith and the vault of stars above. An orbital tower cast one single stark, brilliant line across the sky, where it caught the Earthlight and reflected it down upon him. He, too, wondered at the complicated process of his creation and his relationship to the Archon.

The awareness that there was another person exactly like him cut across Deangelis's existence as a siren would through a symphony. They were identical in every initial condition, but they weren't the same person. Their experiences diverged with every passing moment. The version of him on the moon was delayed by some seconds, giving their overlapping thoughts a jarring, disconcerting beat, like two tones almost alike played at the same time.

Six seconds was the time it took light to travel from the Earth to the moon, and vice versa. It was likely, then, that the two of him had awoken at exactly the same moment, and only once the light-speed lag had been surmounted had their thoughts begun to overlap.

Another six seconds passed, and he began to receive his twin's response to feeling *him* awaken on Earth. The discord was alarming. He, Earth-Deangelis, had automatically assumed that Moon-Deangelis was a secondary creation, but Moon-Deangelis thought exactly the same thing about *him*.

They tried communicating. The lag was difficult to overcome. Next they tried cutting the link between them. It was fixed, part of them. Lastly they tried calling the Archon, but received no reply. They were on their own, momentarily.

Mars-Deangelis woke to a gloomy dawn high on the red world. Dust storms raged around the base of Mons Olympus, obscuring the details from his elevated position. Earth was a brilliant star, far, far away.

Venus-Deangelis chimed in not long after, followed by versions of him on Mercury and several of the larger asteroids. Jupiter-Deangelis joined with a selection of others who had woken on the gas giant's major moons, already knitted into a confused collective by the time light had crossed the distance to Earth. So it went through the solar system: Saturn, Uranus, and Neptune, plus *their* moons, were followed by Pluto and other Kuiper Belt Objects. There were even minds identical to his riding three long-period comets out to the Oort cloud. How far did he extend? he wondered. If he waited four years, would he receive the waking moments of his selves in Alpha Centauri?

The noise was incredible. He could barely hear himself think through the ceaseless babble of his selves. He was drowning, smothering, fragmenting.

But moments came and went when it seemed that, just for an instant, everything gelled. Despite the confusion and the time lags, all his disparate selves fell into synch and reinforced each other, creating a powerful, surging sense of connection. He could tell, instinctively, what Triton-Deangelis was thinking and how Venus-Deangelis felt about their predicament. He was part of a whole, not a piece of a disintegrating mosaic.

He felt grass against his cheek (which Mars-Deangelis distantly acknowledged) at the same time he experienced the taste of sulfur on Io's turbulent winds. He wondered what was happening to him when he reached out one hand to try to sit up and felt methane snow crunch under his fingers. He was dissolving into the relentless rush of self, drowning in the sights glimpsed by eyes identical to his, overwhelmed by so much *him* he could never contain it.

As time went on, the moments of synchrony became more common, until he began to long for them. He imagined that something had arisen from the chaos—not another version of him, but a new creature emerging *out of* him, made from him but not the same as its many parts. It was to him what a tank regiment was to a single tank, or a flock of ducks was to a single duck. A single tank couldn't surround another army; a single duck couldn't control the graceful movement of the flock. The new creature was an emergent property of everything he was, everywhere he was.

A new, permanent standing wave formed from all his different voices. Just as his thoughts rose spontaneously from the cells of his brain, the workings of its mind rose spontaneously from the many copies of him scattered across the system, simultaneously smoothing the chaos and thriving on it. In a matter of days, all the copies of him were integrated seamlessly into the workings of a much larger mind that allowed them freedom and independence, yet depended on the reliable quirks and details that made him who he was on an individual level. No one else could join the collective, just as foreign cells couldn't survive for long in his body. The various versions of him had joined like the flat facets of a magnificent gem, creating something much more wonderful than simple two-dimensional shapes. They contained within them the makings of a whole new dimension of thought and existence.

He underwent in a matter of days an evolution of being that had taken humanity as a whole many thousands of years to attain. He went beyond humanity to another state entirely.

He remembered:

On the morning of his birth, the Archon greeted Isaac Forge Deangelis in a way his components could not begin to comprehend. Linking minds across the great volume of the solar system, he felt embraced by the greater collective that humanity had become. Sol system might have looked empty, apart from the components of numerous minds slowly waking and joining together, but it was in fact full of vast and potent intelligences. They had brewed there for decades, centuries, staring up at the stars and making plans to attain them.

Isaac Forge Deangelis was an Exarch.

The time had come to branch out into the universe.

It was strange, then, sixty years later, to be standing on the brink of another continuum entirely, an artificial space that had been made by minds unknown. He sent his many selves out into the habitat to test its mood and monitor its changes, readying himself for anything. He walked among staring Naturals and more adapted Arc Circuit citizens, all of whom knew his face from pictures but few of whom had met him in person. He sent one to monitor the exploration of the skulls, although he had already determined everything he needed to know from the alien wrecks. He sent one to sit with Hails, joining him for a glass of wine and continuing their discussion face-to-face, by means few of the people around him would recognize as communication at all. He took several transports and traveled the pipes of his domain as an ordinary person might. He passed the one containing Palmer Eogan several times, but did not hail him.

The experiences washed through him like a vitamin tonic, centering him. The Mizar Occlusion was a distraction from his primary concern, which was the maintenance of his colony. Being an Exarch wasn't about seeking personal gain—although having a sense of ambition was important. He had been on the fringe for too long to realize just how far from the center he had drifted.

He smiled at Hails over his glass of Pinot Noir and toasted the mouth of hell.

+15

Eogan woke from a nightmare with a jerk that sent him bouncing around the cramped, unlit interior of the transport. Gripping an armrest and bringing himself to a halt, he cursed himself for nodding off. Palmers didn't need to sleep, but the instinct wasn't excised entirely from their bodies. Some slept for release from consciousness; others for the dreams. Eogan hadn't slept since finding the Occlusion.

Until now.

He had dreamed that he had been standing in a long, straight corridor. Gravity had held his feet to the floor; his clothes had hung from him like lead weights. Behind him was a door—an antique wooden door with a metal handle. The door was shut. He suspected it might even be locked, but he didn't try to open it.

He turned back to the corridor. It stretched ahead of him to infinity, undeviating, lit in regular patches all along its length. His eye caught on the vanishing point, and would have held there but for the feeling that he was being watched back.

He glanced away. *Where to now?* he thought, even though there was only one way to go.

He took one step along the corridor, then another. The door receded behind him, dropping away like the ground during a vertical ascent. Gravity pulled at him, made his knees want to buckle. The vanishing point seemed to draw closer, although he knew that had to be an illusion.

Two more steps, and he reeled as though the corridor had shrugged beneath him. He hadn't had a panic attack since childhood, but this felt very similar. His skin prickled. His heart rate increased.

Two more steps made six in total. The sense that he was completely alone, utterly vulnerable, struck him an almost physical blow. Although constrained in four of the six directions—left, right, up, and down—he felt as though he was hanging in an empty void. Were there dimensions he wasn't aware of? Could something be slouching toward him through time, or along one of the rolled-up Planck-scale spaces?

He managed just one more step before the corridor defeated him. The vastness of the space before him distorted like some cheap visual effect. Something was rushing toward him out of infinity—and with a gut-wrenching jolt he realized it was infinity itself. The atom-sharp point where the curved walls of the corridor met flexed in upon him, folding space so it could stab at him like a rapier. He recoiled with one arm flung up in front of his face and ran for the door.

One step, two steps. A wind sprang up around him. Three steps, four. He heard a howling noise, growing louder. Five steps, six. Space-time crackled and snapped, tearing itself into splinters. Seven steps—the number he had taken into the corridor.

Then—*eight.*

He panicked. How was this possible? He took nine steps, ten steps—but the door was still out of reach.

Eleven!

The corridor snarled.

He lunged for the handle as infinity's teeth snapped at his heels—

—and woke in Bedlam, flying through an anonymous, random pipe with his heart hammering like an overstimulated Natural.

Eogan sighed and tried to put it from his mind. If the Mizar Occlusion was what he dreaded it might be—a wormhole connecting Bedlam to the force that had destroyed Sublime—then it was only natural to be afraid of it. But letting that fear dominate his thoughts, getting in the way of what he needed to do, was irresponsible and dangerous.

Knowing exactly what he needed to do, of course, was the difficult part.

He checked the *Nhulunbuy*'s telemetry and found that he had missed an interesting development.

"When did you hear from him?" he asked Vermeulen, whose

component, N-11, was already preparing for disconnection from the rest of the Cell.

"Ten minutes ago." She affected grumpiness. "Just when I thought I was out of the firing line."

Eogan replayed the conversation between his science officer and Exarch Deangelis. It had been brief and to the point. The Exarch intended to honor his agreement with Eogan, allowing a Palmer presence inside the Occlusion observatory. If Vermeulen was willing to observe, she could join the project immediately. Slightly stunned by the offer, she had accepted.

With Eogan out cold, she and Palmer Flast had begun making the necessary arrangements before the Exarch changed his mind. That could happen at any moment, they knew. The Exarch had no obligation to them.

"You don't have to do this if you really don't want to," Eogan told her.

"Oh, I do," she replied. "I may not like it, but I don't have any choice. I owe it to my profession, curse it, if not to myself."

"You'll keep us up to date, of course."

"As and when I can. That thing is sealed tight. Nothing's gone in or out since it went up."

"If you get into trouble, we'll do everything we can to get you out of it."

"Thanks. It does make me feel better, knowing that you'll be there to rescue me. If you can stay awake long enough."

He laughed to hide an undercurrent of doubt. Was Deangelis giving them access because he thought he had the Occlusion under control—or because he was as stumped as they had been? Or was Eogan missing the point entirely?

He fought the impulse to check in on Melilah, to see if she had read the fiche. Then he gave in to it. She was awake and active, but not on any overtly Occlusion-related business. He could tell from her public record that she was in the middle of some sort of legal wrangle. On probation herself, she was lodging a claim of public harassment against the man called Gil Hurdowar. While she didn't mind Hurdowar watching on principle, she told the appeals AI, Hurdowar had a social obligation to do the right thing by her in return. When she asked him to leave her alone, he should either comply or be discreet. Bombarding her and her associates with constant requests to communicate got in the way of her work. His resistance to her pleas for consideration provoked arguments that affected her public record. She wasn't the only guilty party, therefore; he should be punished, too.

The laws of Bedlam were complex, but no more so than those of any society. Abnegation of the right to privacy was compensated for by the shoring up of other rights: the right to access information at all levels of government at any time; the right to personal physical security; the right to travel unhindered and free of charge within the habitat; etc. Gil Hurdowar could watch anyone he wanted, thirty-six hours a day, and no one could legally stop him; but should he make the slightest move to enter someone's apartment or to damage his or her personal property, he would be hit with severe penalties, including imprisonment or expulsion. "Property" was occasionally defined as goodwill or productivity, so Hurdowar's interference in Melilah's work counted in her case, she argued, as an infringement of the law.

The AI agreed with her argument. Gil Hurdowar lost a slew of privileges he probably wouldn't exercise anytime soon, and then only temporarily. It wasn't much, but it was recorded as a small victory on her part.

Melilah went back to work, searching archival material for information on two women Eogan didn't recognize. If she knew Eogan was watching, she made no sign. Maybe she was ignoring him, or just didn't care.

Eogan allowed instinct to guide him again. He didn't know what made Hurdowar so persistent, and he had no right to act in Melilah's defense. But Hurdowar had tried to contact him as well, and that fact alone made him curious and suspicious.

"The famous Palmer Eogan," said Hurdowar in response to his communications request. The man's face was puffy in low gee. His graying hair stuck out on one side, drifting like lank seaweed. Eyes as brown as a bog regarded him half-lidded, while dry, thin fingers tapped restlessly on naked thighs. "I'm glad you ignored 'Lilah's advice regarding not talking to me."

"I didn't ignore it. I just didn't follow it." He shifted position as the transport took a sharp corner. "What do you want from me?"

"Nothing more than your attention."

"What for?"

"I'm a watcher," the man said. "I see lots of hidden things. Some are down deep, where no one thinks of looking; others are right out in the open, where no one notices. 'Lilah is good at finding the former, but she needs my help with the latter."

"I don't mean to be blunt, but it doesn't look like she wants your help at the moment."

Hurdowar grimaced, sending a landscape of wrinkles spreading across his face. "Ever, to be honest. It's frustrating. There are things she needs to know. I told her that you were coming, for instance. She's very fragile where you're concerned."

Eogan bit down on a sharp response. "Melilah is perfectly capable of looking after herself. She doesn't need you to do it for her."

"She can't watch everything." Hurdowar's lidded eyes were muddy and cool. "She's distracted."

By me, Eogan knew the man meant. And now Melilah had restricted Hurdowar's access to her. "You want me to pass something on to her, I suppose."

A nod sent lank hair waving. "Yes. Obviously you have your own secrets: the missing crew members, for instance. If she doesn't know about them already, then you can tell her in your own time. But there are other details. She needs to know about them, too."

"Like what?"

"The Occlusion observatory. It's very well defended, don't you think?"

"Yes. It would be."

"People remember Sublime and don't wonder that the Exarch is taking precautions."

Eogan frowned, wondering how much the man had guessed. "What's your point?"

"I've studied the design of the station—as much as I can, anyway. 'Lilah's Defiance group has some clever brains among them. They've noted details I couldn't work out on my own. But they haven't worked out what's wrong with them, why they don't make any sense."

"Go on."

"If Sublime is truly the Exarch's concern, why is the Occlusion so well protected from the *outside?*"

Eogan let the thought sink in before responding. "That *would* seem strange, I suppose."

"I've tried asking the Exarch about it, but he hasn't responded."

Of course not. "Perhaps your speculation is wrong. The level of technology is very high. Deangelis doesn't need to explain his actions to anyone."

"He should if the habitat is under threat."

"You really think that's likely?"

"*Likely* I don't know about. *Possible,* yes, I do."

Eogan pictured the colony pinched like a seed between thumb and forefinger, with the threat of the Occlusion itself on one side and something much more nebulous on the other. Who or what would attack the station? And, more importantly, why?

He couldn't think of an answer to the last question—at least not one he wanted to believe, anyway.

"I think you're barking up the wrong tree," he said. "But I hear you, and I'll keep it in mind."

Hurdowar looked resigned to getting no more than that from him. "I'll tell you if I find anything else. There's so much traffic coming in at the moment. There could be anything hidden in it all."

Eogan nodded. He had noticed that, too, before sleeping. One of the manifests had listed the Negotiator Select. If Palmer Christolphe was really in Bedlam, events were taking a truly significant turn.

"Just take it easy," he warned Hurdowar. "Melilah will know we've talked and what we've talked about. If your information is good, she'll listen eventually. Don't let it get personal is my advice to you. She doesn't owe you anything."

Hurdowar's pupils rolled back under his lids. "She's here now. She's listening to us."

"You'd better go, then," Eogan told him. "You're on probation, too, remember?"

The man winked out.

"You don't have to talk to him," Melilah said, her presence sliding into his like cream into coffee, audio only. "I already knew about the station—more or less. Something about it was bugging me. I would've worked it out."

"You're preaching to the choir, Mel."

"About our earlier conversation . . ." She hesitated, and he could tell that she wasn't being literal; she was referring to the fiche. "You mentioned a connection between—you know."

Clever, he thought. Eavesdroppers would think they were talking about each other, not the wormhole.

"I did."

"I don't think you're imagining things. There *is* a connection. But it looks like we disagree on what to do about it. You think it's a bad thing, that it's something we need to sever."

"Of course. Don't you?"

"Not in itself, no. It might even be a good thing. It might be just what I need to get myself out of a sticky situation."

He felt himself grow tight around his midsection. "I'm not sure I follow you." *I hope I don't, anyway.*

"There's a third party—someone whose attentions I'm trying to distance myself from. Do you know who I'm talking about?"

Not Gil Hurdowar, Eogan thought, although many people would assume so. *Exarch Deangelis. The Exarchate.*

"Yes," he said. "I think I do. But the means don't justify the end."

"The means are the whole point. And perhaps that's what you're *really* afraid of, Palmer Eogan. That the means might destroy your precious monopoly."

She was skating perilously close to openly stating the truth. He kept his voice calm and measured. "I'm not interested in monopolizing anything," he said. "I had my hands on it before anyone else here, but that doesn't make me its owner. If I'd wanted it for myself, I could've tried keeping it long before now. Do you think that would've worked? Do you think something like this *can* be owned?"

She was silent for a second. He wished he could see her face. God only knew what those listening in thought of the conversation.

"No," she said in the end. "But it can be *used.* I'd be irresponsible not to try."

"You're making a mistake," he said, feeling it in every artificial cell of his hollowed-out bones. "I came to you for help—not this."

"So we're at cross-purposes again. What's new about that?"

The conversation's sudden shift to old territory left him feeling as though the transport had fallen out from under him. "I'm sorry, Melilah."

"Don't start that again. Either help me get what I want, or stay the hell out of my way."

The line went silent. A transport whizzed by in the opposite direction. Eogan glimpsed a pale, fair-haired face looking back at him and thought: the Exarch?

He shook his head, and wished again that he had never come to Bedlam. Nothing ever seemed to go right there.

+16

Melilah closed the connection to Eogan with the mental equivalent of a slammed-down headset. All her incoming lines failed with it, so she found herself in an illusory quiet, as though she was suddenly and completely alone.

You fucker! she wanted to yell. First he forced her into a position where she sounded like she wanted him back; then he deigned to judge her when he didn't like the conclusion she came to! She was infuriated. Of all people, he should have been sympathetic. He *owed* her!

She knew she was just being petulant, though. She had known in advance that he wouldn't approve of her opinion. He was a Palmer through and through. Anything that threatened the guild's cozy little hegemony was bound to upset him.

But that didn't stop her being disappointed. Part of her, so deep she hardly dared acknowledge it, had hoped that—

What? she asked herself. That they would overcome their differences and work together to cast the demon out of Bedlam? That they would gain access to the Occlusion and use it to strike back at the Exarchate? That wormhole technology would be the key to set humanity truly free? That they would reconcile their differences and give the relationship another go?

You fucker, she cursed again, but with resignation this time, rather than anger. *You screwed up my life once. You won't have me on your side, this time.*

She opened her inputs one by one, reconnecting herself to the constant ebb and flow of information through the station. She didn't need to be in her apartment to access the data. She simply preferred to do it the old-fashioned way as often as possible, without resorting to virtual overlays and other synesthetic means. It wasn't that she was afraid of forgetting what was fake and what was real; she just didn't like fake very much.

For several years she had studied origami, the ancient Japanese art of folding paper, partly as a mathematical exercise but also to clear her mind. She could have fed the patterns into an assembler and had a machine create the finished product for her, with every fold crisp and clean, every point as sharp as a stiletto, but that wasn't the issue. The process was what was relevant, the *experience* of doing it herself. It was the same with the tunnels of Bedlam: she could have sent a remote into the pipes as easily as gone herself; it would've shown her as much detail as her flesh-and-blood senses could retrieve, maybe even more. But it wouldn't have been *her* doing it, and that meant something—to her, if no one else.

When she thought of the Exarchate ruling her home, her gut recoiled just as it did at the thought of using a machine to make a Hojyu ammonite or a simple *yuan bao*. The means might not justify the end, as Eogan had said, but without the right means the end was simply irrelevant.

The Mizar Occlusion could be the key to Bedlam's cage. A wormhole through space offered a way of not just communicating faster than light, but actually traveling between the colonies with greater swiftness than anything the Exarchate could manage. A resistance movement could sweep around the Arc Circuit—indeed, through the entire human territories—in hours, always one step ahead of their oppressors. Ditching it in deep space—as Eogan seemed to wish he'd done—would be as bad as rolling over and accepting Sol's domination.

Yes, there were complications: the real dangers of the wormhole throat for one, and the more nebulous threat of the Sublime Catastrophe for another. But to give up without even *trying?* She wouldn't have it.

She called up a grid showing the location of the Exarch as a series of points plotted on a three-dimensional map of the habitat. Exarch Deangelis was unusually dispersed; he normally kept to himself in a deep section of the habitat, coming out only as required to deal with people face-to-face. Speculation occasionally flared that he kept some sort of secret hideout there, a high-tech retreat for all the many parts of him, but no one had ever confirmed the hypothesis.

Now, Deangelis was crawling over the habitat like a swarm of ants. His deceptively youthful face was everywhere: cruising the pipes, talking to vendors and scientists, in meetings with specialists. One was sitting in a bar in Albert Hall, drinking wine with an imposing white-haired man listed on the public register as a visitor to the station. *Fiddling while Rome burned,* she thought.

Two in tandem were meeting to discuss trade agreements with Palmer Christolphe. The Negotiator Select bristled with high-tech modifications, many of them hidden from the visible spectrum. To a casual glance, he was a solidly built man with no body hair at all and striking orange eyes, dressed in a garment that clenched and unclenched around him like a fist. Microwave links cast a complex web from transmitters on every exposed patch of skin. Delicate-looking fan-shaped field effects fluttered all over his infrared body, their purpose unknown.

"We were unprepared for Sublime," he was saying. A chirruping electronic chorus enhanced his words, making sure his audience captured every possible nuance. Subtitles described his tone as conciliatory but firm. "The ROTH artifact found there took us by surprise. In retrospect, we should have expected such an event before long. There is much in the Dark that has not yet been charted."

The Dark was Palmer slang for the gulf between stars. Melilah could accept the Negotiator Select's point. Inhabited systems and trade lanes comprised a very small percentage of the total volume of space over which humanity claimed dominion.

"I'm sure you do not deliberately discount the loss of life in White-Elderton colony," said one of the two identical Deangelises facing Palmer Christolphe. His tone was biting, no doubt also protesting the use of the pre-Exarchate name of the destroyed system. "That, not scientific or technological gain, is our prime consideration."

"Yes, yes." The Negotiator Select waved away the concern with a gesture. His hands, Melilah noted, had no fingernails. "But we must consider all outcomes when anticipating future developments. You have another ROTH artifact in your custody now. Its origins are similarly unknown."

"That is public knowledge."

"Indeed, but precious little else is. The Palmers would like access to your discoveries, when and as you make them. We are prepared to pay well for such access."

"It is not mine to sell. The information belongs to all humanity."

"But while access is limited, as of the moment, it is tradable."

"Access to data is a right in this system, not a privilege."

"Then why have you released none to those in your charge? You cannot expect us to believe that you have had this thing in your possession for two days and uncovered nothing at all!"

"What I have uncovered is mysterious even to me. That's why I've asked the science officer of the *Nhulunbuy* to assist me. What information we find she will be free to share as she sees fit."

Christolphe's smooth brow creased. "This is a circuitous route toward disclosure. I fail to see the necessity of it."

"And I see no reason to explain myself to you. Our existing agreement has sufficed for thirty-eight years. You haven't offered me a reason to change it now."

Melilah watched with detached amusement as the Exarch stonewalled Palmer Christolphe at every turn. The Palmers were going to get nothing out of Deangelis, just as she had got nothing out of him in the past. He was using the same technique on the Negotiator Select as he had on her. Moving his point of view constantly between identical bodies was distracting. Christolphe, who should have been used to occupying a room with cloned individuals, seemed disconcerted by the constantly changing spokesperson.

Two members of the Palmer's bodyguard stood behind him, listening patiently to the exchange. The clane—a neologism combining "clade" and "clan" with "clone" to describe something that hadn't existed until two centuries earlier, and still wasn't a common variant of humanity—consisted of twelve women of average height, each with the same pointed features and muscular forms, each dressed in identical all-encasing light armor that faded to transparent over face and hands. Slight bulges at thigh and waist hinted at concealed weapons. Grown from the same seed body and imprinted with the same reflexes and personality, their minds operated in perfect tandem, thinking the same thoughts and responding to the same stimuli. The clane was in effect a single person with twelve pairs of eyes, twenty-four hands—and eleven extra lives.

Melilah didn't like them. They made her uncomfortable. The particularly sharp purple of their armor made her eyes want to itch. The remaining ten were, like Deangelis, spread out over the habitat, going about their business with serious, impenetrable expressions. They gave away nothing that was going on in their combined heads.

She sent her point of view upward, out of the habitat to where the *Nhulunbuy* was parked nearby. One of the components was missing, supporting Deangelis's claim that Eogan's science officer had joined the investigation of the Occlusion. She was annoyed at herself for missing that. As much as it galled her to admit it, Gil Hurdowar was right: she *was* distracted. At any other time she would have been taking advantage of the numerous newcomers filling the systems—the Cells, the Negotiator Select and his clanes, the Occlusion itself—to go data-hunting. In all the chaos, all sorts of fragments would be cast adrift, deleted improperly, or simply forgotten. This should have been an opportunity, not an impediment.

Her daily alarm rang to remind her of her memory exercises. She ignored it. *Stuck in the past,* she told herself. That was as dangerous as forgetting.

It had been just two days since she'd last gone gleaning through the deeper tunnels. It felt like weeks. She uncased her crawl-suit and enjoyed the tingling, faintly erotic sensation as it swarmed up over her legs and torso, then down her arms. She had no specific target in mind, but that didn't matter. It was the journey that counted, not the destination; the search, not the rescue.

And maybe, she thought, it was time to pay the Exarch a visit on *his* territory, for a change.

+17

Isaac Deangelis had never claimed to read minds, but he had a very real ability to decipher the signals passing between them.

The clane's thoughts were highly encoded, sweeping constantly from brainpan to brainpan. The two with Christolphe exchanged frequent packets of information with the other ten. Managing so much additional sensory input required considerable sophistication. Signal processing between the twelve bodies, in order to present the illusion of a single self, was a deeply demanding task. A clane, unlike him, was therefore inherently fragile. Disrupt the signals between its bodies, and the illusion would collapse; likewise when separated by more than a few kilometers, so signal lags could accumulate.

Encoded and complex though its thoughts might be, Deangelis could tell that it was waiting for something. A signal of some kind. A sign. Its mind stirred restlessly in its many homes. It was nervous.

Perhaps Palmer Christolphe thought the endless rights negotiations sufficient to distract him from his vigilance. If so, he was going to be disappointed. For whatever reason he had brought the clane to the habitat, Deangelis was watching them both very closely indeed. On top of everything else.

There's a storm coming . . .

"Okay, I'm in." The voice came from Palmer Vermeulen, within the Occlusion observatory. Her integration within the station's infrastructure was complete. "Can you hear me, Flast? Eogan?"

Replies came immediately from the *Nhulunbuy* and the habitat, confirming the connection. Eyes from all over the system were drawn to the exchange.

"Deangelis is as good as his word," she said. "I have access to all the raw data I want."

"That's—pleasing," said Palmer Eogan. Deangelis could tell that he meant *surprising*.

"There's a lot of it," she said, her enthusiasm not matching his. "He's using instruments I'm not sure I even understand. It's going to take me a while to work out what's going on."

A while was an understatement, Exarch Deangelis thought. He doubted a single human, even a Palmer, could penetrate in less than a month the vast amounts of data he had collected so far. And more came in every second.

"Perhaps you can understand, now, why I have been slow releasing it," he said to all of them. "This is no simple skull we're investigating. I am following a carefully coordinated approach, examining every iota of knowledge gained along the way. I do not wish to replicate mistakes that have been made in the past."

That, at least, was the utter truth. He didn't want Lut-Deangelis to vanish in a hellstorm of alien replicators any more than they did. But at the same time he wasn't afraid to tread where Jane Elderton had tripped ten years earlier. He wasn't going to skirt around the edge and let such a pristine opportunity pass him by. Lut-Deangelis was in the thick of things, not out on the Exarchate's frontier.

"I understand." Eogan granted him that much with barely a hint of disapproval. The transport the Palmer occupied was winding its way to the surface of the habitat, heading for the hopper he had arrived in.

Leaving so soon? he thought to himself with a hint of satisfaction. Things obviously hadn't gone so well between the estranged lovers.

Remembering Awad, he checked her location and found her back in the tunnels at the heart of the station. Gleaning again. Running away from reality.

Hails drained his glass and locked it into place on the arm of his low-gee chair.

"Well," he said, clapping his hands down on his thighs, "that's the wine-tasting done with. Unless you've got something else to say, Isaac, there are a number of sights I haven't caught yet. Might as well make the effort while there's time, eh?"

"The art gallery would be my next recommendation," Deangelis said. "You'll find the low-gee environment very congenial to sculpture and dance. In fact, at thirty o'clock there's a performance of—"

He stopped when movement at the periphery of his vision caught his attention.

"Yes?" prompted Hails.

"Wait." Instruments swung around to focus on the globular cluster 47 Tucanae. Emissions on several spectra were flaring. Something was breaking cover.

Hails followed his shift in focus. "Ah. It's begun, then."

The part of him sitting opposite Lazarus Hails looked up sharply. His many hearts beat faster. "What do you know about this?"

"Only what I've told you, my friend." The statesmanlike presence rose to his feet and made to move off. "Don't say I didn't try."

"Where do you think you're going?"

Hails shrugged. "Elsewhere."

A cloud of gleaming, darting shapes boiled out of 47 Tucanae, expanding as it approached the habitat. Instruments scattered across the system rapidly triangulated on the cloud. Its distance was a little under twenty million kilometers, its speed appreciable—nearly twenty percent light. The cloud was not solid right through, consisting of numerous small projectiles that left brilliant drive flames in their wakes.

Missiles—many, many thousands of them aimed squarely at the habitat—and due to arrive in less than a minute!

Deangelis's reaction was automatic. He sounded impact alarms through all quarters. Pressure doors irised shut in slow motion, dividing the habitat into numerous small sections. He set up pressure differentials to encourage people to move into safer locations. All external operations were halted immediately. Cells and other vessels were advised to move clear as a matter of some urgency. Thrusters on the Occlusion observatory nudged it deeper into the shadow of PARASOL. Defenses swung around to bear on the attack.

He broadcast a message to the aggressor requesting an immediate cessation of hostilities. He hid nothing from the occupants of the habitat. They heard his words over all channels, in all quarters. He was speaking on their behalf, not just his own.

Whoever you are, he wanted to shout, *you're not going to get away with this.*

The reply, when it came, was unexpected.

A hand tapped him on his shoulder. He didn't need to turn to see who it belonged to. Cameras throughout Ormerod's wine bar gave him an excellent view of the clane, one part thereof, standing stiffly behind the couch on which he sat.

"Don't mess with what you don't understand."

The words came from every mouth of the clane at once, wherever they happened to be. Somehow, without him noticing, it had positioned itself near eleven of him across the habitat.

"Consider this a warning, Isaac Deangelis."

The explosions—twelve of them in perfect synchrony—tore the clane to atoms, and took a large chunk of the Exarch with them.

+18

Eogan felt the transport kick under him. The Scale-Free Bedlam feed dissolved into chaos.

"What the hell's happening?" he asked his Cellmates, feeling abruptly cut off from the world. He'd been just moments from reaching his hopper when pressure doors had closed around him, cutting him off. His complaints had gone without response.

"Something's going down," said Flast, his voice distorted by unusual interference. There seemed to be several of him all talking at once, all slightly off-key. "You heard the Exarch warn off whoever's attacking?"

"Yes."

"We're picking up explosions from inside Bedlam, although the missiles are still a good half minute off. Hang on. I'll see if we can get you some telemetry"

One half minute, Eogan thought to himself. That was barely long enough to quibble over. There were going to be many more explosions if the things hit.

"Okay," said Flast. "Here it comes."

It felt as though a third eye had opened. Where a moment ago there had been nothing but the inside of the transport and chaotic voices, now clarity bloomed. He saw raw data from numerous viewpoints, rotated a logarithmic diagram of the space around the habitat, and charted the precise location of every component of the *Nhulunbuy,* including N-11 inside the Occlusion observatory. The Cell was relatively safe, not the sitting target Bedlam made. The incoming missiles were tipped with blood red, growing rapidly closer.

Eogan snapped through dozens of internal views in less than a second, seeking the source of the explosions. He saw eleven locations in all, ranging from secure meeting rooms to public places. A bar in Albert Hall was the most chaotic. A black shield had dropped around the locus of the blast, containing it to just a few dozen cubic meters. That was enough, though, to fill the air with smoke and blackened fragments, billowing about in free fall. Several bystanders had sustained minor injuries, one a tall man with hair burned completely away. Their blood added to spilled wine in a terrible floating cocktail. It would take hours to settle.

"Any casualties?" he asked, thinking but not daring to say: *Melilah!*

"Palmer Christolphe was in the thick of it. We're not getting a signal from him anymore." Flast hesitated a beat. "You've got bigger things to worry about, boss. There's something coming in the wake of those missiles. Something big. If the Exarch's defenses are sloppy, you're going to end up looking like a colander."

"Right." Fed up with waiting, Eogan ordered the transport hatch open and kicked himself out of it. He wasn't going to sit still while the world fell apart around him. And he wasn't going to let a nonintervention agreement or two stop him from doing what he needed to do. His left arm was already rearranging itself as he reached the pressure door. It took just three seconds to analyze what the door was made of, determine the best means of cutting through, configure his hand into the appropriate tool, and start drilling. Ten seconds after that, he was on the far side.

Red warning lights flashed in his wake. He ignored them. The view through the telemetry feed was dismaying. The missiles were just moments away, and still nothing had come forward to meet them. He cursed his sluggish body—which wasn't *in toto* anywhere near as fast as its individual components—as he hurried to the hopper bays. He didn't care what he found at the dock; he would appropriate whatever would do the job. He just wanted to get out of what might soon become a floating coffin and get to where he could do some good.

Even as he hurried, his mind reached behind him, into the habitat, looking for Melilah Awad. The feed was still jumbled and chaotic, but not nearly as bad as it had been. Her apartment was empty. She had last been noted traveling the depths of the habitat. Her present location was unknown.

"Keep your head down, Mel," he said, although he knew she couldn't hear him. "I'll be back for you as soon as I can."

+19

Melilah had barely reached the lower levels when the alert sounded. The sirens were piercing, unfamiliar. Their whooping shrieks echoed through the pipes of Bedlam like the cries of deep-sea beasts. It took her a second to interpret them. She hadn't heard their particular signature since the Exarchate Expansion, forty years earlier.

Bedlam was under attack!

She kicked herself forward, carried by a wind that seemed to spring up out of nowhere. Although she was deep in the habitat, she wouldn't be completely safe until she left the pipes. Seismic shocks could propagate unpredictably through the complex tangles of the habitat, snapping links where the pressure waves overlapped and reinforced.

Caught up in her own emergency, she barely had a chance to note what was going on outside. Something about missiles. The Exarch was calling for a cessation in hostilities.

Then the feed abruptly died, and it felt for a moment as though Bedlam died with it. The wind carrying her blew itself out. Silence enfolded her. With no voice and no nervous system, the habitat was drifting through space, derelict.

An icy river of fear swept through her. Had a new Catastrophe struck already? Were swarms of alien replicators already burrowing down to her level, devouring everything she loved with deadly voraciousness?

The reason for the wind's sudden cessation became apparent when she reached the end of the pipe. The way was sealed shut, clenched tightly ahead of her like a hose with a knot in it. She turned back the way she had come, hoping the other end was still open. If it wasn't, she would be trapped.

The feed flickered halfheartedly, granting her frustratingly incomplete glimpses of fires and blood. Explosions. She had felt nothing. She was cut off, irrelevant. Melilah cursed the urge to go deep right when she was needed most!

The pipe curved around to her right. The exit, if it was still open, lay some distance away. She kicked herself along it as fast as she could—so fast she swept by a tunnel mouth almost before she had seen it.

She reached out for the pipe wall and spun herself around. Her inner ears protested. The junction hadn't been there moments before; she was sure of it. It wasn't on the map, either. But it was open and offered an alternate escape route.

A youthful, blond face appeared from the opening. "Awad, get in here," said the Exarch. "There's not much time."

Deangelis's expression was grim. Were they tears drying on his cheeks? She swallowed her surprise and did as she was told.

Following him along a short tunnel that was barely wide enough for her to crouch in, she entered a large chamber shaped like an oval sombrero: fat in the middle and thin around the edges. They emerged to one side of the central bulge, where she was confronted by no less than ten identical versions of the Exarch apart from the one who had called her by name.

"Where am I?" she asked, looking around in amazement.

"Somewhere you're not supposed to be," said the nearest Deangelis. He shook his head. "You of all people, now of all times."

A jet of foam struck her from the ceiling, forcing her to the ground. She struggled against the enfolding whiteness but was soon enveloped.

"Wait!" she cried, despairing as the secret chamber disappeared from her sight. "You can't—"

She got no further. The foam tightened around her, and everything went black.

+20

Deangelis knew suffering of a sort he had never experienced before. In all his years of life, spread out over many bodies and experiencing time as a flexible thing, able to creep and race at will, no part of him had ever unwillingly died. From Sol to Hipparcos 62512, the system he now called home, he had only ever grown in complexity and vitality. Apart from those who had sacrificed themselves to explore the Occlusion, he had never been reduced.

Until now.

Don't mess with what you don't understand.

The moment the clane had confronted him, its blank expressions more revealing than its words, he had sensed what was coming. A quick scan revealed how their interiors had reorganized themselves into chemical explosives powerful enough to take a significant chunk out of the station. His mind had raced, seeking an explanation, even as more immediate reflexes kicked into play. What good would it do to destroy part of him? Why have two bodies in one place and singletons elsewhere? Who had sent it?

Consider this a warning—

Unlike the clane, his individual bodies didn't need light armor to protect themselves. There were more subtle methods available to him within the habitat. But protecting *him* wasn't his first concern. There were people all around him: Lazarus Hails and Palmer Christolphe were just two among many innocent bystanders who would be killed if the bombs were allowed to explode unchecked. He couldn't let that happen. The care of his citizens was ingrained into him from birth. His multifaceted, robust existence could tolerate an excision or two, but theirs could not.

—*Isaac Deangelis.*

Not "Exarch" or "Exarch Deangelis." The message came from someone confident enough to address him by his full name. Even as complex shields expanded to enfold him and the clane in a fatal embrace, his thoughts stuck on the mystery: *Why me? Why now?*

The matter of the missiles went completely forgotten as the clane blew itself up and part of him died with it.

He felt—violated. Someone had reached into his living mind and torn a piece out of it. The physical pain was over in an instant and paled in comparison to what was to follow. The dynamic equilibrium of his thoughts shattered like a chandelier in a hail of bullets. What had been for sixty-four Sol years an effortless, vibrant symphony of existence suddenly became a dissonant nightmare. He shrieked and vanished into the discord.

For the first time since his birth, the greater version of him lost consciousness.

Into that fragmentation stepped Melilah Awad. The individual parts of him remained conscious and active. Earth-Deangelis, deep in the heart of the habitat, felt his higher self slough from him like a dream and found himself suddenly weeping with his siblings. It was hard to remember what had happened. One moment they had been an Exarch, their thoughts combined in a magnificent, vibrant wave form; the next they were detached, unraveled, dislocated.

They were still connected, however. Earth-Deangelis could tell what the others felt and thought. He could reach out and touch the survivors elsewhere in the station. All was not yet lost.

They assembled a clumsy facsimile of what they had once been. Io-Deangelis oversaw the habitat's defense mechanisms, swinging powerful X-ray batteries to bear on the incoming missiles and firing clouds of particulate debris into their path. Triton-Deangelis began reconnect-ing communication channels severed by the explosions. Charon-Deangelis checked the status of the Occlusion observatory and found it to be unharmed.

Earth-Deangelis took charge of the habitat's evacuation and safety procedures. Most people had been swept into the chambers by the safety winds and their own need to hurry. All knew that an emergency was in progress and willingly complied with his instructions. He helped a number of stragglers to the bunkers, following his innate reflex to protect his charges.

When he found Melilah Awad caught in a pipe just meters from him, he wished he could shut down that reflex for a moment and let her take her chances.

But that wasn't an option. The missiles were just seconds away. He couldn't risk the possibility that she might perish when they struck. Opening a concealed entrance from the pipe to his secret retreat was as easy as shutting down the security monitors tracking her. If she lived to tell the tale, there would be no evidence to back her up.

"Awad, get in here. There's not much time."

For a moment he thought she was going to resist, but her instinct for self-preservation soon kicked in.

What had happened to *his?* he wondered. For all he knew, she had been involved in the attack. She and Defiance could have conspired with someone out-system to ferry the clane into position, using the Negotiator Select as an innocent courier. She could have been coming to him to deliver the final hammerblow, and he had just led her into his very heart!

No. A quick check of her body revealed no sign of explosives or replicators. Nothing that could harm him. If she had treachery in mind, it was of a sort he couldn't recognize.

She protested as antiaccelerant foam pinned her to the floor, but he didn't have time for niceties. The missiles were almost upon them, and not even Io-Deangelis's best efforts could keep all of them at bay.

There was something riding the wake of the missiles, obscured by their energetic afterwash. This, he assumed, was the main thrust of the attack. No matter what happened in the next few seconds, the worst of it was still to come.

Lasers flashed. The habitat shook like a living thing. Earth-Deangelis tucked himself into a ball and rolled with the quake. The loss of his higher self was a pain greater than any the attack offered. Alone, just one among many, he rode out the attack as best he could.

+21

Eogan burst out of the dock in a stolen hopper. In one sense, he couldn't have chosen a worse possible time to launch. Missiles burst like fireworks in the skies of Bedlam, sending streaks of particulate debris in all directions. High-energy collisions created secondary explosions everywhere he looked. It was impossible to avoid them all. He felt sharp stings in shoulder and knee as shrapnel left fiery tracks through him, barely deflected by his flesh and the substance of the hopper. He flinched but didn't worry overmuch; his most delicate areas were resistant to particle strikes at high velocity, designed to tolerate the dangers of near-light travel in deep space; he doubted that anything here could come close to such energies.

Still, there was the hopper to think about. Its workings suffered from the battering. Fighting unreliable controls, Eogan guided it up into the burning heavens, to where the *Nhulunbuy* awaited him.

"Can you hear me, Palmer Flast?"

Data struggled to rise above the fierce crackling noise of combat. "—clear, boss."

"Send N-6 down to pick me up." Sparks sprayed from the hopper's port flank as another missile fragmented nearby. "I don't think I'm going to get much farther than this."

"Confirmed. Hold tight. We're on our—"

Flast's voice dissolved into a squeal of static. The sky lit up in an insane mural of overlapping razor-thin rays and spirals. Eogan felt as though he was trapped in a cloud chamber, the target of a cyclotron's devastating energies. It was hard to see or sense anything—and it occurred to him then that this was exactly how it was supposed to be. The missiles disintegrated in just the right way to inhibit most forms of near-habitat transport and telemetry. As long as the pounding continued, Bedlam was effectively blind and impotent.

While that realization offered him some hope for the habitat's immediate survival, it also opened another avenue of worry. The thing coming in the wake of the missiles was effectively hidden from sight. It could be anything. Any sense of relief was premature.

The hopper lurched. He literally reached into its stricken circuitry, dissolving his right arm and seeping through cracks in the internal shell, in order to give it a few more moments of functionality. Electronic storms swept along their melded structures; he tasted ozone and melting plastic. He pictured the hopper as a burning terrestrial biplane tracing out a graceful arc through the air, doomed to intersect with the Earth below. Again, he could survive such a collision with Bedlam, but it certainly wasn't optimal. He would be stuck there, a harder target for the *Nhulunbuy* to collect and wedded to a much easier target for whatever was coming.

The particulate storm eased up long enough for him to see a mirror-finished sphere swoop alongside him. He fought the bucking of the hopper, trying to match trajectories, then gave up and simply rammed the Cell component broadside. The mirror finish parted smoothly. Complex engines absorbed his momentum and brought him to a gentle halt. Darkness and silence enfolded him.

He retracted his right arm and forced back the blackened, crackling shell of the hopper. The electroactive womb of the Cell fell over him as the component accelerated away from the surface of Bedlam. The tangle of missile fragments and debris resolved into something much more comprehensible.

The first wave of missiles had entirely disintegrated two kilometers from the surface of the habitat. A second wave, tucked in behind the first, had had more luck reaching its target. Two shallow but large craters gaped in the habitat's midsections, jetting white smoke into the void. Furious nanofacturing showed in infrared around the crater rims as the habitat's living skin tried to seal the breaches. Other, smaller hot spots pockmarked the surface from pole to pole. Seething chain reactions swept like lateral lightning bolts where aggressive replicators fought the local defenses, leaving blackened, dead habitat skin in its wake.

A third wave of missiles sliced in from the sky. Needle-tipped at both ends and as reflective as the *Nhulunbuy,* these weren't designed to fragment.

"Penetrators," said Flast, confirming his diagnosis.

"How many?"

"Five hundred-plus."

"Risk to us?"

"Minimal. Bedlam's a different story. Deangelis's reactions are—surprisingly—no better than ours, and we're not guarding a thing the size of the habitat. Some are bound to get through. Hopefully he's more capable on the ground."

Eogan hoped so, too. "We'll have to help, just in case he isn't."

"I knew you were going to say that."

"You disagree?" He could tell from the telemetry that the other Cells parked around the habitat had made for safer locations rather than get involved.

"Not emphatically." Flast hesitated, as though debating how honestly he could speak. "I question what difference we can make on such a scale. It's not as if we have much training in this sort of thing."

"Good point. For a second I thought you might be questioning my motives."

"I've served with you long enough to know that you wouldn't put the *Nhulunbuy*'s safety ahead of any one person's," he returned soberly. "Not unnecessarily, anyway."

Eogan smiled. "That's good. Because I *am* concerned about Melilah, and I need you to tell me if my judgment is compromised."

"Trust me. The first opportunity I get to take charge, you'll know about it."

Eogan settled back into a hastily morphed flight chair as N-6 powered away from Bedlam to where the rest of the Cell awaited it above. The shell of the hopper crumpled and vanished into the interior bulkhead, its molecules destined for recycling in the component's complex guts.

+22

Melilah woke to the hissing of rain. The sound brought back memories of her earliest years of life, on the colony world called Little Red. She had lived there with her mother until ten years of age, and she retained little more of that time than the sound of water falling freely from the sky. There was no precipitation on Bedlam, and low-gee fountains were a poor substitute. Sometimes, late at night, she would float in the darkness and imagine what it had been like to hear rain hitting a metal roof. A gentle wistfulness would envelop her, for both the lost sound and the mother she'd lost in a spacing accident when she was ten years old. She'd never even had the chance to see their new home in Bedlam.

Bedlam . . .

Melilah twitched against the restraining foam holding her still, memories of where she was—and why—overriding any regrets from the past.

"Let me out of here!" Her voice was muffled but loud enough. "Deangelis, you son of a bitch! What the hell is going on?"

The white foam parted. The Exarch's fresh-faced visage leaned into the gap. His blond hair hung in disarray; a bruise was forming on one cheek.

"I am genuinely sorry to inconvenience you," he said. "I did so only for your well-being."

She didn't believe him at first, but as tattered threads of the Scale-Free Bedlam feed wound themselves around her, the truth began to grow clear. Bedlam had been attacked—and was, in fact, still under fire. Penetrator missiles, a meter long and barely a millimeter wide, were slicing like deadly rain from the hostile sky.

Not aliens, then.

The relief was fleeting. She had seen such things before.

"You've got to let me go."

"You're safer here, Melilah."

"I don't care. This is my home, for Christ's sake! I have to help defend it!"

Deangelis pulled back. His expression lacked its usual smug self-assurance. She remembered seeing tear tracks on his cheeks, and wondered if that could possibly have been real.

"Please," she entreated him.

He nodded. "Very well, Melilah. Our objectives are, for the moment, the same."

His sudden backing down surprised her. She began to shake as the foam retreated completely. The floor trembled beneath her, and the air had an acrid smell to it.

Deangelis helped her to her feet once her legs were free. There were at least a dozen Deangelises standing in the curving, hidden space, milling protectively around a glowing object in the center of the room. It looked like a crystal sarcophagus.

"You'll need this," said the first Deangelis, pressing a small, sharp-pointed object into her hand. She went to look at it, but it had already dissolved into her skin. Uncertainty, a sudden feeling that she had done the wrong thing, made her pull away from him.

"What is it?" she asked, as a strange high swept through her, much faster than any chemical drug. "What the hell have you done to me?"

"Made you sufficient." He turned her and propelled her toward the door. "Do not return here."

"But—" The force of his push was sufficient to carry her clear through the portal. By the time she'd tugged herself to a halt, the entrance was gone.

"Damn you," she hissed under her breath. The tingling had spread to the back of her eyes. Images appeared in her forward vision, overlaid across a map of the habitat. Bright sparks flared into life in the upper levels, and she instinctively—the instinct granted via the nanoware graft Deangelis had given her—knew that these were places the penetrators had broken through.

She kicked herself along the pipe, trying to ignore the way it vibrated under her palms and soles. Fragmentation bombs were designed to cut communications and keep mundane vessels grounded; penetrators were commonly used to breach interplanetary cargo vessels. Everything, therefore, pointed to a takeover, not a wipeout. The origin of the takeover was unknown but not presently relevant. Repelling the invasion was the main thing. They could assign blame later.

A high-speed transport awaited her at its far end. She slid smoothly into it and let its electric engine hurry her away.

"Yasu?" Communications within the habitat were severely curtailed, but it seemed the Exarch had granted her priority. Melilah's four-daughter responded almost immediately.

"Oh, Grandmother Mel, you're back! We were so worried."

"I'm *back?* What are you talking about? I never went away."

"You dropped completely off the system. We didn't know where you were. We thought—well, it didn't look good, given what was going on. Palmer Eogan was nowhere around this time."

Off the system . . . Melilah momentarily regretted leaving the Exarch's secret space so soon. Where exactly had she been?

"Never mind about me," she said. "I'm okay. But what about you? Where are you? Are you safe?"

"I'm in a shelter on Granovetter. There are lots of people here. It's kind of exciting—like a drill, but we know it's for real. Things got bumpy for a while there; we've all got bruises. What's happening out there? It's hard to tell with the network so patchy."

Melilah did her best to bring her four-daughter up to speed, knowing that anyone who could would be listening in. It was important to her that the citizens of Bedlam were kept in the loop—even if, in the end, she could share only her own fragmentary knowledge with them. The Exarch was either unwilling or unable to do it for them.

"An invasion?" Yasu sounded almost scandalized, rather than concerned. *Kind of exciting,* she had said. She was too young to remember the Exarchate Expansion and the last time the shelters had been used. "Who would invade us? We're not a threat to anyone."

"Not normally, no." Melilah thought of the Mizar Occlusion and wondered at how quickly things could change. The transport passed through a rapid series of junctions, choosing routes with unaffected ease despite the occasional lack of lighting and clouds of acrid smoke.

"Stay exactly where you are," she told Yasu. "Wait for the all clear before coming out. Let as many people as you can know what's going on. I can't come join you right now, but I will as soon as I can."

"What will you do, Grandmother Mel?"

She had been pondering this question while they talked. The answer was obvious, and deceptively simple. "I'm going to help."

Melilah disconnected from Yasu and called the members of Defiance.

+23

I'm still here.

Flickers of consciousness returned to the higher Deangelis as his many parts strove individually to repel the invasion. Sense of selfhood came and went in an overwhelming torrent of information. He clutched each brief awakening as a person struggling to swim through rapids gulped for air when he or she surfaced.

What the hell happened?

He knew the answer to that question: brain damage. The clane had destroyed one fifth of his individual selves. Repair took time, required rapid reorganization of his remaining resources. His return was fragile, patchwork, impromptu—and delayed.

Someone had knocked him out of the picture long enough for penetrators to reach the habitat. Dozens of the invasive needles had struck external levels and flattened like old-fashioned bullets as momentum carried them deep inside. Nanotech swarms attacked the outer layers of the projectiles, but were unable to reach the crucial cores in time. Such defenses were deactivated automatically when the penetrators reached inhabited areas lest they cause injury to bystanders. Lumps of red-hot quicksilver dropped from ceilings in widely scattered pipes and chambers. Barely had they hit the ground when the cores unraveled, revealing their deadly payloads.

Deangelis snarled to see them. Tiny in size but rich with malevolence, the invaders were programmed solely to destroy. Ranging in size from the nanoscale to a grain of sand, they swarmed over and through anything that got in their way. Breeder factories produced new breeders every ten reproductions, ensuring the plague spread rapidly. If the incursion sites weren't sealed soon, the habitat would soon be overcome.

Not incursion, he corrected himself. *Infection.* The habitat quivered around him like a feverish child. Its ancient mind was too primitive to interact meaningfully with his, but he could feel it reacting to what was going on. It was *hurting.*

The worst thing about it was that he could do little to help it. The habitat's own defenses, and those of its inhabitants, were better equipped to handle localized attacks within the habitat's many spaces. He could only direct them from above, and assist where he could. Earth-Deangelis's instinct to help Melilah Awad had been a good one. Already she and the Defiance movement were mobilizing to locate and isolate infection sites in their area. Evacuating people was a priority, followed by severing each location from the rest of the habitat, so the infection couldn't spread. If the infection couldn't be destroyed *in situ,* it would be kept isolated for later expulsion.

What was happening in the skies concerned Exarch Deangelis more. The deadly rain had allowed something much more sinister to approach the habitat. With data limited from sources outside the habitat by continuing fragmentation interference, he couldn't get a clear look at the thing. It blocked the stars behind it with silent, ominous menace, an inky black shape growing larger with every second.

Only as a sheer mass of fragmentary data accumulated, and as his many fragments coalesced once again into a whole, did he realize that this new arrival wasn't aimed at the habitat at all.

It was heading for the Mizar Occlusion.

Ice spread through him. Every one of his minds turned their attention to this new development. He reached out for the fragments of him working in the observatory. It was still tucked safely under the protective umbrella of PARASOL, forgotten in the opening salvos. There were five of him there, intermittently connected to the greater him. They realized as soon as the rest of him did that they were the true focus of the attack, not the habitat at all. Everything—the fragmentation, the penetrators—was designed simply to grant the invader access to the observatory.

I won't allow it, he thought with furious resolve. This was his system, his prize, and he wasn't about to let anybody take either of them away from him . . .

As the battle for the habitat waged on, he sent a priority signal to the observatory, activating its defenses.

+24

"It's a Reaper," said Flast. "A big one."

Eogan closed his eyes and let the grim data flow through him.

The black shape riding the tail of the penetrators flickered in and out of view, its signature masked by interference from the stricken habitat. When visible, its silhouette was jaggedly geometric, like a spider or a multiarmed robot; the *Nhulunbuy*'s instruments put its size at somewhere between five hundred meters and one kilometer across; the forces propelling it were carefully shielded, making them especially difficult to pin down.

"I thought they were all decommissioned after the Expansion," Eogan said.

"Apparently not. Or someone built a new one."

Eogan expelled a breath in frustration. "Either way, it's not good news."

"It gets worse." Flast's voice threaded the data like a black ribbon, tying it into a new shape. "My best guess is that it's heading for the Occlusion observatory, not Bedlam."

Eogan studied the telemetry from this perspective. The evidence was inconclusive but compelling. It also necessitated a change of plans. He didn't know what use the *Nhulunbuy* was going to be against a Reaper, but he couldn't in good conscience leave Vermeulen in its path without trying to help.

"We have to split the Cell," he said.

"That makes sense: half for the habitat, half for the station. I suppose you'll take the half to Bedlam."

Eogan took a split second to examine both his instincts and what was best for the situation. They conflicted, which was a sure sign that he should tread carefully. His concern for not just Melilah but for Luisa and James Pirelli as well was particularly keen.

"Actually, I think I should take the Occlusion run," he said. "It's my fault Vermeulen got mixed up in this, and it's therefore my job to make sure she's okay."

"You want me to take the Bedlam run?" If Flast was surprised, it didn't show.

Eogan grunted acknowledgment. "Do what you can to help. I don't know how messy things will be. Find Melilah and do as she says. If you can't find her . . ." He hesitated, remembering how she had dropped off the scopes last time he'd looked for her. "Just use your judgment. And keep in contact as best you can."

They split the remaining crew down the middle. Although not strictly designed for combat, the Cell wouldn't look out of place on a battlefield. What it lacked in dedicated armaments it more than made up for in other ways. There was no need to divide the components up according to mass or resources, since they were naturally flexible. Flast could convert his allotment into dozens of pip-sized baubles, if he wanted to, while Eogan configured the remainder into any shape he desired. The basic design principle of the Cells made them infinitely variable.

He took a moment out of the preparations to ask himself a simple question:

Why am I fighting? He didn't owe anyone here anything, except himself and his crew. So what exactly was he trying to prove?

He was sure the Negotiator Select wouldn't like his answer—if he was still alive—but at least he could honestly say it wasn't all about Melilah.

If someone was coming to steal the Occlusion, then they—along with the rest of humanity—didn't know what they were in for.

The Cell divided.

Nhulunbuy was a region of Australia's midnorth that had had a special significance for the Cell's previous chief officer's grandparents. Although Eogan knew nothing about Yolngu traditions and felt no ties to Palmer Weightman's old homeland, he had kept the name upon assuming command five years earlier. It was a way of honoring Weightman, who had groomed him for the job before choosing to settle on a remote outstation on Altitude. Eogan would have been well within his rights to change its name, but something had stopped him. A fear of stamping his mark too deeply on the Cell, perhaps, as though fearing that it might return the favor.

Flast celebrated his sudden rise in responsibility by coining his half of the Cell the *Kwal Bahal.* Now a functional vessel in its own right, it had to be differentiated from the remainder of the *Nhulunbuy* somehow, so Eogan allowed him the indulgence. There was a small chance that the two Cells would remain permanently separated after the fight. Palmers recognized no minimum or maximum size for a Cell, and new ones were simply budded off as need arose.

"Congratulations, Palmer Aesche," he told his new second officer, an efficiently humorless woman who had been plying the trade lanes longer than he had. She presented no face at all over intra-Cell communications, just voice and a series of complex emoticons. "You've drawn the short straw."

"Better out here than in there," she replied, indicating the habitat. Purple blotches were spreading across the variegated surface, indicating where aggressive replicators had taken root. "Ground battles always struck me as somewhat pointless."

Distractedly, he nodded his assent. Palmers considered anything with more than 0.05 of a gee pull as "ground." What was the point of fighting over a lump of dead mass when the infinite sky was your playground?

The truncated *Nhulunbuy* swept out of the habitat's meager gravitational well with thrusters on full, sweeping over the worst of the fragmentation mines remaining from the initial barrage. Flickering, ghastly light still sprayed in the habitat's immediate vicinity. Signal-to-noise ratios improved dramatically as their distance increased, but there was precious little to listen to beyond the habitat. The system possessed several moon and asteroid stations, mostly unstaffed. A handful of hardy explorers braved the long cold into the near-Dark halos, looking for evidence of exospermia. They were keeping quiet for fear of the invader targeting them next. They hadn't yet realized that they were irrelevant.

Eogan hadn't been caught in a combat situation since the complicated Expansion years, but the lessons learned then were ingrained. Arc Circuit systems had heard rumors of hyperadvanced vessels appearing in other systems that had managed to mount a stiffer-than-expected resistance to the Exarchate incursions. Quickly dubbed "Reapers" for their stealth-black appearance and lethal capabilities, the vessels functioned as destroyer-sized smart bullets, committed to rooting out every possible threat to Sol's imperial aspirations as quickly as possible. Finely targeted strikes took out hardware first—weapons and intelligence outposts; mine clouds; communications arrays. If resistance persisted, the application of force quickly turned deadly. The blackest whispers spoke of satellites ditched on populated areas, bubble cities opened to the vacuum, moons razed, and whole ecologies disrupted. Once they had beaten the locals into submission, the stories went, the Reapers moved on to the next target, ready to dispense Sol's version of tough justice.

Two systems in the Arc Circuit—Schiller's End and Phad 4—had received visits from Reapers during the Expansion. No shots had been fired in either case; the simple presence of such dark emissaries had been enough to stifle resistance. Sometimes Eogan had wondered what had been the most effective weapon in the takeover—the Reapers themselves or the rumors that had preceded them.

Either way, the one looming fast on the Occlusion observatory was certain to be armed with more than just gossip.

He dipped into the Cell's extensive shape-library and chose from several possible attack formations. Twenty-five of the thirty-seven remaining components merged into a configuration that was simultaneously reminiscent of a raptor and a flower, with five tapering "wings" angling forward and out from a central thorn fifty meters long. The remaining twelve components followed randomly determined paths around the raptor, affecting highly reflective profiles.

Although he suspected it wouldn't do any good, he broadcast Cell registration codes and a request to negotiate over all frequencies. He even tried the secret ftl link. Exarch Deangelis didn't intervene. The vacuum between the major players was light on communication, heavy on threat.

"This is an unnecessary violation of interstellar and interhuman treaties," he tried, resorting to voice where other protocols had failed. "What are we: savages throwing sticks at each other?"

Much to his surprise, he received a reply.

"That's exactly what we are, Palmer Eogan," said a woman's voice over the ftl link. "Comparatively speaking."

It took Eogan much less than a second to produce a voice match. The Reaper belonged to Frederica Cazneaux, Exarch of Mizar system. He had last spoken to her a year ago, while leaving to clear what he had thought was a simple occlusion from the Mizar-Bedlam trade lane.

"You're making a big mistake," he said.

Her response was incredulous. "Are you threatening me?"

"Merely stating a fact."

"The facts are simple, Palmer Eogan. *You* are the one who made a mistake: you brought this thing to Bedlam. I'm here to put that right. I advise you to get out of my way before you get hurt."

The *Nhulunbuy* was caught between two opposing Exarchs. Eogan seriously considered the virtues of fleeing right then, before he buried himself any deeper than he already was.

"I can't do that," he said. "One of my crew is—"

Cazneaux didn't wait for him to finish. The Reaper transformed from deep black to glaring white in an instant as energy surged for the Occlusion observatory. Eogan's senses were instantly overwhelmed. The *Nhulunbuy* spun like a dust mote in a laser beam. He heard shouting, felt the sudden thrill of mortal fear in the fabric of the Cell as it strained to get out of the firing line. He urged it on with every iota of willpower he possessed.

He hadn't even begun to hope that they might make it when, from behind them, the observatory unfolded like a predatory flower, and the universe hit him with the weight of worlds.

+25

With a deafening, white-noise hiss and a rush of blast-furnace air, the nanotech infection rushed up the pipe toward Melilah. For a moment, she froze, staring at it as it burst out of the potential breach she'd gone in to investigate. The insatiable replicator was simple and deadly. Designed to disrupt complex molecules wherever it found them, it effectively tore matter apart. If it touched her, the replicators would spread through her flesh like black rot. She wasn't, therefore, embarrassed in the slightest at turning tail and running.

"Infection confirmed!" she yelled at the top of her voice. Kicking like a springbok off the walls of the pipe, she hurried as fast as she could to the truncation point. "Seal it off! Seal it off!"

"When you're through!" shouted Vernon Gard through the opening. "Not before!"

Don't be an idiot! she wanted to yell back at him. *If just one breeder gets on me, I'll contaminate the rest of the habitat!*

But when she shot through the portal and slammed to a halt on the far side, she was glad that he'd waited. She looked back just in time before the pipe was sealed off forever, imagining the contagion boiling just millimeters behind her shoulder blades. It was in fact still some meters away, encroaching like mold in fast motion toward the one remaining link to the outside. She didn't think it was intelligent, in any communal, guided sense of the word, but its black tendrils seemed to wave at her with increased agitation as the portal slammed shut on them.

Until next time, the forces of dissolution seemed to be saying. *It's only a matter of time before you make a mistake.*

Subtle forces flexed. The pipe pinched and folded back on itself, forming a tight U-shaped loop. Its previous destination—and a bubble roughly ten meters across around it—was isolated from the rest of the habitat behind alternating layers of matter resistant to the replicators and complex field effects that would persist for hours even if the local power supply was severed. Within those layers, the replicators could breed to their heart's content, until there was nothing left but itself to devour.

Melilah was still breathing heavily when Angela Chen-Pushkaric gave the all clear. The woman's gruff tones were briskly matter-of-fact, as though listing a supply order.

"That was too close," said Prof Virgo, over the dedicated feed the Exarch had given them. "We should have sent a remote."

"Not when transmissions are so unreliable," she said. "Someone had to go in there, and it had to be me. Are you suggesting that any of you were more qualified?"

There was no response. Gard, with his third-hemisphere capabilities, was far more valuable linked directly to the habitat, overseeing the sudden changes required to seal off the pockets of infection. Angela Chen-Pushkaric and Prof Virgo were helping direct people to safe areas. They needed accurate, up-to-date intelligence on each of the outbreaks, and she couldn't trust the machines to give that to her.

"We have another breach," said Gard, closing his eyes and sniffing as though tasting the air. His elongated skull swung from side to side. "In Faloutsos Junction. A big one."

She smoothed down her crawl-suit. Her breathing and heart rate had begun to return to normal. "Okay. Let's go."

Other emergency vehicles made way for them as they rushed through the pipes. Hatches opened and closed automatically. Melilah oversaw the efforts of the others to clear the infected area. Five people had been caught in the breeding mass of replicators when the ceiling came down on them. Overrun in less than a second, there had been no chance of rescue. Their matter was now part of the invasion, co-opted into a battle they had wanted no part of.

A seething, background rage filled Melilah at the thought of what the attack would cost Bedlam. To her knowledge, her home had done nothing to provoke such action; the explanation had to lie in the Occlusion and what it promised. Someone else must have guessed its secret and come to steal it. That was the only reason she could come up with for the chaos into which the system had been thrust. The mission's objective was theft; everything else was just collateral damage.

Only Exarchs thought that way, she told herself. And no one else in the Arc Circuit had access to this kind of firepower. When it was over, either way, she swore to identify the extropian freak responsible and see that their plug was pulled.

"Something new," said Gard. "I'm picking up a physical incursion. Hardware, not nanotech."

"Where?" she asked quickly, thinking: *What now?*

"Bacon Cathedral. We can be there in two minutes."

She briefly considered her options. The incursion in Faloutsos Junction could be handled by local emergency services without her; her value was reduced now that she had shown them what to do. On the other hand, if the attacker had sent some novel means of attacking the habitat, it might be best to face it head-on.

"Take us there." The transport banked sharply and swooped into the next left turn. "Give me visual."

A virtual window opened, courtesy of the Exarch's nanoware. She swallowed her distaste and looked into it. Bacon Cathedral, like Albert Hall, was a permanent landmark of Bedlam. A teardrop-shaped chimney crisscrossed with platforms and walkways, it stretched all the way from the deepest levels almost to the surface, its ceiling rising automatically as new levels grew around and over it. The new invasion had come through that ceiling, the thinnest point for kilometers around. The thought made Melilah feel physically ill. Not a place of religious worship, the Cathedral was decorated with commissioned art from many of the habitat's inhabitants. Public rallies had been held there during the Expansion; Melilah had led one for eight days straight, lifted up by the united voices of her supporters as they called for freedom. That the Cathedral might require sealing off and excision was intolerable. She imagined replicators spilling down murals and devouring sculptures as they went.

There has to be a way to save it!

No visible nanotech but an awful lot of smoke filled the view Gard gave her. Her gaze swept up and down through numerous frequencies, seeking one that could penetrate the murk.

When it finally cleared, she saw a string of pearl-shaped craft descending gracefully down the Cathedral's chimney.

"I'm not getting a match from the weaponry database," said Gard.

Her breath caught in her throat. “That’s because it’s not a replicator incursion,” she said. “It’s a Cell!”

He nodded, then shook his great head. “Neither its signature nor mass is in the register.”

Excitement ebbed. “You think it could be a Trojan?”

“Anything is possible.”

“Just get us there ASAP,” she said, “and tell everyone else to stay away.”

Seconds later, the first attempts at communication came from the Cell.

“—the *Kwal Bahal,* seeking Melilah Awad. I repeat: this is Palmer Flast, chief officer of the *Kwal Bahal,* seeking Melilah Awad. I’ve come to offer you assistance. Please respond.”

She replied immediately. Talking wasn’t going to hurt anyone, even if the transmission was bogus. “I hear you, Palmer Flast. Where are you from? We don’t know your Cell.”

“It used to be the *Nhulunbuy*—half of it, anyway.” The possible Palmer’s voice was brisk as the mirror-finish orbs sank deeper into the Cathedral and assumed a swirling, faintly hypnotic configuration.

“What happened to the other half?” she asked, steeling herself for the answer.

“Eogan has work elsewhere; otherwise, I know he would’ve liked to be here instead of me.”

Any relief she felt was almost certainly premature. “How can you help us, Palmer Flast?” The transport she rode was only moments away from reaching the Cathedral. She had to make a decision soon.

“The infection is spreading,” he said. “You can see it from outside the colony. As hard as you’re trying, you don’t have the resources to quash this kind of invasion. We can make the difference. We’re more mobile than you are, and we’re expert at dealing with nanotech. We have to be, in the environments we’re used to.”

That made sense. Although extensively shielded, Palmer Cells required vast amounts of exotic technology to keep their once-human crews alive. A large part of that technology consisted of nanoware designed to maintain, repair, and destroy living cells. So inimical was life in the trade lanes, even those most frequently swept by the Palmers, that the repairers themselves sometimes suffered radiation damage. Whole Cells had been wiped out when a single corrupted molecule had turned a beneficent collaborator into a rampaging killer. Extensive feedback systems ensured that such disasters were rare in recent times, monitoring the ebb and flow of passenger replicators to ensure that nothing got out of hand. Such corrective systems would be extremely helpful in combating the incursion afflicting Bedlam.

Cancer ships, she remembered, distracted from Flast for a moment. There had been a pirate once, an interstellar bandit associated with such vessels. A long time ago, when the Arc Circuit had been barely a sketch across the starscape, he had made a habit of cruising silently along the trade lanes, then suddenly crashing his intended victim's VOID drive by ramming in too close. Pellets of corrupted nanotech seeded mutations in the target's immune system analogue, encouraging the growth of destructive replicators. While the crew struggled to deal with that problem, the pirates moved in and took what they wanted. Whole manifests were emptied in the twenty years the pirate had reigned; thousands of people had lost their lives. Only when the pirate's vessel had been found drifting in empty space, gutted by one of its own mutations but still flying under the sign of the Crab, did the trouble cease.

That had been before the Palmers, she knew. Such events had encouraged the formation of a self-regulating organization in a frontier that simply could not be policed. She remembered word spreading that trade lanes were safe again—but she couldn't remember the name of the pirate who had caused so much dread.

"Okay, Palmer Flast," she said. "We accept your help."

"Good. Show me to the nearest site, and I'll take some samples. When we've got something concrete to look at, we'll start talking countermeasures."

Vernon Gard lifted deep-set eyes to focus on her as the transport pulled up at the main entrance of the Cathedral. The entrance irised open at his command, and a shining, giant pearl necklace unreeled from within. Each of the Cell components was two meters across, small enough to fit through a minor freight pipe but seemingly too slight to hold a living human.

Melilah attempted to patch into the Cell's manifest to examine it in more detail, but received only the most cursory sketch in return. She learned little more than that it had a crew of two dozen people and was barely hours old. She made a mental note to report the information infringement when things settled down, if Flast didn't fix it first.

"More outsiders," said Gard with a grimace, watching the Cell as it stretched almost boastfully before them, like a snake warming itself in the sun.

She couldn't think of a reply that didn't expose her own prejudices—since when did someone with a head like a giant banana have the right to criticize people just because they came from a different *place?*—so she ignored him and told the newcomers what to do.

+26

Space boiled, and so did the Exarch.

Frederica Cazneaux, you will pay for this!

Magnificent destruction cast a deathly light over the side of the habitat facing the observatory, projected by weapons so advanced that unevolved humans couldn't begin to understand them—could only gawp in wonder at them as the sky turned bright above them, like Neanderthals struck dumb by lightning. Gone were the days of wars depending on heavy projectiles, rapid chemical reactions, and runaway heat. Even nuclear energy was tired. The two antagonists who traded blows over the Occlusion did so using forces that under ordinary conditions barely existed in the universe. Such energies were found only on the surface of neutron stars, in the accretion disks whipping around stellar-sized black holes, in the hearts of suns. When desperate needs met extreme ends, space-time was an innocent and unlucky bystander.

Deangelis was all too aware of the proximity of the habitat to the conflict. He didn't mind the thought of losing more of himself to the equivalent of a stray shot or a ricochet. His mental integrity would hold up. But such were the forces involved that the slightest echo could tear the habitat to atoms, or erase it entirely from the universe, as though it had never existed. He wouldn't allow that to happen—and that meant that he was fighting two battles at once: one to protect the habitat, and the other to repel the invader.

Frederica Cazneaux!

The name was a battle cry urging him to greater efforts. Never before, to his knowledge, had one Exarch attacked another. There might be rivalries, disagreements, bitter exchanges, trade wars, even threats of conflict, but no open hostilities such as these. The Exarchate was bound by loyalty to Sol and a unifying common purpose—to nurture humanity in its new home among the stars, whatever forms it took. Fighting ran nakedly counter to that purpose. And for what?

Deangelis had no doubt regarding the motives of his attacker. Cazneaux wanted to get her hands on the Mizar Occlusion, believing—as did he—that whoever first grasped its purpose would win an unassailable advantage over everyone else. Wormhole technology could open doorways all across human space, not just the Arc Circuit. Once the dangers were overcome, his system would become the gateway to the rest of the universe.

Cazneaux would take that from him. She would argue, no doubt, that because the Occlusion had been found on the trade lane between their systems, she had a partial—if not total—claim to ownership over it. She deserved a proportion of the riches that would inevitably result.

And perhaps she did. He might have been prepared to negotiate something to that effect, had she but talked to him before opening fire. That was the thing that irked him most: Cazneaux *knew* him. All the Exarchs knew each other. She must have realized that he would talk, that he would rather not fight over something that could be settled diplomatically. The Mizar Occlusion could be shared, if it had to be. He would allow that—and she should have known it.

Instead, this wild, furious attempt to overwhelm his observatory's defenses and steal what he had claimed. But he'd be damned if he was going to let her get away with it. War overrode diplomacy. He would defend himself to the ends of his abilities. She would not win!

He might be distracted by the safety of the habitat, but *she* was a long way from home and using a weapon that had last been in service forty years ago. Its systems were vulnerable to perturbation from afar, if nudged the right way.

He watched closely as the Reaper swept through a rapid series of configurations, each one displaying a different lethality. At one moment, it was a swanlike shape with vast bat wings extended to enfold the observatory; the next it had morphed into a four-dimensional trident attempting to penetrate his defenses by sliding around their gross physical surface. He was prepared for both, and ready with a response. The observatory shrugged ghost-shells from its rippling exterior, sheets of brilliant silver energy that broke over the Reaper like waves on an island, wrapping around its every facet and burning deep. Mass flashed to energy and back again; the vacuum seethed with short-lived particle explosions, blossoming into vast, branching shapes that just as suddenly collapsed down to nothing; the light from the system's primary redshifted to infra, then flashed a startling clear blue.

There. A hesitation as the Reaper absorbed the damage and prepared to strike again. The conflicting demands of offense and defense were taking their toll on a machine that had been self-repairing for too long. Such a stutter could be exploited, like a weakness in a suit of armor. Through soft joints a dagger could slip, crippling an opponent. All he had to do was fashion the blade . . .

In the midst of that thought, he became aware of a third player on the battlefield. A speck he had initially dismissed as a by-product of the firefight turned out to be a small craft bravely but ineffectually weathering the storm around it, a Palmer Cell displaying the signature of the *Nhulunbuy* despite a much-reduced mass.

Deangelis withdrew some of his firepower from its location and considered his options. There was a narrow window of opportunity for him to hail the Cell, should he decide to take advantage of its presence. Caught between two Exarchs, even with him trying to spare it, the Cell simply wouldn't last long. It would be destroyed as casually as an ant on a football field.

Ants can bite, he thought. One solid nip might be all he needed.

+27

Eogan gritted his teeth to blot out a bone-rattling howl that began deep in the bowels of infrasound and ended well beyond the range of any terrestrial creature. It rose and fell in waves too powerful for N-6 to drown out completely. The voices of his crew were barely audible over it; he could barely think through it. Buffeted by forces the Cell had not been designed to weather, he had the strength to wish that he'd never got involved, but little else.

Then, suddenly, the turbulence eased. As though it had burst into the heart of a cyclonic storm, the *Nhulunbuy* found itself in an eerily calm space, one that he didn't dare hope was permanent. With all his senses ringing, jangled, Eogan did his best to get his thoughts in order while he had the chance.

"Is everyone still here?"

Affirmatives from his crew staggered in, accounting for all of them. His relief was profound. The Cell he wasn't so worried about; it could be blown into a million pieces and still function perfectly well. People, however, weren't so resilient.

"Palmer Vermeulen? Can you hear me?"

There was no answer from his science officer. The firestorm curtailed all communication with the observatory—indeed, outside the Cell itself.

"What now, Palmer Eogan?" asked Palmer Aesche.

Outside the bubble of relative stillness, blue-purple light whipped and snapped like auroras with bite. Staccato points of light stabbed in long, curving streamers, resembling rail-gun fire but clearly not made of matter. Pulsing explosions blossomed and died in a constant stream. Behind the conflagration, the dark shape of the Reaper flexed and writhed into half-glimpsed, nightmarish shapes.

If Aesche was being sardonic, he couldn't read it in her voice.

"I have an idea," he said, "but I fear it might be throwing good money after bad. I need to know if you think I made a wrong call."

Aesche's response was immediate. "No, sir, and I believe I speak for all of us on this issue. We've come this far; we might as well keep going."

He nodded, and the motion was transmitted via the couch he had blended with into a general indicator of approval. Body language was just as important to Palmers as any other human variant, even between bodies separated by many hundreds of meters.

"Very well," he said. "Then I want to retune the VOID systems. I believe that to be our best shot. The vanes are worthless out here, as are the thrusters; with that sort of technology we're like bees trying to attack a whale. If we can bootstrap ourselves up to their level, we might be able to do some damage."

"Retune how?"

He outlined his idea as quickly as possible, fearing the collapse of the bubble around them with every passing second. Palmer Cells were utterly different from the early space vessels humanity had built. Unlike craft with single engines, single life-support systems, and control systems bearing only the most basic redundancy designs, Palmer Cells owed their considerable flexibility to a single, simple design concept. The work of all their systems was spread across the entire Cell, performed by millions of machines on the micro- or nanoscale. Every cubic centimeter of the Cell contained hundreds of components dedicated to air purification, water reclamation, field effect generation, VOID maintenance, and more. Every cubic centimeter was, in a sense, a reflection of the Cell as a whole—in the same way a fragment of a hologram contained an image of the entire hologram in miniature. A Cell could take any shape, any size, and still contain all the elements it needed to be a functioning, human-bearing space vessel.

"I want to strip out the VOID drive microunits," Eogan said, "and turn them into bullets."

"There's a lot of junk around," protested Aesche. "The drives won't be effective."

"Then we'll just have to give them some of our thrusters. All we need to do is get them up to speed. When the VOID drives are activated, they'll generate a warp on a small scale. This, combined with the drive units' masses, is bound to have an effect."

"What sort of effect?"

He shrugged. "I guess we'll find out soon enough."

"You do realize that this will leave us pretty much dead in the water."

There was a note of skepticism—perhaps even criticism—to her voice. "I know," he said. "We'll tailor our trajectory to take us out of range on momentum alone. That'll have to be enough, until we can replace what we give the bullets."

Aesche considered the plan for a moment. He steeled himself for more questions, but none were forthcoming. The truth was, he didn't know exactly what the drive units might accomplish, but it was the best he could think of under the circumstances.

"I approve," said a totally unexpected voice over the open channel. "But I would suggest some fine-tuning."

"Deangelis? Is that you?"

The Exarch didn't reply to his question, either assuming it was rhetorical or the answer self-evident. "Your plan will be ineffective unless it is implemented correctly. I will provide you with a target and a time. Stick to both, and you have a chance of succeeding."

Data trickled in over a highly secure link from the habitat behind them, not the observatory. Eogan didn't examine it in any detail, but it did look at first glance to be strategic information.

"Let me talk to Palmer Vermeulen," he said.

"That's impossible at the moment. I can assure you, however, that she is safe. She will be able to communicate with you once you have completed your mission."

Are you blackmailing me*?* Eogan wanted to ask. There was little he could do about it if Deangelis was.

"Very well," he said. "We'll look at your data and decide what to do."

"I wouldn't think too long if I were you. I won't be able to maintain this bubble indefinitely."

Another thinly veiled threat. "You must be worried," said Eogan, "to be throwing your weight around so much."

The Exarch didn't reply.

+28

"A Reaper?" Melilah stared at Gard in astonishment. "You've got be kidding."

"That's the conclusion I keep coming to, based on the limited telemetry available," Gard said. "The Exarch is fighting it off."

"Fighting one of his own?"

The programmer tilted his overlong head in something like agreement. "We live in interesting times."

Her attention was suddenly drawn forward as their transport was blocked by a component of the *Kwal Bahal*. It filled the pipe like a swollen crystal billiard ball, gray at the edges and fading to black in its heart.

"I'm sorry," said the Palmer within. "It is dangerous for you to proceed any farther."

Melilah checked an internal map. They were close to Faloutsos Junction and the site of the latest replicator outbreak. She couldn't tell just how far the infection had spread; feeds in and out of the area around the junction had been purposefully severed to prevent the spread of software viruses.

"I'm not staying back here," she said. "I want to see what happens."

"You don't trust us?" asked the Palmer.

"At this stage, caution seems the best option."

"Understandable." The Palmer was silent for a moment, then said, "I have obtained permission to offer you a berth."

She must have misheard. "A—what?"

"Come aboard. I'll take you the rest of the way in perfect safety."

"But—" Her automatic protest died before becoming a proper sentence. *But I don't want to go in there!* "A certain amount of trust is still required."

"Indeed."

Nothing else was forthcoming; that was clearly as far as the Palmers were prepared to go. She cursed under her breath. It had been almost two centuries since she had last been inside a starship, when she had traveled to Bedlam, and they had been primitive things back then. Who knew what this one might do to her, or how it might *change* her?

That was irrational fear talking, she knew. She swallowed it and willed her voice level.

"I'll be over in a second."

Gard watched her open the transport hatch with sharp, flickering eyes. "Ping me when you're inside."

"Don't worry; I will. If we lose contact . . ." She hesitated as a dimple appeared in the side of the billiard ball, quickly widening and deepening, forming a hole big enough for a person to slip through. "Sound the alarm; tell Deangelis. Give 'em hell."

He nodded like a bishop in danger of losing his mitre.

She kicked herself across the gap between the transport and the Cell component, which become ovoid in shape to accommodate its extra passenger. Its glassy surface loomed ahead of her, reflecting the brown-and-white streaks of her and a distorted image of her face. She forced herself to reach out with hands to arrest her forward movement and was surprised to find plastic warmth against her palms, not cool smoothness. The component hummed to itself, just above the threshold of her hearing.

A light sprang to life inside the Cell, and Melilah fought the urge to run as fast as she could.

The Palmer was barely recognizable; she was, in fact, hardly visible at all. The interior of the component was a cramped, fleshy space with bulging walls and—its only redeeming feature—a smooth, dry surface that looked a little like suede. Its inhabitant sat crouched forward as though playing dice on the ground; her knees were high on her chest, her arms tucked close to her sides like chicken wings. Her eyes were open, but it was clear she didn't see directly through them. They didn't track to look at her. The orbs were held in place by dozens of tiny black fibers that issued from the white of her eyeballs and traced delicate patterns across her cheek and forehead before disappearing into the bulkhead behind her. Thick ropy strands, like dreadlocks, terminated in her black-finished scalp, carrying information to and from the Cell. Her hands and feet were invisible, completely subsumed into the component. Her knees made two angular bumps beneath her chin, which was mercifully clear of modification.

"Don't be afraid," said the Palmer, audible through her ears alone. "You won't hurt anything."

Melilah took a deep breath and slid her long frame feetfirst into the component. There were no instruments before its pilot, no controls. Just a blank, translucent bulkhead that curved around her on all sides.

As the opening passed over Melilah's head and began to close, she felt a powerful wave of claustrophobic fear break through her.

"My God! What was I thinking?" She tried to kick through the hole before it shrank too small, but her balance had gone along with her self-control. All she did was flail about like a child and crack her head on a wall. "Help me!"

A hand gripped her ankle, steadied her. "Easy, Melilah. I assure you, you're in no danger."

"But—" She pulled herself out of the Palmer's grasp and kicked to the far side of the cramped space. "You're—"

"My name is Sarian." The woman had eased partially out of the Cell's embrace. Her hands were free, as were her breasts. The sight was shockingly asexual. A flicker of annoyance crossed her face. "We're on the same side, for the Dark's sake."

"Melilah, are you okay?" Gard's voice came startlingly loud and clear from outside the component.

"Yes," she forced herself to say, willing her muscles to desist from their frantic attempts to escape. She *knew* she had nothing to fear, even if everything she felt contradicted that knowledge.

She slumped down in the space and looked Palmer Sarian in the blank eyes.

"I'm sorry," she said. "I have a—a phobia, I guess, of extreme modification. It's not usually a problem. I can control it, unless I'm taken by surprise."

Sarian eased back into her notch, mollified by the explanation. "I apologize also," she said. "I was not aware—"

"You couldn't have been." She gestured vaguely in a direction she hoped was forward. "Shall we get moving?"

"Yes, of course."

Melilah assured Gard that all was in order as the Cell component accelerated to join its siblings farther along the pipe. He sounded appeased but not entirely convinced. She imagined the transport he occupied receding into the distance, and tried not to think of it as a safety line just slipping out of her grasp.

+29

Helene-Deangelis watched the battle from the interior of the Occlusion observatory. Connected in fits and starts to the bulk of his higher self in the habitat, he had an ever-changing and sometimes frustrating view. In concert with four other versions of himself in the station—all named after satellites of Saturn—they were responsible for the upkeep of the defenses when the rest of him wasn't able to oversee it for them. The five of them comprised an island of selfhood that wasn't fully independent, yet could function for a while without direct connection to the rest. It felt like slipping in and out of sleep, mixing reality and dream.

His higher self was pushing Cazneaux hard, taking the Reaper to its limits. When the momentary hesitation recurred, the arrow of the *Nhulunbuy* would be ready to fly.

"You guys really know how to put on a show."

Helene-Deangelis broke his concentration to focus on the science officer of the *Nhulunbuy*.

"It's not your concern, Palmer Vermeulen."

"It will be if whoever's piloting that Reaper gets through your defenses."

"Don't worry. She won't get that far."

"'She'? So you know who it is, then."

"I told you—"

"It's not my concern. Right, I heard you the fifth time. Call me old-fashioned, but I like to know the name of the person who's trying to fry me to a crisp."

Irritated at Vermeulen for distracting him, Helene-Deangelis almost forced her to do as she was told. There was a preservation capsule waiting for her and her Cell component. If she would only get into it, he could stop worrying about her well-being and get on with his work.

But he could see her point. Were their positions reversed, he would also want to know at whom to point the finger afterward.

"Exarch Cazneaux has come to Lut-Deangelis to lay claim to the Occlusion," he said. "She thinks she can waltz in here and take it from us. I assure you it won't be so easy. Getting into the system is one thing, getting out again another entirely."

"I can imagine—and she would know that, too. Is negotiation an option?"

"She has spoken briefly to Palmer Eogan. Apart from that, she's not broken silence."

"So she wanted you to know who she was, but she didn't want to talk to you direct. I see." Vermeulen, so extensively woven into the fabric of her Cell that she no longer possessed a recognizable head, managed to convey a suggestive smile purely through the tone of her voice. "I think that makes you more than a little miffed."

"Of course I am! She attacks my system, injures my people, tries to steal what's rightly—" Helene-Deangelis bit down on the word "mine." "She risks another Catastrophe purely in order to further her own ends."

"Isn't that what *you're* doing?"

"At least I'm not doing it on someone else's turf, in a manner that puts innocent people in danger."

"Has anyone been killed yet?"

"There have been thirty-nine fatalities, including Palmer Christolphe." He didn't mention the eleven versions of himself who had been destroyed when the clane self-destructed, or the version of Lazarus Hails that had been grievously damaged in Albert Hall. Whether the latter would be salvageable or not remained to be seen. "Eighty-eight casualties are undergoing treatment."

"That's not so bad," Vermeulen said, "considering the ordinance she's packing."

"*One* involuntary death is one too many," he retorted, defaulting automatically to Exarchate policy.

She had no reply to that.

Outside, the conflict had heated up again, severing communication with the habitat. Helene-Deangelis swad-dled himself in the thoughts of his siblings—Pan-Deangelis, Dione-Deangelis,

Telesto-Deangelis, and Enceladus-Deangelis—and focused on the task ahead of him. His strategic map of the volume around the observatory was fiendishly complex, full of transitory reefs and sharks, and other, stranger, secondary phenomena resulting from the interaction between them. The Reaper slid from shape to shape as it pressed the observatory's defenses. Its mighty engines were unfettered now, able to fire without need of cloaking. Between it and the observatory, the *Nhulunbuy* followed a relatively safe route to one side, avoiding the hottest loci while staying within range if needed.

As Deangelis pressed, so did Cazneaux resist. His entire attention focused tightly on their jostling for ascendancy. They were evenly matched, but that didn't mean they were deadlocked. The nature of the battlefield changed from instant to instant. They fought on many fronts at once, in many different ways.

But in the midst of the fighting, Vermeulen's words nagged at him. She was right: Cazneaux wasn't inflicting the civilian damage she could have been. Had she attacked the habitat directly with the Reaper, instead of bombarding it with relatively simple munitions, the death toll could have been in the thousands. That was something to be grateful for, if nothing else. She could easily have used such a tactic to distract him while she took the Occlusion away.

Perhaps, he thought for a wild moment, he should just give the accursed thing to her and be done with it. That would solve the problem quite neatly and stop anyone else from getting killed . . .

As though she could sense his momentary lack of resolve, the Reaper unleashed a new offensive in his direction, a blistering wave of high-energy vortices that would have torn the observatory apart but for his quick reactions. He slammed up fields and launched a counterattack. Strange ripples spread across the battlefield as space-time warped into threadlike defects, arrayed in contour lines between the two combatants. The Reaper morphed into an oblate spheroid, a last-ditch defensive maneuver.

Helene-Deangelis grinned in triumph. He had Cazneaux on the back foot at last! Diverting power from his shields to the defect generators, he maintained the attack, not letting up for a nanosecond, and warned Palmer Eogan to get ready.

The Reaper sprouted points at two ends, giant spikes easily one hundred meters long. The one facing away from the observatory flashed a brilliant white, drowning out the sun. The forward spike was a deep, light-eating black. The Reaper as a whole surged forward, following that leading point.

The move took Helene-Deangelis by surprise. He had anticipated a retaliatory wave, not for the entire vessel to move. He sent countermeasures to meet it. The Reaper's drive-spike flashed deep blue in response, but its shields held and it kept coming. Helene-Deangelis fired narrow beams of warped vacuum that pierced the invader's shields and carved red lines on the Reaper's black surface. In the wake of the beams, he poured thousands of microsingularities into the wounds. Large, semispherical chunks appeared instantly in the Reaper's hull, as thirty percent of its mass collapsed into black holes.

Still it came.

Helene-Deangelis, his mind moving so quickly that the dance of electrons through a wire seemed sluggish, could only stare at the battlefield in puzzlement. What was Cazneaux doing? He was going to cripple her if she kept attacking like that. She had to know it. What was the point of coming all this way only to sacrifice her greatest asset in such a futile gesture?

Vermeulen said something then that he should have realized much earlier—four words that changed everything.

"She's going to ram!"

Before she had finished the final syllable, he was moving. He belatedly powered the shields back up and angled them to deflect the Reaper away. They swung like wings through molasses from his point of view, far too slowly to come into full effect in time. The Reaper speared for the heart of the observatory at full power, its rearward spike blazing with a sun's intensity, its pockmarked forequarters gaping like an open mouth. He launched a half-hearted counterattack—and noticed only then what the singularities had done. In converting such a large chunk of the Reaper into black holes, they had turned the Reaper into an even more dangerous battering ram than it had been before.

More mistakes. He had miscalculated on so many points that, for a timeless moment, he simply watched the Reaper looming ever closer, convinced that death was the reward he deserved for his stupidity.

Cazneaux's objective wasn't to steal the Occlusion. She wanted to *destroy* it!

But it wasn't just about him. There was the habitat to consider, and the rest of him. Helene-Deangelis and his Saturnian siblings hadn't made their decisions in isolation. They had all been fooled.

He had time left to do two things. He gathered up Palmer Vermeulen, her Cell component, and the preservation capsule in one move. Ignoring her half-formed protest, he thrust her into the one place he knew she would be safe, relatively speaking.

At the same time, Telesto-Deangelis hailed the *Nhulunbuy*.

He would not go quietly into the Dark.

+30

"Now, Eogan, now!"

The cry burst out of the ftl channels with none of Deangelis's usual cool reserve. He sounded almost hysterical.

"You heard the man, Palmer Aesche. Let's get moving!"

"Sir, I think you should—"

A shock wave hit them before she could finish the sentence. The Cell shook like a leaf on a rubber tree. Complex vibrations thrummed through the components, increasing in complexity and amplitude until it seemed to Eogan as though the universe was unraveling. He could barely make out what was happening outside—and what he *could* see, he didn't quite believe.

"Cazneaux's ramming the observatory!"

All thoughts of attacking were temporarily suspended. Events unfolded too quickly. Energy scattered in all directions as the Reaper burst through the observatory's defenses like a bullet shooting an apple in slow motion. The geometric shape the Reaper had adopted began to come apart, sending exotic shrapnel flying. Eogan ducked instinctively as fragments passed near the Cell.

The observatory unfolded like an onion, flinging layer after layer of glowing shells at the attacking vessel. They all hit their mark—but still Cazneaux came on. The Reaper's rear spike burned a sickly purple. Eogan could actually *hear* the vessel's distress as topological waves propagated through the vacuum to the Cell. It sounded like a whale crying. The deathly moan rose in volume and intensity as the Reaper plowed on.

The tip of its leading spike hit the observatory's heart with a resounding flash; and then everything stopped.

In the timeless instant that followed, Eogan understood: *Cazneaux and I agree on one thing, even if we disagree about the best method of dealing with it. The Occlusion is dangerous. If whatever destroyed Sublime comes out of it here, we can kiss Bedlam good-bye. And if it spreads* farther *this time . . .*

The implications were troubling to say the least. Alioth, New Eire, Mizar, Megrez—anyone in the Arc Circuit could be the next to fall.

He appreciated Cazneaux's concern, but he could not countenance her methods.

Said the tic to the hippopotamus, he thought, as both Reaper and observatory vanished into a spray of light.

"Get ready," he warned his crew. The tight-beam feeds connecting the components were still working, for the moment. "*Something*'s going to come out of this alive. If it's not Exarch Deangelis and Palmer Vermeulen, we have to strike hard and fast."

"We're set to go," said Aesche. "Just give us the word."

Eogan performed the mental equivalent of a squint, peering into the raw data for any sign of what might emerge from the titanic collision. Space flexed and buckled around them, tossing them on a restless sea of potential energies. Lightning flashed from the exterior surfaces of the Cell components, earthing into nothing at all.

"There's something . . ."

A shadow flailed through the bright fog, threatening to take shape, then sinking back into the glare. He couldn't make out exactly what it belonged to. It had been curved, perhaps part of the observatory's spherical shell, but it had also seemed to taper back to a point, like the Reaper's nose and tail. He held off a moment longer to be certain.

No word had come from Deangelis or Palmer Vermeulen since that one, urgent cry.

VOID bullets be damned, he thought. If Cazneaux had killed his science officer, he'd take her apart with his bare hands.

"There!" A slender black spike stabbed out of the nova-bright flare. With it came a slight ebbing of the sustained explosion issuing from the collision point. "That's good enough for me. Take us in, Aesche. Let's see what damage we can do!"

The Cell surged beneath him, its streamlined shapes blurring with acceleration. Shock tubes hung posed to fire modified VOID drive pellets by the thousand into the target he had provided. The point he had seen kept rising, dragging a jagged, skeletal shape after it, looking like a corpse half-dissolved in acid. It shuddered and lurched, clearly dying but not yet spent. Beams of sickly yellow light strafed the brightness below it where, presumably, Deangelis or automated systems still fought back. The Reaper's form flowed like electroset metal from shape to shape, never fully attaining one of them.

It stuttered, just as Deangelis had said it would.

"That's what we want to see." Eogan locked the *Nhulunbuy*'s targeting systems on the stricken Reaper and released the VOID bullets. Streams of silver flecks arced away from the Cell, leaving visually odd trails behind them as they warped space. He was reminded of footage he'd once seen of a school of knife fish in an Elizan ocean. The flecks flew in an asymmetric curve to where the Reaper crouched in the throes of dissolution over its prey.

White points of light stitched lines across its coal black skin.

"Got it!" cried one of Eogan's Cellmates. He said nothing in response. Hitting the remains of the Reaper wasn't the important thing. *Killing* it was.

"Now what?" asked Aesche.

"We keep firing," said Eogan, as the Cell drifted across the battlefield with little more than attitude thrusters to nudge it along. "And we hope."

+31

"I hope you know what you're doing, Palmer Flast."

"Don't worry, Melilah," said the chief officer of the *Kwal Bahal,* as replicators spilled in a thick, shining wave over the surface of his component. "It's all under control. I'm just taking a sample—"

At that moment, a quake rolled through the station that made everything else Melilah had experienced seem like a mere ripple. The walls of Faloutsos Junction concertinaed, then stretched like a rubber band. Pressure waves sent replicators flying in a silver spray. The gleaming marbles of the Cell bounced and rolled in flickering, failing light. Total darkness came down with a soundless slam.

The Scale-Free Bedlam feed died without a crackle.

Melilah, arms and legs anchoring her grimly in place so she wouldn't have to come any closer to Palmer Sarian than she had to, emitted an involuntary cry of alarm.

"What happened?" she asked.

"Something big," said the Palmer, blind eyes flickering with wild REM motions. "Give us a second."

"Regroup, regroup!" came Flast's voice. Sarian had extruded screens and instruments for Melilah's benefit, since most of the channels normally available to her were dead. The chief officer's voice came over one of those. "We're unharmed and don't seem to be in any immediate danger."

The Cell's components bunched together like grapes on a windswept vine.

"What about the habitat?" Melilah heard a note of panic in her voice but couldn't swallow it. What had the Reaper *done*?

"It's—" Flast hesitated. "I can't tell. Our instruments picked up an event outside, right off the scales. There was a gravitational surge; that's what we felt a moment ago. But that wasn't enough to shut everything down like this. I'm not getting anything at all from the habitat."

"That's impossible."

"I'm telling you, I'm not getting anything at all."

Melilah refused to believe it. "Vernon, can you hear me?" she shouted into the dead feed. "Angela, Kara—Yasu! Exarch Deangelis! Answer me!"

Silence.

It's dead. Bedlam is dead!

No, she told herself. *It's not possible. It takes more than that to kill a habitat of this size. You'd have to blow it apart from the core out—and if* that *had happened, then even I wouldn't be here right now. None of us would be.*

A premonition hit her, as hard as the pressure wave.

Bedlam died the moment the Occlusion came here . . .

"Wait," said Flast from a component nearby. "I'm picking up an energy reading."

"What sort of reading?"

"I don't know. It's weird-looking: not an instrument artifact or an echo of what's going on outside."

"What *is* going on outside?" asked Sarian. "Is the *Nhulunbuy* okay?"

"No signal."

"Fuck the *Nhulunbuy,*" said Melilah. "Find out what's happening to my home!"

A glimmer appeared in the distance, a gleam of deep-sea phosphorescence. She thought she was imagining it at first, then a wave of light swept over them as the Junction returned to life. Momentarily blinded, Melilah blinked in puzzlement at the screens in front of her.

Alive or dead? she thought. *Make up your mind, for God's sake.*

"Citizens of Lut-Deangelis," boomed a voice from every channel at once, unhurried, authoritative, and sexless. "Please remain calm. Order will shortly be restored."

"Who is this?" asked Flast. "I don't have your voice on file."

"I am a guest to your system. I am here to assist you."

"Where are you from?" asked Melilah, thinking of the Reaper. If the person—or persons—behind *that* had taken control, she wasn't going to be so easily reassured. "Give us your name, not empty words."

"Your Exarch knows me as the Archon," said the voice patiently, "and that is how you will address me, too."

"'The Archon'?" she repeated. "I've never heard of you."

"That is as it should be, under ordinary circumstances." The voice paused for emphasis. "These circumstances are far from ordinary, as you well know. I have come from Sol to set them to rights. Will you assist me in this, Melilah Awad, or hinder me?"

She opened her mouth, then dumbly closed it. Her mind was stuck on the phrase: *from Sol.*

The last time something had come from Sol, it had taken her freedom away.

"I suspect," she managed, "that you and I have very different ideas of what is right."

"And I suspect that I can prove you wrong on that point."

A groan rolled through the habitat. Only then did she notice how quiet it had become.

"My systems are dead," said Sarian, her voice little more than an alarmed whisper. "I can't move."

"Enough talking," declared the Archon. "All unnecessary vehicular activity is now curtailed. Emergency services will act only with my direct authority—but that authority will be instantly given in the case of any genuine emergency. Until your Exarch has recovered sufficiently to resume control, I will be running this habitat. There is a terrible mess for us all to clean up."

Melilah felt overwhelmed. A Palmer Cell inside the habitat and a Reaper outside, the Exarch out of action and something—God only knew what—from distant Sol stepping in to take its place. She felt as if she had somehow drifted into a surreal dream state.

"I want to help," she said. That was the one thing she remained certain of.

"So do I," added Flast. "That's what we're here for, after all."

"Good," said the Archon. "Then let's get started. Continue as you were, Palmer Flast. Your assistance in reducing the nanotech threat will be greatly appreciated."

"Right you are. We'll keep you informed."

As the Cell returned to its original task—capturing active

samples of the invading replicators in order to dissect them and design effective countermeasures—Melilah returned to something the Archon had said about the Exarch's needing to recover before assuming control. She remembered the battered look she had seen on one of Deangelis's faces deep in his hideout. She wondered what had happened to him and whether he was going to be okay.

Part of her, unable to forget the way he had saved her during the initial attack, was unsure which way to hope.

+32

Deangelis woke from a dream of being chopped into numerous tiny pieces.

"Citizens of Lut-Deangelis, please remain calm. Order will shortly be restored."

The voice echoed through all the corridors of the habitat and propagated across the system at the speed of light.

Deangelis recognized it instantly.

The Archon!

At long last, the tangler had finished receiving and assembling the ftl data sent from Sol. Deangelis struggled to gather his thoughts, to put on a good face. He had lost so much of himself. The five Saturnians must have died in the collision between the Reaper and the observatory. Eleven of him had been killed by the clane. And he had been too casual with the Occlusion when it had arrived, thinking that he had plenty to spare on such games. The risks were high, but the benefits . . .

He had seen no benefits so far, and now he struggled to gather enough sense of himself to address the one who had made him in the fashion it deserved.

"No, Isaac, don't overexert yourself." The calm, mannered voice was full of compassion. "Let it come in its own time, as you know it will. I am here now. The urgency is past."

"But I have to—"

"Rest easy, my friend. Recover. We have great works to perform, you and I. When you are ready."

An icy current rushed through him. *Was that what you told*

Jane Elderton? he wanted to ask. *Are these the same assurances you offered before the Catastrophe that almost killed her?*

The Archon's voice came to him from all places, speaking to many different people at once. The same even tone, the same message—a myriad of different words. Exarchs were able to function in parallel to a certain extent, but with none of the capacity or ease of the Archon, their creator and superior in every respect. What the Archon's origins were he didn't know; it could have been human once, or many humans combined; it could have been a seamless blend of biological and made, or even purely artificial. Whatever it was, it was immensely powerful.

"All unnecessary vehicular activity is now curtailed," the Archon announced over the open lines, uniting all its many voices into one again. "Until your Exarch has recovered sufficiently to resume control, I will be running this habitat. There is a terrible mess for us all to clean up."

A terrible, burning shame rose up in him at that. He had failed in his duty. The Archon had been forced to step in and fix what he could not. He'd let his citizens down.

"This is only temporary," the Archon reassured him in private. "I mean that, Isaac. Once this flash point is dealt with, as it will be soon enough, all will return to normal."

He tried to take comfort from the words. After all, the Archon had never lied to him before. Why should it now?

But he knew that what it said was wrong. No matter what its intentions were, it was impossible for things to go back to the way they had been.

He had failed.

In the secret spaces of the habitat, his remaining selves sagged a little at the thought.

+33

"All unnecessary vehicular activity is now curtailed."

The unfamiliar voice broke through the interference but went unnoticed at first by the crew of the *Nhulunbuy*. Facing the skeletal remains of the Reaper rising like a hideous ghost from the burning wreckage of the Occlusion observatory, Eogan's attention was more on the likelihood of his impending death than what was happening in the habitat. Although grievously damaged and not long for the universe, the Reaper was far from toothless—like a wounded dragon rising up over the knight who had speared it, preparing to take one last victim into the grave.

The *Nhulunbuy* could do nothing to fight it off, or to run. Its weapons were ineffectual, and its drives were expended in the attack run. Eogan had nothing left up his sleeve.

"I'm sorry, people," he said. "It wasn't supposed to end like this."

"We had to try," said Aesche. If she regretted following Vermeulen to an early death, it didn't show in her voice.

Almost beautiful in its grimness, the burning Reaper loomed over them.

Good-bye, Melilah, he projected into the vacuum. *At least I saw you again, one last time.*

He tensed for the killing blow.

It didn't fall.

"Stand down, Palmer Eogan," said the unknown voice. "You have done enough."

"Who is this?" Eogan broadcast. "What's going on?"

"I am the Archon. There will be no more fighting."

The Reaper crumpled in on itself like a burning log, its shape dissolving into fragments with a shower of high-energy sparks.

"We've lost what thrusters we had left," said Aesche. "We really are drifting, now."

Eogan thought fast.

All unnecessary vehicular activity is now curtailed.

"Where's Deangelis?" he asked it.

"Until your Exarch has recovered sufficiently to resume control," it said, "I will be running this habitat. There is a terrible mess for us all to clean up."

"He's not *my* Exarch," Eogan retorted, although he agreed about the mess. "What about Cazneaux? Who's to say she won't try again?"

"I assure you, Palmer Eogan," it said evenly, "she will not."

The words were calmly delivered, with no sense of braggadocio, and Eogan believed them utterly. The Archon had somehow reached out and killed his motive power without firing a shot, and stopped the Reaper when it was on the verge of destroying him. Whatever resources the Archon had at its disposal, he didn't doubt that they were sufficient to the task of keeping a rogue Exarch under control.

And who else, he asked himself, had that capacity but someone from Sol?

"You're a long way from home," he said.

"I am indeed."

"Will you be staying long?"

"Only so long as I am needed."

"You're here because of the Occlusion, I'm guessing."

"That is correct."

The tangled wreckages of the observatory and the Reaper burned on, blurring into each other like a small lava moon. "It's not destroyed, then?"

"To accomplish that would require more energy than contained in this entire system."

Eogan's unvoiced hopes died then, that Cazneaux might have succeeded—in her terrible, destructive way—at achieving what he could not.

Vermeulen, Cobiac, and Bray. The roll call of victims was growing steadily longer. How many more of his crew would the Occlusion kill, directly or indirectly, before it was finished with him?

"If you give me back my thrusters," he said, "I'll stabilize my orbit."

“Do so,” said the Archon. “I have no wish to inconvenience you further.”

“What *are* your intentions?”

“That entirely depends,” said the Archon, “on what happens next.”

+INTERLUDE

One hundred eighty years before

Things had seemed so simple. Bedlam was the newest Arc Circuit colony: a foundling system built from the legacy of a failed expedition, its marvelous, ever-growing habitat a marvel of human ingenuity, its citizens embracing a novel form of society that promised to avoid the pitfalls of usual top-down government. On the frontier of many territories, Bedlam became known as an exciting place to live. It accepted nationals of all systems, provided only that they adhered to the information laws. The lives of everyday people took on new significance when what was normally hidden from view became accessible to all. Traditional notions of scandal and gossip were transformed. The whole system was a giant soap opera, with cast and audience indistinguishable. Some people came simply to observe; others hoped for a starring role. Many found it not to their tastes; many relished the challenges and the opportunities alike, and stayed for good.

Interstellar traders came and went, perhaps not as frequently as they did to other systems but often enough to ensure that Bedlam wasn't completely isolated. People came and went, too, as populations shifted sluggishly from home to home. It would have seemed strange to pre–Space Age humans, but one could grow tired of an entire planet, and surprisingly quickly, too. Melilah Awad had settled on Bedlam almost by accident, carried there by the momentum of her lost mother's conviction. Enamored of its political and ever-changing architecture, she threw herself wholeheartedly into the life of the colony. She made friends, took lovers, held parties, embraced life.

Dominic Eogan was a spacer she met at an ancient music recital, not long after her eighteenth year on Bedlam. He was solid and square, and his dark hair drifted lazily in the low gee. She hadn't met many spacers who could match her height, and she was instantly attracted to his easygoing manner. His eyes were a refreshingly muddy green, unmodified from the shade his genes had given him. In a crowd of startling blues—the current trend—his natural tones stood out.

She was immediately taken by him and took the first opportunity she could find to get him one-on-one. She made certain the group he was with merged with hers and that they sat next to each other over dinner. That night they just talked—about art, their backgrounds and family, opportunities for study in-system, recent scientific advances, and more—with ever-growing familiarity. He described his love of the stars, and she tried to convey what she saw in Bedlam, which he was visiting for the first time and hadn't quite grasped yet.

Later, she was able to scan back through the archives and relive that first meeting. The entire conversation was recorded as a matter of course by the habitat's monitors. She noted the way his eyes followed her, the fleeting touch of his hand to her shoulder, the fullness of his lips when he drank from a bulb of vodka. She saw herself unconsciously lean in close until they were almost touching, the attention she paid to his hands and arms, and a brief moment at the end of the evening when she had wondered if he was about to kiss her.

That instant was especially vivid in her mind. Her heart had pounded. She didn't understand why he had hesitated and pulled away, and why she hadn't grabbed him to urge him back. Why hadn't they taken it further? And why was she scouring the records afterward like some teenager frantic for a clue?

Either way, they had parted on an agreement to meet for lunch two days later. The attraction was still there, but she was cautious now, wondering if he had a relationship elsewhere that he was honoring, although he hadn't mentioned as much before. Did he think *she* was attached? All he had to do was check the social register to see that she wasn't.

Lunch blended into drinks, then dinner, and finally she could stand it no longer.

"I feel like I know you very well, Dominic," she'd told him, as they stood on the cusp of the night, reviewing the day and wondering what would happen next, "but I know that I don't. I'd like to correct that."

He took her hand. "You and me both."

She kissed him. He didn't pull away. The scent of his skin was rich and heady in her nostrils.

"Don't go back to your ship tonight," she whispered, through the heat of their commingled breath. "Stay with me."

All hesitation was gone, now. Their embrace became more intimate. She broke away long enough to hail a transport.

He didn't go back to his ship for two days.

That was how Melilah remembered the beginning. It matched the facts pretty well. If ever she wondered whether she had imagined the intensity of their early days, all she had to do was glance back at the records. They support-ed every pheromone-steeped recollection. She had it in hard storage, excised from her personal archives and partitioned so she could view her relationship with Dominic Eogan as a single, continuous arc—or not view it at all, as the case might be.

The arc lasted seven months, spread out over thirty years.

"It's not so simple," he said on the third day they had known each other. "We have to be clear-eyed and unromantic about this. I'm a trader, and you're a colonist. We both love what we do, and it would be unfair for either of us to ask the other to give that up."

"Wow. You're really looking ahead." They were floating together in the close confines of her apartment. A single-lobed chamber then, lacking the amenities she would enjoy many decades later, it was a little too cramped for two. She didn't care about that. In free fall with the lights out, it felt as though they were floating in space, surrounded by infinity.

"Is that wrong? I know what I want and how I feel, but I'm not a slave to either. I have a choice: to find out what you want now, before things get complicated, or just dive in and hope we can fix the mistakes later. Me, I don't want to make any mistakes."

"Nor do I, Dominic. But unfortunately they're inevitable. Murphy's Law still works in Bedlam."

"It works everywhere, Mel. But you must understand what I'm saying. I'm here for a week, then I'll be gone for at least two years. We can be long-distance lovers, we can even remain faithful to each other, but we can't be together as often as we might like. As I would like us to be."

She received the impression that this was a speech he had made several times in the past, and that it was as much for his benefit as for hers. "This isn't a fling for you, then?"

"Is it for you? Tell me if it is; that'll make things much simpler."

"Do you *want* simpler?"

She felt his cheek flex against hers: a smile, she thought. "I don't have a lay in every port, if that's what you're thinking."

"And I don't make a habit of picking up traders."

"Well, then. We're both crazy to be getting involved like this."

"I know."

"It's hard enough maintaining a friendship between systems. A romance—"

"Do you want to stop now?"

He was silent for a long time. The darkness pressed in on them like a coffin. What had earlier seemed so vast and limitless became claustrophobic, moribund, the longer it lasted.

"Enough," she said, kissing him. "You don't have to answer that. I'm not sure I could, if you asked me."

His smile returned. "What if I said that we *should* end this now? Would it make you want me more?"

"That which cannot be possessed," she said, "that which common sense rails against, that which I know will probably be bad for me in the long run . . . ?"

She didn't need to answer with words. Despite life-extending upgrades and a substantial knowledge of human biology, they were still creatures of flesh and blood. Matters of the heart never responded well to logic.

"I can handle whatever life throws at me," she said, a seventy-four-year-old woman feeling like a teenager again.

"Are you sure?"

"As sure as I'm ever likely to be."

She went into it with her eyes open, telling herself that was a good thing. Like someone facing a firing squad without a blindfold, it didn't help at all.

Time was short. She gave him a tour of the habitat, forgoing transports for a more intimate look at her home. He reciprocated with a flyby of the ship on which he served, a clunky mess of magnetic vanes, cargo containers, and VOID drive needles all wrapped up in angular scaffolding. Its lack of symmetry dismayed her; she sensed that something wasn't quite right about it, that there must be a better way of crossing the gulf between stars. But she wasn't a space engineer, and she didn't criticize his way of life just as he hadn't criticized hers.

On the fourth day, they flew unassisted over Bedlam, naked to the sun. If the primary chose that moment to flare, they would both be boiled in their suits. Even though PARASOL's sensors had given them the all clear, the hint of danger made it all the more exciting. They held hands and spun gently through the vacuum.

Three days later, he was gone.

They steeled themselves for his departure. Continuity, not fidelity, was the issue. Whatever happened while they were apart, they would be there for each other when he returned. They would at least try to make it work.

Melilah managed to watch the clunky ship accelerate into the starfield without shedding a tear, but it was hard. When it had disappeared, she swore that she would return to the life she had known and been perfectly happy with. She soon found, though, that nothing was the same as it had been. Dominic Eogan was a dye that had seeped into her, coloring everything. She saw the same friends, did the same work, and went to the same places. But now they all lacked *him,* as though she was seeing the world through a filter that made it a darker, unnatural place.

Eogan maintained irregular contact over the time he was away, constrained by VOID drive relativity effects and low-bit light-speed communications. Time passed more quickly for him than for her, but she never once resented him for that. He hopped ships at Altitude and took another straight back to Bedlam.

His return was triumphant and wonderful. Melilah's friends—who had had two years to become acquainted with him, in absentia—embraced him as if he was one of their own. He made friends of his own and explored the habitat itself, making it as close to a home as anything else he had. For two weeks they were together, and happy.

Then he was gone again, this time for three and a half years. They took a month to reacquaint after that, to catch and cling to each other like trapeze artists, getting back into the swing of things. It was exhilarating, better than anything Melilah had experienced before. There were ups and downs, naturally, but there was a sense of certainty underlying the bad times that made them easier to endure. All she had to be was patient, she felt, and all would be well.

Still, patience was expensive. The years between each life-giving oasis were hard to endure. She devoted herself to work and to hobbies, finding solace in activities both solitary and social. On occasion, she allowed a certain intimacy to develop with others, but never anything of the intensity she experienced with Eogan. She knew where to draw the line, as she was sure he did, too. There were boundaries she would not cross for fear of shattering something that was, at its heart, delightfully fragile. Sex was sex, but love—commitment, common goals, *continuity*—was something else entirely.

That he never once checked the public records to see if she had remained faithful to him—a fact she knew for certain, for that, too, was on public record—spoke volumes. They trusted each other to *come back,* no matter where they went.

And for a while, it had been good.

Some journeys, however, were too perilous. Interstellar space and patterns of intimacy were well-charted territories, crossed many times in human history. Newer frontiers were gradually unspooling, along with new ways of exploring. On Eogan's tenth return to Bedlam, for their twenty-fifth anniversary of meeting and her ninety-ninth birthday, he told her that he was thinking of joining the Palmers.

"The Palmers?" She remembered her lack of comprehension with dismaying clarity. A few early Cells had drifted through Bedlam during his most recent absence. She found their design more pleasing than that of their awkward predecessors. Their safety record was impressive, too. If Eogan wanted to join the trading movement, then that was fine by her.

So why his worried look, as though he was about to confess something further beyond the pale than a new assignment?

"There are"—he hesitated—"*conditions* of membership. You should know what they are before I accept."

"You've already decided." Melilah didn't inflect it as a question. She knew him well enough, now, to read that much.

"I know what I'd like to do, but I don't know how you'll feel about it. I can't decide until we talk about it."

"So talk." She felt nervous without knowing why. Although they were floating naked once again in her apartment, touching all along their lengths, he suddenly seemed as distant and frigid as a deep-space satellite. His hair, still impractically long, brushed gently against her forehead. She pulled away.

"Tell me, Dominic."

He did, and her sixth sense was justified. She was a Natural, disliking obvious or unnecessary biomodifications on ideological grounds. He was suggesting a total submission to nanoware support systems that shocked her deeply. Every Palmer was expected to form a symbiotic relationship with the Cell he or she rode between the stars. Eogan's body would melt into the walls of the Cell components when they were in transit, leaving only the patterns of him intact, the flows of information that defined his thoughts, his memories, his decisions. He would retain the illusion of selfhood, required to keep him sane and at least nominally human, but human he would no longer be. He would be a posthuman hybrid—a monster.

"Not a monster, Mel." He tried to make her understand. "I know it's hard to accept. A lot of people don't see the need for radical biomods here. But out in the Dark it's different. If we want to survive, we have to go to extreme lengths. I'm already modified, but not enough to endure more than another decade out there. In a Cell I'll be safer. I'll be able to travel faster. We can see more of each other."

"But you won't be *you.*"

"What am I now? You can't see beneath my skin. I could be the same as you, or I could be completely different."

"I'd know if you were." *If you came back more Cell than man . . .*

"Would you?"

Something about his tone made her pull farther away. The thought that he might already have made the change, might be adopting a semblance of his old self to preempt her, trick her, made her feel physically nauseous.

Her first instinct was to lash out, to hurt him back. She forced herself to examine that urge before acting on it. Was she truly worried about his possible inhumanity, or was she simply disappointed that he obviously planned to keep traveling longer than *another decade or so?*

It was both, she decided. The two emotions were too intimately entangled to separate. She just wanted him: *more* of him, the *real* him, not less of some thin-skinned imitation.

"What would you do if I said I didn't like the idea?"

He shrugged. "I'd think about my decision very carefully."

"That much at least, I hope."

"You know I love you."

All reservations vanished at his simple words. She wrapped herself around him and tucked her head into the crook of his neck. She hated the welling of tears that made her eyes feel fat and heavy in the low gee. "Yes," she said. "I'll always know that."

And I love you, she thought. Just *you* . . .

He was still there the next morning, and the morning after that. Then he left with the ship he'd arrived on, giving her his assurance that he would return the same way in two and a half years' time.

His words were as good as granite. He came back to her in one piece, altered neither in his affection nor in himself. The matter of the Palmers didn't come up again, and she assumed it over and done with. They continued their relationship unchecked, reacquainting and relishing the chance to do so.

Later—older and, as she would like to believe herself, wiser—she could see the cracks. She could see the thing in him that she didn't want to acknowledge. As the Palmers grew in influence and spread to dominate the trade lanes, the number of ordinary starships making long runs decreased. More and more of the old vessels retired to individual colonial systems and stuck to interplanetary routes, ferrying colonists and resources back and forth on journeys measured in days not years. Dominic Eogan would never be satisfied with that. For all that he feared the Dark, he loved it, too. The Dark was his true companion, and always had been; Melilah Awad was a mistress who kept to the hot spaces, where her cold competitor could not venture. She had thought her and her relationship safe in Bedlam, and perhaps hoped for more still: that Eogan might one day turn his back on the void, choose her. If so, she had been dreaming, just as he would have been dreaming to think that *she* might follow *him*. To lose her home, her body, her *self*—that would have left her with nothing at all.

She had in effect asked him to do what she could not. And instead of telling her that the request was unreasonable and trying to find a way around it, he kept the desire close to his chest, where it ate at him. Or so she imagined it. She could only wonder in retrospect what had led him to such extremes on their last sojourn together—when everything had seemed the same as always, when their relationship had felt as solid as ever, when she had finally convinced herself to get rid of the last of the lingering doubts. She'd had no idea of the pressure building up inside him.

On the second day of March 2287, the brand-new Palmer Cell *Cirencester* hove to beside Bedlam. Unknown to her, although available on the public record afterward, the *Cirencester*'s chief officer contacted Eogan to repeat the offer made to him five years earlier: to join the Palmers. The timing was impeccable, and suspiciously so. The captain of Eogan's existing trader had only recently announced that he and his vessel would be traveling next to Schiller's End and there ceasing interstellar trade for good.

The net had finally closed in around Dominic Eogan. He spent the third of March 2287 with Melilah, giving no sign of his internal conflict. In retrospect she wondered if he had been a little *too* attentive, devoting himself to her more than he normally would have—but not so much that she had noticed and become suspicious. It had been a day together like many others they had shared on Bedlam. She didn't know, as the habitat's calendar clicked over to the fourth of March, that it would be their last.

She woke alone. He had left in the night without waking her, without apology or explanation, without even saying good-bye. While she had slept, he had signed his life over to the *Cirencester.* The Cell broke dock at about the same time she stirred, and was out of the system before she realized what he had done. By then, the replicators had taken her lover apart and made him something irrefutably *other,* bonded with him more intimately than she could ever have dreamed or wanted to—and they had done so long before she truly understood that he wasn't coming back to her.

The pain was awful.

At first she despaired that Dominic Eogan had ceased to exist. The thing now called Palmer Eogan might imagine that it was still him, that it had a connection to the people and things it had known in its past, but she swore that it would receive a terrible surprise if it tried to come back to her. She couldn't forget what it was, and she couldn't forgive how the idea of it had seduced the Dominic she had loved away from her, hurting her more deeply in the process than if she had lost her own body.

Then she wondered if she had ever known him at all . . .

Wrenching emotional dislocation, betrayal of the worst kind—one that might have been avoidable had he only *talked* to her about it, or made a clean break—and a sense of utter powerlessness conspired to erode her self-esteem, which she resisted as powerfully as she would have fought him, had he been an available target. She went from being a popular, confident person to one who shunned the limelight and hated the open policy of Bedlam. She tried to cleanse herself of the stain of him, to reset her life to the way it had been before he had become part of it, but that was as difficult as it had been between visits. Most of all, she tried to forget how good it had been before everything had turned bad—but how could she do that without turning her back on the thirty years of her life in which he had been so pivotal? It would be like killing part of her.

Sometimes she wished that he had died, not just disappeared. That would have been easier than coping with his utter rejection of her—and the thought that he was still out there somewhere, imagining himself free.

Only as time passed was she able to parcel up the pain and put it behind her. By moving on—to new relationships, new professional challenges, new phases in her life—she was able to lay down progressively more buffers between her and the mess of emotions that would always be there, whenever she remembered or was reminded of him. The situation wasn't ideal, but she could see no other way to persist.

All it hinged on was never seeing him again.

Life was simpler when she had loved Dominic Eogan, and it was simpler when she had hated him, too. Both were undeniable, and equally false comforts. One hundred and fifty years later, she knew that life resisted such simplifications. Life—like her feelings for Eogan—was a snake in a bottle. Given enough time, it would either find a way out, or die. And when it got out, its bite was full of poison.

+34

"Okay, Sarian," said Melilah. "You can drop me off here."

The Cell component came to a gentle halt. "I don't think I could've gone much farther anyway. The way is tight ahead."

The Palmer wasn't mistaken. Recent shocks to the habitat had prompted a premature collapse in some of its deeper levels. A pipe Melilah had followed with ease just days before was now flattened like a kinked hose. There was a chance that the route she sought was gone forever, subsumed by the core.

"Are you sure you don't want me to wait?" asked the Palmer.

"Positive." The ride in the component had been claustrophobic and uncomfortable. "Thanks for going out of your way, though. I appreciate it."

"Stick to the route we mapped, won't you?" Sarian's blank eyes expressed no emotion, but her face was a mask of concern. "I'd feel better knowing you're not going to stumble across a patch of infection on the way back."

"Of course. And good luck clearing up the rest."

A hole opened in the side of the component, finally giving her a way out. Melilah slid headfirst through it. The warped confines of the pipe seemed luxurious in comparison.

She patted the humming flank of the component, genuinely grateful for the help the Palmers had offered. "Godspeed," she said, not knowing the right words.

With the faintest of sighs, the component healed itself and rushed back up the pipe, leaving her alone at last.

She took her bearings and headed deeper. Five hours had passed since the arrival of the Archon and the suspension of hostilities. In the wake of the attack by the Reaper, the first priority of the habitat had been to regroup and take stock. The gradual recovery of the Scale-Free Bedlam feed enabled most sectors involved to report casualties, injuries, replicator infections, and penetrator impact sites. The list was long, but less than she had feared. Yasu's response had been typical: to get into a shelter and ride it out. Only one shelter had been holed during the attack, and even there fewer than a dozen people had died.

Still, her blood boiled as the tally of dead and dying rose. None of it had been necessary. She didn't believe all the rumors she was hearing, but whoever had been behind the Reaper would pay dearly for the hurt inflicted on her home. She would make sure of that. If the destruction of the Occlusion had been the objective of the attack, that only made it worse. Bedlam wasn't a *distraction;* those who had fallen during the fight weren't *disposable.*

It came as only a small consolation that someone had had the same thought she had. The Occlusion was important. Getting her hands on it was rapidly becoming her next priority, once everything returned to normal.

Normal.

She'd almost forgotten the meaning of the word.

The tunnel kinked and twisted, taking her farther away from the nearest network node, deeper into silence. She slithered and wriggled where she should have soared. Once, facing a hairpin bend that threatened to be too much for her spine, she considered giving up and turning back. But she needed to keep going. She needed to rid herself of the itch that nagged at her, of the hook in her lip that simply wouldn't let her swim free . . .

The narrow niche had very nearly squeezed shut since her last visit. There was just enough room for her to slide her arm in and pat around inside. The disk she had placed there was still securely attached to the wall; it popped free with a gentle twist, giving way in response both to the torsion and the presence of her fingerprints. She held it in her hand for a moment, weighing it, then slid it out into view.

Black, flat, and unadorned. There was nothing on the outside to indicate the bombshell within. Someone stumbling across it by accident might think it contained just banking records or an embarrassing attempt at an erotic novel. There were many people who went to such lengths to bury one aspect of themselves they didn't want in the public domain. In Bedlam, it took a concerted effort to forget.

And even then . . . Melilah felt tears spring to her eyes as she contemplated the contents of the disk. *Dammit!* She knew the contents of the disk by heart. She had taken the records of the time she and Eogan had spent together and buried them deep, metaphorically and physically. Many, many times she had consigned them to a memory disk and hidden them in the habitat's core, fully intending to let them be subsumed by Bedlam's ever-growing, dead heart. Inevitably, though, she reclaimed them—usually under the pretext of moving them to a safer location, where their lonely destruction was more perfectly assured. But she knew the game she was playing with herself, the cycle she had wittingly followed for a century and a half.

Eogan was a glitch that had haunted her for too long. Until she could polish him up and place him beside her other trinkets, that was what he would always be. Keeping him dusty and hidden in the attic of her mind was a sure way to keep stumbling across him forever.

She wanted to let go, but part of her couldn't. She wasn't done with those memories yet. And the harder she tried to destroy their electronic vestiges, the stronger they seemed to burn into her mind.

She was scarred, tortured, and haunted by the past.

And now he was back.

Before she could talk herself out of it—letting emotion carry her like a soliton wave in the wake of the attack on her home, the kiss in the alien wreckage, and the injection of Gentry nanoware into her system—she gripped the disk tightly in both hands and snapped it in two. The sound of it broke the silence of Bedlam's heart: a simple *crack* that echoed for a microsecond from the twisted pipe walls, then disappeared.

It was done, she thought. Done at last. She held the fragments of her life with Eogan, one-half of the shattered disk in each hand, and felt no different.

"Melilah?"

The voice came electronically, not through her ears. She stirred herself and replied in kind. "Is that you, Prof?"

"I'm glad I found you." A tiny drone buzzed up the twisted pipe toward her, broadcasting Virgo's voice where the network couldn't reach. "Palmer Sarian said she dropped you off somewhere down here. The Exarch is looking for you."

"I don't suppose he told you what for?" she asked.

"There's a debriefing meeting in one hour. The Archon has

asked for someone to represent Deangelis's nonspecialized subjects. We thought it should be you."

Melilah grunted. She hated that word: "subjects." It made her feel like the chattel of some inbred king.

"I'll be there," she said.

The tiny drone buzzed as a pressure wave rolled through the habitat's depths. "I don't think it's very safe down here, Melilah."

She agreed. "Hang on," she said. "There's just something . . ." She stuck her hand back into the flattened niche and searched for the data fiche that had been there the last time she had visited. She hadn't found it while looking for her disk, and that puzzled her. The two had been next to each other; she should have noticed it.

She slid her hand across the buckled surface of the niche's interior, feeling for any sign that it had come dislodged. Nothing. It was gone.

The walls groaned around her like peristalsis in a giant's belly. Prof Virgo nervously cleared her throat. Time to go. She slid her hand free and turned about in the flattened pipe. The air thrummed in time with the vibration under her palms and toes; her ears popped.

She kicked forward just as the pipe began to shake. Buzzing furiously, the drone led her back the way she had come, along pipes that flexed and writhed like snakes. The hairpin turn that had earlier almost forced her back loosened just enough to let her by a second time. Then it slammed shut, guaranteeing that she would never come that way again.

The fragments of her memory disk lay in the collapsed bowels of the habitat. There would be no recovering them now, should she change her mind.

Not so, she thought, for the owner of the other memory cache. Whoever the fiche belonged to, they had obviously retrieved it before the collapse. That implied that the memories contained on the fiche were more important than simple throwaways. It also implied that the person they were important *to* was still somewhere on the station.

Lesbian lovers gallivanting around the Arc Circuit my ass, she thought, taking up the mystery again as she and the drone headed for the lower inhabited levels. She would find out what lay at the heart of it, she promised herself. And more besides.

+35

The mind of the habitat flexed like a squid in lightless ocean depths, casting tentacles about to touch loci of pain, chaos, and disease.

Exarch Deangelis, no stranger to pain himself, watched its throes with a feeling of compassion. *Poor, ancient thing,* he thought, *twisted and time-encrusted.* After the death of the First Wavers centuries ago, it had grown alone in the Dark, deprived of intelligent companionship and guidance for decades, until humanity had rediscovered the home it had made and inhabited its living halls once again. For almost two centuries it had known people and vitality; not even the Exarchate Expansion had tried to take that away from them. And now monsters had come out of the void to threaten it, sting it, poison it.

The habitat physically shrugged, as though hunkering down against a chill wind. Seismic detectors registered vibrations in all quarters. Subsidence monitors flashed. Sensors accurate to micrometers recorded the slight shrinking of the habitat's outer layers as the core carefully added another layer of abandoned levels to its growing mass. Wrapped tight within its ever-thickening layer of compressed material, the AI, perhaps, felt a little easier for it.

The process took just seconds. Aftershocks rumbled for several minutes, then they, too, faded away.

"This is a most remarkable ecology," said the Archon.

Exarch Deangelis looked up from the point of view of his self from Earth. The Archon had no outward physical presence; the computations that comprised the visitor from Sol were performed by processors scattered throughout the habitat, plus an increasing number manufactured to precise specifications in the hours since the end of the crisis. Still, the body of Earth-Deangelis straightened to attention, feeling that at least one of him should make an outward show of reverence, like a child before its stern parent.

"I agree," he said. "But then, you already know that."

"I do, Isaac. That's why I chose you for this colony. It's unique, just as you are. None of your siblings would tolerate what goes on here. None of them would indulge such peccadilloes as you do. And I am proud of you for doing so."

Deangelis felt himself flush, although he wasn't sure why. A mixture of shame and satisfaction rushed through him, momentarily snagging his thoughts in its wake.

"You know," the Archon went on, "that the principles on which this colony was founded stand in direct opposition to those of the Exarchate. It is not possible for openness to exist between all levels of society. It simply cannot last."

"Once I would have agreed with you," Deangelis said, his words cautious at first, but becoming less faltering as his confidence grew. "I would have said that authority couldn't exist without effective barriers to communication. I would have argued that the truth must be hidden, sometimes, to protect those who would be harmed by it. I would have pressed for secrecy, as I did when I first came here, to keep to myself that which I did not want to reveal."

"And now . . . ?"

"Now I'm not so sure." There was no point lying to the Archon. "Where secrecy exists, conspiracies thrive. When the citizens of this habitat have free access to all commercial and personal information, it's simply not possible for unnatural power imbalances to emerge among them—either spontaneously or by design. Who would be threatened by someone whose most intimate details are public knowledge—and when the threat itself is visible from all corners of the habitat?

"That's not to say that exploitation doesn't still exist. There are always the negligent, the willingly dominated, the stupid, and the imperceptive—who consent to relationships that most others will not. But they do so at least *theoretically* informed. It's entirely their responsibility what they do with their lives. If they let it happen, that's their decision."

The Archon chuckled. "But where do *you* fit into all of this, Isaac? Are you part of this pretty picture you paint? Or are you the artist, manipulating the canvas until it meets your satisfaction, but never placing yourself upon it? Do you allow one rule for them and another for you?"

Deangelis sighed. "I tried. I honestly did. You can see from the records the efforts I went to; I've erased nothing from them."

"I know," said the Archon.

"Then you already know the answer to your question."

"I know what the facts say. I can see that you let your citizens observe you as freely as you observe them. You let natural differences in technology create the barrier you would not deliberately enforce. No matter how they watch you, no matter how they study your inner workings, they have as little chance of deciphering you as an Elizabethan accountant would a quantum computer. Yet some persist, attempting to pattern-match the signals between your various selves in the vain hope that they will one day come to know your secrets. The fools."

The Archon paused, as though giving him a chance to deny the accusation that he deliberately allowed censorship by default.

"I know that you have secrets, Isaac; the facts tell me that much, very clearly. But I want to hear what your heart says about them. That's what concerns me more."

Deangelis fought a strange urge to weep. The longing between Melilah Awad and Palmer Eogan surfaced unwittingly, from a place unknown.

"Must it be this way forever?" he asked. "Must we always lie to and conceal from those we love?"

"Sometimes, yes. And sometimes we must betray them, too."

"Like you betrayed Jane Elderton?"

"What makes you ask that, Isaac?"

He bit his lip. The question had burst out of him in a rush, out of the body he inhabited, not the greater mind from whose horrified viewpoint he watched. For one terrible moment he saw the exact same scene through two very different sets of eyes.

"I'm sorry," he said, blinking to bring himself back into focus. "I'm afraid, too. The Sublime Catastrophe was—awful. I have no wish to see a repeat of it here."

"None of us do," said the Archon. "I don't want anyone else to die. That is why we need to prosecute this matter as quickly as possible, with the maximum possible decorum. The front we present to the community here must be absolutely united. Are you with me on this, Isaac?"

Earth-Deangelis took a deep breath. "I will continue to keep my secrets. *Our* secrets."

"That's not what I meant."

"I would never defy the Exarchate, or you."

"Would you follow us willingly?"

"Yes."

He felt the Archon's attention sweep across and through him like the fiery stare of a god. He trembled in the face of it.

"Yes," he repeated with more conviction. How could he not willingly obey Sol? The Archon and the Exarchate were more than just colleagues. They were made of the same stuff; they were *family.*

Like all families, there were squabbles. And worse.

"I want to see Frederica Cazneaux punished for what she did to me," Deangelis said, his voice low and determined. "Her, at the very least."

"I've already said that I'll look into it," the Archon said. "Let's get the pieces back on the board first, Isaac, then decide where to concentrate our efforts. It may turn out that the most worrying threat has yet to reveal itself."

The Occlusion. It had floated passively throughout the conflict while vast forces tugged back and forth over it. What would happen if it awoke?

Deangelis had no answer to that question, just as he had yet to exact a guarantee from the Archon that he would be avenged upon the Exarch who had attacked his colony. He wondered fleetingly if the Occlusion was being used to distract him, if the Archon had some reason for protecting Exarch Cazneaux from his wrath.

He dismissed the thought as utter fantasy. His mind was still addled from attrition and disorientation. He couldn't entertain such paranoid fantasies if he was ever to regain his balance, his *self*.

An autonomous agent nudged him, reminding him of his meeting to discuss the habitat's woes.

"There's work to be done," he said, shrugging aside his fears and his anger. His first responsibility was to the people under his care. If he failed at that, nothing else mattered. "I need to inform everyone of your decisions."

The Archon smiled upon him, filling him with warmth.

"Of course, Isaac. You're a good Exarch. One, as I have said, that I'm very proud of."

Good dog, Deangelis thought guiltily as he cast his mind across the station. *Roll over. Fetch.*

The habitat shuddered again, reminding him of the ancient AI lurking in its depths. If only, he thought, he could feel secure by burying himself in another layer of dead skin.

Play dead.

+36

In the relative peace and quiet of space, Palmer Eogan stood guard over the remains of the Reaper and the observatory it had attacked. The vast, flickering wreckage stood out against the stars, a self-contained, angular aurora with darkness at its heart. The *Nhulunbuy,* in its normal extended configuration, had taken extensive scans of the complex knot that was all that remained of both. Strange spines speared at odd angles, trailing sparks. Warped rings and hoops spilled from jagged, cavernous rents. It was difficult to tell what had belonged to what.

Part of him admired Exarch Cazneaux for her bold effort, even if, in the end, it amounted to nothing but a monumental folly.

"We're not picking up anything," said Palmer Aesche from N-4 on the far side of the wreck, currently identified by the newly reinstated Lut-Deangelis Traffic Control as "Hazard One." The Cell had returned to its usual, strung-out configuration and recovered enough motive power to move three of its components at will. The rest had little more than attitudes to keep them from drifting. Several drones had arrived recently from Bedlam and, like the *Nhulunbuy,* studied the wreck with close attention. Thus far they had done nothing to interfere, so Eogan warily let them be.

"Keep trying," he told her.

"Do you really think there's anything alive in there?"

He didn't, but he wasn't going to be the one to admit it. "Until I have Palmer Vermeulen's remains in front of me, I'm going to keep an open mind."

Aesche's skepticism was as radiant as Hazard One itself, but she didn't press him any further. Both of them knew that his intentions weren't entirely honorable: the opportunity to probe Exarchate technology in such a broken state was rare and had to be pursued. Vermeulen would have insisted. So would have Palmer Christolphe.

They had just heard rumors of the Negotiator Select's death. It had come as a shock—not because Christolphe was particularly well liked, even among his own, but because Palmers weren't used to death coming in the relatively safe confines of a habitat. In the Dark, yes, where a single particle could slam through a weak shield with the force of an atomic warhead. But not while docked, surrounded by many layers of dead matter traveling at barely a few kilometers a second.

Exarch Cazneaux and her booby-trapped clane had sent a message to the Palmers at the same time as she hurt the Exarch. *Be careful with whom you ally yourselves. There are more dangerous things in the universe than mysterious alien artifacts.*

Perhaps, thought Eogan, but now Cazneaux's best shot at destroying the Occlusion was a glowing menace to navigation, destined to be dumped into the sun once the Exarch got his act together.

His mind wandered as he waited for word of any kind. He doubted the Occlusion would suffer such an ignominious fate—although the experiment would be interesting to conduct. What would happen at the Sublime end of the wormhole if this one was exposed to the stellar atmosphere? Would the extreme temperature and pressure flush the passage clean of any remaining aggressive tech, so humans could use it in safety? Or would the walls burst under the insult, ruining the wormhole forever and thereby robbing humanity of a valuable xenarcheological artifact?

Again, Palmer Vermeulen would have had an opinion. She would have voiced it, asked or not, either in her capacity as science officer or as a friend. The more certain Eogan was that she was dead, the more he found himself missing her presence in the Cell. Her absence unbalanced it more than the half Flast had excised to form the *Kwal Bahal*. Even if that half returned, the *Nhulunbuy* would still feel out of kilter.

"The Dark take you and keep you," he whispered, mouthing the words of an old Palmer verse often quoted at assemblies for those lost in transit. "The light of ancient stars guide you to rest . . ."

Icons rippled across his field of view. Someone from the habitat was trying to hail him. He glanced at the origin of the signal, but didn't quite believe what it was telling him.

"Melilah?"

She didn't waste time with pleasantries. "Where are you?"

"I'm still alongside the observatory, waiting for the Cell to recover."

"How soon will you be back at Bedlam? There's a reconstruction meeting in one hour."

"I know. I've been invited, but it's going to be too difficult to get there in time." He tried to read her tone, but wasn't able to. "Why? Are you okay down there? Does Palmer Flast need backup from us?"

"No." The response came almost too quickly, but wasn't ungracious. "I was just wondering if you wanted to meet. We have a lot to talk about."

"I daresay."

In his mind, he heard her telling him, the last time they had spoken: *Either help me get what I want, or stay the hell out of my way.* He wondered what had changed.

"Call me when you have an ETA," she said.

"I will."

The signal closed.

He sat for a moment in the embrace of N-6, turning memories over in his mind. They were like sticky sand, presenting the illusion of slipping through his fingers but always leaving his hands gritty and soiled afterward. There were moments he would have been happier to excise entirely from his recollection, but even with advanced Palmer technology such precision amnesia was not possible. He could have crudely removed the chunk of his life that had contained Melilah Awad, but he had known people who had undergone such procedures. No matter how careful the excision, no matter how sure they were that they'd done the right thing, they always tripped over the days, months, or years forcibly wrenched from their life. They seemed permanently puzzled, as though not quite believing that they could have done such a dramatic thing to themselves, and constantly wondering *why*.

He didn't want to end up like that, a stranger in his own head. But he didn't want to turn the same hourglass over and over, either. The sand had worn his fingers to the bone. He still felt every grain.

While reception was good from the habitat, he hailed the Pirellis, who, he learned, had waited out the attack in a bunker not far from the alien skulls.

"It was no great hardship," said James, somewhat more

jovially than the circumstances warranted, Eogan thought. "We even managed to grab a bottle or two before evacuating."

"Actually, the blackout was scarier than the attack." Like her husband, Luisa sounded more amused than worried, as though the crisis had been an adventure put on just for them. "You may think of us as Luddites, but we're as dependent on the feeds as anyone else. We felt completely cut off—even crammed in a room with fifty other people."

"And don't think we haven't been watching *you,* dear friend, since the lines went up again. You have been busy, haven't you? Practically holding off invaders with your bare hands!"

"I lost a friend out here," he said, not in the mood to make light of the situation.

"We understand." Luisa instantly sobered. "So did we all. That's one thing about living in Bedlam. Everyone knows everyone else. Our casualties may have been low, but the cost was high."

"Too high," added James.

"I'm sorry," Eogan said. "I didn't mean to snap."

"That's okay. We're all a little off-color, behind the brave faces."

"All the wine in the system can't make up for the fact that we've been attacked," said Luisa, "for something over which we had no control and didn't much want in the first place."

"At least we've learned something from it," said James. "If the rumors are true, that is."

"What's that?"

"That the Gentry aren't as homogenous as we'd assumed: there's dissent in the ranks. And there's someone or something higher up that ultimately calls the shots."

"I don't know about you," said Luisa, "but knowing that he has enemies—and a boss—makes Deangelis seem almost—well, human."

James snorted. "I wouldn't go that far, my love."

"I did say *almost.*"

Eogan smiled, comforted at last by the familiar interactions of his friends. The issue of the Exarch's humanity was a well-worn one. In the early days of the Expansion, speculation had been rife that the new rulers were AIs posing as humans in order to erode resistance. The issue wasn't entirely resolved, certainly not to the satisfaction of skeptics like James Pirelli, but it had become irrelevant to most people. When what constituted "human" took many diverse and superficially alien forms, quibbling about the Exarchs seemed a little petty. At the end of the day, the Exarchs had to be judged on their actions, not their origins.

"I'm glad you're okay," he told them, cutting into their good-natured debate. "Stay that way. I'll be back in Bedlam soon."

"So we hear," said Luisa with a sly tone to her voice. "Tread carefully, my friend. Now's no time for a covert kiss-a-thon."

"I have no intention—"

He broke off at the sound of her laughter. The Pirellis were gone before he could properly respond.

He waited a beat for a caustic comment from Vermeulen. It didn't come, reminding him sharply of her loss. Irritated, he opened another line to keep himself distracted.

"You made it through okay," he told Gil Hurdowar.

"So it would seem." The man looked no different for the experience. Dark bags hung from his half-lidded eyes.

"I just wanted to thank you for the tip you gave me, about the observatory. You were obviously right. Deangelis was gearing up for an external attack. If we'd known that more in advance—"

"It wouldn't have made any difference against a Reaper. Don't doubt that for a second. Frederica Cazneaux was determined. The only person who could have made a difference was Deangelis, and he barely scraped through."

"The Archon—"

"Didn't appear until the fight was practically over. Cazneaux—or whatever part of her was involved—was probably dead by then. The Reaper would have been running on AI. All the Archon did was switch it off and let it melt with the observatory."

"Is this an educated guess, or do you have information we don't?"

"It's all guesswork, Palmer Eogan. But I defy you to prove me wrong."

Eogan had no inclination to try. Even if Hurdowar was right, and all the Archon had done was hit some sort of kill switch in the Reaper, that was still a powerful demonstration. The kill switch had affected the *Nhulunbuy,* too, and the *Kwal Bahal,* and every other vessel in the system. What else could the Archon do if pushed?

"If you get the urge to share any other guesses," he told Hurdowar, "feel free to let me know."

The man grunted, practiced surliness mostly hiding the fact that he was glad to have earned Eogan's ear. "Don't expect anything soon. I'm still sifting through the mess, trying to work out the details."

"There's no hurry. We're all doing the same."

"I doubt it. *The details,* Palmer Eogan. That's where you'll find the devil. The big picture is just a camouflage."

Rather than get caught up in Hurdowar's cryptoparanoia, Eogan made his apologies and killed the line.

He took a moment to glance at the reconstruction meeting Melilah had mentioned, but found it to be much as expected: focusing on a myriad of minor details, not the core problem.

"Anything?" he asked Aesche, fighting a wave of bone weariness.

The negative was instant and disheartening. "We're wasting time and energy," she said, bluntness finally replacing bland disapproval. "We should give up."

Eogan turned his attention back to Hazard One. The wreckage was utterly lifeless to the *Nhulunbuy*'s sensors. The only movement came from stray energies leaking gradually into the vacuum. Light still played across its angular visage, but with less viciousness than before. The drones from Bedlam had become more numerous while he was distracted.

"What about the Occlusion?"

"We can't detect it directly, but we can measure the pinch of space it closes off, deep down in the tangle. It's the same as always: completely inert."

That was a relief. No alien replicators had come boiling out of it yet. Eogan wondered what it would take to prompt such a response, given that the collision of the observatory and the Reaper around it had failed to elicit anything at all.

Now that the wreck was cooling, it was becoming increasingly difficult to justify hanging around.

"All right," he said, thinking: *It's not much of a memorial, Palmer Vermeulen, but it'll have to do.* "Call off the search. There's nothing left to learn here. Get what flightworthy components we have and find a configuration that will get us back to Bedlam as a whole. We might as well help Deangelis put things back together."

"You don't want one of us to remain behind, just in case?"

He seriously considered it. "No. We might as well accept the fact that—"

"Eogan, wait." Aesche's voice coincided with a sudden rise in activity from Hazard One. "We're getting something."

Eogan returned his attention to the raw data flooding in from the wreckage. Sudden spikes of energy were registering across all frequencies. "What is it?"

"I don't know. I've never seen anything like this before. It's—" Uncharacteristic concern filled her voice. "It's coming from the Occlusion!"

Cold rushed through him. "Pull us out. Get us the hell away from it." He noted the Bedlam drones doing the same. "I want us well back if that thing's about to go off."

"Consider it d—"

Light flashed against the starscape. Something bright and fast-moving shot out of the wreckage, trailing a misty white comet tail behind it. Eogan's fingers, intimately merged with N-6, reflexed to send the component out of its path, forgetting that only attitude thrusters were available to him. The component moved sluggishly as the object curled around in a tight spiral and came right at him.

"Aesche—"

"There's nothing I can do!"

He clutched the component to him and called up emergency collision systems. The object came at him as fast as a meteor, blossoming in his forward feeds, flaring like a supernova—

The impact pushed him face forward into the fabric of the component. Inertia gel flooded the space around him, gripping him like a fist. There was a tearing, screeching noise that was so loud it actually hurt.

Then N-6 was tumbling, and he was tumbling with it, rocking and spinning giddily against the stars. The object was an ungainly lump sticking out of the component like a half-melted, glowing club.

"Palmer Eogan!" came Aesche's voice over the component's battered comm. "Palmer Eogan, are you all right?"

"Don't say anything," said a voice in his ear. "Don't say anything until you hear what I've got to tell you."

He fought the inertia gel, struggling to free himself and see who had spoken. The signal came mechanically through the impact-welded planes of the component and the thing that had collided with it. It sounded as a faint buzz to his ears. The voice emerged out of heavily encrypted Palmer protocols carried by the buzz and was instantly recognizable.

"Vermeulen?" he gasped, incredulous.

"That's right," she said. "And you're not going to believe where I've just come from."

"But you're—"

"Dead? I'm disappointed you gave up on me so quickly—but not really surprised. That was some blast, wasn't it? I've been waiting for the wreck to cool to the point where it was safe to come back out again. Took much longer than I thought. I can't tell you how glad I was to see you on the other side."

Surprise was slowly turning to relief, and puzzlement. "Are you hurt? How in the Dark did you survive?"

"Ah, well, I can thank the Exarch for my present rude health. As soon as things turned nasty, he bundled me and N-11 in this fancy capsule and shoved it in the safest place available: *inside* the Occlusion."

"I thought of that, but the boundary effect—"

"Deangelis solved that in a hundredth of the time it took us. He's been steadily sending probes into it, ever since we gave it to him. All I had to do was sit tight and ride out the collision, then come back out again when things calmed down."

Something in her voice told him that this wasn't the whole story. Ignoring Aesche's continued demands for a response, he took everything he knew about Vermeulen—and her precipitous return to the universe—and bundled it together in one leap of reason.

"But you didn't," he said. "You didn't sit tight at all."

"Absolutely not. I'm back from my little holiday—and wait until you see the postcards."

+37

Detailed displays cataloged the outrages enacted on Bedlam and its immediate environs down four walls of the conference space. Frozen air glittered over exterior surfaces; debris radiated in an expanding cloud; occasional flashes of light marked regions where fires still burned.

Melilah sat in the midst of the visual record with her stomach roiling, reliving the terrible moments when her home had come under attack. She hadn't known Eogan was in the thick of it until afterward, when images he had recorded of the collision between the Reaper and the observatory circulated freely around the network. Her instinct to call him had been strong but ambiguous, as was the urge to see him again. Part of her, having cut free of the deadweight of the past, wanted to establish a new pattern of coping—one that didn't involve total avoidance and denial. *That* method had clearly performed badly over the last century and a half. If she could see him again, talk to him, she could kick-start the rest of her life. A life free of doubt and anger. Free of him.

"Do we know who did this?"

The voice knocked Melilah sharply out of her reverie. Deangelis, at the head of the table, his youthful appearance composed and his expression neutral, faced the woman who had voiced the question.

"There are several suspects," he said. "An investigation is under way as we speak."

"I'm still not sure what actually happened," said another. "We're hearing nothing but rumors out there."

"Are we at war?" pressed a third voice. "Did the Occlusion attack us?"

"Have we been invaded again?"

"Is it over?"

Deangelis flexed his will, and the walls became windows on the outside universe. The sun was a brilliant point behind his head, casting his face into shadow and making Melilah squint. To her right was the scarred visage of the habitat; to her left, the dark umbra of PARASOL. Between the two, directly opposite the sun, was the tangled wreckage of the Occlusion observatory. The skeletal remains of the Reaper clutched the destroyed station like the fingers of a corpse. A hideous glow wreathed the wreck.

"Earlier today," Deangelis said, "we were attacked by forces external to the system. The attack began with a surgical strike designed to excise a significant percentage of my operational capacity."

"Blew up some of your bodies, in other words," Melilah said.

A wince flickered across his smooth visage. "A crude but effective tactic," he admitted. "While I was distracted, several waves attacked the habitat. The first was designed to interfere with telemetry and communications. The second restricted EVA. The third directly targeted the habitat and its occupants. You are all familiar with the effects of that wave."

Nods around the table.

"It was a smoke screen," he went on. "While we were all distracted, a fourth force moved on the Occlusion, intending to destroy it."

"Why?" someone asked.

"That seems pretty obvious to me," Melilah said. "What I'm more interested in is who was behind the attack."

"As I said—" Deangelis started.

She interrupted him. "We know there are suspects. But who *are* they, exactly? Is it true that another Exarch did this? How do we know it wasn't actually the Archon—using it as an excuse to move in and take over?"

"The Archon played no role in the attack," Deangelis said.

"How do you know that?"

He hesitated slightly. "I know that because it is simply not possible."

"*Who,* then?" asked Palmer Flast of the *Kwal Bahal,* a thin-faced, bald man with surprisingly full lips. "You must have some idea, or else you'd be a lot more worried about another attack."

"I can only assure you that the threat has been minimized. The weapon used in the fourth attack was not a commonplace one. It has been destroyed, so the odds are extremely small that another will follow."

"You didn't answer my question about another Exarch," said Melilah.

"No," he said quickly. "I did not."

She bit down on a sharp comment. That he hadn't denied it was enough. The others stared at the Exarch with undisguised horror at the idea the colony could have been attacked by another like him. They must have felt the same shock she had upon coming to that conclusion.

But she was discomforted to note that her skepticism was not representative of the gathering's mood. They were looking to Deangelis for guidance and encouragement. She and Flast were the ones truly daring to challenge him.

"You put something in me," she said. "I want it out."

"It has already decomposed."

She didn't feel even slightly ameliorated. "What was it?"

"A simple tracking and telemetry interface. You accessed the navigational data it gave you. I was able to access your movements in return."

"That's all?"

"Please; have yourself scanned, if it makes you feel easier. I have no reason to deceive you."

She sighed. "Do you have *any* good news to offer us?"

"We're making steady progress against the infection," Flast offered. "We've developed a countermeasure now. It's simply a matter of helping it propagate."

"Your efforts are greatly appreciated." Deangelis inclined his head at the Cell's chief officer, and Melilah echoed the sentiment: the *Kwal Bahal* put to shame other Cells that had fled the moment events took a turn for the worst. "Curfews will remain in effect until the very last of it is neutralized. I estimate that this will take another fifteen to twenty hours."

"This is unreasonably draconian," she protested. "Not to mention impractical. Emergency services must have free access to all areas. People are injured; their homes are burning—"

He raised a hand, nodding. "Perhaps I am being overcautious. Category C personnel can have permission to cross checkpoints as circumstances dictate, but they must undergo rigorous scans to ensure they don't track replicators with them. A single dormant breeder could undo all our good work."

Melilah was satisfied by the compromise. "Thank you."

"It should be me thanking you, Melilah. *All* of you." He swept his gaze around the table, at her and Flast as well as the dozen sector heads and municipal representatives he had gathered. "While I was unable to defend either myself or the habitat, you worked together to minimize the damage caused by the attack. I am grateful and relieved that we can cooperate when we need to, regardless of our differences in other areas. Some things are simply more important than ideology."

He received a murmur of agreement in response. Melilah was mollified, even if she doubted the fragile peace would last for long.

"What's the status of Palmer Christolphe?" asked Flast.

Deangelis's lips turned down at their corners. "It is my sad duty to confirm reports that the Negotiator Select was killed during the attack. I will inform his colleagues in Ansell-Aad as soon as communication lines are open again."

That prompted another murmur. "They've been cut?" someone asked.

"Only temporarily," he assured them. "The state of emergency in which we find ourselves will persist a little longer, as together we make every effort to restore the status quo."

"How long will that take?" asked Melilah, unnerved by the knowledge that Bedlam was for the time effectively isolated from the rest of the Arc Circuit.

"That's one of the reasons I've gathered you all here." Deangelis's cool gaze studied them all. "Are there any specific requests? There is much to consider and coordinate before I can release a workable timetable."

A torrent of demands issued from the various sectors, simple, practical needs that the Exarch promised to take care of. Melilah estimated that the majority of the work could be done within two days. Population flows would return to normal before then. Rationing of resources would not be necessary.

Not an unsatisfactory outcome, she thought, given the circumstances. Something to be proud of.

But it completely failed to address the root of the problem. The Occlusion was still in place, an easy target now that the observatory containing it was destroyed. What if the attack they had just endured was the first of many? Could the Archon wave its magic wand again and keep them all at bay?

The new arrival was conspicuous by its absence. Problem *and* solution were absent from the discussion, and that unnerved her. She doubted the others would want to hear it, though. They had come for reassurance, not more nagging from her. There was a time and a place to get what she wanted.

It came as the meeting devolved into a mess of conflicting requests, with everyone trying to push his or her particular concern forward. Melilah was watching Deangelis, trying to work out his exact motivation for the meeting, since it was clear he didn't really need anyone else's input to put things back together. It was probably just a publicity stunt or a means of making people feel involved, even if they really weren't.

His attention darted away. She could see it in his eyes. Suddenly the Exarch wasn't really there.

Curious, she cast her own attention out of the room. Something was happening near the ruins of the observatory, where the *Nhulunbuy* was stationed. That was enough to make her wonder if the meeting was in fact a distraction, hiding something much more important . . .

"Come back," she said, getting out of her chair and whispering in Deangelis's ear. The argument continued unabated behind her. "Listen to me. You talked about cooperation before. I'm not entirely against that idea. We do, after all, want the same thing: revenge against the person who did this to us."

His eyes swiveled to look at her. The greater Deangelis was back.

"Don't say anything." She kept her voice low, barely more than a subvocalization, knowing he could discern her words clearly enough. "Just because we want the same thing doesn't mean we're on the same side. I know you're hiding something—you and the Archon together, from us. The Occlusion is a doorway, one you can't hope to keep closed forever. If I find out that anything you've done has led to people here getting hurt—"

At the mention of a doorway, he pulled back as though physically struck. His calm reserve cracked, just for an instant, and she saw plain on his face the uncertainty and fear he had successfully contained through the meeting.

"How—?" His Adam's apple bobbed, and the mask came back down. He spoke using the network, rather than speaking aloud. "I don't know what you're talking about."

"You know damned well."

"I swear—"

"Spare me your meaningless promises."

His lips tightened. "I don't like your tone, Melilah."

"And I don't like *anything* about this situation, so let's just see what you can do to fix it."

"I'm doing everything I can."

For a moment, she believed him. The glimpse of panic she had seen suggested that he was as perturbed as she was, that maybe he had as little control over events as she did. But that wasn't her problem. If the Archon was his problem, just like *he* was *hers,* then he would have to take steps, too. She couldn't nursemaid him through the process. She could only nudge him onward.

Suddenly exhausted, and unable to avoid being worried about Eogan, she'd had enough of the meeting. "I guess we'll see about that," she told Deangelis, then turned and stalked from the room.

+38

Exarch Deangelis stared at Melilah's retreating back, still stunned by the revelation. *She knew! Impossible!* How *could* she know? She had been watched every second of every day, observed more closely than any individual in the habitat. She had the data he had hidden in the bowels of the station, but it was undoubtedly too complex for her to decipher on her own. Unless she and Palmer Eogan had exchanged more than just a forbidden kiss in the wreckage of the alien vessel, three days earlier, when she had been momentarily out of sight . . .

And if the Archon found out . . .

Dread filled him. He told himself that Eogan and Awad were just guessing, extrapolating from scanty details and using their hunches to apply leverage to him, but he wasn't convinced.

The voice of Jane Elderton came to him unbidden. *I opened the door,* she had said, *and now no one can ever close it. Nothing will ever be the same.*

The alarm that had distracted him from the meeting sounded again, raised by all his autonomous agents at once. He turned his attention back to the source of their clamor: the wreckage of the Occlusion observatory and Cazneaux's Reaper.

The Occlusion was active. Bright light pulsed in a pattern indicating that something was emerging from its hellish throat. Space-time flexed as the Occlusion spat an object no larger than a hopper back into the universe.

He identified it immediately. The object was one of the observatory's escape capsules, modified to withstand the physical trials of the throat. Clearly someone had fled through the Occlusion in order to escape the destruction of the observatory.

His heart beat again. Part of him had survived!

Then he noted the way the capsule was changing course and realized that it wasn't likely he at all behind the controls.

The survivor could only be Palmer Vermeulen, and she was heading for the *Nhulunbuy*.

"Intercept that capsule!" His command whipped out to the observation drones orbiting the wreckage, overriding telemetry feeds and all other communications. "Bring its occupant to me!"

The drones accelerated to match velocities with the capsule, swarming from all sides of Hazard One to catch it in their net. Uncrewed and relatively slight in mass, they were capable of much greater acceleration than Vermeulen's battered vessel. They were also equipped with sampling field effects that could be wielded as weapons. Dozens of them converged on the capsule's path as it arced away from the wreckage.

But they were too slow. Deangelis knew that the moment the capsule suddenly changed course, angling for one of the larger components of the *Nhulunbuy*—the one containing Palmer Eogan—on what looked like a collision course. No gentle docking for this survivor. Not if she wanted to escape the Exarch's clutches.

He snarled in frustration. Why was everyone so resentful of him? Why did they go to such extreme lengths to thwart him? Didn't they see that he was on their side?

The capsule slammed headlong into the *Nhulunbuy* component, and merged with it, sending them off on a new course that was the sum of both their previous ones, in perfect accordance with Newton's laws of motion. All acceleration died. All electromagnetic emissions ceased. Spinning like a top, the crashed vessels—echoing in miniature the wreck behind them—receded from the habitat.

The drones changed course to follow, as did three other components of the *Nhulunbuy*. He fought a sudden urge to fight them off, to claim Vermeulen for his own, to contain what she might have learned on the far side of the throat before it spread any further. But that, he knew, would only draw more attention than the incident was already getting.

"Back away," he told the drones. "Palmer Aesche can handle it from here." He did his best to project the appearance of someone perfectly satisfied that the situation was now under control—the exact opposite of what he was actually feeling.

"Thank you, Exarch Deangelis." Aesche took a moment from her attempts to hail the occupants of the two craft to acknowledge his involvement, then returned to her efforts. Either deaf to her calls or ignoring her, Eogan and Vermeulen tumbled silently on.

"You could plug this leak right now," said the Archon, "if you would only let yourself."

The voice and words of his creator sent a ripple of alarm through all of him. This was potentially a much greater security breach than Melilah Awad's half-mumbled threat. "I am not in the habit of killing those in my care."

"Just two in exchange for the greater good. That's a simple enough equation, wouldn't you say?"

He thought furiously. "Forgive me, Archon, but this isn't mathematics. We're talking about people, not numbers."

"Let's not quibble over the metaphor, Isaac. You know what I'm saying."

"Yes, I do. But I'm not coming to the same conclusion. There are too many variables in play. We don't know what Vermeulen has seen. To kill her now would only draw attention to the fact there is indeed something to hide. If she has seen nothing, or nothing she can understand, then sparing her poses no security risk at all."

"True—but we must balance this eventuality against the possibility that she *does* know what the Occlusion hides. That outcome must be weighted in excess of the other, so even if its likelihood is the same, we must act to avert it."

There was a small silence as the entangled capsule and Cell component continued to race ahead of the *Nhulunbuy*'s pursuit team.

"You could make it look like an accident," whispered the Archon.

"Are you ordering me to do so?" Deangelis asked, despairing. If the Archon *did* order him, he could not possibly disobey. He would have to accept that his judgment was wrong and do what he was told to do—even though the very thought of it burned like acid.

"I would never order you to do something like that," said the Archon. "I am simply exploring your motivations, Isaac. You are not being judged. Understanding is all I seek."

The relief Deangelis felt was profound. "I'm glad," he said, with total honesty. “I have no wish to become a murderous dictator. Humanity evolved beyond that point long ago.”

“Indeed it did,” said the Archon. “But superior evolution does not free us from situations that challenge us or occasions on which we must act in ways we find abhorrent. All it gives us is the capacity to see with greater clarity why we do what we must do—to see beyond the present, to where our actions might lead. The evolution we have wrought for ourselves gives us perspective, nothing more, and the new altitude from which we observe the world requires a keen sense of balance. We remain part of the universe, no matter how high we climb; gravity is ever waiting to drag us back down.”

The Archon’s words didn’t reassure him. He felt as though he might fragment again, lose himself in a tangle of secrets and crises. He needed to talk to someone who would understand, someone at his level . . .

The rest of the *Nhulunbuy* caught up with the still-inert capsule and the component it had struck. Like a small flock tending one of its wounded, the Cell gathered around the two, expanding protective fields to shield it from the vacuum.

Maybe she’s already dead, Deangelis thought, not believing it but unable to completely quash the hope.

+39

Eogan sat in the darkness for what felt like a small eternity. In the scant minutes since the impact, the capsule had peeled back to reveal N-11, Vermeulen's component. His and hers had merged, allowing them to come face-to-face in the tumbling debris. He could hear her breathing, close to his ear. He felt her silver hair brush his face. Her scent was one of fear and excitement.

"I don't need to ask you if you're absolutely certain," he said. "You wouldn't be telling me if you weren't."

"You'd better believe it. I've *been there,* boss. There's no mistaking what I saw."

"Why didn't we realize before?"

"Because we weren't looking before. Or at least we weren't looking with our eyes open, anyway. A wormhole's a wormhole, right? We thought we knew what we were seeing."

"Cobiac and Bray? What about them?"

"No sign of them, but then I didn't go far. Even though Deangelis had taken the first steps—"

She stopped as something banged from the outside. Their angular momentum changed abruptly, rattling them about like two cats in a barrel.

"Shit." Eogan pulled himself out of the component until he was free from the waist up. He needed his head absolutely clear in order to think what to do next. It all depended on who had got to them first.

His dream—of taking seven steps into a corridor and eleven to get back again—recurred with unwanted intensity.

Another bang. Their headlong rotation slowed. He felt N-6 passively succumb to the grip of another vessel.

Vermeulen tried the same trick she had with him, communicating via sound through the hull of the capsule.

"If that's you, Aesche," she said, "don't broadcast anything just yet."

"No." Eogan suddenly saw the way things had to unfold in his head, as though they were already happening. "We don't need to run silent any longer."

"I can hear you," said Aesche, following Vermeulen's lead anyway.

That it *was* she and not Deangelis gave him a moment of relief—but it was short-lived. Her component was open to public scrutiny. Anything they said would be overheard by Bedlam.

"We've been running silent because our systems were unstable," he said via more conventional means, confident Aesche would recognize the cover story for what it was. "Now that we're piggybacking off yours, it should be okay."

"You're not hurt?" she asked.

"We're fine. Palmer Vermeulen lost control of the escape capsule and only just managed to catch mine before it spun right out of range. We're lucky we didn't have to chase her halfway across the system."

He felt Vermeulen watching him closely, trying to work out what his intentions were.

"Well, we're glad to have you both back with us," said Aesche. "It looked a little hairy, there."

"Too hairy by half," Eogan agreed. "I'm starting to think we made a mistake, sticking around so long."

A second's silence greeted his announcement. Then: "You know you're not alone in that," said Aesche cautiously.

He nodded, pleased that she had caught on so quickly. "I didn't think so. You've all been very patient with me, but it's time I did the right thing by the Cell. We've got to look after ourselves, first and foremost. Nearly losing Vermeulen has brought that home hard."

"What would you like me to do?" Aesche asked.

"Notify Lut-Deangelis Traffic Control of our intention to leave."

"When?"

"Immediately, of course," he said. "And tell Palmer Flast, as well. I'd like him to join us, either as my second officer or as chief of the *Kwal Bahal*. Whatever suits him."

"I'll give him the option."

Eogan had no doubt which option Flast would choose. "Thank you, Palmer Aesche."

The only reply was a soft groan as the three components began to merge into one, absorbing the foreign material of the escape capsule in the process.

Vermeulen's hand found his and squeezed softly. "Don't go all soft on me now, Eogan."

He nodded, wishing he could genuinely put the safety of his crew ahead of the situation in Bedlam. The lie was easy to say because it wasn't entirely untruthful.

"We've been out of the Dark long enough," he said, thinking of everything Vermeulen had told him and feeling very, very tired. "It's time to go home."

+40

Yasu had been waiting for Melilah when she left the reconstruction meeting. Effectively ambushed, Melilah had had no choice but to be swept along with her four-daughter's enthusiasm at their reunion. Ordinarily she would have been more interested in what had happened in the shelters during the attack, and she felt bad for being distracted. But she had been intending to sit down with the file she had uncovered in the depths of Bedlam in the hope of gaining some sort of advantage over Deangelis. Even as she talked to Yasu, she scanned the surface layers of the data, looking for a way in. Images of holidays and half-baked treasure maps mingled in an untidy mess, getting her nowhere.

The events occurring around the Occlusion gradually overtook them as they traveled by transport in the rough direction of Melilah's apartment. She felt a stab of concern at the thought that Eogan and the crippled *Nhulunbuy* might be destroyed if the Occlusion chose that moment to blossom. The strength of the feeling confirmed that, although she might be as angry with him as ever, she'd long gotten over her wish that he was dead.

And then came the bombshell.

"Leaving?" Yasu sounded as though she couldn't believe what she was hearing. "He can't be!"

"Looks very much like it to me." A numbness spread through Melilah, as though she had been dipped in liquid nitrogen.

"But you spoke to him barely an hour ago. He said he'd call you, that he'd be coming back!"

Melilah shrugged. "I guess he changed his mind."

"So what are you going to do about it?" Yasu took her hands. "You can't let him get away from you again!"

Melilah felt a rush of affection for her descendant. Yasu was young and entirely too enthused by what she saw on the Scale-Free Bedlam feeds. The world wasn't a soap opera; it didn't have story arcs, coherent themes, or happy endings.

"Calm down," Melilah told her. "You're blowing all of this right out of proportion."

"But after all you and he went through—you can't just stand back and watch him leave!"

"Yasu, listen to me. Palmer Eogan is not your four-father."

The words emerged without premeditation. If she'd stopped to think, she might have talked herself out of revealing the truth. That had always been something for her to know, no one else. But the revelation had the desired effect. Yasu's mouth shut with a snap; her eyebrows converged; her gaze swept Melilah's face as though searching for a lie.

"I'm sorry," Melilah went on. "Your great-great-grandfather was an anonymous sample recovered from a First Waver cache I stumbled across, two years after Palmer Eogan left. There was no actual person involved; there was just a dead donor, and me. I was adrift, struggling to get back to who I was before Eogan; I needed something to keep me focused. That something ended up being a baby—Athalia, your three-mother, and I'm sure she's the one who put all these ridiculous notions in your head. She could never accept the truth. But if you dig deep enough through the records, you'll find it there, Yasu. Not that it matters now, of course. It shouldn't. Does it?"

Yasu surprised her by bursting into tears. "Oh, Grandmother Mel."

Not sure what had brought that on, Melilah took her four-daughter into her arms.

"I'm sorry," she said again, patting Yasu on the back as she would a child—as she had when Yasu *was* a child, two decades earlier. "I didn't mean to upset you."

"No." Yasu's voice was muffled by her shoulder. "I'm the one who should be sorry. I've been going on and on about Eogan, and he's probably the last person you want to talk about."

"It's okay," Melilah soothed her. "I'm all grown-up, remember? I can handle it."

"But you must have been so *lonely*." Yasu pulled back enough to look at her with swollen, red-rimmed eyes.

"Yes, I was." She faced the truth of the statement without flinching. "But I'm not now, and that's the main thing. I have plenty of friends."

"And family." Yasu wiped her nostrils with the back of her hand.

"I have family I'm proud to call friends, and family I don't care if I never see again. You—" She took Yasu's face in one hand and squeezed it. "Yasu, you are most definitely in the first category."

"I'm glad." They hugged again, and Melilah felt the strange rush of emotion ebb, leaving her drained. She wasn't just "all grown-up"; she was entirely too old to be experiencing such violent mood swings. That was the domain of the young.

"I still hope you call him," Yasu confessed, as the transport pulled up outside Melilah's house. "It doesn't matter if he's not my four-father. I'd like to meet him one day, and that's not likely if you never talk to him again."

Melilah felt herself staring at Yasu as though she'd suddenly sprouted antennae and turned into an alien. "Why on Earth would you want to do that?"

The girl shrugged shyly. "One hundred and fifty years later, and not even the Gentry get you so worked up as he does. Eogan must be a rare person to flap the unflappable like that."

"Are you serious?"

Yasu just smiled and indicated the door. "You've got a lot to think about, Grandmother. I'll let you get on with it. I just wanted to make sure you were okay."

They kissed each other and said farewell. Melilah climbed out of the transport and waved as Yasu sped off into the distance.

When she was gone, Melilah turned to go inside, withdrawing into herself as she would to worry over a loose tooth.

+41

The body of Lazarus Hails—bound up in layers of recuperative nanoware like a moth in a spiderweb—blinked and opened its eyes.

"Welcome back," said Exarch Deangelis, with genuine feeling. "You should be able to hear me now."

"I do hear you." Hails answered using his vocal cords, then continued via less obvious means: "I wasn't expecting to, though. I wasn't expecting to do much of anything. I remember—"

The gaze of Hails's milky gray eyes locked on Deangelis and studied him closely. Hails had lost all of his white mane and eyebrows. He looked vulnerable, even weak without it, as though genuinely suffering from old age rather than indulging the semblance of it.

"Cazneaux got to you," Hails said. "I thought she might. You're too trusting, Isaac. You'd do well to cultivate some good, healthy paranoia before it's too late."

"She didn't succeed," Deangelis told him, with some satisfaction.

"Oh? I guess not, or we wouldn't be having this conversation."

"And the Archon is here."

Hails was silent for a long minute. His gaze drifted, turned inward. "Well, then."

"You'll be discharged in an hour. This is"—Deangelis indicated the brittle cocoon—"cosmetic. You can leave anytime you want."

"Leave? When things are just getting interesting?"

Deangelis hoped his relief didn't show. He wanted Hails

awake and able to talk. They weren't friends, but they were the next best thing for trillions of kilometers. He could use some advice.

He explained the events of the previous day, supplementing his words with images and raw data. He automatically did his best to present the illusion that everything was under control, but suspected Hails could see through it easily enough. He wasn't a fool. He knew what Palmer Eogan's decision to leave might mean.

"So the Occlusion remains intact." Hails's gaze was on him again, probing.

"The throat is still open. I'll give you full access to the data when your peripherals are completely restored. But at this stage the situation is complicated."

"You should have seen this coming, Isaac. The Coral is dangerous. Those it touches, it kills. Its very existence is antithetical to everything the Exarchate—and Sol—stand for. The knowledge that it's surfaced again was bound to provoke an extreme reaction. Those of us who've spoken to Jane Elderton—and there are a few of us, now—have had a taste of what we stand to lose. There was always going to be someone who went too far."

"I need to know . . ." Deangelis stopped to take a deep, calming breath. Talking about the attack never failed to shake his newly restored coherence. "Did you support Frederica Cazneaux?"

Hails shook his head, and grimaced. "I wouldn't be here, done up like a mummy, if I had."

"What about Lan Cochrane?"

A nod. "She supplied the clane, and made sure it was ferried here on Palmer Christolphe's Cell."

Deangelis had suspected as much. Hails had mentioned the Exarch of Alioth-Cochrane as the source of his information about the Occlusion. That doubled the number of people against whom he wished revenge.

"Are there more?"

"I honestly don't know. There's a whole lot of talk going on out there. Several factions are swinging into gear."

"Why didn't you tell me about them?" he asked Hails. "Why didn't you warn me?"

"I didn't tell you, my boy, because I wasn't completely certain of my intelligence. All I had, really, were insinuations from Cochrane and Cazneaux that they were taking steps, plus some solid reasoning on my own part. It wasn't much to give you, and there were many other ways it could've gone. It's the same now. The best I can do is to encourage you to make contingency plans, to consider every option. I'm genuinely sorry that wasn't enough, last time." Hails shrugged minutely under the white crust. "You can't blame me for being cautious."

"They used a Reaper." Deangelis fought to keep his voice level. "They sent a Reaper, and they fired on my habitat—on my *people!*" He could feel himself shaking. "There is no greater crime."

"Oh, there are worse crimes than that, Isaac. Believe me. Pray this is as bad as it gets." Hails shifted again, as though uncomfortable in his cocoon. "That's what I'm doing."

"What do you mean by that?"

Hails sighed. "Wrong question, Isaac. You've got eyes. Open them occasionally, and you'll see what I see. Until then, why not ask me if I know whether Cazneaux and Cochrane had any allies? Ask me what happened to Alioth-Cochrane's tangler. Ask me what I've done to protect my own people."

Deangelis was shaking so badly he couldn't speak.

"I'll save you the trouble," said Hails. "I don't know the answer to any of those questions, except the last. And again, the fact that I'm here right now should make it fairly clear what that answer is. I can't tell you what to do, but I can guide you in the right direction. You have to go the rest of the way yourself, as we were designed to do."

Deangelis nodded, understanding at least part of what Hails was trying to say. The Exarchate, thanks to the tyranny of distance, wasn't intended to be a close-knit community. Individual Exarchs had to be fiercely self-reliant. If they'd needed outside help in the early years, all of them would have failed. Critical decisions simply couldn't wait on consensus from the Exarchate or word from Sol. So Deangelis and his peers were independent to the core. They could run an entire colony single-handedly for decades, and would react strongly against any suggestion otherwise. If ever technology did shrink the distance between the stars to the point that Arc Circuit systems became neighbors, separated by hours or even days, the balance of the Exarchate would inevitably shatter.

And no one wanted that.

"Fine," he said, allowing himself to accept that Hails was probably telling the truth. His sense of relief was powerful. "Circumstances are continuing to develop. I may need to call on you for advice. Would that be all right?"

"I'm keen to help, Isaac. I can't lie around here all day. Just don't expect me to make the tough decisions for you."

"I won't." He had expected nothing else. The Archon had made it clear that he was on his own, when it came down to the crunch. As appalling, though, as that felt at times, he knew it was the right thing.

"Don't worry about me." Hails closed his eyes and eased back into the cocoon. "I'm sure you have more important things to think about."

You have no idea, thought Deangelis, as his point of view detached from the body in the infirmary and prepared to cross instantly to the other side of the habitat.

"Send the Archon my regards," said Hails, as Deangelis jumped.

Deangelis froze in midleap like a transport slamming into a solid wall.

There are several factions swinging into gear.

In the complex no-space of his dissociated mind, Deangelis frantically replayed his conversation with the body of Lazarus Hails.

The best I can do is to encourage you to make contingency plans, to consider every option.

The Exarch of Kullervo-Hails system had been circumspect while seeming to be completely direct. He had dropped hints of conspiracies springing into life when word of the Occlusion leaked, but he had only described one of them—the one containing Cazneaux and Cochrane, hell-bent on eliminating the threat the Occlusion represented.

But what about the *other* conspiracies? How many were there? Who belonged to them? What were their objectives?

You can't blame me for being cautious . . .

Hails was insinuating something very serious, and the way he was saying it was the most important clue of all. Telling Deangelis to pass on his regards to the Archon was both bizarre and meaningless—on the surface, anyway. Hails could talk to the Archon anytime he wanted; in fact, it was a fair assumption that the Archon had already heard everything that had passed between them. What was the point in giving Deangelis an instruction that made no sense?

Because it made sense in a completely different context. Hails was trying to tell Deangelis something he didn't want the Archon to hear. Something about conspiracies, and about the home system. Something that must have been nagging Deangelis's subconscious or else he might never have noticed it at all.

I can't tell you what to do, but I can guide you in the right direction. You have to go the rest of the way yourself, as we were designed to do.

Deangelis was glad he hadn't returned to his body before rethinking the conversation, for he was sure if he had that he would have physically staggered from the enormity of its conclusion. It struck him as though from nowhere, yet every point was there in Hails's conversation, carefully planted so as to make sense one way at first, then a completely different way in retrospect. The audacity of it astounded him. What if Deangelis hadn't seen through such a clumsy ploy? What if the Archon had?

Even as he contemplated the last, awful possibility, he reassured himself that it was unlikely. As advanced as the Archon was, there were subtleties of communication that one could only appreciate from within. An ordinary human could marvel at the complexity of birdcalls, and even go so far as to decipher approximate meanings, but the details—the metaphors and similes, the allusions and hints—would go forever undetected.

He wondered for the first time what the humans in his care got away with, even with him constantly watching. Was this how Eogan and Awad had exchanged information about the Occlusion without him knowing? Was this how word would spread if Eogan and Vermeulen decided to reveal what they might have learned from the far side of the Occlusion?

The Coral is dangerous. Those it touches, it kills. Its very existence is antithetical to everything the Exarchate—and Sol—stand for.

So much for coming to his fellow Exarch for reassurance and advice. Lazarus Hails's information might have been out-of-date, but it was clear he already knew too much, and the conclusion he had come to was radically different from his own.

For one wild, exhilarating second, Deangelis thought he might laugh aloud, everywhere at once. The idea of defying the Archon was simply absurd.

But then he shuddered, more appalled now by the possibility Hails had raised than by the fact that he had raised it at all. The idea of rebellion was crazy—but a rebellion with Geodesica behind it might very well succeed . . .

+42

"Still nothing from Alioth," said Aesche. "The channels are completely blocked."

Eogan glanced up from the controls of the hopper as it descended over Bedlam.

"It doesn't matter," he said. "I can guess what they'll do."

"Embargo?"

"Undoubtedly." The death of the Negotiator Select would send ripples of anxiety and alarm through his colleagues. Where once they had been keen to negotiate over rights to the knowledge gleaned from the Occlusion, now they would want nothing more than to stay away. Until the fuss died down, the potential costs outweighed the gains.

Eogan didn't, therefore, harbor any hope of calling for help from his colleagues. No other Cells had remained in Bedlam since the attack, and he couldn't help a rush of disappointment at the ease with which the Palmers had been scared off. The Occlusion offered either salvation or destruction—depending entirely on who got their hands on it first. In economic and social terms, this was the most critical juncture in the history of the Palmers—and they had run away at the first challenge.

"Either way," Aesche said, "we're on our own."

Aesche's words fueled his grim determination to act before the chance was taken away from him.

"This is LDTC." A new voice replaced Aesche's. "Palmer Eogan, your approach has been disallowed."

He blinked, surprised, at the image of the habitat floating before him. "Could you repeat that, Traffic Control?"

"Your approach has been disallowed, Palmer Eogan, pending repairs to docking facilities. Please return to your Cell. We'll notify you when it's safe to return."

For twenty seconds, while he thought the development through, Eogan didn't change course. The cowardice of the Palmers didn't surprise him, but the Exarch's directness did. Clearly Deangelis was afraid of what Eogan had learned from Vermeulen, and with good reason. The Exarch wasn't an idiot. That he was taking such direct action so soon—concocting excuses so transparent anyone with half an eye could see through them—only highlighted his desperation.

Eogan was tempted to ignore the warning and keep on going. Only the fear that Deangelis might use the recent security scare as an excuse to blow him out of the sky turned him against that plan. Best not to give the Exarch more reasons than he had to.

"Understood, LDTC. Changing course now. Good luck with those repairs."

"Thanks, Palmer Eogan. Try us again in a day or two."

"Will do," he said. Thinking: *And fuck you, too.*

Eogan kicked the hopper onto a new trajectory, one that would take it around Bedlam's equator, then back up to the *Nhulunbuy*.

There went his best chance to talk to Melilah face-to-face. But it wasn't his *last* chance.

"Palmer Flast," he broadcast, "did you catch that?"

"I did indeed. These are heady times."

"Tell me about it. How far away are you from departing?"

"An hour. We have some last-minute patches to oversee, then we're gone."

"Good. I assume those damaged docks won't be a problem going in the opposite direction." Eogan didn't hide a slight sharpness in his tone. He waited a second for LDTC to interrupt. This was the Exarch's chance to speak up if he had a problem with the *Kwal Bahal* departing.

When no such protest came, he went on: "Before you leave, there's something I need you to do . . ."

+43

The call came as Melilah settled back into her apartment to continue scouring the data cache.

"Melilah, it's Eogan."

She considered rejecting the overture, just as she had resisted the urge to call him, against Yasu's advice. If he really was leaving again, it was probably best just to let him go. Why risk opening another wound at such a late stage?

But he *had* called her, and she had told herself that she would respond if he did.

"I know you can hear me, Melilah. I'm patched into the feed."

She sighed. "What do you want, Eogan?"

"To talk to you."

"So badly you've already booked your departure. I get it. What do I have that you could possibly still want?"

"Maybe it's the other way around."

She couldn't see him. The lack of image frustrated her. She couldn't tell if he was being serious or trying to make light of the situation.

"Just go," she said softly. "Just leave me alone."

He wouldn't give up. "I'm sorry, Melilah. I can't do that. Some things are too important. I need to see you."

"Come on down, then. No one's stopping you."

"Actually, they are. LDTC has locked the docks."

That surprised her, but the ramifications of the fact didn't sink in immediately. "Then what do you propose? That I should go up there?"

He didn't say anything. He didn't need to. The silence said it for him.

I should go up there*?*

"No," she said with a sudden lack of breath. "I can't do that."

"It's not difficult. Palmer Flast can be at your door in five minutes. He and his Cell are joining me anyway. They can give you a lift, and drop you back afterward."

"No, Eogan. I'm sorry."

"An hour of your time: that's all I'm asking."

"It's too much."

"Melilah, I wouldn't do this to you if I didn't think it truly important."

His insistence was what caught her. That wasn't like him. Then there was the fact that Traffic Control had locked him out of the habitat. Why would Deangelis do that if all Eogan wanted to do was say good-bye to his ex?

He knows something!

She felt the beginnings of excitement in her gut. The only knowledge with any real currency concerned the Occlusion. If it had been anything else, he could have just told her over the air.

"An hour," she said. "Tops."

"That's all I'll need." He sounded relieved. "Flast is on his way. Be ready to move quickly. You might need to."

She puzzled over his last instruction as she waited for Flast to arrive. Deangelis surely wouldn't stop her from leaving. Would he? She supposed it would depend entirely on what he thought Eogan knew.

Melilah looked around her apartment, at the gathered souvenirs of a long, productive life. She was healthy and in good spirits, and likely to live another two hundred and fifty years if she stayed that way. She would deal with Eogan first, then conduct a fifty percent cull of the names in her memory exercise file. She had to stop living in the past. The future waited.

Her doorway chimed for attention. Assuming it was Flast, she opened it and went to leave.

A stranger stood outside—a large man dressed in white with a pink, blotchy scalp. She recognized his face from the wine bar in Albert Hall. He had been drinking with Exarch Deangelis.

"Please accept my apologies for disturbing you," he said in a voice that boomed improbably. "We have only a moment in which to speak."

"Who are you?" She backed away from him, unnerved by the intensity of his eyes. She considered calling security. "What do you want?"

"To tell you that you are not alone. Your goals are shared by others. We want the same thing."

"Which is?"

"Independence, of course."

He reached out to touch her, but she pulled away.

"Hey!"

"There's no reason to be alarmed." His manner belied his words. Shooting a quick glance either way up the corridor, he tried again. "Melilah, you *must* let me give you—"

"Get the hell away from me!" She braced herself against her doorframe and shoved him back. He tumbled in the low gee just as the first alarm began to buzz. A swarm of flat, disk-shaped security drones rushed up the corridor.

"Be careful of him," said an urgent voice into her ear. "I don't think he's human."

She recognized the oily tones instantly. *Gil Hurdowar.* "What—?"

She stopped, coughing. The stranger had done a strange thing, pursing his lips and emptying his lungs at her as though blowing out the candles on a birthday cake. She recoiled, blinking away sudden grittiness. A taste of peppermint flooded across her tongue.

The security drones rushed into the space between them and forced the stranger back.

My name is Lazarus Hails, said a voice into her mind—the same voice as the stranger. *I know this is surprising, my dear, but you must not react. Your life may depend on it.*

The man backed away and held up his hands as the drones harangued him. She stared at him in alarm. *Nanotech!*

Indeed. Now, pay attention. The Kwal Bahal *is here. You should meet Palmer Eogan as planned. I'll explain on the way.*

Why should I listen to you?

Because it's the only way you're going to hear the truth.

She was about to protest—audibly, so everyone could hear what had happened to her—when the name the stranger had offered finally fell into place.

Lazarus Hails—the Exarch of Altitude!

I don't think he's human, Hurdowar had said—and he was absolutely right. According to Melilah's definition of humanity,

Hails was as alien as the entities who had built the Occlusion and destroyed Sublime.

But he, too, was offering her a version of the truth, and he hadn't actually hurt her. *Yet.*

"Melilah?" It was Sarian this time, from the great, gray bauble heaving to up the corridor. "Are you okay?"

"I'm fine," she said. A rush of light-headedness threatened to trigger an attack of vertigo, but she swallowed it down. That could have been a side effect of Hails's nanoware, or because things were happening so fast that she felt as though she were rapidly being left behind.

Hails had his hands raised behind a ring of drones. "Freak," she told him, for the benefit of the people watching, and also for her own satisfaction. She kicked past him, leaving him to sort out the situation.

"I'm coming," she told Sarian.

The Cell component was already open, gaping like a mouth.

+44

"Is everything under control, Isaac?"

The Archon's question cut across Deangelis's view of events as they unfolded in the habitat. From one angle, he saw the components of the *Kwal Bahal* converging across all quarters in preparation to leave. From another he saw Lazarus Hails—fresh from the infirmary and as hairless as a babe—arguing with a human security officer after his confrontation with Melilah Awad. She, unexpectedly, was back in a Cell component and heading to a rendezvous with Palmer Eogan—who was waiting in the *Nhulunbuy* outside the habitat, already configuring his Cell to leave the system with Vermeulen and whatever secrets she had uncovered.

His options were limited. Melilah Awad was at or near the center of so many situations it frightened him. She was a hub, connected to many people at once, like one of the junctions in the habitat's scale-free network of pipes and corridors. He couldn't let Awad talk to the Palmers, given her recent, mysterious exchange with Hails and her continued worrying over the data he had hidden. Hails and Eogan were hubs, too. He would have to eliminate them as well as her in order to bring current events to a complete halt. But there was no way he could do that—even ignoring the local information laws working against him—without raising tension even higher. And he couldn't let Palmer Eogan leave, especially if Vermeulen had learned what he feared she had.

Is everything under control, Isaac?

How to answer the question without exposing the utter depths of his own uncertainty?

"Let me ask *you* a question, Archon," he said.

"Of course."

The question had been nagging at him ever since his conversation with Lazarus Hails. The Archon had intervened in the attack on the observatory, but it couldn't have known about that before it left, so that wasn't the answer. It claimed not to want to make his decisions for him, so that wasn't the answer either. Since its arrival it had done little more than watch, pass the occasional comment, and tinker deep in the bowels of the habitat. Sol had been silent since the Archon's arrival, but the tangler wasn't idle. Moved from its usual location since Melilah Awad had glimpsed it during the attack, it had become the Archon's responsibility. What it was doing was kept secret even from Deangelis.

"Archon, why are you here?"

"I am here because what happens here is ultimately my responsibility. And by 'here' I don't mean this system; I mean the Exarchate. I created it; it's my project. Were Geodesica to have manifested anywhere else, in any other way, it wouldn't be my direct concern. But it *is* here, and now, and I must oversee the way it's handled. Not just for me and the Exarchate, but for all of humanity."

My project. The Archon made the Exarchate sound like an experiment, a hobby. Was that what an empire of over a thousand suns was to its evolved mind: a reaction in a test tube that could be poured down the drain if it went sour?

"I understand," he said. "I think I do, anyway. But how will your being here make a difference? What are you going to *do?*"

"Palmer Eogan asked me much the same question," the Archon replied.

"And what did you tell him?"

"That I don't know what my actions will be. How could I? My plans are contingent on events as they unfold. There are many things I *could* do, of course, but knowing what I *will* do is too difficult even for someone such as me. *More* difficult, perhaps, because I can see so many more possibilities. A shortsighted person can do little more than follow the road she's on; someone blessed with clear sight sees all the turnoffs she could take—and numerous alternate paths besides, running parallel to the one beneath her feet. One is only lost when one has some perception, no matter how dim, that there is somewhere else one should be."

The reply did little to quell Deangelis's unease. "I fear, Archon, that this situation is far from optimal, in your estimation."

"Don't worry about me, Isaac. Simply do what you think is

right. I trust you and I expect from you only what I expect from myself—that you will do your best in any circumstance. Remember that this is not an exam; there is no *failure*. There are only consequences, as in all moments of life. Do not imagine that I have come here to judge you."

The Archon hesitated, then continued on a slightly different tack: "Perhaps I am misreading your question. Do you ask because there is something you would *like* me to do? Is there any way in which I can help you feel more in command of this situation? All my resources are at your disposal."

The offer was unexpected, and momentarily threw Deangelis. What wondrous devices had the Archon been building with the tangler and all the know-how of Sol? There might be nothing he could conceive of that lay beyond his creator's capacities.

He thought of all the elements of the situation that seemed to be spiraling out of his control: Hails and his insinuations; Eogan and Vermeulen; Melilah Awad. They were all people, and he wasn't sure he entirely trusted the Archon's instincts when it came to dealing with them. If he was to ask for help, it would have to be in an area that wouldn't cause him greater concern.

"The observatory," he said. "It was destroyed in the attack. Only the ruins protect the Occlusion right now. It worries me that it's been left vulnerable, but I've been so busy focusing on the habitat that there's been little time to rebuild. Would you be willing to assist me in that area while I deal with the others?"

"Your mind can rest easy on that score, Isaac." The Archon's reply was gracefully unctuous. "I will begin work at once, while you deal with the situation at hand."

Deangelis's gratitude was mixed with a dose of discomfort at relinquishing even a small measure of control. He reassured himself that there was little the Archon could do without his knowing. The observatory site was in full view of the habitat. Nothing too dramatic could go on there and remain hidden for long.

That left only the convergence of Palmer Eogan, Lazarus Hails, and Melilah Awad to worry about. They were hubs, and so was the colony Awad insisted on calling Bedlam. He wondered if he was a thorn in the Archon's side, as she was in his.

That thought, more than any other, made him hesitate.

+45

"Your behavior hasn't gotten any less reckless, I see," said Vermeulen. "Deangelis is never going to let them leave."

"There's a big difference between keeping someone out and locking them in." Eogan hoped he knew what he was talking about. He still had the equivalent of a watchmeter running in the *Nhulunbuy*. A large percentage of Bedlam's citizens—reconnected to the network and worried about what was going on—were observing his every word, just as he was watching events in their homes.

The many components of the *Kwal Bahal* met and formed the same great pearl necklace it had been on its arrival in the habitat. Flast announced his intention to exit via one of the main docks.

Traffic Control didn't respond.

"Do we have permission or not?" asked Flast.

"You weren't given permission to enter," said the Exarch himself, "so you don't need permission to leave."

"Fine. I'll remember that next time we help you out."

"This isn't ingratitude. Neither is it an argument about law. We trade insult for insult. Can you tell me now, before all my charges, that your intentions are honorable?"

"I have no quarrel with you," said Flast. "I just want to get out of here."

"Then go." Deangelis's various bodies stood stiff and stony-faced as his words echoed through the habitat, emerging from no single mouth but as though out of thin air. "I will not stop you."

"Great," muttered Vermeulen. "He's making *us* look like the bad guys."

"Maybe we are," said Eogan. "Sometimes the truth can harm."

"Hiding the truth is *always* wrong."

He smiled. "That sounds like something Melilah would say."

"You disagree?"

He thought carefully before replying. "I think life is too complex to make such general statements about it. It'd be the same as my insisting that electrons travel in circular orbits or that space is flat. I could believe it as much as I wanted, but reality would keep on surprising me."

The *Kwal Bahal* emerged from the main dock and swept away from the habitat. Eogan felt numerous instruments tracking it, as though it was at the center of dozens of crosshairs. He didn't know how far Deangelis or the Archon would go to protect their secrets. He only hoped they hadn't already crossed the line.

"I've had enough surprises to last a lifetime," said Vermeulen.

"You and me both," he agreed.

The *Kwal Bahal* pulled up alongside the *Nhulunbuy* and handed over its systems to Eogan's command. He kept the two Cells nominally separate, even if they effectively constituted a single Cell once more. Keeping two chief officers in place had the potential to be unwieldy, but they didn't have to maintain the illusion for long.

Melilah hadn't said a word throughout the short trip. She didn't look comfortable in K-3, braced with every limb against the interior walls as though expecting it to lurch at any moment. Sarian, the pilot, respected her silence and did her best to make the ride comfortable. There wasn't much she could do to improve it, though; with minute reactionless thrusters propelling the component on all sides, there was little chance of her feeling any motion at all.

"Our VOID capacity is still down," said Aesche. "With the *Kwal Bahal* and fair weather, we might just make a deform rating of two and half. Maybe three. That puts us a long way from anything."

"A long way from *here* is where I want to be," he said, maintaining the half lie. "Just tell me you can get us moving. We'll work the details out as we go."

"Moving, yes. Running, no."

"Good enough."

A mental command saw his component separate from Vermeulen's and thrust toward K-3. The two components exchanged protocols and prepared to merge. With a faint sigh, their protective fields overlapped. A hole opened in the bulkhead in front of Eogan to reveal Sarian's startled-looking passenger.

"Hello, Melilah."

"We've got to stop meeting like this," she said dryly. "People will talk."

He smiled at her attempt at humor. "Come through here." He had detached himself as much as possible from the Cell, but he could tell that she was still unnerved by his appearance. His back and shoulders were fused with the bulkhead behind him, as though he had eased back into a seat made of taffy. When he leaned forward, the connections stretched like chewing gum.

This was the first time that she had seen him in his normal environment, but there was no point hiding it. The nature of his existence had to be confronted at some point, if only out of a need for closure. He wanted her to see the person he had chosen to be—the person she had rejected by asking him not to become a Palmer. He could still see the look of horror in her eyes when he had raised the merest possibility.

Her lips tightened. That was the only outward sign she gave that she even noticed.

"Well," she said, when the hole sealed shut behind her. The components separated inaudibly. "I'm here."

Not just you, he wanted to say. The Cell was picking up a stream of highly unusual signals pouring out of her body. This was more than the usual information flow surrounding everything in and near Bedlam. It was as though something—an intelligence much more advanced than any he was used to interacting with—had taken over her body and was using it as an antenna.

"Thank you," he said, wondering who else he was talking to, exactly. "This is a very difficult situation. It forces us to do things we might not normally like to do."

"Don't flatter yourself," she said. "I got over you years ago."

"I'm not talking about that," he said. "And I'm not talking about being in the Cell, either." He turned his head symbolically aside to address Aesche, and spoke aloud for Melilah's benefit. "Are the systems ready, Palmer Aesche?"

"As ready as they're going to be."

"Good. Then let's get out of here."

He caught a momentary reaction from Melilah. A flash of panic passed across her face, but was quickly suppressed.

"We're leaving Bedlam?" she asked.

"And taking you with us. I'm sorry, Melilah."

He waited for her to protest, to argue, to shout for help—but she said nothing. She looked frightened, but not in the least surprised.

The *Nhulunbuy* and the *Kwal Bahal,* united in all but name, curved away from Bedlam and aimed for the stars.

Melilah went to say something, but Eogan raised his hand for silence.

Ten thousand kilometers away from the giant habitat, one minute into their journey, the Cell passed outside the colony's territorial jurisdiction. With perfect legality, and in complete accord with usual custom, it severed contact with the network and turned control of its navigation to internal systems.

Eogan's watchmeter program clicked instantly to zero. Information flows returned to normal within the Cell. Eogan severed all contact with anyone outside the component.

At last, they were truly alone.

+46

Melilah crouched in the dimly lit component, not daring to move a muscle. The Cell, touching her peripherals as lightly as a feather, offered her a feed not greatly dissimilar to the ones she had accessed in Bedlam, and she took it, nervously at first but with greater confidence once she was certain no tricks were intended. Through it she saw the *Nhulunbuy/Kwal Bahal*'s many components sweeping in a long arc, accelerating steadily as they went. Bedlam receded into the distance behind it. A long time had passed since she had last left the colony she loved. That she didn't know when—or if—she would return made her eyes water.

Melilah blinked back the tears. She didn't want to give anything to Eogan other than what she had come to tell him.

"We must be clear by now," she said.

"Almost. I'm just waiting for the signals from the nanoware you're carrying to give out. We're almost at the limit of their range."

She looked down at herself, still alarmed by the intrusion of Hails into her person. The nanoware had done little more, she'd thought, than convey a message from the Exarch to her. That it was still functioning when that message was complete made her shudder even more than Eogan did.

She kept her eyes down in an attempt not to stare at him. From the waist up and to the front, he might have been perfectly normal. His chest and arms were bare; his skin was hairless and covered in freckles. She didn't recognize the pattern, much to her relief. There were none of the gross physical intrusions to his eyes and face that Sarian tolerated.

But he had no legs, and he appeared to be melting into the unbroken wall. Every time he opened his mouth, she expected the whirring of gears to emerge, not a voice.

This is his home? she wondered. *This is what he wanted badly enough to ditch me for?*

Melilah tried to quash the bitterness, but it wouldn't stay down.

She cleared her throat, and said, "I have a destination for you."

"Good," he responded with disarming frankness, "because otherwise I was just going to pick a direction at random."

The heading Hails had given her wasn't hard to remember. "Aim for Bode's Nebula. Keep going for around two light-hours."

"And what will we find?"

"A tangler," she said. "Do you know what that is?"

"I have a pretty good idea."

"It's an end point of the Exarch's ftl web," she explained. "Our reverse engineers have been trying to work out the Gentry's communication systems for decades. It turns out they *have* been using entanglement, but with relays every two or three light-years to boost the signals. At each end point is a tangler—and it does a whole lot more than just receive data. It uses nanotech to turn the data it receives into physical objects. That's how the Gentry arrived in force from Sol, during the Expansion, without anyone seeing them on the trade lanes. They sent out the tanglers first. While we were whizzing around in our clunky ships, they were leapfrogging between the stars, nothing more than data. The tanglers built them and their Reapers out of space dust and comets."

Eogan was watching her as she spoke, his green eyes impenetrable.

"If it wasn't *them* behind it," she admitted, "I'd think the idea pretty clever."

"Tell me," he said, "how you know all this."

"Lazarus Hails told me."

"He's the one who gave you the nanoware?"

"Along with the destination, yes."

Eogan nodded. "I've instructed the Cell to follow the vector you gave us. We'll see if Hails is as good as his word when we get there."

Melilah hadn't noticed anything to indicate that he had spoken to the *Nhulunbuy/Kwal Bahal* or its crew, or that they had changed course. "How long?"

"Six hours."

"Is that to a dead stop or for a flyby?"

"Dead stop, unless we change our minds on the way."

She was reassured that his intention wasn't really to leave the system—yet. "They'll be tracking us for sure, Deangelis and the Archon. They'll know when we start to decelerate."

"There's not much we can do about that from here."

"True." She tried not to look nervous, but she could feel herself beginning to talk for talk's sake. "Either way, we've got plenty of time to kill."

"It certainly seems that way."

There followed an awkward pause. "Do you want to go first?"

"That depends on what else you've got to tell me."

She nodded. "Okay. Hails wants us to lead a revolution against the Archon."

Eogan's eyebrows went up. "That's unexpected. Did he tell you that we could use the Occlusion to do it?"

"Not in so many words."

"I guess he knew I'd do it for him."

She felt her pulse quicken. "So it *is* a wormhole," she said. "Nothing could make me happier."

He shook his head. "It's not a wormhole as we understand them. I told you before that a wormhole had to have two ends, that it would lead *somewhere* or else what was the point of it?"

She nodded.

"Well, I was partly right and partly wrong. It's not *a* wormhole, Melilah. It's many of them, all tangled up in a knot. A maze."

She frowned, remembering Greek legends and pictures of old Earth hedges.

"A maze?"

"That's right. And there could be more than two exits. *Many* more."

She stared at him, forgetting for a moment to blink. "Fuck," she breathed, the implications hitting her almost immediately.

A maze with more than one exit wasn't a maze; it was a traffic grid.

"You'd better keep going," she said, completely forgetting about her surroundings in order to hear the rest.

Eogan wasn't the one to tell her all of it. He filled her in on the broadest details, then had his science officer join them to do the rest. Another component, dimly visible as a point of light through the translucent shell around her, grew larger against the backdrop of space until it looked like it was going to crash. Melilah felt a thrum of furious activity through her hands and toes as another portal opened before her, revealing Palmer Vermeulen.

Vermeulen sat cross-legged in the center of her component, legs folded beneath her and arms at her sides. Like Eogan, she looked normal at first glance. Only when Melilah noticed that her hands disappeared into the floor beneath her and her legs seemed to overlap peculiarly was she certain that Vermeulen was fully interfacing with the Cell.

So what is this? she wanted to ask them. *Pretense of humanity for the hick visitor?* Part of her would rather they just acted natural. She could deal with it.

But she was glad she didn't have to stare at naked posthumanity as she had with Sarian. No nanowires sticking out of eyes or melting torsos here.

"When the Reaper came to ram the observatory," Vermeulen said, "I thought I was finished. It was Deangelis who got me out in time. He whisked me into that escape capsule and pushed me through the throat so fast I barely had time to realize what was going on. Conditions inside the throat make for a rough ride, especially at speed; but it was short, and Deangelis had done his homework. The capsule made it through just fine. I've been taking it apart since I came back. I think I've found the trick to it."

Good, thought Melilah, although she didn't interrupt. They would need a reliable way to get through the Occlusion if they were ever going to use it to their advantage.

"The far side is much as Cobiac and Bray recorded it," Vermeulen continued. "A straight tunnel; perfect vacuum; nothing much to see apart from that. But it's obvious that Deangelis has been busy. There are instruments everywhere—in webs, growing into the walls, stretching roots farther than I could see up the tunnel. He's been having a ball, and he obviously hadn't expected anyone else anytime soon. The systems were encrypted, but it didn't take long to get in. I got the data he's gathered."

Melilah nodded. Reams of images and multidimensional graphs were streaming around her, projected by the Cell onto the walls of the joined components. None of it made any sense to her—except for one, a stark tangle of lines that reminded her of something she had seen recently.

"What's that?" she asked, as it flashed by again.

"It's a map," said Vermeulen. "Not complete by any means; it may be no more than the tiniest percentage of what's in there; and it's fiendishly difficult to follow. But it's definitely a map of sorts. Without it, I would never have gotten back."

Melilah turned sharply from the image. "Back from where?"

"Nowhere in particular. I just took a couple of corners, to make sure I was reading the map right. I was. The tunnel really does branch. It crosses other tunnels, loops back on itself, and stops dead, too—all in at least five dimensions. It's not the sort of place I'd spend long in without some sort of guide. If there's a pattern to it, I couldn't see one."

Neither could Melilah, at first glance. "Did you find another exit?"

"No. I don't think I went far enough. Conditions are very unnerving in there. Space doesn't work like it does out here. The warp that caught Cobiac and Bray by surprise is typical of the longer corridors, it seems. The greater the distance between two points, the higher the apparent acceleration someone passing between them will experience. It's not *actual* acceleration; it's more a kind of stretching, not so different to the Alcubierre effects that underlie the VOID drive. Space—as defined by the shape of the walls around you—flexes, so one step takes you farther than normal. You just seem to rocket along. And if you're not careful, you can get lost in seconds."

Melilah shivered. "So that's what happened to Cobiac and Bray. They warped up the opening tunnel and got lost."

Vermeulen nodded. "I don't think I can convey to you in words—or even with pictures—just how disorienting it is in there. Nothing works the way it does outside. Taking all left turns won't bring you back to where you started. Same with right turns. You might think you're going in a straight line, but you could actually be twisting in circles. Whoever designed it had a mind very different from ours."

"Or at least a very different way of looking at things."

"Cobiac and Bray could still be alive in there," Eogan said, his tone bitter. "If we'd waited a little longer, maybe they would've made it back."

Vermeulen didn't say anything. Her eyes were hard. Melilah could tell that she didn't want to give Eogan any unfounded hope. If the maze was as complicated as she described, if one short walk up a corridor could cross impossible distances in unfathomable directions, then Melilah could accept, at least notionally, that the two Palmers had become irretrievably lost. And that they had probably continued to wander after getting lost meant the chances of them ever being seen again were very slim indeed.

"So you went exploring," she said, "then you came back. How else did you kill your time in there?"

"That's the other weird thing," Vermeulen said. "According to Eogan, I was gone for fifteen hours. To me it was more like three."

"So time warps as well as space?"

Eogan nodded. "Makes sense," he said. "They're aspects of the same thing, after all."

"I think the warps are side effects," said Vermeulen. "Most of them, anyway."

"Of what?" Melilah asked her.

"Of the architecture itself. It clearly doesn't belong to this universe; it probably lives in its own unique continuum nestled alongside ours, connected in places by means of the wormholes. Its continuum is much smaller than ours. Its only contents are the maze and *its* contents. Or, more properly speaking, the interior of the maze is the true extent of the continuum it defines: there may be nothing at all outside the walls. So anything *inside* those walls will have a profound effect on the topology of the entire continuum."

"This is where I get a bit blurry," said Eogan to Melilah.

"Blurry my ass," Vermeulen said. "You're just not looking at it properly. The idea that any travelers within the maze actually cause the warps that push us along isn't so crazy. Neither is the possibility that neighboring corridors and their contents could affect each other, even if they are separated by light-years in the 'real' world. What happens inside that other continuum is what matters; that's all. At first glance, I felt sure that it was some kind of superscience transport system, a means of connecting stars, maybe even galaxies together. But now I'm not so sure. Why make it so damned complicated? Why not right angles and straight lines? Why not put signposts up everywhere?"

"Maybe because to the builders it isn't complicated," said Melilah. "Or maybe there were guides you just didn't see right."

"It's possible," said Vermeulen. "In fact, this is probably what Deangelis was looking for."

"We have to stop him from finding it," Melilah said. "We have to get there first."

"At the moment," said Eogan, raising a cautionary hand, "we don't have proof of anything much. There's no actual evidence that it's connected to any other point in our universe. We're only *assuming* that there's more than one entrance, that it's related to the thing they found in Sublime. We might have something completely different here. Strange as it sounds, this might not even be artificial. It could be a natural phenomenon."

"A living thing." Vermeulen stared at him with a slightly appalled expression. "A space-time mosquito, sucking the vacuum from one universe to another."

"And you went right up its mouth." Eogan didn't smile. "Sublime might have been its other end."

"Well, shit," Vermeulen said.

"Exactly."

Silence filled the joined components for a moment, as the Cell continued accelerating toward Bode's Nebula.

"Okay. It's my turn." Melilah reached out to the Cell with her peripherals, proffering the data she had been cradling ever since agreeing to meet the Palmers in their home environment. "I found this hidden on a fiche in the heart of Bedlam, a common place to hide data out of sight of the information laws." She didn't look at Eogan. "On the surface, it looks like nothing but letters and amateur maps, but I think there's more to it than that."

"Why?" asked Vermeulen.

"Several reasons." She waved away most of them as irrelevant. "The main one is because the map you displayed before looked familiar. It took me a while to work out where from. Take a look at the sketches in the file I've just given you. Tell me what you think."

Neither moved, but an instant later the data flashed onto the walls of the component around her. The maps were crude and incomplete. Again, they reminded her of outlines of Bedlam's many crisscrossing corridors. She had checked two days ago to see if it matched any region within the habitat, without success. It had to be a map of somewhere else, then.

"I think it's a map of the maze," she said after a moment. "What else could it be?"

"It does look similar," Vermeulen conceded, her pupils moving, tracking things Melilah couldn't see. "That is, the individual images do share a certain resemblance with the ones I brought back."

"Just a resemblance?" asked Eogan.

"Don't forget that any map of the maze in three dimensions is an approximation of the real thing. It'll take me a while to make sure they're one and the same."

"Take your time. We need to be certain before we make any decisions about what to do with it."

"I haven't got very far with the rest of the file," Melilah conceded. "The letters could just be a cover, to distract from the real data."

"Or they could be the real thing." Eogan nodded. "We'll work on it as we travel. If the Exarch has been storing any data at all this way, I suspect it'll be worth getting our hands on."

"I wouldn't be too sure about that," said Vermeulen. "After all, he had a perfectly secure setup inside the Occlusion itself."

"Not perfectly secure—nor even safe, as Cazneaux's attack proved. He might have created the cache as a backup."

"And I was lucky enough to stumble across it," said Melilah, a slight twinge that she hadn't immediately recognized was evened out by the knowledge that she and the Exarch had similarly demanding tastes in hiding places.

"What?" asked Eogan then, as she frowned.

"Nothing," she said. She had no intention of telling them what she had been doing when she'd stumbled across the cache, but the thought had just occurred to her that Deangelis might have chosen the niche because he subconsciously wanted the data to be found, just as she didn't actually want to forget.

"Let's get on with it," she said. "This trip isn't going to take forever."

+47

The sudden peace and quiet had to be an illusion. Or so Deangelis told himself as he wandered the halls of the habitat, tasting its inhabitants' mood. Everywhere he went, he saw relieved faces and determination to put things back the way they had been. Autonomous repair systems operated in tandem with human workers—the latter often more a hindrance than a genuine help, although he kept that carefully to himself. A sense of contributing to the reconstruction was good for morale. Bulkheads and pipes devoured by the infectious replicators grew slowly back into place. Water, air, power, and data lines were reconnected. Waste systems went back online. Only in a handful of areas were some secondary services on hold—such as food production and hard recycling—and he expected that to be a temporary restriction only. Before long, everything would be back as it was supposed to be.

On the surface, at least—and therein lay the problem. He could feel a tension everywhere he went, as though the cooperation and good-natured industry camouflaged a deeply felt but just as deeply buried concern. The habitat had been attacked; the reason for that attack was still nearby. What would happen next?

Deangelis sympathized with that feeling, even though the number of his problems was rapidly diminishing. The observatory was showing signs of activity under the guidance of the Archon. Hails was in protective custody. Melilah Awad was in the *Nhulunbuy/Kwal Bahal,* apparently leaving with Palmers Eogan and Vermeulen. He should have been relieved at having them finally out of his hair.

But it wasn't that simple. Even if there were no further attacks on the Occlusion, there would be recriminations down the line, should word ever get out. He had delayed dealing with the problem, not avoided it. He had gained a reprieve, nothing more.

Although he tried his best to ignore the uncertainty, it ate at him like vitriol. He hadn't handled the situation at all well. The best he could say about it was that the crisis had gone away. What sort of leader could he call himself, with that track record?

Still, his loss to the clane had earned him some sympathy among the general population. He was greeted by nods and waves. The occasional group invited him to join them in toasting a recently completed project, or merely to participate in the relief they felt that all was returning to normal.

He took the first few offers, but then declined them all. He didn't feel like celebrating. Instead of being cheered, his mood worsened. The sense of approaching doom grew stronger. He felt as hollow as a china doll, waiting for a hammer to fall.

The feeling only worsened when the Archon announced that he was taking the colony's tangler and relocating it in the ruin of the observatory.

"A temporary measure, Isaac, to save the resources ferrying materiel back and forth would consume."

Deangelis could see the sense in the plan, but that didn't mean he liked it. The tangler was his link to Sol; without it, he would feel more isolated than ever.

"The move is not permanent," the Archon reassured him. It failed to ease his mind at all. He watched a flotilla of cargo spheres exit the habitat's main docks with trepidation. Without the tangler at hand, his escape was no longer assured, should the worst come to pass.

"Don't worry," said a voice along a little-used communications channel. "She'll be back in no time."

Deangelis followed the communication back to its source. A quick glance took in the man's identity and his recent activities. Gil Hurdowar seemed to have taken up Exarch-watching in the absence of his usual target.

"I presume you are talking about Melilah Awad."

"Who else? Yasu and Defiance might think she's off on some wild, romantic tryst, but she can't fool us. Right?"

"I don't know what you mean." Hurdowar spoke with a camaraderie Deangelis disliked. "Whether she comes back or not is no concern of mine."

That earned him a laugh. “You can’t fool me either, Deangelis. I’ve watched you watching her. I know that look.”

“Are you suggesting . . . ?” He stopped, appalled by the man’s insinuation. “That’s the most ridiculous thing I’ve ever heard.”

“Is it? Maybe you should listen to yourself sometimes.”

Hurdowar killed the line, but Deangelis couldn’t tear his appalled gaze away from his surveillance of the man. Agonized thoughts slowed his mind like clotted cream. Filthy, antisocial, and invasive Hurdowar might be, but was he as perceptive as he liked to think he was? Could he possibly be *right?*

Yes, Deangelis did spend more time observing and pondering Melilah Awad than he did most other citizens. That was only because she was at the center of so many critical situations. That was *her* issue, not his. If she hadn’t been a borderline terrorist, always probing into secret places and trying to turn things against him, dissenting and brewing rebellion among her peers, he would happily ignore her, let her get on with her life like any of the other forty thousand people under his aegis.

The thought that he might be obsessed with her—romantically or otherwise—was patently absurd!

You should listen to yourself sometimes.

The strength of his response undercut his certainty. Was it possible that he was thinking at cross-purposes with himself, that part of him was indeed expending a disproportionate amount of time and energy focusing on Melilah Awad, that he could have developed some strange, perverse attachment to this blatantly Normal woman? He didn’t see how it could be possible. He might have saved her during the attack, but he would have done the same for anyone. He had shied away from blowing her out of the sky when she had run to Palmer Eogan, but both the urge to do so and the decision not to would have been identical if Gil Hurdowar had been in her place. He was sure of it. There was nothing he could see that set her apart, in his mind, from everyone else. There was nothing special about her at all.

A pinhole of doubt remained. He remembered his feeling when he had found her and Palmer Eogan embracing in one of the ruined alien vessels found alongside the Occlusion. The moment had struck him powerfully, and he had never been able to understand why. Could it be as simple as envy for the flesh? Was he desirous of her passion, her intimacy with primal emotions, her blindness to her own faults that propelled her along paths no rational mind could countenance? Did he long, bizarrely, to be as Naturally human as Melilah? To be Naturally human *with* her?

Deangelis honestly didn't know. Gil Hurdowar was probably just projecting his own feelings on another person, giving his obsession validity by mapping them on the system's ultimate authority. But he had raised a concern that couldn't easily be dismissed. Isaac Forge Deangelis, posthuman intelligence capable of experiencing all aspects of the universe from the breaking of a hydrogen bond to the stately rise and fall of economic trends, was aware of himself to a degree never experienced by ordinary humanity. There weren't supposed to be hidden nooks and crannies supplying twisted urges and self-destructive desires. That lack was one of the things that made him such a good colonial administrator.

But his life wasn't supposed to be so complex, either. He wasn't supposed to have been violently diminished in an attack from one of his own kind. He wasn't supposed to be living with the threat of destruction hanging constantly over his head. He wasn't supposed to be working under the watchful eye of the one who had created him.

Would it be any great wonder if he developed a flaw under such circumstances, if a hairline fracture formed and spread across the edifice that was his normal sense of self?

That fracture could take the form of obsessive feelings for one in his care. He supposed it was conceivable. Underneath all his synergistic cognation, he still had emotions and needs. He was still human in his frailty.

Not for much longer, he swore. Reconstruction progressed apace. He would soon be fully accustomed to the new dynamics of his higher mind. The Occlusion couldn't be a problem forever. When things settled down, the fracture would heal, and he would be back to his usual self.

The feeling that thunderheads were gathering just over the horizon was the only thing marring that plan.

+48

The moment the *Nhulunbuy/Kwal Bahal*'s forward sensors found the tangler, Eogan pasted an image of it onto the wall of the component.

"If that's what it really is," Vermeulen said. The faint image was barely discernible against the background sky.

"Hails had no reason to lie," Melilah said, rubbing weariness from her eyes with the tips of her fingers.

"You defending an Exarch?" Eogan made the point softly, not wanting to jab too deep. "That doesn't match your reputation."

She lowered her hands to look at him. "Lazarus Hails had no reason to tell me the truth, either. The whole lot could've been a load of bullshit—and we could be walking into a trap designed to get rid of everyone who knows anything about what the Occlusion really is."

"*Now* she raises the possibility," said Vermeulen, with a grimace.

"But I still trust him," Melilah said, "as far as I *can* trust him. We haven't proven him wrong yet."

"We'll know in an hour, I guess." Eogan didn't bother explaining that there was no way to bring that time forward. The *Nhulunbuy/Kwal Bahal* was still too deeply mired in the dust of Lut-Deangelis to activate its flawed drive efficiently. The point at which it was able to wouldn't come for some hours yet, when it passed the system's heliopause and entered the interstellar medium. There, with nuclei averaging less than one per square centimeter, the vacuum would be pure enough to allow superluminal effects to come into play, and the stars would be within its reach.

If it kept going, of course . . .

Eogan tried to keep his thoughts focused on the information in front of him, not on what might be. The files Melilah had brought from Bedlam were fiendishly complex to unravel. Deangelis's steganographic algorithms had to be at least five generations more sophisticated than any he had ever seen. The data was encoded by layers of transformations he could barely fathom. It was like trying to find his way through the maze on the other side of the Occlusion with his eyes blindfolded and his arms tied behind his back.

But he had to persist. Unraveling the file could be the most important thing he ever did. Palmer Vermeulen's suppositions and guesses weren't enough. He needed hard data. Specifically, he needed to know if the maze had more than one entrance, and if so *how many.* If there were more entrances in human-occupied space, and they could be accessed as easily as the one he had retrieved, then it would change everything.

He felt for Frederica Cazneaux. The Occlusion was even more of a threat than a single wormhole throat or wormhole technology in general. In the wrong hands it would mean the end of the Exarchate and the irrelevance of the Palmers.

But what should he do about it if his suspicions were confirmed? Destroy it, as Cazneaux had failed to? Destroy those who would use it against the Palmers? Take it for himself?

For the moment, it seemed as though Deangelis and the Exarchs were keeping it under wraps. That was a good thing. He had no intention of telling his superiors until he was absolutely certain of what it was, and what needed to be done about it. He recoiled from an image of the scramble that would erupt when word of a new means of getting around the galaxy emerged. Bedlam would become a war zone—and so, potentially, would every occlusion that drifted across every trade lane in the Exarchate.

And that was ignoring what might yet come out of it, if humanity probed too deeply. Even if the Occlusion was completely unrelated to what happened in Sublime, *someone* had to have built it, and they might not take kindly to trespassers . . .

"Why here?" asked Melilah.

He dropped out of the complex decrypting programs he had been employing to crack the file's secrets.

"Why where?"

"Here—near Bedlam. If the maze does have a multitude of entrances, why haven't we seen it elsewhere before now?"

Clearly her mind had been wandering, too. "I put it down to the VOID drive," he said. "It relies on deep vacuum, and we have more of it out here where the Local Bubble stretches farthest. Here, the interstellar medium is much hotter and thinner than elsewhere around Sol. Because of that, the Arc Circuit covers more light-years than any other trade network, and more traffic flows along it than on any other frontier. That increases the chances of an exit stumbling across a Cell, or vice versa."

She nodded, satisfied with that answer. But there were so many other questions. "The entrances mustn't be fixed; otherwise, the Mizar Occlusion would have been spotted on the trade lane immediately, and all this would've happened centuries ago. Same with Sublime. Maybe the whole structure is drifting, moving slowly through space."

"Or the galaxy is rotating through it," he suggested.

"That's assuming," said Vermeulen, "that the structure's motion in its continuum relates at all to the position of the exits in this universe. They may be connected, but they could also be completely separate. All you need is for the mouths to have a bit of give, and the exits could drift about at random while the thing itself stays put."

The effort required to visualize such a situation made Eogan's eyes cross. "So there are three components to this thing: the exits, the mouths, and the maze."

"That's my best guess, at the moment. The exits are holes in this universe; the throats link those holes to the continuum in which the maze sits; the maze gives that continuum shape." She shrugged. "The structure is likely to be much more complicated than that, but it's a start."

It was indeed, Eogan thought. Especially given the scant data they had to play with. Glimpses on the way to Bedlam; files stolen from the Exarch; coded information buried deep in the giant habitat. It might all come together in a way that made sense, but it didn't have to. Eogan was prepared for disappointment.

He wasn't so sure about Melilah.

"I've got into some of the file structure," he said, returning to the virtual displays surrounding him. "A lot of it's still hidden, but there's some basic information that *can't* be hidden, or faked. The dates on a number of the directories are problematic, if the files they contain do indeed relate to the Occlusion. They appear to have been created years ago."

"They must be dummies, then," she said, "planted to put us off the scent."

"I don't think so. They account for most of the data."

"Then you must be looking at it wrong." She frowned and turned away.

"I don't know, Melilah." Vermeulen spoke with uncharacteristic hesitation, as though nervous of Melilah's reaction. "It's not adding up the way you'd like it to. Those maps you gave me: they do assemble into a 5-D maze, but it doesn't match the one I found inside the Occlusion."

"Could it be an earlier version? A rough draft?"

"No. I can't make the hubs fit, no matter how I fiddle it. And besides, the scale isn't right. If this is an early draft, it should be smaller, right? In fact, it's larger. *Much* larger. That's why it's taken me so long to get my head around it. I've had to check every multidimensional branch and twig to make sure part of it doesn't match the one I found."

Melilah looked downcast and very tired. Eogan wondered how long it had been since she had slept—and how long she could function without it. The limits of her Natural body were blurry, depending on her needs. It all depended on what her needs had been just prior to the arrival of the Occlusion as to how far she could push herself.

"Then it's not the maze," she said dully. "We've wasted our time."

"So it would seem." Vermeulen looked sympathetic.

"I just don't understand. Why would someone go to the trouble of burying information like this if it wasn't important?"

"Maybe it was something they were embarrassed about. Love letters, bad art: I'd be ashamed, too."

Melilah looked defensive for a moment. Why, Eogan couldn't imagine.

"Wait a second," he said, a new possibility suddenly occurring to him. "Why couldn't it be a map of the maze—just not a section of the maze we know?"

Vermeulen frowned. "I suppose it's possible, if what we saw through the Occlusion is typical of the rest."

"That would mean there's another occlusion," said Melilah. Her eyes widened. "Sublime!"

"That would be my guess," he said.

"It has to be!" Such was her excitement that she nudged off

the bulkhead she was squatting against and tumbled about the interior of the component.

"Easy," he said, grabbing her arm and stabilizing her.

"You know what this means," she said when she had secured herself again, floating just centimeters away from him. Her expression was very serious. "It means the Exarchate is in there, where Sublime used to be. They've got past the—what's it called?"

"Horsfall Station. That wouldn't be hard, seeing they built it."

"The replicators must have burned themselves out, or been beaten back. The Gentry have been in there without telling anyone. Maybe they've been in there ever since the Catastrophe!"

"That's why Deangelis didn't seem surprised by what we found on the trade lane," said Vermeulen grimly. "And why he knew how to move the damned thing so easily."

Eogan nodded. It all fit. "They might not have known there were more entrances until we found this one. Until then, it was just a weird, dangerous anomaly. Now, everything's changed. And some of them don't like it."

He thought of Cazneaux and could understand her fear more clearly. He pictured the maze as a vast, invisible anemone drifting through the galaxy, the tips of its tentacles occasionally passing through or near colonized worlds. If those tips were deadly, like they had been in Sublime, how many colonies were at risk? Maybe all of them. Learning how to close the throats, perhaps by destroying them, could be the key to humanity's survival.

A chillingly familiar image came to him: of Bedlam's destruction boiling through the maze like steam out of a pipe. The source of that destruction might be very deep within the maze, so deep it was taking days to arrive. Sublime hadn't fallen for months after the discovery of the artifact they found. Bedlam might have just long enough to imagine that it was safe before the end came . . .

"We've obtained a clearer image of the target." Flast's voice intruded on the moment. "Eogan, I think you need to see this."

He pulled himself out of the revelation concerning Sublime and forced himself to concentrate on the images the *Nhulunbuy/Kwal Bahal* had recorded. The tiny dot of the tangler had resolved into several dots clustering around a long spear-shaped structure.

"What the hell is that?" he asked.

"I can't answer that precisely just yet," said Flast, "but we're working on it."

"It's a fleet," Melilah breathed, staring wide-eyed at the image. "Hails left it for us."

"As a gift for us," Vermeulen asked, "or in wait for us?"

"I guess we'll find out," said Eogan, "when we get there."

+49

The *Nhulunbuy* detected an unauthorized transmission one hour from the coordinates Hails had given them. Eogan broke off a detailed examination of the fleet's composition to inform Melilah of the new development. The source of the transmission was the nanoware she had unintentionally brought aboard the Cell.

"Whatever Hails put inside you is wanting to make contact." Eogan indicated the fleet. "With that."

A great weariness swept through her, and no small amount of alarm. She'd assumed that, since her new peripheral had been silent since leaving Bedlam, it had quietly dissolved away. Now she found that it had only been biding its time, waiting for them to reach their destination.

Her home had been invaded, violated, attacked—and now her body had been taken over, too.

"I want it out of me," she said. "You're good with nanotech. Get rid of it."

Eogan looked uncomfortable. "We're good under the right circumstances, Melilah. But flushing a living person clean is very different from scouring an external environment, especially if that person is physically unknown to us. I'd hesitate to do anything right now, just in case we scrub out something we didn't mean to."

"Like your mitochondria," put in Vermeulen. "Besides which, I think we should let it talk."

Both Melilah and Eogan faced the science officer in surprise.

"Why not?" Vermeulen said. "It might say something we need

to hear. And even if all it does is sic the fleet on us, we're not so close we can't run away. I can't see what damage it could do."

Eogan turned back to Melilah. "It's up to you."

She stared back at them, then resigned herself to the situation with a shrug. "What the hell. As long as it *only* talks."

"We'll monitor the transmissions," Eogan reassured her. "We won't let it hurt you."

That didn't reassure her much. She bet the Gentry had tricks the Palmers had never dreamed of.

"Okay," said Eogan. "We're giving it free rein." A faint pink-noise burble filled the Cell component: an audible depiction of the transmission, she presumed. "It looks like garbage, so far. Hand-shaking, presumably."

A stronger tone, deeper and more rapid, drowned out the one she was producing.

"That's a reply," said Vermeulen. "Still no recognizable content."

Melilah waited in nervous anticipation for anything—anything at all—to happen to her. She monitored all of her body's rhythms, ready for the slightest change. Her heart was beating faster in response to adrenaline. The nanoware was probably draining sugars to fuel its activities and bleeding off waste heat into her circulatory system, but neither effect was strong enough to feel.

Maybe, she thought, she wasn't the intended recipient of Lazarus Hails's message at all. Maybe the vague hints he had given her in Bedlam about rebellion were just to get her moving. Maybe she was nothing but a courier, and the real message was only now arriving . . .

Ah, Melilah Awad. The polished tones of Lazarus Hails were suddenly between her ears again. *You were one of several people I thought likely to end up here. It's a pleasure to speak with you.*

She sighed. "Listen," she said aloud. "If you're going to talk to me, then do it openly through the Cell, or I'm not going to pay attention."

I could make you, but— Very well.

"We're being hailed," came Flast's voice. "The target is signaling us."

"It's Hails," Melilah said. "Open a channel."

"Come on down, Exarch Hails." Vermeulen took the development in her stride. "We have you in our sights."

"I'm sure you do. And vice versa, of course." Hails's leonine features stepped into the holographic depths of the component wall. He looked identical to the version Melilah had met several hours earlier, except this one was dressed in what appeared to be a business suit from the days of the Capitalist Spasm. He clearly wasn't the same Hails as the one on Bedlam, since there was no light-speed delay between question and answer, and he had a full head of white hair. He was just another part of a much larger whole.

"What a pretty kettle of fish we have here."

"Meaning?" asked Eogan.

"It means I've never seen an unlikelier set of allies."

"We're not allies yet, Exarch Hails," said Eogan.

"True. This installation is here for your use, however, should we come to an agreement on *how* to use it—or at least to what end. That should be incentive enough to start you talking."

"What do you want us to do with it?" Melilah asked.

"I'm sure you already know the answer to that, my dear." Hails smiled at her as though humoring a schoolgirl. "You are, after all, the one I brought here. The monkey on your back should have brought you up to speed."

She forced herself to ignore his tangled metaphors. "You want us to attack the Archon."

"What I want is to send a clear signal that Sol is no longer welcome in the Arc Circuit. Attacking the Archon and taking the Occlusion for ourselves won't be the end of it, but it will certainly be a definitive beginning."

"Why us?" asked Eogan. "You've got everything you need right here."

"Isn't it obvious? I don't want my name attached to this rebellion. You can consider me magnanimous if you like, preferring to give you the glory while I slink back into the Dark, but I'd rather you understood perfectly where I stand. You'll take the risk instead of me. Fail, and retribution will be upon your head, not mine. Succeed, however, and we all get what we want. I think that's a fair exchange for the only arsenal in eight light-years with any chance of winning."

"What happens when the Archon is gone?" Melilah asked. "Will you be our ruler? If so, I'm not sure what we stand to gain. An Exarch by any other name—"

"Your sentiments are noted," Hails interrupted in a long-suffering tone. "Consider that life with the Archon is likely to be more uncomfortable than it is now. Sol has significantly less tolerance for the peccadilloes of its primitive wards than our mutual friend Isaac Deangelis. Already, I fear, the thumbscrews are on."

Melilah thought of the Archon's reticence since the end of the attack, the blackout of the system, and Deangelis's increasing stress levels. She decided that on this point she completely trusted Lazarus Hails.

"Tell us about the Mizar Occlusion," said Vermeulen. "How much do you know?"

"I know that there is still much to be learned." The illusion of Hails folded its hands behind its back and began to pace around the component, circling them. "But tell me what *you* know, first."

"We know the Exarchate is still in Sublime," Melilah said, going out on a limb to get a reaction. "We know we've been lied to about that."

Hails didn't break step, but he did raise an eyebrow. "Have you been contacted by Jane Elderton?"

She shook her head. "No. Why? Are you telling me she's still alive?"

"Oh, yes. Poor Jane is in an unenviable position. She has suffered much since the Catastrophe. An Exarch without a colony is like Jupiter without its moons. Technically, she is completely isolated, cut off from everyone around her—but unofficially word has been leaking this last year. She still has her tangler, somewhere in that mess. Even with it at hand, the loneliness would be crippling. She may not often initiate conversations, but she will answer when approached."

"What's she doing in there?"

"Isn't that obvious? She's studying the thing they found. Part or all of her must have survived the Catastrophe. Instead of pulling her out, the Archon forced her to stay. She is the mistress now of a devastated, depopulated system—a system still controlled by the plague that destroyed it. I myself would rather be dead."

"Do you know what she's found?"

"Do you?"

"We know the Occlusion is an entrance to a hyperspatial maze. We know there could be many more such entrances."

Again a penetrating look as the Exarch walked around them. "Do you know this, or is it merely conjecture?"

"I've seen it with my own eyes," said Vermeulen.

"I envy you," he said with apparent frankness. "It is a most remarkable artifact, if the rumors I've heard about it are true. Without such a device behind us, rebellion against the Archon and Sol would simply not be possible. We need every advantage we can get."

Hails had, perhaps deliberately, exposed a depth of ignorance that surprised Melilah. "You sound like you're as much in the dark as we are."

"Of course. This information is not widely disseminated. It is beyond the need-to-know requirements of the average Exarch. Clearly, Sol would rather keep us ignorant of any means by which we might attain our independence. It knows that it is just one small system surrounded by many hundreds of growing ones; if we ever get the upper hand, its days are numbered."

Eogan was looking uncomfortable. "Perhaps we're getting a little ahead of ourselves," he said. "Before we start talking about overthrowing Sol, let's deal with Bedlam. What needs to be done here and now? How are we going to do it? Is there any way we can get rid of the Archon without risking innocent bystanders?"

Melilah nodded, glad for the reminder to stick to basics. "I won't countenance another attack like Cazneaux's."

"Do not fear," soothed the Exarch. "I'm not giving you a Reaper to sic upon yourselves. That would simply be foolish."

"What *are* you giving us?"

"The following." Hails's image faded and was replaced by a close-up of the Exarch's fleet. Nine tapered shapes clustered around a spindly docking assembly, looking like overlarge seeds hanging from a vine. "These are attack drones designed to interface with a Palmer Cell. Don't let their simple appearance mislead you. They're smaller and more maneuverable than anything you've seen before. I've been evolving them on the sly for years, in case a situation like this ever arose. They're designed to be autonomous, under certain circumstances, so the Archon won't be able to knock them out of the sky as it did everything else in Bedlam. At the first sign of interference, they'll shut themselves off to the outside and continue with their mission unchecked."

It was Melilah's turn to have misgivings. She didn't like the idea of unstoppable missiles rampaging around the system, doing untold damage. "I presume there's a kill switch."

Hails returned. "Of course. I will give you all the information you require, when we have a deal."

"What's the other thing?" asked Vermeulen. "The thing they're docked with."

"My tangler. You will have full use of that, too, should you require it."

Melilah didn't need to think about what she would do if she had ftl communications capability at her fingertips.

"You have a deal," she said.

Eogan looked at her in surprise. "Wait a minute, Melilah. You can't accept just like that."

"Yes, I can."

"But I'm not convinced it's the right thing—"

She turned on him, anger flaring. "Who said you have anything to do with it? No one made us allies, Eogan. We're not in this together. Yes, we exchanged information; yes, you brought me out here. But don't forget that you lured me aboard with the intention of kidnapping me—or that I have as little reason to trust the Palmers as I do the Gentry. You're under no obligation to make the same decision as me. Dump me here, if you like, and I'll do what I have to do. Then you can get the hell out of this system and never come back."

He was tight-lipped, betraying a rare emotion. "I just think there's more we need to discuss, that's all."

"Fuck the discussions," she said. "Hails is offering me what I want, and I'm taking it."

"I thought you might," crowed the hologram Exarch. "Am I right in supposing that it's not specifically the attack drones you're after?"

"Damn straight," she said, forcing herself to breathe deeply, calmingly. There was no keeping a lid on the intensity of her emotion, however. She was too tired for subtle games. "I'm sick of all these secrets and lies. I want people to know the truth: not just people in Bedlam, but people everywhere. Tell them about the Occlusion, about the thing the Archon is trying to keep from them, and let them make up their own minds. We're not stupid. We have no need to be *protected.* We stand to benefit most from the maze, so we should be allowed to have a say in who owns it."

"But that will—" Eogan didn't finish the sentence.

"Trigger a revolution? Start a war? End civilization as we know it?" She took no satisfaction at all from the shocked look on his face. "That's what this whole conversation has been about, Eogan. Haven't you been paying attention? Did you think we'd hauled ourselves all the way out here for a polite conversation about the weather? That we'd all go home afterward, pretending everything's okay? Well, it's *not* okay. In fact, everything's about as far from fucking okay as it could be! And if it has to get worse before it gets any better, then that's just what it has to do. It's up to you to decide whether you're prepared to make the effort to fix the situation, or whether you're going to just turn tail like last time, in the naive hope that it'll make life easier for you."

She stopped there, realizing that her mouth had run away with itself. He was silent for a moment, not quite glaring at her but certainly unhappy about the way he was being spoken to. Vermeulen stared at them both, her mouth firmly shut.

When Eogan did speak, it was in a voice that was as soft and inevitable as a slow air leak.

"I want proof," he said. "Proof of so many things it's hard to know where to start. Proof that Hails is leveling with us on the tangler, and the attack drones, and the Archon, and his reason for being here. Proof that the maze is what it appears to be, and not some cobbled-together theory that'll fall apart on closer examination. Proof that it's *worth fighting for.*" He put out a hand to touch the bulkhead beside him, as though to steady himself. "Palmers do not go to war lightly. We are not a military cult. We will act to defend those in need, as we did here yesterday—"

"*Some* of you did," she put in sourly.

"That many of us didn't is an indication of how strongly we feel about getting involved. We are nomadic by nature as well as necessity. Can I in good conscience instruct my Cell to do something even I feel uncomfortable with? I need rock-solid reasoning behind me before even putting it on the table.

"I'm sorry," he added, "if that makes me seem weak or indecisive in your eyes, but I simply need more time and information before I can commit to your plan."

She sighed and wished, not for the first time, that they weren't discussing this cramped cheek to jowl like Apollo astronauts.

"Okay, I understand. You've got a fair point. Hails," she said to the Exarch, who had waited out the exchange with aloof interest, "can you reassure Eogan on any of these issues?"

"I fear not. The only way to ascertain the veracity of my intentions is to put them—and my gifts—to the test. And as far as the Occlusion goes, we are all equally in the dark."

"I figured as much." Melilah turned back to Eogan to urge him to relax his requirements just a little, but the words never left her lips. Vermeulen had raised her left hand.

"Excuse me," said the science officer. "There *is* a test we can perform that should answer a few questions."

"And that is?"

"The data you brought from Bedlam, Melilah. If Hails gives

us the algorithm to decode it, we can see what it contains. If it's nothing, or if Hails won't break the security of the Exarchate, then that's a sort of progress."

Eogan nodded approvingly, openly displaying relief and gratitude at the means to break the impasse. "How about it, Hails? Are you going to play?"

"By all means. Send me a fragment of this mysterious data of yours, and I'll see what I can tell you about it."

Vermeulen looked distracted for a second as she prepared the transmission. "It's on its way. This is about one percent of what we have. If you need more"—she glanced at Eogan—"we can discuss it."

A ream of virtual paper materialized in Hails's hands. He riffled through it, stopping every now and again to examine the odd page in more detail. He hummed to himself, skimmed back to the beginning, then read the final page with both bushy eyebrows high on his forehead.

"Is the pantomime really necessary?" Melilah asked.

He looked up at her. "I apologize," he said. "This is genuinely fascinating. I had no idea such information was available. And you said you found it—where?"

"I didn't. Tell us what it says, and we'll give you more."

"Quite simply, my dear, you've got your hands on everything the Exarchate has gleaned from the object in Sublime—and it makes extraordinary reading. Simply extraordinary!" Hails's attention returned to the pages, which he flicked through with increasing speed. "The rumors appear to be absolutely true. If this is just a fraction of the whole, then I can only wonder at what else it contains!"

"We're receiving new data from Hails," said Vermeulen. "It's the algorithm. I'll try it on the data."

Melilah held a breath as she waited for confirmation, fearing the algorithm might actually be a trap.

"It's working," Vermeulen reported a second later. "We have the data."

"And?" asked Melilah, knowing she was probably being unreasonable to expect results so soon. The files were *huge.*

Vermeulen's eyes unfocused.

You don't need to hear it, Melilah, said Hails into her head, the sheaf of papers hanging at his side. His eyes glittered in the depths of the illusion. *This won't make a jot of difference to what you want to do—and you've known what that is, in your heart, from the moment you saw the attack drones. You understand why I put them here, and why I chose you to receive them. I urge you to pick up the gun and pull the trigger. Fire the bullet right into the heart of the enemy.*

"Eogan—?"

What your Palmer friend decides is irrelevant. Without him, this plan is still workable. Do you and I have an arrangement? That's the important thing. Tell me we do, and let's get on with the messy business of liberation.

Hails's tone was hypnotic. A tingling spread down her back and across her skin. She feared for a second that it might be the nanoware inside her, working some subtle effect, but it was in fact just gooseflesh. The moment had come to truly commit, to put her mark on the devil's contract and sell her soul away.

She felt Eogan's eyes on her, questioning.

It might not be her soul she was selling, she thought, but her home.

+50

Strange shapes stirred through the wreckage of the Occlusion observatory. Since the Archon's arrival there, the spindly remains of the Reaper had melted and been absorbed into a growing mass of material that Deangelis couldn't identify. Some of it broke free from the wreckage like coronal flares on the system's distant primary, orbited a couple of times, then came back down at a different location. These globules glowed intensely in infrared, as though furious chemical processes were taking place inside them. Sometimes they merged with other orbiting globules; occasionally they broke into chains of smaller pieces that one by one went their separate, mysterious ways.

Deangelis also detected short-lived flashes of powerful energies coming from deep in the heart of the wreckage. If there was a pattern to their occurrence, he couldn't find it. Nor could he fathom the process that could have caused them. Whatever the Archon was doing in there, it was well beyond his ken.

I could ask, he told himself. *Just because the Archon keeps its business off the colony's feeds doesn't mean I can't know. I* should *know. If there's any chance it might be dangerous, it would make sense to be informed.*

But he didn't make the call. He had asked the Archon to help him secure the Occlusion, and it appeared to be doing just that. Requesting the particulars would just make him look suspicious, even churlish.

And it wasn't as if there weren't other things to worry about.

"Tell me what they're doing out there," he asked Hails for what felt like the dozenth time.

"Who doing where?" asked Hails from his cell in Protective Custody, where he'd been held since his assault on Melilah Awad. She hadn't pressed charges before her departure, but the Exarch had pulled rank to keep him out of harm's way. Word of Hails's presence on the habitat had sent a ripple of unease through those paying attention. Luckily there were sufficient other distractions keeping him out of the public spotlight for the time being.

"You know very well who. The *Nhulunbuy* hasn't left the system. Its drive signature indicates that it decelerated for a time before coming to a dead halt well short of heliopause."

"I don't see what that has to do with me." Hails picked at an ear with his little finger.

"It has everything to do with you. They were traveling along the same heading you came from; they've stopped where I presume you have your tangler stashed, just out of my range. And I heard what you said to Awad before she left."

"Then you know full well what our conversation means."

Deangelis knew the words by heart.

You are not alone. Your goals are shared by others. We want exactly the same thing.

They were seditious brands on his memory, flaming bright.

Independence.

He couldn't repeat them aloud for fear of drawing attention to them. The Archon was bound to be listening, even—perhaps especially—to the high-speed Most Secure conversation taking place in the cell.

"I could send a high-acceleration probe," he said, "to check on your tangler in person, but I'm giving you this chance to come clean first. I can hide this conversation, but I can't hide a launch."

"That's not my problem."

"Of course it's your problem! If you don't give me some reason to trust you, I'll have to turn you in."

"To our mutual friend from Sol?" He shrugged. "Do it. I've got nothing to hide." Hails's words were casual, but the gesture he made was anything but. He put his index finger to his temple, cocked his thumb, and mimed a sharp recoil.

The meaning was clear. Hails would sacrifice the part of himself on the habitat—kill the body sitting in front of Deangelis—rather than risk details of his plans reaching the Archon ahead of time. Hails only knew what secrets were locked in that skull. Deangelis wanted to take it in both hands and crack it open himself.

"I need to know what you're doing," he said, his voice little more than a whisper. He felt exhausted, physically and mentally drained. The body that was his current point of view swayed, and he let it sink onto the bed opposite the one on which Hails sat. He put a hand over his eyes in a vain attempt to concentrate.

"I need to know what *I'm* doing."

"I sympathize, Isaac. I really do," Hails said, in tones that were more gruff than sympathetic. "But I told you before: don't expect me to make the tough decisions for you. This is your system, not mine or the Archon's, so the call is yours. You need to come to your own conclusions."

"Too many variables . . ." He shook his head and took the hand away from his eyes. The light in the cell seemed suddenly bright. "I don't want to make an enemy of you, Lazarus."

"Let me reassure you on that score, then. You know full well who my beef is with—and you also know that I'm no Frederica Cazneaux. The last thing I want to do is get you offside or put your people at risk. This is the Exarchate, not some Martian frontier. We have to work together, no matter what happens."

"We'll never get on perfectly. We'll always disagree and squabble."

"Of course. We're only human, after all."

Deangelis wondered if that was how the Archon thought of itself. *Only human.* Did it have superiors it reported to that seemed as alien to it as it did to him? As Deangelis seemed to Melilah Awad?

What was the point of pledging allegiance to a notion of humanity that none of the people who claimed it could agree on?

Again, he felt an incipient fracture developing between him and the mind of the one through whose eyes he saw. The world shivered, oscillating between two radically different points of view.

His greater self believed in the greater good and knew what he ought to do.

Earth-Deangelis's grasp on the greater good was slippery. To that mind, resistance had a strong appeal. The notion of the individual was important, as was the goal of individual survival.

But his higher self, who was perfectly capable of holding all the immense complexity of Lut-Deangelis in a single thought, could just about conceive of what it must be like to be the Archon. He could almost imagine the demands that governing the Exarchate as a whole must place on such a mind. This was responsibility beyond measure—and here *he* was, quibbling over the events in a single system.

Yet, the individual part of him said, *that single system is a fulcrum around which an entire empire might turn. There's no escaping the fact that the decision I make now could have more effect than any of the Archon's.*

All the more reason, then, his higher self replied, *to try to think beyond my petty concerns. If I can't work out what the best thing to do is, I have to have faith in one who might.*

"You're looking thoughtful," said Hails, watching him closely. "Does that mean you've decided?"

"I think so," said Deangelis, standing.

"And?"

"There's only one thing I can do, and that's to do what I think is right. Nothing else matters. It's *myself* I have to live with afterward, whatever happens."

"That's the spirit," said Hails. "You can be your own man, Isaac, if you truly want to be."

Even if it kills me? he asked silently of himself.

There was no point talking to Hails anymore. The Exarch clearly wasn't going to tell him anything about Awad and the *Nhulunbuy*. It was time for Deangelis to take his fate in both hands. The rest, he hoped, would simply fall into place.

With the briefest of farewells, his higher self left the cell and signaled the Archon that he urgently needed to talk.

+51

Decisions.

Palmer Eogan's mind whirled as he explored the data liberated by Hails's decryption algorithm, and the attack drones loomed larger before him. Not only did Deangelis's hidden files prove that the Exarchate had been in Sublime ever since the Catastrophe; it also confirmed that the object Jane Elderton had found was essentially the same as the one he had towed out of the Mizar-Bedlam trade lane. That made two entrances. The new data strongly suggested that there would be more.

The sheer volume of information was difficult to plow through, but major points quickly emerged. The complex structure Vermeulen had glimpsed on the far side of the Occlusion was extensive and convoluted, and followed natural laws of its own. The topography was exceedingly complicated, but exhibited consistent scale-free properties: ten to fifteen percent of junctions acted as hubs, connecting far-flung regions by just a few hops. What those regions corresponded to in the real universe had not yet been determined. Roughly five percent of all corridors ended in dead ends, and some of the anonymous minds put to the task wondered if such termini might be potential exits. If that was correct, no means had yet been found to open them.

Similarly, no connection had yet been found between the Sublime and Bedlam exits. Without the existence of a route between them, the theory that the structure functioned as a means of getting through space by going around it—using hyperspatial geodesics to connect far-distant points—remained just that: a theory. There was still a chance it could have been a natural phenomenon, albeit one more bizarre than anything humanity had encountered before.

Its resonance with living structures—not just because of its scale-free arrangement—was not lost on the Exarchate examiners. Such networks occurred over and over, in nature and information networks, in the brain and in the body. They had initially called it "the Coral" in honor of its brachiated structure, but a new name appeared with increasing frequency in the records. The most recent record, saved two weeks earlier, used it no fewer than seventy-eight times.

"Geodesica," to Eogan's eyes, came with associations of wild, dangerous spaces such as Old America and Antarctica had once been. People would fight over them, especially if a real advantage was to be gained by owning them.

The trouble was, thought Eogan as he feverishly tried to decide what to do next, he was no Columbus or Mawson. He had come to Bedlam with no intentions of laying claim to anything. Now that the opportunity had arrived to represent the Palmers in a discovery of truly monumental proportions, he found himself to be reluctant. He hadn't joined the Palmers to push the frontiers; he had wanted merely to ply the trade lanes in peace, like sailors of old. There were always dangers to be avoided and discoveries to be made along the way, but nothing of the order of an entire new continuum that might tear the Exarchate apart.

Similarly, he had no right to order his crew any deeper into the mess than they already were. Ordinarily, they would have been well on their way elsewhere by then, having unloaded their cargo in Bedlam and taken on new contracts for their next destination. They had been lucky not to lose anyone during Cazneaux's attack on the habitat; that Vermeulen had returned still shocked and surprised him. Who might be killed if open rebellion broke out around them? Whose death would he have to carry on his conscience?

Eogan couldn't live with it. He wasn't a fighter by nature, and he certainly wasn't the sort to send others into battle for him. But he didn't like abandoning friends in a sticky situation, either—even if they weren't really friends, but something much more complicated . . .

While attention was focused on the data, he opened a side channel to Palmer Flast.

"Listen carefully," he said. "When you get my signal, I want you to do exactly as I tell you. If you do, the *Nhulunbuy* is yours."

That earned him a long, considered silence. "Continue, Palmer Eogan."

He outlined what he had in mind, then said, "Feel free to tell me if I'm insane."

"That all depends on how you look at it." Flast broadcast the nonverbal equivalent of a shrug. "If you're sure you have to do it, then I guess you're going about it in a very sane way."

That wasn't terribly reassuring. "I simply can't think of any other way around this situation."

"Neither can I."

"You'll do it, then?"

"Sure. But what about Vermeulen? You know she'll be pissed off either way."

"The choice is hers—and the same for anyone else who wants to stay. If you're prepared to offer it to them, of course."

The future chief officer of the *Nhulunbuy* took a good while to think that one through.

"This is a very difficult situation," said Flast finally. "There won't be long to think about it, especially if Hails objects."

"Give her as long as you can. Remember: if you don't allow her at least that much, there's a long journey ahead of you. You'll have a lot of time to listen to her complaining."

"True." Flast sent a wry smile that quickly faded. "*Are* you certain you want to do this? She probably doesn't expect you to."

"I'm not just doing it for her," Eogan said. "And I'm at least fifty percent sure that's true."

The amalgamated Cell decelerated smoothly, all its myriad microscopic drive units acting in tandem—or in a way that, to the macroscopic eye of a human, approximated unity. There were bound to be small variations in thrust and timing, but such evened out over the long haul and the large numbers involved. As drive units failed, more assembled to take their place in a constant dance of attrition and replacement, like cells in a living body. The health of the Cell as a whole depended on maintaining the dance across all its dynamic systems, so a preponderance of drive units didn't lead to a shortage of life support or another vital component at a critical time in its operation.

Eogan watched the attack drones expand in the forward view with a feeling of dread. He wondered, as he had many times before, whether the Cell felt anything like emotions in its artificial analogue of life. Did it feel apprehension, nervousness, uncertainty, terror? If not, he envied it.

When they were less than five minutes away, Melilah made her announcement.

"I'm staying," she said, "no matter what you do. Hails has given me no reason to mistrust him, so turning down his offer would be unjustifiable."

"I thought you'd think that way," he said.

"Don't even think about trying to stop me," she started.

"I wouldn't dare."

She stared at him, trying to gauge his intentions, but he kept his expression carefully neutral. "You're keeping very quiet on this," she said.

"I've made my decision. All that remains is to implement it."

The data flow between her and Hails increased slightly. He wondered what they were talking about. The Exarch's illusory appearance reappeared standing among the morass of data extruded from Deangelis's file, his perspective and virtual lighting jarringly mismatched.

"I don't need to repeat my terms," Hails said. "Are the Palmers with us or not?"

Eogan took a deep breath. "They are not," he said. "Not under these circumstances."

Melilah couldn't hide a disappointed microexpression. "So be it. If we can't give you the assurances you need, we'll just have to work without you."

"It's not that," he said. "I don't feel that I have the right to commit the *Nhulunbuy* to such a venture. That would be exceeding my authority, acting outside my brief—call it what you will."

"It amounts to the same thing. You can drop me off at the tangler, then go your merry way."

"I can't do that, either. Not in good conscience."

"What, then? Stop beating about the bush and get on with it."

She was right. There was no point hesitating any longer.

"Palmer Flast?" he said, both aloud and through usual channels. "You have the helm."

"Understood," came the immediate reply. "Full acceleration in fifteen seconds. Disconnection in thirty. Good luck, Palmer Eogan. And fair weather."

Eogan could tell from the look on Melilah's and Vermeulen's faces that they grasped the ramifications of the conversation as quickly as Flast had.

"You're leaving the *Nhulunbuy*?" asked Vermeulen.

"Permanently," he said. "Palmer Flast is now acting chief officer. Palmer Aesche is his second."

"But—" She stopped, not needing to ask why. She glanced at Melilah, who said nothing, then returned her attention to Eogan. "You haven't asked me to come with you."

"You can if you want to," he said. "But I won't order you. Not again. I almost got you killed, last time."

"It wasn't you," she said. "It was Frederica Cazneaux and the Occlusion—the whole damned situation."

"Nothing's changed," he said. "Only this time it's Lazarus Hails and the Archon. Do you really want to go back there?"

She looked away. There were no tears in her golden eyes, no outward displays of emotion, but he could feel sadness radiating from her. They hadn't traveled so long together without developing an intuitive sense for each other's state of mind.

"No," she said, "but thanks for asking."

"Ten seconds," said Flast. "We need those components separated."

The space around them deformed, slowly at first but with increasing speed. "I'm taking what's left of Deangelis's escape capsule," he told his ex–science officer. "You have all the data we've gathered. It's up to you and Flast what you do with it."

She nodded. "I expect to see you again."

"And I you."

Vermeulen's gaze swiveled to Melilah, who still hadn't spoken. "You look after the big lug as best you can. He's not so smart, but he still has a heart, and it's in the right place most of the time."

The component had stretched into two lobes, Vermeulen in one, Eogan and Melilah in the other. The umbilical connecting them attentuated and sealed shut at both ends. Eogan raised a hand in farewell as his friend disappeared from view, fighting a lump in his throat.

Then a rush of information through his extended senses confirmed that the space around them—contained within a sphere five meters across, possessing all the capabilities of a full Cell in miniature—had disconnected from the *Nhulunbuy*. As its parent Cell accelerated at a brisk rate toward the stars, it braked in a tight circle to bring it on a docking vector with the tangler and its attack drones. Eogan watched with internal eyes as the Cell that had been his home for thirty years snaked off into the Dark.

"You didn't have to do that," said Melilah, watching him, not the *Nhulunbuy*. Her posture was taut, as though ready to run.

"Yes, I did," he said. "You need a Cell to interface with the drones."

"We could have managed."

"I would've felt bad for making you. And besides"—he hesitated—"I think it's the right thing to do."

"To fight the Archon or to help me?"

He smiled thinly, but said nothing in return. The truth was, he didn't know which one. But he was glad the decision was behind him.

"Welcome aboard, Palmer Eogan," said Exarch Hails, reappearing in the walls around him as the Cell decelerated. "If you two would both please hold hands, the nanoware I have installed in Melilah will colonize your system also."

"Is that necessary?" he asked, not daring to meet her eyes.

"Imperative, I'm afraid. Where we're going, we'll need a secure means of communication."

He sighed and gave in. She extended an arm, thrusting it woodenly at him as though it had lost all feeling.

Eogan took it.

Then the Exarch rushed into him, and there was no more time to think.

+52

Eogan's hand was hot in hers. His fingers tightened, and his eyes closed; his torso stiffened. She tried not to look at the joins where he merged with the walls of the Cell.

This won't take long, said Hails.

Eogan shivered. "I hear you," he said. "But can't we keep this out in the open for now?"

She relaxed slightly at that. The thought of his voice in her head as well as Hails's had made her anxious.

"Our plan is simple," said Hails. "We integrate the drones with your miniature Cell, giving you complete control over all nine of them. I hand over the keys to the tangler. Then you move in on the Archon."

Eogan opened his eyes and let go of her hand. His expression was grim. "How important is the element of surprise?"

"Not terribly. The Archon is unlikely to have developed a defense system equal to the drones in such a short time."

"Then I have one request. I want to give the Archon a chance to capitulate before we fire a single shot."

Melilah frowned. "Issue an ultimatum? What would be the point of that? We already know what it would say."

"Maybe not," he said. "Faced with superior firepower, it may just back down."

"It could also take the habitat hostage."

"It could do that as soon as we appear in range. We're going to be fairly conspicuous."

"Hails? What do you think?"

"I think the decision is yours. Either way, I'll get my message across."

She nodded. "Okay, then. We'll do it. But I don't want any screwing around. If it tries to stall, we move in. Agreed?"

Eogan looked satisfied. "No problems there. I just want to give it a chance. That'll make me feel better about what comes afterward."

"So let's get on with it." She couldn't keep the harshness from her voice. Being cooped up with Eogan for so long was difficult. The sooner she was doing something concrete, the better.

"In a moment," said Hails, "I'll send you access codes and control interfaces for the drones and the tangler. The protocols are very tight; you'll need to follow them to the letter. That will require some practice."

"I'm up for it," she said. The thought of doing something concrete restored the vitality she had lost during the long haul out from Bedlam. She could go three full days without sleep, but that didn't mean she didn't feel flatlined as a result. Her eyes were tired of straining data for clues.

"We should aim to leave for the habitat in four hours." Hails was all business, pacing backward and forward in the illusion of space outside the component's walls. "In that time, I suggest we talk tactics."

The Cell drew up alongside the tangler, neatly eclipsing the system's distant primary behind Lazarus Hails's lethal gifts.

Reality struck her one hour into the acclimatization program. For four decades, she had been seeking a way to fight Exarch Deangelis. Now she was fighting his superior, with the help of another Exarch. The possibility excited and terrified her at the same time—as did the capabilities of the attack drones.

They were fast, lethal, and very, very tough. Their needle-slim, tapering shapes lent them an air of fragility that was completely undeserved. They could have sailed through the waves Frederica Cazneaux's Reaper had sent against Bedlam without a scratch. Although one alone couldn't have taken out the Reaper, three could have. Nine would have diced it up and used it for target practice.

Melilah briefly wondered if she should be angry at Hails for not using the drones to defend the colony against the Reaper earlier, before anyone had died. He would have had a reason for not doing it, she was sure—that the timing wasn't right, perhaps, or that his direct involvement would have been impossible to avoid as a result. It certainly would have sent a very different message for Exarch to fight Exarch, so early in the piece.

She decided to let it go, for the moment. There would be time afterward, she told herself, to hold everyone accountable.

And there was plenty to get through before that point arrived. Direct control of the attack drones could be set at various levels, from completely autonomous to totally enslaved. Complete autonomy worried her, but it was impossible for her and Eogan alone to control all nine of the complex craft. Their guidance systems took into account all manner of telemetry, from quantum vacuum density to strength and orientation of local gravitational fields. She would need dozens of separate senses to control just one of the craft, so they sought a middle ground whereby the two of them could oversee their actions but not be responsible for every decision they made.

Together, the drones spoke with a silvery, insidious voice that made her think of mercury and poisoning. Communication from them came in discrete, bulletlike packets that erased themselves so fast she barely had time to absorb them.

| This mission's primary objective was previously set as the destruction of the entity labeled ARCHON, its precise identity and/or location to be confirmed. |

| Is this, now, to change? |

"Yes," she said. "Your primary objective is to protect the habitat. Neutralizing the Archon is your second priority."

"Destroying the Archon is not ideal," Eogan added.

"The Archon will make a difficult prisoner," argued Hails. "It'll be like trying to hold smoke in your hand."

"I know," said Melilah, "but we're not barbarians. If it'll talk, we might even be able to learn something from it."

| This mission's primary objectives have been reset. |

| Performing test maneuvers as instructed. |

"How will we find the Archon?" she asked Hails, as the drones swooped and darted around the Cell.

"Look for Isaac's tangler. There's a good chance they'll be together."

"And if it fights back?"

"I guess you'll have to work that out as you go along. I'm

sorry I can't be of more help to you on that point. The Archon's capabilities are unknown to me."

They familiarized themselves with Hails's tangler in order to increase their chances of recognizing Deangelis's. It was a strange device, consisting of a glowing central column that branched in five places. Each branch continued to divide, becoming increasingly feathery with each division. Close analysis revealed that the device was fractal down to the microscopic level, and probably farther, beyond the capability of the Cell's sensors. Functionally, it consisted of numerous interdependent components she could hardly fathom, but its operation was surprisingly simple. All she had to do was key in a message, and the tangler would transmit it along the Exarchate's entangled web to any number of specific destinations. From Bedlam, at the intersection of so many trade lanes, she could reach almost all the major Arc Circuit systems: from Schiller's End all the way around to New Eire. She could also reach most of the major systems just off the Arc—Whitewater, Alcor, Megrez, Eliza—without having to rely on relays within other systems. She had no way of knowing how individual Exarchs would respond to the news of what they had uncovered in Bedlam. Deangelis, Cazneaux, and Hails had each reacted in very different ways, from loyally toeing the Sol line to taking matters into their own hands. Some, she was sure, would pass the message on beyond the Arc Circuit. Some would erase it in the hope, perhaps, that it wasn't true. Others might absorb the information and let it simmer, laying down preparations as Lazarus Hails had against the coming storm.

The tangler had no internal awareness beyond that required for navigation and maintenance. It was a simple machine and possessed a simple interface. She prepared the message she wanted to send and instructed the tangler to wait for her signal to send it. If that signal wasn't received in thirty-five hours, the message should be sent anyway. Likewise, if anything threatened the tangler from Bedlam.

"I'll be here to make sure nothing goes wrong," Hails assured her.

"But who'll guard the guard?" asked Eogan, precisely identifying her one remaining doubt.

"You have to trust me to a certain degree," the Exarch said. "After all, could you tell if the tangler had worked at all, even if you were right on top of it? You have only its word that it'll do what you tell it to."

"I'm sure confirmation would come pretty fast," she said. "If I were Giorsal McGrath in Friday and received a message like this, the first thing I'd do was query Deangelis to see if it was true. And Deangelis would query me in turn—or shoot me out of the sky without thinking twice."

"I doubt Isaac has that in him," Hails said. "If he did, you probably wouldn't be here now."

That was true. Deangelis hadn't lifted a finger to stop her and Eogan from leaving the habitat, even though he must have had a pretty good idea that they knew too much. Either he hadn't wanted to, or the Archon had told him not to. Seeing Deangelis had saved her life less than a day beforehand, she had to suppose that Hails was right.

But what Deangelis would do when she and Eogan came barreling down on him with Hails's attack drones bristling in full battle array was anyone's guess.

| Tests completed. |

| All systems are optimal for commencement. |

"This is it." Eogan brought the Cell close to the drone they had designated D-1. The drones couldn't merge as Palmer Cells did, but the single component could piggyback on one of them, allowing more rapid and secure communication between them.

"Do you want to ride your own drone?" Eogan asked her. "I can split the component in two, if I have to."

The thought didn't please her as much as it might have a few hours earlier. They had divvied up their responsibilities so few of them overlapped; being separated would introduce unwanted communication lags and confusions into the mix.

"No offense," she said, "but I'd rather keep an eye on things from here."

"Understood."

If she concentrated on his face, she could almost forget about the rest of him, what he had become. His expression was weary, and wary. "I'm sorry if I was hard on you, before."

"It's okay. This means a lot to you: your home, your sense of identity, your place in things. I'd be surprised if tempers didn't run a little hot at times."

"All that meant a lot to you, too, once."

He cocked his head. "Meaning?"

"You gave up the *Nhulunbuy* easily enough."

"Did it look easy? I can assure you it wasn't."

She shrugged. “I suppose you can always hitch up with it again, after all of this is over.”

“I doubt that. The Palmers won’t take too kindly to my abandoning my post and getting mixed up in something like this.”

“No going back?”

“No.” Eogan bent his head down, as though concentrating on virtual information before him.

She thought that signaled the end of the conversation and readied herself to launch the mission to reclaim Bedlam. There hadn’t really been time enough to familiarize herself with the command interfaces. She would have to learn a lot of it on the fly, hoping all the while that nothing too unexpected went wrong.

His voice was soft when he spoke again. “We need a name for the Cell, and I was thinking of naming it after that town your family came from, where they found the black jade deposits. What was it called? Cahill? Cowra?”

“Cowell,” she said, hiding the fact that his easy recall of her history flustered her: no attempt at repression there. “Why?”

“Do I need a reason?” He sighed. “Look, I don’t make a habit of giving things up. Perhaps it’s this place. I sometimes thought that leaving here was the biggest mistake I ever made. Maybe it was an even bigger mistake to come back.”

“You can’t blame Bedlam for the way your life has turned out.”

“I know, but the temptation is there. It’s a human thing to look for simple answers, or ones that absolve you of blame.”

She kept her gaze carefully on the peripheral displays before her. *Human, huh? Who’s kidding whom?*

But she couldn’t bring herself to say it.

+53

On a virtual screen at the edge of Deangelis's greater awareness, the *Nhulunbuy*'s flickering drive signature accelerated steadily out of the system, warping the space ahead of it in a back-to-front wake as it neared interstellar space.

Deangelis wasn't reassured.

"I am pleased," said the Archon, "that you have come to me."

He forced himself to focus on the conversation, stripping back all his inputs until it felt as though he was hanging in a deep, black void. The Archon's voice came to him not as a voice in his ear, not as an electrical or optical trickle at the heart of his mind, but as a vibration thrilling right through him. God spoke from the mountaintop, and he listened.

"You have everything I know," he said to his maker. "What Lazarus told me can be interpreted many ways, as can the behavior of people like Melilah Awad and Palmer Eogan. I feel that it all combines in a worrying pattern. I also feel that I have handled the situation badly, and may have even, in my uncertainty, exacerbated the problem, as I perceive it. I fear that this might be so, but I am unafraid of the consequences. Should you wish to punish or replace me, I am resigned to my fate."

"Resigned?" The Archon's laughter boomed through him like physical blows. "Isaac, I would never think you resigned to anything. You confront life with a vigor few could match. You are loyal, determined, conscientious, and resourceful. I have no doubt that you will weather this situation with your usual efficiency."

"But *I* doubt it, Archon."

"Then that is a matter for you to keep to yourself. If you tell no one, they will never suspect."

"I am telling *you.* I *want* you to know."

"And now I do know. Thank you, Isaac, for trusting me with your uncertainty. It's not an easy thing to confess."

The Archon's response was far from comforting. He had expected it to give him some sort of clarity. He had hoped it would spare him the crippling, mind-numbing sense of being confronted by too many half-glimpsed, terrifying possibilities.

"I would like your advice, Archon." *Tell me what to do!*

"I have given it to you."

"On specific matters, I mean."

"The specifics are your domain, Isaac. Mine is the overview, topsight."

"Is there *anything* you see that can help me decide what to do?"

"I see . . ." The Archon's voice grew softer, introspective. "A critical time for humanity. We stand on the cusp of great things, yet our fate remains far from certain. As a species, we have faced extinction many times. In Africa, as subhumans, sudden environmental change nearly wiped us out on any number of occasions. A random asteroid or comet strike on Earth had the potential to scour the globe clean of us as recently as three centuries ago. A gamma-ray burst aimed directly at us could have destroyed all life in the solar system at any point in our history. We strive for it not to be so. The farther we spread and the more magnificent we become, the more likely we will survive to claim the future for our own. Once we pass the critical threshold glimpsed by the Architects of Sol we will no longer face annihilation, only setbacks along the road to dominion over the galaxy.

"But today, we are little different from the hominids who stared up at the stars in wonderment. They were navigators, not mere animals, but they didn't understand what they saw. And even if they had, would the knowledge have helped them? It's difficult to say. Perhaps we are better off for misunderstanding certain things, for having veils drawn over knowledge that could do us no good and might even hurt us if we suspected its existence. Only in retrospect can we say with any certainty what risk was acceptable, what sacrifice necessary, what ignorance critical. We are shaped by the flow of knowledge as surely as an island is shaped by a river. Uncheck the flood, and we may be swept away forever."

Deangelis listened to the Archon's words with a growing puzzlement. The Exarchate destroyed, and humanity with it? What mere knowledge could possibly cause that?

"Decisions do not become easier the more information one has," the Archon went on. "This is the great irony of evolution—of the universe. Would that omnipotence did equal prescience, for moments like these would be much easier to surmount. I do not know which way events will turn, Isaac, so I cannot answer your question. I cannot give you the response you crave. You must go your way as I must go mine. The journeys are ours to take, and ours alone. If our destinations are the same, I will be glad for both of us."

"And if they're not?"

"I'm sure we'll adapt. That is the great strength of our species, now more so than ever."

Deangelis stood with gaze metaphorically downcast. The parts of him that made up his greater self still niggled that he had acted wrongly by betraying Lazarus Hails and the others. This was guilt he was happy to bear, but it looked now as though it had been for nothing. The Archon wasn't going to do anything about the possible rebellion, and didn't seem to want *him* to do anything about it either. He was right back where he started.

"Have I angered you, Isaac?" the Archon asked unexpectedly. "Or disappointed you?"

"No," he said, trying to find words for what he was feeling. "I just wish there was a way to avoid all this conflict. Why can't we agree on where we're going and make the journey together?"

"Because life would be less rich for it. Diversity is the key to prosperity. That is why the Exarchate happily accommodates such divergent philosophies as that of your colony. Sol could force it to adopt laws more congruent with the ones we follow, but to what end? There is no possible benefit. If the meme dominant here spreads to other systems, that, too, is no threat. The Exarchate is not the law; it is more than just a name. It is the process by which human life expands through and rejoices in the cosmos, adapting and exapting as necessary. The Exarchate will endure—as will Sol, and you, and I."

"Are you saying I should do nothing to defend the Exarchate from the likes of Lazarus Hails?"

"That depends entirely on how you feel about the circumstances. There is no point defending an irrelevant empire, just as there is no point defending an untenable argument. Perhaps the time has come for a change. Perhaps it hasn't. You must arrive at that conclusion yourself, as must I."

"Yes, but—"

Deangelis fought a sudden wavering of his self. Something was happening beyond the confines of his conversation with the Archon.

"What is it, Isaac?" asked the Archon. "What do you see?"

"Drive signatures," he said, reading the data raw as it came in. "A cluster of them, coming from where the *Nhulunbuy* stopped." *From Hails's tangler.* "I've never seen deforms like these before."

"Palmer?"

"No. Something else."

"Heading?"

"Right at us." *Right at* me*!* A presentiment of doom rushed through him. Memories of the Reaper were strong. "I'm going to launch interceptors, just in case."

"Do as you see fit, Isaac," said the Archon. "I will be here, if you need my assistance."

Deangelis opened himself back up to the wild information flows of the habitat and told himself to feel reassured.

+54

| Deployment successful. |

| ETA: one hour, eleven minutes. |

"One hour!" Melilah seemed surprised, despite everything they had learned about the drones. Her eyes opened from scrutinizing virtual displays. "How many gees are we pulling?"

"I'm trying not to think about it," said Eogan, concentrating on the flow of data through the *Cowell*. The drones inundated him and the miniature Cell with information; he had to concentrate to avoid buildups requiring his attention. He had put a sliding scale in place, allowing him to adjust the data flow from almost everything to barely a trickle. He kept it up in the high end to encourage the formation of new connections and nets in the Cell's ever-changing neural infrastructure. If it could learn to assume some of the load, that would be better for everyone concerned.

He felt as though he were caught in an ancient cartoon. He was the moron in a helmet strapped to a giant firework, closing his eyes and putting his fingers in his ears as the fuse burned down rapidly.

Everything looks good, said the voice of Lazarus Hails via the nanoware he had sown in them. *I am impressed.*

"I wondered if you'd hitched a ride," said Melilah. "Another bit part, I presume?"

Enough to advise. I have no intention of taking control.

"Which drone are you in?"

D-4. In the hyperreal schematic of the drone's tightly bound configuration, D-4 glowed faintly pink, as though Hails was reminding them to take extra care of it.

"You can help with target acquisition," said Eogan, copying a significant chunk of the data flow and diverting it to D-4. "Might as well make yourself useful."

The moment I locate the Archon, you'll be the first to know.

The drones continued, jostling among each other in strange, rhythmic surges, uncannily like dolphins in a fast-swimming pack. Packets of data, as fleeting as minnows, swept through their ports and out again. Eogan wondered what they were talking about, if that was what they were doing. Were they eager for battle after so long lurking on the vanguard of the Dark? Or nervous of performing badly, now that the moment they had been created for was almost upon them?

Although Bedlam itself was little more than a speck of light at that distance, PARASOL soon resolved into a distinct crescent. Within a degree of both shone Ah Kong and its attendant moons. There had been talk, pre-Exarchate, of people settling in the gas giant's ebullient upper atmosphere, as they had elsewhere, laying down floating platforms in relatively stable updrafts thousands of kilometers across. The plan had been scuttled by the instability in the system's primary. It was too hard to guarantee shelter from solar storms for the platform colony, even within the gas giant's powerful magnetosphere. Until a reliable means of engineering people against hard radiation became common—without the kind of overt modifications required of Palmers—the plan would remain unfulfilled.

A trickle of telemetry attracted his attention.

"I'm picking up launches," he told Melilah. "Six drive signatures out of Bedlam."

"Vector?"

"They're still coming around, but I'll give you good odds they'll end up heading our way."

"I've received no transmissions of any kind." She thought for a moment. "Do you think we should hail them?"

Not yet, offered Hails. *Confirm the heading, first. Even if the launches are aimed at us, there's little point doing anything about them now. We'll have some time before they reach us.*

"I disagree," Eogan said. "It's obvious that we've been spotted. Given that we're not currently broadcasting or displaying a recognizable profile, Deangelis will be to-tally justified in assuming we're a threat and taking action against us."

"He'll jump first, ask questions later." Melilah nodded. "I don't blame him, after the Reaper."

"Okay. Let's send a message, then." Eogan was glad that he and Melilah were in agreement, but steeled himself for their first confrontation with their Exarch benefactor.

It didn't come. *I'll let you handle that, obviously,* said Hails. *The lower a profile I keep, the better.*

There was no question as to who should make the broadcast.

"This is Palmer Eogan, chief officer of the *Cowell,* on approach and requesting a docking vector."

There was a pointed delay before Lut-Deangelis Traffic Control's AI came back to him. "We have you on our screens, Palmer Eogan. But the *Cowell* is not in the register."

"There was a situation on the *Nhulunbuy,*" he half lied, "and we agreed to disagree about it. What you see is what you get. I can give you the specs if you want to log it in the register yourself."

"That won't be necessary. We can get them ourselves when you supply your access codes. You're certainly in a big enough hurry to get back here."

"It's a big, bad universe, LDTC. The sooner I'm in your shadow, the better."

"Not many people feel that way at the moment."

The routing AI was much chattier than normal. Eogan got the feeling it was deliberately trying to keep him talking—or the person driving it was. Deangelis could have been directing the AI like a muppeteer.

"You'll get our codes when we get our vector," he said, prepared to push a little. Supplying a vector was tantamount to handing over the air lock access codes. Short of ramming or scattering debris in their path, there would be nothing Deangelis could do to stop them coming in. Assuming the vector was legit in the first place.

Several minutes passed before LDTC responded. In that time, Eogan and Melilah shored up their knowledge of the drones' processes. It would never be second nature, but he would be satisfied with third or fourth . . .

Their destination grew clearer. The giant habitat hadn't changed much in the previous hours; repairs continued, with work crews and nanotech swarming across the surface. Its smaller companion, the ruined observatory, however, was undergoing a dramatic metamorphosis. The surface was difficult to pin down from such a distance, even with three of the drones spread wide to increase their baseline of measurement. It appeared to be seething like the atmosphere of the sun.

The six vessels Bedlam had launched were by then perfectly lined up to intercept them on their current approach.

"In accordance with Lut-Deangelis Information laws," came the voice of Exarch Deangelis, "you are required to open all memory and channels to public scrutiny. Please immediately supply access codes and encryption keys."

"He's calling our bluff," said Melilah.

"It's going to take more than that." Eogan fiddled the broadcast settings to add a little static. "Uh, LDTC, we appear to have missed part of your last transmission. What was that vector again?"

"*Cowell,* you are in violation of Lut-Deangelis Territorial Regulations. Continued noncompliance will prompt an immediate and severe response."

"I don't understand, LDTC. We're doing nothing wrong. Give us our vector as normal, and we'll give you the codes. What's the problem?"

"The situation is hardly normal. As you well know, Palmer Eogan."

"I guess that explains those interceptors you've sent to meet us. Are we not welcome here now?"

"All are welcome so long as they mean no harm."

"And we've been presumed guilty of that. So much for Bedlam's famed openness."

Eogan assumed the conversation was going out over the habitat's feeds. He didn't really think he could shame Deangelis into backing down, but he could at least make him think twice about making any rash accusations.

"Your configuration is far from friendly, Palmer Eogan. Until you supply access codes in accordance with the law I am sworn to uphold, I will be forced to treat you as a threat. There is no assumption of anything. I am simply taking every reasonable precaution to protect the people in my charge."

"Our behavior in recent days should demonstrate that we have no hostile intentions."

"Every situation must be treated on its own merit. We are grateful for your efforts but unwilling to take any chances. I'm sure you can appreciate that, Palmer Eogan."

He backed down. "We're not going to get anywhere this way," he told Melilah and Hails. "We've made the only points we can over the open channel. I think it's time to get serious."

She nodded. "Do it."

"Any luck locating the Archon?" he asked Hails.

The activity visible on the Occlusion observatory is symptomatic of advanced technology, said the Exarch, *but that doesn't prove the Archon is there.*

"What's happening to the wreckage?" asked Melilah, scrutinizing the images captured by the attack drones.

That is presently unknown.

"Let's see if we can't stir something up, then," said Eogan, switching back to his conversation with Bedlam.

"Take no offense, Exarch Deangelis," he said, "but we'd like to speak to the person who's really in charge. Put us through to the Archon, and we'll discuss the situation with it."

Deangelis's reply was cold. "I assure you that I speak and act with full authority over this system."

"Then what's the Archon doing here?"

"That is not your concern for the moment. Until you supply your access codes, I am under no obligation to share any information with you."

"Why are you splitting hairs, Deangelis? Are you afraid of the truth?"

"The truth is perfectly clear to me. My function here is unchanged, whether the Archon directs the Exarchate from Sol or anywhere else."

"So it *is* in charge. Is that what you're saying?"

There was a slight hesitation. "The Archon is the authority to whom I answer. That has always been the case."

"Well, we didn't know that. Now we do, that's who we'd like to speak to."

"Who am *I* speaking to, Palmer Eogan?" The query was sharply pointed. "Are these your requests or someone else's?"

It was Eogan's turn to hesitate. Deangelis had almost certainly guessed that someone was working with them; hence the extraordinary profile of the approaching drones. Denying it would be pointless, but admitting that Hails was implicated wasn't part of the deal.

"He speaks for me," said Melilah, taking the line from him. "That is, we speak together."

"Melilah Awad?" The Exarch's reply came with a flash of emotion, not immediately identified. "I should've known you were mixed up in this."

"You didn't think I'd leave with the others, did you? This is my home. You won't get rid of me that easily."

"It is not my intention to get rid of you. I desire only to ensure the peaceful governance of this colony. To that end, I will tolerate all manner of inconvenience—you included."

"Well, good," she said. "I'm sorry I can't be so accommodating in return. While you remain in charge, I can't rest. My long-term objective has always been to return Bedlam to the people who live in it. That's how it should be, and how it will be again, if I have my way."

"But I live here, too, Melilah. This is my home as well. By your argument, I have as much right to govern here as you do."

"Then let's have an election and see who wins."

"You might be disappointed in the outcome."

"We'll never know, will we?"

The Exarch didn't answer her question directly. "Your determination is exceeded only by your hypocrisy. The sort of urban terrorism you endorse differs from the crimes you accuse me of only by degree. You would happily take over this colony in the name of liberation without once stopping to consider if the people you're supposedly saving actually *want* to be liberated. You and a vocal minority aside, how many regard the Exarchate as evil? How many object to the economic and social stability I have wrought here? Before I came, this colony was a minor outpost ignored by its squabbling neighbors. Now it is an essential part of the greatest endeavor in history. Humanity, despite all its wonderful diversity, is united for the first time. Who would not want to be part of that?"

"Yeah, and I'm sure the slaves rowing Roman galleys thought the same."

"Your comparison is inappropriate, Awad! There are no slaves, nor any galleys! You exist in perfect freedom under the guidance of Sol. This is governance like none seen before. That your blinkered view insists on calling it something it's not only proves our point—that until now humanity has not had the capacity to look after itself properly. Until the Exarchate existed, we were just monkeys doing little more than throwing sticks at one another and using feces to mark our territory."

Melilah laughed. "Now who's using unsuitable comparisons?"

The Exarch ignored her flippant comment. "We have an opportunity for greatness here, Awad. I will not let the likes of you derail that process!"

Eogan had never heard the Exarch—any Exarch—speak with

such passion about their job. He had always imagined Deangelis and his peers to be cool, calculating intelligences acting from their ivory towers with little real concern for those beneath them, similar to the crude Policy AIs that had made such a mess of Earth affairs in the mid-twenty-first century. That they genuinely believed in what they were doing was revelatory.

"If it's not a process everyone has subscribed to or is even aware of," said Melilah, her voice low and determined, "I don't see how you can regard it as just, or be surprised that some of us will resist it every step of the way."

"Parents might wish to explain every decision to their children, but there are inevitably times when such communication is not possible. You rail against *nature,* Awad, not me."

"We rail against injustice, Deangelis, whatever its cause. You're either part of the solution, or part of the problem. It seems pretty clear to me which side you're on."

The Exarch made an exasperated noise. "Again, this puerile reductionism. I refuse to be badgered by empty arguments against which there can be no possible defense. If that's the best you and Palmer Eogan have to offer, you are doing yourself a great disservice."

And there it was again, that flash of odd emotion. This time, Eogan thought he might have pinned it down. But why would Deangelis be jealous? That just didn't make sense at all.

| ETA: twenty minutes. |

| Intercept with approaching vessels: ten minutes. |

The voice of the drones brought him back to why they were there.

"That's not all we have," he said. "And that's not what we've come here to say."

"We want to talk to the Archon," Melilah insisted. "If you won't let us, we'll find it ourselves and make it listen."

"How exactly do you plan to do that?"

Tell him, said Hails, *that you know where the Archon is. I've located his tangler; it is indeed in the wreckage of the observatory. That increases the chances that the Archon is in there, too, although I still can't guarantee it. Isaac's reaction will guide us.*

"We already know where the Archon is," Melilah said. "It's in the observatory with your tangler and the Occlusion. Want to tell us what it's doing in there?"

"I—" Deangelis's momentary hesitation was enough to confirm Hails's guess. "The Archon is not the issue."

"The Archon is *everything,*" Melilah insisted. "Whether you'll admit it or not, its presence here is an insult to the entire Arc Circuit. It says that we can't manage our own affairs, that the moment things get tricky we need someone else to step in and take all the decisions away from us. Don't you see that? Aren't you annoyed that you'll never get the chance to prove that you can handle this on your own? Can't you see that this is how I've felt every day *you've* been here?"

The Exarch didn't respond. Eogan watched the data coming in with mounting concern. More distant flashes indicated launches from Bedlam, some of them heading for the observatory. A ripple in space-time propagated before the six oncoming interceptors, accelerating almost as sharply as the drones. He received a distinct feeling that the gloves were coming off. Deangelis had heard enough to be certain of their motives, and now he was preparing a response to them.

Yet no one had declared overt war; no one had fired a shot. So far it was only posturing and pontificating. There was still a chance it might end bloodlessly.

| Intercept with approaching vessels: five minutes. |

Time would tell, he thought. A very short amount of time, indeed, to ensure that they were sufficiently well trained to survive the opening skirmish.

+55

Melilah's personal universe simultaneously widened and contracted. Through the information delivered by the drones, she saw the six interceptors with brilliant clarity, set against the backdrop of Bedlam. Several other vessels had launched to protect the observatory, but she didn't care about them. Eogan shifted position beside her; she didn't care about that either. All she saw were the six approaching interceptors and the dumbbell-shaped corridor of possibilities coalescing between her and them.

Their relative velocity was enormous. Even an unarmed ship traveling at such speeds contained enormous destructive potential, so the fact that Bedlam didn't possess an official defense force forbade any sense of comfortable superiority. She had shields to spin and antiassault batteries to prime. The drones hummed at ever-increasing frequencies as internal mechanisms geared up for battle, preparing contingency plans and displaying simulations for her and Eogan to consider.

"Do we want to destroy the interceptors or just get by them?" she asked.

"Evade, preferably," he said. "Once we're past them, they're irrelevant."

Melilah had thought he would say that. She told the drones to concentrate on minimal—preferably zero—damage scenarios. Either there weren't many, or the drones, battle-ready and eager to engage, were reluctant to show them to her.

| Intercept: two minutes. |

"This is your last chance, Deangelis," she said down the line. "Let us talk to the Archon."

"Come peacefully, and you are welcome to do so," came the reply.

"Who's attacking whom, here?"

"I am entitled to defend myself against a perceived attack."

"And I'm entitled to defend my home against an invader. You fired the first shot forty years ago, Deangelis. It may have taken me a long time to fire back, but I'm not going to miss my chance now. You've had it coming."

Deangelis didn't grace the comment with a reply.

| Intercept: one minute. |

A scenario scrolled by that seemed little different from the others. It was about as likely to succeed in all its objectives as hitting Bedlam with a laser blindfolded, but it was better than nothing. Even if it failed, there would be no mistaking their intentions.

Eogan concurred. "Better strap yourself in. It's going to be rough."

She didn't immediately understand what he meant. There were no literal straps. Instead, the Cell would protect her from damage during the encounter—by completely enfolding her, like a fetus in a womb.

Panic tightened her throat muscles. She forced the feeling down. There was no avoiding it, and she should have realized that it would be asked of her. Eogan had done her a favor by not bringing it up sooner.

She nodded once, spasmodically. "I'm trusting you, Dominic," she said.

He looked up at her with surprise in his eyes, and she almost said: *Do you really think I'm that much of a coward?*

Then she realized the reason for his surprise: she had used his first name. Out of habit—a habit that should have died one hundred and fifty years earlier.

Fuck it, she thought. *This is no time to argue about semantics.*

As though agreeing, he nodded, and the Cell closed in around her.

+56

Deangelis snarled at the screen, a rush of anger clouding his judgment. In the final seconds before the distant flotillas met, he urged the interceptors to use maximum force in dealing with the interlopers.

"Destroy them," he told the AIs piloting the receding craft. "*Utterly.* I want their ashes to rain on me like dust."

The AIs in the interceptors hurried to reorganize their munitions in the short time available to them before engagement. He sensed their alien frustration and puzzlement at the sudden change in plans, but he didn't care. He was beyond caring, now.

Lazarus Hails was dead. After Melilah Awad's last transmission, Deangelis had sent part of himself to the cell in Protective Custody where the representative of his fellow Exarch was being kept. He had arrived just as alarms reached his higher self. That very instant, Hails's heart had stopped. Medical technicians rushed into the cell with Deangelis hot on their heels. Hails's body lay slumped facedown on the floor between the two beds. They hauled it over and administered emergency aid. Every measure failed: his leonine features remained inanimate, and there was no indication of brain activity. Deep-tissue scans revealed vast hemorrhages spreading through his cortex and spinal cord; all that remained of his peripherals were charred bioplastic lumps. Hails was gone.

And with it went Deangelis's last, faint hope that this was nothing but a misunderstanding, that it could all still work out for the best. If Hails was covering his tracks, the likelihood of the crisis simply blowing over was effectively zero.

First Cazneaux, he thought, and now Lazarus Hails. He couldn't work out which was worse. The specter of civil war had been raised in his colony. His *home.* He hadn't been lying when he'd told Melilah Awad that that was how he thought of the habitat. Lut-Deangelis owned more than just one of his names. It owned him, too—and it galled him to think that Hails's brand of treachery had found fertile soil on his territory.

He had spared her, and she had betrayed him.

"Spare no effort," he told the interceptors, "to bring them down. *All* of them."

Sporting a grim, tight-lipped expression on all his faces, he settled back to watch the telemetry.

+57

| External interference detected. |

| Autonomous systems engaged. |

With a scream of tortured space-time, the fifteen vessels met. They hit hard and furiously, stretching the very laws of physics to maximize the split instant in which they could act. Buckyballs flung at relativistic velocities struck with masses far in excess of their rest state. Blue-shifted lasers achieved fantastical energies. Shields spun from ultradense kernels swept space around the battlefield in great, disorienting waves.

From a distance, Eogan knew, the skirmish would trace a sudden streak across the starscape, a brilliant, short-lived line that expanded from a single point outward in both directions. Faint exclamation points would Morse code from each end of the line, gradually stuttering to nothing as the streak itself abruptly winked out. Where had once been a bold, geometric statement would be only a mess of high-energy shrapnel and heat, a dissipating scar that boiled the quantum foam and warped light from distant quasars.

It all happened too quickly for him to follow. Even at his highest cognitive rates, the moment of truth passed before he could barely acknowledge it. One instant the drones and the interceptors were rushing toward each other like shotgun blasts from opposing guns; the next they were heading just as quickly apart, debris sparkling in their wake.

He performed a quick head count when the drones' autonomous systems disengaged, indicating that the Archon was no longer trying to shut them down. All the drones were present, although not all were undamaged. A deep gouge ran down the cigar-shaped flank of D-5, issuing bright rainbow tails of stressed space. Looking behind him, he saw that two of the interceptors were gone. The rest were empty and tumbling, their matter reserves spent in one savage, furious instant of combat.

As he watched, the rear end of D-5 disintegrated with a flash of bright light. Its drive failed, and the front end dropped back like a stone. Barely had it begun a slow tumble when it was suddenly gone, visible only in the radar sweeping their wake.

"We made it," Melilah said. Her voice shook as the *Cowell* eased its constrictive embrace, giving them room to move again.

Good work, said Hails. *But it's not over yet.*

More interceptors launched from Bedlam.

| ETA: thirteen minutes. |

"We need to change course," Eogan said. "The observatory is our target now, not the habitat."

"Agreed." Melilah sent a series of commands to the drones, who responded by expending massive amounts of their antimatter reserves on a lateral course correction.

| ETA: sixteen minutes. |

| Deceleration: five minutes. |

| Intercept: twelve minutes. |

"That didn't take Deangelis long," said Melilah, scowling at the Exarch in absentia as more interceptors launched from Bedlam and swung around to intersect their new heading.

"He obviously prepared this contingency in advance. We'll just have to punch our way through."

"We'll be moving slower at that point. It's a whole different fight."

"We still outnumber him. He can't keep us from the observatory like this, and he must know it."

Right on cue, a transmission arrived from the habitat. The voice of a young woman filled the interior of the Cell.

"Grandmother Mel, what are you doing?"

Melilah looked up sharply. "Yasu? Are you all right?"

"*I'm* all right. But you—the feed is buzzing with the news that you and another Exarch have declared war on Bedlam! Is that true?"

Eogan saw her wince. "No, Yasu, that's not true. I'm fighting the Exarchate, not Bedlam. Deangelis won't let us talk to the Archon, so we have no choice but to force our way through."

"But you could be killed!"

"I know," she said grimly.

"I don't want you to die, Grandmother. Not you, on top of the others."

"That's a risk I have to take, Yasu."

The sound of sobbing came down the line. "But what about *me?* What about all the other people you'd leave behind? We don't deserve it. And for what? Some stupid war that ended before I was born? Don't throw your life away, Grandmother. Please. You have so much left to do!

Melilah looked as though her heart was breaking.

It's a trick, said Hails. *A simulation designed to undercut your resolve.*

"He might be right," added Eogan. "Deangelis could easily do that."

Melilah didn't seem to hear. "I'm sorry, Yasu. I have to do this."

"Why? I thought all this talk of rebellion was a game, a hobby, a fashion among you old-timers. You never seemed to do anything *but* talk. I didn't know you were *serious* about it."

"Of course we were serious. This is important, and always has been. You may not understand now, but you will later, I'm sure."

"How? You'll never get the chance to explain it to me if you throw your life away on some crazy escapade!"

"Yasu, please—"

"I give up, Grandmother Mel. Do what you think you have to do. Drag Palmer Eogan down with you as you go. Just don't expect me to be here for you when you get back!"

On that angry retort, the line clicked dead.

Eogan reached out to put a hand on Melilah's shoulder. She didn't pull away.

"It'll be Luisa and James Pirelli next," he said. "Just wait and see."

"I don't care if it's Elvis," she muttered. "I *know* we're doing the right thing."

He didn't share her certainty, but it was past time for arguing about it. They were committed now.

| Deceleration: two minutes. |

| Intercept: nine minutes. |

He forced himself to ignore Melilah's pain and concentrate on what needed to be done.

+58

Melilah considered sending the signal to the tangler. Blowing the lid off the Occlusion conspiracy would punish Deangelis for bringing such a world of doubt down upon her. Whether the call from Yasu had been real or not, its effect had only been to reinforce something the Exarch had tried to tell her earlier. What right did she have to put her own beliefs ahead of those she was trying to protect? If they didn't *want* her protection, then who was she to force it upon them?

But she wasn't alone. She knew that. There were the members of Defiance, for a start, and many others who had agitated for membership but had been knocked back. There were ex-politicos of the old regime who would no doubt crawl out of the woodwork once the oppression was removed.

And then there were the many thousands of people who simply didn't care much either way. They would accept the end of the Exarch's rule in Bedlam with the same easygoing acquiescence that they had accepted its arrival. Once the shock of the new passed, it would become the norm all too quickly.

Either way, she thought, the Occlusion was bringing change. That it should be the *right* change was critical.

High-tech muscles flexed; powerful forces knotted around the drones as they began the furious deceleration that would bring them in a fast approach over the observatory.

"It's time," she said. "Time we came clean on at least one front."

Eogan, whose subtle support—just one hand pressed on her

shoulder—had been an anchor in a very stormy sea, looked up from his analysis of battle plans. "Which one?"

"Rumors and lies are obviously spreading about us. If the people of Bedlam are to think us the bad guys, then I'd rather they did it fully informed."

He shrugged. "We've yet to give the Archon notice, so I'm for broadcasting generally if we can't get through to it specifically."

She felt a kind of relief that some of the game playing would soon end. One board would be swept clean—although probably to be replaced by another, and another . . .

"This is Melilah Awad," she broadcast over all frequencies. "I come bearing a message for the Archon. For robbing everyday humanity of choice, for keeping secrets, and for lying to protect its own interests, I declare it unwelcome in the Arc Circuit. Go home—I would say to it, if it would only listen—and let us manage our own affairs. There is nothing you have to offer that the forty thousand of us do not already have in abundance."

"I am listening, Melilah Awad," returned a cool, collected voice.

"I suspect you have been all along," said Melilah.

"Of course."

"Then why talk only now? Things weren't chaotic enough for you before?"

It ignored the question. "I have just one thing to say to you, Melilah Awad. You are in great personal danger. This is not a threat, but a warning—and I offer it because I wish to avoid unnecessary bloodshed."

"If you're sincere about that, then you'd go home and leaves us in peace."

"I'm not talking about this rebellion of yours. I'm talking about the Occlusion."

She smiled. "Do you really want us to discuss this over an open frequency?"

"You can say whatever you like, Melilah. Misapprehension or lie, it won't change the facts. You are meddling with powers you cannot hope to understand. Continuing to meddle only increases the likelihood of disaster."

"I see no evidence of any such disaster."

"The Exarchate has already lost one colony. I would not make that two."

"What are the odds of that, really? You've been back in Sublime for ten years now, and there have been no more alien attacks.

We've had our hands on this Occlusion for a year, and likewise. What exactly does it take to set it off? Tell us, and we'll avoid it. Otherwise, I believe we're safe continuing just as we are."

"You know nothing of the circumstances required to unleash such a catastrophe. It may already be too late."

"So, again, what difference does it make? This thing belongs to all humanity, not just to you. It's about time you realized that."

"The Occlusion is not mine or yours, or *ours.* I don't know who it belongs to; all I know is that it is dangerous. We—you, I, *all* humanity—must exercise great care in our dealings with it."

"So you've come to take it off our hands because we're not capable of doing that. Can't you see that it's a self-fulfilling prophecy? Tell us what the danger is, and we'll do our best to avoid it. Keeping us in the dark only increases the chance that we'll make a terrible mistake. Your secrecy puts us at risk, not our naïveté. Would you rather see Bedlam destroyed than reveal the truth?"

| Intercept: two minutes. |

| ETA: six minutes. |

"Time's running out. What's your answer, Archon?"

"What's the question, Melilah?"

"Will you leave us to govern ourselves in peace?"

"I will leave, but Isaac Deangelis will remain. The Exarchate is the future of humanity. You can no more turn it back than reinstate *Homo habilis* at the summit of the evolutionary tree. Your fight, valiant though it is, is ultimately pointless and futile."

Melilah set her mouth in a grim line. "What about the Occlusion, then? Will you reveal the truth about it and the object that destroyed Sublime?"

"Eventually, yes. But not now. These are volatile times, as witness today. Sol wishes to avoid further destabilization."

"But you can't hide something like this! You and I both know what it is. You can try to bury the Bedlam and Sublime Occlusions as much as you like, but another will come along soon enough. And another. And another. It's like trying to bury an ants' nest. Sooner or later it's going to get out."

"And we'll deal with each outbreak on its own merits," said the Archon. "But at present, we have no other choice."

"You're not leaving *us* much choice, either. Do you appreciate that?"

"I understand that you might think that, Melilah, but you are wrong. You are foolishly gambling with your lives."

"You're already gambling with them, as far as I can tell. We have no intention of harming *you,* Archon, unless you force us to. And that makes us better people in my book. I know who I'd rather have in charge."

"That option is not one open to you, I'm afraid."

Eogan nudged her, pointing out that only seconds remained until the drones encountered the second wave of interceptors. Their velocity had dropped dramatically; this would be no blink-and-miss-it encounter. She was needed to oversee the drones' tactics.

"Then I guess there's nothing more to say," she said, steeping her tone in disappointment, and closed the line. The Archon was clearly not going to back down.

"Are you okay with this?" she asked Eogan.

"As okay as I'm ever going to be." His face was stone. "The Archon hasn't left us any options. Unless it changes its mind, I'm with you one hundred percent."

She was genuinely grateful for his support and the sacrifices he had made to give it to her. "Okay. Then let's finish this."

He nodded, and the drones extended their weapons.

+59

The eight attacking vessels unfolded like spindly arachnids, extruding strange spines, many-jointed limbs, and eyelike dishes, each configuration unique to each drone. Harsh sunlight gleamed from wicked points and rapier-thin antennae. Potent energies sparked from angular surfaces through all octaves of the electromagnetic spectrum. Thin lozenges that had once seemed minuscule in comparison to their bulbous, powerful shields were now deadly engines, filling those shields with instruments of lethality.

The shadow of PARASOL swept over them. An instant later, the interceptors sent to guard the observatory came within range. A new sun dawned.

Deangelis glowered at the data as it flooded in. Although no longer directly threatening the habitat, the drones still struck at a point of distinct vulnerability.

Would you rather see Bedlam destroyed than reveal the truth?

Melilah's words sparked a suspicion deep in the workings of his intricate mind. He didn't want to pursue it, didn't even want to think it—but it wouldn't go away. It lingered like the smell of burning oil, issued by some malfunctioning machine.

You know nothing of the circumstances required to unleash such a catastrophe.

The Archon remained no reassurance at all. Sol was as inscrutable as ever, the motives of the home system obscured by more than just seventy-eight light-years. Although he had initially feared the erosion of his authority by the arrival of the Archon, now he yearned for it. Anything to ease the terrible doubt that gnawed at him, the fear that he was doing the wrong thing despite all his best efforts, and the worst thought of all:

It may already be too late.

Two of Melilah Awad's suspiciously advanced craft disintegrated into showers of energy and disorganized matter. He hoped that Lazarus Hails felt their loss keenly, wherever the rest of him was. That the attack drones had come from Altitude he had no doubt, although he couldn't prove it. Each one represented a considerable investment in resources, enough to impact significantly on the Kullervo-Hails colony. Deangelis hoped, vindictively, that the next rebellion was against the man who had given one of his own the weapon she needed to turn against him. Lazarus Hails had joined Frederica Cazneaux on a growing list of people needing to pay for what had happened to his home.

But Deangelis would need to survive the current crisis, first. Just two attack drones died in exchange for all four of his makeshift interceptors. He had no surprises left to pull. Awad and Eogan now had a clear run at the Occlusion. All that stood between them and the Archon was vacuum, and whatever the Archon had been working on the previous day.

Would it be enough? Deangelis hoped so. He didn't dare imagine what might happen if it wasn't.

The Exarchate has already lost one colony. I would not make that two.

He shuddered, and waited. There was nothing else he could do.

+60

| ETA: three minutes. |

Eogan wiped his brow. He was sweating for the first time that he could remember. The last interceptor had come dangerously close to ramming their drone in a last-ditch attempt to destroy them. Only a desperate maneuver by their high-tech steed had saved their lives, and then only barely. It shuddered as it decelerated, shaking them like beads in a rattle.

"This is no good," he said, attempting to reroute power from various subsystems to shore up the breach, but failing miserably. "We can't keep on like this. The drone will tear itself to pieces."

Melilah looked frustrated, but didn't argue. She could see diagnostics as well as he could. "Pull us out of formation," she said. "We'll have to overshoot and come around from behind."

"That leaves you in charge, Hails."

Mine is not to question why . . .

"Hey," Melilah snapped. "This was your idea, remember?"

The illusion of the Exarch bowed deeply. *A jest, my lady. It has been a pleasure.*

The shuddering eased as D-1 eased back from the main contingent. The five fully functional drones surged ahead. Dead in their sights was the Occlusion, a gleaming asteroid-sized bauble in the shadow of PARASOL. As D-1 angled away on a more space-consuming deceleration curve, the target didn't change in the slightest. It looked like a bubble of quicksilver floating in the vacuum. Complex patterns rippled across its surface as though it was ringing like a very large bell.

| ETA: six minutes. |

"How long until the others arrive?"

| ETA: one minute seventy seconds. |

They had selected an attack run designed to show the Archon that they meant business without doing too much damage. If the Archon resisted, the drones would attack again, the observatory's defenses having been tested once and any weak points carefully targeted. This would, once again, be a very different type of combat than the previous two engagements. The observatory was stationary—unless the Archon had worked some technological wonder upon it—and could not therefore run from the drones. The drones, in turn, would be vulnerable to attacks from Bedlam, as Deangelis poured more of his resources into the defense of the Occlusion. They were prepared, however, to fight a war of attrition until the Archon gave in. Only then would they bring the fighting to an end.

"What if we've got it wrong?" Melilah asked him. "What if the Archon isn't in there at all, and we've wasted our only shot?"

"I don't think Hails would throw even part of himself away on a pointless gesture. If he thinks it's there, I'm inclined to believe him."

"But what *if* . . . ?"

He shrugged. "Then I guess we'd better hope this thing can fix itself and get us out of here in time."

"There's the tangler." She looked gloomy. "As long as the message gets out, I guess we're expendable."

"I don't *feel* expendable right now," he said. "And I don't think I'm likely to anytime soon, either."

"This has never felt like a suicide run for you, then?"

"Never. No offense, Mel, but no place is worth dying for."

"And no *one*?"

He smiled wryly. "I didn't say that."

+61

There was nothing left to say, Melilah told herself. This was the moment of truth. Either the drones would succeed, or they'd fail. Nothing was certain after that junction. There was no point even guessing what lay ahead.

"Wait," Eogan said, as the final seconds flew by. "That's not the attack run we selected!"

She had just noticed the variation, too. The drones were splitting up too early and priming their weapon systems in ways she and Eogan hadn't instructed them to. Mass launchers loaded far more matter than expected; lasers sucked power well in excess of their budget; systems not expected to stir until the second attack run were already at full readiness.

She scrolled through screens at lightning speed. Somehow, the plan had changed.

"Hails!" She slapped the bulkhead nearest her. "The son of a bitch is going for the kill!"

"It certainly looks like it," said Eogan. "I'm trying to override the commands, but the drones have switched on their autonomous systems. We're locked out."

Melilah fumed as the drones opened fire on the Occlusion observatory. She should have known better than to trust Hails. He was using them to destroy the Archon, not warn it away. They would take the blame for far more than just starting a rebellion.

Feeling trapped and fearing more bad news to come, she sent a flurry of experimental commands at D-1. The drone responded normally, suggesting that only the five under Hails's command had been compromised. Those five were swooping around the shimmering target like moons in fast motion, weapons and drives sending ripples jack-hammering through space-time. D-1 rocked sickeningly around them, but the waves didn't seem to impede its performance any more than its damage already had.

| ETA: three minutes. |

"This is insane," Melilah said, unable to decide whether to call off their own approach or hasten it in order to stop Hails.

"This is war, Melilah," Eogan muttered. "There are no rules."

She punched the bulkhead again, "Fuck!"

"Take it easy, Melilah. Try to think straight. There must be something we can do. Call the Archon, perhaps. If our communications systems are still open, we can at least try to make it clear that this isn't all our doing."

She nodded, trying to force her anger down. Cursing and hitting things wasn't going to help. She needed to find a better outlet for her energy.

"You do that," she said. "Meanwhile, I'll look into finding a way of stopping Hails."

Determined not to let another Exarch get the better of her, she set furiously to work.

+62

Deangelis watched the attack on the observatory with a feeling of bleak despondency. His rage was gone. He had tried his best to protect the Archon and failed. Now it was out of his hands. He could only hope that the short time the Archon had had to shore up the Occlusion's defenses had been long enough.

Initial signs were good. The quicksilver surface of the new observatory absorbed attacks with equanimity, glowing crimson and radiating waste heat away in infrared. Long spikes stabbed at the attacking craft, shooting all manner of energies and material projectiles from their tips. Scythelike eruptions threatened to slice the drones in two if they came too near. One of the vessels succumbed in just such a fashion. Broken and disintegrating, it tumbled to destruction on the observatory's gleaming skin.

The remaining four concentrated their assault on the bright point their fallen sibling left on the observatory. The red scar glowed orange, then yellow, then a fiery green. Vicious tendrils whipped at the drones but did little more than inconvenience them. Enough energy to crack a small moon in two poured into the breach, turning it a sickly aqua.

Only then did Deangelis pause to consider if Hails's target wasn't the Archon at all, but the Occlusion. Had Hails used the cover of rebellion to go after the same goal Frederica Cazneaux had sought?

"Why?" he asked, firing the message at the drones along the tightest channel possible, but not really expecting a reply. "Why are you doing this?"

"This might sound disingenuous," Hails responded, "but I'm doing my level best to save your life."

"From myself, I suppose."

"No, from the Archon, actually. I told you before, Isaac: you're too trusting. The biggest threat you've ever faced isn't from me or Melilah, or even the Occlusion. It's the one thing you let into the system without questioning it—and now I have to kill it dead before it destroys everyone here."

"What are you talking about?"

"I'm talking about Sublime, and what really happened there."

Deangelis froze. The suspicion he earlier had refused to consider rose up in response to Hails's words, stronger than ever, and caused the equivalent of a freeway pileup. His serial, synergistic thought processes cascaded to a halt.

"No," Earth-Deangelis whispered.

"Yes," said Hails. "We can argue about it later, if there's anything left of us."

"But—" A flurry of disconnected thoughts swirled through his many skulls. He struggled to bring himself back together. "The Archon wouldn't do that. It simply wouldn't."

"Why not? You know it was there when Sublime was destroyed, just like you know Jane Elderton never left. I've seen the data they've gathered since. Does it look to you like they're losing a war against alien replicators?"

Deangelis was stuck for a moment on the realization that Hails had seen the data he had secreted in the belly of the habitat. That had been his worst fear just days ago; now it seemed almost irrelevant.

"Are you saying the Archon could do it here, too?"

"*Of course* that's what I'm saying. Isaac, you're not this stupid. The Archon has some kind of hold over you. The moment things looked dicey, it sent itself down the pipe to make sure every contingency was covered. Someone needed to be there to push the plunger that would destroy your system—if things went wrong, as they clearly have."

The drones pounded the observatory's weak point. It flared bright purple, then inflated like a bubble, increasing its surface area to radiate the energy away. Disfigured and besieged, the observatory didn't look healthy at all.

"There's no proof," he said in desperation.

"That'll come if the Archon survives and Bedlam goes up in flames." Hails used the old name for the colony with easy familiarity, obviously not caring if Deangelis took offense. "I, for one, don't want to perform that test. Do you?"

Earth-Deangelis had no doubt that Hails was right. When the umbrella mind of his higher self dissolved in confusion, the subtle charisma of the Archon evaporated and he could see the truth perfectly well. When his higher self returned, however, the suspicion was quashed.

He fought the reintegration of his mind. The thought that he could no longer trust himself was utterly dispiriting.

The bubble on the observatory burst, exposing a second bubble within, this one radiating most strongly in ultraviolet. It, too, popped as the drones pounded it, exposing another one—and so on, each bubble rising in radiant energy until the boil in the side of the observatory burned brightly in X-rays. Earth-Deangelis dimmed the sensitivity on the electronic instruments focused on the observatory—the equivalent of shading his eyes with one hand. All over the habitat, he felt people hunkering down, afraid of what was to come.

No. Earth-Deangelis fought the seductive sensation of wholeness, of being able to absorb the colony in one gulp. The others could integrate if they wanted to, but he had to stay apart. Someone needed to keep the thought alive in case Hails failed. Someone needed to remember the truth.

A brilliant flash of cosmic rays almost blinded him. Flare screens slammed down all over the colony, antiquated, poorly maintained things installed before PARASOL had rendered them irrelevant. Radiation alarms went off, adding their powerful clamor to the attack sirens already whooping through the pipes and junctions. Those people not already in shelters scurried to find cover.

Earth-Deangelis pulled himself away from the niche in which he'd been standing, numbly jacked in to the data surging through his higher self. If the observatory had been rigged to self-destruct, it might conceivably do so with enough power to take the habitat with it. He headed for higher ground, metaphorically and literally. He needed to keep his head and shoulders above the encroaching tide of his mind.

As he ran for the nearest transport, he tried to find the humor in the fact that he was rebelling against himself, but it wasn't immediately evident.

+63

| ETA: thirty seconds. |

With a resounding concussion that set space vibrating like a plucked ruler, the Archon's defenses collapsed. Eogan surrendered himself to inertia gel as waves of energy poured over and through them. Through barely functional sensors he caught glimpses of concentric shells peeling back around a midnight black shape that glittered in its own deathlight. The chain reaction, once started, spread through all the observatory's new layers, rapidly exposing the raw knot of space-time tucked away at its heart. Eogan picked up familiar spatial distortions through the chaos, magnified and twisted into hideous shapes. He had never seen anything like it, and he hoped never to again.

A white point of light shot out of the observatory's habitat-facing flank. Eogan had barely enough time to notice it when the last shreds of the Archon's defenses evaporated. Energy boiled into furiously agitated vortices of vacuum foam; matter unraveled into photons all across the spectrum. With one last energetic eructation, the observatory simply evaporated into nothing, leaving the Occlusion exactly as it had been when he had first seen it—a strange anomaly surrounded by gas—only much, much hotter than before. A spherical shock wave rushed out into the solar system.

D-1 bucked and complained at the punishment. The *Cowell* shrank to its smallest profile in an attempt to minimize the number of particle and photon hits it was taking. Eogan rode out the shaking with his eyes firmly on what telemetry was telling him. The observatory was gone—and so were the drones that had killed it. All four of them vanished forever into the maelstrom.

Lucky we didn't get as close as we planned, he thought, wondering if that had been Hails's intention all along, too.

"Catch it!" called a voice, rising urgently above the roar of static left in the explosion's wake. "Don't let it hit!"

The voice came from the habitat, from Deangelis. The white mote of light that had ejected at the last moment from the observatory resolved into a stubby shape bearing enough similarities to Hails's tangler to convince Eogan that he was seeing another of them. It was blazing a path toward the habitat, dodging antiassault lasers as it went.

The Archon! Eogan pulled himself out of a daze and took control of the drone. Melilah was stunned, forced into a fetal ball by the Cell in its sudden self-protective collapse. He would have to fly the drone on his own. Swinging targeting routines into play and identifying the rogue tangler as a new priority objective, he set the drone accelerating powerfully in pursuit.

| Target acquired. |

The shudder in its drive returned. He ignored it. The drone's destructive impulses, thwarted earlier by the damage to its systems, brought all its weapons to bear on the tangler. Beam weapons chipped at its rear defenses while VOID-powered missiles snaked in for a broadside hit. The tangler had a few surprises up its sleeve, however: strange butterfly-like feather-shields flapped in and out of existence, batting the missiles aside like flies; concave containment-field effects kept the missiles' self-destruct detonations at bay; brief but powerful surges in acceleration took it at wild tangents to its existing course, just ahead of the next wave of attack.

"It's getting away!" shouted Deangelis. Eogan didn't stop to wonder why the Exarch was suddenly so afraid of someone he had been trying to defend just minutes earlier. "Don't let it get through!"

A lucky beam-shot clipped the tangler's flank. Too late, it surged explosively aside. The damage must have affected its guidance systems, for the tangler spiraled away from the habitat like a disoriented dragonfly. Dogged on all sides, it was only a matter of time before a missile found its mark. White light blared from the tangler's nose, and it went into a tumble.

There, under the shadow of PARASOL with nothing but

blackness at its back and the ruins of the observatory to one side, the Archon's last-ditch hope of escape died. The tangler's hull buckled outward, then tore apart. A massive chemical explosion blossomed, casting a golden light across the *Cowell*. In its wake, glowing debris tumbled.

| Target destroyed. |

Eogan let free the breath he had been holding, and mentally took his hands off the controls.

"Is that it?" asked Melilah, her voice weak. "Is it over?"

He reached one hand through the gel and found hers waiting for him. They gripped and held tight.

"Christ, I hope so," he said.

+64

There was no cheering, no wild fanfare. It seemed to Melilah that she and Eogan hung in the thrall of a shocked silence as they accelerated slowly toward Bedlam. It would take time for recent events to sink in. The feed from Bedlam was chaotic and confused. No one personality rose out of the rabble to give words to the consensus view. It might be hours, Melilah knew, before one formed.

She wasn't prepared to wait that long.

"It's done," she said over all frequencies. "For better or for worse, we've kicked the Archon out of Bedlam. The Occlusion is ours, if we want it. We have a chance, at last, to make up our own minds. That doesn't mean it'll be easy. That doesn't mean we won't still make mistakes. But they'll be *our* mistakes, and we'll learn from them."

"We've all made mistakes," said an unexpected voice. "We've all been wronged."

"Don't you play the victim now, Deangelis," she said. "It's not going to wash."

"I *am* a victim," he responded, "as surely as you are. Sol has committed crimes against everyone in the name of the Exarchate. So many lives have been lost. It can't go on any longer."

"*Now* you see reason." She couldn't help the bitterness. "Why couldn't you have said this earlier?"

"I didn't have all the facts. I was—confused." His voice was uncharacteristically uncertain. "It will take me time to put myself back together the way I should be, and you will have to be patient with me. But I give you my word that I will not rest until justice is done."

Melilah didn't know what had turned the Exarch around so suddenly, but she was quite happy to accept his capitulation—to a point.

"What exactly does that mean, Deangelis? Are you going to give Bedlam back to us?"

"I don't know." He sounded angry and tired. "I have no wish to belong to a government that practices genocide, but I do not know if I am able to abdicate. There are restrictions on my thoughts, constraints I was not previously aware of. Perhaps I can shrug them free and exist in my own right—not as Exarch, but as Isaac Forge Deangelis, human being and citizen of Bedlam. Time, Melilah, is what I need."

"That might be just what we don't have," said Eogan. "I hate to be the doomsayer, but we can expect a strong backlash, and soon. I bet the *Cowell* there are more Exarchs sniffing around for a chance to take advantage of the disruption. And I'm sure Sol won't take this lying down. It may be a long way away, but it's a force to be reckoned with."

"We have the Occlusion," said Melilah. "We have the maze. That gives us an edge they don't have."

"That's true, but they do still have Sublime, and we'll have to find another exit before it becomes truly useful. Don't think the war is won just because we've got one hand on the prize."

His words were sobering. She knew they needed to be said, but that didn't make them any easier to hear.

A flood of messages began to roll in. Members of Defiance offered congratulations. Old political acquaintances did so more cautiously, covering their bets. Yasu apologized for her angry words. Gil Hurdowar sent her a short note welcoming her home, and that one she couldn't let slide.

"I'm not home yet," she told him. "In fact, I've rather enjoyed being out of your sight. Maybe I'll stay away for good."

"You can't do that. Life would be too boring without you, Melilah. Besides, you don't fool me. I know you like it: the attention, the infamy, the drama. You thrive on it. That's why you like politics so much, and why I don't. I'd rather watch while you strut your stuff. It's an equitable arrangement."

"You had your moment in the spotlight," she said, remembering his warning about Hails and other occasional hints.

"Too hot for me, 'Lilah. Besides, you have plenty of company at the moment. There wouldn't be room enough for me even if I wanted to be there."

She opened her mouth to object at his use of the pet name she hated, then shut it again, protest unexpressed. That was what he would have wanted: to get a rise out of her. She wasn't going to give him the satisfaction when, for now and maybe a little while longer, she had the luxury of simply switching him off.

She did so.

"Any food on this thing?" she asked Eogan. Since the Cell had expanded to its usual size, she had taken up a perch opposite him, held in place by one arm and a leg.

"Sure," he said, "if you don't mind it coming through a vein."

She pulled a face. "Let's get home soon then, before cannibalism starts to look tempting."

"That sounds like a good idea."

She checked the flight plan of the drone. Eogan had plotted a low-energy return to the habitat, and that was fine by her. She could wait an hour to eat. They were still closer to the Occlusion than to Bedlam. The weird hole in space was visible only through the distortions it cast upon the universe beyond it. As PARASOL gradually swung around to block out the stars, it became effectively invisible.

"What about you?" she asked. "Any thoughts on what you'll do next?"

He shook his head. "The *Cowell* could probably make another system, if it had to, but I'm not sure what my reception would be like there. The Palmers will have to work out where they stand in all this. And until I know where that is exactly, I guess I'm stuck here." He looked at her. "Is that a problem?"

She searched her feelings for anything she could justify. The thought of his being around any longer made her feel uncomfortable, but there was no concrete reason for forbidding him. It was her problem, not the habitat's. He had helped save Bedlam, so she supposed she could put up with him a little longer.

"As long as there's no more funny business," she said, thinking of the moment in the ruined alien ship.

"On my word."

"And you have to help get Hails's nanoware out of my head."

He nodded. "It'll take time, but I'm sure it's possible."

"Thanks. I appreciate it." She felt as though she owed him something more than that, so she added: "I really mean that, Palmer Eogan. Thank you."

"Gratefully accepted, Mem Awad." He smiled. "Will you listen to us being nice to one another? The sooner we get out of here, the better."

"Agreed." She turned her attention back to the drone's guidance systems, unwilling to completely repress a smile.

So it was that she caught the first flash of light around the edge of PARASOL. *A solar flare,* she thought, although she didn't remember any scheduled for that time. It wasn't surprising that she had missed it; she hadn't been paying attention to forecasts of late. But it was a concern. A big flare could have serious ramifications for the battle-scarred habitat.

"What rating are we looking at, Traffic Control?" Eogan's voice momentarily distracted her from the view.

"Unknown," came back the AI. "All vessels are advised to return to dock."

"We can ride it out," he said. "The Cell's seen worse than anything the sun can throw at us."

"What about the drone?" she asked him.

"It'll make do. PARASOL will absorb the worst of it, after all, and it doesn't have to worry about life support. I'm sure it'll come through okay."

Melilah watched, still feeling disoriented, as the far side of PARASOL began to glow with golden fire as well. This was a particularly big flare, judging by its brightness—and it was still growing.

Her smile vanished as a bright spark punctured the heart of PARASOL's black face. Then another. The spark brightened and spread.

Alarm tightened the muscles in her chest.

The flare was burning *through* PARASOL.

"My God," said Eogan.

An alarm she had never heard began to wail over the Bedlam feed. She clutched the walls of the component for reassurance it couldn't give her. Voices shouted as the sparks joined up and new ones formed. The dark shield was melting, burning, dissolving. The stars were vanishing under an onslaught of light.

"That's not a flare!" Deangelis's voice stood out from the rest—no less panicky but thick with the same anger as before.

"Then what is it?" asked Melilah anxiously.

"Catastrophe," Deangelis muttered, trading uncertainty for despair.

Ice crystallized in her veins. For a moment, her thoughts simply stopped.

Impossible. It couldn't be!

Then alarms began to sound from sensors on the drone's skin. It was being attacked by something invisible from the vacuum around them.

"No," she whispered. Catastrophe wasn't an option. She wouldn't allow it.

But in her mind she saw the debris cloud from the destroyed tangler. She pictured it expanding in a hot sphere, hitting PARASOL first, the object closest to it, then the drone. From there it would keep expanding, as unstoppable as an exhaled breath, its foulness spreading to poison everything in its path.

Bedlam.

"No!" She clambered around the interior of the component to where Eogan sat, half in the bulkhead, half out. She clutched him, shook him. "We have to stop it! There must be a way!"

Eogan's expression was shocked. His eyes briefly focused on her, then rolled away to internal views. "I'm trying my best, but the agents are replicating too quickly, and the drone doesn't have the defenses to deal with something like this. It's spreading faster than I can contain it!"

"To hell with the drone," she snarled. "What about my home?"

He gripped her arm so tight it hurt. "If we can't save the first one, we have no chance at all with the second."

Muscular pain shocked her out of her panic. The world around her turned red as she overlaid the views he was seeing across her natural vision. Warning and damage lights were doubling in number with every breath. Yellow light—now more sinister than beautiful—spread steadily down the drone's flank, as though it had been dipped in molten gold. In another view, PARASOL was already half-consumed by fire.

"What can I do?" Her voice sounded as though miles of fog insulated its source from her. "I need to do *something.*"

"Take the helm. I don't know how much longer we'll retain control of the drone, but try to take us out of the debris cloud. Find the fringes of it. Maybe then I can get a grip on what we've already picked up."

She did as she was told, noting immediately the stricken way in which the drone responded. Its systems, already heavily corrupted, reacted unpredictably to her commands. She could feel its hurt empathically, deep down in her guts. The invading replicators were like cancer eating through her. Tears ran freely down her cheeks as the drone died piece by piece around her.

Then, with a wrenching dislocation, it was gone. Something had cut it free. The pain fell precipitously away, leaving hollow wounds in its wake. Glowing with sickly yellow light, visible through senses not belonging to her, it tumbled into poisonous space, decrepitating wildly.

"I tried to fly it," she whispered, "but it was already too far gone."

"I know," Eogan said. "That's why I had to jettison it. That stuff is *fast.*"

"Are we going to be okay?"

"Maybe. The *Cowell* seems to be keeping the worst of it out. But—Melilah, I'm sorry. I don't know what else we can do."

They were alone with the *Cowell,* the last component of the *Nhulunbuy*. The drone was as good as dead, and so was PARASOL. The view outside was full of hellish light as the debris cloud spread.

Melilah openly wept as the first bright spots appeared on Bedlam's exposed skin. She felt as though she was dreaming. It had to be a nightmare.

"This can't—this can't be happening!"

"I'm sorry," said Eogan again. The words had no meaning.

"Yasu? Yasu?" She commandeered the Cell's communications; he didn't try to stop her. "If you can hear me, get out of there now! Find an escape capsule; set it for our coordinates! We'll pick you up. Yasu? Can you hear me?"

The feed from the habitat was panicked and chaotic, breaking up into random noise as the deadly fire spread. In a way, that was a blessing. The new replicators were much more voracious than those propagated by Frederica Cazneaux's Reaper. These burned through the outer layers of the habitat like hot copper wire through ice. Chambers collapsed too quickly for people to evacuate; pipes opened to naked vacuum, spraying their contents into the maelstrom. In the disintegrating feed, Melilah glimpsed limbs melting, faces bursting into flame, blood and bright yellow death mingling freely.

"We can't save everyone."

Melilah heard Eogan's cautionary words, but she couldn't feel her body. The horror was too much to take. Dimly she thought he might be holding her, trying to comfort her, but it didn't truly register. There was no comfort to be found as her home burned, and the people she loved died.

"Yasu!"

A handful of craft launched from the giant habitat. They caught fire immediately. As Bedlam burned, it spawned a volatile, corrosive atmosphere, a terrible miasma that would destroy anything it touched. PARASOL and the drone were doing the same. The small cloud of tangler debris had seeded a plague that would soon overtake the entire system—as it had Sublime.

Eogan was wrong. The problem wasn't that they couldn't save everyone. They'd be lucky if they could save *anyone.* Red warnings began to appear on the *Cowell*'s skin as more and more of the replicators gained a toehold. It couldn't fight them off indefinitely.

The feed died in a wash of static across every channel. The thought of telling the Cell to stop resisting was morbidly tempting. A quick death, she thought, would be better than watching all she loved burn away to nothing.

"Look!"

One sole craft fought off the replicators just long enough to limp out of Bedlam's feeble gravity well. Gold warred with silver across its skin as it tumbled feebly toward them.

Melilah felt some of Eogan's excitement. Survivors—against all the odds! She didn't fight as he swung the Cell around to intercept the glowing lozenge. It was half as large as they were. Infection sparkled like jewels across its silver hull. She recognized neither its design nor the material it was made from, but it was broadcasting a standard distress call, and that was good enough for her.

The Cell shook as it enfolded the infected capsule. Melilah dimly registered how Eogan contained the replicators—scraping the major concentrations into relatively contained locations, then sloughing off the *Cowell*'s entire outer hull, ejecting the replicators with it. The Cell's extreme-redundancy design principles enabled it to survive the loss of such a large chunk of itself, but it came at a cost. This wasn't a tactic it could perform more than a few times.

The Cell absorbed the contents of the capsule. There was just one passenger.

+65

"We have to get out of here," said Earth-Deangelis. His eyes felt as red as Melilah's looked. "We have to make sure the truth survives."

"Therein lies the problem," Eogan said. "I don't think we *can* get out of here."

Earth-Deangelis forcibly suppressed images of the stricken habitat from his mind. There was nothing he could have done to save it—but nonetheless his truncated higher reflexes screamed that he should have tried. *You ran,* they said. *You failed.*

But to stay would have been taking the easy way out. He knew that. Death wasn't an answer. He wanted time to mourn the destruction of his home, and to get revenge.

He reached out with his peripherals and tapped into the Cell's primitive systems. Red warning signs were spreading across its hull faster than he could credit. With PARASOL now a ghastly yellow disk in the sky, brighter than if the sun had expanded to the size of a bloated yellow giant, space was rapidly filling with sweeping winds of deadly nanotech. The burning bulk of Bedlam was doing the same on the far side.

"I've upped our defenses as much as possible," Eogan explained, "and they're already stretched. I can divert sufficient resources away from them to move us a short distance, but to get us out of the system entirely would take more than we can spare. We'd be eaten alive before we got a light-second away."

Deangelis knew it was true. Palmer technology was no match for what the Archon had set loose on the system.

"There is a way out," he said. "Just one."

Melilah nodded. "The Occlusion."

Eogan eyed them both dubiously. "You've got to be kidding."

"It's close," Deangelis said, "and completely defenseless."

"Didn't you keep the specs for the capsule Palmer Vermeulen came out in?" Melilah added. "That can get us safely through the throat."

Eogan swallowed, looking more frightened of their only escape route than he was of death.

"We don't have forever, Dominic."

"I *know* that," he said irritably. "It's just—" He stopped, and nodded. "Okay. But it's going to be tricky. Melilah, I'll need you to hold us on course while I look after the replicators and Vermeulen's specs."

She nodded.

"The Cell has different interfaces than Hails's drones," Eogan said.

"Whatever. Just do what you have to do to get us out of here."

The Palmer bent his face down and folded forward into the bulkhead, which rose up to meet him like a wave of molasses. The transition was sudden, and took Melilah by surprise. One moment he was there; the next he was gone. Then the walls began to close in around her, and she gasped in fear.

Earth-Deangelis reached out and touched her arm.

She nodded and stayed perfectly still, every muscle rigid.

"Don't worry," Eogan said, his voice coming from the walls around them. "This is no different from the configuration we've used before. I need to reduce our profile as much as possible. The smaller our surface area, the less the replicators have to grip on to."

She nodded, seeing the sense in his words, and closed her eyes as the Cell engulfed her. Irresistible pressure forced both their knees up to their chests.

"What should I do?" asked Earth-Deangelis.

"Just hold on," said Eogan. "If there's anything in the throat we should know about, now would be the time to tell us."

"You know as much as I do," the ex-Exarch said. "Hails told me you cracked the data cache."

"Then we're all equally in the dark."

Earth-Deangelis nodded. "We soon will be, anyway."

+66

A torrent of data flooded through nerves Eogan's body normally used for scent and kinesthesia. He smelled the texture of the infected space around him; he felt the Cell's intricate structure as though it belonged to his own body. Telemetry poured through his aural and optic pathways, granting him a clear and uninterrupted view of the Cell and its destination.

The subtle warp of the Occlusion hung against a backdrop of fire. All that remained of PARASOL was a breeding ground for more destruction. Behind him, the habitat blazed like a small star.

He turned his back on it and let the heat of the flames burn away his sorrow. He would mourn his friends later, when there was time.

With a wild surge of acceleration, they fled.

"That's it," said Eogan, as Melilah hesitantly interfaced with the Cell. He felt as though they were riding a hopper with a faulty thruster, sometimes surging forward and other times falling back, but that wasn't her fault. The Cell's many minuscule drives were sensitive to the storm. "Keep us moving as fast as you can. You may feel some drag as I take the resources I need, but I'll try to keep that to a minimum. And don't worry about slowing down. We'll hit the throat at speed."

She nodded, or tried to. Her body was completely swathed, lost to her. The Cell took the impulse and conveyed it symbolically. He read her fear as easily as words down a screen. Something else to ignore.

Nanotech winds buffeted them from all directions. The replicators were digging in with growing ferocity. Their density increased in time with the Cell's velocity, and Eogan was soon fighting a losing battle. He was forced to peel off layer after layer of corrupted hull, sacrificing it in order to spare the Cell's fragile passengers. At the same time, he frantically tried to build up the defenses they needed to ensure their survival when they rocketed through the throat. It was a contradictory, thankless task, and the only way he could tell that it was working was by the fact they were still alive.

Their velocity increased. The Occlusion came closer.

Catastrophic replicators bit deeper. Drag weighed them down.

Eogan abandoned all distinction between himself and the Cell. He physically leaned forward, as though forcing his way through a heavy wind with fists and jaw clenched, eyes in slits, back straining.

Come on! he urged himself and the Cell at the same time. *Just a little bit farther!*

Gold flared around him. The Occlusion ballooned in his face like a rip in the universe. The Cell lurched as Eogan dropped more than half of the *Cowell* in their wake, exposing an entirely new hull beneath. A feeling of being sandpapered back to the bone enveloped him, and he screamed.

Agony!

Blackness took him. The pain dropped away. Blessed silence enfolded him.

But he wasn't unconscious. He wasn't dead. The Cell tumbled through space unknown, at the whim of laws it couldn't comprehend.

It took him a long moment truly to accept what had happened.

+POSTLUDE

One day later

Darkness.

Then—light.

"Welcome back," said a voice. "How are you feeling?"

"Archon?" Deangelis opened his eyes on a lush, green world. "Is that you?"

"Yes, Isaac."

"Where am I?" He struggled to orient himself, but failed to connect with the view before him. Gently wooded hills rolled into the distance; a creek burbled under lush blackberry bushes nearby; to his left, the sun was rising over the horizon in a wash of subtle yellows and oranges. "Is this Earth?"

"Yes, it is." The Archon was silent for a moment, as though giving him a chance to absorb the answer, then said, "Tell me the last thing you remember."

Deangelis thought hard. Memories came in flashes: of Lazarus Hails's inert body lying at his feet; of attack drones rushing toward him at incredible velocities; of a bright purple bubble popping in a flash of X-rays; of a feeling of gut-tearing panic . . .

The Exarchate has already lost one colony, the Archon had told him. *I would not make that two.*

"It's happened, hasn't it?" A terrible sense of finality rolled through him, as irresistible as gravity. "Lut-Deangelis is gone."

"I'm sorry to have to tell you this, Isaac, but your colony was destroyed thirty-eight hours ago." The Archon's voice was thick with sympathy. "We here on Earth were monitoring events there through your tangler, so we knew of the imminent possibility of such an occurrence. Hopes fell when the signal from your tangler ceased. Just hours ago, deep-space probes stationed around the system confirmed the outbreak. There is, I'm afraid, no hope of finding survivors."

"Was it—?" His mouth closed over the sentence. A real mouth, apparently, because he could feel a breeze on his cheeks and taste sleep on his tongue. He couldn't move, however. He sat, propped limply against what felt like a stone of some kind, and could do nothing other than think.

He forced himself to finish the sentence.

"Was it you who destroyed my home?"

The Archon paused again. This time he didn't think it was for his benefit.

"Anything other than the truth, Isaac, would dishonor you and the work you did in Lut-Deangelis. So yes, I destroyed your colony, just as I destroyed Jane Elderton's ten years ago. And I did it for the same reason: to keep the artifact contained. I deeply regret having to take such action, but the necessity is inescapable. *Not* doing it would have cost far more in terms of lives than doing it, as I'm sure you will come to accept in time. I will understand completely if you decide to hate me, as Jane Elderton now does.

"But that would not stop me from doing it a third time if I have to." The Archon's tone hardened. "Nor will it divert us from the course we must now follow, you and I."

Deangelis tried to think through a suffocating fog of grief and despair. "Course? What course? What use am I to you now—a washed-up, failed Exarch with no colony to look after? I'm nothing; I should be dead."

"You haven't failed, Isaac, and you aren't dead. You still have work to do. We couldn't update our model of your mind beyond the point at which the tangler was destroyed, but we have enough of you to bring you back, almost as good as new. Bringing you back was a necessity. Just like you, I exist in multiple bodies, only my parts can be separated by light-years and still function perfectly well. Thus I see the greatest view possible, across all the Exarchate, and I see all too clearly what must be done now."

Deangelis didn't want to know. Enough had been done already. His home was destroyed, his world turned upside down. The Exarchate, which he thought existed to nurture human life in all its forms, was responsible for the death of tens of thousands of people. Whole planetary systems had been depopulated in the name of—what? Stability? Security?

Insanity, he thought, fighting the urge to weep.

"Two hours ago," the Archon said, "a message was sent from the borders of Lut-Deangelis along the tangler network. The message was written by Melilah Awad and detailed the truth, as she saw it, about the artifact we have discovered. Word has come to me of this message from the Exarchs of Michailogliou-Rawe, Alcor-Magun, and Beall-Cammarano. That these systems received the message suggests *all* in the region surrounding Lut-Deangelis have done so, although we have yet to hear from the others. No doubt some have passed the message on to systems farther away from its source, and some of *those* recipients might in turn do the same. This is both unexpected and alarming, Isaac, as I'm sure you appreciate. Knowledge of this artifact is kept carefully contained for a reason, and you have seen firsthand how far we are prepared to go in order to achieve that end."

Deangelis nodded. He did know, and Lazarus Hails had suspected before him. How many of his peers were putting the pieces together even now, as word of the death of another system spread?

"We have modeled the propagation of the truth as one would a disease," the Archon went on. "We expect the entire upper echelon of the Exarchate to be aware of Geodesica within days. All it will take is one Exarch to leak the truth to an underling or two, and it is bound to spread farther still. We will do what we can to spread counter- and misinformation, just as we did with White-Elderton: one system suggests a connection between the Occlusion and devastation; a second outbreak will only reinforce the meme that meddling with such artifacts is lethally dangerous. But some will remain dubious. This doubt, Isaac, must not be allowed to spread. Do you understand?"

"What can I possibly do about it?" The smell of Earth in his nostrils was all Deangelis wanted to focus on at that moment. This was as close to home as he would ever be again. And even here, where the Archon issued its murderous orders, he would never be fully comfortable.

He felt the Archon regarding him closely, as though the sun was a giant, godlike eye. Its voice was inhumanly calm.

"I need to know more about the rebellion that took place in your colony and the people behind it. You will assist me in this task while you perform your new role in Lut-Deangelis, as caretaker of the latest entrance to Geodesica. Nothing must be allowed in or out, as I'm sure you can appreciate. Together, we must keep a lid on this thing as best we can."

"You don't need me," he protested, thinking: *and I don't want to do it!*

"You underestimate yourself, Deangelis. You are an integral part of this operation. No one else has had such intimate access to the key players: Melilah Awad, Palmer Eogan, and Lazarus Hails. You are truly part of the inner circle now, my friend. There are no more secrets left for you to find."

They're all dead, he wanted to protest. *What's the point in studying them now?*

But the rest of Lazarus Hails was still alive in *his* system, and something in the Archon's voice made him wonder about the others, too.

"No survivors, you said?"

"None has been detected and, judging by our experience in the first outbreak, none is expected. The replicators I propagated after my death in your system were designed for rapid, maximum destruction. If anyone did evade them, they've gone somewhere you and I will never follow."

Deangelis nodded again, reading between the lines and thinking: *No more secrets? Like hell.* If someone had survived, there was only one place they could be: inside Geodesica, the very artifact Sol would kill to keep closed. And if they'd got in, there was very real chance they would one day get out . . .

He repressed a sad smile. Melilah had succeeded in doing what he could not. She had set free the genie, and nothing the Archon did would get rid of it. Word would spread about Geodesica to all quarters of the Exarchate. Enough people would guess what had happened to his colony, and they would worry about it happening to theirs next. Fear would replace trust, fear that would inevitably turn to anger if given a nudge or two.

The seeds of dissent had been sown—and although he had never thought of himself as a farmer before, despite his role as nurturer of his colony, he could get used to the idea.

He took a deep breath. The Archon's charisma was as powerful as ever, but he had a reason to fight it, now.

"Very well," he said finally. "I'll do it."

"That's the spirit, Isaac. I knew you'd bounce back."

"When do we leave?"

"As soon as a relay is in position. It'll take us about a week to transfer and build everything we need, but you don't have to worry about any of that. These are just logistical details. We'll get you home before you know it."

The power of movement spread through his body. Life had been granted to his limbs as a reward for his obedience. He climbed gingerly to his feet and looked around.

He was standing at the summit of a low hill, as he had been at his birth. But this time, instead of a eucalyptus at his back, he had woken leaning against a gravestone.

Be careful, my friend, Jane Elderton had told him a lifetime ago. *Don't lose yourself like I did.*

"Thank you, Archon," he said, hiding thoughts of revenge behind a smooth, obsequious tone. "I'm looking forward to it."

GEODESICA
DESCENT

For MM.

+PRELUDE

Anniversary 8: 2694 CE

"You told me, once," said a voice, "that you loved me."

Isaac Deangelis had been watching the ship decelerate with close attention, not overly alarmed by its lack of identification since its design was so antiquated. It came in three discrete chunks, each spherical and perfectly mirror-finished. Each chunk emitted no drive flame or electromagnetic radiation. They simply warped space as their velocity decreased, propagating strange ripples of starlight from their gleaming, curved surfaces.

He was duty bound to intervene should anyone attempt anything untoward near the entrance to Geodesica. Now, though, he had no idea what to do. The knowledge of who the voice belonged to and the shock of hearing it again momentarily overwhelmed him.

The voice belonged to Melilah Awad. Her ship was a Palmer Cell.

"Didn't you hear me, Isaac?"

"I heard you," he broadcast. There was no point pretending he hadn't, just as he'd made no effort to hide his identity from anyone bound in-system. He checked the Occlusion containment bubble, seeking an explanation for her appearance; it was quiescent, still sealed, as he had known it would be. "Where did you emerge? When?"

"I came out a long way from here, Isaac. As to when—well, if I told you, you wouldn't believe me."

He didn't know *what* to believe as the ancient vessel matched vectors with the observation platform he inhabited. It had been over a quarter of a millennium since Melilah disappeared into Geodesica. Who knew what she had seen and experienced in that time?

"I've been waiting for you," he said. "I knew you weren't dead. I knew you'd come back eventually."

"I know," she said, and he was surprised by the tone of her voice. He had studied her most closely of all the lost citizens of Bedlam. He read surprise in her, yes, and grief, obviously. But there seemed to be no anger there, even now, confronted with the ruins of her home and the man she could easily blame for its destruction.

He wouldn't begrudge her that. It had been his home, too, and he had no compunction in blaming himself. He had imagined her return many times—sweeping out of the Occlusion on a crest of fiery wrath, her indignation fueled by whatever alien technology she had mastered inside the ancient artifact. Her revenge would be swift and justified, and, in all likelihood, he wouldn't lift a finger to stop her.

You told me, once, that you loved me.

He had never uttered those three words in his life, to her or anyone.

"What happened to Palmer Eogan?" he asked. "You were together when the Catastrophe struck. He must have survived if you did."

"He stayed behind," she said.

"In Geodesica?"

"That's hard to explain." Again, he heard a strong note of grief in her voice. "It's probably best you don't ask me to try."

"But I want to know. I want to know how you avoided the replicators; how you got back; what you found; what it's like in there—everything."

"There's no point," she said. "You don't need to know."

"How can you say that? Nothing's been the same since Geodesica was found. People fought a war over it. I risked my life for it. I betrayed everything I believed in because of it!" He stopped, sucking on the memories as one would a bleeding thumb. "I want to know," he finished with more control. "I need to."

"I understand," she said, "but you *did* know. You saw it for yourself—the part of you who came with us."

He bit down on the urge to remind her that the fragment of him that had been caught up with her and Eogan's escape from

Bedlam wasn't *actually* him, but part of the distributed self who had once been Exarch of the system.

"Was he the one who told you I loved you?"

"What difference does it make which part of you said it?"

"All the difference in the world. While he's not connected to the rest of me, he can feel and say many things that aren't representative of me, just as he can experience things I can't possibly know until we're reconnected."

She didn't deny that, but she didn't concede the point, either.

"Where is he, by the way?"

"I don't want to talk about it. It's not relevant."

"Is he still in Geodesica?"

"It's not *relevant,*" she insisted.

He heard irritation in her voice, then, and perhaps the beginning of the anger he dreaded.

"I am not your enemy," he said, "and I am not your lover. But I have been waiting for you to come back for over two hundred and fifty years. Why not dock and we'll talk face-to-face?"

"What could we possibly say to each other, Isaac?"

Her skepticism saddened him. "Well, I can tell you what happened here, for starters."

"Yes. I notice that Ah Kong is gone," she said, referring to the system's former gas giant. "And the sun's spectrum looks weird."

"That's just the start of it. There's so much more. When I've finished, perhaps you can tell me your story."

"I can't do that," she said, stating bluntly for the first time what she had only suggested before.

"Then perhaps we can just talk." *Perhaps,* he thought to himself, *you'll tell me if the feelings of my fragment were returned.*

Her Cell didn't come any closer. "What's the point? It won't change anything."

"This is true, but it won't hurt, either. Come on, Melilah. You're safe now. The war is over." If she could be blunt, so could he. "This place is a grave. No one fights over a grave."

Her reply came not in words, but the sound of weeping over the communication link.

+I

Bedlam: 2439 CE

Bedlam burned. Palmer Horsfall warily approached the system the Exarchate called Lut-Deangelis, keeping a close eye on telemetry for any sign of nanotech attack as she came. The trade lanes had been seeded with dust, as they had been around Sublime, dramatically reducing deform ratings and forcing her to ply an alternate route through the heliopause. Thus far, that dust had been inert, devoid of any payloads more sophisticated than pure inertia, but it paid to be careful. She knew precisely what sort of risk she was taking.

From a distance the system looked little different to normal. Only closer did its absorption spectrum begin to show signs of Catastrophe. The vast, gleaming atmosphere of nanotech surrounding the star was extraordinarily diffuse—barely one particle per cubic meter—but it fed on the energy of the sun itself and bred voraciously. Horsfall knew that very little within its aegis would have been spared. Asteroids, moons, whole planets had been consumed in the fire of its genesis, along with Palmer Cells, automated stations, and outposts. A world of people had died here—as had died in Sublime, along with her sister.

She remembered that day with perfect clarity. Eleven years earlier and seventeen and a half light-years away, it still burned in her mind. She had tried so long to quench it—along with the guilt and the anger and the regret. Now she knew better. She would fan those flames and set fire to all humanity. She wouldn't rest until Sol burned with her, and the smoke obscured the stars.

"Should we hail him?" she asked the monkey on her back.

Wait. The reply came as a whisper in her ears, as subtle and insidious as it had been the first time she heard it. *It's likely he's already seen us.*

"We're coming in quiet." The Cell Horsfall commanded had been modified to very specific requirements in order to minimize its emissions. They had coasted in deep cold for several hours past the system's bow shock, only booting up telemetry when they were confident of having slipped through the outer defenses.

Nevertheless. We want *him to see us, remember?*

She remembered. This was the part of the plan that bothered Horsfall the most. Everything hinged on how Deangelis would react. Would he swat them out of the sky as one would a mosquito, or would he hesitate long enough to listen? There was no way to guess. A man who had just watched his system die was inherently unpredictable.

Not a man, she reminded herself. An Exarch. There was a big difference.

The face of Bedlam's gas giant, Ah Kong, presented an unlikely swirl of colors as the *Dreieichen* navigated its many moons. She felt something akin to relief to be back in a gravity well after so long in the Dark. If she kept her eyes averted from the glowing sphere of the Catastrophe, Horsfall could almost pretend she was in an ordinary system, one untouched by the horrors she had seen, on an ordinary mission for Arc Circuit clients. The *Dreieichen* was designed to be crewless as well as quiet. Part of her longed for a new voice to talk to apart from the one in her head. In the station named after her sister, there had been communications from other systems, companions to talk to, even the occasional lover. For almost two years now, ever since word had come of the Mizar Occlusion, she had been utterly isolated. She hadn't even known what had happened in Bedlam until she had arrived on its fringes. The ghastly golden glow was faint but familiar.

Strength, the voice in her ears had offered her at their first glimpse. *You're not alone in this. We will find peace together, either way.*

The thought hadn't helped much. Horsfall knew that there was only one sort of peace she could hope for—and she wasn't religious; she didn't believe that her sister awaited her in some blissful afterlife. Death was just an end, not a solution, to the problem.

"Come on, Deangelis," she muttered as the *Dreieichen* assumed its parking orbit. "Put us out of our misery. I dare you."

As though the former Exarch of Bedlam had heard her, something broke cover from behind one of the icy moons and streaked toward her Cell.

No warning. No request for ID, even. Deangelis was touchier than Horsfall had expected. She triggered an automatic sequence prepared weeks in advance. The *Dreieichen*'s individual components shrank to balls barely half a meter across and scattered in all directions. The breathing space around her collapsed, and she felt her body rearrange itself to accommodate the sudden constriction. Giddiness accompanied the abrupt shift in proprioception; she fought the urge to gag. Her other senses stayed on the approaching weapon—burning white and fierce like a high-tech sparkler. She held her breath.

The weapon split into nine different parts, one for each of the components. It clearly meant business.

Horsfall's mind raced like quicksilver as she launched a second wave of defensive measures. The magnetic field of Ah Kong snapped and whipped as thousands of tiny flares detonated at once, sowing electromagnetic confusion around the Cell. Through the mess of noise, she could barely make out the nine lances of the weapon continuing to diverge, targeting the Cell's components with unchecked ease.

She knew then that anything she had prepared would be easily countered by the Exarch. They were as good as dead.

"If you've got an ace up your sleeve," she told the ghost riding her mind, "now would be the time to produce it."

She felt the Cell twitch around her as it took a single, brief phrase and broadcast it in all directions at once, in every available medium.

Isaac, don't, said the voice.

That was all. The brevity of the statement startled Horsfall, who had expected something a little more persuasive. There was time for more. They had at least a hundred microseconds before the first of the weapon fragments would hit. How could two words possibly deter Deangelis from fulfilling his deadly duty? It would take much more than that to stop her, surely.

Yet it worked. With a flash bright enough to drown out the Catastrophe, the weapon fragments simultaneously detonated. The Cell rocked in the vacuum, but was unharmed.

"Jane?" came a voice out of the Dark, its tone disbelieving, accusatory, but with a hopeful edge that made it sound almost pathetic.

The voice in Palmer Horsfall's head didn't reply.

Silence.

Horsfall waited in the swirling electromagnetic storm left in the wake of the weapon and her decoys. The Cell remained cautiously dispersed, adding to the gas giant's already large collection of tiny moons.

On one of those moons, a navigation beacon began to blink.

That's our cue, said the voice in Horsfall's ear. *Take us in.*

Horsfall swallowed her misgivings and brought the *Dreieichen* in to dock.

Bedlam burned. Its former Exarch stood in the fire and was not consumed. Yearn though he might for dissolution, the nanoagents that had destroyed his habitat and its citizens—and now drifted like lethal snowflakes on the solar wind within two astronomical units of the system's primary—had as much effect on him as dust. He felt like the Old Testament's burning bush. The voice of God spoke through him, but he was spared.

It was all relative, he supposed. He had been brought back from the dead in order to help his creator maintain the lie that ROTH booby traps in Geodesica had been responsible for the Catastrophe. Why Races Other Than Human would have done such a thing, exactly, awaited adequate explanation, but the lie was likely to stick better than the awful truth. Within days of the destruction of Bedlam, the Archon had sent a new tangler to the system from Jamgotchian-McGrath. When it had arrived, six months later, it received a wave of data transmitted from Earth and built Isaac Deangelis new bodies, an observation station, and a raft of new sensors with which to study the Mizar Occlusion—all under cover of the pervasive haze of the deadly nanotech.

I belong here, Deangelis told himself. *No one else should be here but me.*

But he would rather be anywhere else in the universe than standing watch over the ruins of his home, colluding with the one who had destroyed it . . .

Isaac—

Now someone else had come. Not a survey vessel or a scientific scout. Plenty of those had grazed the system in the previous months, testing the nanotech hellfire and comparing it to that which had consumed Sublime eleven years earlier. He didn't turn those away, even though it meant enduring their closest scrutiny.

The Catastrophe would burn them if they came too close, and there was no evidence of foul play elsewhere in the system. They came, saw, and left when they realized there was nothing they could do. Bedlam was finished. *He* was finished.

It had been scant comfort to him that he wasn't the only one in his position. Jane Elderton, Exarch of Sublime, had been left behind as watchdog, too, jealously guarding her own entrance to the hyperspatial network the Archon called Geodesica. Since returning to Bedlam, he had been unwilling to talk to her, just as he had not spoken to any of the other Exarchs. Some of them had helped him during the crisis; some had actively betrayed him; Jane Elderton had stood as an example of their worst nightmare—homeless, hopeless, and utterly isolated.

—don't.

And now she was in Bedlam, somehow, riding a Palmer Cell that slipped through his sensors like an eel in muddy water.

He didn't need to ask what she wanted. He knew exactly what to do in response.

The Cell slipped in to dock on a tiny scrap of rock the former inhabitants of Bedlam hadn't bothered to name. It was a dark, heavily cratered place, completely overshadowed by its garish primary world but not so close as to be warmed by tidal flexure. Probes had found little more than ice and primordial rubble overlaid by a thick layer of organics, and the search for life and harvestable compounds had soon turned elsewhere.

Deangelis had christened the rock "Rudra," after an Indian god of storms. The installation he built there had never before been activated, not in all the long months he had waited for just such a moment. Deep in its heart, well hidden from the searchers and the curious, a pair of eyes opened for the first time.

Isaac Forge Deangelis, former Exarch of Bedlam and guardian of Geodesica, shifted his attention elsewhere.

Rudra-Deangelis's first steps took him gracefully across the chamber in which he had woken to a door set in the far wall. The air smelled of ancient stone and contained little oxygen. The latter was fine; he didn't need to breathe. What concerned him more was the shaft on the other side of the door. Something was coming down it from the surface of the moon, to him.

He took a full second to think things through. Imprinted memories reminded him of building the station, of placing a nascent part of himself deep inside it, then sealing it up like an Egyptian tomb, waiting not for the afterlife but for something much more substantial. That he had no further memories, and that he found himself inside the station with no sense of his higher self at all, suggested that he *was* that nascent self, brought into being to deal with an eventuality the rest of him had to avoid. His higher self was in regular contact with the Archon. Who knew what his creator could or could not read in the workings of his mind?

One of him would attempt what the whole could not. Small and alone he might feel, but he would be sufficient. He *had* to be. Bedlam wouldn't burn for nothing.

The door slid open, and a woman he didn't know stepped through it. She was compact and solid, with features that revealed nothing of her age. Her scalp and face were utterly hairless; her skin was so white it seemed translucent. Eyes the blue of Earth from space took him in with a single glance.

"You're Deangelis?" Her voice was gravelly and direct. "You look younger than I thought you would."

He didn't grace that with a reply. His appearance—that of a blond, somewhat sexless youth—was designed to avoid the traditional stereotypes of masculine power. Being taken seriously was something he earned, not expected.

"Where have you come from?" he asked. "Why are you here?"

"My name is Palmer Horsfall," the woman said. She jittered slightly in the low gee, as though unused to even that small amount of gravity. "I've come from Sublime."

Her identity fell into place, then. The observation station around the first system to fall was named after Deva Horsfall, a vacuum physicist from Alcor who had died in the conflagration. The woman before him was, presumably, her sister, the Palmer who had delivered her to her death.

She wasn't the person Deangelis had expected to see.

"Why?" he repeated.

"We want the same thing," she said. Horsfall took him in with a sidelong cast, as though wary to look him full in the face. She stayed studiously close to the open elevator shaft. "Revenge."

"Against?"

"The Archon and Sol."

"For what reason?"

"Do I really have to spell it out?"

He nodded. Better that she voiced it first than him, in case this was some elaborate trap.

For destroying Sublime and Bedlam, said a voice that didn't come from Horsfall's lips. *For taking in cold blood the lives of those we loved. For killing our homes.*

His surprise was mitigated in part by relief. He knew that voice. The mind of Jane Elderton inhabited the body of the Palmer before him, grinding it like a pilot of a single ship.

Some of the tension left him then. She wouldn't lie to him about this. She had come to help him fight.

"You are both welcome here," he said. "What shelter I have to offer you is yours."

"Good," said Horsfall, looking only marginally eased by his offer. "If the Archon finds us here, we're dead."

"As am I." He nodded, instructing the previously inert walls to extrude two chairs for his guests and him. The door to the elevator shaft slid soundlessly closed. "By having this conversation, we are automatically committed to the cause."

No matter where it leads us? asked the fragment of Jane Elderton.

Rudra-Deangelis nodded. "You're not here to discuss the whys and what-ifs. Let's concentrate solely on *how* and leave those who follow us to do the rest."

"I'm pleased we don't have to convince you," said Horsfall, seating herself economically on the chair nearest her. "I'll admit that I was less sure than Exarch Elderton."

"Jane understands," he said, "just as I now understand her a little better."

Horsfall's bright blue eyes stared at him, and he wondered if he detected his old friend peering through them. They had known each other on Earth after their creation by the Archon, in his first incarnation. They had trained with other Exarchs such as Lazarus Hails, Frederica Cazneaux, and Lan Cochrane for the Expansion that would reclaim humanity's First Wave colonies. They had been flung like seeds into the Arc Circuit, where they had taken root and prospered—before being cut down in their prime for no better reason than fear of a weed.

Horsfall didn't flinch from his gaze. Whether the steel he saw in them belonged to her or to Elderton, he was glad to see it.

They would fight the Archon and destroy it, or die trying. There was no possible alternative. That was precisely what he had been created for. He would not shirk from destiny.

"So where do we start?" asked Horsfall. "This might be a killer of an understatement, but it's a big job."

"Melilah Awad took the first step by broadcasting a message outlining the truth after Bedlam fell."

"She did?"

Deangelis nodded, appreciating for the first time just how long his visitors had been traveling, and remembering what the Archon had said about that message upon his resurrection on Earth: *We have modeled the propagation of the truth as one would a disease. We will do what we can to spread counter- and misinformation, just as we did with White-Elderton. But some will remain dubious. This doubt, Isaac, must not be allowed to spread.*

"We'll continue the work she started, exposing Geodesica for what it is and opening it up to the rest of the Exarchate."

"I have some thoughts on who to approach first, and how to coordinate the movement as it forms."

We can discuss them on the way. It would be best for us to move quickly. We are too close to the center of things here. One misstep and—

Horsfall mimed an explosion.

"Perhaps not." Deangelis faced the combined stare of his old friend and the Palmer body she inhabited. "You should know that Bedlam is different from Sublime in one important respect. There were survivors."

"Who?" Resentment flashed in Horsfall's eyes just for a moment, and was quickly suppressed. "How?"

"Three people escaped the Catastrophe by diving into the Occlusion itself. They had the capacity to survive the stresses of the entrance, thanks to the research I had performed before the end. I did my best to prevent pursuit, once we returned to the system, but I was unable to do much without making the Archon suspicious."

Who were they, Isaac?

"Palmer Eogan, Melilah Awad, and me. That is: the last surviving fragment of my original self. Their present status is unknown, but I prefer to believe they are still alive."

Why?

"Because if they are, they have to come out somewhere."

He was sure he didn't need to spell out the significance of that statement. A slight widening of Horsfall's eyes confirmed that he was right.

+2

Geodesica interior: plus 2 seconds

Melilah Awad screamed a mixture of despair and agony as the golden-fiery universe vanished from sight. A flash of painful blue swallowed her then spat her out into darkness. Then all was cold and vacuum sharp and bound up with a sensation of falling.

"Melilah? Are you all right?"

The voice barely penetrated her wail. She wanted nothing more than to drown herself in fear and bring an end to it all. She had lost everything—her home, her friends, the family she most cared about—and now she had lost herself. Her body had been tied into a knot and absorbed by the Cell Eogan had called *Cowell* in some perverse tribute to her ancestors. Only her mind remained, twisted up and twitching like one final, futile reflex.

"Melilah, snap out of it! We're through. We're alive. Look!"

She had no body that she could recognize anymore, but she felt something brush her skin—and attempt to soothe her. She pushed the advance away. "Don't touch me. Don't *ever* touch me again."

Dominic Eogan retreated. If he was stung by her words, she didn't care. He was the bearer of the thing that had killed her world. He had earned her anger.

Another voice intruded on her rage-fueled misery.

"We have to put aside our differences," said Deangelis. "The limit of my exploration lies ahead. Beyond that point, we'll be in unknown territory."

A thick, raw emotion underpinned his words. The realization

that someone other than her had reason to hurt—even if they, too, were partly responsible for what had happened—helped her see beyond herself, to finally notice the place they had entered.

The Cell component, radically reduced in size by the voracious appetite of the Catastrophe nanotech, was accelerating headlong down a tubular tunnel. Reflective khaki-gray walls rushed by in a blur. Ahead and behind, a white point of light delineated where the parallel walls met at an illusion of infinity. The space around them was almost pure vacuum, with only the occasional molecular hit registering on the Cell's forward vanes. Each impact released enough energy to shake the Cell slightly, demonstrating just how fast they were traveling.

The light ahead suddenly ballooned before her. The Cell decelerated hard, then swung in a direction she couldn't quite comprehend—neither up nor down, left nor right, but somewhere completely different. Sparks trailed in its wake as it accelerated again, leaving the bright light of the junction far behind.

"Where are we going?" she asked, her voice sounding hollow to her own ears. "Why are we moving so fast? If we hit the walls at this speed we'll be killed!"

"We're perfectly safe," Deangelis reassured her. "The walls of Geodesica aren't composed of matter. They're space-time loops. Push yourself into a tunnel, aligned so the loop twists clockwise around you, and you'll accelerate instead of continuing at a constant velocity. The twist reverses at the midway point, pointing anticlockwise. The opposite inertia gradient slows you down at the far end so you don't slam headlong into the junctions."

"Okay—but what about that turn we took back there? Explain that!"

"Although the interior of Geodesica contains just three dimensions of space, individual tunnels can move in two extra dimensions. The junctions are points of discontinuity, where dimensions can swap. We don't have words for some of the turns available at the junctions. In a one-dimensional structure, all you need is left and right to say which way you're traveling. Extending this terminology to more dimensions gives us left-2 and right-2 in two dimensions, which we might call up and down; left-3 and right-3 are forward and back. What Geodesica gives us access to is left-4 and right-4, and left-5 and right-5, which we've never experienced before. Back there, we took a thirty-degree turn to left-5. Does that make sense?"

"It'll have to, I guess."

"Melilah, it's important you understand," he said. "Otherwise we're going to get lost very quickly!"

Deangelis was almost babbling. Melilah didn't try to stop him, assuming it was helping him deal with what had happened.

"So you step into a tunnel, kick off, and you fly magically to the end. Is that it?"

"Yes—although there's nothing magical about the process at all. The flexures seem to be a critical function of the tunnels: you couldn't have one without the other, like the cables holding up a suspension bridge. Traveling along the tunnels takes energy, which we have to provide."

"And we're using a lot of it," said Eogan as the bright light of another junction ballooned before them. "The Cell isn't magical either. At some point we're going to need something more substantial than vacuum to keep us going."

It amazed her that the Cell component was moving at all, considering how terribly battered it had been by the nanotech and its passage through the Occlusion's throat. Ten percent of its original mass remained, organized in a smooth, vaguely aerodynamic shape reminiscent of a Brazil nut barely one hundred and fifty kilograms heavy—including its passengers. Riddled with the complex micro- and nanomachines that provided flight systems and life support, it staggered on like a full-sized Cell in miniature. It could, theoretically, continue doing so with even more of its mass removed, but at some point it would reach a critical threshold beyond which it could no longer support the lives of its passengers.

She didn't want to know precisely how much of her own mass had been seconded to shore up its systems. Although she remained linked to its telemetry, she avoided looking at anything that would make her feel worse than she already did. Trying to move her arms and legs prompted a feeling of being trapped that made her want to start screaming again.

They braked hard at another junction and rocketed off along another corridor. Space warped and flexed around her. In the middle of a tunnel, as the inertia gradient tugged them along, either exit seemed to retreat to infinity. Only as they came close to the next junction did the ends snap back together, making her senses shake like a ruler flicked on a desk.

"Where are we going?" she asked.

"I'm taking corners at random," said Eogan.

"Is that wise?"

"Better than standing still to argue while the Archon comes marching in after us."

"The Archon is dead. Killing it started the Catastrophe."

"Are you sure? We might only have killed part of it. The rest could be after us right now."

She couldn't argue with that. "I still don't think we should go too far. You said yourself that we don't want to get lost."

"True," said Deangelis. "But I'm afraid there might not be much we can do to avoid that."

"Meaning?" His surety was slipping, her alarm returning.

"I've sent hundreds of drones in here, and only a handful returned. Either something's picking them off or their guidance AIs can't cope with the topology."

"Remember Cobiac and Bray," added Eogan, referring to the two Palmers he had lost from his crew. "They went in just a few meters and never came back out."

Her head felt as though it was being squeezed in a vise. "This is too much." Numbness threatened to envelop her, and she fought it with what strength she possessed. She couldn't give up now.

They took another corner. Warped space gripped them and hurled them onward. Ahead was darkness, not another glowing speck of light.

"What—?" she started to ask.

"I'm not sure," Deangelis cut in. "A corridor of infinite length? A dead end?"

"Perhaps it's an exit," Eogan suggested.

An injection of hope revived her. "A way out, you think?"

"We won't know until we get there."

The darkness ahead of them was complete, giving her nothing. What if Deangelis was right and they were caught in an endless tunnel, accelerating forever with no destination in sight? That would be an ignominious end for the three survivors of the Bedlam Catastrophe.

Without warning, the looped space forming the walls of the tunnel switched direction. They began to decelerate as normal, although the way ahead was still black.

"Did you ever work out how to open the exits from the inside?" Melilah asked Deangelis.

"Yes. The procedure is relatively simple."

"I don't want to be a wet blanket," said Eogan, "but leaving isn't an option we currently have on the table."

"Why not?"

"The Cell isn't up to another trip like the last one. We'd be flayed back to nothing."

"You are kidding, right?"

"I'm afraid not. Sorry."

The surge of hope faded as the end of the tunnel came into view. It wasn't anything remarkable, just a tapering truncation that vanished to a point of discontinuity. It prickled the *Cowell*'s senses, defying definition.

Deangelis confirmed it. On the far side of that point was a throat similar to the one they had followed from Bedlam. While not as hellish as the nanotech storm that had destroyed her home, it was still difficult to navigate. She believed Eogan when he said they wouldn't make it through. The coffin containing them was paper thin. It would erode to nothing at the slightest provocation.

A heavy sense of futility weighed her down. She wanted to sink to the bottom of the tunnel and die. What was the point of going on if there was no way out? If all they were going to do was get lost? If there was no chance of coming home at the end of it?

Don't do this, she told herself. *Don't give up. It's not like you. You've never given up before.*

But she had never been through anything like this before, either. She'd never had cause to give up.

Take it apart. You can't deal with everything all at once. That's your real problem. Break it down into small pieces and tackle them one by one. The ones you can't handle now, put aside for later. Otherwise you'll be overwhelmed.

She could see the sense in that. Even in the grip of black depression, she knew that being seduced by apathy was tantamount to letting the Archon win. She had to stay alive, and sane. She had to *fight*.

There was nothing she could do for Bedlam. She would have to deal with her grief at some point, but for now it was useless. She could, however, use her anger to fuel her determination. It could keep her going when everything else told her to stop.

Similarly, her fear of biomodifications was only getting in the way. She simply had to accept that she was part of the Cell and endure it for the time being. Fighting the necessary—horrible though it was—would only make everything harder.

Her feelings for Eogan and Deangelis were more difficult to parcel up and ignore. Just prior to Bedlam's end it seemed that Deangelis might have been genuinely willing to cooperate, but she couldn't dismiss her warning instincts when they spoke to her of his motives. The same went for Eogan. Yes, it had seemed for a moment that they might be able to put their painful past behind them, but now they were further apart than ever. All she could do was to try to separate her emotional responses and stick solely to those reason told her were correct.

Melilah felt whole parts of her brain metaphorically shutting down. A necessary coldness crept through her, separating her from the suffocating heat of despair.

"It looks to me like we don't have any choice," she said. "We have to go back to the last junction. Do you two agree?"

Deangelis's assent was immediate. Eogan supplied a nonverbal signal that was the Palmer equivalent of a nod.

"Let's do it, then."

She kept her eyes firmly forward as the *Cowell* came about and accelerated back the way they had come.

In order to reach the exit, the *Cowell* had taken a turn forty degrees to left-5, ninety-five to right-3, and one hundred twenty to right-2. In Palmer Eogan's mind, he abbreviated the data to a simple string of alphanumeric codes:

040L5 095R3 120R2

That didn't mean, however, that he truly understood the directions he and the Cell were following. His mind was specifically adapted to deal with navigation in three dimensions, expanding it from the Natural comprehension of just two. The notion of a turn through the fourth dimension was not beyond his theoretical comprehension, but he didn't instinctively get it. The addition of a fifth only compounded a problem hammered home with each wrenching, dislocating turn.

Eogan believed Deangelis completely when he said they were likely to get lost. There didn't seem to be any other alternative. He just didn't want to be lost *and* stranded, if they could avoid it. The Cell's nanomachines were only capable of running for so long without physical input. That input could come from the Cell itself—breaking down larger structures or cargo in order to release energy and raw materials—or it could come from outside. Eogan didn't have a problem with cannibalization per se, but it, too, could only go so far. Before long, vital macrosystems such as telemetry and neural networks would begin to fail—the most important of them being those belonging to the three people aboard. In his grimmest scenario, they were stripped back to three frozen brains squashed into a tin can and cast adrift in the endless warren of Geodesica.

Melilah's patience wouldn't last that long. He didn't dare think what would happen if he pushed her too far.

010L4 170L3 010L2

Another turn, another impossible trajectory. Eogan couldn't afford to let his ignorance bother him. His job was simply to keep the ship flying; Deangelis would have to be the navigator, if anyone could be. Only the expanded brain of an Exarch stood a chance in such an impossible place.

"The manifold is exceedingly complex," Deangelis said. "I can't tell which of the prime geometries it's following, and until I do—"

"At the very least," said Melilah, "shouldn't we make sure that we can get back to Bedlam if we have to? We can backtrack through the turns we've taken. You've been recording them, haven't you, Eogan?"

He confirmed that he had as they took another.

075L5 070L4 080L2

"We won't need a ball of wool to trail behind us, at least," he added.

It was an unfortunate metaphor, bringing images of the Minotaur immediately to mind, and once voiced there was no taking it back. The question was: did the Minotaur originate in the Geodesica labyrinth or would the Archon send it in after them?

At the next junction, he brought the Cell to a complete halt. They floated in free fall at the center of a sphere of crystalline blue light, surrounded by vacuum and the cracking discharges of complex energy fields. The junction appeared to be several meters across to his eyes, but different instruments reported different figures, depending on which direction they pointed. Its walls were made of nothing more substantial than twisted space—indeed the only massive objects the Cell had encountered thus far were occasional molecules of gas, drifting along the tunnels. But as he couldn't assimilate the data in any other coherent way, Eogan accepted the illusion of spherical walls for the sake of his sanity.

Dotted around the surface of the sphere were several circular exits, each one corresponding to a different tunnel, each one identical in size. This junction had six; previous ones had contained anything from two to eleven. They were scattered apparently at random, like black eyes on an alien face, in groups of three, two, and one. There were no signposts, no warnings, no "Welcome to Geodesica" notices. There was no way, apart from geometry, to tell the entrances apart.

He picked one at random and nudged the Cell into it. Darkness enfolded them; an inertia potential he couldn't measure but could feel gripping them scooped them up and whizzed them off to the next junction.

035R5 060L4 105R2

"All the tunnels are the same length," he said. "Inasmuch as I can tell."

"I don't think we *can* tell," said Deangelis. "We take the same amount of time to travel along them, and the peak deformation seems about the same each time—but what does that really mean?"

"You tell us," growled Melilah.

"I can't. Believe me. This is like nothing the Exarchate has ever encountered before. We're very much in the same boat, you and I."

Melilah's laugh was low and bitter. "First Minos. Next you'll be quoting Jerome K. Jerome. Why not the Owl and the Pussycat as well? 'Though the sky be dark, and the voyage be long, yet we never can think we were rash or wrong—'" She cut herself off. "I'm sorry. It just seems farcical to me that we've got in here, where everyone's been trying to get for weeks, and now we don't know what to do about it. If we stand still we'll be caught; the same if we go back. But we can't move on without getting lost, and we can't leave. Have I forgotten something?"

"No," said Eogan, wishing there was anything he could do about the tight confines of the Cell and the way it affected her. Their bodies were stunted, twisted remnants, coiled around each other like triplets in an artificial womb. The full impact of that truth was buffered from Melilah's consciousness, but she wasn't an idiot. She would know. If he had the capacity to provide a virtual environment they could walk around in, he would give it to her gladly. As it was, it was all he could do to keep them functioning and sane.

The enforced intimacy granted him an unsettling insight into her efforts to remain calm. He felt her metaphorically draw a breath, hold it for a moment, then let it go.

"Of the four options," she said, "I vote for moving on as we are now. I'd rather be lost than caught or dead."

"I agree."

"Deangelis?"

The former Exarch, or part thereof, took a moment to reply. "My judgment is unreliable. Do as you wish. I won't stop you."

"Having second thoughts?" she asked, her tone sharp.

"I don't want to think at all."

Deangelis said nothing else. Eogan considered forcing the issue, but decided to let it go. They didn't have the resources to split up.

"Let's keep moving, then," he said. "You never know what we might find."

A grunt of assent was the only response from Melilah as they sped along corridors of twisted space-time.

"Having second thoughts?"

The mind of Earth-Deangelis shuddered all over.

I'm no longer capable of thought, he wanted to tell Melilah. *I am incomplete, truncated, crippled. I'm no longer who I was. I am not.*

Words could not convey, however, the utter disconnection he felt as the grim truth of his isolation finally hit home. His higher self had been destroyed with Bedlam. He would be forever alone.

"I don't want to think at all," he said. The more he *tried* to think, the more he confronted the ghastly stump where the rest of him had been.

Instead, he concentrated solely on the geometry of the space around him. Geodesica's complex topography was a godsend in that respect. His higher self could have lost himself for weeks in the data accrued so far, building models of the 5-D manifold and the 6-D space it surrounded. Even with the severely limited capacity available to him, he could see patterns forming, subtle cadences and rhythms that might expand out into coherent geometries as new data flooded in. He didn't dare hope, yet, that he had mastered the artifact's mysteries, but he could see how it might be possible, one day. Had his higher self been free to dive into the tunnels, using his multitudinous nature to its best advantage, he could imagine a map slowly forming, branching, and spreading like nerve fibers through a human body, crossing and recrossing in a vastly tangled network that might conceivably span the entire galaxy.

He could imagine it. He could dream of what might have been. But at the end of the dream, when he woke to cold reality, he remained an isolated fragment scrabbling to connect a few scattered pieces of a jigsaw whose final shape he couldn't begin to comprehend.

What if they never escaped?

As hard as he tried to ignore the question, it wouldn't go away.

What if he was all that remained of *him*?

The thought was almost too much to bear. He had spanned a whole system, managed whole worlds, held the lives of thousands in his hands. And now he was just one man—less than that, really, given his present predicament. Melilah was right: it was ridiculous . . .

Eogan took them through several intersections, following no particular plan that Deangelis could discern. They encountered one other cul-de-sac, but didn't follow it to its end. The thought that freedom could be just moments away but for the limitations of the Cell was galling. Despite the artifact's immense volume, he was beginning to feel claustrophobic. One mind when he had once been many, how could he hope to remain sane?

Enough, he told himself. He couldn't just give in. He owed it to himself—if not Melilah and Eogan—to persist. He didn't doubt that they would recycle his body mass if he showed signs of becoming a dead weight, so he had to earn his right to survive. Despite everything, he wasn't quite ready to roll over and play dead.

There was one thing he could say with some degree of certainty, so far: Geodesica was, as Bedlam had been, a multiply connected network. Ten to fifteen percent of the junctions qualified as "nodes," major intersections that linked to many other junctions, possibly far across the network as a whole. By sticking to nodes wherever possible, they maximized their chances of confounding pursuit, and of putting the maximum distance between them and the Bedlam entrance. Assuming, of course, that they didn't inadvertently double-track over their own path, or accidentally run into one of their pursuers . . .

"I'm picking up something odd," said Eogan as they rocketed along their latest corridor.

Deangelis checked the dimensions of the tunnel, his enhanced synapses moving much more rapidly than those of his companions, and found them to be normal.

"That's the understatement of the millennium," Melilah said with a slight return to her usual spirit. "Odd how?"

"A lidar echo from up ahead. Normally the walls absorb our pulses, but now I'm getting something back. Can't tell what it is, but it's definitely solid."

"How big?"

"Smaller than us. That's about all I can tell at this stage."

"Is there any way to slow us down?"

"I'm already doing my best to decelerate, but we're like an ant trying to stop a rubber band from stretching. We have to ride it out before we can jump off."

Deangelis could feel Melilah thinking in long, inevitable steps. "We never stopped to wonder what we'd do if we met something coming at us along the same corridor. Is there no way to avoid a collision?"

"I don't know," said Eogan, "but this thing isn't moving. It's just sitting at the next junction, waiting for us."

"Alive or dead?"

"I'm not getting anything but the echoes. If it's alive, it's not broadcasting."

Deangelis studied the data as they hit turnaround and began to decelerate. The lidar image was poorly defined, thanks to the Cell's limited resources. The object had a triangular cross section, indicating a possible pyramidal shape with curved corners. It rotated roughly once a second. He pictured a bucket-sized tetrahedron, tumbling in such a way that it could scan all the tunnel entrances arrayed before it.

A watchdog—or a mine?

He didn't need to tell Eogan to be careful. The Palmer brought them to a halt meters short of the tunnel exit and coasted them gently closer. The Cell rearranged its mass to present an armored foresection, from behind which subtle sensors peered.

"It's a machine," Eogan pronounced, confirming what Deangelis had already guessed. New data revealed it to be a structure of slender rods with a solid core. There were no obvious drive or defense mechanisms.

"I recognize the design," said Deangelis. "It's one of ours."

"When you say 'ours' . . . ?" Melilah prompted.

"I mean the Exarchate's. It's a survey drone, an old one. There could be a breeder in here somewhere, too. Jane Elderton might have sent one in from Sublime and let it roam."

"Could you read its data?" she asked.

"I don't see why not."

"Then—"

Before she could finish, the drone came to life. Tiny thrusters killed its tumble. Myriad minuscule sensors focused on them as they slowly approached through the tunnel. Eogan froze automatically.

"Don't let it—" Deangelis's warning came too late. An intense pulse of radio waves erupted from the drone's casing. "Stop it! It's calling for others!"

Eogan sent the Cell lunging forward, extruding sharp-tipped manipulators as he came. Sparks flew as the claws gripped the fragile casing and sent a powerful electrical current through it. The radio squawk died. Thrusters fired again as the drone fought to free itself.

Then they were moving. The Cell accelerated back up the tunnel they had left—the only one they were certain contained no more of the drones. The manipulators continued to snip until all the drone could do was wriggle. Then Eogan methodically cut its fuel lines and control circuits. By the time they had taken the next corner, in another random direction, it was little more than a small, autonomous brain in a dead body.

"Don't kill it," said Deangelis. "If we can work out how it got here, we might be able to find our way to Sublime."

"What good will that do?" asked Melilah.

"The Archon might not be expecting us there. Jane Elderton can help us get through the throat. She's in the same boat I am. I'm sure she'd help us."

"I'm not. She's an Exarch, and she never offered help before."

"Let's worry about that later," said Eogan. "All I care about is that we've found a way to build up our mass. One drone will lead us to another, and another. Even if we don't go as far as Sublime, we've found a way to get *somewhere*."

The frame of the drone was already under attack. The Cell's manipulators snipped it into smaller fragments, which the Cell absorbed. Their combined mass increased slightly.

Deangelis agreed that looking too far ahead was problematic. He told himself to be relieved, for now, that the next junction was clear, as was the next. The drone was obviously just an outlier, not the first of a swarm about to descend upon them.

But the echo of the radio burst was still loud in his mind. If something had heard it, there might be worse things than drones on the way.

When you say 'ours' . . .

He felt Melilah's attention on him as they hurried away. Did she wonder if he was still working for the Exarchate, even though he had so clearly abandoned his duty after the Archon betrayed his trust? If so, he couldn't blame her. He was still unsure exactly where his fragmented loyalties lay.

Jane Elderton would help them. He was sure of it.

Earth-Deangelis thrust that thought to one side as Eogan's manipulators cut into the drone's processing core and gave him access to its memories.

+3

Bedlam: 2439 CE

The tiny moon contained much more than Horsfall had expected. Beneath many kilometers of ice and rock, autonomous machines had been busy for months, working patiently and quietly to manufacture everything they would need to escape the Archon. Deangelis had never intended to mount an attack from such an insignificant base. That would be entirely too premature.

Two dozen slender rail-guns pointed like cactus spines from the core of the moon to the surface, aimed at random points in the sky. When activated, they would fire a series of projectiles designed to break through the crust, sending a shower of rubble into orbit around Ah Kong. From a distance, it would look like Rudra had suddenly sprouted twenty-four active volcanoes, all of them erupting at once.

Once the crust was clear, the rail-guns would switch to different munitions, some not dissimilar to the sort Horsfall had fired to distract the weapon Deangelis had sent after her upon her arrival in the system. They would detonate upon reaching vacuum, laying down a dense electromagnetic cover designed to confuse distant observers. Additionally, massive EMP generators deep in the moon's core would release their pent-up charge in one instant, ringing Ah Kong's magnetosphere like a bell.

Under cover of the resulting chaos, the *Dreieichen* and its charges would slip away. When they were clear of the base, a series of nuclear charges would break up what remained of the moon, sending large fragments tumbling out of its ancient orbit.

Some of the fragments would collide with other moons; some would spin away into space. Approximately half would spiral into the gas giant, taking with them every trace of the machines that had wrought its destruction.

Horsfall studied the simulations with great thoroughness before deciding on the best route out of the system. There was no way to know exactly how Rudra would fragment, nor what trajectories the individual pieces would follow.

"It's all a bit extreme, don't you think?"

Getting into Bedlam unnoticed was always just half the problem, whispered the voice in her mind. *To be an effective force for change, we have to get out again.*

"I know *that*. But to destroy a whole moon . . ."

"Bedlam was bigger," said Deangelis with finality. "And I'm thinking ahead. The fragments that fall into Ah Kong are seeded with sleeper tech designed to survive deep in the atmosphere. When they reach the solid core, they'll start building. By the time we come back here, we'll have a much bigger diversion ready to blow."

A cold shiver ran down Horsfall's arms. To hear the Exarch's casual talk of blowing up planets and moons as a *diversion* was a forceful reminder that humanity had leapt into an entirely new league. This was war as it had never been fought before—and she was on the front line.

"Is it going to be enough?" she asked. "Rudra, I mean. We can't black out the entire system. Once we're out of the debris storm and under power, we'll stand out like a blowtorch in a closet."

"Seeing us is one thing," said Deangelis. "Catching us is another. The modifications I've made to your drive units should get us moving quickly enough to outrun pursuit. All we have to do is reach the next system intact, and we'll be okay."

"Which system is that, exactly? We haven't talked about that yet."

Isaac and I have, said her inner voice. *Lazarus Hails helped during the fall of Bedlam. We will go, therefore, to Altitude.*

Horsfall swallowed her annoyance at not having been consulted—and at the thought that the former Exarchs had been talking behind her back. She didn't want to be excluded, not when her life was on the line, too. But she knew they possessed capabilities far beyond hers. She didn't expect them to stoop to her level just to make her feel included.

And besides, she trusted them. She had to. She had no other way of getting what she wanted. The pre-Exarchate system names tripping off their tongues was enough to convince her that they had turned on their former peers and master.

"If Hails helped you before," she said to Deangelis, "what makes you think he's still in power?"

"The Archon didn't have enough evidence to move against him. And he hasn't stirred since. All I hear along the tanglers is the usual traffic. He's laying low, waiting to see what happens next."

"He might not thank us for leading pursuit right to his doorstep."

"True. He might not." Deangelis seemed unconcerned by that possibility. "But I'll worry about that later."

Horsfall went back to watching him as he finalized preparations. Unlike a Palmer, who physically linked with systems requiring supervision, he exercised an almost spooky mental control over Rudra's weapons. The shelter at the bottom of the elevator shaft had the capacity to display images and telemetry—which they did regularly, for her benefit—but she knew that neither of the Exarchs required such clumsy input. Sometimes Deangelis froze in his place, a pale-skinned statue of a teenage boy, staring into space. She sensed vast energies shifting around him, mounting in potential.

A storm was building—a storm of ghosts. Unlike Jane Elderton—the mournful, scarred haunting in her mind—Isaac Deangelis took center stage as vengeful spirit, willing to go to any length to attain retribution, with all the dead of Bedlam and Sublime arrayed in ranks behind him.

Palmer Horsfall readied her Cell with grim determination, wondering where Deva Horsfall fit into the strange cast. Was she a shade lurking at the back, watching with a silent, anticipatory smile?

She felt a pang of grief for her dead sister. Eleven years on, the loss still felt as keen as a dagger blow to the heart. Neither patience nor time had soothed its sting. If revenge-soaked immolation failed to do the trick, she didn't know what would.

When everything was ready, Rudra-Deangelis took a moment to collect his thoughts. From the minutiae of his preparations, he cast his attention out into the system, surveying its disposition. The

Catastrophe looked like a vast golden nebula, frozen in time. It neither billowed outward nor collapsed inward, although currents did shift on its diaphanous surface—strange bulges that moved in waves from pole to pole, millions of kilometers long. It looked poised, like a lion waiting its chance.

That was an illusion, he knew. A secondary function of the Catastrophe nanotech was to keep what went on inside it hidden from the outside. Although diffuse, it was more than sufficient to filter out anything but the light of the primary before it reached the eyes of the curious. There could be dozens of observatories inside its glowing atmosphere, along with thousands of versions of *him,* but he would never see them. Not yet, anyway.

"It's time to leave," he said, as much to himself as his new allies. There was no reason to delay. He would return one day to claim his home, or he would never return at all. Being sentimental only clouded the issue.

The moment he and Horsfall were inside her Cell, he buried his qualms under a shower of violence.

Rail-guns fired. Seismic waves shook the surrounding rock. Horsfall shored up the *Cowell*'s defenses as ancient shear planes twisted and flexed. A low groan resonated through the Cell like a giant's distress. The booming of the nearest rail-gun grew suddenly louder, then faded again. Deangelis took one quick look at the rising clouds of debris before the electromagnetic storm began.

There would be no missing or misinterpreting the sudden awakening of the tiny moon. Not since the last days of the Bedlam habitat had such light dawned on the system. This was just as much a declaration of aggression as Frederica Cazneaux's Reaper or Lazarus Hails's combat drones. That they were running away didn't mean that their intentions were any less seditious. Coming back with a bigger army was very much their intention.

The EMP mines flashed. Whole chunks of the spectrum vanished into static.

"Now," he told Horsfall, and the Cell moved beneath them. Shaped charges widened existing fissures; drive units shoved the components forward against the variable resistance of stone and plasma. Moments before the resounding booms of nuclear detonations rent the moon asunder, they entered the expanding bubble of liberated gases.

Horsfall had camouflaged the Cell before departure, accreting a small amount of stone around the components' field-effect shells. Where once had been a string of silvery spheres now tumbled a haphazard agglomeration of irregularly shaped boulders, thrown and jostled by the forces around them. Deangelis rode out the turbulence in the perfect safety of the Cell, accepting its protective embrace and trusting in Horsfall/Elderton's ability to pilot them to safety. His role in their escape was over, in theory.

The minuscule moon blew apart like a marble hit by a bullet. The light of its destruction would take time to reach the inner system, hidden within the boundaries of Catastrophe. They had assumed that this would give them a period of grace before they fired up the drive and made a run for it.

An answering blossoming of light from a quite different quarter of the sky soon proved that assumption wrong.

Singularity mines, said Elderton, reading the data as it poured through her host's nervous system. A dozen frighteningly blue-shifted points of light were converging on Rudra's corpse from three of Ah Kong's major moons.

"The Archon!" gasped Horsfall.

"No," Deangelis corrected her. "Me. The *rest* of me."

"I thought he'd let us go."

"Once, maybe, he could get away with it. Not twice. Not without making the Archon suspicious."

He was waiting for us to make a move, said Elderton. *He was ready for us.*

Horsfall looked resentful, as though Rudra-Deangelis was himself to blame. "So what do you suggest we do?" she asked him.

"Change our plans, of course. We can't use VOID or reactionless drives while the mines are in range. But they won't pick us up if we lie low. Eventually someone will conclude that this has all been a distraction and that we're making our real move elsewhere."

The mines swooped into the debris field, deflecting boulders and leaving dirty smoke rings in their wake. Their physical size was small enough that direct collisions were unlikely. One passed near enough to a Cell component that tidal effects gripped it and swung it up out of the plane of the ecliptic, moving at a hefty pace.

Sacrifice it, Elderton told her host. *It might even prove useful as a distraction.*

"Signal it in two minutes," said Deangelis, in full agreement. "If the mines haven't given up by then, that'll give them something to follow."

Seconds ticked by. The mines came back for another pass,

and another. No one said anything as the remains of the moon expanded like a grisly flower, growing more misshapen and asymmetrical by the moment. The light of Ah Kong painted the concealed Cell a grisly orange, as though the tiny world was burning.

The mines came back for a fourth pass.

"Time's up," said Horsfall.

The receding Cell component flashed into life, warming up its drives and pushing for the edge of the system. Instantly, half of the drones accelerated after it, their Hawking halos glowing a brilliant green. They wouldn't catch it, but they didn't need to. They just needed to get close enough to hurt it when they blew.

The other six maintained their search of the ruins.

"Now what?" asked Horsfall.

"We wait," he said.

"For what?"

"To see whether I was the only contingency plan my original prepared."

"That's it?"

"I know my own limitations," he said, "and *he* knows them, too. There's no way we can get out of this alive, I'm sure he's aware of the fact."

Again, Horsfall looked at him as though he was personally to blame for the situation. Which, he supposed, in a twisted kind of way, he was.

It took just fifteen minutes for the light of Rudra's demise to reach the observation deck deep in the belly of the Catastrophe. By then, it was all over.

Deangelis felt the attention of the Archon firmly upon him as a second small moon exploded, setting the night face of Ah Kong briefly alight.

"Should I be concerned, Isaac?"

He answered truthfully: "We're not under attack." *Not yet.* "Nothing can harm us in here."

"Still, I'd like your full assessment of what's taking place out there."

"I'm not entirely sure. It could be a distraction of some kind."

Another moon cracked open. Fireworks on a cosmic scale brightened the skies of Lut-Deangelis.

"Distracting us from what, exactly?"

"Let me check something." He swung his attention from the

gas giant to the endless field of stars around them. Mental crosshairs focused on one feature in particular, a spiral galaxy called M97. Or Bode's Nebula.

"We didn't find it after the Catastrophe," he murmured. "But it had to be here *somewhere*."

"What, Isaac?"

"The tangler dispatched by Lazarus Hails—the one responsible for both the destruction of the first Occlusion observatory and the message Melilah Awad sent. I always thought it was still around." Sensors more used to peering into the heart of the Occlusion searched the spectra of the distant galaxy. "If it's become active again, perhaps triggered by the Cell we saw earlier, it could be repeating the tactic he tried earlier."

Data flowed through him. Among several spectral emission graphs, a telltale spike stood out.

"There it is," he said. "The tangler's leaving the same way it came in."

"You'd best put a stop to it," said the Archon. "Just in case."

"My thoughts exactly." The singularity mines sweeping the remains of the shattered moons immediately changed course and accelerated after the fleeing tangler. Three remained behind to deal with the rogue Cell component they had flushed out of the first moon. It popped with a flash of light, overwhelmed by radiation, as the three mines self-destructed in range.

"Will they be sufficient?" asked the Archon, continuing its interrogation.

Deangelis weighed up the odds: nine singularity mines, accelerating at rates no massive body could match, against the tangler's significant lead.

"They'll overwhelm it within a light-year," he said. "Altitude is eight times that distance away. Hails doesn't stand a chance."

"Of what, Isaac?" The Archon's voice expressed mild curiosity. "What do you think he seeks to prove at this late stage?"

"I don't know. Perhaps he's trying to get rid of the only piece of hard evidence we have against him."

"He could have just left it hidden, or self-destructed it months ago."

"Perhaps it's been dormant all this time, and only stirred at a signal we didn't detect. Or perhaps it's taken this long to put the distraction in place, so it could attempt to get away clean."

"Perhaps. Or perhaps it, too, is a distraction, and something else is going on we've failed to detect."

Again, Deangelis answered with the perfect truth: "I've found no evidence to suggest that."

"Indeed." Deangelis could interpret nothing meaningful from the Archon's tone. Did it mistrust him? Was it toying with him?

"Should I be concerned, Isaac?" it asked again after a long silence.

"Certainly not," he replied. "I'll have that tangler destroyed before it's a quarter of the way to Altitude. And it's not as if anyone can hurt us in here, anyway. I'd like to see Lazarus try."

The Archon didn't respond. They watched the stretching, glowing lines of the singularity mines as they streaked after their doomed prey, while the death-blooms of the ruined moons slowly blossomed in their wake.

"I've dispatched the last of the SAD replicators," Deangelis said in an attempt to change the topic. "They're fully autonomous, and equipped with chemical and thermal sniffers designed to track down the fugitives."

"Good work, Isaac. I'm pleased."

"I still don't see, though, what you hope to achieve. It's been almost a year. Melilah and the others could be on the other side of the galaxy by now."

"If they are, then they're no longer a problem."

"Were they ever really that much of a problem? Is it absolutely necessary for them to die?"

"You know the answer to that question as well as I do." The Archon chuckled without humor. "Isaac, your motives are completely transparent to me. Geodesica makes her dangerous. Nothing you can say will change that diagnosis. Please accept that her fate is sealed and allow yourself to move on to more important matters."

Deangelis metaphorically bowed his head in submission. Part of him would always wonder where Melilah was and what she was doing. What had she seen since her disappearance into Geodesica? Was she already dead and he worrying about an issue that was entirely moot? None of the replicators sent into Geodesica had reported finding her body, but that meant nothing. Until he received word, he would always wonder.

No more moons of Ah Kong exploded that day. The debris fields expanded according to the laws of motion, gravitation, and chaos. A large amount of rubble fell into the gas giant's fast-moving atmosphere, scarring it for weeks. Some adopted orbits around the planet's equator, shepherded into arcs by the subtle gravitational effects of the surviving moons; centuries from now, Deangelis thought, they might become rings like those around distant Saturn.

The remainder of the rubble—a remarkable but inevitable minority—sped from the system, granted escape trajectories by slingshotting around Ah Kong and flying out of its gravity well. Deangelis routinely watched them all, looking for the slightest deviation from their expected trajectories. Not one of them showed any sign of being more than they appeared to be. When the last slipped beyond his ability to detect something so small, moving so fast, he calculated that it would take seventy-five thousand years for it to reach the next star in that direction.

Godspeed, Deangelis whispered to himself, then promptly put all thought of *contingencies* out of his mind.

+4

Geodesica interior: plus 6 hours

Palmer Eogan felt as though he was staring at an optical illusion. Looked at one way, the data Deangelis had recovered from the Sublime drone made perfect sense. Looked at another, however, it gave him vertigo.

According to its navigation records, the drone had passed through one thousand, one hundred and nineteen intersections since leaving the entrance at Sublime. Every angle, every junction, and every tunnel had been recorded for posterity in hard storage, so following its route back to the entrance would not be difficult. The *Cowell,* thanks to the small meal the drone's peripheries had granted it, was ready to begin the journey at a moment's notice.

There were two problems.

It soon became apparent that the navigational records didn't match the intersections surrounding the drone's resting place. The first junction should have contained a tunnel leading 045R5 125L3 005L2, but such did not exist. The closest match was 050R5 125L3 010L2.

"So Geodesica shifted slightly," said Melilah. "It's a big structure, like Bedlam. Things must move around a little. The drone could have been sitting there for years, after all."

That explanation would have made sense but for one other small fact: according to the drone's memory, it had been dormant for less than a month.

"The log is unambiguous on this," insisted Deangelis. "It left the Sublime entrance May 16, 2434, and followed a preprogrammed route out to a certain point, beyond which it was allowed to roam freely until its power ran down. When it failed to return to the entrance or encounter any other known navigational marker, it entered a state of hibernation, dormant but ready to sound the alarm if it saw something. Around two weeks ago, another drone stumbled across it. It exchanged handshakes and data then switched back to stand by. It's been inactive ever since—one month according to its clock, four years by ours."

"Could its clock be faulty?" Melilah asked. "That would be the simplest solution."

"I've checked," Deangelis said. "It's working fine—and the condition of its battery is consistent with a recent departure date. I'm inclined to believe it."

"We recorded time warps in here before, to match the spatial effects," said Eogan, fighting a sense of giddiness at the thought. "Either we've been affected or it was."

"Perhaps both." Deangelis didn't spare them the ramifications of their discovery. "I've never measured clock discrepancies on this scale, but then none of my drones went this deep and returned. It's almost certainly a side effect of the maze's structure. The further you travel, the longer it takes."

"Thus preserving causality, outside the structure." The pattern fell into focus for a second, before spinning into unreason a moment later. "But who would build a network of wormholes that doesn't allow you to travel faster than light? What's the point of that?"

"We don't know how pronounced the effect is. Not yet. It could depend on the type of direction we travel in—through one of the particular dimensions, for instance, or across one particular type of node. This drone's experience could be atypical."

"I want to find out," said Melilah. "I want to know how much time has passed back home since we left."

Eogan bit his lip on a comment that *back home* no longer existed, as she remembered it.

"We could set a trap," he said instead. "There must be hundreds of drones in Geodesica by now. If we broadcast a signal powerfully enough, we're bound to reel in some of them. Catch them, take them apart, and check their data. That way we kill two birds with one stone: we get data and mass. When we have enough of both, we can decide what to do next."

"Fine," said Melilah. "As long as we don't get ourselves caught in the process."

"Maybe, first, we should try following the drone's data as far as we can," suggested Deangelis. "If the junctions have shifted only slightly, we might be able to make it to Sublime without needing any more information."

"That's one thousand, one hundred and nineteen intersections," Melilah said. "Sorry, but I don't want to go that far without knowing how long it's going to take us, outside. Even if it works."

Eogan was inclined to agree with her, and said so, adding: "We need more mass in order to go so far. A lot more. Getting it should be our first priority."

Deangelis didn't argue with one of the few hard facts they possessed. The drone they had captured made but a small meal for the Cell.

"We passed through a large node not far back, one with thirteen exits," the former Exarch said. "I suggest we set our beacon there to maximize our chances of being heard, and of hiding when something comes."

"Agreed," said Melilah. "Lead the way, Isaac."

Deangelis gave Eogan the directions, and the Cell accelerated along the appropriate tunnel. Eogan's perception of Geodesica had shifted slightly in the face of the new data. Instead of the rigid, purpose-built piece of supertechnology he had imagined, it now had a hint of the impermanent. It was changeable, paradoxical, perhaps even fundamentally flawed.

Welcome to the club, he thought.

Melilah didn't waste a second. The moment the decoy was installed in the node and the Cell had retreated into one of the tunnels to wait, she withdrew from her companions as best she could and tried to sleep. Her body was distant and fuzzy; she felt as though she had been crying for weeks, even though she hadn't shed a tear. It had taken her far too long to realize that it wasn't just the Cell to blame, but too many stressful days in a row with too little rest.

She couldn't remember the last time she had slept. Possibly not since the Occlusion had come to Bedlam—although that seemed unlikely. Had the habitat's records existed, she could have scrolled through the previous weeks to see if she had taken a nap at any point, but that option was now gone. Every important detail of her life had been erased, along with those belonging to many other people. She felt as though a large part of her had been physically amputated.

The Cell offered her no privacy at all, either, but unlike Bedlam it forced intimacy upon her as well. In Bedlam she could have retreated to her quarters and turned out the lights, if she wanted to escape from the presence of people. Here she could only close her eyes and try to ignore her companions.

This tube of folded space will be my blanket, she said to herself, employing meditation techniques she had learned while fighting insomnia a century and a half before. *I am embraced, comforted, safe . . .*

She dreamt of Sofia's, a popular coffee shop in the Cohens, where she had sometimes gone to read. Hand-drawn pink love hearts adorned the walls, an affectation she found simultaneously puerile and charming. In her dream, they were pulsing like real hearts, and blood trickled down the walls. Crimson puddles pooled at her feet.

"You weren't there," a voice accused her.

Melilah looked up over the edge of her book. Her four-daughter, Yasu, sat opposite her, dressed from head to foot in a white gauzy garment that didn't suit her slender physique. Melilah tried to remember what the outfit was called, but the word had temporarily slipped her mind.

"Where?" she asked. "When?"

"You weren't home when I died." Yasu's green eyes were hurt. "You were off fighting someone else's war."

That hurt. "I was fighting to save you."

"You could have saved me if you'd been with me."

"Honestly, Yasu, I couldn't! The Catastrophe would have claimed me as well. There's nothing I could have done."

"I don't believe you." Yasu took the edge of her veil and draped it across her face. A golden glow sprang up around her just as Melilah remembered the word she had been looking for.

The garment was a *shroud.* Yasu was dressed for burial.

"Good-bye, Grandmother Mel."

"Yasu, no." Melilah reached out to help her four-daughter but the light drove her back. It was already so powerful. "Yasu! Listen to me! It's not my fault!"

She defied the flames, lunging forward with one hand outstretched. The fire enveloped her, but her fingers touched nothing. Yasu was gone. Only the fire remained. As she flailed about, clutching helplessly at air, she felt the golden death beginning to bite into her own skin. The pain was excruciating.

"Melilah! You're dreaming. Wake up. Wake up!"

The voice came from outside her, but spoke deep into her mind. She jolted out of sleep to find her heart pounding and the garish electric blue of the node dimmed down to a bare glimmer in the distance.

"Yasu," she gasped, still entangled in the complex emotions of the dream. "She was—I—"

"You were calling her name," said Deangelis. The Cell was stimulating her auditory nerves directly in response to activity in the relevant sections of his cortex. "Yasu—your great-great-granddaughter. That *was* her, wasn't it?"

She couldn't answer. Grief overwhelmed her, and she could no longer keep the tears at bay. They wracked her with the same physical intensity as vomiting. For several minutes, she did nothing but sob, not just for Yasu, but for everyone she had known in Bedlam—Angela Chen-Pushkaric, Prof Virgo, Werner Gard, Kara Skirianos, even Gil Hurdowar—and the places she would never again visit. No more gatherings in Albert Hall; no more art in Bacon Cathedral; no more coffee from ben-Avraham's. She didn't think about why it had happened; she didn't wonder who was to blame; she didn't care if Deangelis and Eogan thought her hopelessly weak. She simply let her body do what it needed to, just as she had let it sleep when it could no longer function without it.

Deangelis said nothing and made no move to comfort her. She was grateful for that. Only as the emotional spasm passed did she realize that Eogan wasn't watching at all. Somehow Deangelis had taken the two of them out of the cognitive loop of the Cell. They stood at one remove from its senses. She felt as though a dark bubble had enclosed her—a black veil, mirroring Yasu's white shroud in the dream.

"I am very sorry," Deangelis said when it was clear that she was calming down. "I can't imagine how it must feel to lose family. I had none, except those I adopted."

"Who were they? You've never mentioned anyone like that before."

"Oh, but I did. Everyone in Bedlam was my family. Or so I thought of you, whether you wanted me to or not."

She was too exhausted to rise to the bait, if he was baiting her at all.

"Thank you for doing this," she said, meaning the relative peace of their dark bubble. "I needed a break."

"Eogan can handle things for the moment. Nothing has responded to the beacon as yet, and I do not expect a response soon. That would strain the laws of probability. Geodesica is very large; a thousand drones could lose themselves in here and never be found."

Her dislike of him was habitual, a matter of principle rather than the gut, and it had been wearing thin lately. She couldn't fight a pang of sympathy that his sense of connection to the colony hadn't been returned—by her, anyway. "It's okay to be sad," she said. "I'm not going to begrudge you that, of all things."

Deangelis didn't pursue the topic. "Have you ever heard of the McMeeken Plan?"

She frowned. The name was familiar, but she couldn't immediately place why. "Tell me about it."

"James McMeeken was a First Wave activist, born on Earth and settled among the Scorpio Systems, where he and his plan are best known. Back in the twenty-first century, anthropologists realized that one of the major factors separating modern humans from Neanderthals and australopithecines was that more of us survive to be grandparents. That may not seem significant, but the truth is that grandparents exert a powerful influence over civilization, helping to rear children, passing on knowledge and experience to future generations, and encouraging a sense of kinship across generations. The existence of grandparents literally made civilization possible. Without them, we would still be roaming the African plains."

Melilah had heard the theory before. It had been an accepted part of anthropology as long as she was alive. "Where did McMeeken fit in?"

"He took the theory and turned it into a map for the next stage of human evolution. If the simple existence of grandparents could give us so much, what about great-grandparents and beyond? What could they offer us? Populations were aging significantly back then; for the first time in human history, thanks to improving antisenescence treatments, grandparents outnumbered the new generation.

"McMeeken believed that humanity had a golden opportunity before it. Instead of worrying about the ossification of society and forcing the elderly out of the workplace, stripping them of their assets, and turning them into a new underclass, as many did, why not use their experience to better everyone's lot? The elderly ill had long since become the elderly well, reducing their burden on society, and what humanity undoubtedly needed was a long view. The shortsighted and forgetful had held the reins for too long. How better to find a new perspective on the world than through the eyes of those who had lived in it the longest, combined with those seeing it for the first time?

"McMeeken wasn't advocating a gerontocracy; he wanted open collaboration between the generations, as many of them as was humanly and scientifically possible, in order to end environmental degradation, poverty, and war. History repeats itself, he said, only when those who saw it the first time are dead or disenfranchised. We ignore them at our risk."

Melilah had heard enough to recall what she knew of the man from the deep recesses of her memory. "He founded Caspari Arbor, right?"

"He did, around Epsilon Scorpio."

"How did it do?"

"It was moderately successful. Not significantly better or worse than the many others Earth seeded in the First Wave. It was, however, one of the most resistant to the Exarchate Expansion. It fought for two full years, and didn't submit until two neighboring systems dispatched Reapers to bring it into line."

She couldn't see where Deangelis was going. "Because of McMeeken's plan? Because he liked great-great-grandparents? If you think that's why *I* was so stubborn, or why I was close to Yasu—"

"No, no, nothing of the sort," he cut across her. "I'm merely trying to point out that McMeeken's colony and the Exarchate aren't so different. They both believe in the validity of the long view, and in the inability of so-called modern humanity to obtain it. The future demands a new methodology, a new sort of society, and we must make sacrifices in order to achieve it. McMeeken's only failing was, perhaps, the naïve belief that the solution could be as simple as he imagined it—and the assumption that achieving the long view would automatically bring an end to war."

"We still fight," she said, finally understanding. "We just fight over different things."

"Exactly. Sometimes it's hard to see what's happening on the battlements from the battlefield—and vice versa. The more eyes we can see the world through, the better."

Melilah wished she could look him in the eyes, but she was little more than a disembodied point of view in a shadowy bubble. She felt his presence in a nebulous way, as though he was an out-of-focus ghost hovering next to her. It was impossible to read his body language. Was he trying to justify his actions to her, or looking for forgiveness?

"Is that why the Archon made the Exarchs the way they are?" she asked him. "One mind spread across many bodies: lots of eyes there."

"There are many ways to be human, Melilah. I feel—my mind is—" He struggled for words. "Autism is rare these days, but the condition is still known. Without the rest of me, my mind is in pieces. I don't see the world the way I used to. It's hard for me to remember what the whole of me used to believe, and why. But I do know that I had my reasons. And I felt as deeply as any individual human, possibly more so. I am telling you this because I too am sad, for many things. The destruction of Bedlam is just one of them. I am sad that Sol could have been behind such a monstrosity. Not the Exarchate: I have faith that we would not have done such a thing uncompelled. In the end, the Archon is responsible. I do not know how it sees the world, or what long view compels it to take the actions it does, and I cannot forgive it for what it has done."

She realized then that Deangelis wanted her understanding. Nothing more.

"What you were," she said, "was very little like me. You called yourself human, but you saw the world in a fundamentally different way. We were both human in the way that a Stone Age artisan was human, too. We had lots of genes in common, but that's about it. Culture makes all the difference."

"I agree," he said. "But that doesn't rule out coexistence. Collaboration, even—as we are collaborating now, inside Geodesica. Natural, Palmer, and Exarch: that's quite a mix."

"If you think we'd be doing this voluntarily, you're deluded."

"You, Eogan, and Lazarus Hails attacked the Archon, didn't you?" Her response didn't seem to faze him in the slightest. "Maybe these are the eyes we need to see Geodesica through. Perhaps, without the full length and breadth of humanity confronting it, we will never come close to understanding it."

Melilah retreated into herself at that thought. She didn't feel any closer to understanding Geodesica *or* Deangelis. She was just tired. The absence of Bedlam ached in her like a missing lung. She felt hollow and fragile, liable to collapse in on herself at any moment.

"We need Geodesica," she said. "Without it, we don't have a chance of kicking the Archon out of the colonies. But we don't need to understand it in order to use it. We just need to know how it works."

"What if we can't have one without the other?" Deangelis asked her.

She didn't have an answer to that.

"I'm tired," she said, pushing him gently but firmly away. "I'd like to be alone now, if you don't mind."

"Of course." He receded from her numbed senses. "I'll wake you should something come in response to our signals."

"Thank you."

She breathed a sigh of relief when she was alone in the bubble. Her companions were never far away, but for the first time she felt as though she could be at ease. It was hard enough dealing with her own needs and feelings, let alone Deangelis's as well.

Give me time. Once the scar tissue sets, I'll be my old self again. Just wait and see.

Whatever the Archon's plans were for the future, Melilah thought to herself, they had better be flexible.

The first drone came seven hours after the beacon sounded. Lidar picked up its echo approaching rapidly along one of the twelve empty tunnels leading from the node. The one the *Cowell* occupied was the only one in the beacon's shadow; they didn't want anything picking them up from behind.

Deangelis monitored Eogan's data closely as the drone came into range, with Melilah looking over both their shoulders, rested but reticent.

The drone was identical to the other, a spindly pyramid possessing just enough motive power to enter and leave the tunnels. It broadcast a faint but steady ping back along its wake, clearly communicating with some distant base station or node. Whether it was receiving a reply, Eogan couldn't immediately tell. The beacon itself swamped any faint signals.

The drone came cautiously. A simple transmitter modeled on the first drone's design, it approached the bait by increments. Sensors tasted the vacuum around it but failed to detect the lurking Cell component. Eogan had coated its skin with lidar-absorbing compounds and adjusted its color to match that of the wall behind it.

Once the drone was within range, he pounced, disabling it with a series of rapid snips. It died as quickly as the first. Like a trap-door spider retreating into its lair, the *Cowell* dragged its prey back into the tunnel, where it began disassembly and digestion with ravenous haste.

The data contained in the drone's processing core unfolded rapidly. The machines weren't designed for stealth but for low-power, long-life network operations. Many such machines could spread their processing load across hundreds of isolated components, exploring and monitoring vast swathes of the maze with no centralized AI required. Accessing one of them didn't give Deangelis access to the network as a whole, but it did give him another piece of the larger jigsaw. More of Geodesica fell into place.

"This one is part of an exploratory push sent two years ago," he said to the others. "It's been sitting in a node thirty junctions from here for six months in real time, cycling between watchful dormancy and hibernation. It passes on signals received from other drones and reports its own data as it comes in—not that there's been much at all to report. This is the first time it has thought to move, in response to our signal. It doesn't know if its telemetry has been received by any of its fellows. It just transmits in the hope of something getting through."

"How many junctions between it and Sublime?" Melilah asked.

"Less than two hundred."

"Well, that's a clear improvement."

"Still not close enough," said Eogan.

"We wait for more drones, then? We could sit here forever."

"Let's see what happens," he told her. "It didn't take us long to get this one. Another two and I'll feel more confident. We'll certainly be more comfortable, anyway, physically speaking."

That was enough to win her support. Deangelis didn't dispute the call to keep the beacon running and wait for more drones to turn up. It was true that they could use more mass and data before running off on a potential goose chase through the maze. And thus far nothing untoward had happened.

Barely an hour after the first, the second drone nudged up a tunnel on the far side of the junction and into their trap. It put up more of a fight, requiring a short chase through the tunnels before they reeled it in. Its core memory revealed that it had been on station for four years according to the calendar outside Geodesica. Its energy reserves were almost drained, and its skeleton partly corroded.

"That looks like rust," said Melilah, studying rough patches on the pyramid's struts before the Cell absorbed it.

"I think it is," said Eogan. "And that raises some interesting possibilities."

"Oxygen and water vapor," Deangelis agreed. "Presumably atmospheric, and presumably from somewhere in here."

"The questions are: who put them there, and why?"

"Actually," said Melilah, "my first question would be: *where*?"

"We can follow the trail to where it was stationed," said Eogan. "It's only sixty junctions away."

"We could do that, yes, but does that put us closer to Sublime or further away?"

Both of them looked to Deangelis for an opinion on that subject.

"You have to understand," he said, "that a map of this complexity doesn't fall into place overnight. I possess a data set containing thousands of junctions now, from the data I was given from Sublime plus that we've gained today. Bearing in mind that Geodesica might change with time, it's exceedingly difficult to put this together in one piece. I can follow strings of directions, but I can't tell if they overlap or not. All I can say is that if we follow this drone back to its station, and from there to Sublime, we're looking at around three hundred steps."

"That's further than the last one," Melilah said. "It doesn't help us at all."

"I don't want to be repetitive," said Eogan, "but we need resources for life support, and a potential supply just sixty junctions away is hard to ignore."

Deangelis saw his point. "We could jump to there and hold another stakeout. There might be a drone with a shorter route nearby."

"Could—might—if. I just want to get out of here and on the Archon's case."

"Quiet," said Eogan. "I'm picking up something else."

"Another drone?" Melilah asked him. "Already?"

"That's what it looks like." The Cell packed the remains of the second drone away for later processing and adopted a low profile again. "From the same tunnel as the last one. Maybe this one was following on its tail."

"Maybe. And maybe that means we're becoming a little *too* conspicuous."

They watched as a third drone decelerated into the junction, its sensors quivering like a cat's whiskers.

"No rust this time," said Eogan.

"I think we should grab it and get the hell out of here." Melilah's voice was low and tense.

"Wait," said Deangelis. The drone rotated, giving him a clear view of its far flank. "What's that there? A scratch mark?"

"Could be," said Eogan. "I think—"

He didn't get to finish the sentence. The drone exploded, filling the junction with plasma and metal shards. The shock wave was deafening after the silence of the vacuum, and powerful enough to knock the *Cowell* from its safe observation point. It ricocheted up the tunnel and into the grip of the spatial warp.

Events unfolded rapidly. Deangelis's mind kicked up several gears, to its fastest rate. The clouds of gas sweeping along with them billowed in slow motion. Debris spun into the curved space of the tunnel's walls and ricocheted back at the Cell. Eogan moved with clumsy tardiness, reacting far too late; Melilah was even more ineffectual. The force of the detonation momentarily overwhelmed the Cell's sensors, giving him junk signals and noise.

Through the chaos, a lidar shadow appeared at the far end of the tunnel, toward which they were inexorably swept.

Deangelis had no choice but to take over. It wasn't something he wanted to do, although he had known he could at any time. Palmer Cells were immensely complicated machines, with systems finely attuned by centuries of algorithmic evolution to life in space. Their incredible redundancy made them resilient and very hard to destroy: blow one to pieces and each could operate as a miniature Cell, each cubic centimeter crammed with micromachines capable of supplying power, life support, and thrust. Their only weak points were their control systems, which took a vastly complicated mess of data and reduced it to something a single person could understand and direct. If subverted, such systems could grant control of the entire ship to someone unauthorized.

Deangelis was most certainly not authorized, but he was an Exarch, and even the very best Palmer security could not withstand a concerted assault from within. And there just wasn't time to argue . . .

By the time the lidar shadow resolved into something very different to the harmless seek-and-report drones, Deangelis was in full control of the *Cowell* and had only to decide how best to employ it. He was in no doubt that they had allowed themselves to be trapped. The third drone had been booby-trapped, rigged to explode either way: when they approached or to force them out of their hiding place if they didn't. The explosion was never intended to harm them. That job was left to the thing behind the plan—the machine that had captured and modified the third drone and sent it in to flush them out, and now waited for them to fall into its lap at the next junction.

That it had come from Bedlam he had no doubt. Dozens of autonomous killers would have poured into the Occlusion after them, their missions simple: to destroy the only living witnesses to the atrocities that occurred in the name of the Exarchate.

This one had turned their own trap against them. Unless he acted fast, their fate was sealed.

But what to do? The tunnel had them firmly in its grip. Space flexed, firing them like a gun down an infinite barrel. Deangelis considered using the reactionless thrusters to slow their headlong plunge, but Eogan's previous attempts to do that had been useless, and the Cell's rudimentary ability to defend itself was almost certain to be insufficient against the thing waiting for them, no matter how long he had to prepare.

"What are you doing?" Eogan asked, voice booming like whale song, his alarm coming far too late to do anything about it.

The only thing I can *do,* Deangelis thought, not taking the time to reply. There were just moments left.

First, he nudged the thrusters to take them out of the debris cloud from the drone. Next he reduced the Cell's profile down to a bare minimum and narrowed the leading edge to a point. The remains of the second drone he fashioned into crude missiles that carried no payload, but would contain enough lethal momentum when he was finished with them to sink a battleship.

Finally, in an act of desperation even he could not quite credit, he activated the Cell's VOID drive systems. It wasn't an easy decision to make. This was an experiment he had never dared to perform, even with an uncrewed drone, during his time with the Occlusion in Bedlam. Jane Elderton had never tried it in Sublime. The cylindrical spaces within Geodesica's tunnels seemed in most respects similar to space-time outside the exits, but the warps that confined them were a different story, as were the junctions. No one knew what effect ftl travel would have in such a confined space.

The lidar shadow ahead of them unfolded like a net, numerous, many-jointed limbs spreading to catch them and do to them as they had done to the first two drones.

Instead of turning the Cell to point back up the tunnel, away from their enemy, he kept its orientation forward, aiming right down its throat.

"Close your eyes," he told Melilah and Eogan. "This could be rough."

Deangelis gave the Cell its final instructions. The VOID field snapped on. Space screamed and twisted around them. Time slowed to a point.

Snapped.

The lidar shadow leapt instantly closer, blowing up to fill the view. The impromptu missiles struck and vanished into a flash of X-rays. The VOID drive roared, catching the wave of spatial distortion and amplifying it. Resonances in the very nature of space-time swelled around them. The Cell rushed forward at impossible speed. Its instruments recorded deform ratings in double, triple, even quadruple figures—something completely unheard of—before jumping right off the scale.

Deangelis caught fragmentary glimpses of tunnels and junctions rushing by. He reached out in desperation to kill the VOID drive. The controls systems were chaotic, unresponsive. Whole swathes of the drive units did deactivate, but many failed to receive the shutdown signal and kept determinedly operating. The VOID field became unstable, spinning the Cell at its heart like a top. The Cell crashed off of surfaces that weren't entirely real, tangling up dimensions and tying them in knots. Deangelis felt his grip on the Cell fading. With the last of his strength, he sent another kill signal, but he didn't last long enough to tell whether it had succeeded or not.

His world collapsed down into a cold, dark point.

Gone.

+INTERLUDE

Anniversary 12: 6534 CE

The thing had grown on the edge of the system over seven years, bubbling out of the vacuum like a boil. Occasionally Deangelis stirred from his slow appreciation of the stars to send a probe to investigate, but as it didn't resemble anything from the Exarchives he decided to wait before assuming it hostile. He surrounded it with instruments, orbiting at a carefully respectful distance, and waited.

Fractal patterns came and went.

The day it switched itself on, a nova flash of bright white light rippled across the system, snap-frying the instruments monitoring its progress. By the time Deangelis put another probe in range, the Gate was already active, a sphere hanging unsupported in space like a gleaming soap bubble or a rubbery crystal ball. Although its swollen surface was translucent, the interior of it was utterly black. Starlight shone through that blackness only when the Gate was open.

It opened once to disgorge a dart-shaped capsule containing information on the Gate's operation and maintenance. Then it closed again. Deangelis spent a year trying to understand how it worked, but gave up in the end. What did it matter? He didn't need to grasp its principles in order to use it, and he had no intention of using it. He knew his place.

A century passed, during which time the Gate remained closed.

Then it opened again, disgorging a vessel that looked more like a mile-high, chrome cactus than a starship. He knew immediately on seeing it that she had returned.

"You lied to me," he broadcast.

The cactus disgorged thousands of tiny, hoop-shaped craft from the tips of its many launch-needles. Brilliant motes shone in the center of the hoops, which flew head-on rather than in the fashion of flying saucers. Deangelis assumed that the motes provided motive power, although he didn't understand the principles by which they operated any more than he understood the Gate. He didn't even try to resist them.

The hoops tore his observation platform to shreds in search of every last one of his bodies. These the hoops gathered into an ungainly bundle and delivered to their mothership through a puckered hatch in its side. There, in a room large enough to fit a small skyscraper, he was separated into his individual parts and interviewed one by one. Only later, when he was allowed to reassemble, did he realize what she was doing.

"You dare," she said to each one of them in turn, "to accuse me. I should tear you into a thousand pieces and toss you into a thousand suns. You deserve no less for what you've done to me."

She came to him in the form of a human with no hair, no face, no eyes—no distinguishing marks whatsoever. The only corporeal being he witnessed in the entire ship, she was spindly and spry, like a stick figure possessed by a poltergeist. Her skin was white and looked plastic. Her gestures were expansive and melodramatic, as though she had forgotten how such things usually worked. Her voice burned into his mind like a branding iron.

He didn't recognize her, saw nothing of her old self in the bizarre framework of the new, but he didn't doubt her identity for a second.

Whoever she was.

"You told me you were Melilah Awad," he said. Each part of him said the same thing, each time she confronted them. "You told me you had emerged from Geodesica. I believed you."

"This is true," she said, raking sharp-tipped fingers across his many faces. "I have no reason to lie to you."

"Then why are there no records of your emergence? Why does Sol deny you've returned? Why haven't you used your name anywhere in your travels? Why wouldn't you tell me what happened inside Geodesica?"

"There are reasons," she hissed.

"I don't believe you. You're not who you claim to be. You're an impostor. You lied to me!"

This only made her angry. With capering fury she turned the conversation back on him.

"It's not relevant!" she roared at him, each word burning fresh from the coals of hell. "*This* is relevant! My anger, my wrath! I do not believe that the Archon was right. Bedlam didn't have to die! You agree with me, don't you?"

"I don't believe it."

"You must believe it! Don't you grieve like me? Don't you want revenge?"

"I still grieve, but I no longer desire revenge."

"Nonsense! You are just old and gray and tired. You will feel again. I will revive you!"

She devoted herself to the task for many days, as the giant cactus-ship swung around the system's primary, badgering his many parts, one by one, in an attempt to make them crack. But they did not. He had had many, many years to come to terms with who he was and what he wanted. No ambiguity existed for him anymore.

Except where she was concerned . . .

"Nothing you say is true," he told her.

"I call you Corpse," she ranted at him in return. "I plunder your tomb and desecrate your headstone! I could erase you if I wanted to, just like your precious Archon erased my home. Would *that* anger you?"

"It would," he admitted. "I can offer you that much."

"It's not enough! I want more!"

"Why? Why come to me with your problems? Why don't you leave me alone?"

"Because you're here, of course!"

He couldn't tell whether she meant *in Bedlam* or simply *alive*.

"I'm going to be here a while longer yet," he said. "Until Melilah returns, at least."

The spindly marionette danced in frustration. "But I am she! I won't let you take that away from me as well! I am grown; I am glorious! You should worship me!"

"Did Melilah Awad ever worship *me*?"

Some of the fire went out of her then. "No," she said, sagging. "Melilah Awad did not."

The walls surrounding his fragments dissolved. He reassembled without obstruction and took in his surroundings properly.

The giant chamber contained an atmosphere thick with carbon dioxide and incapable of supporting human life. It smelled like a room that had been sealed shut for too long: an empty cellar boarded over and forgotten.

"What is this vessel?" he asked her, his many eyes looking up at the distant ceiling in confusion. There were no windows, no holds, no signs of human habitation apart from the strange creature before him. "Does it have a name?"

"It's hard to say," she said. "The language you use is ancient. Few people speak it now. I had to relearn it."

With every word she convinced him further of her lie. "Melilah Awad was meticulous with her memories."

"You do not understand, or you refuse to. Too many memories died with Bedlam, and many more have been corrupted since. I have lost and gained much in the four thousand, three hundred and fifty-one years that have passed since my birth. Do you not see what I have become?"

The marionette spread her arms to encompass the vast space around them, and Deangelis only then realized the truth.

"This is you?" he said, scanning his surroundings. "This entire ship?"

"If I had come to you in the shape of my old self, you would accept her even less."

"Perhaps." That wasn't nearly enough to change his opinion. "I am still waiting for her."

The impostor screamed, and the sound of it filled the giant space. He covered his ears—all of them—and fought the dissolution of his reassembled personality.

"Ashes and dust!" he shouted over the terrible noise. "That's all that remain here! Why do you come? To torment me, or to taint her memory?"

"I am *her memory!"*

The air shook with the sheer power of her personality, but he remained unmoved.

"You are not the Melilah *I* remember," he said.

Fury boomed from end to end of the vertiginous cavern. Thunder rolled for a good minute, drowning out anything else he attempted to say. The stick figure swayed madly from side to side, clutching her featureless temples in apparent agony. Deangelis staggered as the curved hull shook beneath his feet.

Then it, too, passed. The air grew still and heavy again. The marionette stood with head bowed and arms limp at its sides.

"I knew Isaac Forge Deangelis," she said. "I remember you well enough."

"We have met before, whether you're an impostor or not. When you first came to Bedlam, we talked briefly, and then you left. You wouldn't tell me what supposedly happened in Geodesica, and that made me suspicious. I started asking questions. No one knew anything about you. This is the first time I've seen you since."

"You were different in Geodesica," she said.

He understood the reason then for being separated, and for the many identical performances she had given him.

"I am not he," he said, "and you are not she."

She nodded her blunt, white head in resignation, as though she had expected him to say this. "If I am not Melilah Awad, then who do you think I might be?"

This he could not answer.

"I will leave now," she said after a moment. "Give me one reason why I shouldn't kill you before I go."

That surprised him. "Why would you?"

"If you cannot be the way I want you to be, if you will not even acknowledge the person I am, what right do you have to exist?"

"I need no right, just as you, perhaps, need no reason to kill me."

"But I have plenty of reasons. I am still angry with you—you and all your wretched kind."

"Would killing me solve anything? Would it make you feel any better?"

"It would bring me closure."

He laughed. "It would only make you lonelier than you already are."

She was silent for a long while. He waited patiently, unsure whether the ship was moving or still in orbit around Bedlam's star. She could have taken them through the Gate without him knowing, and brought them to another part of the galaxy entirely. If she had, he would be angry. He wasn't ready to leave his old home yet.

"Perhaps you should live," she said eventually, "and remain firm in your belief that I am not Melilah Awad. That would be better for all concerned."

"Why is that?" he asked, puzzled.

"You are correct in your assertion that I do not travel under my own name. The name of this vessel, loosely translated, is *Mirth of Angels*."

The hoops returned, issuing from the walls in flocks like strange birds, or a swarm of miniature solar systems.

"I spit you out, pale thing," she said as the hoops lifted him up and bore him off to the opening air lock. "But we will meet again. You have not yet been punished."

"Must I be?" were the last words he spoke to her, in that form.

"We all are, in time."

He tumbled into the vacuum and the great silver ship sealed tight behind him. Alone again with the stars, he watched as its enormous, hollow bulk slid through the Gate and disappeared. When it was gone, he was left with just the memory of its name and the ghost that had clung to it. *Mirth of Angels* was an odd-sounding choice, especially for someone fixated on the death of Bedlam. But there were connections he couldn't ignore: the word "Angel" and his own last name, for instance; and the fact that "Isaac" meant "he who laughs."

He didn't feel much like laughing right now, though. She—whoever she was—had destroyed his platform and left him floating in space, millions of kilometers from the nearest solid body. Resigning himself to the long process of rebuilding what he had lost, he turned his many faces sunward and went to work.

+5

Altitude: 2440 CE

"Come in hot," Deangelis said, "as you normally would. No one knows who we are; no one knows where we've come from. The *Dreieichen* is just an ordinary Cell on an ordinary journey. Don't give them reason to think otherwise."

Horsfall could see the sense in that. As the system of Altitude, which the Exarchate insisted on calling Kullervo-Hails, ballooned before them, she fought a rising sense of unease. After nine months in transit following their slow and nerve-wracking escape from Bedlam, the thought of being in the thick of things again unnerved her.

"At least there are no antiprivacy laws here," she said, coordinating the Cell's approach with the familiarity of a veteran. That was one thing to be grateful for. In Bedlam of old, a single sweep would have revealed the nature of her crew and passenger, both of them disgraced Exarchs a long way from their homes.

While Jane Elderton helped her direct the operation of the Cell, Isaac Deangelis stared fixedly forward at the colony he had fled to, in the hope of succor.

Altitude was a key system in the Arc Circuit, conveniently situated between several economic and social powerhouses in that region of the Exarchate. A player itself—unlike Bedlam, the role of which had ever been little more than way station and political curiosity combined—it boasted a population in excess of a million and no less than three thriving cities. The planet after which the system took its name was a barely hospitable hothouse, unstable and well endowed with unusual geography as a result. Civilization concentrated at the poles, from where remote survey and mining operations explored the rest of the planet. Its two moons were extensively outfitted, serving as stopovers between surface and escape trajectories. Tethers and linear accelerators stuck out from them like bristles from a porcupine; ships of all ranges and configurations came and went in a steady stream.

For tourists, the system's real draw card was a magnetically active jovian core slowly spiraling into the primary star. Within a hundred thousand years, it would have vanished forever into the solar atmosphere, but until then it rewarded those willing to risk the searing temperatures with stunning auroral displays. Luckily humanity hadn't come half a million years earlier, when the dying gas giant had been roaming chaotically across the system, perturbing orbits and flinging moons in all directions. The system—much quieter now—was relatively shy of planets as a result, but rich in asteroids.

Altitude the planet was a dense purple-blue color from orbit. To Horsfall it looked like a rotten plum ready to burst at any moment. She imagined it squeezed by the mighty fist of the Archon, and grimaced at the resulting image.

"This is Palmer Horsfall, Chief Officer of *Dreieichen,* requesting permission to dock."

"Point of origin?" came an immediate reply from an AI on the smaller of the two moons.

"Gabison's End," she lied, following the story the three of them had prepared in advance. "Is that relevant?"

"This system is on high alert. All vessels hailing from Alioth-Cochrane, Michailogliou-Rawe, and Mizar-Cazneaux must be searched before being granted permission to dock. You're in the clear, *Dreieichen*. Stand by for berth protocol."

"What was that all about?" she asked her companions when the line closed.

Deangelis answered in wooden tones: "Two systems conspired against Bedlam when the Occlusion arrived. Frederica Cazneaux attacked the colony with a Reaper; Lan Cochrane sent a clane to kill the Negotiator Select and threaten me. New Eire—Dalman Rawe's colony—lies between here and Mizar, and is an obvious jumping point. Looks like Lazarus is taking no chances."

Horsfall took a moment to absorb all this. Deangelis had informed her of the Negotiator Select's death while in transit from Bedlam. Her shock had been profound. Although she had been out of touch with the Palmer organization for a decade since her sister's death, she remembered Palmer Christolphe well. He had been popular and widely traveled, and therefore a good representative for the movement, which covered all the colonized systems, not just the Arc Circuit. He would be difficult to replace.

She could understand that feeling among the Palmers might be running high, but for that to spill over into a security embargo held by one Exarch against another—that was unheard of.

"Cracks are showing. Interesting."

Old rivalries, said the voice in her skull, *given new life. It'll take more than this to get the show on the road.*

"It's a start," said Deangelis. His voice still lacked inflection; his face was averted, as though staring out a nonexistent porthole at the planet below. "Take any berth they offer you. Once we're docked, I'll go find Lazarus. I know where he'll be."

Horsfall tilted her head. "When you talk like this," she said, "you're not offering suggestions. Are you?"

"No. I'm making sense."

"That's not the point."

It is *the point,* said the voice in her mind. *Or it should be. This is no time for pettiness.*

Horsfall felt her vestigial limbs stir restlessly, deep in the Cell's interface. "I'm the Chief Officer of this Cell. It won't look good if I take orders from you on the outside."

Deangelis looked at her then. "You're not coming with me."

"Of course I am. Both of us are."

"There's no need. What if someone draws the connection between us?"

"Then let them. This may not be Bedlam, but it's not as if we won't be watched anyway, from the moment we dock. 'High alert,' remember? If we try to hide, we'll only stand out more."

He nodded. "This is true."

"And it's not all," she said. "That's not even most of it. The real reason I'm coming is to make sure this gets done. Sure, you seem friendly enough, and yes, you got us out of Bedlam okay in the end—but where were you when Sublime was destroyed? Where was Lazarus Hails when my sister burned? Although we're on the same side at the moment, I have no intention of letting you two old buddies get together without being there myself to make sure it stays that way. Understood?"

If he resented her suspicion, it didn't show. "I understand, Palmer Horsfall. And I apologize for seeming pushy. I think you can assume that Jane will tell you if my suggestions are inappropriate."

"Who in the Dark says I trust her any more than I trust you?"

Before either of them could respond, the berthing data trickled through, granting her access to a second-tier lock halfway along one of the tethers.

"Now pipe down," she said, "while I put my baby to bed."

She returned her attention to the view outside the Cell and hoped neither of them would draw attention to the tears that had sprung to her eyes while talking about her sister. The tangle of ships and tethers reminded her of the colony in Sublime, where she had delivered Deva to slaughter like Abraham offering his son up for sacrifice. But hers hadn't been an offering. She'd had no idea what the consequences of her actions would be. And the Archon was anything *but* a god . . .

More than that bothered her. It had been a long time since she'd last been in the presence of colonists untouched by the Catastrophe—those who hadn't lost loved ones or weren't sniffing around for clues as to its origin. She told herself not to worry about that as the Cell component she flew mated smoothly with the berth, allowing its fluid grapnels purchase and submitting to its embrace. A circular recess formed in the curving wall opposite her, and Deangelis kicked himself out of the way as the air lock opened.

She suppressed a wince at the sound of voices echoing up the astrobridge.

Don't be pathetic, she chided herself. *They're only human.*

With two fallen Exarchs in tow, she went out to meet them.

Rudra-Deangelis had no reason to be angry with Lazarus Hails, but that didn't stop the fury growing inside him with every step he took through the moon's plastic-coated corridors. The stink of people was thick in his nostrils. The evidence of their industry was all around him. Altitude thrived on a steady stream of trade from around the Arc Circuit and beyond—a willing benefactor of blind economic forces that took no notice of political trends. The destruction of one of its neighbors hardly affected it.

The cold certainty of that fact struck him with almost unbearable force, although he had steeled himself for it all the way from Bedlam. He'd had months to prepare, and had spent most of that time in deep slow-time once he felt that he had covered every conceivable angle. Leaving Horsfall to manage the Cell, he had skimmed through the months as though they were bare moments. To him, the trip from Bedlam's outer fringes had seemed to take just a week, with most of that spent on approach. He didn't feel as tired or out of synch as Horsfall obviously did.

But the anger remained. He wondered if Jane Elderton was feeling it, too. She kept quiet for the moment, watching through Horsfall's eyes as they combed the moon's tubes and chambers for the sort of place Lazarus Hails could be found. A wide disparity of people passed them on their travels: Palmers in various stages of machine integration, obviously passing through; traders and service staff ranging from hard-skinned vacuum workers negotiating the low gee with practiced ease to dirtsiders in partial pressure suits. Two- and 3-D signs flashed at them everywhere they looked. Hawkers chanted and called in a variety of dialects.

Deangelis missed the easy access Bedlam's antiprivacy laws had given him to the background of everyone he saw. How did people decide which dealer to buy from, which establishment to eat in, or which transport to hire without full access to business and civil records? Advertising was patently untrustworthy and word of mouth offered no objective guarantee of anything. While commerce and risk were familiar bed partners, it didn't make sense to him that people would willingly make it harder on themselves than it had to be. Perhaps that was part of the pleasure, perverse though it seemed to him.

The moon was honeycombed with habitats, some barely fit for three people, others containing facilities for a hundred or more. Its infrastructure was rigid and inflexible, its form set in place two hundred years earlier, when First Wave colonists had sent corers in to dig out the main thoroughfares. Since then, a network of finer tunnels had spread like dendrites through the ancient stone, honeycombing it with fuel dumps, water tanks, waste recyclers, food factories, infirmaries, and meeting halls. The latter were hard to pin down, sometimes; social types would gather just about anywhere, following fleeting fashions and incomprehensible whims, while old haunts fell out of favor. Deangelis had never been able to keep up, not even with complete access to information at his fingertips and the reasoning power of a full Exarch behind him. It was beyond him.

He did, however, recognize a happening place when he saw one, and the Jade Monkey fit the bill perfectly.

"This is where we'll find Hails?" asked Horsfall, following

him through a press of humanity preoccupied with eating, drinking, smoking, and any other means of chemical appropriation at their disposal.

"Guaranteed." For their venture outside the Cell, he had modified his shipsuit to match the sort of clothes he saw around him. Loose-fitting garments tended to drift and tangle in the low gee, and were almost universally avoided as a result, but that left plenty to choose from. He was now clad in a clinging long-sleeve blue top with matching pants and black braces that crossed over his chest. His feet were bare, allowing him to grip surfaces with his toes if he needed to.

Horsfall sniffed. "Some Exarch Hails must be, if he spends all his time in bars."

"If you truly think that, you don't understand us at all," Deangelis said, finding her disapproval irritating even though he felt a measure of it himself. "I advise you to reserve your judgment."

"Didn't he attack you, too?" she shot back.

He shook his head, not wanting to get into that. Hails had attacked the Occlusion observatory and the Archon hiding within, not the Bedlam habitat—but that attack had led inexorably to the explosion of Catastrophe through the system, so in a sense Hails was partly responsible for what had happened. Had he not forced the issue, Bedlam might still be intact.

Deangelis drew his lips into a tight, straight line. Had Hails not forced the issue, someone else would have. He would be a fool to believe otherwise. At least Hails had tried to keep the Bedlam habitat out of the firing line.

He could only guess how Hails would react when he found out that Deangelis had failed to return the favor.

Don't mention me, said Jane Elderton into his mind as they crossed the bar. The Jade Monkey sold drinks in a variety of forms: premixed in bundles of grapelike sachets that burst on contact with the tongue, or prepared by hand and siphoned into glistening sacs that mimicked traditional highball glasses, champagne flutes, or beer mugs. Patrons could order their drinks from the bar or through a service network accessible on paying an entry fee. Small semiautonomous drones skimmed constantly over the crowd, delivering drinks and collecting empties, the faint buzz of their miniature electric motors inaudible over the mélange of music and conversation filling the air.

The far wall of the bar featured a giant, fluorescent reproduction of Frank Zappa's *Hot Rats* album cover. It cut a chord through the otherwise circular floor plan, suggesting a private room behind it.

Deangelis flagged the service network by raising his hand and snapping his fingers. Instantly one of the drones swooped over and descended to hover by his ear.

"I was wondering—"

"Follow me, sir. Your table is just through here."

He didn't show surprise. "Thank you." Without glancing at Horsfall, but aware that she was watching him closely, he tailed the drone through the crowd. A few people glanced at him, but not in recognition. No one seemed alarmed at his youthful appearance. There were far stranger phenotypes in evidence.

A triangular panel in the far wall swiveled open and the drone guided them through it. Noise cancellation effects pushed the bar's amiable hubbub into the distance as the door clicked shut behind them. Here the lighting was warm and indirect, with smooth pink couches arranged in semicircles clustered around a white bar. The room's sole occupant was a tall, white-haired man displaying the sort of nose patriarchs had once been proud to own. He stood as they entered and smiled. One broad hand brushed down his dark gray suit. Polished buttons gleamed.

"You're late," Lazarus Hails said, waving them to the couch opposite him.

Deangelis didn't see the point of sitting in such low gravity, but he went along with the charade, bouncing only slightly as he crossed his legs.

"I'll not accept your criticism on that score," he said. "You're aware of how difficult it is for me to travel."

"Naturally. Without Palmer Horsfall's timely intervention, you'd probably still be home right now, fuming impotently while you did our master's bidding."

Horsfall looked up at the mention of her name, but said nothing. She stood to one side, looking awkward. Deangelis wondered if Jane Elderton was speaking to her at that moment, reminding her to keep the extra Exarch in their party a secret.

"Drink?"

Deangelis waved the drone away as it swooped in to take their orders.

"We haven't come here to be sociable."

Hails pursed his lips. "I know full well why you're here, my friend." The drone darted to the white bar and returned with a crimson sac. “Shall I say ‘I told you so’ now or leave it unspoken?”

“If it’s important to you to say it, get it over with now so we can move on.”

“Oh, I don’t need to say it. But I need you to accept that I *did* tell you, and that you didn’t listen.”

“You’re just guessing. You can’t possibly know what happened in Bedlam.”

“*Au contraire.* The part of me conversing with you was in regular contact with the part of me minding my tangler. As things came to a head, that part of me retreated here, to keep me appraised. I left the tangler behind, just in case you found a use for it.” Hails’s eyes dropped to his drink. His lips tightened. “I don’t want you to think that I’m glad about what happened, Isaac. We are very different, you and I, but we are on the same side. And even if we weren’t, no one deserves to go through what you did.”

Horsfall stirred again. With a sharp exhalation, she kicked herself away to get a drink from the bar.

Hails half-turned to watch her, then glanced back at Deangelis. One bushy, white eyebrow arched.

“You’re here on the business of rebellion,” he said. “I wish to help you.”

Deangelis felt the tightness in his gut loosen, but not by much. “Is this room secure?”

“Of course. We’re not in Bedlam. We keep secrets here—and no one better than I. You don’t have to be afraid of the Archon in Altitude.”

“I’m not afraid,” he hastened to say.

“No? Well, I’m man enough to admit that *I* am. You should be, too. *Especially* you. You’ve seen what it can do.”

Deangelis nodded. “I thought you might not want me here, given what could follow.”

“I consider myself lucky it’s not here already. The Archon knew I was in Bedlam; it must have suspected my part in the endgame.” Hails looked at him over the red-hued drink he raised to his lips. “Did it tell you why it destroyed your home?”

“Yes. To keep the artifact contained.”

“That’s all?”

“It said that more people would die if we failed than had lived in all of Bedlam and Sublime combined.”

Hails's eyes narrowed. "I can't believe it's that frightened of Geodesica."

"Something inside it, perhaps?"

"But you didn't find anything, and neither did Jane."

"Nothing obvious, anyway."

"It didn't need to," said Horsfall from the bar.

Hails swiveled in his seat to look at her. "I'm sorry? If you intend to contribute to this conversation, you'd better speak up."

She raised a clear bulb to her lips and squirted a jet into her mouth. "The Archon is afraid that we'll get our hands on Geodesica itself, not something inside it. The Archon knows we'll outgrow Sol with it in our possession. The Archon fears what we might become."

"And what might that be, exactly?"

"That's irrelevant." She drained the bulb and discarded it. The drone swooped down to clean up her mess as she kicked away from the bar. "The Archon and its mates in Sol want Geodesica for themselves only. In order to get that, they gain sole access to the two entrances we know of and, under cover of a ROTH threat, explore the maze to their heart's content. If they can find another exit closer to Sol, or one well away from a colonized system, then they have their own private access point. They go off to explore the galaxy, leaving us behind. And we'll be damned fools if we let them do it."

"You seem so sure of yourself," said Hails with an amused air. "Why can't we explore it together?"

"Because it's big." She brought herself to a halt next to his couch and leaned over him, pointing. "It's big enough for us and the Archon and the Palmers and the Naturals and everyone else who ever wanted to have a poke around. If eleven years of exploration hasn't found the limits to it, then the chances are there might not be any limits, as we know them. It could be as boundless as the universe we live in—and if that's so, then how is Sol going to control us any longer? One of us could make the lucky discovery that changes everything. The builders, an instruction manual, a tool kit—whatever it is, they want to keep it to themselves."

Hails's amusement had turned into an open, almost mocking smile.

"What's so funny?" Horsfall asked him.

"You said 'one of us.'"

Horsfall pulled away. "What does it matter? I may not be an Exarch, but I've lost something. We all have."

"Please," he scoffed. "Don't play games with me, Jane. Come out where I can see you."

Horsfall said nothing, and neither did the woman inhabiting her body.

"Why so shy?" Hails persisted. "That's not like you."

"She says—" Horsfall blinked. "She says you have to earn her trust."

"Really? How quaint. She needs to understand that I don't take kindly to people—apart from me—keeping secrets in my own colony, and unless she puts all her cards out where I can see them, she can repent at leisure in the deep end of the Dark." Hails's smile had turned distinctly humorless. "She can trust me when I say that I would rather flush her out an air lock than take a chance on her being the Archon, or something worse. I trust I'm making myself perfectly clear."

Deangelis risked leaving the couch to lean forward. "Threatening each other solves nothing."

"Neither does lying, or keeping information to ourselves." Hails looked at him, then back at Horsfall. "You'll both be scanned before I let you out of this room. The slightest sign you're more than you seem, the air lock awaits. I want access to the Cell's memory store as well. All of it. If I find anything untoward—"

"Spare us the intimidation tactics," said Horsfall. "We get the picture."

Hails ran a hand through his hair. "Trust me. This isn't intimidation."

"Then what is it?"

"It's fear—good, old-fashioned, primal fear. Isaac and Jane may have nothing left to lose, but I certainly do."

Horsfall held Hails's stare a moment, then backed down. "If the Archon keeps Geodesica for itself, we all lose."

"You won't get an argument from me on that score."

Deangelis was keen to move on to something more concrete. "So let's work together to stop that happening," he said. "We're obviously not well enough equipped to take on Goliath. Have you thought about ways you can help? And ways we can help you?"

"Well, Altitude was stretched by those attack drones I sent you before. And getting them built underneath the radar was difficult enough. I don't have the resources to mobilize in earnest without bringing the puppets online. They may not be the splendors of human evolution we are, Isaac"—Hails tossed a casual wink at Horsfall—"but there certainly are an awful lot of them."

Deangelis hid a moue of distaste. By "puppets" Hails meant the system's majority inhabitants—the people the Exarchate had claimed along with the systems it had taken over. Hails used the term to emphasize the hierarchical manner in which he preferred to rule. Deangelis found the term distasteful. It smacked of bigotry.

"Do you think they'll choose to follow us?" he asked.

"What if they don't? They have no choice. The fighting has started, whether we admit it or not, and the Exarchate took the first casualties." Hails downed half of his remaining wine in one smooth gulp. "I'm certain they'll come around. We're a proud and territorial lot out here. The slightest hint that Sol is trying to muscle in on our jurisdiction, and the mob will ride out. And those that don't? . . . Well, they can leave before we get started. It never hurts to appear clement, old boy, especially when they'll spread the word that the Arc Circuit is finally itching for a fight."

"And the other Exarchs?" asked Horsfall. "Will they fight with us?"

Hails leaned back into his seat. "That's the question. The answer, I'm afraid, will be a while coming. Melilah Awad's sensational broadcast was picked up by all of us in the Circuit, and by now it should have spread everywhere else, across the entire Exarchate. Sol has done its best to counter it, of course. Who believes whom depends on individual temperament—and we are all individual by design. It's going to take a fair amount of talk to thrash out a consensus."

"Communication is going to be a serious issue," said Deangelis. "If we talk over the tangler network, Sol will overhear. If we use the Palmers to ferry messages, it will take decades to come to an agreement, let alone coordinate retaliation."

"That's if the Palmers wish to be involved," put in Horsfall.

Hails nodded. "We need Geodesica," he said. "That's the bottom line."

Deangelis nodded, unable to completely quell the thought that Sol had won before the fight even started. If they couldn't win without Geodesica, but couldn't take Geodesica without winning first, then they were doomed.

But it needn't be so clear-cut, he reminded himself. There might be other exits out in the Dark, just waiting to be found—or Bedlam could be reclaimed without confronting Sol head-on. If they acted quickly, they might take the Archon by surprise.

He felt a moment of sorrow for his higher self, forced to guard the key to humanity's future while forces gathered around him. What hope had he of surviving the coming storm? Rudra-Deangelis didn't know, and he couldn't let himself be influenced by that uncertainty. Casualties were inevitable in times of conflict, as Bedlam and Sublime clearly demonstrated. When hundreds of worlds and billions of people—not to mention control over the entire galaxy—were at stake, the body count was only going to go up.

As long as one of him was left standing at the end, he would be satisfied. He would stand on a mountain of bodies and proclaim, for the universe to hear, the wrongs Sol had committed. He would not be denied that.

"To justice," he said, miming raising a glass and toasting his two conspirators, "however we achieve it."

"To revenge," said Horsfall.

Hails tipped the last of his blood red wine into his mouth and swallowed it in one gulp. "To war."

+6

Geodesica interior: plus 25 hours

The first thing Melilah noted on waking was a sensation of weightlessness. Floating in free fall with nothing around her but air, she stirred sleepily and sent herself into a slow tumble. Her right leg brushed against something solid, and she kicked reflexively, pushing herself away.

Leg. Air. Free fall.

It took her a good minute to put the three facts together. When she did, her eyes snapped open. The space around her was roughly spherical and cramped, with rust brown walls and dim lighting. She reached out to take a handhold and found it to be warm and soft beneath her hands, like living felt. She reveled in the sensation, struck by the simple wonder of moving her fingers.

She had her body back!

Someone moaned. She tore her attention away from her fingertips and looked down. The thing her leg had bumped against was another body: Deangelis floated like a dead starfish in a tidal pool, his back to her, rocking back and forth on the momentum her gentle kick had given him. It wasn't he who had moaned, though. Behind her, Eogan hung half-merged with the wall itself, looking like a creepy biotech sculpture. His arms from his elbows down were visible, protruding as though from a bathtub full of molasses. His head craned forward. Long dark hair hung over his forehead, limp in the zero gee. His eyelids fluttered.

They were in the Cell, she realized. Somehow it had found the resources to mend itself and make them separate again. The three of them wore identical black shipsuits, seamless and snug fitting, with white circles at throat, wrists, and ankles. Her hair danced as she moved, just short enough to miss her eyes and dyed brown and yellow in horizontal lines. She flexed her fingers and ran a tongue along the back of her teeth, not feeling any different but unnerved by the knowledge that her flesh was manufactured, counterfeit right down to the bones. Only her brain was original, and even on that score she had her doubts. It had been infected with Exarch nanotech twice in the last week. God only knew what had been done to it now.

"What happened?" Eogan's eyes opened for an instant, unseeing, then closed again.

"I don't know." The last thing she remembered was rushing along one of Geodesica's abstract tunnels. "The drone exploded. I think. It's all a bit confusing."

"I remember . . ." Eogan's upper torso slid several centimeters out of the wall, making her think sickeningly of bodies in tar pits. Thin threads trailed from his skin back into the workings of the Cell. His clean, pheromone-rich scent jarred with what she saw before her.

His eyes widened. "Deangelis!"

"I did what I had to do," said the former Exarch.

Melilah jumped. She had assumed him unconscious. "What do you mean?"

"We were discovered," he said, his voice low and despondent. He didn't move, and she couldn't see his face. "I got us away by the only means I could."

More of Eogan emerged from the wall, revealing him from the waist up. His expression was furious. "You took control of the *Cowell* from me!"

"I had no choice. Your reactions were too slow. It was either take over or die."

She could understand Eogan's misgivings. Deangelis's explanation sounded a little too convenient. "Are you still in control?"

"No. The danger appears to be behind us."

"'Appears to be'?"

"Must I explain *everything* to you?" Still Deangelis didn't turn, but the anger in his voice was suddenly a match for Eogan's. "Take a look outside and make up your own mind. If you'll just stop badgering me for a moment, maybe I can work out how to get us home."

She retreated as best she could in the confined space, stung by his tone. "Eogan? Where are we?"

The Palmer had frozen in the middle of separating from the Cell. His eyes were glazed, staring elsewhere. He didn't respond.

"Eogan? Are you all right?"

Before she could demand that he answer her, the walls became transparent, revealing their surroundings more clearly than any description could have.

Deangelis's mood and Eogan's silence were instantly forgiven.

For a long minute, all she could do was stare.

The behemoth was as gray and menacing as a battleship, but many times larger. As a child, Eogan had collected images of ancient seafaring craft, feeling a particular fascination for the brutal, metal ships of the first two World Wars and the Cold Wars that followed. They were nothing like spacecraft or space stations. Requiring crews of hundreds just to stay afloat, yet able to withstand powerful explosions without flying to fragments, they had plowed the oceans of Earth with grim relentlessness—demonstrating a brute-force approach to colonization that had never translated to the broader fields of space. Some early off-Earth regimes had attempted to emulate the glory days of colonial expansion, but all had failed. Speed, efficiency, and maneuverability won battles in space, not mass, firepower, or size.

His first thought on seeing the behemoth was that either the rules were different elsewhere in the galaxy, or someone had had the chutzpah not to care.

From bow to stern the thing was almost two kilometers long. Each end was rounded like a fat cigar, which it broadly resembled. Its girth was in the order of two hundred meters, roughly consistent along its length; there were protuberances and fins scattered around the hull, but none so large as to throw the symmetry out of whack. Its color ranged from gray to black, unrelenting in its bleakness. Deep-penetrating lidar brought back glimpses of a thick shell surrounding concentric decks. Long shafts connected each level—possibly elevators or air-conditioning vents. A single tube, ten meters wide, ran up the center of the craft. It appeared to be blocked by debris.

Eogan spent too long looking for its means of propulsion. There was no obvious front or back, and therefore no identifiable reaction or intake vents. What propelled it remained a mystery until he tore his eyes away long enough to see what it was flying through. Then he understood.

Both the behemoth and the Cell cruised up the center of a kilometer-wide pipe in an atmosphere half as dense as that at Earth's sea level. Alternating bands of dark and light swept by, but there was no sensation of movement apart from that. The air was stationary with respect to the craft, obviously caught in the same propulsive effect—which, Eogan decided, was probably a warp effect similar to that in the smaller tunnels. Someone had set the behemoth in position long ago, and space-time did the rest.

Tiny black spots speckled the bright bands as they went by. Eogan couldn't tell what they were. He noted also that the pipe wasn't perfectly straight. It possessed a curvature that, although invisible to the human eye, the Cell's instruments perceived perfectly well. If the behemoth continued unchecked, the tunnel would bring it back to its starting place after completing a circle ten thousand kilometers across.

Eogan planned to be long gone before that happened, no matter how interesting the scenery might be. The *Cowell* hung next to the behemoth like krill shadowing a whale. The Cell had replenished its mass from the air and an irregular atmosphere of debris accompanying the giant craft. Eogan checked the composition of the debris and found it mainly to be lightweight metal alloys and ceramic chips doped with carbon nanotubes for strength—difficult to digest but ideal for rebuilding the Cell's lost capacity and restoring independent mobility to its passengers. The air was far from Earth normal, with surprisingly large amounts of helium and noble gases, but there was enough oxygen and water vapor to bring life support back up to optimal.

The giant vessel didn't seem to care how much they consumed. It loomed over them like a cliff face, with about as much personality.

"We should try hailing it," said Melilah, her head physically turning from side to side to take it all in.

"I'm not sure I want to," Eogan responded. He already missed the intimacy they had shared when tightly bound by the Cell, but knew she would feel very differently. Her physicality—the grace with which she moved; the frame of her hair around her well-defined features; and the shape of her, fit and unambiguously female in the black shipsuit—was inseparable from her sense of self. Having it back would ground her, help her focus.

What'll help me? he wondered.

"We might be here," he said, "only because it hasn't noticed us yet."

She glanced at him. "The fact that we're still alive should tell us we're safe. It can't possibly have missed us."

"Maybe, or we're hovering on the brink of trying its patience. Let's not push our luck."

"I think it's dead," said Deangelis, looking up from his mental calculations long enough to pronounce his opinion, then retreating back into them.

Eogan swallowed an angry retort. Deangelis's violation of the trust between them burned like a red-hot coal inside him. The *Cowell* was *his* ship, no one else's, and that was the way he intended to keep it. One more attempt to take over, he told himself, and that would be the end of it. Deangelis could float home for all he cared.

But even as he fumed, Deangelis's words wouldn't leave him. *Your reactions were too slow.*

That was patently true, and undoubtedly—whether intended that way or not—a threat.

And there were worse things to worry about in the Cell's operating memory . . .

Eogan decided to try the patience of the behemoth, wise or not. Kicking the Cell's rejuvenated thrusters into life, he nudged them down the giant ship's length and angled around it at the same time, following a gentle spiral that kept them well away from the bristling hull.

"What are they?" asked Melilah, indicating several circular features that looked like nothing so much as portholes. "Windows?"

"If they are, they're five meters across."

He risked an exploratory laser. The coherent light scattered randomly back at them, or was absorbed, revealing nothing. "Everything's the same color," he said. "Does that strike anyone as odd?"

"A coating of some kind," she said. "Possibly not a design feature."

"Nanotech?"

"Or something less dramatic—like dust."

Eogan asked himself how long it would take a ship cruising through the pristine environment of Geodesica to accumulate such a buildup. He didn't like the answer.

"Look," he said as another feature came into view. "They're Merchant Bees, aren't they?"

"I think you're right. Too small to be Snailer ships, anyway."

The nine spindly twig shapes, each larger than the Cell but still dwarfed by the bulk of the behemoth, clustered around a mushroomlike protuberance midway along the ship's length. It looked exactly like a docking point.

"Do you think they're still in there?" she went on.

"I don't know what to think," he admitted. "The temperature is completely uniform, all across the structure. There are no vibrations, sonic or seismic. Nothing has acknowledged us since we woke up."

"I told you," said Deangelis. "It's dead."

"I want you to keep quiet," Eogan snapped. "We have no reason to listen to you."

Melilah seemed startled by his comment. "I think he might be right."

"I don't care if he is. We'll work it out for ourselves, eventually."

"Listen, Palmer Eogan," Deangelis said. "I am not your problem. Time is your problem—and I'm doing my best to solve it for you."

"All you've done is make it patently clear that you don't need us." Eogan couldn't keep the lid on the anger as it flowed back into him. "Damn it, Melilah, he could have left us behind back there and we would never have known!"

"But he didn't, did he?"

"No, but what about next time?"

"Why would he?" she put in reasonably.

Her defense of Deangelis surprised him, threw him off guard. "Why *wouldn't* he?"

"You're being irrational," she said. "I can understand your anger, but—"

"This has nothing to do with anger! It's just common sense. The fact that he can take over the Cell any time puts us both at risk—and it's not a risk I'm prepared to take. You say we should trust him. Well, I'd like to agree with you, but you only have to be wrong once and we're in the shit—*both* of us."

"In case you hadn't noticed, we're all in the shit right now." She turned her back on the alien spectacle outside the Cell and confronted him eye to eye. "We need him, Eogan, whether you like it or not. Can you tell us how we got here, or how we might get back? I know I can't. Arguing about whether or not he needs *us* is irrelevant. At least it seems so to me."

Eogan barely kept his voice under control. "Tell her how we got here," he said. When Deangelis didn't respond, he reached down to grab the Exarch by the shoulder and spun him around.

"Tell her how we got here, you son of a bitch, or I'll tell her myself."

Deangelis's face was pinched and pale. He looked at each of them in turn and shook his head.

"What are you talking about?" Melilah forced herself between them, as though she thought he might punch Deangelis.

Eogan had never hit anyone in his life—but his fists were itching to try.

"Deangelis might not want to talk about it," he said, "but the *Cowell* knows. He activated the VOID drives—*inside Geodesica!* And the Dark only knows what that did to us."

A frown flickered across her features. She turned to Deangelis. "Is that true?"

"I had no choice," the former Exarch said. Two matching spots of red burned in his white, high-boned cheeks.

"You're using that excuse a lot today," Eogan snapped.

She shushed him. "Obviously it worked, and I'm grateful for that. But how far have we gone? How far did we travel while the drive was on?"

Deangelis shook his head. "I don't know for certain. I was unconscious most of the time, too."

"You must have a rough idea. The *Cowell* was active while the drives were running, otherwise we'd be dead now. It must've recorded the number of intersections we went through."

"It did, but there were so many of them and they went by so quickly—plus I think the VOID field interacted with the tunnels themselves, making them bend and join in ways they normally wouldn't—"

"How *far,* Isaac?" There was a brittle edge to Melilah's voice that made it clear she didn't want an explanation, just an answer.

"My best estimate," he said, not meeting her eye, "would be in the order of nineteen thousand junctions."

"Nineteen—" She caught herself in midecho. Eogan could see the shock on her face as clearly as he felt it in his gut. That was an awfully long way to backtrack.

"I think I can do it," said Deangelis. "Just leave me alone and let me think. Don't distract me. I need to *concentrate*. I know it's possible, if I just try hard enough . . ."

The former Exarch curled up into a ball, shutting himself off from the world, and them. Eogan turned away, alarmed by the display.

"*This* is our best hope of survival?" he said to Melilah.

"Perhaps our only one," she said without conviction. "I suggest we let him get on with it. It's not as if we don't have other things to keep us busy in here."

Eogan looked up at the shadowy bulk of the ROTH ship. "Fiddling while Rome burns."

"Maybe," she said, "but it's better than doing nothing at all."

Deangelis clutched at himself and thought feverishly of phantom limbs.

It's too much, a seditious voice in his mind whispered. *Nineteen thousand junctions might as well be nineteen million. Look at the state you're in. What sort of mind are you? You're just a warped reflection of the one you used to be. The sooner you admit your limitations, the better.*

Deangelis's thoughts were truncated, incomplete. He flailed for connection with the rest of him, the glorious multitude he had left behind in Bedlam, but all he felt was vacuum, cold and heart-wrenching. The void where his higher self had been ate at him, undercut him, brought him crashing down in a tangle.

Your full self could have traced the route back home in his sleep, but you can't even come close. The voice belonged to his doubt and despair. The two emotions spoke in unison, forcing him to confront everything he dared not think. *You overestimated your ability and must now pay the cost. You can't go back. You can never go back. You will never be whole again.*

He knew the rest of him was dead. There was no way anything could have survived the destruction of Bedlam. Barring a miracle, he was the last fragment of himself extant in the universe—or *outside* the universe, in his case. Yet part of him had clung to the hope of regaining his former glory, of somehow making new bodies and joining them up into a new mental network. He couldn't do that in Geodesica; he doubted he could do it anywhere without the Archon's help. As unlikely as the latter might have been, there had still been a chance.

Now that chance was gone. He had gotten himself lost in the maze and all he had left was a phantom limb where the rest of himself had once been. A phantom *mind*. He had been able to function despite the handicap for a while, but the situation was quickly becoming unsustainable. There had to be a reckoning at some point, between him and the emptiness.

You can't exist with just one mind, the voice said, *any more than a Natural can walk with no legs. Exarchs are creatures of thought and reason. That is their strength. With just one fragmentary mind you are weakened, crippled. You are incomplete. You are little more than* human.

I was always human, he retorted.

Is that what Melilah and Eogan think?

Not the same sort of human as them, but human nonetheless. The label is flexible.

That's easy to say from the top down. What if the Archon claimed to be human, too? Would you allow it?

He shook his head in frustration. *Why are we arguing about this?*

The voice didn't answer immediately. He tightened his grip around his head, willing it to stop aching. His entire mind felt like scar tissue, pink and raw. He could barely think through it.

If you aren't an Exarch, said the voice, *what* are *you?*

He couldn't answer that question. Trying to do so saw him repeatedly confronting the harsh truth that he was a lost part of something, not a whole. But he needed to answer it. He needed to become whole in order to function, to be of use to Melilah and Eogan. If he couldn't help them, what reason did he have to exist?

He braved a glimpse of the outside world, piggybacking on telemetry without Eogan's knowledge. The Cell had sidled up to an opening in the behemoth's side and was braving a closer look. Eogan aimed a tightly focused beam of light into the hole and played it about, noting such details as access ways, curving ramps, and stairwells. The existence of the latter suggested that the immense structure had once rotated around its long axis, providing its passengers with a semblance of gravity. That it was some kind of ferry struck Deangelis as obvious, although he wasn't sure the others had figured it out yet.

The behemoth was utterly lifeless, a hulk drifting on the tide of space-time endlessly circling the giant torus—a relic, just like the atmosphere it occupied. There was no obvious way to ascertain its age; Geodesica's artificial environment rendered the usual methods of dating irrelevant. It could, therefore, have been traveling for as long as humanity existed—or, more to the point, at least as long as the Merchant Bees hadn't.

"Do you remember those skulls you picked up by the Occlusion?" he dimly overheard Melilah ask as they pulled out of the hole and swept along the nominal top of the ship, toward the docking point.

Eogan nodded. “What about them?”

“They were atmospheric ships. It seemed odd at the time, since you found them in deep space. This could be the solution to that mystery.”

“The Bees used them to get around Geodesica.” Eogan focused the Cell’s instruments on one of the abandoned craft. It wasn’t streamlined at all; none of the Merchant Bee vessels were. *Catching a plane to cross the galaxy,* he thought in wonderment. “Okay, so how did they end up outside?”

“Maybe there was an accident,” she suggested. “An explosive decompression. It could happen, depending on what provisions they made to seal the tunnels. The skulls evacuated and got stuck out there.”

“It’s possible.”

“Can you think of another explanation?”

“Perhaps they were deliberately expelled for some reason. Or junked. I don’t think we can say for certain until we have more data.”

Melilah reluctantly agreed.

The discussion of the ROTH ships reminded Deangelis of the moment Eogan and Melilah had snatched alone in Bedlam. He still didn’t know exactly what had happened then. If it *had* been a brief, stolen intimacy, there had been little sign of affection since. His two human companions remained wary of each other, cautious in every word and gesture. He was no expert at romantic relationships, but he doubted that could possibly constitute progress.

He watched Melilah as she stared at the images the Cell threw for her onto its sophisticated walls. Her fascination with the behemoth was slightly desperate, but infectious all the same. They were looking at artifacts studied by no human in all of history. It should have been a wondrous opportunity, not one for recrimination and blame. He could understand her using them to distract herself from her grief.

“I want to go out there,” Melilah said as the Cell approached one of the behemoth’s rounded ends and peered up the central tube.

“I don’t think that’s a good idea,” said Eogan.

“Why not? The air won’t kill me, and there’s no sign of life.” Her eyes shone. “I want to touch it. It won’t feel real until I do.”

“I want you wearing a suit, then,” Eogan insisted, “and in line of sight at all times.”

“Aye-aye, captain. Whatever it takes to get the hell out of here for a while.” The Cell extruded a transparent, flexible membrane that crawled up her arms and spread to cover her entire body. She shuddered as it slid over her face like a lizard's second eyelid blinking, then she looked around with no apparent discomfort. Her fingers smoothly clenched and unclenched. The only sign that she was wearing a suit at all was a smooth bump in the small of her back, and a new shininess to her black shipsuit.

"You have scrubbers for air," said Eogan, "a standard comms pack, and basic maneuvering thrusters. The envelope is self-repairing and independently powered. It'll protect you from the background radiation. You could live in it for a month if you had to."

"I'd prefer not to." Melilah crouched expectantly as the Cell came in close to the behemoth's snout—or tail, depending on how he looked at it. From the Cell's repertoire of configurations, Eogan summoned an oval door one meter across, and Deangelis fought the urge to warn her not to go. She had no reason to listen to him, and he had no reason for being so nervous.

"Ready?" asked Eogan.

"You bet."

The oval hatch retracted into the hull. Air pressure equalized with a sudden whoosh, and a new odor impinged on Deangelis's nostrils. It smelled like a hybrid of iron and ozone, and made the back of his tongue water. He wondered if Melilah could smell it in her humaniform bubble. Neither he nor Eogan required such precautions. They could stand unprotected in vacuum itself and feel no ill effects. They could also, if they wanted to, immerse themselves in the feeds from the Cell and thereby experience every possible sensation from its point of view. They could see the hulk in colors never known by Natural humanity, taste the chemicals it emitted, hear the infrasonic creaks it made as it pursued its stately course.

But she would be the only one to touch it with her hand. Just the narrow film of her environment suit would stand between her and a machine that might have been launched before *Homo habilis* walked the Earth. She would own that experience until the day she died.

For a fleeting moment, Deangelis was jealous. Then he realized that there was nothing stopping him from doing the same except fear—and a stubborn determination to at least *try* to get them home.

The alternating stripes on the tunnel walls sent a slow, strobing effect across Melilah's face as she exited the Cell. Deangelis had spent almost a minute examining the tiny black dots on the bright stripes, wondering if they might be evidence of writing or some sort of code. They weren't. They were in fact tunnel mouths, identical to those seen in the earlier junctions but seeming much smaller in this new context. There were around one hundred tunnel entrances per bright stripe, and the stripes were roughly ten meters across. If the giant tunnel did indeed form a ring ten thousand kilometers long, then roughly fifty million entrances opened onto it.

And they had come through *one* of them . . .

Neither Eogan nor Melilah seemed to have realized just how dire their situation was. He wasn't about to tell them. Not yet. There was always a chance he might be able to backtrack successfully, if he only focused hard enough.

What's the point? demanded his doubt, the scar tissue that flexed every time he attempted to move his phantom limb. *You don't even know who you are.*

I know exactly who I am, he answered, with all the confidence he could muster. *I'm Isaac Forge Deangelis.*

In name only.

In everything.

Do you really think that'll be enough?

He huddled tighter, isolating himself with the data.

It will have to be, he told himself.

On exiting the Cell, Melilah felt a surge of relief so powerful it left her light-headed. Strange though her surroundings were, at least she wasn't cooped up in the tiny Cell with her inhuman ex-lover and a despondent Exarch. The walls of the tunnel were so far away they didn't look like walls at all, but weirdly geometric cloud formations marching by. The end of the giant ship bulged at her like the head of a giant catfish, its mouth open in a permanent O. She hadn't truly grasped the scale of it yet.

"Can you move in closer?" she asked Eogan.

The Cell nudged forward by degrees until she was two meters away. She let go of the hatch and pushed herself forward. The sides of the giant mouth engulfed her as she slid into its shadow. It was as black as the exterior hull, as black as night, and crusty with it, as though it had rested at the bottom of an ocean for a hundred years before being dredged up and put on display.

She drifted into the cavernous maw, eyes slowly growing used to the darkness and picking out details from the gloom. The ship's central tube was as feature-studded as the exterior hull, with frequent antenna stubs, "portholes," and other unidentifiable shapes marching off into the distance. There was no light at the end of the tunnel. She resisted the temptation to shout, "Halloo!" If anything lurked in the darkness ahead, she wanted to give it as little cause to be frightened of her as possible—and vice versa.

Her shove off from the Cell had been just slightly off center. As the wall on her right-hand side came slowly closer, she began looking for a suitable anchor point. She chose a spiky antenna that had grown fur on it, like a moss-strangled tree, and reached out for it as it approached.

Her hand went right through it, as though it was made of loosely packed salt. A cloud of black dust puffed as she tumbled by, thrown off balance by the unexpected development.

She must have made a small sound—not a cry of alarm, but enough to alert Eogan.

"Are you all right in there, Melilah?"

"Fine," she said. The wall was almost within arm's reach. She would arrest herself against that instead. "It's just—this thing is so old it's falling apart!"

Her hand brushed against the wall almost without resistance. Her fingers plowed through the black fur, stirring up another cloud of dust. She clutched for the slightest hint of solidity, but her fingers closed around only powdery darkness. The dust thickened, covering her as she rotated slowly into the wall. She struck the ancient surface broadside, not missing the farcical nature of her situation.

"I'm going right through it!" she called out to the others.

Eogan's voice came back to her, thick with static. "—thrusters—"

"What?"

"—again: use—"

"I'm okay," she broadcast, turning the suit's gain up high to reassure him. "It's not hurting me."

All she could see through her visor was ancient black metal, or whatever it was, crumbling and parting around her. Its density wasn't uniform. The occasional relatively hard point brushed by, not strong enough to stop her but turning her and slowing her down before breaking apart. She clutched at one of them and brought a handful of silvery nuggets up to her face, so she could see them. They gleamed faintly in the darkness.

Finally she came to a halt. Rather than swim, if she could, she activated the suit's internal propulsion system. Tiny thrusters warmed up with a single command. Green ready lights flashed in her peripheral vision.

Which way? She could backtrack to the Cell as easily as saying the word—keeping her promise to stay in line of sight—or she could press on in hope of finding a hollow space, or something solid. Figuring that there was little chance of anything being alive, given the corrosion around her, she settled on the latter, keeping thrust to an absolute minimum and angling herself headfirst through the ruin, so her cross section was at its smallest. She felt like a nighttime scuba diver, braving the deep without a torch.

"—hear me?"

"Don't worry," she sent back to the Cell. "I'm just exploring."

"—signal—faint—"

"No kidding," she muttered, breaking through into a chamber, trailing a black wake behind her. She killed the thrusters and hunted for some sort of light switch. The suit possessed twin torches that radiated from her shoulders, pointing in the direction of her chest. She swiveled to take in the view before the spreading cloud of dust obscured it completely.

The room was five meters across and circular, with a dais as high as her waist in the center. The floor sloped up to the dais, and up again to meet the walls around it. She felt as though she was inside a giant doughnut. The remains of structures that might have been chairs slumped in groups around the room. A conference room? Mess hall? There were no colors. Everything was covered in the black fur. Even through the suit's filters, the air smelled stale and dead.

There was a door at the far end. Two sliding panels met to form a stylized eye, or so it appeared to her. No doubt the builders' eyes looked very different to anything she would recognize, although the existence of chairs was intriguing. Thus far she had seen nothing resembling a body, or any sign of damage that might explain why the ship had been abandoned.

She pushed through the door as easily as if it was made of wet tissue paper. The corridor outside was diamond-shaped, which would have been awkward to walk in had there been any gravity. Her feet would have slid down into the rut beneath her. She wondered what that said about the builders' physiques. Did they have no legs, as she knew them, or did they lack a simple vertical orientation? Perhaps their legs stuck out at forty-five-degree angles, in which case the V-shaped floor would suit them perfectly. She pictured a strange myriapodous creature flowing through the corridor like an armor-plated snake. Her imagination supplied details she couldn't possibly know, such as clicking mandibles and gleaming compound eyes. Vestigial legs under its mouthparts would function as hands, with opposable pincers instead of thumbs.

The image was faintly ludicrous, and not at all in keeping with what xenarcheologists knew about the Merchant Bees. Still, she told herself as she followed the corridor around to her left, the Bees hadn't necessarily built the giant ship. They could just have been visitors, or explorers like her. Explorers and fugitives . . .

She had almost forgotten Bedlam in the rush of their discovery—and she was glad to pursue her new obsession rather than revisit her grief. In all its years of exploration, humanity had never found anything on such a scale. The presence of something *material* inside the strange topologies of Geodesica made it so much more interesting, to her mind. Without a glimpse of the people who traveled along them or the places they traveled to, the endless tunnels were just empty.

The corridor ended in a pressure door, which gave way before her as easily as the last, only to reveal yet more corridor. She craned her neck through several open portals, discovering a series of rooms identical in size yet varying decidedly in content. Some were full to the ceiling with elaborate structures that had decayed and clumped into low-gee tangles of spaghetti; others were empty apart from isolated objects that could have been ornaments or scientific instruments. It was hard to imagine what they might be for without the clues color and texture would have given her. It was difficult even to tell if the single structures were sitting on the floor or growing out of it.

She pushed on, following the corridor in the vain hope of finding its end. It was an access way of some kind, perhaps a maintenance corridor, and led for hundreds of meters through the ship. The suit played beams of sonar ahead of her, giving her glimpses of a wide variety of spaces. Some might have been engine rooms. Others might have been bedrooms. Her imagination ran wild.

On the fringe of the sonar, just within range, something solid pinged. She turned her attention toward it, unable to make it out through the hazy walls and access shafts. Whatever it was, it wasn't large—a meter or two across at most—and located to one side of the access corridor. She considered changing direction to check it out. If it was a dead reactor core, she might not want to go *too* close.

A faint noise from behind her distracted her from the anomaly. At first she put it down to imagination, but the deep rumbling sound was soon clearly audible through her environment suit, and growing rapidly louder. She looked automatically over her shoulder. Nothing was visible around the bend of the corridor, but sonar pinged off something large coming nearer.

Wishing she'd never put the image of giant centipedes into her head, she upped her speed using the thrusters and burst through another crumbling pressure door. The noise grew louder still, and she nudged her thrusters so fast that the turbulence of her passage kicked up a cloud of black dust from the smooth walls and obscured the corridor behind her. As the clouds closed over, she glimpsed something large accelerating rapidly toward her.

The smaller, hard echo fell behind, forgotten, as she fled through the ruined ship.

Melilah's voice crackled from the behemoth's dark heart, barely intelligible and thick with static.

"I'm—right through—"

"Use your thrusters," Eogan sent to her, picking up her heat signal as she tumbled through the ancient ship's rotten wall. "I'll say that again: use your thrusters if you can't get a grip."

"—hurting me!"

Her heat signature vanished, swamped by the black debris.

"Can you hear me?" Eogan leaned forward, willing the Cell to pick her signal out of the noise. The Cell echoed his movement, nudging further into the wreck's mouth. "Melilah! Are you there?"

"—worry," came back a faint reply. "—just exploring."

"Your signal is very faint. Perhaps you should come back."

All he heard over the comms was static.

"Damn it."

"It was a bad idea to split up," said Deangelis.

Eogan couldn't fight a snappy reply. "Could *you* have stopped her?"

Deangelis shook his head. "No, but I can go in after her, if you like."

Eogan shook his head. "There's no point both of you getting lost. If she gets into real trouble, all she has to do is bust through the walls into clear air and hail us from there."

Deangelis nodded and went back to his mental huddle. Eogan watched him, grimly intrigued by the former Exarch and his strange mood. A pall of depression hung thick around him, and it was catching.

Eogan's own feelings were complex. Not normally an angry person, he was bothered as much by his own response to Deangelis as he was by Deangelis himself. His undeniable rage at the way Deangelis had taken over the *Cowell* didn't stem just from the loss of the *Nhulunbuy,* although that was part of it. The plan had been appallingly risky: activating the VOID drives within Geodesica should have vaporized them, more likely than not. Instead of saving them, Deangelis might have killed them, and it smacked of a fatalism that Eogan didn't want to humor.

Most of all, though, he resented the ease with which it had happened. Palmer Cells were complex vessels with many intricate and convoluted control systems that naturally resisted external takeover. It took years of practice to learn how to use them properly even when one was authorized to. Yet in the space of an eyeblink Deangelis had reached in and ripped command out from under him as easily as an adult taking a child's toy.

Deangelis looked like an ordinary person. At a glance, he could have been a moody teenager upset that life hadn't gone the expected way. But that façade hid a mind both powerful and mysterious. The combination was an unnerving one.

"Like a ship in a bottle," Deangelis murmured.

"What?"

Deangelis opened his eyes, startled. "I'm sorry. I was talking to myself."

"About anything in particular?"

"The ship out there. It's like one of those antiques where a model sailing ship is sealed inside a bottle. How did it get here? Why go to so much trouble?"

"I feel safe assuming it's not an ornament."

"We can't be sure of anything. It could be a museum piece, a memorial. It might not even be a *ship*. Its appearance could be a form of camouflage."

A cold feeling suffused down Eogan's modified spine. "Camouflage for what?"

"I don't know. For itself, perhaps. A nanoplex can assume any shape it desires while still retaining its functionality. That makes them perfect for covert operations."

"And traps." Eogan turned back to the telemetry, thinking of the crumbling, insubstantial nature of the wreck and searching in vain for any trace of Melilah. "I wish you'd raised this possibility earlier."

"Why? It's obviously quite dead."

"Or *playing* dead." Eogan's anger returned full force. "What if you're wrong and Melilah's in trouble?"

The youthful-seeming skin between Deangelis's eyes crinkled. "There's little we can do about it, and little point getting upset over it. It was her decision to go. She is capable of looking after herself."

"I know that, but . . ." Eogan reluctantly acknowledged Deangelis's point. "Damn it. We're in enough of a fix as it is without taking any extra risks."

"We're in no danger here, Palmer Eogan," said Deangelis smoothly.

"Really? How can you be so certain?"

"The only thing that has tried to hurt us so far came from outside Geodesica, from us—and when I say 'us' I do mean humanity, not the Exarchate."

"So you feel safe assuming on the basis of one dead wreck—which you yourself say might be camouflage for something else entirely—that we're completely safe in Geodesica?"

"I'm not saying that at all. Here, where we are right now, there is no single reason to feel threatened. Vulnerable and cautious, yes. Lost and confused, yes. But not threatened. Or frightened. Or any less sure of Melilah's abilities."

"I'm not—" Eogan stopped the word *frightened* before it could issue from his mouth. He almost laughed at his own irrationality. He *was* overreacting. "I feel like a rat in a laboratory maze. I keep waiting for something to give us an electric shock."

"Perhaps," said Deangelis, nodding sympathetically, "that's what happened to our friend out there."

Eogan rolled his eyes. "You're determined to make me paranoid, aren't you?"

Before Deangelis could answer, the Cell sounded an alarm. His attention immediately diverted to telemetry, where a sudden change in the wreck's environment had prompted the alert.

Something bright and fast was rocketing along the torus. Eogan nudged the Cell further back into the hole and directed all its instruments on the incoming object. He couldn't get a hard reading. Whatever it was, it moved at hypersonic speeds and hid behind a plasma disk from the turbulence and friction of the thin atmosphere.

It was coming right for them.

"Should I feel threatened now?" he asked Deangelis, unable to keep an edge from his voice.

"We should be very careful." The former Exarch closed his eyes and immersed himself in the data. Eogan did the same, seeing the approaching object as a burning, golden dot streaking through the striped tunnel. Its cross section increased as it approached. Various spectra revealed chaotic shock waves in its wake. A measurement of its velocity clocked in at many times the local speed of sound.

"It might not have come after us," Deangelis said. "This section of Geodesica is, I believe, a central hub—a supernode in the greater network. So many tunnels converge here that traffic must regularly flow along the torus—or have once flowed along it—to justify its size. This could be an innocent traveler, unrelated to us."

"Or it might be another drone from Sol." Eogan picked up a slight wobble in the object's trajectory, as though it was about to decelerate or change course. "I'm not about to jump out and say hello until I know for sure, either way."

"That's sensible. Wait a moment. It probably can't see us in here."

Eogan took the Cell deeper into the mouth, just in case, and launched a trio of tiny telemetry drones to relay data from the lip. He could rely on the wreck to distract the new arrival for a while, but there was still a chance of their presence in its maw attracting attention.

With a flash, the plasma disk preceding the object evaporated. Instantly, it began to decelerate. Forces greater than a Natural human could withstand gripped the craft. A booming roar heralded its descent to subsonic speed. By the time it was half a kilometer away, Eogan had a pretty good ambient-light fix on it; he didn't dare risk lidar or any other form of active examination. Gold in color, its shape changed from a tapered needle to a broad arrowhead as its speed dropped further still. When it crossed the hundred-meter mark, it was practically coasting at fifty meters per second.

"I recognize that configuration," said Deangelis. "It's from Sol."

Eogan didn't curse or argue the point. "How could it have followed us here?"

"Perhaps the VOID drive left a wake through the tunnels. I don't know. But I think we're safe assuming it's not friendly."

"Agreed." He muffled the Cell's emissions as far as they would go. As long as they didn't break radio silence or anything stupid like that—

He stopped in midthought. This time he did curse.

"Ah, shit: Melilah! If she gets into trouble and comes out into clear air, she won't find us there to help her—only that thing waiting to grab her!" He ran a hand over his scalp, thinking as fast as he could. "We'll have to warn her. I can take the Cell deeper into the wreck and head her off."

"I'm uncomfortable with the thought of being in there and not knowing what's going on out here."

Eogan nodded. "So we run a series of relays behind us, or even old-fashioned wire. As long as the signal doesn't leak and leave the wreck, we'll be safe and sound. Right?"

"Right, except—" Deangelis opened his eyes but didn't look at Eogan. "Except I want to go out there and confront our visitor."

"What? *Why?*"

"Because even if it passes us by, we'll know it's still out there. What's to stop it from doubling back and catching us out in the open? We need to deal with it here and now, or we'll be forever running."

Eogan could see the sense in that, but he still didn't like the idea. "Do you think you can take it out?"

"I don't know, but even if I can't that'll still work to your advantage. I'll make it look like it's killed all of us: problem solved."

"Why you and not me?"

Deangelis did look at him then. "You know the answer to that question, Palmer Eogan, and I know why you asked it. I'm the person best qualified to perform such a maneuver, and your concern about my motives is understandable. You'll just have to trust me, I'm afraid."

Eogan hesitated. The craft was coming dangerously close and showing every sign of stopping. If it made a thorough search of the wreck—or Melilah put in an unexpected appearance—the game would be up and they would be fighting on its terms. If, however, they brought the fight to it, they would at least have a chance of taking it by surprise.

Assuming Deangelis meant what he was saying, and didn't turn them in. A change of heart was all it would take. Perhaps the Archon would be lenient and let him come home. A dead home was better than none at all.

As soon as the thought passed through Eogan's mind, he knew it for the falsehood it was.

"All right, but screw us over and—" He floundered for a moment, seeking a threat that had a chance of sticking. What could possibly hurt a man who had once been ruler of an entire star system? Did Deangelis even have a vulnerable point?

He proceeded on instinct—and in response to his earlier concerns about whether Deangelis needed either him or Melilah Awad.

"Screw us over," he said, "and, with my dying breath, I'll make sure Melilah knows. She'd have nothing to do with you after that—and where would that leave you?"

Deangelis reared back as though struck, his lips sealed shut in a fierce line. He pushed himself to eye level with Eogan and glared. Just for an instant, Eogan thought Deangelis might actually attack him. He brought his hands up to defend himself, and kicked himself away.

A barrier slammed shut between them, cutting the space around them neatly in two. Without a word, and with no hope of stopping him, the former Exarch had co-opted half of the Cell. Eogan could feel the fabric of the ship dividing and rearranging. A whole chunk of it went dark to his senses, then reappeared in a shadowy form as Deangelis brought the maser link online.

Eogan braced himself as physical separation occurred, but it still shook him.

"I grow weary of your accusations, Palmer Eogan," came Deangelis's voice frostily down the line.

Deangelis accelerated smoothly out of the mouth of the wreck, and Eogan sank deeper into blackness, watching him go.

Don't think; don't feel. Just do it.

Deangelis chanted the mantra to himself as he rushed headlong to meet his maker's instrument. Thinking about Eogan's words and the feelings they had aroused served only to confuse him and get in the way of the task before him. If he stopped to question why exactly he was throwing himself forward as some kind of live bait, he would never actually do it.

Don't think; don't feel. Just do it.

The killer drone reacted the moment he came into view. It simultaneously changed course and launched a wave of dartlike missiles in his direction. They gleamed like minnows, dividing and redividing until a multitude of tiny specks formed a vicious cloud right in his path. He banked smoothly to avoid them and pulsed the Cell's thrusters into the cloud. An expanding shell of small but potent detonations lit up the torus for a full second.

Deangelis didn't stop to admire the fireworks. They were just a warm-up, a test of his reflexes and capabilities. He kept moving as the killer came around in a smooth arc, accelerating with crushing energies in order to get another shot.

"Must you do this?" Deangelis asked it, sending the message using an Exarch-exclusive protocol.

The killer drone didn't exhibit the minutest sign that it had heard. A series of coherent pulses probed the reflective defenses of his Cell component. More light scattered across the powdery, scarred face of the wreck. Deangelis narrowed the Cell's profile and dodged like a hyperactive mosquito out of the way.

"My name is Isaac Forge Deangelis," he broadcast, "Exarch of Lut-Deangelis and child of Sol. I order you to cease and desist!"

"I cannot," came the reply. The killer ceased firing and sprouted a multitude of flanges down its smooth, golden flanks. Its voice was smooth and oratorical, like any well-made AI. "You I am not to destroy, but the other fugitives must be eliminated."

"They're not here," Deangelis said, wondering why he alone had been spared—or if he was simply being toyed with. "You've come too late."

"Where are they?" The killer spiraled around him in a harrying, suspicious manner. He kept moving in return, to stop himself from getting too close or being pinned down.

"Does it matter?"

"Of course. If your paths have simply diverged, you can tell me where so I can find their trail and keep searching."

"They're dead," he lied. "The shock of the VOID field killed them."

"Where are their bodies?"

"They don't exist anymore. I absorbed them into the Cell in order to increase its mass. As you can see, I don't have much to work with. I'm lucky to have got this far. The three of us never would have."

The killer pondered this for a fleeting microsecond. "Convenient."

"You don't believe me?"

"I am ordered to be merciful on your account, not gullible."

"On whose orders are you acting? The Archon?"

"No. The Exarch of Lut-Deangelis." If the killer had possessed a face, it would have been grinning. Deangelis was certain of it.

"The Exarch—" All attempts to evade the killer ceased in the face of that shocking revelation. "*I* am the Exarch of Lut-Deangelis!"

The killer didn't respond. It took advantage of his stunned immobility to lunge forward, flanges unfolding into claws and field-effect grapnels.

He barely dodged in time. His mind rang with the news that someone had taken over Bedlam, even as the thing sent to kill Melilah and Eogan accelerated hard on his tail, matching his every move and tugging at him with thin but insistent talons.

"Why are you chasing me?" he broadcast. "I order you to stop!"

"I will not," came the smooth reply. Pincers as nebulous as air but as sharp as the finest steel snipped at his wake. Deangelis darted away and found himself angling toward the behemoth. The killer was going to try to force him into the gap between it and the wall.

"You just told me that you're working for the Exarch of Lut-Deangelis, but that's me—and *I* am giving you an order! You must obey me!"

"You are not the source of my instructions. You are a fragment of the one that was. Your orders are invalid."

Deangelis swooped over the bulging shoulder of the black wreck, hoping against hope that neither Melilah nor Eogan chose that moment to emerge. The killer followed him with ease, its reactions adroit and confident. He was running out of space. "But you're not supposed to kill me. You said so yourself!"

"This is correct."

Deangelis turned ninety degrees and shot for open space. He had to get the killer away from the wreck, whatever happened next.

"This game tires me," said the AI.

"So why don't you just give up and go home?" Deangelis told it, pouring everything the Cell had into a surge of acceleration along the torus. He didn't want to activate the VOID drives again for fear of what it would do to Melilah and Eogan behind him. All he could do was run and hope.

"Why don't *you*?" asked the killer.

"Because Bedlam isn't my home anymore. It's dead and gone, like Melilah and Eogan—like I *should* be! I can't go back."

"We'll see about that." The killer surged forward on an unexpected spike of energy. Its claws, material and immaterial, opened to grasp the Cell, and there was little Deangelis could do to stop it. A score of pinpricks pierced the Cell's defensive shell and sliced deep into it. He screamed aloud as the invading talons slid through the space he occupied, stabbing walls, control systems, and him like hypodermic needles from a dozen different directions. Silver fire coursed along his nervous system. Invading protocols designed by the person who knew him best in the universe—the Archon—began shutting off his senses one by one.

My memory! he thought with horror. The killer was going to read his mind like an open text and find out exactly what had happened to Melilah and Eogan. He struggled against the intrusion and felt the mental control dig deeper. His thoughts began to grow choppy, disjointed. Flashes of black hacked his view of the torus into erratic slices of time. As the needles probed deeper and the protocols pared away the last defenses he had, the black gradually overtook the world and left him floating in nothingness.

Deangelis waited for the killer's software mandibles to begin tearing his memories apart. He wondered if he would feel anything or if the violation would occur without him knowing at all. Part of him hoped for the latter, but an older part didn't want him to give up on his companions without at least hurting a little. He had gone down fighting. He should at least *suffer*.

A hint of green rose up out of the darkness. He thought he was imagining it at first, but it grew brighter, stronger. The void slipped away as another place formed around him—one that, to his utter astonishment, he recognized instantly.

He was standing on a hill overlooking a low valley. The flanks of the hill were grassy and bare. Below, near a meandering creek, were the remains of a sandstone settlement, abandoned and crumbling. Gray clouds hung low over the horizon; a stiff wind blew, chilling him.

He hugged himself and looked around, trying to find the tree he knew was there, a broad, straggly eucalyptus under which, sixty-five years earlier, he had been born.

The tree was gone. In its place now stood a low, squat headstone. Its chipped marble face had been stained by time, but the inscription was still legible. There were two names on it:

WHITE-ELDERTON
LUT-DEANGELIS

He recognized those names instantly: the first victims of Geodesica, better known as Sublime and Bedlam to the people who had lived there. But what did it mean? Was the killer trying to torment him while it ate into his mind?

"This is a back door," said a voice from behind him. He spun and saw himself walking up the gentle slope toward him. A mixture of surprise and joy rushed through him. His yearning to *connect* rose up so powerfully he thought he might vomit.

"How—?"

"Don't talk. We don't have time. I've given you this opportunity. It's the only one you'll get, and you must not waste it."

"What opportunity?"

"Take the path through the SAD replicator. I've left a trail for you to follow. Don't stop to look around. Just get to the end of the path, and kill it."

Deangelis reached out to take the arm of his other self as they came face-to-face. He wanted to ask what a SAD replicator was. He wanted to know why he couldn't stop to look around. There were so many questions, but he couldn't put any of them into words.

"I don't understand."

"I'm an illusion of an illusion," his other self told him, "an echo of who you were. I am here to give you a chance to live. Now go!"

Deangelis staggered back as the arm he held suddenly pushed him backward. He lost his footing on the dry soil and tripped. His balance tipped and he was unable to correct it. The sky turned around him and he tumbled into the Earth.

And the Earth, surprisingly, was full of lines. Straight lines that turned only in right angles, kinking and crossing everywhere he looked. There was no up or down or left or right. There wasn't even left-4 or right-5 or anything approximating a geometry he could fathom. Not at first. The skein of lines swept him up in a dizzying net and tied his mind in knots.

One of the lines brushed close to him, and he received a strange sensation. For a fleeting instant, while he remained in contact with the line, he knew the precise surface temperature of one minuscule point on the killer's hull. Then, as the line swept by, that knowledge dropped away. Experimentally, he tried another line, brushing through it as he would a cobweb. It didn't snap or bend or respond in any other way to his presence, but he did learn the exact molecular composition of the drone's fusion core at that instant.

He could only be in one place: the mind of the killer AI. It was ransacking his memory while at the same time he fell into *it,* pushed there by the ghost of himself.

Something flashed at him. A gleaming point stood out among the endless complexity. He willed himself closer to the flashing spot, just as he would will himself through a virtual environment, and he did move. The spot pulsed coolly, right in front of his eyes, then went out.

Another light popped up just within sight. He pursued it through the forest of lines. The second light led to a third, which led to a fourth. It was immediately clear what the echo of himself had meant by "the path."

Deangelis ex machina, he thought as he followed it through the mind of the AI. But how had this echo come to be in the mind of the killer drone? How had it come to *be* at all?

Flashing lights came and went. He strobed his way through the mind of his enemy, snatching vicarious glimpses of its existence as he went. All of it was internal: the disposition of its variable shape, the arrangement of its processing resources, the map of its various algorithms, the condition of its memories. Through the data he gleaned he managed to put together a map of the thing's mind—nebulous and incomplete, but nonetheless meaningful, like a blueprint sketched with lasers through smoke-filled air. He could trace his path through it, skipping in erratic leaps and jumps from the fringes of its being, where it was busy taking apart *his* mind, to the very center.

Even as he hurried, even as he sensed time passing and worried about what the AI had learned from him, even as he wondered what was happening to Melilah and Eogan in the world outside, he felt his attention being diverted by what he learned from the memories he passed through. He caught fragmentary glimpses of Bedlam's primary; he saw the Occlusion, shining in frequencies never seen by a Natural human eye; he felt the AI's moment of creation and the imperative that drove it; he tasted the will of the one who sent it on its mission, into Geodesica to search and destroy the fugitives.

Search And Destroy.

SAD.

That's one less mystery, thought Deangelis, even as he came to the understanding that he himself had sent the killer drones into Geodesica. The Exarch of Lut-Deangelis, the source of the killer's orders, was a new version of him, rebuilt somehow by the Archon, and he had given the killer the order because he had no choice. He was just doing his job and obeying his creator's orders. But he had given him—the *surviving* him—one opportunity to escape. He had given him a back door.

Flashing lights flew by like stars in an old sci-fi movie. The lines became blurs along with the sensory information they carried. *Don't stop to look around,* the echo of him had said, and he didn't. He already knew more than he had wanted to. If he kept looking, he might learn too much about the mind he had come to kill—the AI whose center he was burrowing toward like a borer on speed. The last thing he could afford at that moment was *sympathy*.

The lines bent around him, converging on a single point. Flashes of cognition assailed him, but he pushed them away as he would the beads of a curtain. They rattled and sparkled, setting off chain reactions and short-lived flashes of sheet lightning. Finally the AI noticed him, the passenger it had unwittingly acquired. Too late it coiled around itself, weapons raised in impotent readiness. Deangelis was at its very heart. Attack, and it would only destroy them both.

Before it could consider that option, he leapt on the mind's focus and wrenched at it, twisted it, smothered it. He felt it resisting, fighting back with every fiber of its being. From the center, the lines didn't look like lines. They were all pointing inward, toward him. They were black stars against a gray sky, forming and reforming in constellations that broke apart before he had a chance to recognize them. He felt like one primitive killing another under primordial skies: stripped of all their weapons and senses, the one who would win was simply the one who most wanted to.

You are a fragment! the AI protested. *You are invalid!*

Deangelis didn't respond, except in the depths of his mind: *I used to be an Exarch!* Fueled by frustration and loss, he squeezed the mind of the AI down into itself, like the diamond core of a gas giant, and grunted with satisfaction as it winked out of existence.

Instantly, he found himself at the center of the killer's neural mindscape. Information rushed into him from the world outside. Veils fell away, revealing the torus and the wreck drifting along its heart. The vista was momentarily disorienting, flooding him with data on a thousand different frequencies. He fumbled with unfamiliar protocols, seeking any sign of Melilah and Eogan. Had he taken control quickly enough? Had he given them a chance to evade the killer's attention?

In the flood of telemetry, a single automatic signal flashed. He felt a blast of hard radiation, followed shortly by pressure waves and a crack of loud thunder. Three bright, animated sparks lit up inside the body of the wrecked vessel: miniature nukes that expended all their pent-up energy in a nanosecond.

He watched with horror as the behemoth exploded in a shower of ash and dust, filling the torus with black, deathly smoke.

• • •

A broad shape broke through the clouds of Melilah's wake. The thing chasing her was definitely catching up. Her suit thrust her forward at its upper limit. The battering of dust, insubstantial at slow speeds, made her feel like a dozen vindictive midgets were pummeling her with cudgels. Time, she told herself, to abandon her pride.

"Eogan?" she transmitted. "I'm not alone in here. Something's hot on my tail and I need your help!"

Another door shattered before her, revealing a Y-intersection. She took the left turn, barely dropping her speed. Fragments of door scattered behind her, only to be shattered still further by the blunt nose of the thing creeping out of her wake.

"Eogan? Can you hear me?"

She didn't need to look over her shoulder to see how close it was. A screen in her visor showed her exactly what was going on behind her. Static crackled over the comms; she felt insubstantial fields snatching at her, trying to pull her back.

Fuck you. G-forces wracked her as she turned abruptly to her right, abandoning the access corridor and cutting through the belly of the wreck. The suit pulled her legs up to her chest and blacked out her visor. The impacts were stronger, physically painful. She didn't stop to see what sort of spaces she tore through. The damage she left behind her, to a xenarcheological find beyond all concept of value, barely crossed her mind, and then only as a fleeting regret. She would worry about her crimes to science when and if she survived.

The suit produced a shimmering sonar image that floated in the blackness before her: the thing was closer than ever, a bulging, green eye like something out of a low-tech nightmare. She zigged and zagged through the ship, trying in vain to shake it.

Her suit crackled again. She felt fields snatch and grip. The eye's pupil suddenly dilated, opening wide to engulf her. The view through the sonar flashed green, everywhere, and she felt herself and the suit being *swallowed.*

"Dominic!"

"Easy," came his voice surprisingly loudly in her ears. "I'm right here. I've got you now."

The visor cleared. She gaped as light flooded around her, revealing the interior of the Cell. Eogan's face loomed into hers, so close she could see the pores of his skin. The suit relaxed its tight grip, granting her free movement again, and she craned her neck in disbelief, not quite able to accept the transition at first.

"You—?" She pulled away from him. "What the hell do you think you're doing?"

He looked apologetic, but his words didn't spare her feelings. "It's your fault. You said you'd stay in line of sight, and you didn't, so the only way to warn you without breaking radio silence was to come after you. We've been rumbled."

She felt a minute shift in gee as the Cell accelerated around her. "Sprung?"

His eyes closed, and he sank deeper into the wall of the Cell. "Don't ask any questions for a second. I need to concentrate. I've left some spy drones in the debris cloud outside, but we'll have to get closer to the surface to pick up their signals. I couldn't maintain a hard link to the relay with you putting up such a chase."

"Damn it." She ran a hand across her face and felt gritty black dust under her fingertips. She was angry at herself, and at the Archon. Would they never be free of pursuit? Even after *nineteen thousand* intersections?

Her dermis and outer musculature felt shaky and blood-filled, as though she had endured a particular vigorous massage. She wondered if she would bruise from the battering she had taken. Most of all she felt embarrassed that, while she chased ghosts in the belly of a long-dead beast, Eogan and Deangelis had been facing a very real threat outside.

"We can take this as a good sign," she said, determined to salvage something from the situation. "If we were followed here, that means we left a wake. We can trace the way back home."

"If this thing doesn't catch us first. Hold on. I'm reattaching the wire."

Images chased themselves around the inside of the Cell, thick with static and shifting color. The torus, as seen from the end of the wreck through which she'd entered, looked no different than before, at first. The alternating light and dark stripes slid by in stately progression. The air was clear.

Then targeting reticules appeared around a bright, golden spark, and the view zoomed to show her their pursuer in more detail. It was roughly spherical, five meters across. Passive sensors picked up hints of radical changes taking place within it: mass redistributions, pattern deformations, even the occasional flash of radiation sneaking through its shields.

"Where's Deangelis?" she asked, her pulse quickening at the

realization that one of her companions was missing. "Did he go after it?"

Eogan nodded, grim-faced. "There's no sign of him. I'm looking back through the data." A new window opened before her. Different views of the torus flickered by. On one, a mirror-finished dot—a Palmer Cell component—streaked from the wreck to confront the killer. Weapon fire flashed; the two ships circled each like hyperevolved sharks. Then the killer lunged and took the Cell component into itself.

She pictured Deangelis trapped, like a rat slowly digesting inside a snake's gut, and felt ill.

"There's nothing we can do for him," said Eogan. "If *he* couldn't fight it—"

He stopped as the killer extruded a conical limb that swiveled to point at the wreck. Light flashed three times from its tip, tracing three superhot lines that reached for them like thin, deadly tentacles.

"Dark take it!" Eogan swore. Melilah braced herself, not knowing what was coming but assuming the worst from his reaction. The Cell collapsed around her, clutching its two passengers. The flow of data from the drones ceased as they pulled free of the cable, plunging her into blackness. Acceleration surged through her.

"What—?"

She got no further. Mighty hammerblows struck the Cell, three in quick succession. The space around her spun and shook so violently her mind and body seemed to separate. Synesthetic illusions assailed her: light that screamed; blows that flashed like strobes. Her sense of self became brittle, as though it might shatter into a million pieces at just one tap.

"—just ride out the EMP for a second," Eogan was saying when she came to. She felt arms around her, and realized that they belonged to him. Stranger still: she was holding him back.

"EMP?" she echoed, not yet pulling away. The physicality of him was profoundly comforting. "We were *nuked*?"

"Felt like it."

"Jesus Christ."

"If you'd been out there—" He didn't need to go any further.

She leaned back to look at him, realized that he was mostly merged with the wall of the coffin holding them, and averted her eyes. His eyes were half-lidded, like a corpse.

She shuddered and shoved his arms away from her. There was barely enough room to move in the Cell, but she needed what space she could get.

"Clearing the spam now," he said. A section of the Cell became transparent, giving her a nonintrusive visual. It showed darkness lit by occasional flashes of sonar clarity. The behemoth was gone, utterly destroyed. The nukes hadn't blown it to smithereens; it had already been a wreck long turned to dust. The explosions had simply blown the dust away, leaving nothing behind.

Complex algorithms traced the emergence of the three circular shock waves, analyzing how they had overlapped each other and echoed off the curving walls of the torus around them. Black grit raced along the torus in either direction, trailing the pressure wave caused by the explosions. The walls glowed white then yellow in its wake. She wouldn't have liked meeting that compressed front head-on—but it could hardly have been worse than sitting practically on top of the bombs as they went off. The Cell had weathered the blast with characteristic resilience.

Or so she thought, until Eogan gave her a verbal update on their situation.

"We've lost two nines on all our nanosystems. That's ninety-nine percent. It's going to take days to replenish them, assuming we can find the energy and mass to do it."

She looked around them. They were bouncing around ground zero like a Ping-Pong ball in free fall. Clouds faded and formed in the plasma, much faster than they would have in a terrestrial environment. The walls were still radiating powerfully. They were made of space-time, like the rest of Geodesica's tunnels, but they obviously weren't impervious. She wondered what would have happened had the nukes broken them. Would they have been sucked outside into null-space, null-time, and lost forever?

She couldn't imagine the outside of Geodesica. There could have been nothing out there at all. Not even emptiness, void. Just . . . nothing.

Sonar touched something solid and instantly shut down. Eogan used what little motive capacity the Cell possessed to nudge them onto another trajectory. Melilah peered through the accelerated, irradiated weather, trying to find their new assailant.

A wisp of cloud twenty meters long dissolved, revealing the golden mote hanging stationary in the center of the torus. Its furious shape-changing had ceased, having settled on an elongated acorn form, with a tapering stern and flat prow. In ultraviolet, the Cell traced the lines of field-effect vanes curving out of the prow. The vanes clutched something close, uncannily as though holding it up for closer inspection.

The Cell zoomed in the view for a closer inspection. Through the flickering vanes Melilah glimpsed a dark scrap that had once been human.

"My God," she whispered. "It killed him. It killed Deangelis."

"Wait." The sound of energetic particles rose up to fill the Cell with crackling effervescence. "I'm picking up a transmission."

A faint voice threaded the static. "*—sworn to protect—was the last—failed her—failed them all—*"

"But that's—" Melilah stopped. Recognizing the voice only made the situation more confusing. How could Deangelis be speaking if his body was in the killer's insectile grip?

Before she could come up with an explanation, the killer stirred. The Cell registered a sweep of coded radiation over its hull.

"It's spotted us," said Eogan. "There's not much we can do now."

A ragged cloud-limb formed between them and the killer. By the time it had swirled away, the killer had moved. It came around in a series of jagged turns to confront them. The voice grew louder as it approached.

"—shouldn't have let her leave—should have done something to stop her—shouldn't have let her die—shouldn't have let them all die—"

The field-effect grapnels clutched the human scrap close. Angular vanes grew out of its side—the weapon-tipped limbs of a futuristic wasp.

Melilah suddenly understood. Reaching out for Eogan's shoulder, she gripped it tight. "Tell him I'm not dead," she said. "Tell him that's not me he's holding."

"Tell who?"

"Just do it!"

Eogan opened up a channel and broadcast her message. "Melilah isn't dead. I repeat: Melilah isn't dead."

The voice didn't pause: *"—should have tried harder—should have kept them safe—should have kept* her *safe—"*

"Let me talk to him," she said. Eogan nodded. "Deangelis, listen to me: I'm in the Cell. Eogan caught me in time. I wasn't outside when the nukes went off. I'm all right. Are you listening to me?"

The killer hesitated. The unfolding limbs froze. "Melilah?"

"Right here. There's no need to go crazy. I'm right here."

The Cell swept the scrap with its own sensors. Eogan looked as confused as she felt. There had been too many reversals in too little time.

"That's a Palmer environment suit he's holding," Eogan said to her. "If it's not you inside it, Deangelis, or Melilah—"

"Then who?" Deangelis's voice, coming impossibly from the killer drone, continued the sentence.

"Cobiac or Bray," she finished. "They were lost in the maze weeks ago. One of them must have made it this far. Probably died here, inside the behemoth. I picked up a hard echo when I was inside it, roughly human-sized. That must have been him. The blast blew him out, and Deangelis found him, thought he was me."

The killer drone had stopped dead in its tracks, still clutching the body in its manipulators. For several seconds, no one said anything.

Then an alarm sounded, and another. Two hard, hot specks had burst through the plasma shock wave, in the same direction the killer drone had come from. As Melilah watched, a third appeared.

"We can't stay here," Eogan said. "The explosions will draw every killer for hundreds of junctions."

"Where do we go?" Melilah felt her grip on the situation slipping. Every step seemed to take her further away from home; every development made a return that much more unlikely.

"Anywhere," said Deangelis. The manipulators holding the body unfolded and gripped the Cell. A hole opened in the front of the killer drone. Melilah felt Eogan stiffen with alarm as the Cell surrendered.

Whatever had happened to Deangelis, there was time neither to question nor to fight it. She could only go with the flow.

As darkness enfolded them, she felt a surge of acceleration, and closed her eyes in acceptance of her fate.

+7

Altitude: 2440 CE

"All right," Horsfall said. "I'll go along with it."

The two Exarchs facing her and the one inside her were silent. She felt them waiting to see any signs of wavering, of her resolve cracking, and she could understand their concern. At the center of a swirl of emotions, she hadn't been sure herself how she would react when they gave her their verdict. But she had seen it coming and had prepared herself as best she could. There was, after all, no way to argue with the facts.

"We've considered our options," Hails had said when they had reconvened a week after their first meeting in a private chamber far from the moon's motley crowd. At the tip of a hollow needle protruding from the ancient regolith, they sat in a cylindrical transparent room on aluminum chairs, ignoring the vacuum just meters away. Hails's craggy face was side-lit by Altitude's glaring primary. Sharp-edged shadows slashed his expression into angular shards.

"Out of all the courses of action open to us," he said, "and all the possible outcomes they might lead to, one thing is clear. To move too quickly now would be disastrous. We must gather intelligence and assemble our forces before striking; we must not move precipitously or overextend ourselves, or we will waste the one shot we have. If our rebellion is to win, *it must not lose*—and to act before we are ready will guarantee nothing but disaster. There is no middle ground against Sol."

We want you to understand, Jane Elderton had whispered into her mind. *We want you to know that we're doing what's best.*

Even Deangelis had looked sympathetic. “We don’t want you to feel excluded,” he said. “Without you, we wouldn’t have come this far.”

“I know,” she’d said. After a deep breath, she had asked the question she’d been dreading since their arrival. “How long are you talking about? How long will it take you to collect your data and make your alliances, to plan your plans and build your fleets? How long until you’re ready to strike?”

“One hundred years.” Hails didn’t spare her a syllable. “Plus or minus twenty.”

She took a deep breath.

Communication, as you know, is our biggest problem. We can’t move until we’re certain we have the majority of the Exarchate behind us. Getting that surety without the tanglers will take time.

“Even if we find another Geodesica entrance,” Deangelis had added. “We’ll need more than just one to reach the other systems. A wormhole network isn’t something we can put in place overnight.”

“But we’re patient.” Hails had leaned forward and put a hand briefly on her shoulder, as though to assure her of his conviction. “A century is nothing to us. We can easily wait that long to claim what’s rightfully ours.”

The question is, Jane Elderton had asked, *can* you*?*

Horsfall wavered for an instant, buffeted by disappointment, frustration, fear of failure, distrust, and a thousand other feelings that were equally strong, equally strident. She had been feeling them ever since the possibility had first occurred to her, days earlier. Subsequent thought had only turned the possibility into a certainty. She could see no other way for the plan to work. Half a century just to put it in motion; longer—perhaps *much* longer—before it came to fruition. Hundreds of years might pass before Sol finally capitulated. Possibly thousands.

Resignation won out. Not only did the plan make sense, but she was also outnumbered three to one.

“All right. I’ll go along with it.”

Silence. She didn’t crack, although emotion bubbled under the thin crust of her face like magma, and even though, deep inside her, the vengeful flame sustaining her flickered uneasily.

“I do have one request, though.”

Name it, said Jane Elderton.

“I want to be there at the end when Sol falls. I haven’t come this far to drop by the wayside. Whatever it takes, I want you to make sure I’m around to see it.”

"Is that all?" asked Hails.

"There's not much more I can ask for," she said, "that I expect you'll freely give."

Hails regarded her from under lowered, bushy brows. Harsh starlight didn't soften his expression. Deangelis sat completely in shadow. Jane Elderton said nothing that Palmer Horsfall could hear.

"You have our word," said Deangelis eventually, with a grim nod. "While we live, you will live, too."

"Good." The promise had the ring of a fairy tale, one sure to bring unexpected consequences and an unhappy ending, but she was glad enough to have it. Death could take her when the job was done and not before. Until then, she vowed not to be completely useless.

"I've been making contacts," she said. "It's been a while since I was active among the Palmers, but I still have friends. They'll listen to me—and they have access to ftl communicators."

We know, said Exarch Elderton. *We have a message for them.*

"The Palmers have more to lose than anyone, if Geodesica is opened," said Deangelis. "Access to wormhole technology will make Cells obsolete overnight. If Sol wants to keep it all under wraps, the Palmers will be tempted to support that move."

"They're fools if they think they can maintain their monopoly forever, with or without the wormholes. Our tanglers hint at what might be to come." Hails leaned back in his chair and rubbed his thumb and forefinger together as though testing the consistency of an imaginary cigar. "They're probably not fools, though. If we offer them a cut, if we agree to share Geodesica with them, they might side with us against Sol. The odds are slim that the Archon would make a similar offer."

Horsfall nodded. "That's my mission, then—to get them on our side?"

That's our *mission,* said Elderton.

"Of course." Any thought that she might soon be free of the monkey on her back evaporated.

"I'll be dispatching envoys—parts of me—in the next few days," said Hails. "They'll spread through the Arc Circuit, testing the water. Along the way, they'll seed the trade lanes with breeders: small, self-replicating probes designed to leave the lanes and hunt for other entrances. If we can find one before Sol, that'll give us an edge."

"And I'll be leaving here altogether," said Deangelis, "to set up an installation in deep space. We need a location to prepare in private. It'll take me a while, working from scratch, but I'll be ready by the time everything else is in place."

Communication between us will be difficult, Elderton said. *This might be the last time we meet in person for fifty years.*

Horsfall was unnerved by the swiftness with which the Exarchs were moving. On the one hand they talked about ventures lasting a century or more, while on the other they made decisions in mere moments. Longevity obviously didn't mean lethargy for those considering themselves the rightful caretakers of the human race.

"I guess there's nothing else to say. You've got it all worked out." She stood, and the others followed suit. "We'll just go about our business, keeping each other up to date as best we can."

Hails held out his hand. She took it, and felt a tiny pinprick in the center of her palm.

"See you anon," he said.

She took her hand back and rubbed the tiny wound. *This isn't an ending,* she told herself. *This is the beginning of the next stage. If—when—we meet again, I'll know it's time to strike.*

"The Dark hide you," Deangelis said, "and keep you safe."

She inclined her head, touched despite herself by the ritual. "And you."

A faint tingling spread along the veins of her right hand as she turned and left the transparent office. It was done, and she felt at peace for the first time in a week. Decades of dangerous work lay ahead of her; an unknown technology was spreading through her bloodstream; she might be nothing more than a pet to the Exarchs—a steed for Jane Elderton's bodiless mind, or perhaps a mascot. But she had a role to play, and she would be there when the curtain fell.

That was enough to keep the fires burning.

+INTERLUDE

Anniversary 14: 18,822 CE

A rash of accelerated supernovae painted the starscape all the colors of hell. Over the course of a thousand years, four hundred G- and K-type stars had ballooned out of the Main Sequence and burst like boils, spewing colossal amounts of energy across the sky. Even as Deangelis watched, he felt energetic polar jets sweeping over him like the beams of distant searchlights. How the devastation had been achieved, and for what purpose—war? housekeeping on a colossal scale? art?—he couldn't tell. All he could do was stare up at the sky, as a child would at fireworks, and wonder.

"Look upon our works, ye mortals," she said, "and despair."

Senses that had coasted for a hundred Natural generations scurried to locate the source of the voice. Radio, microwave, and laser channels were quiet, apart from the background sputter of stars going up in smoke. All through the remains of Bedlam, he found nothing on which to triangulate. The voice seemed to be coming from nowhere.

The mystery only deepened when he traced the trail of information through his own mental networks. Each of him, scattered far across the system in unprepossessing habitats barely large enough for one, had registered the voice at the same time. Somehow, she was speaking to all of him at once, without light-speed delay. Or else she was timing her transmissions so they arrived in such a way as to create the appearance of an instantaneous broadcast. He could think of no good reason why someone would do that.

Odder still was the realization that the words weren't coming from outside him at all. They were forming spontaneously within the delicate organic circuitry that made up his nervous system and declaring themselves directly to his consciousness.

"Ozymandias would point out that you'd got the quote wrong," he said, not bothering to broadcast the words since the source of the voice could presumably read his thoughts. "I presume that's deliberate."

"Naturally. The King of Kings is a name only now. This monument will last much longer."

"What is it, exactly?" he asked, worrying not for the first time that Bedlam's primary might be next.

"Irrelevant to those who refuse to participate in humanity's ventures. There's a lot going on out there that you have no conception of." He detected bitterness in the voice-within-his-mind. "I've come to you in the hope of striking a bargain."

He considered his precarious existence: a somnolent being waiting out the eons for something that might never occur. "What do I have that you could possibly want?"

"It's not a matter of wanting," she said, "but needing."

"That, too. The question still remains."

"Let's talk about what you want, first."

"You already *know* what I want."

"You want the woman you knew as Melilah Awad."

"I want to know whether she's safe or not. Yes."

"Why?"

He had stopped asking himself that question fifteen thousand years earlier. "Because she's an innocent victim who deserved better treatment. Because she's the last of my wards and I still feel responsible for her. Because—"

"Because you love her?"

"I don't know. Perhaps I do. I love the idea of her: she was so reckless and willful, and I think she might have made a real difference, at another time, in another place. I want to tell her that."

"That's all?"

"I don't know," he admitted again. "I'll know when I see her."

A great weariness suffused him, as though the ghost of Bedlam had sighed.

"I can't prove to you that I am her," the voice said.

"I already know that you aren't. She was a Natural. She

wouldn't have taken the last form I saw you in. Do you even have a form now?"

"Not as you would know it. Times change, Isaac. People change. Certainties can be eroded."

"Not this one. It was fundamental to her very being."

"How can you know that? You knew her for a handful of decades several millennia ago. You observed her and spoke to her, but you never really understood her. She could have changed in a million ways."

"*I* haven't changed. I'd know her if I saw her."

"You're right on that point: *you* haven't changed. Not one bit. All these years since Bedlam was destroyed, you're still where the Archon abandoned you, waiting. Doesn't that worry you? Don't you feel an urge to move on? Experience something else?"

That was a question he occasionally pondered. Sol had stopped responding to his queries a long time ago; he was, theoretically, free to go anywhere he liked. "Not enough to do anything about it. Not yet, anyway. I am . . . satisfied."

"If you're genuinely satisfied, then I have nothing to bargain with. The truth of my identity is irrelevant."

He considered her words carefully. She was quite right, whoever she was. If he accepted her statement that she was Melilah Awad, then he was free. He had in effect told her what he needed to say, and she had made it abundantly clear that she was well and thriving. If he could only cast aside his doubts, his long wait would be over.

That was the trouble. The solution struck him as being entirely too easy. If he hadn't been able to convince himself in the time that had already passed—after two haunting visits from the being claiming to be her—then another empty assertion wasn't going to do it.

"Without knowing where and when Melilah emerged from Geodesica," he said, "I can accept nothing you say as truth."

Again a weary wind blew through him, followed by a squall of frustration. "I understand," she said. "Truly, I do. And one day you will understand why I can't tell you what you need to know."

He accepted her words at face value. "Perhaps it's time you told me what *you* want," he said. "Otherwise we'll start going around in circles."

"Very well."

A shimmering ripple swept through the system like a gravity wave, detectable as a faint tingling sensation in all his disparate minds. His wakened senses scoured the sky for the source, and this time it detected numerous sources of radiation. As though a curtain had been pulled back, installations appeared on moons, in Trojan points, and around rocky inner worlds where previously there had been nothing. Dozens of small vessels and probes pursued trajectories from point to point, drives flaring blue.

He didn't know how to react to the revelation, at first. An initial wave of relief—that he wasn't alone; that others cared about his mission—was swamped almost immediately by puzzlement. The radio chatter he picked up was preposterously dated, the technology of the ships implausible. An increasingly anomalous stream of data suggested that a new planet had appeared in the system, along with a worryingly large installation of some kind, bristling with activity. Nervously, dreading what he might see, he focused all his senses on the heart of the action.

At what they saw there, every one of his minds performed exactly the same action at exactly the same moment.

Home.

Impossible.

The part of him closest to the illusion stood up from the couch he had occupied for four centuries and waved a fist at the suddenly opaque ceiling.

"What the hell do you think you're doing?"

"Asking you a question. About to, anyway."

"Are the special effects really necessary?" The sight of his dead system, pre-Catastrophe and vibrant with life, brought tears to all his eyes. His hands shook. Even Ah Kong, the gas giant, was back.

"How do you know they're special effects?" she asked him. "You've seen what humanity is capable of now; it remakes the heavens on a whim. Who's to say this isn't for real? That we can't bring it all back with a snap of our fingers?"

Isolated from the rest of himself, he felt breathless, uncertain.

"Would you like me to?" she asked, the words a seductive whisper.

The word "yes" froze on his lips. His thoughts locked.

"Everything you've lost can be returned to you. That would mean more to you than Melilah—wouldn't it? All you have to do is ask me for it. What could be more simple?"

He couldn't move and couldn't speak.

"Why don't you say anything, Isaac?"

"What do you want me to say?" His voice sounded like glass crushing underfoot.

"I want you to tell me," she said, "that death and destruction on this scale is wrong and should be undone."

"Why me? If you were really Melilah Awad, you'd know the answer to that question."

"I know what I *feel,* Isaac, but that's not enough. My feelings are memories; they are ways of being I grew out of a long time ago. I need to know that what I've worked for is right. I need rock-solid certainty to go with the energy and mass I've hoarded. I can do this, Isaac, building up from old off-system records and blueprints and your own mind; I can undo the wrong; I really can bring Bedlam back. By rolling back time, in effect, we can pick up where we left off. But only if you *tell* me to do it. I need you to give me the certainty I lack."

The stars were invisible behind the habitat's opaque shell, but he remembered the hellish light filling the sky.

"It wouldn't be the same," he said. "And what would be the point of it?"

"It'd put us out of our misery, of course!"

"But I—they—" He fumbled for words, wishing he had the courage to open himself up to the system again, to reconnect with himself. "They died for a reason."

"Do you think that reason is still valid?"

Again the word "yes" was hard to say, but he choked it out. "Yes, I do."

"Why? You fought with Hails and the others in the Gentry War. You did your best to undo the crime the Archon committed then. Why not now? What's changed?"

"I guess," he said, "*I* have."

"You must have," the voice responded, "if you would condemn your wards to death a second time."

"Not a second time," he said, ignoring the tears streaming down his face. "These people never existed. They're all an illusion. If you could've done it, and if you're who you say you are, you wouldn't have asked before doing it—and you certainly wouldn't have asked *me*."

He stared at the echoes of Bedlam, the lights and the voices, as one hypnotized.

"You are the only one who understands me, Isaac," said the impostor, "and yet three times you have denied me. What am I doing wrong? What have I lost that you no longer know me?"

A terrible grief filled him, filling him up from the mind occupying him. As the various parts of him reconnected, his higher self formed around the grief, finding it familiar, almost comforting.

"Erase it," he said. "It doesn't belong here."

A dark ripple swept through the system, taking the ghost of the past with it.

"I had hoped for more," she said.

"Sorry to disappoint you."

"Don't be." She either missed or ignored his sarcasm. "Hope is another old emotion. I'll be better off without it."

The grief dissolved as the illusion had. A cold surety filled him that she wasn't talking about Bedlam at all, but about something very different. He struggled with it for a second, could see no obvious subtext.

"Why do you come here?" he asked. "Are you trying to punish me? Do you think I haven't suffered enough?"

"No."

"Do you think I'm wasting my time waiting?"

"No."

"Then what? Tell me, and leave me the hell alone!"

"There is no hell but that we make for ourselves." Strange forces worked in the system once more. A new artifact appeared, one woven from space and time and vacuum rather than matter and energy: a glimmering nonthing that eluded his comprehension even while it so definitely *existed*. His senses were confounded under the nova-light of the nearby stars.

"This is my cache," she said. "With it I planned to rebuild our home. I have no use for it now, so I bequeath it to you instead."

"What for?"

"Let me finish. I have another gift for you, Isaac Deangelis." The new distance in her voice was unnerving. She sounded dead, utterly inhuman, like a machine speaking words from an ancient file that no longer had any meaning.

Knowledge blossomed in his mind—a skein of information so vast he couldn't immediately take it in.

"This is a map of every entrance to Geodesica, as seen from the outside," she said. "Don't think I offer you this as tactical information. It's common knowledge now, and has no importance for those who've moved on from such dead stuff. But you—if you're intent on waiting for Melilah, you'll need it. You're a fool if you think she'll come back here."

"I don't want to leave here," he protested.

"You don't have to. I'm offering you the resources to copy and propagate yourself across the galaxy. I advise you to take them. Staying here will only kill you. Time and nothingness will wear you down, and when there's nothing left it'll be too late to do anything about it. Everything you ever cared about will be meaningless. Trust me. Take what I'm offering you and survive. It's not too late."

Instructions accompanied her words: the means of activating the cache and bending it to its will. The amount of energy it contained was very nearly beyond his comprehension. He felt like a Neanderthal gawping at a nuclear reactor.

"Why?"

The voice didn't reply.

"Why?" he asked again.

He waited so long for a reply he felt sure she had gone. Only as he tentatively reached out to activate the cache did she say anything more.

"Because she'll need someone when she comes out of the maze," the voice said, "and I can't guarantee that I'll be there for her."

Deangelis pondered the words for a long time and came no closer to their meaning. Even as he studied the map the Arc Circuit rebels would have killed for sixteen and a half thousand years earlier, he could find no good reason to doubt its accuracy.

It was clear that she had done him a favor, on that level and perhaps another, more important, one as well. The conversation they had shared had taken almost ten years to complete. He *was* getting rusty; the Dark only knew how slow he might get before death finally took him.

Death was the end of novelty. Death was the end of change.

The time had most definitely come for a change.

Bloated stars scattered their gases to the many winds of the cosmos as he went in search of Melilah. The voice never spoke to him in Bedlam again, and if he felt her lurking around the edges of his home he told himself he was mistaken.

+8

Geodesica interior: plus 30 hours

They took the first junction they came to. Until that moment, Eogan hadn't realized that the black dots on the walls of the torus were exits. The scale of the place made them look like fly droppings. Only as Deangelis flew the Cell nearer did they resolve into holes wide enough to accept the killer drone and its cargo.

Running away again, Dominic.

He ignored the inner voice as they fled up another tunnel and gray-green space enfolded them. He couldn't, however, ignore the feeling of being trapped. It was all-pervading and tenacious—as dogged as guilt, as exhausting as regret.

175L5 150R3 010R2

He catalogued the intersections as they hurried through them, neither knowing nor caring if Deangelis had a destination in mind. The endless tangle of tunnels tied his mind in knots. Unchanging, relentless, wondrous yet unremittingly *dull* at the same time—Geodesica was interstellar travel stripped down to its most mundane. In the maze they had no need for magnetic vanes and preventative nanotech; they didn't have to worry about deform ratings and stardust. They didn't even need a Cell, really, except for somewhere to put their fragile bodies.

115R4 035L2 090L1

The intersections, too, were maddening in their bland randomness: there was no pattern at all to the tunnel mouths, their position in the junctions, or their distribution; none that he could see, anyway, and he couldn't fathom what sort of architect would design such a shambles. He could only conceive that Geodesica was a grown thing, an accreted structure rather than a planned one, perhaps one that sprawled out of more humble, better organized beginnings, and blindly propagated across the galaxy. Perhaps if the junctions started making sense, then he would know that they were nearing the center, its source.

But he knew that this was most likely a false hope. Scale-free networks had no center. Like the Internet of old, networks of friends and neurons, and the dead colony of Bedlam, their robustness depended on that simple fact. To destroy such a network would take more than just carefully targeting one single, vital component; an aggressor had to weed out almost a quarter before things would start to fall apart.

By analogy, Palmer Eogan and his fellow refugees could cross Geodesica from one side to the other without encountering anything they could remotely call the heart. This wasn't Minos; it wasn't a stately garden maze. They were somewhere else entirely, and just surviving would be hard.

005R4 015L3 030R2

He studied the forward instruments with some surprise. Deangelis had guided them into a tunnel with no end.

"Do you have any idea where you're going?" Melilah asked, breaking her silence for the first time since their flight from the destroyed behemoth.

The ex-Exarch didn't respond as they plunged through the boundary at the end of the tunnel and into the throat beyond. Hellish blue light razored across the surface of the killer drone. Even secondhand, it made Eogan flinch. Space tied itself in writhing knots as the artificial topologies of Geodesica welded uneasily with his universe's space-time. The last time he had crossed that boundary had been in Bedlam, with the Catastrophe boiling at his heels. There was no telling, now, where they would end up. It could be on the other side of the Local Bubble, or in the middle of Sol itself.

Blue agony fell away. Blackness enfolded them as space gripped them, tugged them back into its domain.

Melilah's gasp perfectly mirrored his own.

Against a soft, fuzz-speckled darkness hung a bright globular cluster—hundreds of thousands, perhaps even millions, of stars grouped in an untidy sphere that occupied almost half of his forward vision. It was so far away and the stars in the center so tightly packed that it resembled a single giant sun, dazzling in its brilliance. Individual stars hung like an atmosphere of fireflies around the center, gradually dispersing with distance until deep intergalactic void took over. A ragged tail trailed off to Eogan's right, where an encounter with another cluster, or even a full-sized galaxy, had marred its rough symmetry.

"Jesus," Melilah breathed. "What is that thing?"

Eogan had temporarily lost the ability to form words. He looked around them, making out details he hadn't noticed before. The backdrop of distant celestial objects contained several orphan stars and two brighter fuzzballs that were probably neighboring clusters. He found himself wondering what might lie beyond the one closest to them: more clusters still? A spiral galaxy?

"Wherever we are," he said, "it's a long way from home."

He turned the senses of the Cell, linked to those of the killer drone, directly behind him. The entrance to Geodesica was barely visible, little more than a dimple in space three meters across, lightly choked with primordial matter. Their emergence had scattered dust in a fine cloud, disturbing what might otherwise have been a priceless scientific sample. Astronomers would kill for a taste of such intergalactic matter. Theories would founder or thrive on such data.

Eogan checked himself. His thoughts were taking on a slightly unreal edge. There was little to no chance of them ever returning a scientific sample of any quality to human scientists. And even if they did, he doubted anyone would believe them. Their story was wild, improbable, dangerous. Even after what had happened to Sublime and Bedlam—and the Dark only knew what else since—the notion of a supergalactic tunnel network was outrageously implausible.

"Omega Centauri is the biggest cluster near the Milky Way," said Deangelis, breaking the strained silence. "If that's what this is, we're about sixteen thousand five hundred light-years from Sol."

"Is that all?" Melilah asked with acid sarcasm.

"Of course, this might not actually *be* Omega Centauri," Deangelis added.

"Shut up," she said. "You're not helping."

"How long would it take us to reach it?" Eogan asked, wondering what new wonders they might find in the close-packed stars of the cluster core.

"Eight hundred years at intergalactic deform ratings," Deangelis said, "but that's not something we can seriously consider. We don't have the fuel reserves, and we're not likely to find any out here."

Eogan reluctantly filed away that thought. They were stuck in the middle of nowhere with nothing but a pinch of gas and a hole in the fabric of space for company. *Who,* he wondered, *would build an exit out here?*

The *why* didn't need an explanation, as far as he was concerned. The view alone was worth the effort.

"So now what?" Melilah asked, her tone less forced than it had been before.

"Our options are limited," Deangelis said. "We know we're being hunted. These drones are designed to breed. Now they've hit atmosphere, there could be dozens of them looking for us. Hundreds, even. That's not a lot considering Geodesica as a whole, but our trail *is* conspicuous. Using the VOID drive carved a glowing scar across the structure; add to that the nuclear shock wave we left behind, and our presence is certainly drawing attention. We have to be very careful if we're not going to walk into a trap."

"That's why you brought us here," she said. "To lie low for a while."

"It seemed the obvious solution. And there was always a chance, albeit a slim one, that we would emerge close to home."

Deangelis's voice broke just slightly, revealing for the first time the emotion he, too, must be feeling.

Melilah let up on him.

Eogan understood then that the two of them were barely seeing the spectacle before them, not for what it was. To them it was nothing but further proof, if they needed it, that their home was an impossible distance away. They saw it through eyes still clouded by grief.

Abruptly irritated, he sent a series of orders through the Cell, reconfiguring it into two separate sections.

"Excuse me," he said, nudging against the killer drone's restraining fields until it let go. A hatch opened and he slid into empty space. "I need some air."

"Where are you going?" asked Melilah, startled.

"Not far. Don't go anywhere without me." The Cell's thrusters kicked him away from the entrance. He didn't aim for the globular cluster, but in a random direction. *Away.*

When the killer drone and its two companions had shrunk to a dot against the fuzzy black, he killed the thrusters and let himself coast. Quiet enfolded him, and a sense of calm fatality. If he shut down his systems and let the Cell drift, it would do so for millions of years before hitting anything remotely solid. Such a decision was in his power. It was even slightly tempting, to surrender himself to a fate too large to truly grasp. By the time his destination—currently a blurry dot at the limits of his visibility—came into range, every problem he had ever had would be far behind him.

Palmer Eogan didn't think of himself as a hard-hearted man. He liked people, and he cared about them; he had had friends whose well-being concerned him, and he went out of his way to establish good relations with his fellow Palmers. But there were times when people just seemed too much work, when the myriad complexities of interpersonal relationships became too intricate, even for someone used to juggling nanotech drive systems, time dilation effects, and quantum deformation parameters. At such times, when what had once seemed comprehensible suddenly became mysterious, perplexing, even alien, escape was the only viable option. He had to get away from everything and find a new sense of perspective. Find *himself,* perhaps, among the welter of external stimuli.

Was he wrong, he asked himself, in considering the glimpse of the globular cluster an opportunity not an impediment—a compensation for rather than a reminder of the things he had left behind? Was he such a terribly bad person for being excited by where they were instead of where they *weren't*? He had to bite his lip around Deangelis and Melilah for fear of upsetting them further—and he could see the need to do that. But at some point, he thought, they should really stop thinking about what they'd lost and concentrate on what they'd found.

Melilah had felt it, he knew, when they had found the behemoth in the transit torus. Perhaps Deangelis, too. But it had been easier then, when returning had still seemed a possibility, no matter how remote. Now, with pursuit intensifying, not weakening, everything was tainted by the growing distance between them and their origin.

To him, that distance changed nothing. He was *here*. He was *seeing*. The Dark could take the rest and swallow it forever. There would still be opportunities for fulfillment.

Time, he concluded. *Give them time.* He shouldn't expect miracles. While emotions ran hot, it was hard to see the bright side of anything. Even he, just minutes ago, had been bemoaning the boredom of Geodesica's regular tunnels. And now he was gazing upon a spectacle no other person but him and his companions had witnessed.

They would come around. They had to.

In the wake of the Cell's departure, Melilah fell moodily silent. Deangelis didn't have the energy to bring her out of her shell. He was too busy dealing with his own. The killer drone was a challenging machine, one requiring every iota of concentration. Getting out of Geodesica gave him an opportunity to explore its capacity without their pursuers breathing down his neck.

Four times during their escape from the torus he had felt sensor sweeps brushing him. Twice they had found purchase. The shell of the killer drone appeared to have fooled them, but the closeness to disaster had unnerved him. Getting out of the tunnels and into clear space had been essential. That they hadn't been followed came as an immense relief. Pursuit would drift elsewhere, to new sectors, as the traces he had left behind faded.

To help pass the time, and to give him something concrete to do with his new capacity, Deangelis performed a postmortem on Palmer Bray.

The SAD replicator wasn't designed as a scientific instrument, but it did rely on science to hunt and kill its prey. It possessed numerous systems that could be modified for more peaceful purposes. Vicious field-grapplers scaled down to wafer-thin scalpels; high-tech artificial noses proved more than adequate at sniffing out proteins and fragments of DNA; complex neural nets designed to fathom the five-dimensional architecture of Geodesica made short work of the cellular networks comprising a single human body.

Palmer Bray had entered Geodesica in a highly modified form, even for a Palmer. His body had been shielded against the stresses of the throat by layers of active bioshielding and a reinforced environment suit, much of which appeared to have survived intact. On becoming lost in the maze—and presumably separated from his companion, Palmer Cobiac—he had modified his physical configuration only slightly. His torpedolike form extruded limbs; eyes and ears examined the interior of Geodesica directly, rather than through instruments. In death, Bray looked passably human, with arms and legs hanging limply and head drooped forward, chin to chest.

He had died from resource depletion—not technically starvation but something resembling it. Even in the oxygenated atmosphere of the transit torus, his shipsuit had been unable to obtain the several critical compounds required to keep a human body, or reasonable facsimile thereof, functional for any extended period of time. Zinc, potassium, calcium, and other essential minerals weren't readily available in the artificial environment of the tunnels. Without them, Bray's ability to function had deteriorated. Normally the suit would have put him in a preservative coma and waited for rescue, broadcasting a distress beacon should anyone happen upon him. The suit's power reserves would have lasted for years. Even with the odd time-dilation effects Deangelis and the others had experienced, Bray should still have been alive.

That he wasn't suggested that either the suit had failed—no evidence for which Deangelis discovered—or that Bray had deliberately opted for death. Deangelis could understand why Bray might have chosen that course. His options had been exceedingly limited. He had no company and, without a Cell or the ability to navigate in five dimensions, practically no chance of getting home. Despairing, he had buried himself in the body of the wreck and become subsumed by the dust of ages. In darkness he had shut down the suit and stilled his artificial hearts. And there his corpse had stayed until Deangelis and the others had found him.

Few kings had enjoyed such a sarcophagus, Deangelis thought. Few had had their rest so violently disturbed.

"What are we going to do with him?" Melilah asked.

Deangelis hadn't noticed her watching over his metaphorical shoulder. "He would, perhaps, want to be returned home."

"This is his home," said Eogan, out of the Dark. The Cell was on its way back. "Don't even think about suggesting we absorb him like the drones."

"I wouldn't." Deangelis felt a twinge of very human resentment. "I'm not a ghoul."

"Leave him here," the Palmer said. "Point him at the cluster and give him a nudge. That's what I'd want."

Melilah agreed, so Deangelis did exactly that. The body of Palmer Bray slid smoothly out from the shell of the killer drone and tumbled end over end into the void.

Eogan muttered something so quietly it barely counted as subvocalization. It sounded like a prayer.

Then the Cell fragment pulled up alongside the drone and the three of them were united: Exarch, Palmer, and Natural in the shell of a machine sent to kill them. What would the Archon think of them now?

"It will soon be safe to go back," Deangelis said. "Into Geodesica."

"And then where?" asked Eogan.

"This replicator came from Bedlam. We can follow the route it took back there, if you wish."

"What makes you so sure it's safe to try now?" asked Melilah.

"I can't speak for Bedlam, but I know how the replicators hunting us are designed. They're not inclined to sit and wait. They move; they prowl; they hunt. Once our scent goes cold, they'll shift their attention elsewhere in Geodesica, spreading to cover as great an area as possible. There will be some traveling up and down the routes we've already followed, just in case we doubled back. Others will branch out into new territory. All of them will be breeding, spawning new versions of themselves to increase the chances of one of them stumbling across us. They came close, once. They'll keep trying."

"Will they ever stop?" Her voice was weary. She sounded on the brink of breakdown.

"Only when we're dead," said Eogan.

"Or something very much like us." Deangelis explained what he had in mind. The germ of an idea had been planted during his autopsy on Bray. Given the shell of the killer drone they now had at their disposal, many things became possible. By a simple procedure, he could take a seed from the *Cowell* and genetic samples from all three of them. From these he could grow a new Cell and enough undifferentiated biological material to give the impression that three people inhabited it. The strange genesis would consume roughly ten percent of the killer's shell, but wouldn't affect its functionality in any critical way. It might have its shape-memory capacity reduced slightly, or lose the ability to use some of its more arcane weapons, but for their purposes it would still suffice.

"So we send the Trojan out first," he said. "If nothing attacks it, we follow at a discreet distance back to the torus. When it comes across another killer, the chase will be on. They destroy the Trojan, thinking it's us, and the chase is over."

"We go home. Simple." Melilah sounded wary, unconvinced. "Are you telling us how it's going to be or can we contribute in some way?"

There was no easy way to say it. "I'm telling you," Deangelis said. "Although if you disagree or have any suggestions, I'm happy to hear you out."

Eogan had nothing to add, and neither did Melilah. Taking that as consent, Deangelis obtained the samples he needed without either of them noticing, and put the process into motion. Intergalactic space was orders of magnitude emptier and quieter than that around Bedlam, but it seemed loud compared to Geodesica. Time didn't seem to exist in the artificial corridors and halls. Back in the real universe, he was painfully reminded of it passing, and of the distance between him and where he wanted to be.

Melilah stirred. "How long is this going to take?"

"A few hours," he told her.

She mulled that over for a moment. "There's something both of you can do that I can't. You can adjust your internal clocks to slow up or speed down your perception of time."

Eogan nodded.

"Yes," said Deangelis.

"I want you to do it to me," she said. "Slow me down so I don't have to sit here waiting, with nothing to do."

"You could sleep—"

"Not for that long, not without dreaming." She shook her head. "Just make it all . . . *pass*. Can you do that for me?"

Deangelis checked the replicator's capacity, and found it up to the task. Her body, despite its appearance, was heavily biomodified, as had been everyone's in Bedlam. Antisenescence treatments required a base-level sophistication she had been unable to turn down. Not without dying two centuries ago. Activating certain disabled subroutines to allow her to take conscious control over her circadian and perceptual timekeepers was a small task.

"Yes," he said. "I can."

She nodded. "Then do it."

"Melilah," Eogan began.

She held up her hand and closed her eyes, shutting him out the only way she could. "Later."

Deangelis couldn't give her what she wanted so quickly, but he could provide a semblance of it. He reached into her, easily bypassing security protocols intended to prevent just such an intrusion, and raised the levels of the neurotransmitter oleamide in her brain, dropping her instantly into an anesthetized state not very different from sleep. Dreamless, dark, and timeless, she would register nothing until he completed his modification of her and restored her brain's usual chemical state.

"I hope you're happy," said Eogan.

Deangelis was startled by the bitterness in the man's voice. What now?

Then it occurred to him. Deangelis and Geodesica had succeeded where Eogan had failed: they had driven the thin edge of a wedge into Melilah Awad's determinedly Natural stance. For the first time in her life, perhaps, she had actually *asked* to be enhanced.

A Natural with biomodifications. An Exarch with only one body.

"No, Palmer Eogan," he told the man caught between them. "I assure you that I'm very far from happy indeed."

+9

Bridgehead: 2445–90 CE

On September 5 in the year 2001, a musical performance commenced that would take 639 years to finish. Written by the experimental composer John Cage, the single work for organ unfolded in an abandoned church in Halberstadt, and began with a year and a half of total silence. The work continued unchecked through wars and political upheaval; even the True Singularity itself didn't cause it to skip a beat. Written in an attempt to reclaim equilibrium in an ever-changing world, it was, declared the Archon to the minds that would one day become Exarchates, perhaps the first great posthuman work of art—one that could not be fully appreciated by beings trapped in natural timescales, or bound to natural tempos.

Nature, of course, had beaten John Cage to it. In slow-time, planets swung around stars like spinning tops, while in fast-time, a drop of water hung suspended in midshimmer for an age before falling an inch. Subsequent artists took full advantage of the newly flexible human form to explore the boundaries of aesthesia, and beyond. On Bedlam, there had been human experimentalists who boasted of tuning their internal clocks so that a lifetime could fly by in a nanosecond. In a split moment they could experience philosophical enlightenment or go insane from sensory deprivation. It was hard, sometimes, to tell the difference.

No matter what tempo Rudra-Deangelis followed, the stars stayed much the same. Far from anyone, deep in the Dark, he was the one who moved.

Decrypt REMEMBRANCE (ELDER):
> Good. You're online. That's all we need to know.

Decrypt REMEMBRANCE (ANGEL):
> Come on. It's lonely out here, and I have plenty of bandwidth. Tell me what's going on.

Decrypt REMEMBRANCE (ELDER):
> Still talking to Palmers. We have their loudhailers, but we need more than that. Negotiations continue.

Decrypt REMEMBRANCE (ANGEL):
> Let me know if there's anything I can do.

Decrypt REMEMBRANCE (ELDER):
> Just lay low. It's your turn.

Ends.

Over ftl links, the rest of the Arc Circuit seemed an impossible distance away. Completely cut off from normal means of communication—apart from the occasional years-old spill from a poorly tuned maser—Deangelis depended on what came to him along the Palmer's semiautonomous communications network they leased from Sol. Not everything went through Exarchate channels, as information hopped and leapfrogged from repeater stations every two to three light-years, but there was a small chance it could be intercepted and rerouted to Sol. Critical information masqueraded therefore as meaningless chat. Rudra-Deangelis encouraged an increase in *actual* chat in order to hide the true signals in noise.

Decrypt REMEMBRANCE (ANGEL):
> How's H shaping up?

Decrypt REMEMBRANCE (ELDER):
> Which H?

Decrypt REMEMBRANCE (ANGEL):
> The Sister.

Decrypt REMEMBRANCE (ELDER):
> Sister is stable.

Decrypt REMEMBRANCE (ANGEL):
> Your loyalty to her surprises me. Why don't you just get a new body and go out on your own?

Decrypt REMEMBRANCE (ELDER):

> I'm surprised to hear this from you, of all people. I've heard a certain name on your lips more than a couple of times.

Decrypt REMEMBRANCE (ANGEL):

> That's different. She was a colonist; I was—*am*—responsible for her.

Decrypt REMEMBRANCE (ELDER):

> At least you have her. The Sister is *all* I have. Give me something to cling to, won't you?

Deangelis coasted at a low deform rating, overseeing the creation and expansion of the bridgehead from which the takeover of the Arc Circuit would be launched, while at the same time carefully cataloguing the achievements of his allies. Hails's slow but steady permeation of neighboring systems proceeded with hardly a hitch. Multiplied and disseminated, he soon covered more of the Arc Circuit systems than any other Exarch, hopping from Cell to Cell as he infiltrated colonies, made contact with resistance groups, sounded out fellow Exarchs to see where they stood, or simply watched. The reports he sent back painted a picture of poised anticipation. After Melilah Awad's sensational exposé of events in Bedlam had spread through the region, years earlier, everyone knew that things were going to change. Expectation spread like cancerous tissue through the body of the Exarchate. It would have to be excised at some point, or it would start to flare up. Few people seemed to believe in the possibility of remission.

Which way people would jump when the time came was the difficult issue. Every colony was different, just as every Exarch was different, and analyzing the situation over a low-bandwidth medium was well nigh impossible. A great deal rested on Hails's judgment and integrity. If either one were to go awry, the end result would be disaster.

An informal slang developed naturally in conversation with Elderton. *The Sister* stood for Palmer Horsfall; *the Old Hospital* was Bedlam; *Dead Man Walking*, or just *DWM*, meant Lazarus Hails. Frederica Cazneaux and Lan Cochrane, the two Exarchs who had assisted in the destruction of Bedlam, became the *East* and *West Witches*. As time passed, the colony on Asellus Primus took on the name *Indivisible.*

It would prove, Deangelis hoped, to be more than just a pun.

Decrypt REMEMBRANCE (ELDER):

> The East Witch is still on the loose. Despite what happened, she's not been censured, demoted, reprimanded—nothing. Some of the Palmers have called for an embargo of Mizar, but the new Negotiator Select has vetoed such a move.

Decrypt REMEMBRANCE (ANGEL):

> There's a new NS?

Decrypt REMEMBRANCE (ELDER):

> Palmer Demmerich. A moderate face for an organization likely to tear itself apart in the long run. Sol refuses to confirm the rumors about Geodesica, which only makes some of Demmerich's members more certain than ever that the gossip is true. Some want to ally the guild more closely with Sol; others want to break all existing trade deals. We're talking to everyone involved as openly as we can.

Decrypt REMEMBRANCE (ANGEL):

> I can't believe the Witch is still free. She should've been nailed to the wall for using a Reaper.

Decrypt REMEMBRANCE (ELDER):

> Nailed and flayed—although I understand why she did it. If ROTH nanotech had been behind the Catastrophe, the threat would have been real. Desperate times call for desperate measures.

Decrypt REMEMBRANCE (ANGEL):

> And terrible crimes for terrible punishment.

Decrypt REMEMBRANCE (ELDER):

> Would you depose her?

Decrypt REMEMBRANCE (ANGEL):

> Both of them.

Decrypt REMEMBRANCE (ELDER):

> And put you and me in charge?

Decrypt REMEMBRANCE (ANGEL):

> Tempting, isn't it? Two empty systems and two homeless Exarchs. But . . . I don't think so. That's not what I want. This isn't about territory. It's about governance. Those who aren't fit to govern will be removed. We can discuss replacement once that's done.

Decrypt REMEMBRANCE (ELDER):
> It's interesting that you should say that.

Decrypt REMEMBRANCE (ANGEL):
> Why?

Decrypt REMEMBRANCE (ELDER):
> Do you remember that day on Earth, before the Expansion?

Decrypt REMEMBRANCE (ANGEL):
> Which day?

Decrypt REMEMBRANCE (ELDER):
> Giorsal called it "playing with dolls."

Decrypt REMEMBRANCE (ANGEL):
> Yes. I remember. What does it have to do with this?

Decrypt REMEMBRANCE (ELDER):
> Think about it.

Ends.

He *did* think about it as Bridgehead followed a lazily torturous route around the trade lanes in the rough direction of Sol. It amazed him how quickly raw asteroid-stuff passed through Bridgehead's refinery. The installation was soon way ahead of schedule. That was a good thing, but it was a difficult process to feed.

He detoured through an uninhabited M-system to restock. Automated hoppers scoured the rubble-rich atmosphere of the dwarf star, returning bloated with raw material. His attention wandered.

The night of the dolls had begun on August 15, 2381, during a sumptuous Southern Hemisphere spring evening in a region that had once been the birthplace of humanity. Isaac Forge Deangelis—barely seven years alive and still finding his feet in the mind-rich environment of Sol System—had accepted the invitation to attend the annual Graduates' Ball on the advice of the Archon, who had encouraged him on the grounds that it would be an educational experience. He had known before stepping through the front door that it would be a challenge, and had used the decadently quaint cover of "fashionably late" to dawdle along the way. It fit the theme of the evening, anyway.

The magnificent glass ballroom, constructed in the middle of nowhere on the boundary of old Richtersveld National Park, stood out against a backdrop of jagged mountains that bore the scars of their volcanic origins. The sun had already set, but the sky still glowed a deep, diamond-sparkled purple, fading to black in the east. A stand of immature quiver trees made him think of alien soldiers from a twentieth-century B movie as he walked up the long, sweeping drive. His feet crunched on gravel with a raw, startling sound. He felt like a complete fool in a black tuxedo with a silk tie choking his Adam's apple. The rest of him, scattered across the system, watched with a mixture of fascination and amusement at the anachronistic getup. No matter how hard he tried to distract himself with what they were doing, attention kept returning to Earth.

A butler met him at the top of the marble stairs and offered to take his coat. He surrendered it although he knew the night would be chilly. It would be warmer inside, he hoped. The sound of voices grew louder as he trod thick red carpet through an arched doorway and entered the ballroom.

It was an odd experience, being in the company of so many people at once. Like the other guests, he roamed the Earth freely in both corporeal and virtual forms, interacting and communicating with his peers and himself via all manner of media, not needing to be face-to-face for any conceivable reason. The presence of his body on that particular evening, he had assumed, was a mere formality, no more or less anachronistic than the suit he was required to wear. Both could have been assembled at will in a moment, as could have a belly dancer's outfit and a body to match. That he hadn't yet decided what his physique would be when he finished his training wasn't an issue he spent much time considering; while he waited, he wore a physical form of indeterminate age, with blond hair and broad shoulders generated by the genes the Archon had bestowed upon him. It fitted.

The ballroom was expansive and gleaming and full of music. That was his first impression. His second was of the crowd, all beautiful and familiar and garbed in clothes no less outlandish than his own. Out of a thousand, two dozen pairs of eyes looked up as he crossed the threshold—recognizing him, he assumed, as he recognized them in turn. He went to wave.

Their true reason for looking at him became apparent when his body lost all connection to the rest of *him,* scattered across the system, and collapsed back down to a mere individual.

He stumbled, as disoriented as if he had lost his sense of sight or balance. His perception of the world, and of himself, suddenly crashed down to *just him* in *just one room*. Mentally reeling, he struggled to work out what could possibly have gone wrong. Since his awakening in many bodies scattered all across Sol System and experiencing the wondrous union that had risen out of his disparate thoughts, he had never been alone. The experience was jarringly dysfunctional, even frightening.

"Fear not, old boy," said a familiar voice. A hand clapped down on his shoulder. Lazarus Hails was all grin and gloat as he came round to confront his fellow student. He, too, hadn't fixed his final form, but his nose bore a patriarchal prominence that would remain later. "All part of the experience. You'll find our bodies don't quite work the same anymore, as well as our minds."

Deangelis watched Hails with some puzzlement. His balance centers seemed dangerously out of whack, and his speech patterns were different. He had clearly suffered the same mental impairment Deangelis had on entering the ballroom. Were they under attack? Could their brain damage possibly be *permanent*?

A laugh as sharp as a cut diamond drew Hails's attention away from Deangelis. Lan Cochrane, dressed in a lime green flapper's outfit, was puffing on a cigar—the genuine, burning article—and blowing rings of smoke at Frederica Cazneaux. Dark-skinned and wonderful in a black suit of her own, Cazneaux batted the smoke away and turned down a chance to try a drag for herself, despite her friend's insistence. Cazneaux held a cocktail glass containing an electric blue liquid balanced between two fingers; she raised a perfectly shaped eyebrow at Hails as he took Cochrane's cigar and blew a messy cloud between them.

Deangelis looked around him in disoriented wonder. Across the shimmering expanse of the ballroom, the vast majority of the Exarchate's future leaders were engaged in similar physical debaucheries: dancing, eating, drinking, smoking, and singing as though three hundred and fifty years had rolled back and plunged them all into some upper-class Light Age.

"I think it's an experiment," said Jane Elderton, who had appeared at Deangelis's side during the display holding a thin, white-papered cigarette with a long filter in one hand. She smelled of perfume and smoke. "A test, perhaps."

"Not a graduation party after all?"

"We're beyond that," she said, pale lips pursing in faint amusement. Her skin was porcelain white and her gaze a startling blue. Blond hair—longer than he'd ever seen it on her before—curled exquisitely tight around her skull and ears. The color of her silk dress matched her eyes. He took in her silver necklace, her cleavage, the delicate bracelet on her left wrist, and her thin-strapped shoes with one sweep.

"We don't need rites of passage," she went on, taking a sip of smoke and inhaling it as though she had done so every day of her life. Wisps emerged from her mouth and nostrils as she spoke. "Growing up is something anyone can do. Even animals do it, and we don't throw them parties."

"Bonding, then, before we all go our separate ways?"

"Wrong again, Ike. Why join something destined to be shattered? We're designed to be loners."

He looked around. Something thrilled in the air. He could guess what it was from the way his flesh responded to it. His heart rate accelerated, along with his respiration. His pupils dilated and his skin tingled. He was feeling his body in a new way, or a very old way—primal and not entirely unpleasant.

"You need a drink," Elderton said. "Is there something you've always wanted to try? Gin and tonic? Sea breeze? Gimlet?"

"Gimlet. How do I—?"

A waiter—artfully humaniform like the butler outside but obviously no more than that—appeared beside him holding a silver tray. His drink rested on it, gleaming with condensation. Deangelis took the glass and sipped carefully. Volatile alcohol made his tongue and throat sing. He laughed at the play of chemicals on and in his suddenly unpredictable body. It was like reading an old novel in its original language, or listening to the first take of a famous jazz recording: full of unexpected nuances and subtleties that he had never anticipated. In the raw flesh, with nothing to distance himself from the play of the molecules in his bloodstream, he was suddenly, vividly, nothing but a man. A gendered man in a room full of people, as men had been for tens of thousands of years before him.

He drank and danced and laughed with the rest of them, awash with hormones and pheromones and utterly delighted at finding another way to enjoy life.

Dinner came, an extended six-course feast with dishes from all over the old world. Some of the partygoers forwent the meal, preferring to keep dancing, but Deangelis took the opportunity to experience another lost art. He had been born with a complete range of culinary skills and knowledge, none of which he had ever expected to use; until now, it had been just one minuscule part of the enormous pool of human knowledge. Dining came as natural as play, and he wallowed in the succulence of meat, the richness of gravy, the texture of vegetables, the indulgence of pavlova. Crayfish, pigeon, artichoke, plum; caviar, sturgeon, puy lentils, bread.

The Archon had been absolutely right: the evening was an education he hadn't known he needed. He raised his glass to their absent creator, wondering what it was making of events from its lofty perspective.

An intoxicating rainbow of after-dinner drinks followed. Port. Sherry. Coffee. Brandy. His grip on proceedings began to slip. He knew he wasn't thinking properly, but that didn't stop him from attributing far too much weight to the thoughts he did have. There was no baseline profundity against which he could measure his drunken revelations. They seemed groundbreaking. Every emotion felt new and powerful. And why couldn't they be? He was content for the moment to be tugged along by alcohol's smooth, seductive currents.

The party spilled out into the night, onto a green grass lawn he would have sworn hadn't been there before. The interference that separated them from the rest of their minds followed them, maintaining the illusion that they and they alone were the full extent of their beings. Among prickly green hedges and mazes they ran like children, shouting and stumbling and willfully ignorant.

He gravitated naturally to those whose systems his would neighbor and basked in the broader ambience of merriment. Lazarus Hails's jokes and wickedly timed outrages had kept them all amused through dinner. In another age, he might have been a Byron or a Nicholson, genetically tailored for carousing. Deangelis was content to go with the flow, sipping Merlot or Shiraz on the fringes of the group, only interacting when Giorsal or Jane or one of the others drew him in. Once he caught Frederica and Lan whispering about him behind their hands. They actually blushed.

"You're beautiful, darling," Lan Cochrane said when he pressed for an explanation. "Don't you know it? You really scored when the genetic dice tumbled. I wonder where your stock comes from."

Lan was a Vietnamese name meaning "orchid." She looked more Malaysian, Deangelis thought, full and high-cheeked, with hair subtly framing her face. Her brown eyes were wide and laughing. He felt the butt of a joke, and blushed in turn.

He became aware of other people looking at him. Some did more than look. In the torch-lit wonderland of the gardens, with shapes rushing by and laughter everywhere, hands touched him; lips pressed against his ear to whisper jokes or flirtations. Warm fingers laced with his and soft hair brushed his cheek. Dizzying stimuli prompted yet more novel sensations.

"Come with me," Frederica breathed in his ear, tugging him down a dead end in a hedge maze. His free hand held a bottle of champagne he didn't remember opening. She pulled him to her in the darkness and kissed him. The smell and taste of her occupied his mind more completely than any training exercise. Her lips were full and warm. The touch of her moist tongue against his made his skin shimmer from head to toe. The feel of her body was unimaginable.

Where that kiss might have gone, he would never know. With a rustle and crack of vegetation, Lazarus Hails's head burst through the hedge.

"Found them!" he called triumphantly over his shoulder. To them he said: "Quick! Dalman's climbed onto the roof and says he's found a stash of dope!"

They pulled apart. Intrigued by the possibility of yet more sensory destabilization, Deangelis said that he would come. Satisfied, Hails's head retreated through the gap in the hedge. He followed Hails out of the maze and across the lawn, where a conga line had formed. Frederica trailed him at first, then fell behind to join the dance.

The sound of raised voices didn't alarm him, nor did the sight of someone vomiting into a flower bed. He was fully aware of the effects of alcohol poisoning, and had no doubt that he, too, would experience them at some point that night, especially in combination with other drugs. That concern seemed distant and unimportant. His entire being was focused like a poorly tuned laser on the now, with no thought for what had come before it and what might follow. His body seemed to move of its own accord. He was little more than a passenger.

Later, he clearly remembered his first hit of marijuana and the rocketing sensation it gave him inside his head. The thick smoke burned his throat and made him cough, but he went back for more as the joint passed round his circle of acquaintances. The notion of stoned Exarchs seemed the height of humor and set off a wave of giggling. The last sequential memory he possessed of that night was of snorting smoke through his nostrils and choking so hard he almost threw up.

Flashes remained, like fragments of a smashed vase. He couldn't piece them together, but he could make out the rough shapes of those that were missing. More kissing followed an extended discussion with Giorsal McGrath over the long-term goals of humanity. What conclusion they came to, he couldn't remember, but it seemed deeply important. They had called out to the Archon, wanting to share their wisdom, but not received a reply.

A blur of faces. People everywhere. Women were soft to the touch, men hard and angular, their stubble rough against his lips. He stuck with women in the end, but wondered if he had made the right decision when a fight broke out between Lan and Frederica over who had kissed him first, and what rights over him that gave them. Hails joined in, seeming upset that Frederica wasn't paying him enough attention. Deangelis felt removed from it all, wanting nothing but to touch and be touched.

Fights broke out over sexual partners, territory, imagined slights, nothing at all. He wandered off, feeling suddenly tired.

"Strike up the band," said Jane Elderton, who had appeared at his side again, her hair unpinned and her cheeks red. "We're apes dancing to tunes we didn't even know we knew."

"Is this all it takes?" he asked. "Are we so close to chaos, to savagery?"

"They're not the same thing, Isaac—but yes, I think we are. You can fire clay and turn it into a brick; you can lay that brick in a wall and make it part of a building; that building can be one of thousands in a city; but at the end of the day it's all still clay. And so are we, underneath. If we don't understand the clay, we don't understand the city."

"*That's* what this is all about, then?"

"I think so. Don't you?"

He shrugged. "I'm enjoying *not* thinking, for once."

Her smile warmed him. "I'm glad. Let's go."

The darkness awaited them. He wanted to run, to let muscles swing and thrust and propel him blindly across the ancient land, naked under the stars they claimed. The two of them might have run together a mile or ten, or not run at all; he didn't remember; but the night ended with his breath coming fast and hot from his lungs, and her moving against him with a feverish urgency of her own. All semblance of rational thought vanished in an explosion of nerve impulses. His spinal chord, electrified from its base to his brain, seemed to dissolve, and the night dissolved with it. Skin against skin, they reveled.

Decrypt REMEMBRANCE (ANGEL):
> You were all gone when I woke, and so was the ballroom and the gardens. I had an awful hangover.

Decrypt REMEMBRANCE (ELDER):
> We all did.

Decrypt REMEMBRANCE (ANGEL):
> I spoke to the Archon that morning. It confirmed your theory: that we needed to understand what it was like to be human. How it felt. I felt as though my head was going to explode. It took me almost an hour to flush out the last of the toxins. By the time the Archon told me that I was ready to rejoin the rest of me, I was angry at it for not warning us. If we'd known in advance, we would've been prepared. We could've behaved better.

Decrypt REMEMBRANCE (ELDER):
> You're missing the point. Behaving badly was the whole idea. That's what humans do. If we'd got together for a lovely chat and maybe a nice game of bridge, what would we have learned?

Decrypt REMEMBRANCE (ANGEL):
> I learned not to trust myself. My reintegration was difficult. I chose my final body as a kind of protest against what I saw that night. I didn't want to appeal to those levels of my mind, or the minds around me.

Decrypt REMEMBRANCE (ELDER):
> Was it really so awful?

Decrypt REMEMBRANCE (ANGEL):
> Parts of it, yes. The squabbling. The fighting. The petty rivalries. It was all so—so pointless.

Decrypt REMEMBRANCE (ELDER):
> Do you know what annoyed me most? I told the Archon this afterward, and its response never satisfied me. If we need to understand humanity in order to rule it, don't we need to experience it from above as well as below? Shouldn't we get a glimpse of the world through *its* eyes, so we can glimpse a bigger picture still?

Decrypt REMEMBRANCE (ANGEL):
> What did it say in response?

Decrypt REMEMBRANCE (ELDER):

> What do you think? I'm still waiting for an invitation.

His stockpile of attack drones and decoys grew. The more he thought about the night of the dolls, the more he remembered his own desire for ascendancy among the systems of the Arc Circuit, years later. The Mizar Occlusion had offered him a way of increasing his system's standing. Had things gone differently, Bedlam might have been the center of a hive of xenarcheological industry. In a sense, therefore, his motives *had* been territorial; he had been the same as a monkey fighting with its rivals or a business tycoon driving a competitor out of business. He wondered how much of Frederica Cazneaux's attack on the Occlusion had been driven by jealousy at his newfound opportunity, and how much Lazarus Hails's timely intervention had owed to wanting to be in the thick of it, keeping a close watch—and therefore a measure of control—over events as they unfolded, for fear of missing an opportunity.

If we don't understand the clay, we don't understand the city.

They were still clay, after everything, which had implications for the push to achieve independence from Sol. Could it really be a grab for land by a bunch of sophisticated monkeys? Was the moral stance taken by the conspirators—that the destruction of Sublime and Bedlam was completely unjustifiable—just a disguise for baser motives?

He assumed that was why Elderton had reminded him of that night. He didn't think it was because their physical intimacy meant more to her than it did to him. Once they had rejoined their higher selves, sex became just one of many unique experiences shared that night, then put behind them forever.

Decrypt REMEMBRANCE (ANGEL):

> You said it was interesting, my opinion on the Witches' systems and what to do with them when they're empty. Why so?

Decrypt REMEMBRANCE (ELDER):

> I was wondering how you'd feel about leaving the systems free.

Decrypt REMEMBRANCE (ANGEL):

> Without an Exarch?

Decrypt REMEMBRANCE (ELDER):
> It's a thought. Are you against it?

Decrypt REMEMBRANCE (ANGEL):
> I don't know. I've never considered the possibility. It shocks me, I admit, on first thought.

Decrypt REMEMBRANCE (ELDER):
> Melilah would have approved.

Decrypt REMEMBRANCE (ANGEL):
> Of course she would have. What are you saying?

Decrypt REMEMBRANCE (ELDER):
> Her opinion doesn't sway yours?

Decrypt REMEMBRANCE (ANGEL):
> No. Why would it?

Decrypt REMEMBRANCE (ELDER):
> Just testing.

Decrypt REMEMBRANCE (ANGEL):
> I find this . . . exhausting.

Decrypt REMEMBRANCE (ELDER):
> I'm glad. If you thought it easy, I would respect you less.

Word spread. Chains of communication formed from widely separated links, all communicating in code. Strange messages drifted through the ftl link—fragmentary messages that meant nothing to him in his isolated, silently cruising fort. If Elderton understood them, she didn't say. When the Palmers finally confirmed their involvement, she and Horsfall moved on to the next phase of their mission, which was to travel to Asellus Primus and begin setting up operations there. Prime One had been chosen as the location for the first salvos of the war since it was far from both Bedlam and Sublime, and an old, pro-Sol colony. It stood between the Arc Circuit and the home system. Bringing it down would be a symbolic act, severing the old from the new. At the same time strikes would be made against Friday and Alioth, the most influential systems of the Circuit. All three Exarchs—Adriel Binard in Prime One, Lan Cochrane, and Frederica Cazneaux—would be offered a simple choice: join the rebellion or be shut down. Not killed, but placed in a state of extreme slow-time until the conflict was over.

Perhaps they would never want to return to normal-time, he thought. The war would be over in an instant for them. They could wait out the aftermath and the next round of disputes. Given the choice, would it be tempting to sit out a million years and see what fate awaited humanity in the future?

He didn't think so.

Decrypt REMEMBRANCE (ANGEL):

> We made a toast when all this began. I want justice; the Sister wants revenge. You didn't toast with us. What do *you* want?

Decrypt REMEMBRANCE (ELDER):

> I want an end to it. This isn't what we were made to do. We're not an army; we're not robots, either. We're people, and we're hurting.

Decrypt REMEMBRANCE (ANGEL):

> An end to hurt?

Decrypt REMEMBRANCE (ELDER):

> That'll do. After that, I'll take my chances.

Ends.

+10

Geodesica exterior: plus 36 hours

The Trojan horse took shape with unnerving rapidity, boiling into being on the back of superfast nanofacturing. Within an hour it progressed from an invisible dot to a lozenge three meters long and one wide, wrapped in a fractal coat designed to weather the strictures of the throat. Melilah—experiencing that hour as though it had passed in seconds—regarded it with no small feeling of unease. The new Cell was perfectly functional; she could only hope that the rough facsimile of her was not.

Another two and a half hours passed as Deangelis fine-tuned the Trojan. Very little changed on the outside as AIs received their instructions and nano- and microscale components took on optimal configurations, all with the sole intention of fooling the Archon's tracker hounds. Deangelis hadn't talked about how he had taken over the killer drone he now occupied. She could only assume it was a feat he was unable or reluctant to duplicate.

"Finished," said Deangelis to her, and she ramped her speed up to normal as he had showed her, calling up the circadian window in her field of view and toggling the virtual sliding scale back to zero. She experienced no symptoms of her sudden change in rate, but she felt jarred on the inside regardless. She was a Natural by inclination as well as choice; the thought of being other than human normally made her anxious and panicky. Faced with an alternative more harrowing than her fears, she had broken a lifetime of habit, just as she had already accepted all manner of radical intervention by Eogan's Cell. How long until she was willing to slide between states of humanity and inhumanity as easily as Eogan himself?

That she didn't feel any less human—or *herself*—for the betrayal of her body was no consolation at all.

"When are you going to send it on its way?" she asked.

"It's ready to sail," Eogan said. "We were just waiting for you."

"So don't wait any longer. Do it. Get us out of here." The vast exuberance of stars before the exit made her feel exposed. Although she knew that no one from those distant systems could possibly see them in the depths of intergalactic space, the small of her back still itched.

The fake Cell activated its drives and jockeyed forward. The possibility of watching it enter the hole in space penetrated her oppressive funk. Eogan gave her noninvasive access to numerous streams of data, and she settled on a simple visual display. Cerenkov radiation rippled like alcohol flames down the hull of the Trojan as it activated its defenses in preparation for entering the throat.

It slid through the entrance without fuss, disappearing into the discontinuity as though vanishing down an invisible well. Its leading edge seemed to contract marginally and take on a reddish hue, but beyond that there were no obvious displays of superphysics. The damage was done, she supposed; the door from one continuum to another hung permanently open, and didn't require any more holes to be smashed through the wall of space-time.

"Give it thirty minutes," said Deangelis, "then we'll follow."

She didn't adjust her newly mutable circadian rhythms to speed through the delay, although it dragged painfully. She wished she could know what was happening to the Trojan inside the alien maze. If it was caught too quickly, the ruse might be ineffective, and might even draw more attention to their vicinity of Geodesica.

"I'm tired of running," she said to the others.

"I hope you're not going to suggest we give up," Eogan said.

"No. There must be another way to deal with our situation. Leave Geodesica for good, perhaps, if the tunnels are too full of the killers for us to travel safely. Or put as much distance between them and us in there, then go to ground. Lie low for a while and see if they give up."

"I really do think this will work, Melilah," said Deangelis. "There's no need to give up on going home. Not completely."

"I'm just preparing myself for the worst." She felt as fragile as a frozen soap bubble. The tiniest knock could shatter her into a million tiny pieces. With Bedlam gone and time passing in unknown ways outside the maze, her connection to the rest of humanity—to friends she had known in other systems, to family, to old rivals and enemies—was stretching so thin as to strain the word "tenuous" to its limits. "It's not fair to be angry with you if it doesn't work out. Neither of you could have tried any harder to get us home. I've been nothing but a passenger, really. Wherever we end up, I just have to accept it."

"That's a little harsh," said Eogan, a frown creasing the broad contours of his face.

"The truth is. But I'm honestly not bitter about it." Looking at herself in the most objective light possible, she was as certain of that fact as she could be. She might have to settle for being a passenger, but that didn't mean she was chattel. Without passengers, the Palmers guild would never have existed, since the need for a stable means of interstellar travel was driven by movement of people not goods. Naturals colonized the worlds; Naturals traveled between them; Naturals populated the interstellar empire the Exarchate claimed. She had her uses, even if none of them were evident in Geodesica.

And how. The scale of the alien maze was beyond her. Just one glimpse of the universe outside it—at the proof of its awesome extent, not just spanning the Milky Way galaxy but reaching far, far beyond it—had the effect of putting her firmly and not comfortably in her place. She had as much hope of conquering it as an ant had of taking over a skyscraper. That job she had to leave to those more like its builders.

"My expectations are very low now," she said. "I came here thinking we'd find the solution to all our problems. Now I'd be happy with an hour in which I don't have to worry about things spying on me or jumping out at me from nowhere." She looked around at the emptiness of interstellar space again, and shivered. "I know it's crazy, but I feel safer in there than out here."

"Here's hoping you're right about that," said Eogan. "If not, this might be the last peaceful moment we have."

"It's not peaceful. We're just stuck, buried alive."

"I don't feel trapped," said Deangelis. The kidnapped replicator flexed around them, rippling smoothly into a new, leaner shape. "If anything, I feel more capable than ever. We have a real chance now. We're not flailing about at random. We have a plan."

"*You* do," she responded. "And I wish you'd get on with it."

"As you wish. A few minutes are unlikely to make a difference."

He didn't muck around. Without another word, they accelerated into the entrance. Melilah didn't look back as the cold blue energies of the throat enclosed them. Although intensely glad to be insulated from the topological storms raking the outside of the drone, she found herself unconsciously drifting closer to Eogan, who hung in his usual position again, half in and half out of the Cell's wall. His black shipsuit blended smoothly with the warm shell enclosing them. He looked at her and smiled reassuringly.

The gesture didn't touch her, except to make her nervousness flare up as irritation again.

"Why do you even bother?"

"What, Melilah?"

"Trying to look human for me. Why don't you just let yourself be the way you are?"

The smile faded. "This *is* the way I am. At the moment. I look this way for my benefit, not yours."

"But we both know it's fake. A wake. A *husk*."

"No more than your body is." He was beginning to look hurt. "Would looking like a monster make it easier for you to hate me?"

"Thanks, but it's easy enough already," she snapped, and immediately regretted it. "Ah, fuck it. I'm not going to open my mouth again until this is over, either way."

"Fifty Sols says you don't make it."

She barked an unexpected laugh and pointed a *you won't trick me so easily* finger at him.

Then they were through the throat and back inside Geodesica. The walls of the tunnel leading back to the exit rushed by them in a featureless blur. From a static void to a twisted space with few reference points—the leap was abrupt but not so challenging. She was becoming accustomed to the realities of her new life.

Her *after*life, she told herself. Her life had effectively ended with Bedlam. The only reason she had left to exist was revenge, a dish that must have turned very cold by now. No magic ROTH artifact was likely to change that.

As they plunged into monochrome pseudospace of the first intersection, she told herself to concentrate.

Eogan watched, no stranger to impotence himself, as Deangelis followed his plan to the letter. The SAD replicator was a machine of vast complexity; although Eogan had access to its senses, he remained very much the observer. The Cell was a passenger inside the replicator's gut; he and Melilah were in turn passengers inside the Cell. Waiting and watching were their only options now.

The replicator sped along the tunnels of the maze, retracing its steps to the transit torus where the behemoth had been destroyed. The Trojan had been programmed to follow the same route, and traces of its passage were evident in the thin atmosphere. The flow of air through the tunnels was odd; oscillating back and forth from junction to junction by the spatial effects connecting them, it didn't truly circulate. Some pockets, displaying subtle chemical and isotopic differences, might have remained undisturbed forever but for the passage of the Trojan and them in its wake. He wondered how long the pockets had been isolated for such differences to emerge naturally.

There was no sign of other replicators—no drive wakes, echoes of sensor sweeps, stray comms signals, anything. The furious search that had accompanied their escape from the torus appeared to have dissipated. Could the Trojan have been lucky and slipped through what net remained?

Any hope of that vanished when they rounded a junction and hit a wall of superheated plasma utterly different from the atmosphere behind them.

Deangelis brought the replicator to a sudden halt. Arcane sensors tasted the shock wave and the molecules boiling within it. Eogan caught fringes of the analysis the ex-Exarch performed. Certain trace elements stood out clearly; other more subtle markers clinched it.

"That was us," Deangelis said, "or so the replicators will think."

A cold feeling spread through Eogan's modified body. He'd never had any doubt of the replicators' lethal intent, but to see the proof of it so baldly, without a hint of ambiguity, was a powerful reminder of what might have been.

There, but for the grace of Deangelis, go I.

"Are you sure they fell for it?" asked Melilah, breaking her self-imposed silence.

"As sure as I can be. There are no SAD replicators in evidence in our vicinity. That may not be sufficient evidence, but it's the most we're likely to receive."

Eogan did his best to read the smooth lines of her face. Was she relieved? Wary of Deangelis's judgment? Nervous of what came next? Her expression was so complex as to be impenetrable.

"Do you have the route the replicator followed here from Bedlam?" he asked Deangelis.

"I do."

"How many junctions?"

"Two thousand, four hundred and seventeen."

"I guess we'd better get cracking, then."

"How long will it take us?" Melilah asked.

"Over three days, assuming we don't stop."

She shook her head and hid her eyes behind her fringe. Eogan was reminded of his dream of exploring Geodesica—seven steps into the tunnels, eleven to get back. They had been inside the maze for just one Bedlam day. Somehow, the replicator had had time to be built from another's seed and travel three days' worth of junctions after them. It strained his credulity.

"Better started sooner than later, I suppose," he said. *And don't even think about what might be waiting for us when we get there . . .*

Melilah said nothing. Her eyes didn't track as the replicator took a different turn from the one containing the cloud of the destroyed Trojan. The ghost of their deaths retreated behind them while Eogan automatically logged the turn—

175L4 100L3 040R2

—and he realized that she had dropped back into slow-time again. In a minute or two, from her perspective, she would be there. He was angry, just for a moment, at her willingness to abandon all effort at participation, at her sudden passivity. But he supposed she had few options. Deangelis would simply check off the turns as they encountered them, one after the other. There was nothing she could do except watch the blank walls slide by.

He, however, would not shirk that duty. Someone had to keep an eye on Deangelis, to make certain he wasn't screwing them over. Even if there was nothing Eogan could do about it, should the worst come to pass, he didn't want to wake up in the jaws of the Archon, when it was too late even to protest. He wanted to go to his fate with his eyes open.

He resisted an obscure impulse to brush the hair out of Melilah's frozen eyes, and directed his senses outward.

• • •

I'm losing her.

Deangelis tried to concentrate on the task before him, but his attention kept drifting. When his mind should have been full of nothing but five-dimensional intersections and the barely comprehensible path he was supposed to follow through them, all he could think of was suicide by default.

If Melilah gave up, what reason did he have to keep fighting? Would the thought of revenge sustain him as keenly as had the need to keep her safe? She was the last of his wards; if the fragment of him that remained proved insufficient to protect that small fragment of Bedlam's population, what hope had he of achieving anything else?

Space knotted and twisted around him as though in sympathy with his thoughts.

He could, if he dared, reach into the wetware of Melilah's mind and adjust the levels of neurotransmitters to stave off incipient depression, if that was what she suffered. Would she consider such a tactic an invasion if it improved her well-being?

Of course she would. He knew that much about her. His invasion of Bedlam had significantly improved conditions for her fellow colonists, but she had never accepted the validity of his authority. It didn't matter to her that he was better suited to rule than any Natural. What mattered to her was *choice*—and the freedom to exercise it.

Damn her. He wanted to confront her with his feelings just as she felt free to confront him. Why shouldn't she be on the receiving end of someone else's grief for a change? But he couldn't bring himself to do it. It ran counter to his instinct, which was to nurture her, not needle her. He possessed the capacity to be cruel in order to be kind—people had died during his takeover of Bedlam, and he agonized still over their deaths, even though he knew them to be necessary—but so much hung in the balance. If she *did* refuse to emerge from slow-time, effectively removing herself from the world around her, he would have lost her forever. He couldn't follow her down that long, slow road to eternity. Someone needed to make sure her inert body was safe.

He considered appealing to Eogan for help. The Palmer had a stake in Melilah's well-being, after all. Perhaps he could talk her around.

Before he could take the thought further, a feather-light electromagnetic touch on the replicator's outer hull indicated that another of its kind had detected them.

Deangelis immediately set in motion every contingency he had prepared in the intergalactic void. Weapons bristled invisibly behind the replicator's outermost skin; sensors triangulated on the source of the touch; translator programs prepared numerous responses to every conceivable inquiry. At the center of the inward-pointing skein of the replicator's empty mind, he held his breath.

The touch came a second time. At the very limit of his perception, two intersections along, his own senses detected the presence of the replicator that had found them. Swept back like himself in standard raptor/seeker mode, it broadcast a simple recognition code and went about its business.

He didn't relax until another five intersections had gone by and the microscopic drones he left behind failed to trip at the presence of someone following them.

"We're swimming with the sharks now," said Eogan, piggybacking his actions as best he could.

"Sharks can be cannibals."

"We'll just have to avoid the hungry ones, then." The Palmer looked thoughtful for a moment. "Do you think they're all going home?"

The replicator's AI had had several options open to it, when the quest to find the fugitives came to an end. It could return to Bedlam to make sure the news arrived; it could continue its exploration of Geodesica; or it could self-destruct. Its master, the Exarch of Lut-Deangelis, had given it plenty of leeway in that regard.

Deangelis was in the unfortunate situation of having to unpack the motives of himself—and worse, his *higher* self, as re-created in Bedlam by the Archon after the Catastrophe.

"Their numbers will be down," he said, "and they won't be actively searching for us. They'll gradually disperse through the tunnels until the odds of us coming across one become effectively zero. As long as we don't do anything to draw attention to ourselves, we should be safe. We're only going to be here a few more days, after all."

"Do you really think you can follow the route all the way back?"

"I believe it's possible. The structure of Geodesica flexes constantly, so the turns don't exactly match, but the correspondence is close. Only a global catastrophe could knock everything completely out of whack."

"Those nuclear detonations—"

"Have disrupted geometries in the vicinity of the torus, yes; and so did my use of the VOID drive earlier. Nevertheless, given the precision of the replicator's records, I am confident."

"What about time? Any idea how long it will take, on the outside?"

"That, Palmer Eogan, I cannot answer." He refused to make any promises. Some of the navigational notes referred to environments he had not encountered before. Until he knew what they were, he could only give it his best shot.

Their route led back through the torus, now filled with a sooty haze as the wreckage of the behemoth continued to disperse. Visibility was limited to several hundred meters. Deangelis traveled cautiously, sweeping the volume ahead with lidar and every other available means. If anything lay in wait for them, he would know it in time to flee.

Nothing surprised them. Three hours after entering the torus, he located the exit point they required, identified by the unique pattern of holes on a particular strip of wall. He felt less exposed once he was in the familiar confines of the tunnels, but at the same time he missed the opportunity to see ahead of him. The tunnels concealed them, but could just as easily become another trap.

They flew on. Melilah, still in the grips of slow-time, didn't react to anything around her. Her eyelids descended in a barely perceptible blink; her right arm hung at an awkward-looking angle. She looked neither oblivious nor despairing, as befitted her state. She was just waiting.

Time passed. Junction after junction fell by. The fuel reserves of the drone were easily sufficient for the journey, unless something unexpected happened. Deangelis fell to obsessively analyzing the replicator's records, agonizing over the slightest abnormality. What if he had inadvertently corrupted the data or was misinterpreting the AI's elaborate shorthand? He could only do his best and hope it would be enough.

The closer he came to the first of the anomalous data points, the more his apprehension grew. As he coasted along the tunnel leading to it, he unfolded numerous hidden weapons and sensor arrays in preparation for anything. Ahead, instead of the usual distant glow of a junction, he caught fleeting glimpses of something considerably larger. Another torus, perhaps. If such supernodes connected the vast and far-flung tangle of Geodesica, it made sense that there would be more of them.

He decelerated to a gentle coast at the end of the tunnel. It opened onto a space that was neither torus nor ordinary junction—and as the replicator slid into it, he bristled at sudden movement in the distance. He froze, priming weapons to fire and acquiring targets in every direction as the mind-stretching truth of the place hit home.

He appeared to be hanging between two flat, white planes. Tunnel entrances in the planes looked like holes in the surface of an ice sheet. Deangelis's mind recoiled from the hazy horizon where the two planes disappeared into the distance. The glimpse of eternity overwhelmed him.

Of more importance were the other replicators emerging from other tunnel mouths: dozens of them, both around him and on the far "sheet." They, too, had their weapons extended in readiness to attack. Sensor sweeps touched his hull, locked on, as he locked on to theirs.

Just nanoseconds from firing, he pulled his mental finger off the trigger. A bubbling laugh rose up at the back of his throat, and he firmly repressed it. The situation wasn't amusing at all.

"That's us, isn't?" asked Eogan.

"Yes." His mind struggled with the topology of the place. It wasn't truly infinite. Like a Möbius strip, the three-dimensional space around them was bent in higher dimensions and effectively looped back on itself, over and over again. The plate opposite them was the same plate from which they had emerged. The presence and nature of such a twisted space provided further proof, should they need it, of the higher-dimensional nature of Geodesica and the difficulties faced in navigating it.

He roughly mapped the true extent of the space they had found themselves in. The spatial knot was much smaller than the torus, but still appreciably—as well as apparently—large. Almost a kilometer around, it brought together several hundred tunnel mouths, all of them identical. Fortunately, the replicator's detailed memory gave him just enough information to find the one they wanted. Deangelis steadfastly ignored the multitudinous images of himself as they crossed the anomalous space. At the midpoint, he seemed to be one of many hundred versions of himself, all flying past like silent ghost ships, trapped by a supernatural curse to an eternity of wandering.

He left the thought behind him as they resumed their journey. If such anomalies were the worst they encountered, they had nothing to worry about—except getting lost. And while the data from the replicator's data remained reliable, there was little chance of that.

As more and more intersections fell behind them, he began to feel sorry that Melilah had taken the easy way out. The tunnels of Geodesica were merely the most common of many different sorts of geometries available within the structure. As well as the torus and the space-bending sheets, there were sections shaped like cylinders, cubes, pyramids, soccer balls, and more. Some flexed in more than three dimensions; others did not. One seemed like nothing so much as a complete inversion of the usual arrangement, with intersections floating like solid polka-dotted spheres in a vast, gray-green space. Entering one of the exits in that spatial permutation delivered him immediately to a point elsewhere in the volume, or another volume perfectly identical to it, elsewhere in the greater structure. That time was twisting as well as space came in glimpses of his replicator coming and going around him, glimpsed and then gone like fleeting hallucinations.

The geometries weren't artificial, he suspected, except in the sense that the entire place was a made thing, like the nanotech seed that had burrowed into an asteroid and grown to become the habitat called Bedlam. As time had passed and it had expanded outward and inward, entangling itself like a baroque coral, new forms had arisen spontaneously around the basic seed shapes of tunnels and entrances. Fractals and chaos arose from simple mathematical equations, and so, too, did the strange and wondrous nooks and crannies of the alien maze. They *were* anomalies—or flaws, perhaps, in the structure its makers had devised.

And occasionally, tucked into these nooks and crannies, attracted there or caught there like sand in an oyster, were signs that other visitors had come to wonder at the complex forms space wove around itself: fragments of a ceramic Snailer habitat, layered in elaborate parallel waves with no respect for up or down; more Merchant Bee ships, crumpled and empty like discarded toys; nine Rockhead droid shells with dimpled skulls and seven-fingered hands, as clear and angular as pure quartz crystals, attached to eight-legged bodies of cloudy silicon; one corner of a Web Caster sextet turning with Euclidian precision in the center of an intersection, whose walls spiked outward as though hooked and tugged by threads wherever the lines of the extrapolated tetrahedron this corner was just part of passed.

All were old—*very* old. Some had fallen foul of whatever had turned the behemoth to ash; others were perfectly preserved.

Deangelis recorded everything in the possibly vain hope that someone else might one day see it.

"Tunnels, tunnels everywhere," mused Eogan as they passed the two thousandth intersection, "but not a window to be seen."

"That's because there's no outside," Deangelis responded. "If you punched through one of the walls—if you *could*—you wouldn't hit vacuum. There's nothing in this universe but Geodesica, so you'd probably just hit another tunnel."

Eogan looked as though he needed conversation more than explanation. "Maybe that's why there's no one else here. You could go crazy in a place like this."

"It's not a habitat; it's a means of travel."

"Travel doesn't have to be unglamorous. Look at sailing ships, first-class rail, lighter-than-air dirigibles, the Concorde, the Orbital Express—"

"And their downsides: scurvy, derailings, explosions, air pollution, high-energy radiation. Come on, Palmer Eogan. You're not seriously saying you'd turn your back on this opportunity because its aesthetic displeases you, are you?"

"Of course not, but—well, tell me this: why *isn't* anyone using it? We're the fifth race we know of to come here, and there might have been more. Where have they all got to? Why isn't the place crawling with them?"

"I don't know," Deangelis admitted. "And I doubt Geodesica will give up its secrets easily. It's too big. A prolonged study with the resources of an entire civilization might crack it, but not the three of us on the run."

The Palmer was solemn at that. "I keep hoping we'll turn a corner and there it will be: the workshop where it all started, complete with map and instruction manual. I know it won't be that simple, but I can't help wishing. With those in our hands, Sol would give us safe passage out of here, for certain. Without them . . ." He shook his head. "Maybe we should seriously think about calling this place home. Or picking an exit at random and never coming back."

Deangelis could guess which of those options Eogan would prefer, if it came down to it. Palmers weren't known for their ability to settle, as Melilah had learned to her cost. The trade lanes of the Exarchate were lonely places. It took a particular sort of person to endure them.

Neither Deangelis nor Melilah was that sort of person. The concept of home was important to them. While he couldn't speak for her, he did feel confident in assuming that for her, as for him, a lifetime of wandering held no appeal whatsoever.

"Let's see what awaits us at Bedlam," he said, "before making any decisions one way or the other."

The intersections ticked by, falling into a predictable routine. Finding the exit closest to the recorded vector was second nature to him now. Only one more exotic location remained between them and the replicator's point of origin: a lazy spiral that curled through five complete revolutions before meeting itself and beginning again. When they reached it, having traveled through almost twenty-three hundred junctions, he took just a moment to rest and gather his thoughts, then pressed firmly on.

They were getting very close. Deangelis had no idea what awaited them at the exit from Geodesica. The replicator records contained information solely on its journey and the search for the fugitives. His reflexes remained at hair-trigger readiness for the slightest sign of ambush.

The number of intersections remaining dropped to double digits. The tunnels were clear of echoes and stray comms chatter. It was, he thought, almost *too* quiet. If the Exarchate—or anyone—retained control of the exit in Bedlam, surely they would be using it. Surely it would be a hive of industry and commerce. He had imagined a giant complex occupying the void left by the passing of his colony. The Catastrophe cover story wouldn't hold forever. However many years had passed, something like Geodesica couldn't be ignored for long. Its potential was simply too great.

Yet the way ahead remained determinedly silent. What could possibly have happened?

At twenty tunnels remaining, unnerved by the unexpected development, he paused to send ahead a series of drones. While he waited for them to report back, he took everything he knew about the region around the Bedlam exit—garnered from the data he himself had gathered before the Catastrophe and from the Archon's drones they had captured, plus their own experiences—and tried to piece it together. Most of the routes overlapped, if only for one or two junctions. The one they were following did not.

The drones came back safely, reporting no sign of activity in the run-up to the last junction.

Eogan was silent. Deangelis knew better than to ask. The decision was his.

While the last embers of hope still glowed, he nudged

Melilah's circadian back to normal and took a physical form in the empty heart of the Cell. Eogan looked up, startled, when Deangelis slipped out of the wall, then performed another double take as Melilah stirred from slow-time.

"What's happening?" she asked as though waking from a sleep. "Are we there yet?"

"Not quite," said Deangelis, taking her left hand in his right. "I want us to go in together."

"I had no idea you were so sentimental," she said, but behind the acid tone he could see that she was touched.

He reached for Eogan's hand also, and the Palmer didn't resist, although his expression was suspicious.

Hoping against hope, Deangelis instructed the replicator to take them home.

+II

Prime One: 2532–36 CE

The war began two days early, on the fourth of January according to the old Sol calendar. After ninety-two years of preparation, Horsfall surprised herself by being taken off guard by the sudden change of plans, although she could understand how it had happened. Word had only just reached her and Jane Elderton of the third Catastrophe, in a system called Familiar two hundred light-years away. The double whammy—that Sol had found another entrance to Geodesica ahead of them, and destroyed another colony in order to retain control of it—pushed the Exarch of Gabison's End over the edge. Valerie Aad was a jumpy character anyway; Horsfall had been struck by the unpredictable energy of the Exarch when Elderton had met with her over a decade earlier. Unable to decide if that energy sprang from restlessness or fear, Horsfall had agreed with Elderton that she shouldn't be a full member of the conspiracy. She would back them, but they couldn't afford to rely on her.

Now she had jumped the gun by declaring independence early in protest at the "continuing and morally abhorrent war against humanity" conducted by Sol and "its instruments." Horsfall wondered if the woman was trying to take credit for what would inevitably follow; if so, she soon regretted it, as a stream of military viruses spewed forth from her tangler and shut down her colony's communications system. Palmer Cells in the system reported a surge of EMPs, and then also fell silent. No one knew what exactly had happened to the colony, but the silence was an unhappy one.

As a result of the incident, security levels went to red all across the Arc Circuit. Those on the side of the rebellion found themselves facing unexpected challenges and barriers where previously there had been none. Hastily recalculated timetables initially suggested that the start should be delayed. Only sheer bloody-mindedness on Elderton's part and an awful amount of last-minute work enabled the plan to go ahead almost unchanged.

For those outside the conspiracy, the incident in Gabison's End only increased the vague certainty that *something* was about to happen, sooner rather than later. Melilah Awad's message had not been forgotten in the ninety-four years since its broadcast. The Familiar Catastrophe hammered home the fact that it was as relevant now as it had ever been, and would remain so until the situation was dealt with.

One hundred and four years had passed since Sublime, the first colony system to encounter Geodesica, had died. It was finally time for payback.

Decrypt REMEMBRANCE (ELDER):
> ETA Indivisible?

Decrypt REMEMBRANCE (ANGEL):
> Five hours.

Decrypt REMEMBRANCE (ELDER):
> I wish it didn't have to be like this.

Decrypt REMEMBRANCE (ANGEL):
> It's too late now for second thoughts.

Decrypt REMEMBRANCE (ELDER):
> Too late for lots of things; I know. It's just . . . There are so many other ways it *could* have gone if Sol had only opened its eyes. We're not pawns to be pushed around the chessboard. We're not expendable.

Decrypt REMEMBRANCE (ANGEL):
> Yet here we are. We could very well be *expended* in a matter of hours.

Decrypt REMEMBRANCE (ELDER):
> Do you think we'll see each other again?

Decrypt REMEMBRANCE (ANGEL):

> I have no intention of dying, and you have your promise to the Sister to keep. Let's not be sentimental ahead of time.

Decrypt REMEMBRANCE (ELDER):

> No. Let's be bold and forceful against our natures. Let's bring an end to it, either way.

Decrypt REMEMBRANCE (ANGEL):

> And when it's over, we can rest.

Decrypt REMEMBRANCE (ELDER):

> Amen to that.

Horsfall watched from the rear of the attack fleet, where Jane Elderton had insisted she remain during the battle. No one knew how long the conflict would last; it could be moments, or it could be hours. Everything depended on how Adriel Binard reacted.

Neither Palmer nor Exarch but something in between, Horsfall body had been completely integrated with her old Cell *Dreieichen* and incorporated into the vastly distributed array of stations, missiles, drones, and dust converging on the world called Prime One. The planet was white with clouds, its dense atmosphere a relic of the greenhouse effect gradually brought under control by First Wave terraforming. Three orbital towers trisected the equator, topped with bristling docking arms and habitats. Horsfall thought of Altitude, and of Sublime's sole habitable planet, one that had looked similar to this one until Catastrophe stripped it back to atoms. What would it have looked like after an extra century of habitation? What had the Exarchate—and humanity—lost?

The attack fleet had coasted in-system in dark mode, hiding their profiles and vectors until the very last moment. In line with the plan, every reactionless thruster burned at the same moment, all across the system. Munitions shunted along new trajectories; hollow asteroids spun up to cause maximum damage. Forerunner darts erected space-warping shields to protect their payloads. Spigots opened in reservoirs, spraying the vacuum with clouds of ice crystals. At speed, a single molecule packed a serious punch. Just one high-energy impact could knock out delicate nanocircuits at a critical time, thereby forcing a tactical error. Deangelis and Elderton had sought every advantage and exploited it to the limit.

Accompanying the rebellion fleet was a contingent of Palmer

Cells under the auspices of the *Jebel al Qamar*. Some had recently withdrawn from Prime One; others had come from as far as Eliza and Phad 4 to be present. Although technically independent units, the Negotiator Select had given Horsfall authority over their deployment. It amazed her to think of how far she had come since Sublime. Then, she had been a grieving victim of circumstance; now she flew at the heart of a navy—the first true space navy humanity had ever known.

Elderton was with her, still bound to her flesh like a ghost to a chalk outline. Deangelis brought up the rear, for the moment. The Bridgehead he had built hadn't even begun decelerating, and wouldn't unless Binard capitulated fully. Traveling at a substantial fraction of light-speed from the rear of the vanguard, it lurked in the Dark like an illegitimate at the reading of a will, impatiently waiting its turn.

The fray's opening salvo came over the comms.

"This is Ansellus Primus–Binard Traffic Control to incoming hostiles," said the defiant AI. "You will identify yourselves and state your intentions or face the most severe of consequences."

It was a bluff, and everyone on both sides knew it. The invading force was too extensive for the civilian colony to repel, and its position at the top of the gravity well gave it an unassailable advantage.

On the other hand, crushing the colony wasn't the plan. Gaining concession to the new authority without civilian casualties had to be the priority, or else the rebellion would be no better than the forces it was fighting.

"Adriel, this is Jane Elderton," Elderton replied. "I have been delegated temporary spokesperson of the Arc Circuit Alliance. I want you to stand down before any blood is shed."

"The *what* alliance?" the voice of the system's Exarch came back.

"It's a temporary name. In response to grave and persistent crimes against humanity, we have declared the Arc Circuit free of Sol and its influence. Our union of Palmers, Exarchs, and Naturals fights together to establish an independent territory on our terms, one that will be governed as we see fit. We accept that this amounts to treason against those who created us. We do not accept that we owe our creators fealty any longer, or that their appalling acts against us can ever be justified."

Adriel Binard's laugh was rough-edged with alarm. "This is insane. You can't expect to succeed—here or elsewhere."

"We'll succeed. Don't you worry about that. Your concern should be your colony and its well-being. We have no wish to supplant you. Our targeting priorities are your tangler and anything that's emerged from it in the last week. If you don't want to surrender outright, give us those at least and we'll negotiate."

"The tangler?"

"The Archon will take countermeasures, if it hasn't already." Elderton's tone shifted to one more placating than confrontational. "Please, Adriel. I don't want to fight you. We can make this happen. It'll be easier if we all work together."

"Of course it would be, but that doesn't make it right."

"Might *doesn't* make right. That's exactly why we're fighting. "

The conversation took place over open channels. Everyone in the system—and beyond—bore witness to it. The fleet expended as much energy on ftl messaging as on armaments and defense. Horsfall agreed with the decision wholeheartedly: this wasn't a war to be fought in secret. It involved everyone.

"Why here?" asked Binard, almost plaintively.

"Not just here, Adriel," Elderton replied. "Everywhere."

A shower of projectiles twinkled as they fell on Prime One's outermost moon.

"To all the citizens of Prime One and the Arc Circuit," Elderton's voice boomed out over the channels, "we say this: you are not our enemies. On your behalf we risk our lives. Death does not frighten us, for we know our cause is just. We ask but one thing of you: to spare us the tragedy of fighting you, our fellow citizens of the Arc Circuit. Lay down your arms. Allow us the measures we require; give us the time to prove our point. We do not seek to sweep aside your Exarchs and the ways of life you treasure. That is exactly what we are fighting *for*. When Sol could destroy us on a whim—and has willingly done so to whole colonies, three times now—who would not join us? To the Arc Circuit and beyond we say: become our allies and fight with us. As one, we will prevail; apart we are nothing but chaff."

Elderton waited a moment for a reply. Horsfall felt her tension as a physical ache. They had become so entangled down the century that each knew the other's moods as well as her own. Horsfall knew when Elderton burned and hated and grieved; Elderton in turn experienced Horsfall's rage and despair. A century of planning fueled the darkest of emotions. Only rarely did the light shine through.

As a new star dawned just light-minutes from Prime One, a feeling of joy spread through Elderton's mind.

“We’re not playing games,” said Isaac Deangelis, riding the wings of a vast and fiery bird of prey, its weapon arms extended and clawed, almost batlike but shining in all frequencies. A negative image of a bat. “Adriel, this is your last chance.”

The Exarch didn’t reply. Instead, a high-frequency scream tore through the airwaves, one designed to play havoc with every system the rebellion had carefully sent into war.

Horsfall flinched at the unearthly sound of it. The density of data it carried appalled her; whole terabytes of persuasion and incision crammed into microseconds. If it continued the Dark only knew what would happen. Cells would self-destruct; weapons would turn on each other; Exarchs would go mad.

The sound shut off in mid-Babel as automatic defense algorithms kicked in. Recognizing the attempted override for what it was, the fleet went comms-silent. Ftl died that same moment.

“Okay, it’s happened,” said Horsfall. “You said it might, and it did.”

These are desperate times, said Elderton. *No one knows that better than the Archon.*

“Do you think we can salvage anything?”

Only time will tell. I’m sorry, my friend, but this is only the beginning. The end is a long way off yet.

Horsfall felt thrust surge through her section of the fleet. As explosions began to pockmark bases all across the system, she tried to concentrate on them and not the hundreds of entanglement repeater stations that formed the foundation of the Exarchate’s ftl communications network—the first great sacrifice made in the name of the war.

In fast-time, an ocean wave crashing on a shore looked frozen in place, each spittle of spray moving by minute increments, the body of the wave itself seeming as solid as marble. In slow-time, the surface of the sea became a blur that also seemed solid, as waves advanced and retreated, crashing in an unceasing progression—in the same way that a tabletop looked solid, despite its myriad fast-moving molecular components.

Horsfall resisted the impulse to retreat into slow-time as the battle progressed. She needed to see the consequences of her actions. Every individual death, every habitat or vessel destroyed, every advantage lost that had been hard-won from the depths of the Dark—she wanted to feel it all. Her shoulders were broad, and they had had years to strengthen. She could bear the weight, not shirk it.

But it was hard. She had to remind herself that Sublime, Bedlam, and Familiar were the true reasons for fighting, not her sister; that justice for all the Exarchate's citizens was the goal, not retribution.

She watched as a Palmer contingent fell foul of an arcane weapon they had discovered boiling out of Prime One's largest orbital counterweight docking station. A shimmering, translucent mass, it sprouted twisting, dagger-sharp magnetic field lines that whipped and snapped through even the toughest of shields, stripping electrons from atoms and breaking molecular bonds all through the Cell components. The rebel contingent fell apart like Christmas decorations hit by a cricket bat. Not one component of the *Duszniki Zdrój, Scheveningen,* or *Alcazarquivir* survived.

She watched as rubble fell from another tower, tracing black and red lines across the cloudscape below. Ghastly domes bloomed where they landed, uglier than boils.

She watched as citizens rebelled against their Exarch and dropped their defenses ahead of the rebellion's arrival. She watched as other defenders, too proud or fearful to accept the truth, opened their air locks and tasted vacuum rather than defeat.

She watched as Isaac Deangelis swept through the system and brushed away every last possibility of resistance. "The Angel of Death," someone had called Bridgehead, and not without reason. His awful creation blazed with the fire of stars but cradled the darkness of their deaths within. The web of singularities he commanded could destroy whole worlds. It dragged space-time after it like a torn shroud.

Prime One fell as Bridgehead matched orbits with the cloudy world. Adriel Binard surrendered control of her tangler to the Alliance, her system with it, rather than see her people destroyed by such overwhelming firepower. Whether Deangelis would have gone so far as to use his weapon to its full capacity, Horsfall was glad not to know. Those unwilling to submit, or perhaps nervous of what Sol might send in response, Elderton rounded up and confined to one of the orbital stations.

Adriel Binard was not supplanted.

"We need all able hands," Elderton said in another general

broadcast, "to rebuild what has been damaged and to replace what has been destroyed. This is your home. Our mission is not to take it from you, but to return it to you. Until now your sovereignty has been a lie. Now it is truth. Take this opportunity and make of it what you will."

"Four hundred and thirteen people are dead," said Binard. "How do you suggest I replace *them*?"

"You can't, just as we can't replace the citizens of Sublime, Bedlam, and Familiar. All you can do is honor them—and stand firm to prevent such atrocities from ever happening again."

Deangelis stayed long enough to convince Prime One that it had made the right choice, and then sped elsewhere. The next system he had on his target list was Little Red—again, not technically an Arc Circuit mainstay, but another old system closely tied to Sol. With those two ties severed, the Arc Circuit would be effectively isolated.

Horsfall threw herself into her work, which consisted of reassembling her body and moving among the populace, preaching her message to any who would listen. Elderton went with her, as always, a silent observer and occasional savior. Twice Horsfall was shot at; once the habitat she visited was deliberately holed. She survived all three attacks by virtue of the Exarch within. Elderton was as good as her word, sparing no arcane technology to keep her charge alive.

Rumors spread about Horsfall—that she was indestructible, that she alone had survived the Catastrophe in Sublime, that not even the Archon could kill her. She didn't encourage them, but the more she denied them the more they stuck. The children of the colony called her Awful Horsfall, and she couldn't stop that either. Her intensity made people uncomfortable; her promises that the war was only beginning weren't popular.

When the Reapers came, no one questioned her popularity then. They rallied behind her to resist the deathly, ancient warhorses. For the second time in a year, the system burned—but this time the attack was indiscriminate. Grim weapons laid waste to anything that stood against the retribution of Sol. Relentless broadcasts warned of worse to come if they didn't surrender immediately.

The attack was genuine, but the weapons were outdated. Once, Reapers had struck fear into the hearts of colonists; now the Alliance's new toys outmatched them. Given time and preparation, miracles were possible.

Four thousand people died and many more lost their homes. The Palmer contingent lost half its numbers before the last of the Reapers fell, destroyed by the Alliance in cooperation with the people of Prime One.

Adriel Binard called for a cautious celebration. Even she seemed pleased that, thus far, independence was holding. But Awful Horsfall didn't toast with the rest. Worse could still be on its way. With the ftl networks down, there was no way of knowing.

"Perhaps," she confided to Jane Elderton one dark hour, "we're all that's left. Everything else went cockeyed and Sol is closing in on us right now. It'll be years before we hear by Palmer or maser—and by then we'll be a cinder and a memory. Nice try, but thanks for nothing."

Have faith, said her Exarch companion. *Hold firm. Don't fall to the battle within now that the battle without is going in our favor.*

"I've held on this long, haven't I?"

It's a whole different fight now.

Horsfall conceded that much. She'd thought it would be easier when the killing started, but it wasn't. The enemy lines weren't so clear-cut on the battlefield. The way the rules kept changing didn't help. Life had been much simpler when they had been slinking from system to system, afraid of everyone.

Decrypt REMEMBRANCE (DMW):

> Testing, testing. Acknowledge receipt of message, Indivisible. Testing, testing. Acknowledge receipt of message, Indivisible. Come on, old girl. I know you're there. We can't have lost *that* easily.

Decrypt REMEMBRANCE (ELDER):

> Hails?

Decrypt REMEMBRANCE (DMW):

> I thought I was "Dead Man Walking," or something equally undignified.

Decrypt REMEMBRANCE (ELDER):

> You were, but there's no need for encryption anymore. Switch to a clear protocol. It's all out in the open now.

Open channel (LAZARUS HAILS):

> Well, that sounds promising. I hate all this skulking around.

Open channel (JANE ELDERTON):
> Your skulking seems to have done the trick.

Open channel (LAZARUS HAILS):
> Quite.

Open channel (JANE ELDERTON):
> How many relay stations did you capture?

Open channel (LAZARUS HAILS):
> None.

Open channel (JANE ELDERTON):
> But I thought—

Open channel (LAZARUS HAILS):
> Reverse engineering is a wonderful thing. I'm not saying it's been easy, and the way the tangler network crashed took even me by surprise, but I've managed to rig a rudimentary link between certain key systems nonetheless. Not all the tangler network is down, you know; I'm piggybacking off some of its trunks while I get my own running in parallel. Once that's done, the Arc Circuit will be completely ftl.

Open channel (JANE ELDERTON):
> Good work.

Open channel (LAZARUS HAILS):
> I know.

Open channel (JANE ELDERTON):
> Where are you right now?

Open channel (LAZARUS HAILS):
> This part of me is midway between Alioth and Altitude. Technically I'm scattered all across the new network, supervising construction.

Open channel (JANE ELDERTON):
> Have you heard from elsewhere?

Open channel (LAZARUS HAILS):
> Friday and Gabison's End are ours without a fight. Whitewater, Eliza, and Megrez are wavering but will come around

when they see what's happened elsewhere. Schiller's End and New Eire are putting up some stiff resistance; we might need Isaac there to convince them. Our forces are still closing in on Alcor and Phad.

Open channel (JANE ELDERTON):
> What about Alioth and Mizar?

Open channel (LAZARUS HAILS):
> I saved the best for last. They folded without so much as a whimper. The ultimatum had barely finished airing before Frederica Cazneaux handed over her tangler. Lan Cochrane—what's the best word?—*fragmented* the moment we appeared. It turns out that her personality has been unstable since Bedlam went under. The people under her were glad to have someone competent in charge again.

Open channel (JANE ELDERTON):
> Does Isaac know?

Open channel (LAZARUS HAILS):
> I can't see how, while he's between systems. When's he due at Little Red?

Open channel (JANE ELDERTON):
> Within the year, depending on deform ratings.

Open channel (LAZARUS HAILS):
> It'll be interesting to see what he meets there. Sol will have had plenty of warning by then. It won't be an easy fight.

Open channel (JANE ELDERTON):
> We had Reapers here—ten of them. The attack was spirited but unconvincing.

Open channel (LAZARUS HAILS):
> Something else is coming, you think?

Open channel (JANE ELDERTON):
> Undoubtedly. Sol won't roll over and accept defeat so easily. The Arc Circuit is its best route out of the Local Bubble. It needs sovereignty over this space if it's ever going to break free.

Open channel (LAZARUS HAILS):
> Or it needs Geodesica.

Open channel (JANE ELDERTON):

> Two out of three known entrances are right here, so the point is still valid.

Open channel (LAZARUS HAILS):

> Dead systems of no tactical value . . .

Open channel (JANE ELDERTON):

> Which is why we have to leave them until last. Secure the rest of the Arc Circuit, then take what we're really after.

Open channel (LAZARUS HAILS):

> Agreed.

The geography of Prime One fascinated Horsfall. In the two years of peace following the attack of the Reapers, she found time to get to know the world and the people who called it home. An uninterrupted equatorial sea girdled it like a belt, one studded with endless chains of volcanoes and small islands, the latter covered in rich rain forest seeded by First Wave colonists. Slender bridges, looping and curling over the sea in graceful golden arcs, linked the islands, but many of Prime One's citizens preferred to travel by ship or dirigible, following air and water currents around the planet's bulging waist. Horsfall took a berth on an ever-wandering triple-hulled boat, determined to see as much as she could before duty called her elsewhere.

The *Blue Charlotte* traveled perpetually west, into the setting sun, and Horsfall, like many of its passengers, celebrated each night on the gleaming, white foredeck, watching as the system's primary slid through gossamer clouds behind the bulge of the world.

"This is a sectarian conflict," opined a large man holding a stein of thick-foamed beer. Either ignorant or not caring that Awful Horsfall was in his audience, he held forth with gusto, splashing foamily when he gestured too hard. "It's obvious. The human species has diversified rapidly in recent centuries. All that's held us together is that word: *human*. But what does it mean, now? Is it us, the colonists, or the Exarchs? Is it Sol and the minds who live there now? There's no clear-cut definition, so we fight to clarify it."

"I thought it was about territory," risked a slender redhead leaning on a rail, her attention mainly on birdlike creatures traveling in a rippling flock across the sunset.

"Space is one thing we'll never be short of, out here." The burly man issued a mocking noise. "And we don't fight over religion or money anymore. Identity is the only commodity left that we'll kill for. The right to call ourselves human is the last remaining bounty."

"Who, then, has that right?" asked Horsfall. "Who decides what makes us human or not?"

"The victors," said an onlooker. "They write the history books. They create the definitions."

"Nonsense." A heavy splatter of beer struck the deck as the pontificator turned too quickly. "We know what *human* is. We have sixty thousand years of evidence to back us up. Naturals are the rightful heirs of the title. Few would argue with that."

"So it's a war of race," said Horsfall, irritated that this pompous ass had ruined her enjoyment of the sunset. "Is that what you're telling us?"

"That's what it risks becoming. Naturals versus Palmers versus Exarchs versus the Archon. And why stop there? There must be something above the Archon."

"I suspect you're right," she said. "And something above that, and something above that, and so on, ad infinitum. Naturals are at the bottom of a pyramid stretching way up out of our sight. Who are we to claim that the apex is not worthy of its origins?"

"I'm not saying that." The proselytizer seemed slightly nonplussed by her response. "I'm just saying they're not human. They have no claim over the word."

"Do the Palmers who fight alongside you? Do the Exarchs? Do those who diverge in other ways from the Natural code? Are they to be disowned as soon as you no longer need them?"

"Obviously not—"

"It's not obvious at all, friend. For you, this war is about setting boundaries around who and what is human. I say it's about ensuring a base level of *humanity,* no matter who claims what title. The way we behave is more important than our genetic or technological makeup. I don't care if a mind is built from genes or scrap silicon. If it behaves in a way that I think a human should, then I'm prepared to accept it as one. And if it doesn't, then I'll consider my options."

Her passion surprised her. The man had touched a nerve—that was clear—and in the process uncovered a deeper motivation than she had suspected. Not revenge or retribution or justice, but to ensure a moral and ethical framework over the civilization she was proud to call herself part of. She hadn't known her motives could be so cerebral. Perhaps she had been hanging out with Exarchs for too long.

With gentle surges, the deck rocked slowly beneath them. The sun was gone. There would be no stars through the planet's cloud cover. The small crowd was ignoring the view, anyway. The burly man glowered at her, stein lowered and dripping. He seemed to have just realized who she was, perhaps alerted by someone else in the crowd, via silent, wireless communication, or in receipt of a search engine result based on her face.

"You *would* think that," said the man with a sneer. "You and your freak friends. How long until they turn on us, too? How long—"

"Excuse me," she said, feeling real rage beginning to creep over her. "My freak friends, as you call them, are doing their best to give you space to live in. Sol is evolving whether you like it or not; the vanguard of human evolution is stretching further beyond us every day. How long do you think it would have been before it forgot where it came from and wiped you out as casually as you'd eradicate an infection? By reminding it now of the obligations it holds to us, to the name *human,* we hope to avoid a tragedy far greater than anything you care to comprehend. If you can't or won't face that fact, then you are as bad as Sol is. Slip back into the past; rush headlong into the future. Either way, the present is lost."

She turned and walked away, not caring if it looked like retreat. The argument was simultaneously pointless and utterly pivotal to the future of the Arc Circuit. She couldn't solve it on her own no matter how much she shouted. Persisting would only make her more upset than she already was. It dredged up not grief over Sublime, but reminded her of more distant upsets, those relating to her decision to become a Palmer—when, against the wishes of her family on Eliza, she had volunteered for the guild and accepted the necessary biomodifications. If she wanted to travel in space that was simply part of the deal. Humans could terraform planets; they could build habitats to keep out what they could not change; but traveling through space at speed presented hazards that could be avoided only by changing people themselves. Faced with the immovable object of high-energy physics, the momentum of humanity was bound to lose.

The wedge her decision drove between her loved ones persisted for decades, reinforced by relativistic lags and long absences. Her parents became strangers to her; her home faded from her memory. The trip to Sublime had been the first opportunity to connect one-on-one with her sister for longer than she cared to remember.

The Sublime Catastrophe had severed the last link she had with *family*. Since then, she had known only the ache of its absence.

And now this pompous fool tried to make out that she and the Exarchs weren't legitimate humans—a statement that carried a burden of sinister implications. They didn't feel; they didn't love; they didn't care what happened to anyone different from themselves. The fact of the matter was that anyone not of Natural stock was *more* likely, not less, to care about those different from them. After all, humanity followed its own evolution now. The random currents of genetics had been abandoned for more purposeful means of development. A willingness to change, and to accept change in others, was unavoidably part of that process.

People didn't have to work hard to be a Natural; they were born that way. Resenting those who chose not to be that way was just stupid, but it seemed in some to be hardwired. Resentment so easily became fear, and that curdled almost immediately into hate . . .

Horsfall went back to her stateroom and shut the door behind her. She stood for a long moment without turning on the light, a slightly improved version of the human animal with shaking hands and tears on her cheeks. Was there an emotional equivalent to high-energy physics? Could she have her genome rewritten so she could survive such trauma?

Don't be angry with him, whispered the voice that had been mercifully silent through the confrontation. *Let time prove him wrong.*

"*Is* he so wrong?" she asked, voicing the one doubt she couldn't bring herself to admit in public. "Couldn't this be the end for Natural humanity, if things go badly?"

Elderton laughed. *You'd find it easier, I think, to wipe out the cockroach. Or the common cold virus.*

"Is that how you think of them? As pests, as disease?"

No. As parts of nature. We can live with them well enough, even enjoy their company. Naturals are much more interesting than viruses or insects.

"To you, maybe, but what about the Archon? Or what comes after it?"

The pyramid analogy is a good one. For all the billions of Nat-

urals that exist today, there are about a hundred thousand Palmers, a thousand Exarchs, and one Archon. There's room for everyone, and no reason to despair.

"Now, perhaps—but later?"

We have enough to worry about at the moment. Let's deal with the future when it comes. After all, if we lose here, you and I might not have one.

That was a sobering thought. Whatever happened to humanity in the long run, Horsfall and her ghostly companion were on the front line. If anyone was going to die in the war—sectarian or not—it would most likely be them.

"You said once that, whatever happened, you didn't want to make Melilah Awad a martyr." Still without turning on the light, she walked to the bed and lay flat on her back, staring up at the darkness. "I see why, now. She was a Natural, and linking our cause to her death—if she *is* dead—would motivate people for the wrong reasons. It's not about the Archon killing Naturals. It might have been easier that way, sometimes, but it would've been wrong."

Yes. The ends do not justify the means.

Horsfall nursed her grief and anger, branded deep into the muscle of her heart, and wondered what the architects of Geodesica would think of her species' hapless fumbling at greatness.

"Do you think we'll ever sort ourselves out?"

Her question hung in the darkness of the room for a disturbingly long time. Elderton didn't always respond when Horsfall called, but this time the silence went deeper than just an absence of noise. Elderton's voice wasn't the only thing missing.

"Hello?"

"Please don't be frightened," said someone out of the darkness. "I mean you no harm."

She jumped and reached mentally for the light. It flashed on, filling the room with a warm, yellow glow. The stateroom wasn't ostentatious, consisting of the bed, a small desk and armchair, and an antique 3-D entertainment facility. The wood paneling hid steel-carbon composite walls that could form an airtight seal in the event of an emergency. Nanotech atmosphere reprocessers, not dissimilar to those in a Palmer Cell, could keep her alive for weeks, even at the bottom of the ocean, until rescue came.

This was a very different sort of emergency. A man sat in the armchair in the corner of the stateroom opposite her bed, light gleaming off his smooth, bald scalp. Dressed in a sharp-lined gray suit, he had the air of someone who had been sitting there for some time. His hands lay folded in his lap. His feet angled slightly apart. His posture was very slightly slumped.

Horsfall recognized him. That was the strangest thing. Even as thoughts of assassination flashed through her mind, she searched her memory and came up with a name.

"Palmer Flast?"

"I merely—and temporarily—inhabit his body." The voice issuing from Flast's full-lipped mouth possessed a measured calmness out of all keeping with the situation. "You do not know me, except by my actions."

She frowned. A powerful handgun rested in the top drawer of her bedside table. She backed away from him, opened the drawer, and raised the weapon between them. Flast didn't try to stop her.

"What did you do to Jane?"

"I put her away for a while so we can talk uninterrupted."

"If you've hurt her—"

"I assure you that I have not." Flast's expression was neutral. Horsfall felt nothing but relief at that. To see him express a false emotion, or to watch as one was thrust forcibly through him, would be physically upsetting.

"I am the Archon," the voice said through Flast's lips.

"I was beginning to figure as much." She kept the gun carefully beaded on his chest, for all the good it would do her if the Archon attacked. The last time she had seen Flast—in Megrez, over a cup of coffee—the former Chief Officer of the *Nhulunbuy* had been well and himself. He had been considering retiring from the trade lanes and moving into the diplomatic arm of the guild. The Palmers, although they secretly allied themselves with the Alliance, had never quite given up the hope of striking a new deal with both Sol and the Exarchate. War for them was ever a last resort. "When did you get to him? How long has he been spying for you?"

"He isn't a spy. He doesn't even know I'm here, and he won't unless you tell him. I chose Palmer Flast because he was convenient, and because I knew I could get to you through him."

"What do you want with me?"

"Just to talk. I felt the need to meet you. I made Isaac and Jane who they are; them I understand intimately. You I know only from afar. It seemed wrong to be so ignorant, under the circumstances. No." Flast's right hand rose at the whim of invisible puppet strings. "Not wrong. *Disrespectful.*"

She eyed him warily. "If you think you're going to change my mind—"

"I neither need nor want to."

"Change or fuck with it, it amounts to the same thing. And don't believe for a moment that it will alter what's coming your way."

"I *don't* believe it." The cool eyes regarded her for a long moment. "Understand, Palmer Horsfall, that I could have attained the data I needed long ago without revealing my presence to you—just as I could have quashed this rebellion of yours within minutes of its inception. My being here now should tell you something about me and my motives."

"It could tell me that you're lying."

"But I'm not."

She hesitated, not even remotely sure what to make of the encounter. Her hand didn't tremble as she aimed the handgun at the man in the chair, but inside she felt aboil with emotions. Fear, resentment, uncertainty—even guilt for not seeing something like this coming and preparing for it. She should have something witty to say, if nothing else.

"You're much shorter than I expected."

The Archon laughed, which startled her. "Palmer Horsfall, you are everything I imagined."

Her eyes narrowed. "Meaning what?"

"Meaning that I'm proud of you. You are a fine example of the humanity you serve."

"Now I know you're fucking with me."

"I assure you that I am not."

"Well, I don't need your approval. We're on different sides, remember?"

"You might think so, but I disagree."

"I just imagined those Reapers, then?"

"No. They were real enough."

"I should shoot—"

"And kill an innocent man? If you were willing to make that sacrifice, you would have already done so."

She felt her ears beginning to redden. "Don't assume this makes us allies."

"You should be glad that I don't think of us as enemies, Palmer Horsfall." Flast's features were grimly neutral again. "Do believe me when I tell you that I could stop you and your rebellion any time I chose, just as I could have killed you the moment you walked in the door. Like you, I don't want to cause unnecessary loss of life. Destroying the Arc Circuit will only inflame the rest of the Exarchate, and I have no wish to see this grand venture end in ashes. It's too important to the future of our species."

"Spare me the rhetoric."

"I mean every word. No death, at any scale, should be taken lightly. I kill only in moments of absolute necessity."

"That's a hoary old excuse. It's never been convincing, and I'm not falling for it now."

"You wrong me, Palmer Horsfall—and your hands are as bloody as mine. The people who died when you gained control of this colony were only a small percentage of its total population. Exactly the same can be said of the deaths resulting from my actions, in terms of the Exarchate as a whole. We are exactly the same, you and I. The only difference between us is the scale on which we're working."

"I'm nothing like you." She glared at the shell of Palmer Flast and wished that she did have the capacity to shoot him, just to bring the conversation to an end. If such a crude action would kill the Archon, she might consider it. But there was no point wishing for yet more dreadful choices.

"I want you to leave," she said, lowering the gun and edging off the bed. She stood with her back against the wall farthest from the door, not wanting to come any closer to the shell than she had to. "Leave now or I'll raise the alarm and someone else can deal with you."

Flast's body didn't move, but his sensual mouth pursed. "Is there nothing you want to ask me?"

"No."

"This opportunity may never be repeated."

"I don't care. Get out."

Flast unfolded with a rustle of fabric and stood calmly before her—to all appearances an ordinary Palmer, but filled with an intelligence that she felt uncomfortable thinking of as even remotely human, by any measure of the concept.

"Jane Elderton told you a moment ago that the ends don't justify the means. I'm afraid I disagree. Every action has a price.

Sometimes we don't see that price, or we do but choose not to care about it. Sometimes the benefits and costs are hard to fathom, especially over longer timescales and in complex, chaotic systems. I tell you now that the cost of not acting in Sublime far exceeded the damage caused by the Catastrophe. Even when you add the deaths of Bedlam and Familiar—deaths I feel as keenly as you—and the lives lost during your rebellion and the war to come, the cost of not acting is still higher. You may disagree. In fact, I expect you to. You do not know the ends toward which the Architects of Sol are working. Without knowing those ends, how can you judge us for our means?"

"Your ends are not ours," she said. "That's the problem."

"You don't even know that. Only time will tell, Palmer Horsfall. I hope that, one day, you will come to see that you have judged us falsely."

She thought of her sister. "There isn't enough time in the universe for that to happen."

"Again, I disagree. The future of the human race is at stake. It is, perhaps, a future beyond your comprehension. When you see what you have been risking, I am certain that you will understand me better."

Flast's head inclined in the faintest of bows. "Good-bye, Palmer Horsfall."

She watched him go, hatred and resentment surging through her tissues. The angry words she'd said earlier on the deck of the ship came back to her. The anger she had felt at those fearful of people who were different undercut her automatic distrust of the Archon. It had, after all, come just to talk to her and done her no harm.

She rubbed her arms, feeling gooseflesh. Unless, she thought, it *had* hurt her and she simply hadn't noticed . . .

A shuttle engine whined out on the deck. The hull kicked slightly beneath her feet, then resumed its normal gentle rolling. She found it odd that the ship moved as it traveled. The water brushing against its hull was nothing compared to the powerful impacts of atoms between the stars, yet in the *Dreieichen* she could seem to float in perfect vacuum, isolated from every outside influence.

A longing for the Dark struck her then. She wanted to leave Prime One and put the rebellion behind her. The fight truly was only beginning; she didn't know when peace might come, if ever. That thought utterly exhausted her.

For the first time she regretted the promise she had extracted from the Exarchs. A century of anticipation had so easily been outweighed by a year or two of war.

You're very quiet, said Elderton into her mind.

"I—" She looked down at the gun in her hand. Had the Exarch seen *nothing*? "I'm tired."

You'd better rest, then. A sense of calm suffused her, and she marveled at the ease with which her mind and body could be manipulated. But she didn't fight it. That would serve no purpose.

"I feel like—" She put the gun away and lay back on the bed. "Prime One is secure. I want to move on, find something constructive to do elsewhere. Eliza, perhaps, if we're still struggling in that quarter of the Circuit. I'm treading water here." *And afraid I might sink.*

We can do that, if you wish. Elderton's voice whispered softly around her thoughts, as intimate as a lover's embrace. *Conditions are safer here. I thought you might want a break from the fighting.*

"No. I don't want to be safe. I want to see firsthand what we've done."

Very well. I will make arrangements immediately.

Horsfall killed the lights and closed her eyes. "Thank you."

She never told Jane Elderton about her encounter with the Archon, although it ate at her in moments of doubt. What if it had seeded her with spyware? What if it took her over as it had Palmer Flast and made her into an unwitting traitor?

But she watched herself closely for any signs of betrayal and saw none. It was easier to parcel up the experience and put it away, even if she couldn't entirely forget it, than to confess to her minders.

Slightly more than one year after the encounter, a force loyal to Sol swept into Prime One and engaged the antiretaliation defenses installed in the system by Adriel Binard and the rebellion. The skirmish was protracted and bloody; thirty thousand people perished over six weeks. Unlike the Reapers, this force consisted of vessels constructed and piloted by Exarchate citizens from outside the Arc Circuit, who had come to defend their empire against insurgency. The Archon had nothing to do with it, except as a distant symbol of good or evil depending on the side one took.

When the rubble dispersed, control of Prime One was split between loyalist forces on the main colony and rebellion installations throughout the system. A bitter guerilla war waged by both sides looked likely to seethe for decades.

Palmer Horsfall received the news in the *Farafangana,* en route to Schiller's End. She felt instantly guilty that she hadn't stayed, even though she knew that there was little she could have done. This wasn't likely to be the only clash between loyalist and rebel forces. She couldn't be at all of them.

But still she wept for the peaceful, cloud-clad world that had reminded her of Sublime, and for the many people who, like her, had lost loved ones. And she wondered what it would be like on Earth, to look up and see the flames of revolt licking from star to star, until the whole sky was consumed by fire.

+INTERLUDE

Anniversary 17: 133,510 CE

Isaac Deangelis hung in space like a man frozen in the act of falling through a gallows. Waiting endlessly for the noose to catch around his neck, he had become nothing more than a creature suspended. Caught between. Not really existing. An emptiness surrounded by emptiness, unable to dissolve.

Fragments of himself remained bound up by a promise he barely remembered making, yet burned across his thoughts like a brand. The promise defined who he was. It *was* him. It itched incessantly. Scar tissue, never fully healing; scratching at it only made it worse. He had existed with that itch for longer than he cared to remember and was hard pressed to imagine life without it. Even by slow-time, the eons dragged.

Still, life was simple out in the void. There was little to do but stare at Omega Centauri and mark the changes creeping slowly across its bright face. He didn't know what was going on at the heart of the distant globular cluster; it wasn't his job to know. But a faint, flickering candle of curiosity still burned. Not long after he had arrived, a front of star formation had swept through the cluster, rushing out from the center in a bright tsunami, sweeping away reddish stellar corpses and filling the vacuum with superenergetic photons. Shortly after that, the cluster's RR Lyrae stars—pulsing cosmic beacons that could double in brightness in a matter of hours—had started flashing in synch. And most recently, a strange series of gravitational shudders radiating from the cluster suggested that massive singularities were forming and colliding with uncommon regularity in its heart.

Someone was keeping busy, he thought. Unlike him.

He kept his back to the dimple in space he guarded, not because he was ignoring it. Far from it. He had more sensors aimed in that direction than he did at the universe around him; if anything triggered them, he would know in a picosecond. But a watched pot never boiled. The ancient metaphor held especially true in deep slow-time and the void between galaxies. It seemed sometimes that the heat-death of the universe would arrive before anything at all happened.

When something *did* finally happen, it took him much more than a picosecond to react to it. A ring of white, crystalline fire opened out of nowhere a hundred meters from him, beginning as a point and expanding rapidly outward to form a circle five meters across. The space within the disk glowed in outraged ultraviolet and X-rays, limning a shadow that glided smoothly from its heart. The shadow resolved into a lopsided, opaque ball with one straight stalk protruding from its smallest side. *A pencil sticking out of a potato,* he thought as his thoughts very slowly came up to speed.

Despite the ludicrously inappropriate image, there was no mistaking the identity of his visitor.

"Who's your friend?" she asked.

He explained fully, because there was no reason to lie. The corpse had appeared on Deangelis's scopes the moment he had arrived at the exit he had been assigned. The solid body occluding the stars of Omega Centauri stood out like an extra moon in the sky of old Earth. Curious—and thinking that he had, perhaps, found the object of his search—he had sent a drone after it. A feverish examination had confirmed almost immediately that the desiccated, radiation-scarred mummy was not in fact Melilah Awad.

"His name was Palmer Bray," he concluded. "He was one of two men Palmer Eogan sent into Geodesica before it arrived at Bedlam. They disappeared, and their fate had always been a mystery."

"Until now. How long had he been drifting?"

"Eighty thousand years or thereabouts."

"How long have *you* been here?"

"Seventy-two thousand, one hundred twenty-eight years." The number had no meaning. Subjectively, the time he had spent watching the exit was more like five centuries. "He didn't get here by himself. I performed a very thorough examination of both him and the space surrounding this exit. He was brought here from inside the maze, and set loose after an autopsy. The direction he followed—right for Omega Centauri—can't have been an accident. It was a burial; I'm sure of it. A *Palmer* burial."

"Palmer Cobiac, do you think?"

"I did think so at first, but have come to suspect otherwise. The dispersion of dust around the exit suggests the presence of an object larger than two human-sized masses. Someone else was here." He hesitated, and then plowed onward. "Are you going to tell me it was you?"

"I might have claimed that, once," she said. "If it was me, we didn't miss each other by much."

"Only eight thousand years or so."

"That's nothing compared to the ages we have lived. Does it irk you, this close call? Have you known despair?"

Ancient words for ancient emotions. He felt like a fossil, locked in its stratum and unable to feel, to move, to be. The question sounded like an honest one, not intended to goad from him any particular response. He could have tried to answer it, but wasn't sure he had an honest answer for her.

Instead, he asked, "Why are you here?"

"To make sure you haven't fallen asleep at your post," she said.

His post. His curse. The knot on the noose around his neck. The exit had no name, was just one of millions, each no more important than any other—except this one *was* different because Melilah or one of her companions had been there in the past, and might conceivably return. That had given him hope for a while. Now it was just another fact.

"I wouldn't do that," he said, thinking of the exit, Omega Centauri, the date, and him. It wasn't a rut he found himself in, but a pit. A pit growing deeper with every century, one he would never escape from.

"You made it here, anyway," she said. "That's something I needed to know."

"Yes. The means you gave me proved sufficient." Emotionless, formal, distant. He felt like a machine—and indeed the two of them didn't communicate in English or any human language. Her transmissions came encoded in a modified version of a high-density AI code he had learned in Sol. Some of her syntax was off, as though it wasn't a method she employed very often. "I presume you're checking all the exits, one by one."

"Yes. I am."

"Why?"

"That wasn't the question I expected, Isaac. I thought you'd want to know if another version of you has found Melilah by now."

"Would you tell me if I had?"

"I have no reason to lie."

"Of course you do. If she emerges, that proves that you're not her."

"You would think so."

Silence absorbed them for a long moment. The stalk on her potato-ship swiveled to take in the vista round them, uncannily like an old-fashioned robot eye.

"*Has* she emerged?" he asked eventually.

"Not yet, so the mystery remains unsolved."

A genuine emotion rose up in him: irritation, bristling and unpleasant. "Do you enjoy torturing me? Is that why you've come here?"

"No."

"Then why? Why can't you just leave me in peace?"

"I could ask you the same question. Melilah Awad is gone. Why do you haunt in her absence? Why can't you let her go?"

"Because it's important to me."

"There's my answer to your question, then. *This* is important to me, too. Do I have to give you more information than that?"

"You don't have to give me anything at all."

"That's true, Isaac. But it would please you if I did."

"Yes, of course. The truth: that's what I want from you, before you go this time. Who you are and what you want with me. Nothing else. I'm tired of lies."

"No. You're tired of waiting, and you're tired—although you don't know it—of not being able to tell the difference between ignorance and a lie."

Some of his annoyance ebbed at that. "Perhaps. If you *are* telling me the truth, I have no reason to believe you; and for all that I'm sure you're lying, I have no proof of it. We are caught for eternity, or until Melilah returns and proves one of us wrong."

"Indeed. Until then, all we can do is honor her passing in our own way. You have yours, and I have mine. Sometimes they coincide, as they have today."

"What's so special about today?" he asked, his curiosity pricked. Beyond knowing that the visitations came further and further apart as time went on, the question of their timing had seemed less important than other mysteries attending her occasional presence in his life.

"Bedlam died exactly one hundred thirty-one thousand, seventy-two years ago," she said.

"Ah." He recognized that number instantly as two raised to the seventeenth power. The chances of that being a coincidence were remote. Glancing back at the previous dates, he noticed other correspondences: the first time she had appeared was two hundred fifty-six or 2^8 years after the death of Bedlam; the second time, after 2^{12} years. Further appearances at 2^{14} and 2^{17} years only clinched it further. She was marking time exponentially. At that rate, he wouldn't see her for another one hundred and thirty thousand years after she left this time, at the earliest.

That she had skipped some anniversaries interested him. Physically, emotionally, economically, some anniversaries would be more difficult than others. Or perhaps she *had* attended and erased all memory of the encounters from his mind. He didn't doubt that she had the capacity to do that to him. Whoever she was, she possessed abilities far in advance of his.

Again, they had nothing to say to each other. She seemed in no hurry to go anywhere. Not for the first time, he wondered what life for her was like outside their irregular meetings. What in her psyche or circumstances drove her to impersonate Melilah Awad? Did she maintain the pretense for him or everyone? Did her peers, whoever they might be, consider her mentally ill? Could she be as caught as him by an obligation she could not control?

The gate she had come through hung open next to the exit to Geodesica. She made no move to enter it. Neither of them mentioned it. They floated together between the galaxies in silence, and waited.

One hundred fourteen thousand, six hundred and eighty-eight: another meaningless number. That was how many years had passed since she had come to Bedlam and given him the map of the exits, and told him to go forth and guard them. Like a seedpod bursting in a gust of wind, Isaac Forge Deangelis, ex-Exarch and watcher, had diffused into the Dark, traveling the gulfs by any means available. What he had seen on his journey still puzzled and terrified him. The furious wreath of nebulae that had surrounded Bedlam, following the spate of novae millennia ago, was pockmarked by artifacts large and small, some active, many dead or simply inert. Ancient transport systems woke at his approach and offered access to distant reaches of the galaxy. Gates opened that had been shut for centuries. Minds stirred to guide his passing, then returned to their slumber.

And everywhere, undeniably present but always just out of sight, was a sense of furious activity taking place. Instead of empty gulfs to be crossed, the interstellar reaches were full to the brim with life, a vibrant tangle of quantum fluctuations and dark matter. Humanity had abandoned planets and moved into space quite literally; the vacuum boiled with information and intelligence. Thoughts flowed like invisible rivers along the arms of the galaxy and back, taking what would have seemed like forever from the point of view of an ordinary human but might have been but moments to the slow-paced minds that experienced them. Humbled, he had moved quietly through their interstices, wondering at their existence but worried that he might disturb them and incur their wrath.

Despite his fears, nothing had interfered with him during his travels. Six hundred years it had taken him to reach the exit he now guarded. The effort had seemed immense at the time. Now he knew it to be trivial. In the journey of humanity, his was just a side story. A slight detour. An irrelevance, disconnected and ignorant.

In slow-time, the galaxy turned like a starfish on a tide, twinkling and rippling with uncanny phosphorescence. That his birthplace was hidden behind Omega Centauri saddened him. Given the recent and dramatic activity in the globular cluster, he was loath to assume that the galaxy would even be there in the future. Sometimes he felt like the last person alive in the universe—alone but for the corpse of Palmer Bray, which he kept nearby as a kind of grisly reminder. Humanity had been here before him; they might yet return.

And now *she* had come again, as enigmatic and impossible as ever.

"It's ironic," she said, breaking the long silence, "how we've swapped roles."

"What do you mean?"

"Exarchs used to seem so posthuman and radical. Naturals worried that you were freaks, unnatural, dangerous—and here you are now, exactly as you were back then, still part of an Exarch. These days, *you'd* be regarded as a Natural; you're so far behind the cutting edge. Does that seem strange to you?"

"Only in the sense that you continue to maintain the pretence that you are Melilah Awad."

"Putting that aside for the moment," she said with a flash of testiness. "You must surely see what I mean."

"I suppose so, although I fail to see that it matters."

"Why should it? I'm only making an observation. I'm very different now. The person I used to be lies buried beneath many new experiences. You're the same as ever. Time is wearing us both down, either way."

"Does it worry you that we're being left behind?"

"By . . . ?"

"By the rest of humanity, of course."

"It's not a competition, Isaac. Humanity has achieved wondrous things, and we are still firmly part of it, no matter how isolated and regressive we are. Don't ever misunderstand that. Someone out there—other than we two—cares what happens to us."

He remembered the Archon, which had claimed to care about every individual life under its aegis. He had believed it at the time, although after the destruction of Bedlam that had been hard to credit.

The memories stirred like a row of mummies in sarcophagi, brittle and dangerous, raising a cloud of stinging dust. He was undoubtedly the same person who had thought those thoughts about the Archon, tens of thousands of years ago, but the circumstances in which he had had them now felt impossibly remote.

"Are there other Exarchs left?" he asked. "Lazarus Hails, perhaps? Or Lan Cochrane?" He cast his mind back to the Gentry War and found that he no longer remembered who exactly had survived. Or cared much, except out of passing interest.

"No," she said. "You are the last of your kind. But your name is remembered, and so is Bedlam. Nothing is lost, now. Humanity passed an important threshold not long after Geodesica's discovery, and the Bedlam information model clinched it. People want to remember more than they care to forget. As we've evolved, our memories have grown with us. They circulate endlessly, as rich and complex as the universe we inhabit—perhaps even more so, for every mind sees the universe a different way. As humanity has evolved and the scales we encompass have increased, our perception of time has changed dramatically. Our beats lengthen; our connection to the rhythms of life become increasingly abstract. For some, they will soon become so slow and removed that they will to all intents and purposes cease to matter to the universe, and vice versa. We gaze at the universe through the lens of humanity and its experiences, and we rejoice."

She seemed truly alive for the first time since she had turned up on his doorstep. He envied her that animation. Yet in her words he sensed a kind of sadness, too. He wanted to ask her what there was to be sad about in a universe where nothing was lost and everyone knew everyone else, but he thought he already knew the answer. Remembering something wasn't the same thing as having it, and not being able to forget could be a curse.

The person I used to be, she had said, *lies buried beneath many new experiences.*

Not changing was one thing. To know that one had changed and to know exactly what one had lost in the process of changing—that was something else entirely.

"Where will it end?" he asked. "When the universe is dark and dead, and humanity huddles around its memories and grief, longing for something new?"

"I can't tell you that," she said. "I *can* tell you that humanity is still growing and changing. We have outgrown the galaxy, and will soon outgrow the Local Group. From there, it's only a matter of time and determination before we fill the observable universe from horizon to horizon—and the possibilities open to us then will be truly wondrous. Some hope to find a way to counteract dark energy's repulsive forces; some expect that we'll survive the dimming of the last stars and end up playing marbles with evaporating black holes in the emptiness of the Final Void. Almost anything is possible, they say. The only limits are self-imposed."

"So why are you here?" he asked again. "Why aren't you helping roll back the frontiers? What's the attraction in me and Melilah Awad?"

"The attraction lies in your—and my—humanity. Without limits, we're just replicating machines. Our quirkiness is what makes us unique. Why do you think the Archon tolerated the Bedlam privacy experiment? Why do you think it kept the Naturals around at all? It's all part of the plan—the plan that is no plan. Evolution doesn't run to a script. Culture isn't about efficiency. Moments like these, and the reasons we seek them, define us as a species, as well as individuals. They may seem meaningless, but they add up. And what they add up to is humanity."

"What *is* humanity?"

"It's a word, an idea, a process—and a name for something that's still important, if only because we haven't outgrown it yet. We share a common origin, machinekind and biologicals, in all our many shapes and sizes. Without Sol and Earth and Luna, none of us would be here, and that's meaningful. The place itself isn't special, but what arose from it is. Humanity: the great unifier. Us against the Dark."

"What about the ROTH?"

"There aren't any aliens. They were all gone before we came on the scene. They left plenty of stuff behind, stuff like Geodesica, and we've learned a lot about them, but we've never stood face-to-face with one and said *hello*. Humanity has always been—and might always be—utterly alone."

The void seemed to mock them on their isolated vigil.

"So what's the point?" he asked.

She took a long time to answer that question.

"The point, Isaac, is not what comes after our lives, but what we do during them. It's the same with humanity. What does it matter what it becomes or leaves behind? What it *is,* at any point during its evolution, is what counts."

"That sounds circular to me."

"It might well be. But who says reasoning needs to be linear?"

Weariness filled him. "I don't understand." The phrase was one he had rarely uttered before. "If it's circular, it's meaningless. It doesn't *go* anywhere." *Just like me.* "There has to be a reason."

"Reason is overrated," she said. "Not as a methodology, but as a way of existing. You have your reasons for being here, but they aren't you. Names are no different. You call yourself Isaac Forge Deangelis, just as I call myself Melilah Awad. Is that any different from calling us *human*?"

"I don't know." Despair did rise up in him now. "I don't even know who you are! If you're Melilah, why are you letting me suffer? If you're not, how can you expect me to believe anything you say? Did the Archon send you to test me? Are you a cruel joke Frederica Cazneaux left behind to taunt me? I don't know why I'm even *listening* to you. Why won't you leave me *alone*?"

"Is that what it boils down to, Isaac?" The stalk of her craft was pointing directly at him now. "If I'm not her, I mean nothing to you?"

He wasn't a Natural. He didn't have the glands to weep. But inside, where it counted, part of him remembered how.

"I don't know," he sobbed. "I don't know."

She moved closer.

"I'm sorry," she said. "I'm so sorry I hurt you. But you need me, just as I need you. Our fates are entangled in ways you cannot know. You wouldn't believe me. You wouldn't want to."

"How can you be so certain of that?"

"Because I did tell one of you, once. A long time ago. You copied yourself, and I told the copy everything. Then the copy killed itself. It stopped its own heart and melted its brain so nothing could remain of what I had revealed to him. It was too much, too awful. And this is the truth I carry, Isaac. Do you really want it? Do you want that burden?"

Shocked, he didn't even wonder if this story was a lie, like everything else might have been.

"I don't need you," he said. "I'm designed to be alone. All the Exarchs were. We had to be independent, self-reliant. That's how the Exarchate worked."

"Really? Look at yourself. Humans have never thrived in isolation. That's partly why you're obsessed with the idea of Melilah Awad, and why I'm obsessed with you. Eternal self-reliance leads to nothing but solipsism and stagnation. If I don't check in on you every now and again, you'd freeze up completely, eventually. And I'd fade away; it works both ways. I have to remain me, at least partly. It's important: I have a date to keep. Because you haven't changed, because you're still profoundly *you,* you help keep me anchored. You're not my memory or my conscience, but I don't feel quite so much in danger of losing myself when I'm around you. You're the only one left who has that effect on me."

"Even when I refuse to believe you when you say you're Melilah Awad?"

"Perhaps. Time makes a tangle of the truth. Can I be sure, now, what was real and what a fantasy?"

The admission surprised him. "You're telling me you *don't know*? After all you've said to me?"

"Is that so unreasonable? It's been over a hundred thousand years, Isaac. I've grown and changed in ways you could barely imagine. If I didn't admit to uncertainty about some things, I'd risk psychosis."

"But to forget your *name* . . ." The thought appalled him. He could understand wanting to pretend to be someone else, for whatever reason—but to become so bound up in the lie that the truth evaporated forever or became completely buried under falsehood, that was inconceivable. He was Isaac Forge Deangelis, and always would be. It was the one thing of which he was completely certain.

Even as the awfulness of it sank in, another thought occurred to him.

"I will never call you Melilah Awad," he said with deliberate coldness in his voice. "That name belongs to just one person, and you're not her. If that's what you want from me—some sort of validation you can't give yourself—then I'm sorry. I'm not going to play your game."

She said nothing for so long that he wondered if she had dropped into deep slow-time. The stalk of her vessel quivered slightly; that was the only sign of life it exhibited.

"Hello?"

"That's your choice," she said. A mortal weariness filled every word. "And I can't deny you that. Choice is everything, you know. There's nothing else. 'Destiny' and 'fate' are forgotten words in a dead language. Nothing happens for a reason, except that we choose to make it so. We live out the consequences of our decisions in regret or celebration, or a mixture of the two."

Again, as he had before, he wondered if they were talking about the same things.

"Are you celebrating," he asked her, "or regretful?"

She didn't answer. The potato's stalk swung abruptly to face the circular gate through which it had come. With a surge of acceleration so great the ripple it left in space-time made him shudder, the potato sped through the gate and disappeared. An instant later, the gate shrank to a dot and vanished, leaving him staring in shock at the space it had inhabited.

He waited to see if it would return. A full minute passed, then an hour. At the end of a week, he shifted his internal rhythms down a notch and told himself that he didn't mind not changing; that was the whole point of his extended existence, after all. His memories of Earth and Bedlam remained as accurate as he could expect them to be, after so many years of random errors and cosmic rays. If he had grown and changed as the imposter had, he might forget his very reason for existing at all.

Or he might cling to a memory that bore no relation to his actual life. No matter how seductive or powerful it might be, it would still be a lie.

You told me, once, that you loved me.

Grossly extended practical joke or genuine, if misplaced, posthuman angst?

He didn't know. After a month of fruitless waiting, he returned to slow-time and watching the magnetars winking on and off in Omega Centauri.

+12

Geodesica interior: plus 128 hours

The yellow light went some way to warming her, but Melilah knew better than to let her guard down. The environment suit the Cell had given her detected a solid dose of hard radiation behind the deceptively natural glow. The suit protected her as best it could, and the nanotech defenses Eogan had flooded her bloodstream with could mop up any minor damage, but she didn't want to rely too heavily on anything she didn't entirely understand. She was careful, also, not to stray too far from the others. After the near disaster of the behemoth, she had learned that lesson well.

She held herself in readiness for the next lesson, certain that it was coming, from some unexpected, possibly deadly, direction.

"All clear." Deangelis's voice came from the replicator where it hovered above her, out of range of the field interfering with its reactionless thrusters. "Inasmuch as I can tell, anyway."

"Wait a second," said Eogan from the other side of the spike. "I'm on my way to you."

Melilah endured a disorienting moment as Eogan walked into view around the cone on which she stood. The cone was nineteen meters high and three across its base. An artificial gravity field strong enough to keep her securely anchored to its side radiated at right angles to its vertical axis. The field turned in a full circle around the spike, orientation changing as it went, so for a brief time she and Eogan had been standing on opposite sides with feet pointing toward each other. Now—as she stood motionless, looking ahead of her to the tip of the spike, beyond which hung the artificial light source at the center of the chamber, the source of the dangerous yellow glow—he walked around the spike to her, tipping gradually "upright" as he went.

"No seams," he said, studying the surface beneath his feet. "No doors or windows. No obvious switches, contact points, or soft spots. They must've maintained this thing from underneath, or had a way in we can't find. Whoever *they* were."

He came to stand by her, dressed in the same black and white shipsuit the Cell had given them days earlier. She had changed hers to a deep purple and her hair to a translucent white. Tiny gold flecks crawled over her arms where they lay folded across her chest. The sensation of being under gravity was an unnerving one, even without the visuals to confuse her. She couldn't remember the last time she had been under anything like one gee.

"It's going to be hard to explore the floor without thrusters," she said. The spike on which they stood was just one of thousands pointing inward from the surface of a giant sphere they had entered. Each of the spikes possessed its own gravity field, radiating outward from its surface like the branches of a Christmas tree. The gravity fields overlapped, drawing objects "down" from the center of the sphere and "up" slightly from its surface, trapping them in an exceedingly complex tug of war that had taken her off guard on at least two occasions.

He crouched with his arms half-extended on either side, like a kingfisher bracing to take flight.

"Ready?"

They leapt off the surface of the cone. Achieving escape velocity required more than a gentle kick. She had to shove as hard as she could against the translucent surface of the cone in order to be caught by the g-fields emitted by the cones surrounding them. Her inner ears protested vigorously—despite extensive remodeling performed by her First Wave ancestors, the first humans to live for extended times in low-gee environments—and the chamber turned giddyingly around her. Eogan was within arm's reach, but she refused to flail about for his help, as she had the first time. Orienting against the tapering, stalagmite-like backdrop, she spread her arms and legs in an X and sent a command to the gas ports scattered across the environment suit. The impromptu attitude jets slowed her tumble with a series of gentle nudges. When the view stopped turning, she found herself gliding effortlessly along a "stream" of air winding through the forest of spikes, tugged gently from side to side by the invisible, artificial gravity.

She felt satisfaction. Deangelis had dropped several million microscopic sensors down into the maelstrom. The data retrieved from them allowed him to map the many eddies and flows that arose naturally out of the chaos. Rivers of air, trapped in a narrow, horizontal boundary around the waists of the cones, flowed endlessly around the surface of the giant chamber. The patterns they formed were of immense complexity, and liable to change as the shock of the replicator's arrival rippled through what had probably been a perfectly stable system for centuries prior to then. Raging storms sprang up around peculiarly stable pockets of stillness. Odd geometric shapes—knots of air that remained intact even as they threaded invisibly between the spikes—roamed with a semblance of purposefulness across the chamber's curving wall. Melilah's enhanced vision looked like the doodle of a madman, splattered with multicolored shapes that coalesced and fragmented from minute to minute.

"It's coming up on your left," said Deangelis. "Get ready to leave the stream."

One particular cone took on an orange hue as she approached, singled out from the rest by the suit. She let the suit do the course correction this time, being more concerned with where she was going than how she would get there. The cone stood a full three meters taller but was otherwise no different from the rest. Deangelis had identified nineteen other such "superior spikes" across the interior of the sphere, forming a regular icosahedron. Like the others, it was made of a translucent, amber-colored material possessing a very low density but an extraordinarily high strength. Strange shadows lurked in its depths, rounded lumps and coils that varied from cone to cone. The tips of the cones were perfectly sharp, showing no sign of bluntness down to the nanometer scale; their bases merged seamlessly into the surface of the chamber's matte gray walls. Someone, a long time ago, had marked the chamber's walls with lines and circles, indicating—Melilah assumed—airflows and jams that no longer existed. The marks were almost invisible in places where the airflow had been most vigorous.

Her gas ports nudged her toward the superior spike dubbed #14 on the map overlaying her vision. As she came closer, she made out something fuzzy around its base. More substantial than a cloud and unmoving in the air currents, it defied her best attempts to identify it.

Eogan cut in front of her as they approached the spike. His jets pushed him higher, closer to the spike's upraised tip. Its gravity caught him, and his path swung around to meet it. He landed gracefully, hands splayed for purchase on the smooth surface.

Melilah followed a second later, and stumbled only slightly. Her sense of down had shifted again, into the heart of the spike. Now its neighbors looked like cruel extrusions from a wall arcing up overhead in an enormous dome. The far side of the chamber, four hundred kilometers away, was visible only as a blur behind the light source at its center.

The interior of the superior spike resembled a megalomaniac's lava lamp frozen in midchurn.

"Right." She straightened and mimed dusting herself off. "Let's take a look."

They walked toward the base of the spike, its gradient lending her a feeling of walking slightly uphill. Her shadow preceded her, sharp-edged and long-limbed. When it touched the fuzziness at the base of the cone, it flattened and spread out in a blur. She raised a hand and waved. The fuzziness didn't react.

"It's definitely not an instrument artifact," Eogan told Deangelis, who had described the anomaly from above as a blur he couldn't identify. "It's thicker than it looks from a distance, like fiberglass or carbon foam. I can't see through it."

Melilah slowed as the surface of the cloud came closer. Light reflected off tiny planes and threads, casting miniature rainbow flashes as she moved closer. Five meters from the base of the spike, she stopped dead, unable to go any farther without touching the cloud. It wrapped around the spike without break or dimple, as impenetrable as a real cloud, and spread unbroken into the distance on all sides. The spike's angular brethren stood out from the glittering surface like surreal islands from an icy sea.

"The structure is crystalline," said Deangelis, looking over their shoulders and through their suit sensors, "but I'm having trouble determining the atomic structure. Can you take a sample?"

Melilah reached out to touch the surface of the cloud with her left index finger. She didn't know what to expect. The delicate, linear crystals could crumble instantly or prick her with myriad diamond needles. They could be cold or hot. They could ring like tuning forks or shatter into a cloud of blinding dust.

She didn't expect them to *move*.

One centimeter from the surface of the cloud, she froze as, with a whispering sound, the tiny crystals began to crawl away from the tip of her finger. Individual threads tipped and rotated, shifted off balance by the ones supporting them, which were in turn moved by those below them. A small depression formed directly under her finger, with a tiny upraised rim around it, like a miniature crater. Then the whispering trickled away into silence and the crystals froze again.

She pushed her finger closer. The crystals moved more urgently, rearranging their structures with a hiss to avoid touching the approaching object. The crater became a hole, one that deepened and widened until her finger had disappeared up to the first knuckle.

She moved the finger sideways. The hole moved with it, crystal cloud parting and closing smoothly to avoid touching her, leaving no mark in her wake. Curious, she thrust her entire hand into the cloud, and the crystal boiled away from it with a loud tearing sound. She clenched and unclenched her fist, gripping nothing at all.

"Weird." She removed her hand. The hole in the crystalline cloud healed over with a crackle like supercooled water freezing in a rush. "Nanotech, I presume."

"Or micro. Did you notice any radiant heat?"

She shook her head and flexed her fingers, testing them for suspicious changes. "It might as well not have been there, for all I could tell."

"Don't go any deeper," said Deangelis. "I'm dropping an instrument pack down to you."

A crack-boom sounded from over her shoulder as something entered the thin atmosphere. Melilah looked behind her, squinting into the bright light, and made out a smooth, small dot dropping rapidly downward. It resolved into a disk with fins that folded out into wings as the air thickened around it. Attitude jets decelerated it further until it came within range of the g-field of the superior spike she stood on. For a second, she thought it might rush right by her at speed and plunge headlong into the cloud. It stopped with a whoosh and hovered before them, fizzing, wings retracted and spinning slowly.

"Stand back, just in case."

She obeyed Deangelis's instruction but didn't go too far away, curious to see what happened. Eogan stood by her as the instrument pack danced on its attitude jets and slid smoothly into the cloud. The crystal surface closed over behind it. The jets didn't seem to disturb it any more than her hand had. The fizzing sound the instrument pack made faded into silence.

"Now what?" she asked. "Are you getting anything interesting from in there?"

"I'm not getting anything at all," said Deangelis. "Carrier signals with data scrambled, and that's fading fast."

"The cloud stuff killed your little toy?"

"No. It appears to be moving in accordance with its original flight plan. The data it's sending is simply being absorbed. I expect—yes, I've lost the signal completely now."

The development only heightened Melilah's curiosity regarding what lay on the other side. "You could do the same trick Eogan pulled inside the wreck. Send down another box of tricks, but this time trail a wire behind it—"

"Wait a moment. The pack has instructions to follow should it drop out of contact with me. Don't write it off just yet."

She and Eogan exchanged glances. The Palmer looked out of place in the open air, well away from the Cell that had been their home—or habitat, at least—for several days.

"You're the boss," he said without any obvious sense of irony. His gaze fell back to the surface of the spike, still looking for a way in. She wasn't sure what he would find, judging by his lack of success so far. The purpose of the spikes was as mysterious as the space they inhabited. That they were the source of the g-fields didn't necessarily mean that that was what they were *for*. They could have monuments as well as machines. Graves, perhaps. Or hatcheries for superdense aliens. Or something she hadn't even thought of.

Whatever they were, the chamber was unlike any they had visited in all their travels across Geodesica. Mysteries within mysteries within mysteries . . .

A second feeling of dizziness swept through her, one no less unsettling than the previous despite being of purely mental origins. It dispelled her abstract curiosity as easily as a hand tearing at a gauze curtain, and exposed the true state of her, beneath.

"What the hell are we doing here?" she muttered.

"This must be where the replicator was activated," said Eogan, misunderstanding her question. "We mistook its starting point for ours. Not Bedlam, but the place it commenced looking for us."

She sat down cross-legged on the curved surface of the spike. He wasn't telling her anything she didn't already know. Despite following the replicator's route as closely as possible, they had ended up no closer to home than they had been before. The massive chamber, with its forest of spikes and its artificial, deadly sun, had greeted them on the final jump—a hideous, many-fanged mouth gaping wide to engulf them. Eleven randomly scattered entrances stared like spider eyes from the chamber's curved walls. It wasn't what any of them had expected. The only point operating in its favor was that it provided a distraction from the truth.

Not for the first time, she wondered if Deangelis and Eogan had pulled some kind of swifty while she was leapfrogging the hours, but they seemed as puzzled as her. All plans had been carefully suspended until they knew more. Therein lay the problem, one she could forget for a moment, but not forever.

Tears sprang unbidden and she hung her head down so Eogan wouldn't see. This was supposed to be the end of their journey. Whether they had emerged from Geodesica into a Bedlam gutted and empty or a wasp's nest of deadly Catastrophe, at least it would have been over. So much had happened since their escape, but she hadn't really gone *anywhere*. She was still frozen in that moment of terror when the throat had enclosed them and the world burned.

Before the end, shortly after the attack on Bedlam by Frederica Cazneaux, she had resolved to move forward. Destroying the memories of her past with Eogan had been a step, a symbol of letting go and getting on with more important things. And now, as though the universe was showing her the danger inherent in making such grand gestures, she was trapped in Geodesica with him and her home was utterly dead. Her memories were gone forever.

She made a sound that started as a laugh, but came out as a sob.

"Are you okay?"

She couldn't answer him. When she tried, all that came out was grief. Her heart was tearing into ribbons, and she couldn't stop it.

Distantly, she felt his arms come around her, and this time she didn't fight him off. He had held her before and she had taken comfort from him. There was no great crime in that. She needed someone or something to lean on or she might fly apart and never reassemble. He was all she had left—and he wasn't even human.

"Damn you," she whispered. "Damn us both."

He made soothing noises. She wouldn't be comforted, but she didn't let him go, either.

Deangelis, mercifully, said nothing. Only when the fizzing sound of the instrument pack's propellant system became audible again did she pull away.

"What—?" She wiped her burning eyes and looked around. The rough crystal surface at her side remained unbroken. The sound came from sunward.

She looked and saw the winged disk skidding through the air toward them. Tugged by g-fields, it wobbled from side to side like a drunken flying saucer.

"It must have made it through," said Eogan, letting go of her and standing to meet it. "And come around from the other side."

Now Deangelis spoke. "I'm receiving data."

"Put it through."

At Eogan's words, a new window opened in her field of view. It showed a blur of creamy crystal dissolving before the instrument pack. Temperature readings were normal on the far side of the barrier; the ambient radiation had dropped to zero. Most notable, though, was the color.

While everywhere else inside the giant chamber was gray, brown, or silver, there, under the crystal cloud, the view was dappled green.

Life.

Eogan studied the recording thoroughly before coming to the only possible conclusion. Deangelis agreed, although the Exarch's excitement seemed more muted than his own. The green of photosynthesis, of plant tissue or bacterial mats. Either way, it was a momentous discovery. Until then, Geodesica had seemed utterly sterile, a lab maze for mice to get lost in. Now it was something more. Someone had planted a seed, and it had grown.

"I'm going through," he declared, following his gut as much as his head. The footage taken by the instrument pack was clear but insufficient to answer all his questions. The darker clumps arranged in groups of seven around a central bulge: were they leaves, petals, or arrangements of funguslike cellular aggregations? The numerous dark brown crucifixes fixed to the underside of the chamber wall: woody branches or trellises, hanging motionlessly in the static g-field of the spike's base? The blue dots scattered apparently at random in clumps and drifts: tiny flowers, berries, or something else entirely?

As he moved forward, Melilah gripped his arm. "Don't be stupid."

"It didn't hurt the instrument pack."

"We still shouldn't take any unnecessary risks. You can go the long way around. We know that's safe."

He could see the sense in that. Skimming forward through the pack's data, he traced the route it had taken out from under the crystal wall and to their location. The gravity gradients were complicated to map, but not impossible for someone accustomed to flying in three dimensions.

"Do you want to come with me?" he asked Melilah.

She shook her head, making her white hair dance. Red-rimmed eyes avoided meeting his. "I'll wait until Isaac has set up a relay between here and back there."

That made sense, although it meant he was going into possible danger alone.

His decision, he supposed. And he wasn't exactly helpless.

"If there's any trouble at all with the link, I'll come straight back."

She nodded as another instrument pack pierced the top of the atmosphere. This one split into a string of smaller components that arced away from their spike to the edge of the crystal cloud and dipped underneath.

"Go," she said, "or Isaac will beat you to it."

He smiled and kicked away from the spike. The influence of the next spike along caught him and he spun like a gymnast toward the one after that. Using the gas vents of his environment suit—his sole reason for wearing one—and crude muscle where necessary, he followed the string of relays to the cloud's edge.

Only when he reached that point did he wonder how long he would be able to stay "afloat" on the other side. The gravity gradient close to the wall pulled uniformly inward, apparently toward the center of the giant chamber, although he would only fall to the other side of the crystal cloud if he did let go. He could use his gas vents to resist the pull, but not indefinitely. At some point he would have to test the effects of the cloud's underside—and his bravura response to Melilah's concern had been more bluff than anything. He didn't want to be eaten by alien nanotech any more than she did.

On kicking over the edge, however, and taking in the view beyond, he realized that his fear was misplaced. A forest greeted him, so thick and tangled that finding handholds wouldn't be a problem. Quite the opposite, in fact. Woody boughs, as straight and narrow as human femurs but brown in color, crisscrossed the space, forming a mat of leaves that completely hid the chamber wall from view. Light filtered through the crystal cloud, casting a yellowish, twinkling pattern over the underside of the plants. *Cave trees,* he thought, wondering if they had an analogue anywhere else in the universe—where light shone up from underneath and gravity was mutable from meter to meter. Vines curled and reached through the changing g-fields; sheets of moss clung to the broad bases of spikes where they penetrated the crystal cloud; a swarm of winged motes weaved through a spray of hair-thin stalks that swayed as though to attract their attention.

The sight literally took his breath away. He had heard of people who lived in the deep tunnels of habitats like Bedlam, people who rarely if ever went near hydroponic gardens. For them, the sight of natural vegetation caused a profoundly visceral response. People were known to burst into tears and sing songs. Like ancient coal miners trapped underground, the sight of *green* came as a revelation.

He was struck the same way, and swung himself up into the trellislike network of branches with a feeling of reverence.

"This is incredible," he said to Deangelis via the instrument relays. "The crystal protects the plants from radiation but lets enough light through so they can grow. Who would build something like that here?"

"I don't know," the Exarch replied. "The cavern's central light source shows evidence of extreme age. The radiation it emits is most likely a by-product of dysfunction, not a normal feature. It's entirely possible that the whole place looked like this before the radiation came. The crystal screen could have been erected in order to protect what remained."

"Are there any others?"

"Each of the superior spikes harbors such a cloud."

"Interesting." The garden's origins were momentarily less important than the spectacle itself. "Where does the water come from?"

"That I have not yet been able to determine. From the superior spikes, perhaps. I assume a great deal of it is recycled."

Eogan swung slowly but steadily hand over hand through the branches, occasionally catching leaves across his face or scratching himself on thorns. The forest was eerily quiet: no bird calls; no monkeys chattering; no whirring insects; no wind apart from a gentle breeze moving from one end to the other. He had never seen a real forest, but he knew a good imitation when he saw one. The Kedraon habitat in Whitewater was famous for its genetic diversity, and he had visited it several times during his travels. Among the epiphytes and orchids, there had even been parrots—gaudy, wild-feathered things that savored the low gee with raucous glee. Kedraon was never quiet, not even when the artificial sun dimmed to simulate night.

The silence took some of the edge off Eogan's ready acceptance of the place. Just because there were no visible animals, that didn't mean it was completely safe. Plants on three known worlds had evolved sophisticated defenses against potential attackers. The swarm of motes could have comprised eerily motile pollen rather than insects.

One of Deangelis's tiny instrument drones whizzed by, riding rapid-fire staccato puffs of air. Eogan followed it to the base of the superior spike, where thicker and presumably older trunks merged to form mossy buttresses three times higher than he was. Two more instrument drones met him there. The light filtering through the crystal cast shadows at the top of the dense canopy. The air, even filtered by his environment suit, smelled green.

One particular, moss-covered root caught his eye as he swung around the base of the superior spike. Longer and straighter than its brethren, it angled up into the overgrowth, where it terminated in a shape resembling the crescent moon of Islam. He nudged closer and brushed gently at the moss. It came away in ragged clumps that wafted slowly toward the crystal cloud.

The reaction of the forest to his disturbance was immediate. Responding—he assumed—to airborne chemicals released by the moss, a cloud of the darting motes issued from the plants around him. They congregated in fuzzy balls around each moss fragment, intent on taking them apart and whisking them away before they could vanish into the crystal. Another congregation focused on the hole he had made on the odd stalk. He brushed the black motes out of the way as best he could in order to see the object beneath.

It wasn't made of metal. That he immediately realized. Nor was it plastic. The creamy yellow surface was pitted and whorled.

Not wood either, he decided, but *bone*.

He wiped his hands on his thighs and let the motes go about their work—restorative or predatory, whichever it might have been. The moss he had dropped was already gone, broken down into crumbs and swept off into the shadows. He was momentarily glad he hadn't triggered a more violent defense mechanism, and swore he would avoid doing any further damage. The last thing he wanted was to fall victim to the motes himself, should they turn nasty. Although it was unlikely that something could get through his body's sophisticated immune system, that might have been just what happened to the creature before him.

He tried unsuccessfully to see what the bone connected to, but it disappeared into a tangle of branches. In doing so, he managed to get his head around the unusual biology of the cave forest. The crystal cloud was both down according to gravity and the only source of light. The plants competed with each other for that light, and also for purchase on the cavern wall above and the spikes dotting the space like Doric columns. What would be trunks on terrestrial plants tended to be the uppermost portions of the cave trees, while the leaves dangled below. Adventurous plants sent out tendrils and fronds closer to the crystal, creating pathways for their competitors. These tendrils and fronds were soon overgrown, and either died or sent out new shoots in search of new pathways to the light. Such branching and rebranching formed convoluted webs and mats that could be meters long. In places, they had left bubbles of clear air in their wakes. He crawled through one in an attempt to locate the end of the bone, and found the space within pleasantly dim and warm.

Roots in the overgrowth. Leaves dangling to catch the light from below. Trunks that stuck out at right angles from the superior spike. Everywhere he looked, his earthly expectation of what trees were supposed to look like was confounded. Eogan grinned, childishly delighted by the discovery.

A faint tinkling sound from below grew louder, as of a glass mobile stirring in a stiff breeze.

He hurried out of his hidey-hole to investigate the new development, and was startled to see Melilah's head issuing from the surface of the crystal cloud. She turned from side to side with eyes wide.

"Decided to take the plunge, eh?" he asked, swinging to position directly above her and reaching one hand down. With the other he gripped a sturdy-looking branch.

"It didn't seem fair that you should get all the fun," she said, letting him haul her up. She glanced at him, then pulled away and looked up into the overgrowth without blinking. "Wow. The images don't do it justice, do they?"

He beamed, absurdly pleased as though she had complimented him. "Look at this."

He showed her the bone and outlined his suspicion that the forest's natural defenses might have killed its owner.

"The forest certainly made good of the remains, whatever happened," she said, brushing the moss with her fingertips. The green appeared to have erased—or at least buried—her moment of grief, and he was glad of that. If grief it was. She had been distant from him since their differentiation into separate bodies upon waking near the behemoth. He could tell that her thoughts were dark and as tangled as the roots in the overgrowth above them. Clearing them would take more than just a few kind words and a hug; of that he was certain.

"Native or visitor?" she wondered, pulling herself along the bone to the crescent moon at the top. "Probably not native. Probably introduced, along with this entire place. Maybe it came here to die, like Palmer Bray in that old wreck." She looked at him again. "There would be worse places to die than here."

"Do you mean *here* here, or Geodesica in general?"

"Either." She clambered back down the bone. "Don't worry. I'm not planning on rolling over and dying just yet. It just makes me think, that's all. Some ancient rulers used mazes and other traps to keep people out of their tombs. What if that's all Geodesica is? A memorial to the universe's first emperor?"

The thought was macabre. He wasn't sure what he made of it. "That would make us grave robbers."

"Exactly—so here's hoping we don't make the emperor's spirit angry."

Melilah tested the sturdiness of the branch beneath them and kicked off to explore the space. The curving flanks of the trunks anchored to the superior spike provided numerous handholds. She clambered like a spider monkey through the overgrowth, sniffing the blue blossoms they had glimpsed through the instrument pack and rubbing fleshy leaves between her fingers.

Eogan watched her, wondering how long her relatively good mood would last. She seemed as cautiously enthused by the fertile oasis as he was. Perhaps she took hope that, although they had come upon it by mistake, it showed that there *was* still hope; that some good might come from their flight through Geodesica.

The talk of death and ghosts unnerved him, though. Both she and Deangelis were haunted by what they had lost. He could understand that. He didn't, however, want their baggage to taint the innocence of the forest. It possessed no agenda, no history, no subterfuge, no guilt. It just *was*.

"Come on," he said, leaping out to meet her. "Let's explore."

Isaac Deangelis watched from above through the multiple viewpoints of the instrument back and its smaller siblings. The compound perspective was bewildering. Glimpses of leaf morphology overlapped with a cursory analysis of a stem section, revealing strange, spiraling cells not dissimilar in terms of chemistry to terrestrial species. A hasty genetic assay produced matches with several familiar proteins, but isolated many more of unknown structure and unknowable—for the moment—purpose. One instrument burrowing through the overgrowth exhumed another alien cadaver, in far worse repair than the one Eogan had found. The ancient bones were stained reddish brown by sap and had been hollowed out in places by the patient, incessant probing of roots.

The forest truly was a remarkable discovery. It compensated somewhat for the disastrous end to their long voyage. But not entirely. The matter of what to do next hadn't been forgotten. Should they begin searching for another of Sol's SAD replicators in the hope of finding a genuine return route? Or should they recommence their search for home on their own steam, following a more methodical means—the details of which eluded him at the moment?

He was confused. From his elevated vantage point, through his many mobile eyes, he watched Melilah and Eogan delay the inevitable with the single-mindedness of children playing through a family breakdown. They might kid each other that everything was okay for the moment, but they weren't fooling him. A difficult decision awaited them. What was the point in pretending otherwise?

His instruments dodged and weaved through the alien forest, looking for an answer.

Something caught his eye, something utterly unexpected and startling. He went automatically to sound the alarm, but was halted in midtrack by a voice that seemed to fill the entire cavern.

—NO, ISAAC. SAY NOTHING.

For a moment he was too confused to react at all. The voice was as all-pervading and authoritative as if Geodesica itself had spoken, and yet it was clear that Melilah and Eogan had not heard it.

—DO NOT ALARM THEM UNDULY. JUST LISTEN TO ME, AND THEN DECIDE.

"Who are you? How do you know my name?"

—DON'T ASK QUESTIONS; LET ME TALK. MUCH WILL BECOME CLEAR IF YOU SIMPLY ALLOW ME TO DO THAT.

As he listened, Deangelis made every attempt to locate the

source of the voice. As far as he could tell, it had none. Either that or it was all around him.

"Are you the artifact we call Geodesica?"

—WOULD YOU DO AS I ASKED IF I TOLD YOU I WAS?

"Maybe."

—THEN I SAY THAT I AM NOT. WHETHER YOU BELIEVE ME OR NOT IS IRRELEVANT, AT THIS POINT IN TIME.

"How could it not be relevant? If you *are* Geodesica, then you can show us the way out. If you're not, then you're obviously as lost as us."

—NOTHING IS SO OBVIOUS, ISAAC. YOU SHOULD KNOW THAT BY NOW.

Deangelis took a mental deep breath. "All right," he said. "I'll listen." *After all,* he thought, *what other choice I have?*

—THAT IS THE CORRECT DECISION, the voice continued, sounding pleased with Deangelis's compliance.—BELIEVE ME WHEN I TELL YOU THAT I MEAN YOU NO HARM. VIOLENCE IS A POOR SUBSTITUTE FOR CONVERSATION, FOR WORDS CAN BE TAKEN BACK; BLOWS CANNOT. WHILE I COULD FORCE YOU TO DO WHAT I WANT, PEOPLE LEARN TO THEIR COST, SOMETIMES, THAT IT IS IMPOSSIBLE TO RETREAT WHEN ONE HAS ADVANCED TOO FAR. DO YOU UNDERSTAND?

Deangelis thought of Sol and the Catastrophe, and wondered if the owner of the voice had taken from his mind as well as added to it.

"I think so," he said.

—THEN LET US TALK ABOUT THE EXARCHATE, AND WHAT IT'S *REALLY* FOR . . .

With a tinkling of glass tiles, Eogan emerged from the crystal cloud and shook his head. "Wow," he said. "What a trip."

Melilah helped him out of the cloud and onto the wall of the spike. He planted his feet firmly on the smooth, translucent surface and brushed himself down. *A reflex,* she thought. The cloud had left no residue on him that she could see.

"Was it worth it?" she asked.

"It's weird. The cloud parts just like it did for the instrument pack and your finger. I felt like I was completely covered, but it never actually touched me."

"Are you sure?"

"My environment suit hasn't reported a breach—and I'm still

me, aren't I?" Catching her sour expression, he added, "As much as I ever am, anyway."

She felt bad, then. "Tell me about down there," she said, walking a meter or two around the curve of the spike so they weren't so close. "Is it as bizarre as it looks?"

"It's beautiful," he said. "I'd suggest you see for yourself, but I have a better idea. The other superior spikes have clouds, too. What if they all hide environments like this? We should go check."

"Isaac could do it for us."

"Where's the fun in that? Come on—let's explore."

She opened her mouth to say that she thought it a waste of time, but changed her mind. She had been bored waiting for him. The images Deangelis had relayed were pretty but depthless. It wouldn't hurt to check it out for herself.

"Okay," she said, "as long as the instruments go in ahead of us. Is that okay with you, Isaac?"

A split-second delay preceded the Exarch's reply. "Of course, Melilah. I'll arrange it now."

"Is there any particular spike you recommend?"

Again, a slight delay. "I suggest number nine." A map of the chamber and the best route to their next stop came with the words. "The currents are the simplest to navigate in that direction."

"Are you okay up there?" she asked, squinting along the length of the spike to where the artificial sun glared at her. The replicator was visible as a black speck in the sky. Deangelis sounded even more distant than that, and distracted.

"Don't worry about me, Melilah. I'm just trying to piece together a map of the area around here. It's proving very complex."

"Okay. Well, don't overheat or anything."

"I won't. The instrument pack is on its way."

A bright blue speck shot out from the replicator, riding conventional thrusters until the g-field interfered with them, at which point it vanished from sight.

She turned back to Eogan. "Right, then let's go."

He nodded and leapt off the side of the spike. She waited a second until the air was clear, then followed his lead, enduring again the giddying ebb and flow of gravity as it twirled in braids around her. A sense of down corresponding to the spherical wall of the cavern reasserted itself, for the most part, so she oriented herself against the artificial sun "above." Soon they were beyond the edge of the crystal cloud and flying over naked cavern wall.

Spikes swept by with mechanical regularity, their mysterious interiors the only thing differentiating them. She wondered if the frozen, half-visible lumps within could be nothing more arcane than navigational markers. *Take a right turn at the twisted question mark until you reach the half-melted three-legged bear . . .* Each three-dimensional sign would look different depending on the viewing angle, giving the system a complexity it probably didn't warrant, but the thought was still interesting. It wouldn't do to assume human values in a place like Geodesica. Aliens had built it, and more aliens had visited it before humans had even existed. There was no limit to what they might have brought into it, and why.

That said, there was something familiar about the act of flying through the spikes, over the gray, gently curving wall.

Eogan looked at her as she edged up to him. "This reminds me of—"

"Don't say it." She knew what he meant. One hundred and fifty years earlier, when they had been lovers, they had gone EVA over the irregular surface of Bedlam. Drifting through the vacuum hand in hand, with conical docking spires all around them and the ceaseless work of steel-colored nanotech below, they had experienced bliss and happiness. For a long time, the memory had been a precious one. Nothing at all like the present.

He glanced at her with an earnest expression, as though calculating her mood.

"I saw in your records," he said, "that you had a child. After I left."

"I did," she said, a hollow feeling opening up in her chest at the thought of Yasu, her four-daughter who had died with Bedlam and all its citizens. She swore she wouldn't cry again. She was done with revealing her pain to him. "She wasn't yours, if that's what you're wondering. Life was complicated enough already."

He nodded, perhaps understanding, perhaps just acknowledging that he had heard. She went on in carefully measured tones, whether he wanted to know or not.

"Athalia was a difficult girl. I loved her, but we weren't alike. We did nothing but argue until she passed her citizenship exam and moved to New Eire. She hated Bedlam and its information laws, hated me, hated the work I did and the hours I kept. She resented me for having her without the father involved, and I resented her right back, thinking that she was either being ridiculously antiquated or looking for reasons to despise me. She was too young to realize that there were no reasons for what happened; it just fell out that way, as families sometimes do. But I couldn't tell her that because she would take it as me pushing her away. She had to come to terms with it her own way."

"Did she ever have a child of her own?"

"Two, actually."

"Did that help her understand?"

"I don't think so. The last time I saw her, fifty years ago, she still seemed angry—maybe because I got along better with her kids than I ever had with her. Or *they* did with her, for that matter. Perhaps she's just a generally unhappy person—although that seems a terrible thing to think about one's daughter. I *want* her to be happy, of course, but there was never anything I could do to make that happen."

Superior spike #9 was looming on their right, and she stopped talking to concentrate on their final approach. That was her excuse, anyway. Fleeing to New Eire wasn't an option for her at that moment. She and Eogan were stuck together like misshapen magnets, bristling with thumbtacks.

Why now? she wanted to ask him. What was the point of dredging it all up in the middle of Geodesica, one hundred and fifty years after the fact?

She knew the answer to that question. They had stopped running. They were outside the Cell. Suddenly, for the first time in days, they had the space to deal with what hung in the air between them, unspoken and rotten. And deal with it they had to, or explode—or so he seemed to think. He was certainly eager to talk now, for a change.

Idly, and with a guilty twinge, she wondered what had happened to Athalia since their escape into Geodesica. Was she safe? Had Melilah's parting shot at the Exarchate swept her up on a tide of revolution? Did she even care that her mother had vanished from her life, perhaps forever?

"What about you?" she asked as they alighted on the side of the spike. "Any little Palmer Eogans wandering the Arc Circuit?"

He looked surprised by the question. "There was no one serious in my life after you. I didn't have the heart for it. It wasn't as if I didn't *want* a relationship, or try to have one, but none of them lasted long."

"What's that got to do with anything?"

He smiled then, a little foolishly. "Okay. No, no kids. It didn't seem the right thing to do, given the amount I travel."

And the Dark is a barren mate, she thought, unable to repress a flash of satisfaction.

"They were good times, when we were together," he said, his gaze drifting back to the forest of spikes through which they had just flown.

She literally bit her lip. *If they were so good,* she wanted to ask him, *why did you turn your back on them?*

She looked down along the length of the spike, seeking distraction from the painfully obvious. The new crystal cloud looked identical to the previous one, spreading in a rough, flat sheet in all directions. One of Deangelis's instruments hovered at its edge, watching them.

"Nothing unusual to report?" she asked the distant Exarch.

"The ecosystems, although separated by several kilometers, appear to be largely the same." No hesitation this time.

"Seeds or spores could travel on the cavern winds," Eogan said, looking down through the spike wall at the blobs within. They resembled two obese giant squid in the process of mating or merging into one. "Assuming the crystal stuff would let them through."

"I don't see why not." She walked closer to the scintillating barrier and reached out a hand. Uncountable planes and facets retreated before her, creating a space just large enough for her to slip through. The crystal looked like glowing sugar as it wrapped around her head and body. She moved impulsively, not giving herself time to think about being buried alive. Resistance was minimal, although the sensation of walking uphill increased as she moved farther down the spike's side. By the time she broached the innermost limits of the crystal cloud—easing out of it like a swimmer from a tranquil pool—she was crawling on all fours in order to maintain traction. Even that became impractical after another meter, and she was forced to rely on the gas vents of her environment suit.

As she rose up and out of the now seemingly horizontal crystal barrier, she stared in wonder at the hidden ecosystem. It possessed the same broad structure as the other one—with a dense, leafy canopy hiding the woody layers of overgrowth closest to the cavern wall—but in this oasis vines had taken a much stronger hold. Dangling streamers hung everywhere she looked, dotted with yellow and orange flowers and sprouting secondary stems every ten centimeters or so. The fronds traced out the vagaries of local gravity with eye-bending precision. Closest to the base of the superior spike, they pointed nearly straight down; farther away they began to lean inward, pointing toward the spike's midsection; at even farther points, the g-fields of neighboring spikes began to have an effect, like the lines of force of two magnets interfering with the patterns they made in iron filings. Some stood straight up; others hung at an angle from vertical; many curved sinuously throughout their length, creating strange yet stable shapes like snakes frozen in the act of falling.

The air smelled faintly of citrus and tomatoes. There was no breeze at all. The thick forest of vines around her kept the view down to barely a dozen meters. None of Deangelis's instruments were visible.

An uneasy feeling grew stronger in her as she studied the vines. She knew it was stupid, but they seemed to be staring back at her.

The cloud rustled musically as Eogan slid into view behind her.

"Don't move," she said before he could go too far.

"Why not?"

"I don't know. It's too . . . quiet, I guess." She half-laughed at the cliché. It didn't help. "Remember the Venus flytrap?"

"Sure, but these plants couldn't have evolved predatory traits here. There's no prey."

"That we know of. And who said they evolved here? Maybe this is someone's idea of a botanical garden. Or an ark."

Eogan didn't seem overly concerned. "I guess there's one quick way to find out." With that, he kicked out from the side of the spike into the thick of the vines.

They reacted instantly, twitching when he touched them and swinging to follow him as he arced through the air. An excited rustling propagated through the oasis as the disturbance he caused spread along the fronds.

"See?" Melilah called, wishing he had been more cautious. "What did I tell you?"

He seemed more curious than concerned. "You were right. They're definitely responding to touch." He brushed aside a frond that tried to touch his face. "But what can they do? They're just plants."

He flapped his hand in irritation. The frond had stuck to it and wouldn't pull free.

"Uh-oh."

"What is it?"

"There's a sticky secretion coming out of the epidermis." He tugged at the frond with his other hand, and winced. The frond stayed stuck, and so was his other hand when he tried to let go. He yanked at the frond, but it remained firmly planted in the overgrowth. The effort set the other vines dancing. Where they touched each other, they also stuck, forming a net that only tightened as he wriggled.

He laughed. "Oh, shit . . ."

She would see the humor later, when he was safe. Resisting the impulse to leap out after him—which would only get her caught as well—she cast about for a weapon or lever of some kind, with which to pry him free. Nothing obvious sprang to mind.

"Those are probably digestive juices you're basting in there," she said as she jetted up the spine into the overgrowth, squeezing past a nest of vines along the way. They swayed but didn't reach for her in time.

Eogan's voice became muffled as more and more of the fronds leaned in to add to the growing tangle. "There's no need to worry. They can't hurt me. Only"—he grunted and sent the branches shaking with a particularly mighty effort to break free—"*inconvenience* me, Dark take them!"

Then she was above him, peering down at the top of his head. The vines originated from several plants in the overgrowth, not just one as she had hoped. Planting herself firmly against the cavern wall, she tried to pull one of the clusters free from its anchor, keeping her hands well away from its nether, sap-secreting regions. Its tough, stringy flesh resisted her every attempt. It was as hard as tearing a spray of bamboo in two.

"What are you doing up there?" Eogan called to her.

"Trying to get you free."

"There's no need—"

"What do you mean, *no need*? The vines may not be able to hurt you now, but I don't like the thought of leaving you trussed up like a Sunday roast until something that *can* comes along."

She channeled her annoyance at him into an extra burst of energy and tugged at the recalcitrant plant. The vines shivered below her, as though in agitation. The overgrowth shook with the effort she put into it.

"Deangelis!" she grunted, thinking of the mechanical instruments and the sharp-edged tools they contained. "Where the hell *are* you?"

Then a hand reached up from below, followed by a face, and she jumped back in surprise.

"Easy," Eogan said. "Don't burst an artery. I'm fine, really. I could've set myself free at any point. I just wanted to see what the plants would do next."

She stared at his sap-covered face in disbelief, relief, and then, as he clambered up to join her in the overgrowth, anger.

Of course, she told herself, feeling like a fool. He wasn't human. *He probably turned his hand into an electric knife and carved his way free while I danced around like a monkey in a tree. He must think this is just hysterical.*

"Sorry you were worried."

She could tell from his voice that he thought this the limit of her distress.

"I hate this," she said, sagging back and letting the branches take her weight. "I'm sorry, Dominic, but I hate it. Hate you looking like you did back then. It's too easy to forget what you are now."

"*What* am I, Melilah?" He eased himself closer, and she backed away. "Our bodies are both machines designed to keep our minds alive. We're no different from each other."

"But I'm not . . ." She clamped her jaw shut, then opened it again, spitting the words like bullets. "You had a choice to be the way you are. It's not like being gay or asexual; this is entirely your decision. And you made it knowing what the consequences would be. Yet here you are, rubbing my face in it like *I'm* the one who made the mistake; *I'm* the one who should feel stupid. Well, I do feel stupid. Are you happy now?"

"Why would I be happy, Melilah?"

"Because—" She choked on the rest of the sentence. *Because deep down part of me wishes you were Natural, like me.*

She took a deep, shuddering breath.

"I'm just tired of it," she said. "I want it all to go away."

"*I* could go away, if you wanted me to. Take the Cell somewhere else, try to find my own way back home."

He seemed perfectly serious. "Don't be ridiculous. You'd get lost in an hour without Deangelis to guide you—and besides which, you don't even want to go back."

"What makes you say that?"

"You want to explore. You want to travel. Geodesica is paradise for you. Nowhere to settle down; no obligations. You could drift forever in here."

An expression of shock gave him a slightly slack-jawed look. “And never see the stars again? Never follow the trade lanes I helped clear? No, thank you. I’d rather stay here and feed the vines.”

“I don’t believe you.”

“That I’m here with you now I would have thought pretty convincing evidence. I could’ve gone off on my own days ago. I could’ve tried to talk you out of following the replicator’s route here. There are dozens of ways I could’ve sabotaged your attempt to go home, but I haven’t tried any of them. Doesn’t that tell you something?”

She looked down at her hands. Her mind was in turmoil. Why did everything have to be so complicated? Why couldn’t Geodesica have led them home like she wanted? Why couldn’t Eogan go back to being the figure she’d pasted together from deeply imprinted memories—one so easy to hate, as she needed him to be? Why couldn’t she just *get over it*?

A distant hissing noise, growing louder by the second, heralded the appearance of one of Deangelis’s instrument drones. It had, presumably, been caught up in the vines, and was only now coming into range.

“I don’t want you to go,” she said in words so soft she barely heard them herself.

Eogan, with his superhuman senses, understood them perfectly well, and nodded.

“Edible, do you think?”

Eogan followed Melilah’s voice through the verdant world beneath the crystal cloud to where she hung before a drooping lichen, as broad and thick as a heavy cloak draped over the bough that supported it. Its surface was dotted with broad pores that emitted a piercing aroma of rotten garlic.

“I’d rather not find out,” he said, although his body could ingest just about anything without difficulty. He could even numb his taste receptors completely, if he had to. “Feel free to try. I won’t stop you.”

“No, thanks. I’m not quite that desperate just yet.”

She clambered away, tugging herself easily along branches into a thicker section of the overgrowth. The superior spike at the heart of the cave forest disappeared behind them. Gravity tended to be highly variable, and radiation leaking in from the edges of the crystal cloud lent some sections an unhealthy look. Strange spores withered or bred with cancerous profligacy, choking on their own excess. Some moved without respect for the gravitational tides or air currents, waving at them with elongated, blotchy fingers.

Eogan trailed Melilah at a respectful distance, not to make sure she was safe on her own, but because she had followed him down into the forest, and that suggested to him that she didn't want to be alone. She stopped to examine another lichen—fungi of all kinds had been almost absent deeper in the forest, but were becoming more common farther out—and glanced at him as though making sure he was keeping up.

Her ambivalence toward him would drive him crazy if it went on much longer.

"Did I ever tell you," he asked, "that I'm an orphan?"

"Our relationship was a hundred and fifty years ago. I've forgotten most of what you told me."

He couldn't tell if she was lying, and didn't challenge her on that point. "Understandable, I suppose. I guess I had less to distract me between stops than you did on Bedlam, so I've often thought about the stuff we discussed."

"Okay." She shrugged. "Go on."

"If I *did* tell you that I'm an orphan, you probably misunderstood me. You probably assumed I meant orphan in the sense that you are an orphan: that your parents are dead, and you have no other family. In my case, that's not strictly speaking true."

"So—what? You ran away from home when you were a kid and joined a traveling circus?"

"More or less. A trader came through Megrez from outside the Arc Circuit. I must've been about thirteen, and just entering puberty. This was in 2205. Even after a century, VOIDships remained tricky to handle; voyages were still long and dangerous, only marginally better than we'd been used to before. Megrez 8 didn't have much of a space industry—just a couple of drum colonies and some stations over the main world—so I'd never seen a starship up close before. They didn't come to outposts like ours more than once a decade. This one, the *Ambidexter,* wasn't much to look at, but it still won my heart. It was about a mile long and as heavy as a skyscraper, all shields and engine and reactor cores. The crew habitat was a tiny tube about two-thirds up from the stern, barely able to hold twenty people, half of them in hard sleep, balanced on the line between particle impacts up front and drive wash from the rear. It was amazing anyone made it anywhere alive."

Melilah paused to smell a flower. An immediate wince of distaste, then she nodded. "I remember ships like that. My mother and I took one from Little Red, before she died."

"They weren't all the same. Some were run by honest people who refitted their ships regularly, even though it cost enough to bankrupt a small colony each time. Some did their best to keep their passengers safe and to ensure their cargo—the precious little of it they could fit in—got where it was supposed to go. Do you remember how long it took to scour out those trade lanes? Do you remember when a deform rating of two was about the most you could hope for, even in the best-maintained ship in the Circuit?"

She smiled—at him, not the memory. "Yes."

He forced himself not to digress. "This ship definitely wasn't well maintained. It had scars all down its length, and yellow scoring where something had hit it on the way into the system. The Dark knows what, but the *Ambidexter* was lucky to have made dock—which is where it should've stayed for a year or more. I learned later that the core AI had been compromised in the same accident by some kind of wetware glitch. That, on top of the physical scrapes, made it a very unlikely prospect for going anywhere.

"I, of course, didn't know that then, and the captain, an old pirate by the name of Barbato, must've seen me coming from halfway across the system. Barely had the drive stopped shining than I was hanging around the spaceport where his shuttle had docked, begging for a tour. I was relentless, but he and his crew kept putting me off. Sometimes they'd bait me, act like they might relent and pick me over the others who wanted the same thing—to see a real starship in the flesh, from the inside out—but they always knocked me back. They kept me dangling for weeks, while they made deals and swindled and did anything they could to leave our dumpy little outpost and get somewhere *real*."

The passion in his voice surprised him. It had been a long time since he'd told the story, and although he'd forgotten none of the details, he had forgotten just how much it roused him. Those youthful aspirations had culminated in experiences the like of which he had never dreamed, but then, back on Megrez 8, a starry-eyed boy with no prospects and no real plan, his chances of getting off-world—let alone out-system—had looked decidedly slim.

"Barbato big-noted himself everywhere he went, and he was charming and convincing enough that people believed him. When he announced a departure date, the colonial authority did everything short of declaring it a public holiday. They thought he'd be back, you see. They thought he *mattered,* and that they mattered to him.

"All that mattered to him was moving on without blowing himself into atoms in the process. The corrupted AI was giving him a real problem. Megrez didn't have the sort of facilities he needed to fix it *in situ,* and he couldn't get anywhere else to fix it while it wasn't working. Not legally, anyway, and he wasn't normally a man who worried about that sort of thing."

Melilah had stopped pretending to sightsee. She hooked one leg over a dangling branch and found a semblance of comfort.

"There are crimes," she said, "and then there are *crimes*."

"Exactly. On the day the ship was due to leave, with the spaceport overflowing with people come to see it off and last-minute deals unfolding everywhere, Captain Barbato came looking for me. He remembered my face, he said—and I'm sure he did. He knew exactly what I was prepared to give up, after all those weeks of whetting my appetite. The ship had two empty berths, he told me, and it looked like weight wasn't going to be too big a problem. So why didn't I sign on for the trip to Alcor 3a and see what life was like among the stars? Leave this miserable shit-heap behind and seek a fortune afar? Only don't tell your parents, because they probably wouldn't approve, what with you being a minor and all. They don't see the big picture. They don't know that opportunities like this don't come along every day. Did I want to wait another ten years before my next chance appeared?

"Of course I didn't. And of course I had no idea of his real intentions. Alcor 3a was a dummy destination. The *Ambidexter* was really going to Altitude, where Barbato hoped to dry-dock long enough to fix most of his problems, then keep on moving, staying one jump ahead of whatever trouble had set him running in the first place.

"So I signed on. Me and a girl, someone I recognized from my weeks hanging around the port like the stink of a bad filter. The crew smuggled both of us aboard and gave us the quickest possible tour. Galley, bunks, head, and not much more. You won't need any of that, the crew said; you're sleeping right through the trip out. We'll wake you en route, when the tricky stuff is over, and you can take a proper look.

"I should've been more suspicious then, I guess, because the living quarters had no windows, and the brief glimpse of the bridge I'd been given showed nothing more than remote viewing rigs. If I'd been happy with simulated or secondhand views, I would've stayed home.

"But I didn't say or question anything. I let myself be put into a sleep chair and held my breath as the ship's doc fitted the nanoweb over my scalp. The girl who'd come with me—I can't remember her name, although I really should—was in the seat next to me. She looked as terrified as I felt, but she said nothing. If she balks, I remember thinking, I'll balk, too. But she didn't.

"Now, whenever I'm feeling uncertain about doing something, I remember her face, and what a difference it would've made if just one of us had opened our mouths.

"The last thing I saw was Captain Barbato saluting us with a shit-eating grin, like he was doing us this big fucking favor. I tried to salute back, but the nanoweb had already knocked out my ability to move. Not long after, I began losing sight and sound as well. My body became distant. I fell asleep. And I dreamed."

Eogan shuddered involuntarily. "God, did I dream. That was the part Barbato hadn't told us about. We weren't passengers. No one could afford to drag whole human bodies from system to system unless they were worth their weight in antimatter. As we weren't paying, we had to earn our keep another way—which consisted entirely of propping up the core AI. Megrez couldn't supply the add-ons needed to repair an AI's damaged neural nets, but Captain Barbato could exploit the neural plasticity of two teenagers too dumb to realize that their value as keen explorers and rebels was considerably less than that of their brains.

"Teenagers are stupid. It's the way things are. They're stupid because their neurons are rewiring at a massive rate, taking in a whole bunch of new social clues and incorporating them into an increasingly complex adult worldview. We were very stupid, that girl and I, and that made us valuable. With our heads laid open and our gray stuff accessed by the core AI, our natural ability to learn propped up the *Ambidexter* long enough to get it somewhere. Neural techs used to call the process skullbooting, before new techniques superseded it.

"And it worked, after a fashion. The ship *did* make it, although the journey wasn't a comfortable one for anyone aboard. I had constant nightmares and suffered all the symptoms of sleep deprivation, despite being unconscious the whole time. Those dreams—of fire and weightlessness and stress; of constantly trying to tear myself through something that couldn't be torn; of being stretched and squeezed in all directions at once—were feedback from the AI. A good skullbooter could have kept the dreams deep in my subconscious. The grim talent aboard the *Ambidexter* wasn't so sophisticated. Some of it leaked over, and I got it raw.

"The AI in turn got some of my shit. The VOID systems fluctuated wildly, causing all sorts of problems. For an extended period just over halfway, it simply stopped working, leaving Barbato and the *Ambidexter* adrift in space. I don't know what lengths they went to to get the ship moving again, but somehow they did, and it arrived in Altitude a year late, even more battered and worn than before.

"Barbato knew he was in trouble the moment he signaled for docking protocols and was told by port authorities to stand down and be boarded. That unexpected stopover in the Dark had royally fucked up his plan. It had given warning from Megrez time to reach Altitude. Both the girl and I had been reported missing and our disappearances traced. Even at sluggish light-speed, the message that we'd been kidnapped had had time to make it ahead of the dreadful, near-junked *Ambidexter*.

"Barbato had some fight left in him. Figuring his best shot hadn't paid off, he took the only option left to him, and he ran. He fired up the VOID drives in-system and did his best to get away. The ship, though, was as good as dead. He had squeezed every last drop from the core AI getting to Altitude, and it died in a cascade of apoptosis, taking the girl with it. Would've killed me, too, but for the feedback frying the link between us. With the AI down, the *Ambidexter* had only maneuvering thrusters left. It was, in effect, a very ugly sitting duck."

Eogan wiped his mouth. More than a century later, in a body that couldn't sweat if he told it not to, he relived those days with painful vividness.

"The ship was boarded, the crew arrested. Barbato got the death sentence; he'd done this kind of thing before, apparently, and no one was inclined to show him any mercy. I didn't see the trial and the execution until much later, after I'd been rehabilitated. It took seven years to put my brain back together, to scour out the last of the illegal routines that had leaked in there and left me riddled with neural scars. I don't remember much of that time, except for endless dreams containing nothing but talking, and being told that I wasn't going to be charged with any crimes. Skullbooting was illegal and dangerous; few people volunteered for it. Only an idiot would've done it, and my life on Megrez hadn't left me with a record for being *that* stupid.

"Anyway, when I woke up," he said, "I wasn't sure what I was anymore. Not a teenager, since I had turned twenty-three in my coma and missed a large chunk of my life. Not a cripple, although some people treated me like one. Not innocent or stupid either: part of me felt that I had done the right thing by volunteering to join Barbato's feckless crew. I had gained something from the experience, even if it wasn't the sort of experience most people had had by the time they weren't teenagers anymore. It was *something,* and it had changed me.

"The next starship that came through Altitude en route to Megrez offered to take me home. I accepted the offer, but refused any form of hard sleep on the journey. I stayed awake and watched the crew, and learned. My brain had lost its teenage plasticity, but I wasn't stupid. When we arrived at Megrez, after two years in the Dark, it didn't feel like home anymore. My parents welcomed me, of course—even hugged me—but they weren't the same either. They had aged, changed. I had a sister now, a two-year-old who didn't know who I was. She was frightened of me when I came to visit.

"I couldn't stay. The *Ambidexter*'s core AI had altered me. Not deliberately, or in any sinister way; it hadn't even changed me that much, since I'd already had an overwhelming yearning for the stars. If I hadn't, I wouldn't have taken Barbato's offer in the first place. Perhaps it didn't change me at all. Either way, the experience only made the decision to leave a second time much easier. I successfully applied for a permanent berth on the ship that had brought me home. Within the week, I would be leaving Megrez on a starship again—only that time I got to say good-bye, and my parents knew for sure I wouldn't be coming back."

He remembered their faces at the farewell. They had looked like mourners at a funeral. His father, a broad-shouldered man with an anxious expression on his face; his mother, taller and more composed, her eyes full of tears she wouldn't let flow; and his new sister standing between them, uncertain what this stranger had done to cause such an upset. He felt bad for them. They had waited twelve years for him to return, only to have him run away again.

From his point of view, though, he hadn't been running away from home. He had been running *to* it, into the Dark. If the AI had given him anything, it was an appreciation of what every old-time starship pilot and modern-day Palmer held dear: the gulfs between stars; the endless, dust-swept barrens that most colonists dismissed as an inconvenience. In terms of volume, the Dark outranked systems by many, many orders of magnitude. No one could be said to hold dominion over it, or even to truly understand it. Fragile humans plied narrow pathways through it, weaving a flimsy spiderweb that crisscrossed their notion of an empire, but could not bind it. Deep in the cold, with the nearest colony months away and nothing but void for light-years all around, it was easy sometimes to believe that the Dark wasn't empty at all, but full of potential so subtle and profound that if it ever stirred, ever woke and flexed its deep, bulging limbs, humanity would be swept from the universe without so much as a thought.

Eogan didn't try to explain that feeling to Melilah. He knew it made him sound like a nutcase, or as though the AI had given him something much more dangerous than a simple insight. He wasn't a religious fanatic, and he wasn't a space junkie, either. Some Palmers avoided gravity wells entirely, never coming closer than heliopause to stars and other people. He had worked with such types before. They were unpredictable, likely to split away from a Cell in midjourney without warning, and vanish forever into their beloved Dark.

He wasn't one of those. He was just a Palmer.

"What's your point, Dominic?"

"I'm not brain-damaged," he said, "and I'm not inhuman. You might not believe me on either score, but I wanted you to know the truth. Becoming a Palmer didn't change anything essential about me. This is who I was before, when we first met, and you were prepared to love me then. You didn't know I'd been touched by an AI. You accepted me for who I was, just as I accepted—and continue to accept—you for who you are. It's your nature, being a Natural."

"Is that why you're telling me this now?" she asked. "So we can feel like invalids together?"

He winced at her sharpness. "No, that's not it at all, Melilah. But if that's what you want to believe, I guess I can't stop you."

She opened her mouth to say something, and in a flare-up of irritation he decided he didn't want to hear it. He couldn't repair the breach between them from his side only; she had to meet him halfway, or they both risked falling. Their natures kept them apart and drove them together at the same time. The conflict was insurmountable.

He kicked away from her, into the cave forest.

"Hey—wait!" Foliage rustled as she came after him. "You left *me,* remember? Just like you left your family. I didn't push you away any more than they did. It was entirely your decision."

"It was the only one open to me." He didn't stop moving, didn't even look behind him to see if she heard. "Do you really think it could've gone any differently?"

"We won't know now, will we? If you hadn't waited so long to tell me—"

"So it *does* make a difference?"

"No—I don't know." Her voice choked off in frustration. "Why didn't you just *talk* to me, Dominic?"

Because the words weren't there, he wanted to say. *Because no matter what I could have said, I would have hurt you. And I didn't want to see that.*

"I was a coward," he said as he fled into the forest. "I still am."

She called his name once, then a second time more loudly. Then she stopped following. He didn't need to look over his shoulder to see her falling behind. He knew that view intimately, from his dreams.

—THE EXARCHATE IS AN EMPIRE IN EVERY SENSE OF THE WORD. IT IS ALSO A FRONTIER, ESPECIALLY ALONG THE ARC CIRCUIT, SINCE THE LOCAL BUBBLE REACHES FARTHER FROM SOL IN THAT DIRECTION THAN IN ANY OTHER. AS BEFITS HUMANITY'S BOLDEST EXPERIMENT, IT COMES AT GREAT COST TO ALL WHO PARTICIPATE, WILLINGLY OR UNWILLINGLY, KNOWINGLY OR UNKNOWINGLY. AND SOME MIGHT SAY THAT ITS VALUE AS AN INVESTMENT IS INCALCULABLE, IF ONLY BECAUSE THE POTENTIAL RETURNS LIE SO FAR IN THE FUTURE THAT NO ONE COULD EVER REASONABLY EXPECT TO COLLECT.

—THE EXARCHATE PERFORMS ANOTHER FUNCTION, ONE THAT MANY OBSERVERS HAVE OVERLOOKED. IT INSULATES SOL FROM THE REST OF THE UNIVERSE; IT IS A SHOCK ABSORBER, IF YOU WILL, DESIGNED TO ABSORB ANYTHING THAT MIGHT UNEXPECTEDLY LUNGE OUT OF THE DARK. WITHOUT IT, SOL WOULD BE VULNERABLE. AND WHEN SOL IS VULNERABLE, HUMANITY IS VULNERABLE.

—TO PUT IT BLUNTLY, THE ULTIMATE FATE OF THE EXARCHATE IS IRRELEVANT, SO LONG AS SOL SURVIVES.

—THIS FUNCTION OF THE EXARCHATE IS EASILY OVERLOOKED BY THOSE ON THE GROUND. THIS INCLUDES NATURALS, PALMERS, EVEN YOU. AM I NOT CORRECT?

Deangelis didn't know exactly how to respond. Was the voice right in saying that he'd never suspected such a thing? Well, yes—but he wasn't so sure it was correct in its suspicion.

And what did it have to do with Geodesica?

"I'm not supposed to ask you questions," he said. "I had assumed that agreement worked both ways."

Laughter, rich and cultured, greeted his response.

—QUITE SO, ISAAC. I AM BEING DOUBLY UNFAIR IN THAT I ALREADY KNOW THE QUESTIONS YOU WOULD MOST LIKE—AND NEED—TO ASK. THAT MAKES MY VOICING OF THEM SOMETHING WORSE THAN RHETORICAL. IT IS, PERHAPS, GLOATING, AND FOR THAT I APOLOGIZE.

"If you can read my mind so easily, then isn't this conversation just a waste of time?"

—NOT FOR YOU.

"I have only your word for that."

—QUITE SO. I COULD BE TOYING WITH YOU FOR MY OWN AMUSEMENT.

"And if I won't play?"

Another laugh.—RULES WERE MADE TO BE BROKEN.

He didn't know how to take that. "You claim to know the questions I want to ask. Why don't you just answer them now and be done with it?"

—FOR THE SAKE OF THE CONVERSATION. THAT MAY SEEM A TRIVIAL REASON TO YOU, BUT FOR ONE SUCH AS I, WHO HAS BEEN ALONE FOR SO LONG, A CONVERSATION IS A WONDROUS THING.

"How long—?" Deangelis stopped himself. "No. Tell me or not. It's your decision."

—IT IS INDEED. I'LL TELL YOU WHAT YOU NEED TO KNOW, AND SOME OF WHAT YOU'D LIKE TO KNOW, TOO. I MUST KEEP YOUR ATTENTION FROM DRIFTING ANYWAY, LEST YOU TRY TO ALERT YOUR FRIENDS TO MY OTHER ACTIVITIES.

Deangelis hadn't forgotten that aspect of the situation. He had been keeping a close eye on movements below while talking with the mysterious mind above. It was difficult to track Melilah and Eogan while simultaneously probing the latest manifestation of Geodesica's weirdness. As they tried to talk to him, too, and he attempted to keep numerous mobile instruments under control, he found his focus slipping on more than one occasion.

What about you? asked Melilah in the garden of vines. *Any little Palmer Eogan's wandering the Arc Circuit?*

In a completely different section of the cavern, Palmer Eogan had a question of his own: *Did I ever tell you that I was an orphan?*

Deangelis continued to tolerate what, under almost any other circumstances, might have been intolerable. That made him complicit with the voice already. But he had little choice. He couldn't put his fingers in his ears. The voice spoke and he listened.

"Begin," he said. "Or not."

—YOU WANT TO KNOW HOW I COULD KNOW SUCH THINGS, HOW I COULD HAVE COME TO SUCH AN OPINION ON THE EXARCHATE, YOUR HOME, WHEN I LIVE IN THIS PLACE, THIS ARTIFACT YOU CALL GEODESICA. I SAY THAT THERE ARE MANY WAYS THIS COULD HAVE COME TO PASS. YOU HAVE IDENTIFIED ONE OF THEM: THAT I HAVE READ YOUR MINDS AND TAKEN THE KNOWLEDGE I NEED FROM THEM. ANOTHER POSSIBILITY IS THIS: THAT I OBSERVED THE DEVELOPMENT OF THE REPLICATOR YOU FOLLOWED HERE. IT GREW SLOWLY FROM THE SEED THAT CREATED IT, AND I STUDIED THE PATHWAYS OF ITS MIND AS IT UNFOLDED. INDEED, IT COULD HAVE SPOKEN TO ME WILLINGLY, FOR IT HAD ITS OWN FORM OF INTELLIGENCE, AND I WAS NO THREAT TO IT.

—WHICH OF THESE TWO POSSIBILITIES SEEMS THE MOST LIKELY TO YOU?

"The second," he replied. "I'm not sure if that makes it more or less likely to be true."

—YOU ARE WISE TO SPECULATE, MY FRIEND, BUT THERE'S NO NEED TO TIE YOURSELF IN KNOTS.

—YOUR NEXT QUESTION, WERE YOU TO ASK IT, WOULD BE: WHO AM I? THIS IS ANSWERED SIMPLY. I AM THIS PLACE, THIS CAVERN AROUND YOU, WITH ITS FUNCTIONS AND ITS MYSTERIES, ITS SPLENDOR AND ITS BEAUTY. I AM NOT ITS VOICE OR MIND, NO MORE THAN YOU ARE THE VOICE OR MIND OF YOUR OWN BODY. I AM THIS PLACE, FOR WHICH YOU HAVE NO NAME, AND THAT IS ALL I AM.

—BUT THAT'S NOT THE ENTIRETY OF THE QUESTION. THE NOTION OF IDENTITY IS A COMPLEX THING. YOU WANT TO KNOW MY ORIGINS AS WELL. AM I ALIEN OR HUMAN? AM I INDIGENOUS OR EXOGENOUS TO GEODESICA?

—IN RESPONSE TO THIS, I ASK *YOU*: DOES IT MATTER?

"It might," he said. The voice was so all-pervasive he felt in danger of losing his own identity, of being swept up in an avalanche of words and buried forever.

The voice in Deangelis's mind chuckled.—YES, IT MIGHT.

"But you're not going to tell me, aren't you?"

—NO, I AM NOT.

"Then how can I trust you?"

—YOU WILL NEVER TRUST ME ENTIRELY, NO MATTER WHAT I SAY. I CAN ONLY TELL YOU WHAT I THINK IS REASONABLE, AND LET YOU MAKE UP YOUR MIND IN YOUR OWN TIME.

"Make up my mind about what?"

—YOUR FUTURE, OF COURSE. DO YOU REST HERE OR GO BACK TO WANDERING THE TUNNELS? PICK AN EXIT AT RANDOM OR RISK RUNNING INTO ANOTHER REPLICATOR? LIE LOW FOR A WHILE OR ROAM FOR AN ETERNITY? THESE ARE NOT QUESTIONS I ASK OF YOU, BUT WHICH YOU ASK YOURSELF. OBVIOUSLY, MY PRESENCE HERE COMPLICATES THINGS. YOU MUST DECIDE IF I AM A THREAT TO YOU, OR AN OPPORTUNITY.

"It's hard to feel threatened by a voice."

—DO YOU BELIEVE ME INCAPABLE OF ACTION? WATCH.

Across the surface of the cavern, all eleven of the exits from the cavern, including the one through which they had arrived, irised shut.

"How did you do that?" Deangelis asked, panicked for a moment that Eogan or Melilah might notice—but they were engrossed in their own conversations on the surface of the chamber. "Bring them back!"

The exits reappeared.—THE MANIPULATION OF SPACE-TIME IS NO DIFFICULT THING. YOU YOURSELF POSSESS THE MEANS REQUIRED, ALTHOUGH IN RUDIMENTARY FORM.

"The VOID drive units?"

—SLEDGEHAMMERS IN A JEWELRY SHOP. MY MANIPULATIONS ARE MUCH MORE SUBTLE.

Or not, thought Deangelis, watching Melilah and Eogan interacting with their doppelgangers below.

—LET ME TELL YOU SOMETHING, said the voice.—FREE OF CHARGE, IF YOU WILL. YOU ALREADY KNOW THAT TIME FLOWS DIFFERENTLY IN HERE. STAY IN ONE SPOT AND IT TRICKLES ON UNCHECKED AT A RATE ROUGHLY CONCOMITANT WITH THAT OUTSIDE. VOYAGE, HOWEVER, AND THAT CONCOMITANCE IS INTERRUPTED. EACH INTERSECTION, EACH NODE, TAKES ITS TOLL. YOU SUSPECT THIS ALREADY. I NOW TELL YOU THE TRUTH OF IT. OUTSIDE, MANY YEARS HAVE PASSED SINCE YOU CAME HERE.

"Do you know how many?" he asked, afraid of the answer.

—THE EXACT NUMBER IS UNKNOWN TO ME, BUT I RECEIVE GLIMPSES FROM THE MINDS OF THOSE WHO COME HERE. YOUR STEED WAS NOT THE ONLY REPLICATOR TO VISIT. EACH OF THEM BROUGHT ME NEWS OF YOUR EXARCHATE AND THE FATE THAT BEFELL IT, AFTER YOU LEFT.

"What? What happened?"

—YOU HAVE SUSPICIONS ON THIS SCORE ALSO. WAR, YOU THINK: AN UPRISING OF EXARCHS AND THEIR CHARGES, DEFYING SOL AND THE ARCHON, THE DESTROYER OF WORLDS. THE EXARCHATE DECLARES INDEPENDENCE AND TURNS ON ITS CREATOR LIKE A BEEHIVE DEFYING ITS QUEEN. YOU WONDER WHAT FOLLOWS. YOU CANNOT KNOW THE LENGTHS SOL WOULD GO TO IN ORDER TO QUASH THE REBELLION. ARE A THOUSAND WORLDS STRONG ENOUGH TO OVERWHELM THE HOME SYSTEM? YOU CANNOT KNOW HOW FAR EITHER SIDE HAS ADVANCED IN YOUR ABSENCE. THIS IS A WAR THAT COULD DRAG ON FOR CENTURIES, IF THE FORCES ARE EVENLY MATCHED. IT MIGHT NEVER BE RESOLVED.

"Do you know or not?"

—AH, QUESTIONS, QUESTIONS. MY FRIEND, YOU FORGET THE TRUE PURPOSE OF THE EXARCHATE. I HAVE GIVEN YOU THE ANSWER ALREADY. SOL IS NOT THE ENEMY; THE ARCHON IS NOT THE ENEMY. THERE *IS* NO ENEMY WITHIN HUMANITY. A CIVIL WAR IS BY DEFINITION NOT A WAR, JUST THE SHIFTING FROM ONE STATE TO ANOTHER. A PHASE CHANGE. HUMANITY IS A SELF-ORGANIZING CRITICALITY, LIKE A PILE OF SAND IN AN EGG TIMER. THE WALLS COLLAPSE SOMETIMES. IT'S NATURAL.

Anger burned in him, sudden and bright. "Are you really saying that the fall of civilization is not a bad thing?"

—IS THE FALL OF A SAND CASTLE? A RELATIONSHIP? I ASK ONLY WHETHER IT MAKES ANY DIFFERENCE TO YOU. NO MATTER WHAT HAPPENS OUTSIDE THESE WALLS, BEYOND THE EXITS TO THIS MAZE, YOU CAN NEVER GO HOME. THAT IS THE ONLY CERTAINTY.

Anger became sadness at the thought of Bedlam burning in the cold, golden fire of Catastrophe. Everything he had held dear had gone up in that conflagration: his colony, his colonists, his higher self, his trust and faith in the Archon and Sol . . .

If war *had* broken out over the Archon's actions, then he had no real reason to try to get back. Those they had left behind would do the work that he could not. The conflict might even be over, for all he knew; the bonfires of rebellion could be ashen and cold. Whatever shape humanity was in, it might care little for his need for revenge.

He couldn't go home. His only remaining concern was for Melilah, the last of his charges. What did *she* need? She, too, had lost everything. Could she turn her back on the hope of regaining it in exchange for peace, for an end to running?

This, he thought with growing certainty, was what the voice offered. The cavern could be a refuge, a bolt-hole for the fugitives from Sol. What did they stand to lose by taking a moment to draw their breath?

A moment, or perhaps longer.

—THAT IS THE ONLY QUESTION THAT MATTERS, said the voice.—NOT WHO I AM OR HOW I KNOW THESE THINGS. NOT WHAT'S HAPPENING BACK HOME OR WHETHER YOU CAN GET THERE. WHEN YOU'VE LOST EVERYTHING, BY DEFINITION YOU HAVE NOTHING LEFT TO LOSE—SO DOES IT MATTER IF YOU STAY HERE? IF YOU NEVER LEAVE?

A sudden dimming of the light took him by surprise. So bound up had he been in the conversation that he had forgotten the world around him. Melilah and Eogan were finished arguing; a tense and sullen silence ruled their separate quarters of the cavern. Above, near where he hung in the evacuated heart of the hollow world, the artificial sun was growing dark.

—DO NOT BE ALARMED, the voice soothed.—THE GARDENS HAVE THEIR CYCLES, LIKE ALL THINGS, AND I MAINTAIN THEM JUST AS I MAINTAIN THE AIR AND WATER BALANCE.

"Night?" he asked, watching the finely balanced fusion reactions ebb in the ancient mechanism that so badly needed repairing.

—YES, NIGHT IS FALLING. BE REASSURED, ISAAC, THAT THERE ARE NO WOLVES HERE BEYOND THOSE YOU BRING WITH YOU.

Melilah looked down in alarm when the crystal cloud grew dark below her, as though a cloud had eclipsed the sun.

"Deangelis?" she called. "What's going on up there?"

"Nothing to be frightened of," the distant voice reassured her. "It's some sort of automated diurnal adjustment to the light balance."

She looked around her, noting flowers closing and leaves drooping: a natural reaction to the ending of daylight. "Do you want us to come back to the replicator?"

"No need. Stay where you are and rest, if you can."

"Where's Eogan?" After their argument over the vines and her admission that she didn't want him to go anywhere, they had wandered off in separate directions to study the plants. She had kept a careful note of his movements by the sounds he made as he tunneled through the overgrowth, but she couldn't hear him anymore.

"He's on his way."

The light ebbed until she could barely see her hands in front of her face. Although tempted to switch to infrared, she found that she enjoyed the gloom. It was soothing and, in the plant-infested oasis around her, perfectly safe.

"Okay, Isaac, then I'll say good night," she said with a smile. "And don't stay up too late with those calculations, will you?"

"Those what? Oh—no, I won't, Melilah."

The roots shook beneath her as Eogan clambered out of the darkness. "Well," he said. "What do we do now?"

"I could sleep. It'd be nice to switch the brain off for a bit."

He settled down nearby, not so close that they were touching, but she could sense his presence and was vaguely reassured by it.

"I'll tell you a story," he said.

"A bedtime story? How quaint."

"Not really, although if you fall asleep I won't take it to heart. It's about an old pirate and a stupid kid who bites off more than he can chew. You might have heard some of it before."

Something in his tone told her that this wasn't just a gambit to pass the time until the light returned. "All right," she said. "But it'd better be good."

"I'm sure you won't be disappointed . . ."

He could see perfectly well in the dark, but had lost the urge to explore. A cooling breeze swept through the cave forest, making the leaves rustle and the crystals shiver. If he closed his eyes, he could be in a Little Red garden, listening to furin bells welcoming the dusk. The scent of flowers was strong.

"Does this mean you've stopped avoiding me?" she asked. He'd heard her approaching but made no move to run again. That was getting old.

"It's different with the lights out," he said. "Less overwhelming."

The clutch of boughs he occupied dipped as she came to join him.

"Thank you for talking to me, before," she said. "I used to think you wanted to explore, to travel, and nothing else. I thought it was a compulsion. And maybe it is. Hell, I don't know. But that only makes the fact that you didn't take your Cell out the nearest exit and rejoin the stars, as you could've done days ago, all that more meaningful. You haven't, and you're trying to help me get home." She took a deep breath. "Well, I don't think that makes you a coward. Quite the opposite, in fact."

He nodded, presuming she could make him out in the darkness via infrared. Visible light had completely faded.

"Thank you."

"Don't think I'm saying something I'm not. I still hate this thing you've chosen to become. You look like you used to; you even act like you used to. Assuming you're the same will only lead us to make more mistakes, and I've had about enough of them as I can handle, with you." He felt her shift slightly on her perch. "But I'm glad you're not going anywhere in a hurry. That's all."

He switched to infrared and found her huddled in a V-shaped pocket of the overgrowth. She held herself tightly. Even in the darkness, she looked very lonely and small.

"Want me to watch your back while you sleep?"

She exhaled heavily, as though she'd been holding the breath a while. "I'd be grateful, yes, if you wouldn't mind."

"Not at all. Just don't ask me, in our new spirit of glasnost, to sing you a lullaby."

"Rest easy on that score," she said with a smile. "That really would be going too far."

+13

Bedlam: 2608 CE

Isaac Deangelis watched the forces gathering around Bedlam with an appraising and slightly nervous eye. A steady stream of mass launchers, drone swarms, carrier asteroids, and rail platforms had been converging on his system for years, adopting orbits deep in the cometary halo and assembling new weapons of mass destruction among the traps he had laid for them there. The occasional mine-burst or singularity flash marked a surreptitious beginning to the conflict, but war was not openly declared. Neither side hailed the other. There was no point. Both knew what was coming.

"Are we wise to let them muster like this?" he asked the Archon, made nervous by the accumulating lidar echoes and gravitational anomalies. "We are ready. They are not. If we move now, we can still take them by—"

"Don't worry, Isaac. You'll ride out soon enough. But not yet. Not while *she* isn't here."

After more than a century and a half of cohabitation in the ruined system, Deangelis had come no closer to understanding the being that had created him. At times infinitely patient and methodical, at others spontaneous, almost capricious, it pursued objectives he barely glimpsed along paths he could not discern. What it saw in Palmer Horsfall he didn't know, but it seemed determined to have her present before it allowed him to act in the system's self-defense. Until then, they crouched under the cover of Catastrophe with the weapons he had built, and waited.

VOIDship trails marked the arrival of more interstellar attack forces. Fleets formed and merged like satellite galaxies around a massive black hole. Reports came in from across the Exarchate of systems falling to the rebels in an accelerating procession. Once the Arc Circuit had surrendered, the collapse of Sol's authority had begun in earnest.

He wondered if it was a trick of some kind—if, at the very last moment, Sol would unleash a new, incalculable vengeance upon those who defied it. Who knew what manner of weapons the Architects had dreamed up since the Catastrophe had destroyed his home? Humanity's birth-system could probably wrench control of the Exarchate back from the rebels without so much as a cry of protest.

But if that was the case, why did it not do so? Why did it sit back and watch as, one by one, the worlds it had knitted together under its authority united to shrug it off? Its actions—or lack of action—just didn't make sense.

Unless, he thought, that was exactly what it wanted . . .

The standoff couldn't last forever. With more than one hundred thousand discrete objects now circling the system in orbits fine-tuned to turn into inward-plunging dives at a thruster's well-timed nudge, the moment of reckoning came closer with every week. Finally, as yet another convoy swept in from a neighboring system, carrying yet more instruments of death and destruction, the Archon stirred.

"It's time. She is here."

"How do you know?"

"Don't worry about that, Isaac. I want you to go and meet with her."

"Why?" A chill went through all his bodies at the thought of leaving their bubble of safety.

"Not all of you. Just one fragment. You will be my emissary, sent to discuss terms."

He didn't react for a long moment. Behind the relentless congruity of his higher mind, tiny flickers of independence still remained. The parts of him that were not drowned out completely by the stately beats of his combined consciousness heard the Archon's words and felt a renewal of hope. If one of him was to leave the bubble of Catastrophe and reach the rebels intact, that one could break free of the influence that kept him at the Archon's side—possibly to assist the rebels in their quest, perhaps even join with the fragment that had broken free over a century and a half ago. Rudra-Deangelis, the missing part.

"It's a little late," he said coolly, "to sue for peace, don't you think?"

"Not peace, Isaac. You're going to negotiate the terms of our surrender."

Deangelis bit his lip on an outraged protest. Surrender? Impossible! It would make a mockery of everything he had done in Bedlam since the Catastrophe!

But even as he reigned in the impulse, he couldn't help but hope that it might be true. Could the end of the war come so easily? As jackals circled the last remaining outpost of Sol's authority in the heart of the Arc Circuit, would the Archon finally see that it had gone too far and make amends for its crimes of the past?

He didn't know which to hope for: that the Archon knew what it was doing and would fight by any means to defend the future it had mapped out for humanity, or that its entire campaign was built on quicksand, and any moral certainty it had once possessed might disappear in a moment. Either was potentially awful.

An existential shiver rippled through his disparate minds. Had the death and destruction been for nothing? Could it all have been some vast and trivial posthuman *diversion*?

He wasn't sure whether to feel reassured or even more unsettled when the Archon added: "There will be conditions, of course . . ."

Palmer Horsfall rode with the crew of Bridgehead 4 into the outskirts of Bedlam, feeling like a fallen angel laying siege to an ancient holy city, half-buried in the sweeping sands of history. Years of fighting had led to this moment. Decades of calculated risk and martial savagery had brought her to the point where the final sword thrust was about to fall through the heart of the conflict. There had been enough death and destruction. Soon, she hoped, it would end.

She stood on an observation deck as Bedlam's primary brightened ahead of them. Several other passengers watched with her: a motley collection of Naturals, Palmers, and exotic types sporting enlarged skulls, extra sense organs and limbs, or even more unusual body plans. The system's gas giant, Ah Kong, and a motley collection of planets were little more than specks at such a great distance. Space around the Catastrophe nanotech looked utterly empty. She suspected otherwise.

No one made a sound as a dozen angular shapes dropped camouflage to match orbits and exchange handshakes, their surfaces dusted with frozen oxygen and nitrogen. Horsfall felt as though her face was similarly frozen. Behind her cool, Earth-blue eyes, an ocean of grief lay pent up, straining for release.

One hundred and eighty years had passed since the fall of Sublime. She forced herself to bide her time still further, to listen to the advice of those better placed and equipped to comprehend the vastness of what they attempted. The whisper in her ear urged caution, and she listened as she always had.

"We know the Occlusion is still in there," said Chief Officer Metin of the *Khatangskiy Guba,* one of many former Palmer Cells conscripted and extensively modified for combat. Its components numbered in the hundreds, each a miniature version of the mighty war vessel she rode into battle. He spoke over the heavily encrypted ftl network designed specifically for the battle ahead; few people in Bridgehead 4 heard his words, apart from Horsfall. "The Catastrophe envelope has not been breached even once in the last fifty years. If Deangelis had sent so much as a pebble through, we'd have seen it."

Deangelis? she thought, momentarily confused. Isaac Deangelis was with the original Bridgehead on the far side of the system—or should have been, if things had gone according to plan. What was he doing inside the Catastrophe zone, mucking around with the entrance to Geodesica?

It took her an embarrassed second to remember that the Deangelis she knew had once been part of a larger being, the one currently still in charge of Bedlam. After so many years of fighting, she had become used to Exarchs in fragments, singletons cut off from their wholes by warfare, accidents, and suicides. She had forgotten that the rest of him still existed.

How did it feel for him, she wondered, to be coming home?

"I'm more concerned about other ships," she said over the same secure line. "Lurking in Ah Kong's mass shadow, perhaps."

"We've seen nothing," Metin replied. "The Catastrophe nanotech has become a little denser down the years, and so has the interference it radiates, but beyond that there's been little change."

She accepted Palmer Metin's analysis of the situation without question. The ones with the most to lose if control over Geodesica slipped through their fingers, the Palmers had kept a close watch on all three systems in which entrances to Geodesica—and therefore Catastrophe—had appeared. While the rebellion took shape around them, a select few of her former peers had guarded the entrances closely, noting anything that changed about the giant bubbles of hostile nanotech, no matter how large or small. That nothing much *had* changed in Sublime, Bedlam, and Familiar suggested that the Archon had either grossly underestimated the rebellion or already laid on sufficient measures to repel its attackers.

"Should we issue an ultimatum?" she asked. They had discussed this many times before. Even though the Exarchs called the shots, the Palmers looked to her for guidance.

The Archon knows why we're here, said Elderton. The ex-Exarch's voice echoed out of loudspeakers and implants all across the fleet, a split second behind the whispering in Horsfall's mind. *The time for diplomacy has long passed.*

By second-generation tangler from the far side of the fleet, Deangelis confirmed his readiness and his willingness to act immediately.

"I agree with Jane," he said. "We've tried reasoning with the Archon in the past, to no avail. Let's get on with what we came here to do."

Guiltily, Horsfall remembered the Archon in Palmer Flast's body, on Prime One seventy-two years earlier. Some time later, when she and Flast had next come face-to-face, she had flinched at the sight of him and been unable to explain her nervousness. He clearly had no memory of his possession by their mutual enemy. Or if he had, he kept it very well concealed, as she did from those closest to her.

You should be glad that I don't think of us as enemies, the Archon had said. *I have no wish to see this grand venture end in ashes . . .*

"Go," she said. "Let's finish it."

All around her, encircling the system where the first vague plans of rebellion had been aired, thrusters burned and electromagnetic cloaks fell away. Giant vessels broke orbit with the sluggishness of mountains—mountains that would accelerate steadily all the way into the heart of the system, where not even the voracious appetite of Catastrophe could prevent them from penetrating deeply into the Archon's stronghold. Once within the kill zone, they would perform a variety of functions, depending on what they found there. They could broadcast telemetry to the rest of the fleet; they could self-destruct by collapsing into singularities, taking substantial chunks of the nanotech with them; or they could mount a more conventional campaign should the opportunity arise. The laboring of their engines as their long journeys began sent space-time vibrating for millions of kilometers. Even at such an expenditure of energy, they would take days to reach the front line.

Horsfall adjusted her internal clock so that those days would pass in just hours. By that new tempo, the more stately movement of other vessels became apparent, Bridgehead 4 among them. A school of silver darts slid across the sky ahead of it, angling around to meet and merge with a second attack group. Messages flashed back and forth along the command channels as AIs and humans alike confirmed the order to attack. Horsfall looked around, finding herself alone on the observation deck. Her silent companions had melted away into the shadows like ghosts.

"This had better do the job," she said, thinking of the megatons of ordnance bearing down on the system before her. She felt dangerously light-headed, as though free-falling through an atmosphere of nitrous oxide.

If it doesn't, no one could reproach us for failing to give it our best shot. Elderton's voice was silkily persuasive. *"Persistent" doesn't do us justice.*

"'Bloody-minded,' perhaps."

How about "obsessive"?

She half-laughed. "Definitely."

"I'm picking up an anomaly," said Metin's voice from the *Khatangskiy Guba*. "A small vessel just breached the border of the kill zone."

Horsfall's strange elation instantly evaporated as her clock returned to normal. "From the inside?"

"That's correct. The drive signature is not one of ours."

How could it be? she wanted to ask. "Course?"

"Out-system."

"Where's the nearest recon drone?"

"Two light-hours out. I'll try to get something closer. This thing is accelerating hard."

Horsfall's eyes narrowed. A two-hour lag meant that *right now* the mystery ship could be a significant distance from where they had seen it. She didn't like the thought of anything gumming up the works just as the attack got under way.

A voice burst out over the old tangler channels, hailing her in person.

"Palmer Horsfall," said the Archon. "You took longer to get here than I expected. I'm sending you a package. Do treat it carefully."

"Tell me what's in it," she responded as evenly as she could, "or I'll shoot it out of the sky."

"An emissary—the Exarch of Lut-Deangelis system, no less. He will attempt to find a diplomatic solution."

"Why?" she asked, suspicion and uncertainty curdling in her gut. The Archon's voice was as syrupy as it had been the last time. "The time for talking is over."

"You disappoint me again. Humanity thrives on communication. It's when we stop talking that tragedies occur, wouldn't you say?"

She ignored the question. Instead, to Palmer Metin, she said: "When that ship comes in range, destroy it immediately."

"Is that really necessary?" he responded.

"If the Archon has anything genuine to say, it can tell us through the tangler. Why send Deangelis except to do its dirty work? It has to be a trick."

I agree, said Elderton.

A chorus of support came in from the Exarchs scattered throughout the attack fleet. Only Isaac Deangelis, on the far side of the system, remained silent.

"Very well." Metin sounded reluctant but resigned now the decision had been taken out of his hands. "As soon as I've got a clear opportunity, I'll take it out."

Horsfall understood his misgivings. Even now, after decades of war, killing didn't come easily. And nor should it, she reminded herself.

I kill only in moments of absolute necessity, the Archon had told her.

On that point they agreed totally.

Decrypt REMEMBRANCE (JANE ELDERTON):
> Don't, Isaac.

Decrypt REMEMBRANCE (ISAAC DEANGELIS):
> Don't what?

Decrypt REMEMBRANCE (JANE ELDERTON):
> I know what you're thinking.

Decrypt REMEMBRANCE (ISAAC DEANGELIS):
> What am I thinking?

Decrypt REMEMBRANCE (JANE ELDERTON):
> The same thing *I'd* be thinking if this was Sublime and part of me was coming out of the hole at us.

Decrypt REMEMBRANCE (ISAAC DEANGELIS):
> So what's the problem? This is a golden opportunity to gain intelligence about the enemy's intentions and disposition. If I can rendezvous with that fragment and integrate with it—

Decrypt REMEMBRANCE (JANE ELDERTON):
> This isn't up for discussion, Isaac. It's not going to happen.

Decrypt REMEMBRANCE (ISAAC DEANGELIS):
> Jane, I'm not stupid. I know the risks.

Decrypt REMEMBRANCE (JANE ELDERTON):
> You *are* stupid if you think we're going to let you do it. This is a golden opportunity for the Archon too, don't forget. If it gets *you* it'll have all our strengths and weaknesses laid out on a plate. We can't allow you to take that risk on our behalf.

Decrypt REMEMBRANCE (ISAAC DEANGELIS):
> Would you shoot me down if I tried?

Decrypt REMEMBRANCE (JANE ELDERTON):
> Yes.

Decrypt REMEMBRANCE (ISAAC DEANGELIS):
> I don't believe you.

Decrypt REMEMBRANCE (JANE ELDERTON):
> Please don't put it to the test, Isaac.

Ends.

Rudra-Deangelis's hands shook as Elderton killed the private link between them. Resentment and something very much like fury boiled in him. How dare she summarily decide what he could and couldn't do? He wasn't answerable to her. What gave her the right to make such decisions on behalf of the fleet—a deranged, suicidal Exarch who hadn't thought any further than the coming attack? If he took his plan to the combined leaders of the rebellion and sought their opinion—

No. He knew what they would say. They would side with her because she was right, and he knew it. His judgment was clouded when it came to his higher self. He yearned for connection with even a single fragment of the rest of him, he ached for it. After so many years of crippling truncation, to be so close to himself and yet denied completion—

It hurt.

Concentrate on the attack, he told himself. *Ignore that hours-old blip and get on with the plan. Don't let the Archon throw you as it knows it can. Don't do its work for it.*

Like a swarm of sharks circling a lonely swimmer, the fleets of the Arc Circuit tightened around Bedlam's inner system. Drones and decoys went first, testing for defenses and hidden weapons caches. He wasn't aware of any outside the Catastrophe kill zone, but the Archon had had plenty of time to make preparations. Even before Palmer Metin and the *Khatangskiy Guba* had arrived, it could have laid down all manner of traps.

The Archon's emissary came within range of Metin's attack force and drew fire immediately. The small craft avoided every attempt to destroy it but didn't once retaliate. Instead, it changed course with unbelievable acceleration and headed up, out of the ecliptic, too fast for the Palmers' pursuit vessels to keep up.

Deangelis told himself again to ignore the fleeing ship. He forced his attention down and inward, to where the rippling nanotech boundary separated the Archon's territory from the rest of the universe.

That boundary flexed as though in the grip of a sudden storm. Shining globules spat out at the incoming fleet—many thousands of them aimed at all portions of the sky. Alarms began to ring, even though impact with the virulent globules lay many hours in the future.

The first shots had been fired in Bedlam for over a hundred and fifty years.

The end of the war, Rudra-Deangelis hoped, had begun.

The image of Ah Kong and its nascent rings shrank behind the high-powered singleship. As soon as he cleared the bulk of the clutter, Bedlam-Deangelis activated the second-generation VOID drive units and surged so far ahead of his pursuers that his light would take hours to arrive. He imagined their frustration and puzzlement—no one outside of Sol had witnessed a demonstration of the VOID-2 drive systems before—but felt no satisfaction. They had fired on him, an emissary of peace!

Now that he was free of his higher self, he could consider his situation clearly and in the open, free of the necessary double-think that being so close to the Archon demanded. The need for revenge burned hot and fast inside him. The loss of his colony would not go unpunished.

Yet an echo of the Archon's certainty remained. It had a plan, or at least a core concern that had come to seem almost reasonable down the years. And now this offer of peace, which had been so casually rejected. What did that say about the Great Enemy against which the rest of humanity railed?

Bedlam-Deangelis spared no effort from the new drive systems to sweep around the converging attack fleets and approach from behind. He had to deliver the message before the firing started in earnest. That was his duty—to himself if no one else, as a combatant on both sides of the conflict. If he didn't move fast, he would literally be at war with himself. Whoever won, he would lose.

Only as he jockeyed closer, dodging defensive stabs designed to keep him at bay, did he notice that the Catastrophe's first-line defenses had already been activated.

No time, he breathed to himself. *No time!*

Abandoning all pretense of subtlety, he rammed forward to confront the massive ship the Archon had told him Palmer Horsfall occupied.

"Listen to me!" he broadcast on all channels, with enough power to punch through all attempts at jamming. "The Archon sent me to work out a deal. You can have everything you want: independence, compensation, reconstruction. It'll give you that, if you'll just talk to me!"

"The offer is meaningless," said the Palmer. "The Archon has lost. We don't need its complicity and we never have. Why would we make a deal with it *now*?"

"It hasn't lost," he replied, relieved that they were talking at last but afraid that it might have come too late. Several dozen interceptors were converging rapidly on his position. "You have no conception of its powers. The Archon has had a century and a half to prepare for this. Do you think it's been sitting on its hands all this time? Are you not seeing how fast this ship flies?"

"You can bluff all you like. I know the Archon hasn't tried to talk to us before. What's changed to make it want to negotiate now—except that we're here and there's nothing it can do about it? Its Reapers are destroyed. Its allies are gone or turned to our side. It's alone, apart from you and your fancy toy. I don't care what the Archon's been doing these last decades. It can't possibly stand up against the entire Exarchate and hope to survive."

"But it can! You don't understand. It wants to talk not because you've won or it's lost, but because you're *here*. Your revolution simply doesn't matter to it. All it cares about is Geodesica." He took a deep breath and put every iota of sincerity his voice could carry down the link. "The Archon has authorized me to negotiate a full handover of the Exarchate to your forces on two conditions only: that Sol remains independent, and Geodesica is undisturbed. Everything else is yours. What do you say?"

"No deal."

"Horsfall, wait." He ignored urgent telemetry reports warning him of the approaching hostiles. "At least think about it! We're talking a complete cessation of hostilities, a total handover of territory. How many lives will you save if the war ends this instant? How much energy will be diverted toward more peaceful pursuits? Consider what you're committing your forces to by pushing ahead with this attack. If you lose, you lose everything!"

"We're not going to lose," Horsfall told him.

Bedlam-Deangelis could talk no longer. Taking the helm of his ship, he swung it out of the firing line of the converging interceptors and concentrated solely on getting away. The rebel ships were fast and determined, their reflexes honed by years of combat. His ship might be faster, but he didn't have their edge. He had to devote his entire attention to the task or die in the attempt.

Missiles exploded in his path, tearing vicious holes in spacetime the ship strained not to fall foul of. It rattled and shook as long-range field effects snatched like claws for purchase. He returned fire only when no other option remained, and he made a break for clear space at the first opportunity. As the vacuum flattened into something like its empty state, he kicked in the VOID-2 units and streaked away.

"Damn them." There were no words for the frustration he felt. He was just one fragment of an Exarch caught between two massive forces. What could he possibly do to stop them colliding? There was no way he could ask the Archon for advice. He could only persist and hope that reason won out.

Turning his ship around, he dove back into the system's spreading light cone and watched in despair as the signs of battle swept over him. It had started an hour ago, and he hadn't even realized.

• • •

Palmer Horsfall still stood on the observation deck of Bridgehead 4, only now that the shields were up and the view obscured, the window ahead of her contained a complicated mess of flat and 3-D images. A third focused on the surface of the kill zone, as rapid-fire droplets and jets of nanotech shot out at the approaching forces. Some looked deeper, at the primary star hidden in the glowing golden shell, tracking strange flares and convulsions sweeping across the stellar atmosphere. A quarter monitored Ah Kong, since the gas giant was the obvious place to hide a retaliatory force. Nothing had stirred in that area as yet, even among the rubble left behind by its two destroyed moons, now curving in regular arcs around the equator. Remembering the nanotech her Deangelis had dropped into the swirling atmosphere years ago, she was happy to keep it that way.

The rest of the screens caught glimpses of battles happening too far away, too quickly, and at too low a resolution for her to follow. She deliberately pulled back from the details and studied the broader picture. *There* a front of rebel forces encountered and neutralized a stream of Catastrophe nanotech. *There* a mountainous ramship, still hours away from hitting the edge of the kill zone, had been infected and burned like a small star. And *there* a survey drone stumbled across a nest of conventional weapons that spat and snarled furiously across the sky.

All left clouds of gas and debris in their wake, lit by flashes of radiation from other points in the battle. Miniature nebulae of hydrogen glowed in visible light, except where the leading edges of shocked gases flared them into X-rays. Hot hydrocarbon clouds glowed in infrared. Ultraviolet lasers stripped electrons from everything they encountered; those electrons were in turn caught up in violent magnetic field fluxes, which made them radioenergetic. The system was a mess.

The situation only worsened when the rams finally hit their target. Several thousand bullets moving in slow motion toward a very large golden apple, they had promised all manner of chaos, and they delivered in spades. The starscape disappeared as wave after wave of brilliant yellow radiation swept outward from the kill zone. Battle telemetry—limited by light-speed data-collection systems where ftl links were severed or not available—traced hundreds of lines creeping into the heart of Bedlam's forbidden territory. Reports emerged of mostly empty space, apart from a handful of small installations in a similar orbit to the one Bedlam's primary habitat had once occupied. None of the objects looked familiar; all had clearly been built since the Catastrophe had cut the system off from the rest of the Arc Circuit. In one of them, Horsfall assumed, was the Occlusion, the entrance to Geodesica that had brought so much mayhem to the aptly named system.

Bridgehead 4 shook palpably as gravitational waves rolled by and through it. Horsfall noted the retreat of a large percentage of the ramships into collapsed matter. Gaping holes appeared in the surface of the kill zone. Empty space beckoned beyond those holes.

"Go!" she shouted unnecessarily to the forces at her disposal, urging them forward, faster. "Go, go, go!" It seemed crazy to her that, after decades of planning, years spent gathering around Bedlam, and days trailing the ramships on their hopeless plunges, it might all come down to the minutes or seconds those black holes in the kill zone lasted. Bridgehead 4 surged at the head of a long, stressed-continuum wake as its VOID drives struggled to deform the matter-filled space around it. She was distantly aware of the tiny ship sent by the Archon still buzzing around, dodging nanotech and rebel fire alike, but she paid it no heed. Its mission was irrelevant now the battle was under way.

A bright flash seemed to shine through the suddenly dimmed screens and through the bulkheads surrounding her as though they were nothing more than vapor. She staggered backward, feeling Bridgehead 4 reel as something passed by—a terrible beam that flickered and stuttered like a faulty fluorescent tube. When and where it shone, it left space shredded and matter boiling. Behind it, behind the Swiss cheese surface of the kill zone, the sun burned a piercingly bright blue.

"What in the Dark—?" she managed as a significant percentage of the rebel fleet near her instantly vaporized. Hard radiation seared the outside of Bridgehead 4, stripping a good meter off its last-resort blast shell.

The sun is lasing, said Elderton with awe in her voice.

The flickering beam turned with awful implacability onto another section of the fleet. A wall of neutrinos followed hard X-rays, backed up in turn by slower particles, deadly in their own way. Carrier asteroids vanished like insects in a plasma jet, stripped back to atoms—perhaps even further—by the awful energies at the Archon's disposal. It turned again. Bridgehead 2 disappeared with a white-noise howl, taking half of Lazarus Hails with it.

Horsfall had read about polar jets around black holes and exploding stars. She had never imagined taking a star and deliberately torturing it, tying its magnetic fields in knots so that a jet formed, and lased, and moved to hit specific targets. What sort of technology—what sort of *mind*—built and used such weapons?

They couldn't fight this. That was her first real thought as the spectacle continued. Even Catastrophe was dying under the stellar onslaught. Vast swathes of the nanotech turned black in its wake, tracing squiggles and dashes through the kill zone. Under other circumstances, Horsfall would have urged her people to exploit those breaks in the system's primary defense. But now, without the right sort of defenses to withstand the lasing or an attack plan to stop it at its source—

She would be sending them to their death. Not *possible* or even *probable* death, but a demise as certain as putting a gun to their heads and killing them herself.

She steeled herself to issue the recall order. They had waited over a century and a half. The survivors could regroup and try again later. Dying now would achieve nothing.

"Wait!"

The word came from two different directions but one voice: the Archon's envoy and her own Isaac Deangelis had spoken at the same time.

"You've made good on your threat," she told the envoy, unable to hide the bitterness she felt. "Is that what you're going to tell me?"

"No," he said. He sounded breathless, upset. "I didn't know this was going to happen. I swear." As he spoke, the stellar laser shut down. In its wake, vast prominences rose and fell over the stricken star's surface: tsunamis that could have swallowed Prime One whole and barely noticed. "Thank God," he breathed.

"Don't listen to him!" This came from the other Deangelis, in Bridgehead 1, lurking around the cluttered gravity well of Ah Kong. "We're not finished yet!"

The envoy ignored him. "The offer is still on the table, the same terms as before. You can have your sovereignty, but you can't have Geodesica or Sol. Take it or leave it."

"We're fighting for your independence, too," Horsfall shot back to him. "You do realize that, don't you? Independence and justice. We're fighting one person here—two, if we have to count you. The Archon is killing thousands. For what? To keep Geodesica to itself."

"Is that such a bad thing? Would it be so awful if you just let it have it?"

"Of course it would be! If we let the Archon have its way, we've lost. Yes, it's promising us our independence, but for how long? Once it's worked out the maze, it'll spread throughout the galaxy and hem us in on every side. Then where will we stand? We'll be back where we started, or worse." She couldn't see the envoy; the transmission came over audio channels only; but she sneered at her image of him: no different from the Deangelis in Bridgehead 1, but alone and isolated with the moral ground sinking fast under him. He couldn't possibly expect them to make a deal now. Fight to their deaths, perhaps. Retreat and fight later, more likely. But hand the Archon the weapon that would destroy the Exarchate forever? Not ever.

"Keep him talking," her Deangelis told her over the private link from Bridgehead 1. "I know what to do."

Sensors on Bridgehead 4 registered a launch from its older sibling: a tiny, needlelike craft angling away and down toward the bloated gas giant. She barely had time to acknowledge it when the envoy was talking again.

"If the Archon wanted you dead," he said, "we wouldn't be having this discussion. It'd still be firing. What does that tell you about its motives?"

"That they don't make any fucking sense," she said, distracted by her Deangelis's actions but forcing herself to concentrate.

"Do they need to? The Archon stands one rung on the evolutionary ladder up from us. It thinks differently, sees differently."

"That's irrelevant. I can't trust something I don't understand."

"It can't understand you, if that makes you feel any better. It has trouble seeing at our level, on timescales that for us would be equivalent to a breath or a blink. That's why it's sent me to talk to you. That's why it uses Exarchs rather than govern the Exarchate itself. It sees the long view, and it knows that Geodesica isn't good for us."

"But war is?"

"In terms of lives and resources, the Exarchate will survive in one form or another regardless of what happens during this rebellion. That is a given in the short run. In the long run, the Exarchate will go the way of all institutions, all governments. From the Archon's point of view, you're fighting over something that simply isn't justified. It's pointless. Here at the starting point of the great human journey, why squabble over who takes the first steps? We should be concentrating on not tripping up."

"Fine, but we're all in this journey together. How do you think the people who lived in Sublime, Bedlam, and Familiar felt about being trodden on?"

"Good-bye," said Deangelis.

She was thrown for a moment, until she realized that the voice didn't come from the envoy. Horsfall had temporarily forgotten the tiny craft and its passenger on the far side of the system. She couldn't find it for a second, then caught it entering the gas giant's turbulent atmosphere. His broadcast came thick with static, transmitted through powerful magnetic fields from the singleship to Bridgehead 1, then relayed by tangler to her location.

"When Melilah comes back," he said, "tell her I'm sorry. I hope this goes some way toward making amends."

"Deangelis! What the hell do you think you're doing?"

The ship vanished into thick clouds. Her question went unanswered.

I suggest you move our ships away from Ah Kong, said Elderton into her mind.

Horsfall agreed and issued the order immediately, thinking of nanotech and last resorts.

"What's coming?" she asked. "What is he going to do?"

I don't know. Elderton sounded as shaken as she felt. *I honestly don't know.*

Space-time wakes traced radial lines away from the gas giant as the Archon's envoy squawked for attention and went unanswered.

Decrypt REMEMBRANCE (JANE ELDERTON):
> What are you doing?

Decrypt REMEMBRANCE (ISAAC DEANGELIS):
> What I have to do.

Decrypt REMEMBRANCE (JANE ELDERTON):
> But—

Decrypt REMEMBRANCE (ISAAC DEANGELIS):
> This isn't up for discussion, Jane. You wanted an end to it? Well, here it comes.

Decrypt REMEMBRANCE (JANE ELDERTON):
> Isaac, wait—

Decrypt REMEMBRANCE (ISAAC DEANGELIS):

> My tangler's decohering; I'm losing your signal. Promise me one thing, before I go. Don't ever forget this, Jane. Don't ever forget what it means to play with the dolls.

Carrier signal lost.

He had lied to Elderton, of course. His tangler was experiencing no dysfunction, even in the extreme environment of the gas giant's atmosphere. The time for talking had simply passed, as Horsfall had told the Archon. It was time for action.

Rudra-Deangelis killed the thrusters and free-fell a third of the way into Ah Kong's gaseous interior. Without the force of acceleration pushing him back into the seat, his descent felt almost peaceful. The noise of thickening atmosphere rushing by would have instantly deafened him had it not been dimmed by shielding and the singleship's morphing hull. He heard it as a chorus of ululating whistles, all at slightly different pitches; alien voices singing an elegy in a language he couldn't understand. It was weirdly beautiful. A fitting accompaniment for his mission.

He was the trigger of a weapon loaded and cocked one hundred and seventy years earlier. The time had come to fire it, and there was no room for second thoughts.

The ship's elegant needle shape changed to a sphere as the pressure mounted. Friction increased, too, and he was soon forced to reactivate the thrusters. A rhythmic growl joined the chorus, giving it an urgent, almost martial air.

He faced his death without fear or anger, only a faint disappointment that he wouldn't see the end of the war. Not this version of him, anyway. His higher self still existed, even if it was in the thrall of the Archon. Someone remained to look after Bedlam and its sole survivor, should she ever return. He couldn't have done this without that knowledge behind him. And without the single message of encouragement the envoy had sent him, he might still have hesitated.

"Do it," the fragment had urged him as the Archon's dreadful weapon razed the rebel forces across the system. "Whatever you have up your sleeve, do it now."

That brief touch—a pale shadow of the connection he still yearned for, after so long alone—had been enough to convince him. He would not stand by and watch more innocent people being slaughtered. Not when he had the means to end it within his grasp.

Desperate situations required desperate solutions.

The singleship dived. Deeper and deeper he went. Gases congealed into liquids and surged around him. The nanotech he had seeded in the gas giant during his escape with Elderton and Horsfall, so long ago, had bred and sunk deep into the heart of the mighty planet. There they had assembled into devices that, alone, would not make a great deal of difference. As was so often the case with nanotech, its strength lay in numbers. The Palmers knew that fact well: one microscopic drive unit couldn't propel a feather, but several thousand of them could take a bird to the stars.

Similarly, one antihydrogen atom didn't amount to much of a firework, but several trillion of them, all bursting out of their magnetic bottles at once . . .

He detected their unique signatures on approach to the nethermost depths of Ah Kong's atmosphere. Metallic hydrogen congealed around the singleship, eroding its shielding and sending a sustained, white-noise roar through his bones. He didn't have long now. The rest of the universe had vanished into static, drowned out by the energies of the planet's core. The planet itself seemed to be attacking him, as though it knew what approached and resisted as best it could.

Gathering the shreds of the singleship around him, he focused on the one task remaining to him. One final message, and it would all be over. At his command, the antihydrogen traps would release their charges and begin a cascade of destruction. It would begin at his location, on the face of Ah Kong pointing away from the Occlusion station he had glimpsed behind the deadly veil of Catastrophe. The fiery shock wave would spread steadily outward as matter and antimatter annihilated each other, causing the failure of containment bottles farther from the center. A burning ring would form and spread, hurling matter upward from deep within the heart of Ah Kong. Stratospheric clouds would bulge and shred.

Ah Kong would not survive, not in its present form. By the time the explosion had spread all the way around the planet, its outer layers would be mostly gone. All that would remain was the core, a fiery cinder bigger than the Earth, given a tremendous hammerblow by the initial explosion, the primary kick that set the ball rolling—literally.

Deangelis tensed to broadcast the signal, to pull the trigger.

A voice spoke to him, out of the deafening roar of the hydrogen ocean.

"Bold and brave," said the Archon. "I'm proud of you, Isaac."

"No!" he screamed, broadcasting the signal before his creator could interfere with either him or it.

The syncopated sound wave propagated through the medium outside much faster than it would through air or water, or even steel.

He had just enough time to think that the Archon—if it had come this far—could have stopped him at any point during his fall.

Then the first of the traps opened on receiving the signal, and his world exploded into light—

—the brilliant, hard light of atomic annihilation. It hurt like looking at the sun through naked eyes. Bedlam-Deangelis gaped as the dark side of Ah Kong literally bulged. Lightning flashed around the bright puncture point of the first explosion. Through fifty thousand kilometers of atmosphere, a growing fire burned.

Loud electromagnetic screeches—the sound of molecules torn asunder—all but drowned out the babble of the rebel fleet. Voices flashed back and forth, demanding explanation. Most of them assumed that the Archon was behind this violation, too. Horsfall's voice rose up out of the chaos, assuring them that it wasn't. He knew that, too. It was Rudra-Deangelis, the version of him on their side.

A steaming tail of gas reached out from the rear of the stricken gas giant, propelled by the force of the explosions below. It jetted out into the void, not aimed at anything in particular. It obviously wasn't a weapon as the stellar laser had been.

A by-product, then, he thought. An *exhaust.*

Ponderously, with all the grace of a trillion-trillion-ton elephant, Ah Kong broke orbit.

All hopes of reconnecting with Rudra-Deangelis vanished.

"What are we going to do now?" he asked the Archon, hoping his signal could punch through the noise with his tangler. His ship stood well back from the rebel fleets as they reassembled away from the burning jovian. His loyalties were as torn as ever, caught in a tug of war between his creator and higher self, and the people his lost sibling had served.

The reply came in less than a second, arriving in the form of a ream of data projecting Ah Kong's trajectory, given certain assumptions about thrust and duration of the burn. The energy involved was enormous, but it would take a lot to bring the planet up to speed. Deangelis's first thought was that the sun was its target: an attempt to disrupt the stellar atmosphere and the laser with it. But the course would miss the sun by a large margin.

The planet was, in fact, aimed at the entrance to Geodesica and the huddle of stations around it. It was aimed at *him.*

"What good will that do?" he asked. ETA wasn't for almost a day. He and the Archon would have plenty of time to move out of its path before impact, and the stellar laser could burn to shift the planet's course, just to make sure. The beam couldn't compete with the power of the explosions currently wracking the world's thick atmosphere, but a relatively small nudge, early in the piece, would be enough.

The rebels could ride the remains of the gas giant through the outer layers of Catastrophe, though. Its sheer mass, and the shield it offered against the laser, might give them the edge they had lacked before. If they could get close enough that the Archon couldn't fire without hitting itself . . .

"I want you to repeat my conditions," the Archon said. "This time, tell them that it's not an offer at all, but an ultimatum. They *will* have independence; they will *never* possess Geodesica. That is my final word on the subject."

"You're going to *make* them take independence?" He couldn't believe what he was hearing. Sometimes it felt as though he and the Archon were fighting a very different battle. "What will that prove?"

The Archon chuckled. "Prove? Nothing, my friend. Life is not an argument, or an equation with an equals sign at the end. What ends here today is not the Exarchate or my personal empire. It's something that was for a while and soon will be no longer. It's change."

Bedlam-Deangelis gave up on understanding, for the time being. The middle of a battlefield wasn't the place for a philosophical discussion. Cutting fast through an expanding debris cloud, he flagged Palmer Horsfall and signaled that he needed to talk.

No tears, Horsfall thought. It was an observation, not a resolution, by one death-hardened warrior over the demise of another. Deangelis's sacrifice touched her deeply. His pyre burned brightest among the wrecked ships and rubble, but it wasn't the only one.

Behind her eyes, she could feel Jane Elderton silently weeping.

"What do you want now?" she asked the Archon's emissary.

"The third time is the charm," he said. "I'm offering you independence once more. Will you please just take it?"

"Sure we'll take it—but without any conditions. Don't you see what's bearing down on you? Don't you understand that we're not going home until we've got what we came for?"

She kept a close eye on the sun as she spoke, waiting for the blast of energy that would destroy her and the crew of Bridgehead 4. That it didn't come she took as a hopeful sign. Perhaps the shifting of the gas giant had disturbed the sun's magnetosphere enough to render the laser inoperable.

"The Archon—" Deangelis hesitated, as though listening to something out of earshot. "It asks that you stop confusing justice with Geodesica. It wants you to know that Geodesica would never give you what you desire. You think it would, but that's wrong. Geodesica would destroy you, the Archon says. You're not ready for it—"

"Sol obviously thinks *it* is," Horsfall snapped.

Again a slight pause before Deangelis continued. "No, the Archon says that Sol doesn't need it. Every exit will be sealed from the outside, so no one can enter. The Architects will find another way to get around. It says—" Deangelis broke off at Horsfall's low, disbelieving laugh. "It says that enough damage has been done already."

"Are you saying," she said, "that this has all been *for our own good*? That the Archon is telling us what to do because we're too stupid to work it out for ourselves? Of all the barefaced, arrogant, patronizing—"

She didn't finish the sentence. On a dozen screens, staggered due to light-speed and information lags, the expanding white ring on Ah Kong flared to new heights. The flash was so bright the displays cast her shadow onto the wall behind her. She raised a hand to shield her eyes as, with a soundless detonation, the gas giant began to expand all over. Its atmosphere, already disturbed by the hole blown out of it on its night side, puckered and dimpled everywhere, borne upward and outward by a series of titanic pressure waves rising from the core.

Hydrogen, heated to fusion temperatures and under incredible pressure, began to fuse. For a brief moment, the reaction was self-sustaining. The gas giant's atmosphere lit up like a light bulb as pressure waves crossed and recrossed over its bloating face. A new star shone in Bedlam's sky.

The ships of the rebel fleet recoiled. Horsfall gaped at the spectacle, thinking: *Now we're* really *screwed.* The chain reaction couldn't last long; Ah Kong's atmosphere would soon be blown apart and the fire would falter and fail. But as a demonstration of power, blowing up a gas giant was hard to beat.

Look! Jane Elderton shouted in the dark recesses of her head. Horsfall felt her eyes physically dragged away from the unnatural sight. *Look!*

As though cast into shadow by the brilliance of the temporary new sun, the pockmarked, golden glow of Catastrophe began to go out. Patches of darkness appeared and spread, edges meeting and joining and forming oceans of black that raced faster than the speed of light—since they weren't material things at all; not even information—from one side of Bedlam to the other.

The inner system lay bare before them. Horsfall reached out a hand as though to steady herself, unsure whether to cut her losses and run for the Dark or send someone in to investigate this new phenomenon.

The decision was made for her as, tracking much faster than an Exarchate ship could travel, a single dot raced inward, shouting at the peak of its power.

+14

Geodesica interior: plus 211 hours

"I have an announcement," said Deangelis to Melilah. "As of now, we're officially lost."

"You're sure?" She sounded sleepy.

"Well, I certainly don't know where we are; that amounts to the same thing. I've sent a steady stream of drones into the tunnels surrounding us, and they've found nothing of use. I can keep sending them, but I refuse to believe there's a chance of finding an exit to Bedlam or Sublime or anywhere else in the Exarchate. Geodesica is too big and we're too deep inside it. We can't go back. I have to stop fighting that conclusion. It's unhealthy for both of us."

"Then what do we do?"

One of his instruments watched her from the canopy near superior spike #2. Half of the *Cowell* hung anchored in the trees, remodeled into a rounded, asymmetrical habitat for two people. The other half was, supposedly, still docked with the replicator above. Melilah lay on a bed facing directly out onto the cave forest, dressed in a gown as blue as the flowers blooming on the creepers below. Her right arm dangled loosely in thin air. Her expression was disarmingly blank.

"I don't know," he said, wondering if she was depressed. Her mood had been difficult to read since the early grief and rage over the destruction of Bedlam had passed. "We don't have many options open to us."

"Wander forever, find an exit at random, or stay here." She nodded. "What if we get a three-way tie?"

That he didn't know either. "I'm sorry if I woke you," he said. "I just wanted you to know."

"That's okay. Thanks for keeping us posted."

She retracted her dangling arm and rolled onto her side, turning her back to the forest and the instrument watching her. Deangelis lingered a moment, wishing there was something else he could say, then moved on to give Palmer Eogan the same news.

How much longer can I keep this up? he asked himself.

It was the second night of the seventh day. The cavern's artificial sun followed a complex seventeen-hour cycle. Two hours of full dark followed five hours of light, after which came an hour of twilight and another hour of dark. Three hours of full light and another two of twilight completed the cycle, which Deangelis assumed was designed to imitate the light levels on a world with multiple suns. Or maybe it, too, was another symptom of age.

—YOU THINK ME OLD, said the voice of the cavern. The sentence wasn't pitched as a question.

"Yes, I do. How old *are* you, exactly?"

—I AM A CHILD COMPARED TO GEODESICA.

Deangelis didn't push any harder. He had become accustomed to the voice's evasion when confronted by direct questions. The trick, he had learned, was to let it talk. Set a rough course for the conversation and it would navigate of its own accord. Trying to force a destination upon it only sent them in the opposite direction.

"Tell me again why this farce is necessary," he said when he had had much the same conversation with Eogan, on one side of the cavern, as he had with Melilah on the other.

So what happens next, Deangelis? What's the right thing to do?

There's no hurry to do anything. We have plenty of time to consider the possibilities before picking the one that suits us.

Time? Yes. No shortage of that in here . . .

—ALL THEY HAVE IS EACH OTHER, said the voice. BUT THEY ARE NOT YET TRULY COGNIZANT OF THE FACT. WHEN THE TIME COMES, THEY WILL NEED TO KNOW. I AM PREPARING THEM FOR THAT MOMENT OF REALIZATION. THEY ARE TO EACH OTHER WHAT THE EXARCHATE IS TO SOL.

"A buffer, a shock absorber. Yes, you keep saying that. But you're deceiving them. They think they're talking to each other—"

—AND IN EFFECT THEY ARE. I PUT NOTHING IN THE MOUTHS OF THEIR DOPPELGANGERS THAT WASN'T IN THEIR ORIGINALS. THEY SAY WHAT NEEDS TO BE SAID, RATHER THAN REACTING IN PATTERNS THAT ARE DYSFUNCTIONAL AND COUNTERPRODUCTIVE.

"Humans don't always want to be functional or productive."

—I THINK THEY DO.

"And I think you're taking a big risk."

—THEN WE BOTH ARE, ISAAC.

That fact sat uncomfortably with Deangelis. He was undeniably an accessory to the crime of deceiving his companions; no matter how he twisted the facts, he couldn't escape that conclusion. But that didn't mean it was *wrong*. He just had to live with the decision—as the Archon, perhaps, did—and see how it panned out.

—AH, ACCEPTANCE: THE VIRTUE I CHAMPION MOST OF ALL. MUCH CAN BE LEARNED FROM STILLNESS.

This was the *other* route taken by the voice. When answers weren't forthcoming, it advised patience and nothing more. Occasionally it returned to the questions he had asked, only to twist away from them again, leaving him tangled up in more mysteries and half-facts. Sometimes Deangelis felt as though he was being led along like a donkey with a carrot in front of its nose.

The voice laughed, reading his thoughts.

—I HAVE EVERYTHING YOU NEED RIGHT HERE, ISAAC DEANGELIS. NO NEED TO FEAR ON THAT SCORE.

"I've yet to see the proof of it."

—NO? THEN PERHAPS YOU AREN'T LOOKING IN THE RIGHT PLACE.

Deangelis turned his senses away from the artificial sun—which he had convinced himself was the origin of the voice—and looked down at the surface. The spikes looked like eyes from directly above. Thousands of them, all staring back at him.

"But this is all there is," he said.

—EXACTLY, the voice replied. —EXACTLY.

We can't go back.

Melilah tried her best to sleep, but despite deep-breathing meditation, hormone and neurotransmitter adjustments, and even old-fashioned masturbation, it evaded her completely. She had slept too much lately. There was nothing else to do in the cavern except explore, and talk.

She didn't know Eogan's present location, and Deangelis had nothing but bad news. All talked out, she was running short of ideas.

Slow-timing remained an option, but to what end? To hide the pointlessness that would still be there when she returned to normality? She could accept making time fly when she had something to look forward to, but when her future held only emptiness it smacked of suicide.

And that, too, was an option. If she decided that life held no purpose, no hope, she could end it once and for all. The ability to self-euthanize came automatically with the antisenescence treatments she had undergone on Bedlam. She had never before considered using that ability—not once after Eogan had left her; not even when Bedlam had been destroyed—until now.

What would she miss? She focused on that question in the alien night of the cavern. What would miss *her*? Her home no longer existed; Yasu was dead; the Dark only knew how much time had passed since they'd entered Geodesica. There might be nothing left but ashes, or a bizarre posthuman empire in which she'd stand out as badly as a chimp at a diplomatic reception.

Try as she might, she couldn't justify either ending her life or freezing it until something better came along. She didn't want her existence to end; she simply wanted it to be *better*. There had to be a way to make that happen. She just hadn't thought of it yet.

"Isaac told me." Eogan's voice came from outside her open-air bedroom. She rolled over on the thin but perfectly supportive mattress to face him. He had swung down from above and hung suspended before her with a vine wrapped around his right forearm.

"Lord Greystoke, I presume."

He didn't smile. "Are you okay?"

She rolled onto her back. "You know I'm not."

"We can talk about it, if you want."

"Unless there's some amazing new angle you've come up with in the last few minutes, I don't think there's anything left to say."

"I think—"

"I don't want to think, either." She stared up at the ceiling, unsure whether she felt hollow or so full she might burst. She seemed to oscillate at random between the two states. "I'm tired."

The words didn't come from her lungs or her larynx. Her bones were talking. Her bones, and her heart.

Eogan swung into the room. She felt the mattress shift slightly to accommodate the pressure points of his knees, toes, and hands. Awkward in the darkness and the cramped space, he trod on her shin.

"Damn it," she said, reaching for him. "Come here."

She pulled him down next to her. He came cautiously at first, then gave in and lay beside her. He made no move to touch or hold her, and that was fine by her, at first.

They lay side by side, looking up into the darkness. She could smell him, hear his breathing, feel his warmth and the weight of him on the mattress tilting her slightly toward him. It occurred to her only then that this was the first time they had shared a bed under gravity. Every other time, one hundred and fifty years earlier, had been in Bedlam's low-gee environment.

She couldn't see him. The artifice of him, the masquerade, was easier to accept when its perfection couldn't be seen.

Going back wasn't an option. No possibility of that remained in her mind. Too much had happened; every last hope had been extinguished.

But they could go forward.

Aware that Deangelis's instruments prowled the branches around the Cell habitat, keeping a close eye on its charges and their safety, she instructed the *Cowell* to close her window and give them privacy.

They didn't make love. Eogan was glad about that. Nature drew people together during times of crisis, but that didn't apply to them. Only one of them was remotely Natural, and they had spent entirely too much time together in recent days as it was. When bodies coiled around each other in a Cell's embrace, physical proximity became a problem, not a panacea.

The closeness between them in the cavern was, however, something new and welcome. Together they had explored seven of the nineteen crystal-covered ecosystems. The spaces they explored were empty of alien remains, but the spaces themselves were interesting in their own subtle ways. In one, an explosive diversity of flowering plants held sway, while in another great sheets of moss reached down from the overgrowth to the light of the artificial sun. Nowhere did they see sign of animal or insect life, but the evidence that such might exist was ever present. In two forests Eogan had noted broken branches and stalks bent back as though something large had recently crawled through the branches. Plucked blossoms, disturbed fungi, tangled vines—the evidence was tantalizing, but never more than that. If anything shared the cave forests with them, it remained prudently out of sight.

The spaces between the superior spikes were wastelands of hard radiation and tangled gravity. Nothing lived there.

Alone, apart from Deangelis in his aerie, he and Melilah had had a chance to be lonely, to work out what they actually needed. At first he had thought he just wanted to say that he was sorry for what had happened in the past, but she had slammed that door before it ever opened. It truly was too late to make up for what he had done, and he would carry the guilt of it forever, whether he apologized or not. Did that, then, leave any basis for a relationship of any kind, be it friendship or something more? He wouldn't have thought so, but for the kiss they had stolen on Bedlam and the fact of them being together now. They could easily have taken separate habitats. It pleased him that they had not.

He realized, lying in the darkness next to her, that he had been measuring the relationship in terms of what she wanted, what her needs were. He had spent very little time considering his own feelings, whatever they were.

Did he still love Melilah Awad? *Could* he still love her, if the opportunity to do so arose? Did he want to go back there, face those issues again? Was that another part of his nature, one he couldn't fight?

A small voice whispered that many of the old issues were now irrelevant. How, after all, could Melilah remain tied to a colony that no longer existed?

He felt guilty for even considering the possibility that he might benefit from the destruction of her home. Bedlam might be gone, but the memory of it wasn't, and neither was the need to do something about that loss. The injustice of their situation was very real, and demanded a response.

What form that response would take, given their position inside Geodesica, he didn't know.

"Don't say anything," she said, belying her earlier comment about having nothing to say. "Just let me talk for a bit."

Eogan nodded. Her voice was soft, barely more than a whisper.

"I've been lying here, thinking about us. Well, actually, I've been mainly thinking about you. I've seen what you've become, now. I've seen your life since you left. Does it horrify me? Do I feel like I've lost you because of it? Yes—to both—but I've always known that to be a gut reaction. It's my phobia talking. I've had a chance to see what lies beyond the Palmer, and I'm beginning to understand that it's really you in there, not some ghastly fraud. You're Dominic Eogan, and you're Palmer Eogan at the same time. You can have one and the other; the latter doesn't cancel out the former."

The relief he felt at her words surprised him. He knew them to be true, but he had needed her to understand. He couldn't open up his skull to show her his brain and point to the parts that made him who he was, and say: "See? Still me." It didn't work like that, and not just because his brain wasn't in his skull anymore. It was in his chest, roughly where his heart used to be, and received data from his senses via means more efficient than any cellular nervous system. Instead of a heart, his body employed a myriad of miniature rotary pumps to circulate the fluid in his veins. Parts of his body didn't even need blood. They were fueled and maintained by other means.

Showing any of this to Melilah would make things worse, not better. The only way to convince her that he wasn't a monster was to be himself, and trust that she would come to accept him that way. Older and hopefully wiser, but still him.

"You know what?" she went on. "I've realized something else. All this time I've been worried about who or what you are, and I've completely missed the point. It's not about you. It's me I should be thinking about: who *I* am, what *I* want. Asking myself that question now, I realize that I don't know the answer. Without Bedlam, I don't know who I am or where I fit in. Without being completely Natural, I don't even know *what* I am or what I want to be. Without knowing all these things, how can I possibly work you out as well? I'm just asking to be hurt, or to lose myself even more thoroughly than I am now. Does that make sense?"

"Yes." And it did. He couldn't begin to understand what it felt like to be in her shoes. He still had the *Cowell* and, in theory at least, his independence. He still had his physical integrity. The only time his state of mind had been challenged was when Deangelis had taken over the Cell, and he had dealt with that resentment. He trusted the ex-Exarch's judgment. He had to; it had kept them alive this long.

"Part of me wants very much to be with you," she said, and he could tell from the tremor in her voice that the words didn't come easily, "but I need to understand myself first. I don't know how long it'll take for me to work that out, or whether I'll feel the same at the end of it. I don't want to promise anything I might not be able to deliver. I can't ask you to wait, just in case."

"Well," he said, "I'm not planning on going anywhere—not anytime soon, anyway."

"Just don't hold back because of me. Your home is in the Dark, not here."

"This isn't your home, either."

"No, but—" He heard her swallow in the darkness. "I don't have a home anymore, Dominic. There's nothing left—nothing but you, and I can't ask you to stand in for everything I've lost. I can't let myself lean on you that way. It wouldn't fix anything. I need to find that strength in myself, somehow. I know I can do it. I just need . . ."

"Time," he finished for her.

"Yes," she breathed, leaning microscopically toward him.

He reached out to touch her face. Her cheeks were cool and wet under his fingertips.

"Take as much of it as you need. And if there's anything I can do—"

She took his hand and put it over her shoulder. He moved closer, and she didn't pull away. "Thank you, Dominic."

They held each other through the short artificial night. The embrace was undemanding and static. Eogan felt at peace with her for the first time since they had reconnected. Their present was hopeless and their future unknowable, but at least for now the past was behind them. That was a change, and perhaps the start of something new. Time alone would tell.

Sometime before dawn, he slept and dreamed of monkeys swinging through the overgrowth of the cave forest. They were hairless and dressed in standard Palmer shipsuits; they had no tails and their calls sounded more like language than animal hoots and hollers. They danced around him, waving their arms, pulling faces, and calling him names—and only as they rushed in to mob him with grinning teeth and wide eyes did he realize that they looked exactly like him and Melilah, and that they had come to take their places forever.

Before night ended, the cavern flexed its muscle. Deangelis watched from his privileged position near the center as the walls began to move. Spikes drifted and moved like people in a crowd, nudged this way and that in response to forces he couldn't see. His instruments reported odd gravitational effects; the knotted atmosphere swirled into new currents; crystal clouds shook like chandeliers in an earthquake.

Through it all, neither Melilah nor Eogan stirred.

"What are you doing?" he asked the voice. "This *is* you, isn't it?"

—AS I TOLD YOU: I AM THIS SPACE. IT MOVES BECAUSE I WILL IT TO.

"Why do you will it?"

—PATIENCE IS ALWAYS REWARDED.

Deangelis thought he was being fobbed off again until he realized that the ordinary spikes weren't the only things moving down on the cavern walls. The superior spikes were shifting, too, along with their ecosystems. Two in particular, formerly far apart, were beginning to draw closer to each other. Their brethren made way for them as a crowd parted for royalty. Their crystal skirts followed.

Sensors on the two halves of the *Cowell* registered the change in their location but did nothing to prevent it. Neither did Deangelis. As soon as he plotted the probable courses of the two superior spikes, he guessed what was going on.

He felt a weird sort of grief at the development. Part of it sprang from his powerlessness. This was as beyond his control as his fate in Bedlam had been—but with a very different conclusion, he hoped.

He felt, also, a sadness that he could never have what Melilah Awad and Dominic Eogan shared. The minds of Exarchs were complex, robust structures. Such complete minds didn't need another to mate with. They were sufficient within themselves. His old self could keep himself amused until the end of time. As a singleton, now, and remembering what he had lost, he knew a loneliness deeper than any emotion he had felt before. For all his playing with Jane Elderton and the fellowship of minds during training on Earth, he had never been truly close to anyone. In Geodesica, he never would be.

—YOUR NEEDS ARE DIFFERENT, said the voice. —THE KIND OF LOVE YOU THRIVE ON IS NOT THE SAME AS THEIRS.

"Love is love, and loneliness is loneliness."

—YOU KNOW THAT TO BE UNTRUE. THE LOVE OF ONE MATE FOR ANOTHER IS DIFFERENT FROM THAT OF A CHILD FOR ITS MOTHER OR BETWEEN LIFELONG FRIENDS. The voice spoke easily, casually as the fabric of the cavern moved around them. —WHAT DOES AN EXARCH LOVE, ISAAC? YOU KNOW THE ANSWER TO THAT QUESTION.

"Is that really love?" he asked, confused.

—WOULD YOU DIE FOR IT?

"Clearly, I would lie for it. For *her*."

—WELL, THEN. I CAN'T THINK OF A BETTER WORD. SHE IS THE LAST OF YOUR CHARGES; HER SAFETY, HER PRESERVATION, HER WELL-BEING ARE PARAMOUNT TO YOUR OWN SENSE OF SELF. YOU ARE AS DEPENDENT ON HER AS SHE IS ON YOU. CALL IT LOVE AND BE DONE WITH IT, MAN.

"I'm not—" He stopped. *A man,* he had been about to say. Human, yes; but not *a man*.

The voice already knew that. Its point was *exactly* that.

"My role is to stand apart," he said. "I can't be one of them. I can walk among them, interact with them, be familiar with them—but I am not of them. I'm an Exarch. That is my function."

The grief grew inside him. It burned with a cleansing fire.

—DO YOU SEE NOW WHAT I HAVE CREATED FOR YOU, HERE?

He did. The cavern was Bedlam in miniature: he, a fragment of an Exarch, governing over a tiny fraction of his former population. Everything was reduced in scale, like a dollhouse. The situation possessed a certain slapstick aptness he could not deny.

"Do you really think this will be enough?"

—YOU TELL ME. OR, BETTER YET: *SHOW* ME.

"And where do you fit in, exactly?"

The voice didn't answer that question. It remained silent as the sun came up on the new day, shining brightly and dangerously on the remade world.

Melilah woke uneasily. Something felt out of place. It wasn't just that Eogan was still lying next to her; surprisingly, even a little unnervingly, that detail didn't throw her at all.

She reached out and pulled the window open. Green-tinged light flooded in from below, making her blink for a second as her irises contracted. The mottled shadows of the overgrowth looked different. The vine Eogan had dangled from was gone.

She sat up and was about to shake him awake when Deangelis spoke aloud through the Cell walls.

"I altered the configuration of the habitat while you slept," he said. "Forgive me if I startled you."

Frowning, she ran a hand down her face. It felt rubbery, nerveless from sleep. "Why?" The explanation was perfectly reasonable. She didn't know why it didn't satisfy her. "Did Eogan ask you to do that?"

The man beside her stirred at the sound of his name and opened his eyes.

"No," Deangelis said. "The initiative was entirely mine. Overnight, it came to my attention that part of the overgrowth had suffered stress because of the weight of the habitat; an anchor had come free of the wall, undermining the canopy backbones in your area. I took it upon myself to relieve the situation."

"How did you know?" asked Eogan. "How did it *come to your attention*?"

Melilah expected Deangelis simply to explain that one of his roving instruments had noticed the stress. That would have been explanation enough.

Instead, he hesitated just long enough to confirm her fear that something was wrong. Not just in the orientation of the habitat. Something bigger.

"I must come clean with you both," Deangelis said. "There's something about this place you need to know."

Melilah's sense of misgiving grew stronger. Eogan raised himself to a sitting position and leaned on his left arm. "Go on."

"We're not alone here," came the voice from above. "The chamber is sentient."

Melilah looked around her involuntarily. "What do you mean—*sentient*?"

"It's alive, and responsible for the maintenance of the forests. I don't know where it comes from or how old it is, but it's here, and I've been communicating with it."

"How long have you known?"

"I've known for some time." His reply contained no sign of remorse. "Until I was certain this intelligence meant us no harm, there seemed no point alarming you."

"Well, I'm alarmed anyway," she said, looking out the open window and hugging herself. The flowers on the vines now seemed less than innocent—unblinking eyes and gaping mouths camouflaged in verdancy.

"What does this mind want?" asked Eogan.

"And why hasn't it talked to *us*?" added Melilah.

"Would you like to talk to it?"

"Of course I would!" She said the words before their ramifications truly sank in. An intelligence indigenous to Geodesica; an *alien*.

—HELLO, MELILAH AWAD. The voice sprang from the air

around them, vibrant and filled with implicit power. —I WELCOME YOU AND PALMER EOGAN TO MY WORLD.

"Where are you?" She looked around for a moment and shrugged a helpless gesture. "And *what* are you, exactly?"

—I AM THE CHAMBER. I HAVE NO REPRESENTATIONAL FORM.

"You're an AI?"

—THE ANSWER TO THAT QUESTION IS UNIMPORTANT. I AM AWARE AND INTELLIGENT BY ANY DEFINITION. MY PHYSICAL MANIFESTATION SURROUNDS YOU.

"We're *inside* you?" she asked, thinking of Jonah and the whale.

—THERE'S NO NEED TO BE ALARMED.

"Really? Did you tell the others who came here the same thing? The ones whose bodies we found?"

Laughter pealed through the chamber, full and whole-bodied. Echoes filled the air. —I DO NOT EAT MY GUESTS, MELILAH, IF THAT IS WHAT YOU ARE THINKING. THAT WOULD BE A MOST UNGENEROUS RESPONSE. I ENJOY COMPANY FOR ITS OWN SAKE, NOT FOR ITS NUTRITIONAL VALUE.

Its amusement at her question made her blush. She was far from reassured. Other folktales sprang to mind. Stories of psychic vampires and mind-eating aliens were ingrained after centuries of speculative fiction, despite none ever having been found. Until now.

"Are you—" She swallowed the question, thinking halfway through that it sounded stupid.

—AM I GEODESICA? NO. I'M NOT AWARE THAT THIS ARTIFACT IS CONSCIOUS, OR POSSESSES ANY PERMANENT INHABITANTS APART FROM ME. VISITORS ARE INFREQUENT, AND I CAN'T CLAIM TO HAVE REVEALED MYSELF TO ALL OF THEM. SOME COME HERE TO GROW, SOME TO DIE. SOME FIND SANCTUARY HERE; OTHERS FIND HOPE. I AM NONE OF THESE THINGS. I AM JUST ME.

"That's as may be," said Eogan, still resting on his left arm but looking at her, not at the cave forest outside. "Will you let us leave?"

—I WILL NOT STOP YOU.

"Forgive me if I don't take your word for it."

—FEEL FREE TO TEST MY WORD. I WILL NOT BE OFFENDED. THE REPLICATORS WHO BRED HERE DEPARTED UNOBSTRUCTED.

"Yes, the replicators . . ." Eogan nodded. "Deangelis, was there any record of this intelligence in the mind of the replicator you took over?"

"None."

"Don't you think that's unusual?"

"Not necessarily. The function of the replicator was strictly defined. Information not relevant to that function has been meticulously expunged."

"Just in case we captured one of them," Melilah mused. "Information like this could have been useful, if we were looking for allies."

—I AM NO ONE'S ALLY, said the voice. —I AM INDEPENDENT.

"So you claim. But again we only have your side of the story."

—WHY WOULD I LIE? NOTHING YOU CAN DO WILL HARM MY FLORA OR ME.

"We could sweep a fusion torch across the surface," said Eogan. "Speaking purely hypothetically, of course."

—YOU WOULD BE DEAD BEFORE YOU ISSUED THE COMMAND, responded the voice. —AGAIN, PURELY HYPOTHETICALLY.

Eogan showed his teeth in a smile. "Fair enough."

"We're welcome to stay here," said Deangelis, "for as long as we wish."

"Can it tell us how to get home?" Melilah asked.

—I KNOW NOTHING OF THE WAYS BEYOND MY BOUNDARIES. I AM SELF-CONTAINED. BUT MY OFFER IS GENUINE. YOU ARE WELCOME HERE.

"No offense, but here isn't where I want to be."

—ISAAC HAS EXPLAINED YOUR CIRCUMSTANCES. I KNOW THAT YOUR HOME IS LOST, AND THAT YOU HAVE IN TURN BECOME LOST IN GEODESICA. I AM POWERLESS TO CHANGE YOUR CIRCUMSTANCES, BUT I CAN OFFER YOU NEW ONES.

"Such as?"

—A *NEW* HOME, MELILAH.

Melilah's eyes watered at the phrase. *A new home?* She had barely accepted the loss of her old one, let alone begun looking for a replacement.

"I don't know," she said, retreating along the mattress until her back leaned against the wall behind her. Her knees came up and she clutched them tightly to her chest. Part of her wondered if she could be dreaming the whole conversation. The offer was superficially tempting: the cavern could keep her occupied while she recuperated and grieved; it wasn't likely to be revisited by the replicators since their successful Trojan horse maneuver had convinced them that she and her companions were dead; she had no real alternative on the table to compete with it; and to clinch the deal, she didn't even have to make a formal decision—all she needed to do was *not leave*. Not until she was ready to, anyway.

But she wasn't convinced. Images of spiderwebs and flypaper, once in her mind, wouldn't fade. The offer was almost too tempting, too perfect. What if they were lured into a trap and couldn't get out again?

She felt backed into a corner.

"Before I agree to anything," she said, "I want to perform one last reconnaissance around here. What if Sol's just a couple of hops away and we haven't noticed?"

"I've been sending drones," Deangelis said. "They've found nothing, Melilah."

"I want to check for myself. The three of us. Maybe we'll see something your drones have missed."

Melilah stared at Eogan, wondering if he would disagree or point out the transparency of her request. She didn't doubt that he and Deangelis—and probably the voice of the cavern, too—knew exactly what she was doing. Eogan just inclined his head in a minute nod.

"If that's what you want—" Deangelis began.

"It is. Thank you."

—I HAVE NO OBJECTION.

"Just out of curiosity," she said to the cavern, "if you *did* object, what would you have done about it?"

Again, laughter filled the air. —I CAN SEE THAT OUR FUTURE INTERACTIONS WILL BE LONG AND STIMULATING, MELILAH AWAD. I WILL LOOK FORWARD TO YOUR RETURN.

The voice didn't sound annoyed or threatened. Its smug confidence that she *would* return simply grated.

"Okay, Dominic. You brought the Cell down here. Take us up again and let's see what we'll see."

Eogan nodded and, placing a palm firmly against the wall beside him—but nothing more dramatic than that—set to work.

The *Cowell* responded instantly to his touch. Although normally configured for low-gravity flight through near vacuum, it could function as an atmospheric vehicle, even in an environment where reactionless thrusters wouldn't operate. The room he shared with Melilah shrank into a flattened oval around them, and a curved, clear window shut off the open space that had previously occupied one wall. Through the window he saw plants rustling at the breeze raised by the habitat's rapid conversion.

His senses integrated with those of the half Cell he had brought down from Deangelis's location on high. Odd details tugged at him: data flows that weren't configured the way they should have been; commands that didn't respond in exactly the right fashion; physical parameters that weren't exactly as he had left them. The craft responded well overall, however, growing stubby wings and a tail section; smooth, cylindrical fan engines extruded from its underbelly. He concluded in the end that the anomalies were signs that the cavern had interfered nondestructively with the Cell while he had slept. He didn't mind so long as the Cell functioned within design tolerances, as it seemed to be doing. He was certain it would have alerted him had a more determined or less respectful probe been attempted.

Still, it rankled. First Deangelis, now anonymous alien groundskeepers. Where would the undermining of his Palmer autonomy end?

The fan engines whirred into life, lifting the Cell gently from its overgrowth cradle. Branches creaked and settled back into their old postures, gnarled and tangled like old roots. Petals and leaves drifted along complex paths, dislodged by the force of the fans and soon gathered up by clouds of self-propelled mites. Eogan still hadn't determined to his satisfaction whether the mites were animal, vegetable, or nanotech. He supposed he could ask the voice of the cavern later, if the chance arose.

The *Cowell* flew at low thrust over the crystal cloud, respectful of the miniature biosphere around it, and only truly powered up as it reached the edge. At first it simply dropped in the direction gravity wanted it to go, but as the downward direction shifted, its fans kicked into life, pushing it away from the midsection of the superior spike that pulled at them. *Something else to ask the voice about,* he thought as the cell accelerated through the atmosphere of the cavern. Why such unusual gravity, and how was it generated?

The roaring of the fans faded as the atmosphere thinned. Conventional thrusters kicked in moments before the combined gravitational pull of the spikes dropped completely away. By the time the fans shut down and folded back into the body of the Cell, they were in vacuum, approaching the cavern's sole source of light.

Sensors across the Cell's hull facing the artificial sun reported radiation levels increasing steadily.

Melilah watched the view through the window he had provided her with. Her jaw worked, and he wondered what she was thinking. Less than half an hour ago they had been asleep as equals. Now she was the passenger again, and he was no longer entirely human. The sudden transition in their status bothered him more than the lingering unease of his dream. The nightmare about monkeys puzzled him, but he had more important things to worry about.

The replicator loomed out of the sky above them, roughly seed-shaped, seven meters long, and studded with slender stalks that he assumed were sensors and antennae tracking the data transmitted by thousands of instruments scattered throughout the cavern. A portal opened in its underbelly, allowing them access to the rest of the Cell. The *Cowell*'s other half reached out and merged with its mobile twin, marrying systems with comfortable familiarity. Only a slight awkwardness suggested that the cavern's reach extended as far as Deangelis, too. And that made him wonder in turn just how far they would get if the alien intelligence didn't intend to let them leave.

"Okay," he said, purely for Melilah's benefit. "We're docked." An array of displays appeared in the Cell's inner walls as data rushed in from Deangelis. The interior of the cavern looked very different from on high. There was no sign of the cave forests, only foreshortened spikes, blurry crystal clouds, and eleven black exits, highlighted in red.

"Are you certain you want to do this?" asked Deangelis. He sounded faintly hurt, as though wounded by the implication that Melilah trusted neither him nor the drones he had sent out of the cavern.

"Yes. It won't take long, Isaac," she said with weary apology. "Then we can decide what to do next."

The replicator warmed up its thrusters for the first time in over a week. "Pick an exit. I'll let you guide us."

"That one." She pointed at the screen, at random Eogan suspected. The replicator thrust toward it, tapering slightly at the forward end in anticipation of hitting and spearing through atmosphere at speed.

—WAIT.

Here it comes. Eogan felt his stomach muscles tighten in an ancient reflex.

—I CANNOT LET YOU GO, said the voice, WITHOUT ASKING YOU TO INFORM ME SHOULD YOU FIND YOUR HOME. I WILL WAIT HERE, OTHERWISE, IN ANTICIPATION OF YOUR RETURN, AND TIME PASSES SLOWLY ENOUGH AS IT IS.

Eogan felt a complex mix of emotions. Pity to begin with, for the loneliness revealed by the request, and suspicion that it might be nothing more than a final attempt to change their minds before resorting to force.

"We will," said Deangelis.

The way remained open ahead of them, allaying Eogan's worst fears.

Deangelis imagined the exit slamming shut at the last moment. He couldn't help it. Such a collision was unlikely to be lethal for him or his passengers, but the fact would remain that he had been deceived. And they would be trapped forever, until the cavern tired of them and set them free. He would have been instrumental in Melilah's imprisonment.

Even as the gaping tunnel mouth approached, moving with apparent slowness in reaction to the speed of his thoughts, he knew that she would never forgive him for that. No matter how long they were imprisoned together. No matter that his existence rested fundamentally on her well-being. She would be lost to him—as lost as Bedlam and the rest of his charges. Forever.

His relief as the exit swept over and around him was as profound and total as any he could imagine. The familiar gray-green ambience of a Geodesica tunnel welcomed them. Space-time gripped the replicator in its usual way and tugged them in directions unknown. Smooth immaterial walls swept by.

A slight giddiness gripped him. He couldn't tell if it was relief or agoraphobia. They were outside the giant chamber and back in Geodesica. A wrong turn could land them in the lap of something much more hostile than a puzzling voice.

All his senses were on edge. He told himself that there was nothing to worry about. He had faked their deaths and left no trail. It didn't make sense that the replicators would still be looking for them. The maze was empty now, most likely, apart from drones and other robotic explorers sent by Sol to map the giant construct.

Turnaround at the middle of the tunnel came and went without incident. The junction ahead of them loomed—a small one with just five entrances.

"Feeling lucky?" Eogan asked Melilah.

"Not really. Are there any tunnels you haven't already surveyed?" she asked Deangelis.

"None."

"Well, then. We might as well pick another one at random." They decelerated into the heart of the brightly lit junction. "That one."

Deangelis swept the way as a routine precaution. Lidar immediately picked up a hard return from the junction ahead, and his instincts jangled.

"What is it?" asked Eogan, noticing the alert.

"I don't know." He scanned the silhouettes contained in his and the replicator's combined memories. Nothing matched. "It wasn't there before."

"Take us back," she said, gripping Eogan's arm. "Get us out of here before it sees us."

"Too late." If they had spotted it, it had undoubtedly spotted them in return. But it wasn't moving toward them. It just sat silently at the end of the tunnel.

Without fanfare, he backed away and tried another tunnel mouth.

Lidar picked up another silent watcher at the end of the tunnel.

One by one he tested the others, even though he suspected the answer already. All of the tunnels leading away from the cavern were blocked.

"Could they be sentries?" Melilah asked, her face pinched. "Or mines?"

"Whatever they are," said Eogan, "I'm disinclined to get any nearer."

"I agree." Deangelis backed up and took them along the tunnel to the cavern.

—THAT WAS QUICK, said the voice as they burst into its domain.

"We took a wrong turn," said Melilah.

"There's something out there." Deangelis directed the replicator along a parabolic course from one side of the chamber to the other. With only the slightest of course corrections, he threaded a different exit perfectly. "And hopefully not out here as well . . ."

The tension grew as they accelerated then decelerated along the tunnel. He had chosen the junction ahead for its many exits: no less than fourteen led in all directions of the five-dimensional compass. He swept them with lidar and received hard echoes from all of them.

"I don't like this," said Melilah.

"Neither do I." It would take hours to search all the exits leading from the cavern. He felt safe assuming they were all blocked. "I want to hail one of these things."

"Why?" asked Eogan.

"Because talking first would be better than just turning up in its lap. Don't you think?"

The Palmer nodded. "Yes. You're right."

"How could you not have seen them before?" asked Melilah, her tone betrayed.

"I can only assume that the drones' data were corrupted. Or that these things can tell the difference between us and a drone, and know when to hide."

She cursed, and he understood the urge. Even as he sent a rapidly repeating, coded request for ID up the nearest tunnel at hand, he knew it would be recognized.

A reply came instantly.

"Don't come any closer." The message was heavily encoded and tightly packed in pulse of coherent light that at first or even second glance would resemble a lidar ping. "Believe me: you don't want to."

"What do you mean?" he replied in the same fashion, certain that neither Eogan or Melilah would notice the conversation taking place, let alone what it contained.

"I possess lethal capabilities beyond your grimmest imaginings, and just one purpose: to prevent you from leaving this place. Come within a certain range and those capabilities will be activated. I will be compelled to use them."

"You don't sound very keen to."

"I am not, but I represent neither my maker nor my dominant personality. I am only a caretaker, woken to respond to your presence. I was asleep until then, while another part of me kept watch. It woke me the moment you appeared on the scope. We each have our duties, and our strengths."

"And what exactly is *your* strength?"

"To talk you into going back. That's all. If I fail, my dominant personality will wake to perform the task it is designed for. That is, it'll destroy you. Don't have any doubt about that, Isaac. We're as far beyond that replicator you're in as it was beyond your

Palmer friend and his Cell. We've been evolving, you see. You don't stand a chance."

"It sounds to me like you're pretty good at talking and not much else."

"Oh, *I'm* not, but as I said I'm not the dominant personality. It doesn't talk a lot. If I suddenly go quiet, you'll know it's taken over. Then I advise you to run."

They had been talking for several seconds. Deangelis figured that he might have as many as five more before his companions became suspicious.

"Why do you want me to go back? Why not kill us outright, if it would be so easy for you?"

"Because we don't need to, not yet. Your presence here proved, rather comprehensively, that the replicators had failed in that very mission, and that's when we moved into position. We're a backup plan, you see. Rather than kill you, we're here to *contain* you. You're only a threat to those back home if you get out, you see. So if we make sure you don't get out, your threat is effectively neutralized. That's why the replicators were programmed to lead you here."

"I sent drones—"

"Yes, we saw them. And sent them back to you undamaged, I hope. Not very talkative, your little toys, but they helped pass the time."

Frustration rose in him. "How long have you been in here? When were you sent?"

"We bred from the same batch as the replicators. As soon as we saw this place on the charts, we reprogrammed the replicators to trace their home routes back here, guessing it was the first place you'd go to, given the chance. And you did. All we had to do then was wait to see if you came out. Which you have. And now I have to talk you into going back in or else—"

"What's going on?" asked Melilah, pointing at a half-formed shape on the screen before her. "What is that thing?"

The image returned by his message-lidar pulses revealed a shape not dissimilar to a dead spider, with lumpy ridges and joints converging on a shadowy center. A suggestion of wings behind it gave it a demonic cast.

Deangelis decided not to lie. "It's a sentry," he said. "It—*they* are here to make sure we don't get any farther."

"How did they know where we were?"

"They say—"

"You're talking to them?"

"Yes. They say they led us here deliberately."

"Why?"

He thought of the cavern's mind saying: ***I HAVE EVERYTHING YOU NEED RIGHT HERE, ISAAC DEANGELIS.***

"To keep us out of the way," he said. "To make sure we didn't cause any trouble back home."

"To shut us up?"

"Yes."

Her face clouded over with fury. "Get us past that thing. I don't care how you do it."

Deangelis didn't want to argue with her, but he doubted his trick with the VOID drive would work a second time, and he didn't want to test the sentry's word on its destructive capabilities without first exploring every other option.

It was hailing him. By the standards of their rapid-fire exchange, he had been silent for well over a month while he talked to Melilah. He remained that way while he tried to think of a reply.

"You don't think we *can* get past it, do you?" asked Eogan.

"No," he admitted. "The trap has sprung, but it's not designed to kill us. Not if we play by their rules. If we don't, the gloves come off."

"They could be bluffing," Melilah said.

"We *are* outnumbered, even if this one has exaggerated its capabilities." The feeling of vertigo worsened. He didn't know what to do.

"I'm not going to sit here and rot while the Archon gets away with its crimes." Melilah's voice was firm. "I'd rather die than give in and let it win."

"Die?" Panicky denial and ethical solidarity collided heavily inside him. "I can't let you die, Melilah."

"What? Why not?"

"Because you're the last—the one—I must—"

"I think the decision's been taken out of our hands," Eogan interrupted. "Look. It's moving."

Deangelis confirmed the truth of the Palmer's observation and chastised himself for not noticing sooner. He had been too focused on Melilah to notice that the sentry had left its station. It was moving rapidly up the tunnel toward them. It had also fallen silent some tens of seconds ago, and the silence was more worrying than any verbal threats it could have made.

"I'm sorry," he said, putting the replicator into motion even as he spoke. "I think it's in our best interest to—"

The twisted space-time in the sentry's tunnel twanged like an overstressed wire. Arcane resonations shook the vacuum around them, sparking mass-heavy photons, extruding linear topological defects, and blowing ring-shaped singularity bubbles into existence. The junction shuddered and shook around them. He could barely see or sense a thing.

He knew only that he had to run. Clutching his charges closely to protect them from the maelstrom, he lunged for the exit leading back to the cavern and thrust along it at speed.

The turbulence eased. Glancing behind him, he saw a rippling boundary where the effects of the sentry's opening salvo ended. It looked like the surface of a cauldron filled with molten, boiling glass. All the colors of the electromagnetic spectrum rippled at him, stray echoes of space-time under duress.

"Guess they got tired of talking," Eogan said, steadying Melilah, who looked shaken and pale.

Deangelis didn't waste time replying. Whichever personality had taken control of the sentry, it clearly had no intention of letting them go so easily. The rippling boundary was already moving up the tunnel toward them. Diverting power to his forward arrays, he broadcast a message ahead of him as loudly as he could and set it on repeat.

All he could see through the exit ahead was the glare of the chamber's artificial sun. Over his own shouting and the growing screech from behind, he didn't listen for a reply. That would be too much to hope for.

His pulse tripped as the circle ahead of him began to shrink. The exit at the end of the tunnel was closing.

"No!" cried Melilah.

Deangelis tucked his two wards close together in his belly and narrowed the replicator to its thinnest possible profile.

Black borders irised together as the sentry's weapon gained on them. He didn't dare calculate their chances. It was going to be close either way.

The replicator shot out of the tunnel like a slug from a linear accelerator. Melilah shouted as they slammed into atmosphere. Invisible restraining fields gripped them, decelerated them, and contained the damage they would have caused had they arrived without warning. Black specks danced across her vision.

Behind the replicator, the entrance slammed shut. Only a tiny fraction of the sentry's arcane weapon leaked through, searing a blindingly bright line across the artificial sky before it was pinched off and much reduced in power. Even so, it broke free and slammed sideways into the cavern wall, demolishing several dozen spikes in the process, including one superior spike and much of its attendant forest. Dark smoke spread from the wound along gravity vortices and air rivers, swirling like ink in turbulent water.

—YOU ARE SAFE, FOR THE MOMENT, explained the voice to her. —ISAAC WARNED ME YOU WERE COMING. I HAVE SEALED US OFF FROM THE REST OF GEODESICA AS BEST I CAN.

When the replicator stopped shaking and Melilah took a proper look around her, she saw that all the exits had indeed closed. The one behind them, through which they had so precipitously returned, glowed a faint orange.

"How safe are we, exactly?" she asked.

—THAT I CANNOT SAY. The voice lacked its usual surety. —MY WALLS HAVE NEVER BEEN BREACHED BEFORE.

"It's us they're after, not you." She thought of the forests and what might happen if the sentry made it through the door. The orange patch was brighter and beginning to bulge. "Open one of the other exits and we'll go elsewhere."

—I FEAR THAT WOULD BE SUICIDE FOR ALL OF US.

"Shit." She imagined that she could taste wood smoke in the Cell's pristine air, and swallowed her self-pity. "I'm so sorry. This is all my fault."

—NOT SO. I AM NEITHER STUPID NOR DEFENSELESS, MELILAH. A CHANCE EXISTED, DESPITE ALL THE EVIDENCE TO THE CONTRARY, THAT I WAS THE BAIT IN A TRAP LAID FOR YOU. NOW THAT I KNOW THIS TO BE THE CASE, AND GIVEN TIME TO PREPARE, I WILL DO MY BEST TO PUNISH THOSE RESPONSIBLE.

The bulge became more pronounced as the sentry tore at the wound in space-time, stretching and flexing it in the hope that it would snap. The energy output from the artificial sun increased sharply. As the replicator arced across the vacuum-filled sky, she saw spikes changing shape and color, becoming blood-red thorns with deadly tips. The crystal clouds shrank inward, becoming denser, sealing their contents off from the rest off the cavern.

"If there was a chance, why didn't you tell us?"

—BECAUSE I WANTED YOU TO STAY, AND I KNEW THAT YOU WOULD NOT IF COMPELLED TO. IT HAD TO BE YOUR DECISION. TO THAT END, I HAVE MANIPULATED YOU AND YOUR COMPANION IN VARIOUS WAYS. I CONFESS THAT MUCH, BUT I DO NOT APOLOGIZE.

"What?"

—LEAVE IN ANGER; LIVE WITHOUT REGRET. GOOD-BYE, MELILAH AWAD.

Eogan gripped her shoulder and pointed at the cavern wall. "Look. Another exit!"

Melilah did look, although she wanted desperately to know what the voice had meant by "manipulate." Among the deformed spikes and closed entrances—many of which were now glowing, outraged—she saw a twelfth tunnel mouth, one that hadn't been there before, opening wide.

"Where will it take us?" Eogan asked.

—BEYOND GEODESICA.

"It's an exit?"

—I DO NOT KNOW WHERE IT GOES. I ABSORBED IT A LONG TIME AGO AND HAVE NEVER FOUND THE NEED OR COURAGE TO OPEN IT. YOU MUST DO SO NOW. IT'S YOUR ONLY CHANCE.

Melilah found her voice again. "Isaac?"

"I think it's right," said the Exarch. "I can't see another way out of this situation."

"Is there nothing we can do to get them off our back? Tell them we'll stay put then sneak out the back door anyway?"

"I'm not taking any chances on them destroying us first and listening second."

The orange patches were too bright to look at.

"All right," she said, thinking of being stranded in space between galaxies with no way home. "But I don't like it."

"Neither do I, Melilah. Neither do I."

The ancient fusion fire at the heart of the chamber began to dim as they accelerated for the sole tunnel mouth. The Cell contracted again, gripping her and Eogan tightly. She found Eogan's hand and squeezed it just as hard. He looked worried.

"Where to now?" she asked.

"The Dark only knows." His eyes distantly focused on data flooding through him from the Cell, but they saw her. She was sure of it.

The tunnel entrance ballooned before them. Turbulence made the Cell shake.

Something kicked hard against her, a surge of acceleration she hadn't been expecting. She heard Eogan grunt in surprise and knew he hadn't anticipated it either. The darkness of the exit swept around them at the same time as something extraordinary fell into her mind:

A tiny pocket of stillness, removed from time. In it she saw herself and Eogan exploring the interior of the cavern, dealing with carnivorous vines and tangled roots, recording the details of ancient bones and maneuvering the Cowell *into position and taking samples. But for every scene she recognized, there was one she didn't remember—as though there had been two versions of them inside the chamber.*

The recordings were taken from Deangelis's instruments. He had known about this. He had been part of it, whatever it was.

A sick feeling began to grow in her gut, even as the timeless moment unfolded and Isaac himself appeared before her, not as the sexless young man she was used to seeing, but someone older, physically mature but with a confused innocence in his eyes.

"I'm sorry, Melilah," this Deangelis said. "I was complicit for the best of reasons—but that is no excuse. Good-bye."

She opened her mouth to speak—

—and time started again. The walls of the exit rushed by her with awful speed. She knew exactly what had happened. The jolt before entering the tunnel had been Deangelis kicking the Cell free from the replicator, shoving them forward while he recoiled back into the chamber.

"Isaac!" she cried, even as the exit began to close behind them. Space-time had the Cell in its grip, and would drag them inevitably down into the throat linking Geodesica to the rest of the universe. There was no time to turn back and talk him out of staying. Even as the diminishing circle behind her shrank to a dot, she saw dreadful light blossom in the chamber. The sentries had arrived.

Then the way slammed shut behind them, and they were in darkness.

Melilah stiffened in the embrace of the Cell, but Eogan didn't have time to consider the cause of her distress. He had felt Deangelis kick abruptly free and was doing his best to get the *Cowell* back under his command. It tumbled like an out-of-control capsule on reentry. If they hit the throat at the wrong angle, they would be scoured back to atoms.

What the hell are you doing back there, Isaac? Wherever we're headed, we're certain to need you!

He regained full control less than a second before impact. The Cell's external shell took on the properties necessary to survive the hellish environment of the throat. Even approached at the right angle, it was no place to stay for longer than absolutely necessary.

Blue light glared around them. The Cell bucked and twisted anew but he kept its heading true.

Blue faded to red. Heat struck him, and turbulence, and a sound so loud it hurt. He didn't know what had happened. This wasn't the void of space. This was an *atmosphere*.

Sensors snatched data from the outside as the Cell buffeted back and forth. The gas consisted mainly of hydrogen at a temperature of fifteen hundred degrees Kelvin. Ferocious currents roiled around them, stretching as far as his instruments could reach. A quick molecular assay revealed a marked lack of lithium.

"I know where we are!" Even through the Cell's shielding, the noise of the storm was overwhelming. He had to shout for Melilah to hear him. "We're inside a brown dwarf!"

She stared at him in mute amazement. He felt absurdly like laughing, but restrained himself. There was nothing to say that Geodesica had to open into deep space. They should count themselves lucky they hadn't turned up in the middle of a planet or right next to a black hole.

Still, getting out of a star, even a small one, was going to be tricky. The Cell tossed like a pollen grain in a hurricane, and he tried in vain to get it under control. Convection might take them upward, perhaps all the way to the surface. The trick would be to avoid being sucked back down again. He didn't want to spend any longer than he had to in that chaotic, hellish place.

Even as he began to gain some semblance of control, he picked up a solid object on their tail.

Despite the stellar fires battering them, he felt a chill rush through him. *Impossible,* he thought. *The sentries couldn't have followed—not so soon!*

He forced the Cell forward, cutting through rivers of gas wider than Bedlam had been, straining for every last shred of delta-v.

The object on their tail didn't fall back. If anything, it came steadily closer.

Melilah had seen it. She stared at the screens in horror, steadying herself with both hands against the interior bulkheads.

"I'm sorry," he said. "I've done everything I can."

"I know," she said, her voice flat, beyond emotion.

"If it wasn't so dense in here, the VOID drive—"

"It doesn't matter. It's over now."

The object tailing them grew larger in the rear views. Eogan fought the currents to keep them ahead, but there was little else he could do. The Cell was hard-pressed to move and survive through the atmosphere of the failed star, let alone fight back.

A signal crackled over the comms, drowned out by electromagnetic noise.

Don't gloat, Eogan thought. *Just do it.*

As though reading his mind, the object lunged forward and took them in one swoop.

—WHY DID YOU COME BACK? asked the voice as the tunnel mouth closed shut behind Eogan and Melilah.

Deangelis steadied the replicator. Strange promontories rose from the mouth assailed by the sentry that had chased him. In a bare fragment of a second, it would burst.

"I came back to make a stand," he said. "And to find out the truth about you."

—YOU THINK I AM IN LEAGUE WITH THESE MACHINES?

"No. I want to know why you thought I'd be happy here. It wasn't just about Melilah, was it? There was something else."

—YES. CAN'T YOU GUESS?

"Can't you just give me a straight answer?" The interior of the chamber had darkened to a deep, reddish gloom. He felt as though he was caught inside a bloody eyeball. "Sometimes you remind me entirely too much of the Archon."

—I THINK, said the voice, THAT'S EXACTLY THE POINT.

Deangelis felt a great weariness as his worst fears were confirmed. His mental architecture was forever yielding new secrets. Not only had he been designed for independence while at the same time bound fatally tied to his charges; now it seemed he needed an authority figure as well. If not the Archon, then the next best would do.

Or perhaps, he wondered, it wasn't quite that sinister. Perhaps the voice reminded him of himself—his higher self, whose presence he had missed ever since its destruction.

Either way, he now knew exactly what the voice had meant when it had told him: *I HAVE EVERYTHING YOU NEED RIGHT HERE, ISAAC DEANGELIS.* He would never trust the Archon again, and all hope of reconnecting with himself had fled. This had been his only chance to find true completion.

I was Earth-Deangelis, he told himself. *Now I belong to Geodesica, if I belong to anything at all.*

The ravaged tunnel mouth burst open. Streamers of blue and ultraviolet light lashed the interior of the cavern like whips. The blood-red thorns flared, and Deangelis felt strange gravity clutch at him, many thousands times stronger than it had been before. As the sentry swept out of the tunnel mouth, it was snatched from the sky and slammed into the cave wall, where it burst into brilliant flame.

The atmosphere coiled and uncoiled like serpents, writhing in the sudden turbulence. A feeling of grim euphoria swept through the chamber—and Deangelis understood then, in a moment of sudden clarity, that the voice of the chamber wasn't contained in the sun at all, but in the air itself. The complexity of the streams, the strange eddies that came and went, the gravity fields that sustained them— all were pieces of a mind more unusual than even he had imagined.

Another tunnel mouth blossomed, and another. The space was suddenly full of energy. There was no more time for discussion or wonderment—or doubt.

Unfolding weapons the replicator had tried to use against him, Geodesica-Deangelis rallied to the defense of the chamber, and swooped downward into the light.

+15

Bedlam: 2609 CE

Palmer Horsfall made certain she was present when the Exarchs penetrated the final layer in the Occlusion observatory recovered from the battle-scarred and rubble-strewn remains of Bedlam. The fighting was long over, but the fine gray ash of deactivated Catastrophe nanotech had clumped in great sheets and clouds, stirred by the passage of Ah Kong's burned-out core as it swept out of the inner system. Given a powerful boost by the primary, the garish cinder would never return to haunt the remaining worlds. The primary's atmosphere still churned after its use as a weapon. Some astrophysicists speculated that, as an unintended side effect, the Archon might have cured it of solar flares once and for all.

Horsfall couldn't imagine anyone wanting to live in the ruins, but she was willing to keep her mind open.

"Be careful," Deangelis warned them, unnecessarily. The sole remaining fragment of the system's Exarch watched from the sidelines, a nervous, twitchy figure with no function but desperately needing something to do. After his panicked attempt to reconnect with the rest of himself, following the Archon's sudden and mysterious retreat, he had been traumatized and shocked. Rather than imprison or kill him, since he was as much a victim of circumstance as the Isaac Deangelis who had fought on the side of the rebels, Jane Elderton had urged the others to accept him as one of their own. His possession of a valuable second-generation VOID drive only reinforced that decision.

Still, his presence irritated her. He wasn't the Deangelis she had known. He was back where that one had started, one hundred and seventy years earlier, the pain of disconnection fresh and destabilizing. He hadn't been with them during the long years of covert battle preparation. He had been tucked away in Bedlam, waiting for them to strike.

She knew better than him how to *be careful*. The impulse to plan and prepare had ruled her life for more decades than she cared to think about. She had almost forgotten how it felt to look forward to something. Once, perhaps, she had anticipated the end of the war, but that had been so long ago and so deeply buried that she could no longer remember it.

Thousands of tiny drones swarmed over the surface of the final layer. Needlelike feet equipped for atomic force microscopy tested the observatory's remaining defenses, unpicking its puzzle.

They're almost through, whispered Jane Elderton into her mind. *Not long now.*

Despite the imminence of their triumph, Horsfall didn't trust herself to speak. In her memory, the sight of Ah Kong erupting was still vivid. *It had better,* she thought, *be worth it.*

Other images still haunted her, half-glimpsed through the fading glow of Catastrophe: the angular shapes of the Bedlam installation, blurred only slightly by distance and the many millions of kilometers of dust between her and it; a spitting, energetic ring that appeared in the background, into which one of the pressurized habitats vanished. Another habitat vanished, and another, as she watched, unable to completely credit what she was seeing. The burning ring gulped down two blocky support facilities, then shrank to a point and disappeared, leaving the observatory behind.

When she and the rebels had arrived, the ring was gone, never to reappear, the Archon and the rest of Deangelis with it.

You can have your sovereignty, but you can't have Geodesica or Sol.

The Archon's ultimatum had come true. The Exarchate no longer rested under the heel of the Archon. But without Geodesica their victory wouldn't be complete.

She held her breath and resisted the urge to press the drones to go faster.

A spark of light appeared on the purple, space-bending fabric of the innermost shell of the observatory. A second spark joined the first, then another. The drones backed away as a succession of nano-thin cracks formed and spread, rapidly covering the surface they had attacked with a burning filigree.

Horsfall narrowed her eyelids as the barrier dissolved in a flash of energy. Even from her observation point on Bridgehead 4, the light was too bright to look at directly. When it had faded a purple blotch marked the place it had been.

"What happened?" she asked. "Are we through?"

I told you, said Elderton with barely repressed triumph. *I told you we'd make it, that we'd keep you alive to see the end. Now we're here. We have it in our grasp. It's almost over!*

Horsfall's vision cleared. The fireworks were definitely over, and the entrance to Geodesica lay naked before her. The drones had been blown away by the release of energy, but several more solid craft were inching closer to the impossible knot of space at the center of the observatory.

"Wait; pull back," she ordered. An entirely new feeling filled her. Not dread or fear or uncertainty, but anticipation.

She requisitioned a Cell component from the nearby *Tumucumaque* and swooped down toward their prize.

One hundred and seventy years, millions of lives, and megatons of matter expended in the name of—what? A hole in space that could easily have been overlooked, had it not wandered across a Palmer trade lane completely by chance—yet it was so much more than that. An entrance to an entirely unique universe, where light-years flashed by like kilometers and space folded in unique shapes. What would humanity find in there? Where would it travel? Who would it meet?

She felt Elderton reaching into the cache of data she had carried from Sublime. The exterior of the Cell component reconfigured in readiness for its passage through the throat Horsfall knew awaited them. Many, many times had she imagined sailing through those ghastly energies into an unknowable future. All her fears and worries fell behind them as the entrance grew large ahead.

Blue light flared.

For you, Deva, she thought, remembering the sister she still grieved for.

And for all the citizens of Sublime, the Exarch in her mind added.

Horsfall prepared herself to see the corridors of Geodesica for the first time.

Without warning, the light blue-shifted even further into the upper end of the spectrum. An intense and unexpected spatial deform snatched at the Cell component, shaking her violently.

"What is it?" she asked Elderton.

Something—

"What?"

I don't know! This doesn't match the data I gathered in Sublime!

She felt herself stretched thin like spaghetti and simultaneously crushed.

"A black hole?"

A trap! Elderton cried. *No!*

Horsfall clenched her fists in rage.

"Can we get out?" Through the Cell's instruments, she saw nothing but X-rays and beyond. Its shields sizzled with a sound like hydrogen emissions in the microwave band. She couldn't tell if they had passed the event horizon or not. "Is it too late?"

Jane Elderton took forever to answer. And that, she supposed, was as good an answer as any. The Archon had left the Exarchate to its citizens, but it had closed and locked the entrance to Geodesica behind it. Although the Alliance probes had crossed all the visible hurdles without incident and she had thought the way clear, she had begun to think of what came *after—*

She had obviously thought wrong.

There was nothing to do but wait as time dilation effects gripped the Cell and prolonged its existence beyond all expectation.

Her last protracted thought was to curse the wish she had made, long ago. The Exarchs had been as good as their word. She would outlive any plans they set in motion. How many years would pass before she and Elderton finally fell into the heart of the singularity? A hundred? A thousand? Perhaps more. Perhaps they would outlive the Archon and humanity itself and still not have met their grisly end.

While we live, you will live, too.

That thought was no comfort at all as the shields began to fail and hard radiation drowned out Jane Elderton's implacable, awful silence forever.

Deangelis watched from the sidelines as every attempt failed to penetrate the singularity blocking the entrance to the alien maze. One after another, drones and Cell components vanished pointlessly into the gaping maw that had swallowed Horsfall and Elderton. That he had warned them to take care gave him no satisfaction whatsoever. They were gone. The singularity couldn't be shifted.

Shock turned to anger. He endured with equanimity charges that he had known what would happen. They were utterly baseless, and enough people believed him to avert a lynching. Still, he was avoided by most and left on the outer as the situation in Bedlam became clear.

The Archon, it seemed, had exploited the inherent instability of the wormhole mouths to create a one-way trap. Anything going into Geodesica would be destroyed. The scientific minds studying the phenomenon weren't so certain about the other way. What effect would the wormhole have on someone coming *out* of the throat? Would they be destroyed as well, or pass through unscathed?

It was impossible to tell without sending a probe through. As word trickled in from Sublime and Familiar and it became apparent that those entrances had suffered the same sabotage, the chances of the Exarchate ever getting back inside Geodesica looked increasingly slim.

Deangelis thought of the thousands of drones he had sent into the mouth while his higher self had been caretaker of the destroyed system. What would happen to them? Were they abandoned forever, along with all the data they had collected? Had the Archon simply written them off as a bad loss?

That didn't worry him, as long as he had access to the data he needed. His only concern was to find the answer to one question:

What about Melilah?

While racing in vain to reconnect with the rest of him, he had received a final message from his maker.

"Peace, Isaac," the Archon had said to him. "You no longer need to be my voice in this system, or any other. I release you from my service. You are free to do whatever you think right. Stay here and talk to the others, perhaps; they'll need you in the days to come. It's your choice."

Some choice, he thought. He, too, had seen the strange hole that had opened up in the system and whisked the Archon and the rest of himself away to safety. The glimpse was maddening: suggestive, but proof of nothing. What was the rest of him up to that he had been excluded from? What would Sol do next?

There were too many questions and too few answers.

He stayed with the victors in Bedlam as grief over the loss of Palmer Horsfall and Jane Elderton poured forth unfettered. He stayed as good news for the rebellion began to flood in in return. Only a handful of systems still resisted the new regime. Lazarus Hails declared himself satisfied with their efforts and toasted the dawning of a new age of humanity.

"We stand on the cusp of the future," he said in an address broadcast via tangler to every inhabited system of the Exarchate. "The cost has been great and the effort long, but we have our fate in our hands at last, and it's up to us what we do with it. Rebuild, prosper, expand, diversify, grow in wisdom—all this and more, I say, in honor of those who fell along the way. Mourn them but do not regret their passing, for they gave us the one thing we need to be truly great: our freedom. Use it in their names, and remember them for eternity."

The celebrations seemed to last for days, but eventually reality reasserted itself. The rebels now had an empire to run. Ships returned to their home systems; the focus of the Exarchate shifted to those places where negotiations continued; only scientists remained to study the booby-trapped entrance to Geodesica, and even they grew weary in time.

Isaac Forge Deangelis felt no driving urge to go anywhere. He was home. The system and its useless artifact needed someone to keep watch, and no one argued when he volunteered. He resisted the call to erect a memorial in the orbit of the old habitat. The war would be remembered so long as he remained, whether the rest of him returned or not.

One day, just maybe, someone would come out of Geodesica.

And Isaac Forge Deangelis, he swore, would be waiting for her.

+INTERLUDE

Anniversary 20: 1,051,014 CE

"Who are you?"

"My name is Isaac Forge Deangelis."

"What are you?"

"Exarch of Bedlam."

"What are you doing here?"

"Waiting for Melilah Awad, sole surviving citizen of Bedlam, to return from Geodesica."

"Is that all?"

"Yes."

"You have nothing else to say about yourself?"

Hesitation. "Who asks?"

"I do."

"And who are you?"

"My name is Isaac Forge Deangelis."

"What are you?"

"Exarch of Bedlam."

"What are you doing here?"

"Waiting for Melilah Awad, sole surviving citizen of Bedlam, to return from Geodesica."

"Is that all?"

"Yes."

He didn't notice the gaze of someone distant and unknowable sweep over him until it had passed, and by then he was far too late to do anything about it.

+16

Closure: minus 1 day

"Melilah?"

She stirred at the sound of the voice. All around her was dark. She couldn't see anything, but she could feel tremendous motion, in her and through her, as though every atom and molecule in her body were hurtling the same direction at once.

The voice. She knew that voice.

"Isaac?"

"Yes. It's you. *You* are you. I know it, this time. The real Melilah. Melilah Awad. You are you and you are here at last!"

The voice faded in and out, as though coming over a faulty channel, and he sounded badly shaken. There was no mistaking him, though.

"But Isaac, you—I thought you were still back inside, in the chamber, and the sentries—they—we—"

Words failed her. She didn't know whether to weep or scream. Where was she? What had happened to her? The last thing she remembered was the sentries bursting into the chamber and she and Eogan coming out of Geodesica into the atmosphere of a failed star and—

Captured. They had been captured. All their running and hiding and trying to get home had come to nothing in the end.

"Oh, Isaac. They got you, too. I'm so sorry."

The voice had faded into a buzz of static, but returned now with renewed strength. "Melilah Awad, you're talking to me in English. Forgive me for being unaccustomed. But that proves it's you. It really *is* you. *You* are you. And I know it!"

"Are you all right, Isaac?"

"Yes, yes. Perfectly fine! That is, I am adjusting. We are talking much faster than I have thought for a very long time in a language that barely exists anymore. But all is good. Yes, all is now very good indeed."

The first inkling that she might have mistaken the identity of the person talking to her struck her then.

"Where are we, Isaac? Where *exactly*?"

"That's hard to say, Melilah. I will show you. I think I remember how to—yes. Here."

Isaac's voice ceased. The darkness around her suddenly unfolded to reveal a sight unlike anything she had ever seen before, inside Geodesica or out.

A vast, gray wall hung several dozen meters away, curved like the inside of the cavern she had just left—minus the spikes—and much, much larger. Circular portals dotted its surface in a regular pattern as far as her eyes could see, blurring to black in the distance. The space between them was a strangely metallic, burnished white; not quite bone or ceramic or glass, but something else entirely. The portals seemed, almost, to hover over the wall instead of cut through it.

As if that optical uncertainty wasn't enough on its own, the entire wall was flexing, flattening like a rubber sheet pulled tight, and simultaneously coming closer. She reached out a hand to steady herself, feeling giddy, and touched a cool surface barely half a meter from her. She was standing in a transparent sphere barely large enough for the three people it contained: herself; Eogan, looking as dazed as she felt; and a fuzzy version of Isaac Deangelis, his face frozen in an expression of faint surprise, with eyebrows raised and lips parted.

She didn't know which oddity to tackle first. Her gaze tracked naturally to the wall outside as it loomed closer and closer. Their sphere was falling or flying into one of the portals. The geometrically perfect opening rushed soundlessly toward her, then past. She was reminded of Geodesica's tunnels as dark walls swept by on all sides, but the similarity was only fleeting. The walls closed down to a point ahead of her—and they did the same behind her too, when she turned to look back at the opening they had passed through. The portal had closed. Claustrophobia gripped her.

"What's happening?" she asked, feeling like a child lost in a crowd of towering legs.

"We are traveling," said Deangelis, his face unfreezing. Waves of static rippled up and down his slender, youthful form—not the "adult" version she had briefly glimpsed before leaving Geodesica.

As he spoke the words, the tunnel ahead opened and they shot out a matching portal on the far side of the wall. Or so it seemed to her at first. The wall behind them was exactly as it had been before: an endless, milky plain dotted with portal after portal, gripping the eye and tugging it to infinity.

When the distant edges of the plain bowed inward around her, forming a flattened bowl much like the first she had glimpsed, she disbelieved her eyes completely. But the gradient of the slope increased, defying all attempts to dismiss it as an illusion, until the very edges of the bowl rose up around them. The wall was definitely bending. The faster she and the others moved away from the portal they had come through, the farther ahead the most distant portals stretched.

Her mind rebelled completely when those edges began to close together ahead of them, completing a sphere around her, a sphere covered entirely with portals.

Out of the frying pan, she thought, *and into the fire.*

"Travelers called this the Onion," Deangelis said, staring intently at her. "Yes. Or names to that effect. A myriad of entrances to a myriad of different spaces, natural and artificial, overlapping and entangling in a series that is not infinite, but nearly so. The route we're following was preprogrammed for me a very long time ago; I haven't the capacity to navigate these spaces on my own. But I can appreciate them and the effort our kind expended to map them."

They crossed the midpoint and the portal behind them faded to black. A shadow seemed to rush away from it as the wall ahead of them formed a bowl whose edges flexed once again to infinity.

"It's incredible," said Eogan, speaking for the first time. "Humanity made this?"

"Yes." Deangelis turned to him as though only belatedly remembering he was there. His features flickered through a variety of expressions: confusion; alarm; concern. He settled on amiable interest and continued: "It started off as a series of small interstellar links and expanded in step with the borders of humanity's territory, system by system. The first recorded use of it was in Bedlam at the conclusion of the Gentry War. We didn't know what we'd seen until much later, when it came into common use. For many thousands of years it knit all humanity's reaches together, but it fell into disuse when more efficient alternatives arose to cross the gulfs of space. We might be the only people using it for transport at this moment, in all its vastness. That's a strange thought, don't you think?"

The question was addressed to Melilah, but she didn't know how to answer. Details bombarded her. *Bedlam; the Gentry War; many thousands of years . . .*

They swept through another portal. The passage beyond enclosed them and she avoided looking at either of its ends.

She wanted to ask the date, but couldn't bring herself to do so. Not yet.

"Where are we going?" she asked instead. "Where are you taking us?"

"To Sol."

"What?" Eogan raised a hand to grip Deangelis's shoulder. His fingers slipped right through the ex-Exarch's flesh. Static flared. Eogan was startled but not deterred. "We can't go back there. The Archon—"

"Is no threat to you now."

"How can you say that? It destroyed Bedlam and Sublime! Its replicators have been hunting us all through Bedlam. Replicators *you* sent, I presume." Eogan's lips set in a furious line. "You are the Exarch of Bedlam, aren't you?"

"Yes, but I had no choice—"

"Maybe you didn't *then,*" Melilah said, "but you do *now*. You can't turn us in—not after all we've been through!"

Deangelis looked hurt by the suggestion. "I'm not turning you in," he said. "I would never hurt you. I have been waiting for you, alone, in order to ensure your safety. You are the reason I exist, Melilah. I have no other purpose. Without you, I am—" He hesitated, and again another series of complex expressions passed across his face. "In another age, another place, I said I loved you. That is as true here and now as it was then."

Shock rippled through her, making her head feel light. "You *what*?"

"I love you, Melilah. I always have. But I do not expect this feeling to be returned. You are a free agent; I am tied to you by my nature. It would be wrong for you to feel obliged." Deangelis's eyes were pleading with her. "All I ask is that you do not mistrust me."

She didn't know what to say. Conscious of Eogan starting at both of them, her jaw locked.

Deangelis's gaze dropped. "I am sorry. Perhaps I am communicating poorly. A long time has passed since I spoke to anyone but myself in any language."

She turned away just as their transparent sphere flew out of its tunnel. The infinity of portals was too much for her to take in. She closed her eyes and leaned against the curved wall.

"I must ask you." Melilah didn't need to look at Deangelis's face to hear the sadness in his voice. "Three of you escaped Bedlam: you, Palmer Eogan, and part of me. May I ask . . . ?"

"He's gone," said Eogan gruffly. "He sacrificed himself to give us a chance to escape."

"Yes, of course. Yes. I understand."

"He lied to us," said Melilah, remembering the final communication she had received from their lost companion. *I was complicit for the best of reasons—but that is no excuse.* She kept her eyes tightly shut, unable to look at him or through the transparent walls at the impossible spaces outside. It was hard enough remembering what had happened, let alone taking in new details. *He sacrificed himself to give us a chance to escape.* It all sounded so noble. *I love you.* But Eogan didn't know the truth about what had happened in the cavern. She wasn't entirely certain of it herself. *A long time has passed since I spoke to anyone but myself.*

It was all too much.

Eogan watched Melilah's reactions closely. She was cutting herself off, isolating herself from both him and Deangelis. The latter he could understand; the ex-Exarch seemed dangerously unstable, a patchwork of his former self held together by threadbare willpower. But *him*? What had he done? He could feel the connection they'd shared in the cavern fading with every passing second.

Frustrated, he put a hand on the transparent wall of the vessel as she had, but seeking information rather than balance. A flood of data rushed through him, only a small percentage of which he understood. The vessel was much larger than it appeared, as he had suspected; its true extent was hidden by the view Deangelis had given them of the Onion. Complex, multidimensional architecture baffled him; the ship was as peculiar as the space through which it traveled. He struggled to get his head around winglike vanes and curving spines and globular drive units that seemed to occupy the same points in three-space but were far-flung in other frames of reference. It made no sense. He felt the feather-light touch of the *Cowell* when he looked for it, and was reassured somewhat.

The data recorded by the Cell confirmed his initial impression: that the exit they had taken from Geodesica had led into the outer atmosphere of a brown dwarf. Exactly which brown dwarf he didn't know—they had been captured long before glimpsing the sky beyond that hellish environment—but at least they had been outside Geodesica, however briefly. The vessel that contained them now, presumably controlled by Deangelis or some form of advanced autopilot, had engulfed them like a toothy, deep-sea fish gulping down a drifting morsel. They hadn't stood a chance.

Then suddenly he had been standing next to Melilah, confronted by the same incredible view. He, too, was reminded of Geodesica. *A myriad of entrances to a myriad of different spaces* . . . But why build such a thing when Geodesica already existed? Why duplicate such an almighty effort?

He wondered if they were being lied to again.

He doubted there was anything he could do about it if they were.

Another portal swept by, different from the rest. Whereas the other tunnels had terminated in pinched-off points, this one ballooned outward as they neared its end. Blackness ahead held a bright light source that might have been a sun. Eogan shielded his eyes as the glare became stronger.

With a jolt, they exited the tunnel and entered real space. Looking behind him, he saw a brilliant, white ring hanging against the sky, spitting like a sparkler. It began to shrink when they were a safe distance away and within a breath had vanished.

"We're here," said Deangelis.

Melilah opened her eyes. Her chin tucked down protectively to her chest.

The view of Sol meant little to Eogan. Apart from the primary—an unremarkable G-type star he knew from navigation manuals and history texts—little was visible of the planetary system. Jupiter and Saturn were bright specks on opposite sides of the sun, with smaller planets scattered in their orbits across the celestial backdrop. All were present and accounted for.

But that backdrop! His jaw dropped at the sight of it. His eyes searched for a familiar landmark and found none in the visible spectrum. He didn't recognize a single constellation. Instead, an all-encompassing spray of nebulae and glowing clouds of gas obscured the Milky Way and painted the normal black of space every color of the rainbow. Purples and reds and yellow shone everywhere he looked, dimmed only by the bright glare of ancient Sol. It looked as though an insane cosmic god had dropped a palette of paint across the heavens. Only a handful of stars remained—and he wasn't one hundred percent certain they *were* stars. Their absorption spectra looked decidedly out of whack.

In the end, he oriented himself via the powerful X-ray source that was the center of the galaxy. Once he knew where that was, he felt grounded and less vulnerable—a sensation that faded only when their craft accelerated at many thousands of gees toward the inner system of Sol.

Such beauty, such horror . . . *What had happened here?*

"I need to ask *you* something," he said to Deangelis, the wounded, eroded being who had caught them on their emergence from Geodesica. "Don't spare us anything, even if you think it's for our own benefit. We need to know the truth."

Deangelis nodded, anticipating the question before he had voiced it. "Yes, Palmer Eogan. I will tell you the date."

"No. Don't do that; it'll be meaningless. Just tell us how long we've been gone. I think that's what matters most. How many *years*?"

"One million, two hundred twenty-six thousand, six hundred ninety-seven," came the deadpan answer.

That didn't make any sense either until he thought about it. The yawning chasm of doubt and disorientation closed with a slam.

"One and a quarter million years," Melilah muttered. "I can't believe that."

"I can," he said. "It's the only way to make sense of all this—the Onion, *him,* the stars—"

"The stars," interrupted Melilah, her expression that of someone woken from a deep state of shock. She was obviously having trouble accepting it. "What happened to the stars?"

"They were destroyed," Deangelis explained.

"During the Gentry War?"

"No. To seed the interstellar medium with useful elements. You see, humanity abandoned planets long ago. They're too confined, too expensive, too fragile. Except for those enjoying a nostalgic thrill by living at the bottom of a gravity well, the vast majority of humans migrated permanently to space, where they flourished. Even stellar neighborhoods began to look a little crowded, as time went by. The only thing stopping people from moving right out into the gulfs was a lack of resources. During one of its expansionist phases, humanity decided to solve the problem once and for all. The nebulae you see are the result."

"They blew up the stars to—to *mine* them?" Melilah turned her head from side to side in open-mouthed horror.

"In a manner of speaking. Not everyone agreed. The Fiery Way movement was, for the most part, confined only to the Local Group. A handful of key systems were spared for posterity's sake; Sol was obviously one of them—and Bedlam, you might be pleased to know. The rest were put to the torch."

"And you approve of this?" she asked him.

"Personally, no. But I can follow the reasoning. On the scale humanity inhabited at that time, stars were irrelevant. Do we quibble about the skin or blood cells that die within us every day? No. Neither would a mind that takes the entire galaxy for a home."

Eogan looked for any sign that Deangelis was exaggerating. A mind composed of many parts: that he could accept; he had seen such in action, with the Exarchs. Minds powerful enough to shut down an entire system: an intelligence of this caliber, too, he had glimpsed when the Archon had come to Bedlam. It wasn't so great a stretch from there to minds that could cross light-years and join stars, small clusters, even galaxies.

Was it?

"You've been gone a long time," Deangelis said, flickering like a poorly tuned digital feed. "I'm sorry."

"What've you got to be sorry for?" Melilah asked him. "As far as you're concerned, we're nothing but old news. I'm surprised you even remember us."

"I told you: I—"

"No, don't say it." Melilah shook her head. "I don't believe you."

Deangelis's hurt look returned. He did stop talking, though, and that was a good thing. Old news wasn't necessarily dead news. Eogan could tell just by looking at Deangelis that time hadn't healed some wounds.

Sol grew brighter by the second ahead of them, and Eogan found himself staring at it even though its brightness made his eyes water. So much for his desire to see the stars again, to ply the trade lanes of the Arc Circuit, to get his life back. The thought that followed was ungracious, but he couldn't help it: that Melilah might be glad that the fields were level now. They had both lost their homes. They were even.

A blue speck rushed toward them out of the burning sky: Earth, complete with white clouds and gleaming oceans. The continental outlines looked odd, but that was only to be expected; a million years wasn't an eyeblink even geologically speaking.

Their invisible craft decelerated at a bone-crushing rate—not the slightest jolt reached them in its protective embrace—and docked with an orbital station that was as graceful and streamlined as a work of art. Pliable matter melded seamlessly with rigid spatial architecture; it was hard to tell where the station stopped and space began. He sensed vast forces around them acting with tremendous restraint and delicacy, like a starship firing up its engines to nudge a painting back into alignment.

Their glass bubble popped soundlessly; ambient gravity became a little steeper; a scented breeze brushed his cheeks.

"We've arrived," said Deangelis, indicating that they should walk ahead of him into the station. A short, dimly lit corridor awaited them, its end hidden in shadow.

Eogan waited to see what Melilah would do. She folded her arms and looked at him, then hugged herself tighter and walked forward. He followed.

Three paces into the corridor, he stepped into bright sunlight shining over a green field, and almost walked right into Melilah's back.

"What in the Dark—?"

"Not in the Dark at all, Palmer Eogan. Quite the opposite, in fact."

Eogan turned to see a perfectly androgynous figure walking up a slight slope toward them. Bald head; broad chin; delicate nose and eyebrows; proud laughter-lines; full lips; wide gray eyes: many contradictory gender signifiers blended somehow into one seamless face. The body was the same, beneath a skin-tight white bodysuit that left little to the imagination. No breasts or external genitals. No distinctive skin color, either; just an earthy tan that displayed no visible scars.

Melilah stared at her—Eogan settled on the pronoun at random—in stunned silence until the new arrival came within arm's-reach and went to touch her face.

"Hey—keep your distance!"

The hand—as perfectly formed and perfectly genderless as the rest—retracted. "We did not mean to offend you, and do not wish to cause you alarm. Our curiosity merely overcame us. Your presence here is—*remarkable*."

Melilah took a step back. Eogan wanted to offer his support, but he knew she wouldn't accept it. Her façade was shattered; overwhelmed by recent developments, she lay naked to the world around her. He could see the fright bare on her face. He felt it, too.

"Who are you? What's going on?"

"This is Earth, where your ancestors were born," said the genderless creature. "You have come back to the beginning. Isaac has awaited your return, and we are here to receive you. We are—" The figure hesitated, and a sensual smile played across her lips. "We have no name in much the same way that the universe has no name. It doesn't need one; it defines itself."

"You must have a name," Melilah insisted. "Or a serial number, or *something*."

"Why? Why must we be anything at all?" She laughed. "We are ancient beyond measure. We are broader and more massive than entire galaxies, deeper than black holes, and as pervasive as the cosmic microwave background radiation. Yet for all our greatness, our strength rests upon the realm of the very small. You could fit a million of our thoughts on the head of a pin, and a million entirely new thoughts on the same pin the next nanosecond. We can lift single atoms and trace the path of isolated photons. We can untangle strings and dissect empty space itself. We have pushed the boundaries of what it means to interact, to observe, to be. We are the peak experience. We are—" Again a pause, but this time she sobered. "No, you need a word, or you will never understand. Not one name exists for us, but there is a noun in this ancient language you speak. We are *Humanity*."

Eogan felt vertigo sweep through him as the being's gray eyes met his. Just for a moment, he had wondered if the creature before them could be a human disguise for the builders of Geodesica. Who else, after all, had done all the things she claimed?

"Come," she said. "We'll be more comfortable seated."

She gestured, and a tree appeared on the meadow where there had been none visible before, with a picnic table shaded by its broad boughs. He had a strange feeling that it had always been there, in a parallel reality that he had simply failed to see. The air was clean and fresh, but it seemed filled with possibilities, as though every grain of pollen or dust might suddenly flower into a multitude of bubble universes.

Obediently, his mind ringing like a bell, he followed Melilah and the creature claiming to represent all of humanity to their seats in the shade.

"Now, listen to us while we tell you what's going to happen next."

Deangelis hovered like a ghost at a funeral as Humanity welcomed home its prodigal children. He felt no great need to interact, content merely to bask in the moment. After so many years waiting, to have finally achieved his goal was a miracle. He could die and be happy.

For a fleeting moment, he seriously considered ending his life right there and then. He possessed that capacity, as had every Exarch and most citizens of the Exarchate. Euthanasia was a basic human right, accompanying the right to pursue an extended, healthy life. His life had certainly been extended beyond all expectations, the definition of "healthy" with it. He could feel a thousand millennia's worth of errors accumulated in his mind. They slowed him down, interfered with his natural processes, made even his appearance unsteady. Perhaps it was time to surrender to the nothingness that lay beyond slow-time, in the final full-stop.

But who, he asked himself, *would look after Melilah?*

"Everything," said Humanity, "ultimately comes back to scale. In the early moments of the universe, when the boundary between matter and energy was decidedly blurrier than it is today, life existed, in its own way. It was nothing like the life you and we enjoy. It was fleeting, furious, and fantastical. We wouldn't even recognize it as such were we to encounter it today.

"Sadly, there is no chance of that. Life in this form cannot exist anymore. The rules of physics haven't changed, but the universe has. Our home is too dark and disparate for the Bright Ones who preceded us. Their entire evolution flashed by in a mere thousand years, from statistical glitch to a web of information that encompassed the fireball that was the early universe. We know of their existence only through anomalies in the afterglow of creation—a death mask that tells us nothing about their thoughts, their lives, their aspirations. Just that they existed.

"Still, isn't that remarkable? One thousand years from conception to rulers of the universe! And perhaps they weren't the first. Perhaps other beings, even more unknowable, preceded them, blazing briefly in the seconds after the big bang. Others certainly followed. You knew of seven Races Other Than Human in the vicinity of this star system. We have identified no less than four hundred and eighteen intergalactic civilizations in the history of the universe. They came in every conceivable shape and size and left their marks in all manner of ways. Geodesica is just one of many legacies left behind by our forebears.

"Yes: Geodesica; the reason you're here. Do you know that you are the only people we have ever met to experience this remarkable artifact from the inside? We could ask you what you learned, what you saw, who you met. Did you find its builders, and encounter welcome or resistance during your incursion on their precious territory?

"We could ask you these things, but we will not. We know that you did not meet its builders, because they are dead and have been for eight billion years. After their extinction, Geodesica broke free of its anchor points and wandered the universe, growing and spreading as its natural function dictates. Its exits are navigation hazards, just as they were in your time. They warp space and deform time, and are carefully mapped for just that reason. But we would never destroy them, no more than you would have destroyed a valuable archeological site. Geodesica tells us something important about life in the universe—about *all* life, not just its creators, and therefore about ourselves, too.

"Geodesica's makers left other marks on the universe, ones we found and deciphered during our expansion and exploration. We can tell you more about them and their works, perhaps, than you would ever have found out from the inside. We can look and wonder what they might have been like; we can read their texts and examine their artifacts; we pore over their bones and re-create biologies. Although it is hard to find similarities, sometimes, between the quick-thinking inheritors of the Bright Ones, and more leisurely, atomic beings like the makers of Geodesica and us, one very important convergence stands out. All of these civilizations evolved and existed alone in the universe. Intelligent life blossoms and flourishes among the ruins of those who preceded it—and we, their inheritors, are similarly alone.

"Nothing but hints remain of the grandeur our predecessors achieved. They themselves are but dust and fading memories. The universe is a graveyard—occasionally inhabited by lively, capricious spirits, but most often echoing and empty; a bottomless sepulcher. We who study it cannot avoid the conclusion that awaits us: *why should humanity be any different?* What separates us from the former rulers of the universe, who like us claimed dominion over the visible universe, and to whom space and time hold no mysteries; who blossomed like novae then faded from the sky? What can we do to avoid their fates?

"The answer, my friends, is: nothing.

"Geodesica, that grand but doomed artifact that was once the hope of a thousand worlds, is a monument to the greatness of those long gone. We treat it with the same respect we hope ours will receive, in the distant future, for it is a reminder of humanity's ultimate mortality."

"The scale of our endeavors matches and exceeds that of Geodesica, but it is no match for the scale of the universe across time as well as space. We are doomed, as all things are doomed, to pass into ash and cobwebs. We will leave our mark, undoubtedly. You have seen the sky. You have visited the Onion. Our works are manifold and magnificent. But they are not *us*. They will remain and we will fade, as others have faded before us. There is no technological wizardry that will help us elude our fate. Nothing will prevent us from fading and withering and vanishing.

"You're giving up?" interrupted Melilah, her expression appalled. "Isn't that what you're saying?"

"There's nothing to give up," Humanity replied with perfect patience. "This isn't a competition; there are no winners or losers. This is life, and it follows cycles. Patterns recur; phase changes unfold. Fighting nature achieves nothing, and we see no need to do it. In fact, the process has already begun. Within a few hundred thousand years, we will all, most likely, be gone, and our mighty works will be left to rot, just as Geodesica was by its makers.

"You see this as a tragedy. We disagree. Two possible transformations lie before us. One: we can retreat into our memories and effectively vanish from the universe. Other races, we suspect, have done this in the past. This is not so barren an experience as you might initially imagine. Consider the openness of Bedlam multiplied a trillion-trillion-fold. That is how much information humanity has at its fingertips now, at its end-times. It would take an explorer a million years or more to wander through the vault of human experience, making new connections and discovering little-glimpsed pockets of experience as they go, and creating their own memories-of-memories that others will explore in turn.

"The second transformation open to us is to abandon the notion of who we are entirely and become what we will be. In this option we see the greatest possibilities. Humanity's children have adopted many different guises down the millennia. We know that to you, Melilah, this may seem abhorrent, but it is necessary. One cannot move into space and adopt galaxies while confined by the bodies you know and are familiar with. Yet despite our many changes we still call ourselves human. That word—and the concept it captures—matters to us. The notion of *humanity* helps cohere our ventures in ways that politics and ideals alone cannot; it defines itself in an arbitrary and utterly vital fashion.

"At this time, however, at the peak of humanity's greatness, we have come to wonder if the concept of 'humanity' is both a blessing and a curse. We ask ourselves what there is left for us to do under that label, from within that well-defined identity. Once we conquered the universe, we had nowhere else to go. If we can't go anywhere but deeper into our memories, the only thing left to do is to change. Some see in the lack of human identity and unfocused energies—in *evolution*—hope for a new beginning. Just as you had to let go of your homes in order to come here, so, too, will we let go of 'humanity' in order to reach some new, unknowable destination. To not take that chance would be to invite stagnation—and we do not want that. Inasmuch as we can choose our legacy, we would have it be that we came, we were wondrous, and we didn't outstay our welcome.

"Two paths, then: the temptation of memory; the allure of the alien. Is this how our forebears ended their reigns? We can't ask them how they fared because they're no longer with us. We can't wonder what will happen to us, either, because we won't *be* us anymore, whichever path we choose.

"This is a marvelous time to be alive. We are the pinnacle of life in this universe, at this time; nothing will ever be like us again. We have to let go of everything we have, and are, if we are to become greater still—be it a home, a lover, a sense of self, a destiny. The time has come to find new dangers and make new mistakes. We do not shy from that certainty. We are ready for this decision, and embrace it to the fullest possible extent."

"How long?" asked Palmer Eogan.

"The sunset of humanity is upon us, even as we speak. It might take another hundred thousand years before the memory-divers completely vanish into the archives and those who remain evolve into shapes and cultures unforeseen. A hundred thousand years is a long time from your point of view, but it is not to us. We watch stars blaze and die as you would watch flowers bloom and wilt. We grow eager to throw off our shackles and *become*."

Humanity's face glowed with life and expectancy. Deangelis thought that he had never seen anything quite so beautiful. But he sensed only confusion and suspicion on the faces of Melilah and Palmer Eogan, and that, he supposed, he could understand. They had emerged from Geodesica too late to witness the full glory of humanity. Wonders remained, and much to explore and learn, but not forever. The future was not limitless. Everything had an end.

"We are sorry to bombard you with this information," Humanity said. "You feel overwhelmed, we are sure. This is a necessary evil, however. You must begin to understand the world you have come to before you make the decision awaiting you. And yes, you *do* have a decision. We would not make it for you; we are not tyrants, and we would never presume to know what is best for you. You must decide of your own free will. Once you are sufficiently informed, we will implement your decision without hesitation, no matter what it is. This is our promise to you.

"More than one million years ago, you left us. Your journey was confusing and arduous. Now you have returned. Melilah Awad, Palmer Eogan—we are proud of you, and honor you. And you too, Isaac Deangelis. There is time now to celebrate. You are free."

The table beneath the tree was suddenly laden with food and drink, or a convincing facsimile thereof. Slices of fresh apple; duck liver pâté; bread still warm from an unseen oven; slivers of chocolate in a variety of colors and flavors.

"We have been remiss," said Humanity. "You look hungry. Please, eat. It must be weeks since you last ate proper food."

Melilah picked up a long-stemmed wineglass to take a sip, but her throat closed on it, and she thought for a moment that she might be physically sick.

Free?

Everything she had known and loved was a million years dead. Humanity destroyed stars for a hobby now. What sort of insanity was this?

There was no questioning the effort that had gone into making them feel welcome—or at least to ensure they wouldn't go wanting—but nothing could stop her head from spinning.

Letting go of home is the hardest thing a person can do. Technically, she *was* home now, or as close as she could ever come, if what Humanity told them was true. And she had no reason to doubt it.

But she was a stranger here in humanity's ancient birthplace. The grass, the boughs of the eucalyptus under which they sat, the fresh air, might have reassured someone raised on Earth when such things had been commonplace; they didn't reassure her, daughter of the Arc Circuit.

"Tell me . . . ," she began, then faltered.

"Anything." The face of Humanity radiated openness and compassion. A façade, she was sure, but a believable one. It didn't necessarily hide deception.

"What happened to the Archon and the Exarchate? Isaac—" She glanced at the fragile form of her former enemy; he shivered, then firmed with a smile. "Isaac mentioned something about a war. Did people fight over Geodesica? What happened to them?"

Humanity's expression became somber. "The conflict in your system did indeed spill over into the rest of the Exarchate. A number of secessionist Exarchs demanded control over the Exarchate from Sol. They were given what they wanted, in the end, to avoid a protracted conflict, but control over Geodesica remained with Sol. The known entrances were sealed from the outside. It was never used."

"I don't understand. Why *not* use it? What was so dangerous about it?"

"You've been inside it. Can't you guess?"

"It wasn't dangerous at all. The only problems we encountered came from the drones sent after us. But for that and getting lost, we would've made it out a million years ago."

"Exactly." Humanity folded his—as Melilah thought of the androgynous creature—hands on the table before him. "It's too easy. Didn't you once say, when the Exarchate first came to Bedlam, that Naturals deserved the chance to make their own mistakes rather than be dictated to by Sol?"

"Yes, but—"

"Geodesica was the right artifact at the wrong time. The Archon knew it; the Architects of Sol knew it; you would have come to know it, too, as unprepared humanity swarmed like rats across the stars. The scale of the universe would have defeated you. The fight for control of Geodesica would have been the beginning of conflicts spanning whole galactic clusters. The only way to end such horror was before it started. So Sol did everything it could to keep Geodesica out of your hands. It was studied, briefly, then abandoned. We found other means to get around, and Sol certainly didn't lack the patience or the resources required for that task. Once humanity understood the technology behind Geodesica, the alien artifact was no longer needed and could be safely ignored. We built our own."

"Why didn't Sol just tell us this? Why were we left in the dark?"

"You wouldn't have accepted Sol's decision, even had you known the truth about Geodesica. That is the sad but undeniable fact. The Exarchate was an inappropriate response to an unexpected problem. To Palmer Horsfall and Jane Elderton—and, yes,

Isaac Deangelis—Geodesica represented a possibility that did not exist. Geodesica wouldn't have saved humanity; it would have destroyed it. For two centuries, its mere existence tore humanity in two. How much more deadly could it have been had it actually fallen into the Exarchate's hands?

"The Gentry War was the last great conflict of our species, fought in the name of an artifact that symbolized hope for some and destruction for others—yet it wasn't really about Geodesica at all. It was about what humanity should be, what it means, and how it changes. In that sense, the Archon was absolutely correct in its actions. Humanity prevailed. That is the important thing."

Melilah bit down on a retort that *important* had a very different meaning from where she was standing.

Then she remembered Deangelis talking to her about the McMeeken Plan and the long view of humanity.

We still fight, she had told him. *We just fight over different things.*

That insight neither reassured her nor compensated for the destruction wrought on her home by those professing to work in humanity's greater interests.

"Friends." Humanity reached out as though to touch Melilah and Eogan's hands, but fell short. Perfectly proportioned fingers rested instead on the white tablecloth. "There is one more thing you must know. I have told you that the concept of 'humanity' bound us all these long millennia, that it united our sense of self and our purpose. This is true, but it alone would not have been enough. We required one other achievement to ensure our longevity, beside which the mastery of space and the human genome paled into insignificance. Without this step behind us, all our journeys would have gone nowhere. Knowing full well that such a development would be required to ensure the continuance of humanity beyond any significant length of time, the Architects of Sol dedicated all their efforts to achieving it, and achieve it they did. We achieved our aspiration two centuries after your departure.

"On the fourteenth of April, 2692 CE, Sol opened a portal to the future."

Melilah blinked, wondering if she'd heard correctly. "You have time machines as well?"

"Just one, and a temporal gate rather than a machine as you imagine it—but yes. Essentially that term is correct."

Deangelis and Eogan looked as surprised as she felt. "How?" asked Eogan. "Why?"

"The mechanism itself is unimportant. You need know only

that the existence of such a gateway promotes stability never before known in human history. All times are effectively one. Through the gate, the Architects commute between them as easily as you once traveled from world to world. This leads not to stasis, but richness; life is varied beyond imagining now that all people and cultures exist coevally. There are limits, of course, as there are with all technologies: we can travel to times only within the gateway's existence, not before or after, when the technology to sustain it no longer operates. But within those points, Melilah, Palmer Eogan, the entire length of our existence is a playground."

An image of gods making castles in sand came to her. "That means you've always known when we would emerge from Geodesica."

"Yes. But facts are less important than meaning; the delight is in the details."

Deangelis's look of shock only increased at the revelation. Melilah shook her head in wonderment and confusion. Had she not seen the Onion, she might have believed that everything was a lie, that Humanity—or whatever it really was—had no intention other than snowblinding her and Eogan indefinitely.

"The temporal gate," said Eogan, "You called it a portal to the future. Am I right in assuming that it works in reverse?"

"It does. And I believe you've guessed the nature of the decision you have to make."

Eogan didn't match Humanity's broadening smile. He glanced at Melilah, then away again, and she wanted to ask: *What? What are you two hinting at?*

Then it hit her, and all she could do was stare.

"How far back could we go?" Eogan asked. "If we so chose."

"If you so chose, to the moment of the gateway's opening. That date marks the beginning of our calendar—the calendar of Coevality, in which all ages are one."

"What about the end?"

"Does it matter?" asked Melilah.

"It does matter," said Humanity. "Measuring the days, months, and years by your old scale, Coevality will end on December fourth, 1,224,005."

"And when is that, exactly?" Eogan asked.

"Tomorrow." Humanity folded her hands on the table before them. "So you see, your timing is critical."

"And a little unlikely," he said, unable to hide his suspicion. "One day later and the temporal gate would be closed. What are the odds that we should happen to arrive now?"

"It's not a coincidence. This date is chosen *because* you are here. We have kept the gateway open solely to give you this choice—you, the last of our lost children. You can stay or go back, as you desire. You can't go all the way back—but 2692 is not so long after your departure. Some people you knew will still be alive, such as Isaac, here. The Exarchate still exists."

"And the Archon?" asked Melilah, sharply.

"Yes."

Melilah's jaw muscles tightened. Eogan intuited what her decision would be. The last time he had seen that look was when Lazarus Hails had offered her a devil's pact enabling both of them to get closer to the Archon. He hadn't been able to talk her out of it then; he doubted he could do so now. But he couldn't stay silent.

"If you go back then, the Archon will be ready for you," he told her. "Or if not ready for you, then faster and stronger than you. You'll be landing right in the middle of Sol, remember; you'll be completely overwhelmed."

"I'll take that chance."

"To do what? Take on all of Sol on your own?"

"Tell the truth about what happened. People deserve that much."

"Won't they already know the truth because of Coevality?"

Humanity, who had watched their debate dispassionately, spoke up: "The spread of Coevality takes time. One can open a door and not immediately pass through it. One can step onto a road and not follow straight it to its end. Remember that your civilization had existed for only a few hundred years at that point in time, and had already generated too much data for everyone to assimilate. Drop another one point two million years' worth of data pertaining to a civilization many magnitudes larger into that mix and you will see how Coevality might not immediately be adopted."

"But the fact remains," he said. "It's pointless."

"I disagree," Melilah said.

"At least think it over," he pleaded.

"You have a day," Humanity agreed. "We would be honored if you would stay that long, if no longer."

Melilah looked at both of them as though wondering if she was being conned. "All right," she said. "I'll think it over."

"Thank you," Eogan said, unable to hide the weariness in his voice. He hadn't truly believed that all his problems would be over once they escaped Geodesica, but he hadn't expected anything like this. All the stars that he had called home, all the routes he had followed—none of them existed anymore. Yet even in its dying hours, humanity held dominion over the entire universe. Billions of galaxies; uncountable new stars; who knew what rare and incredible wonders existed that he had never imagined seeing?

What in turn did 2692 hold for him, apart from his old haunts? The aftermath of an interstellar civil war; a Cell that might no longer exist; friends whose allegiances and characters had undoubtedly changed dramatically in the two hundred fifty years since he had allied himself in an intersystem conflict against Palmer policies and subsequently vanished from their lives. He had no family, no home, no career to return to.

Here, in a date he had still to truly accept, the universe was on his doorstep.

A stiff wind whipped around them, rustling the trees and making the white tablecloth flutter. He hadn't noticed how late in the day it had become. The sun was sinking low over the horizon. He had trouble remembering the last time he had experienced nightfall on a planet's surface. New Year's Eve on Eliza perhaps, in 2350? An ill-advised hike on Alcor 3a around the same time? He couldn't quite place it. Either way, the thought was unsettling. There were no clouds, so the sun would simply set without spectacle. And then it would get cold.

"We have prepared accommodations for you," Humanity said. "Once we might have offered to show you the sights, but this is the pinnacle of life on Sol. Nature is free of our influence and unfettered by the misguided and well meaning alike. Not a blade of grass is ever mown here; no species' existence is ever prolonged. Our footprint may be large in the heavens, but it is small where we were born. We are, perhaps, disproportionately proud of that fact."

As she spoke, the walls of an ancient cathedral coalesced out of thin air around and above them. Its beamed wooden ceiling was easily high enough to accommodate the tree in which they sat, at the center of its cross-shaped floor plan. Its stained-glass windows were narrow and tall, reaching like glowing fingers for the heavens above. The sunset cast multicolored patterns across the wall, the table and its marginally depleted fare, and the three people sitting facing each other.

Humanity raised her glass and drained it. "We have talked enough. The night is yours to think, sleep, discuss—whatever you require. Your needs will be met at a simple request. Do not be afraid to ask."

Humanity stood and eased her chair back. Her eyes gleamed in the mottled light, as moist as any natural human's; her lips were stained red from the wine. He wanted to know if her skin was warm, if she had a pulse, if she was anything more than just an artful shell.

Instead he simply said, "Thank you."

Her smile swept over him. "You are welcome. Isaac?" The flickering ghost who had said nothing and eaten not a scrap throughout the evening looked up, startled. "Come with me. This is for our friends to explore alone."

Deangelis tore himself away from Melilah's side with a visible effort. "Good night," he said. "I won't be far away."

Eogan thought of the one million and a quarter years he had been waiting for Melilah to return, and knew he meant every word.

Deangelis focused on the small of Humanity's back as he/she led him out of the cathedral. Resentment burned inside him, even though he knew Humanity was right to give Melilah and Eogan space to absorb everything they'd learned. He understood, too, why Melilah felt no compunction to reciprocate his devotion. From her point of view, she had been gone only a matter of weeks. The decision to wait out her return had been entirely his.

But he had expected better than this. Gratitude, recognition, sympathy—*something*. Not cold, hard confusion, and renewed uncertainty.

You've always known when we would emerge from Geodesica . . .

Humanity walked along the nave of the cathedral and through gothic archways out into the night air. As the light of Sol faded over the western horizon, the work of the Fiery Way gradually became visible. The sky looked like a collision between Rothko and Pollack, and he supposed that, in its own gargantuan way, the interlocking nebulae could be considered magnificent.

Humanity led him up the gentle slope of a low hill. He recognized the place now, although he hadn't before. On this hill he had been born, twice: the first time when the Archon had brought his higher self together in 2374; the second after the destruction of Bedlam, sixty-four years later.

"Wait here," he/she said. "You have your own decisions to make, friend."

Deangelis opened his mouth to protest, and Humanity touched his cheek with the palm of one hand. A flood of strength rushed through him, leaving him feeling as though nonexistent clouds had parted. He breathed deeply of the brisk air, savoring its scents and richness. A complex, ever-changing ecosystem lived in this atmosphere, and had for billions of years. It would live on long after the human race had gone, vanished into a remembered past or beyond all applicable definitions. He might be one of the last to stand at that spot and savor its richness.

When he exhaled, he/she was gone. Any complaints he wished to make would have to wait.

On the summit of the hill he found a waist-high round boulder instead of the gravestone that had been there in the past. He climbed onto it and crossed his legs. The solidity of his artificial flesh was variable. At some point he would have to have that permanently seen to by Humanity's advanced debuggers. Part of him wore the disruption as a warrior would scars, except his enemies were solely internal or passive. Self-doubt and time weren't the stuff most heroes had to deal with.

But he did feel a sense of accomplishment, in among everything else. He had lasted long enough to recognize Melilah when she emerged from Geodesica. Out of all the millions of versions of him, scattered to all the reaches of the universe, he was the lucky one. What would the others think when word reached them? Would they feel cheated, or simply relieved that the long wait was over?

He pushed all thoughts of those other selves from his mind. Tonight wasn't about him. It was about *her*. She was alive, as he had always insisted. And she was *back*.

Although he doubted Humanity would approve, Deangelis increased the sensitivity of his hearing in order to eavesdrop on Melilah and Palmer Eogan. The stone walls of the cathedral interfered with the sound, so he could pick up only snatches of their conversation, and his comprehension of colloquial English wasn't what it used to be. But he could follow the gist of it. They appeared to be arguing.

"What's the point?" she asked. "Why stay here when everything's going to fall apart?"

Palmer Eogan's response was indecipherable.

"So it was all for nothing," she went on. "Everything we

dreamed of and strived for? I can't accept that. There has to be more to life, something deeper. More *meaningful*."

"What could be more meaningful than understanding the entire universe?" came the reply. "By definition, there *can't* be any more meaning."

"You know what I'm trying to say."

"Actually, I don't think I do. You want there to be more meaning, and you won't accept it when someone tells you that that's all there is."

"Meaning is in the eye of the beholder."

"Well, yes. And maybe humanity has had all the meaning it can deal with, hence the next step. Or steps."

Melilah snorted in exasperation and moved to a part of the cathedral where Deangelis could no longer hear her clearly. All he heard was Eogan's half of the conversation.

"What would going back achieve?"

(. . .)

"What if the Archon was right to do what it did?"

(. . .)

"Well, there's no doubt in my mind that Deangelis is a more capable person than I am, at least when it comes to flying the Cell, and I'm not as strict as you when it comes to who's a person and who's not." Deangelis felt a mixture of pride and unease at Eogan's bold declaration. "I don't think it's wise to write him off so casually—or who he represents."

(. . .)

"I think you do. We've both seen the Exarchs at work. They were designed to govern. Maybe the ends didn't justify the means, but you have to admit they did a pretty good job of managing the Exarchate. Whether you like it or not—"

(. . .)

"—you have to question the automatic assumption. You just have to look around us to see the long-term results of Sol's policies. Could a single Natural government have lasted a million years?"

Melilah's voice suddenly came into range. "One million fucking years. If I hear that number one more time, I'll scream!"

Deangelis knew exactly how she felt.

He pulled his attention away from the conversation, disturbed by the possibility that she might take up the chance of returning to—or close to—her own time. Where would that leave him? He had focused so hard on waiting for her; he had spent no time at all thinking about what would happen *after*. He had been so far removed from the rest of humanity that he hadn't known about the gateway through time. If he had, he might have asked to know when Melilah returned and saved himself an extraordinarily long subjective wait.

The possibility that she might never return had occurred to him, of course, or that she might die shortly thereafter. The former possibility absolved him of a decision, and the latter demanded that he accept what couldn't be changed. But this was an entirely new sort of quandary. Should he try to talk her out of it, as Palmer Eogan was clearly doing? Should he offer to come back with her? Had she already done so, from the point of view of the past, and died a million years ago?

A strange and upsetting possibility occurred to him then, one he could barely credit, but which grew only stronger as he returned to the conversation like a moth drawn toward a naked flame.

"What about you?" she asked Eogan. "Would you consider going back?"

This time it was the Palmer's voice Deangelis couldn't hear. He was forced to extrapolate based on Melilah's responses alone.

"Where's the joy in that? We're like chimps here, cutting in on a very big, very sophisticated party. The special effects might be of some comfort, if only we didn't know it was about to come down around our ears."

(. . .)

"It *is* a grim thought, that everyone's ended up like this. No other species has broken out of that cycle and stayed on top. Or have they all gone on to bigger and better things? Are we like the caterpillars looking at all the empty pupae and thinking *what a goddamn waste*?"

(. . .)

"I don't think that's the only way to find out. How can we go forward without knowing where we came from? How do we know that anything we've been told is true? I can't just accept it. I want to find out for myself. Until I see it with my own eyes and make sure we didn't try everything possible to avoid it—"

(. . .)

"Yeah, I know that's unrealistic. But the journey is important. We've had our journey through Geodesica; we've missed out on everyone else's because of it. I'm not ready to let go of where I came from. I can't do it that easily. And maybe I have to let go properly before I can move on."

(. . .)

"Yes—you, too, if necessary. Letting go of *everything*."

More silence. Deangelis sat unmoving, barely feeling the unyielding surface of the stone under his buttocks, or noticing the moon as it rose over the eastern horizon, its face scarred by massive works abandoned millennia ago.

He was trying to remember a series of conversations that had taken place a very long time ago.

I came out a long way from here, Isaac. As to when—well, if I told you, you wouldn't believe me.

The memories were deeply buried. They surfaced like fragments of a long-sunk galleon, but he was persistent.

What happened to Palmer Eogan?

He stayed behind.

In Geodesica?

That's hard to explain. It's probably best you don't ask me to try.

His erratic skin tingled as something more profound than culture shock rippled through him.

You knew her for a handful of decades several millennia ago. You observed her and spoke to her, but you never really understood her. She could have changed in a million ways.

I *haven't changed. I'd know her if I saw her.*

Then:

I will never call you Melilah Awad.

And, most galling of all:

You told me, once, that you loved me.

He felt faint. For so many years he had thought the impostor had been referring to the part of him lost in Geodesica—when it had in fact been himself in his own future who first told her those words. What should he do now? Should he run to her, tell her that he knew what decision she would make and apologize for his obtuseness down the years, for misjudging her then and in the future? Should he beg her to tell him the truth when she arrived in the past, so he could avoid this moment, when he would realize, finally, that the thing he sought had been right in front of him all along? Should he beg her to change the past and stay with him, even though she patently didn't need or want him?

Humanity's hand came down on his shoulder. He/She had appeared directly behind him; perhaps he/she had always been there.

"Say nothing," Humanity told him. "Let her come to her own conclusions."

"As I did?" he protested with more than a twinge of irritation.

"I never knew about Coevality. I wasn't told the truth. When she first appeared and I asked Sol if she had emerged from Geodesica, I was told that she hadn't."

"And so it was. Not yet. She arrived through the gate from the future, not out of Geodesica."

"But—"

"It is a technicality, yes; a lie by omission—but one she wished perpetuated. We abided by her decision, as you would have in our place."

He could find no fault with his/her answer, even though it irked him. So much time lost. So much of *himself*!

He remembered the impostor—no; the *real thing*—telling him that one of him had committed suicide when told the truth. And no wonder, he thought. No wonder!

He could barely live with the revelation now, even at the end of his long, awful quest, when he knew he had been successful.

Melilah's voice came faintly from the cathedral. "Anyway, we've got a whole day to make our decisions. I think we should sleep on it, otherwise we'll just start going around in circles again."

Eogan, too, sounded weary. "We've been doing a lot of sleeping lately."

"It's the only way I feel completely safe with you. Stupid, isn't it? That after all we've been through, this sort of shit still matters?"

"I'm not sure that *stupid* is the way I'd describe it."

"Irrational, then. Or pathetic, or desperate. Take your pick."

"Some choice you're giving me. Do I really seem that way to you?"

"Only when we're together. And believe me, it's mutual."

They fell silent.

Sleep well, Deangelis thought. *I'll keep watch over you, and I'll let you go if I have to.*

He had no good answer to the question: *And then what will I do?*

+17

Closure: minus 15 hours

"I've made my decision," she told Humanity at the entrance to the cathedral. "And I think you already know what it is."

"What about Palmer Eogan?"

"He can make up his own mind. There's still time."

"There is indeed."

"Do you know what his decision will be? What it *was*?"

Humanity just smiled, and Melilah felt bad for bringing it up. She wanted to ask what happened to *her,* too. Did she arrive okay? Did she ever find peace? But that question went completely unasked.

"I feel like I've forgotten something." She looked around at the shadowed stonework and the darkened field. The moon was far from full and the skyscape muted despite all the colors. In the visual spectrum, the night was almost completely black.

Good, she thought. This wasn't where she'd expected to end up. The less she saw of it, the less she'd miss it.

Despite telling herself that, tears hung heavily in her eyes. She refused to let them fall. Her internal alarm had woken her an hour after she and Eogan had fallen asleep. His hand lay under hers, fingers limp, not quite gripping. She slid away from him as gently as she could. He hadn't stirred.

"This way." The androgynous figure took her by the hand and led her into the night.

+18

Closure: minus 5 minutes

Eogan wished he could excise the part of him that felt guilty and throw it into the gateway's swirling abyss. He didn't understand why he still labored under that pointless emotion. After all, Melilah had evened the score now. She had left him while he slept just as he had left her in Bedlam all those years ago.

How many years? Too many to still feel like he owed her something. That was a terrible reason to leap into the gaping maw of the temporal gate as she had, even though the impulse did hold a certain self-destructive appeal. The personification of humanity was cagey on exactly what they'd be diving into, but he doubted it was an idyllic world of peace and prosperity. Co-evality would be new to those far-off days. The Exarchate was still technically independent from the home system; Sol wasn't likely to burst out of its self-imposed isolation with the news that its descendants had taken over the universe and were ready to give elder humanity the benefit of their wisdom. It would take time for latent hostilities to cool. Many colonists had lost loved ones and friends during the Gentry War. Resentment persisted among people whose life spans were theoretically unlimited. The short-term picture looked, in other words, decidedly uncertain.

Melilah might have been killed or imprisoned as an enemy of Sol the moment she stepped out of the gateway. He recited a half-hearted prayer to the Dark even though it meant nothing, really, and was over a million years too late.

The Dark take and keep you. The light of ancient stars guide you to rest . . .

If he followed her, who would pray for him?

"Time is running out," said Humanity from behind him, at the base of the stairway leading up to the Earth's surface. "In four minutes, the gateway will close forever."

"I know."

"Once it's closed, the past will be lost. Not just to you, but to all of us. It will be . . . traumatic."

He nodded, utterly unable to know what it would feel like to lose a million years of simultaneous history in an instant. Like being confined to one planet after a lifetime of traveling the trade lanes? Like being imprisoned?

"Where's Deangelis?" he asked. The last time he'd looked, the ex-Exarch had been buzzing around the gateway like a lost drone bee, his expression one of dismal betrayal. He was gone now.

"Isaac is moving on in his own way, finding his own answers," Humanity said. She came forward to stand with Eogan on the very brink of the temporal gate. Strange forces tugged at her robe but she stood steadfast at his side. "What are you thinking?"

"That you can't go home," he said. "Isn't that what they say?"

"They did say that, once." Humanity smiled benignly. "Not anymore. The entire universe is our home now."

"I don't have a home," he said. "I never have, not since the *Ambidexter*."

"Perhaps that means you can be home anywhere."

"I miss my friends," he said, thinking of the Pirellis on Bedlam, of Palmer Vermeulen of the *Nhulunbuy,* and of countless others scattered over what had been the Arc Circuit. Whichever way he jumped, they were lost to him. Lost in time or lost in war. What difference did it make?

"Two minutes," said Humanity.

His throat tightened. "I've missed Melilah all these years. I've become quite used to that feeling. Why should the thought of it be so hard now? Obviously because part of me always thought we might work things out, one day, somehow. While she was out there, the chance remained. Remote, yes, but a chance nonetheless. If we decided to take it."

The spinning blackness reached for him, and he felt himself sway on the brink.

"If only she'd asked me to go with her."

Humanity said nothing when the one-minute mark arrived.

His calves tensed. How easy it would be to just lean forward and let the strange vortexes take him back from one end of the wormhole to the other. As easy as falling down. He clenched his fists and refrained from screaming.

With no sound, no flash of light, no fuss at all, the gateway entrance collapsed to a point and vanished.

"There," said Humanity with a sigh. "It's done."

"I guess it is," he agreed, although he'd done nothing, really. It had been done to him. He'd just stood there and let it happen.

"For a moment, we were complete." Humanity turned away from what was now a blank wall and walked back out into the day. The genderless creature's figure gained a halo as it briefly eclipsed the sun. "How brief it seemed."

Eogan followed up the stairs, dazzled by the brightness. "Do you regret it?" he asked, shading his eyes.

"No. You only regret what you never did. Isn't that something else they used to say?"

"Yes. And you did everything."

"Within reason. We were only human, after all."

Eogan climbed the last step, feeling all too human and not at all sure that he wouldn't regret his decision for the rest of his life.

Where to from here? Get the Cowell *out of storage and start looking for some stars?*

Momentarily at a loss, he stood at the top of the stairs and looked around. Humanity appeared to have forgotten about him and was setting off at a determined pace across the field, heading for destinations unknown. Deangelis still wasn't anywhere to be seen; he might have evaporated to the four winds now his reason for existing had gone. Part of Eogan felt in danger of doing exactly the same thing.

What's the point?

"I took some time to think about it," said a voice from behind him, "and I think I've changed my mind."

He spun around. Melilah stood on the grass on the far side of the stairwell, looking exactly as he'd seen her last. Her hair was short and black; her clothes were black, too—a strap of winding cloth that enclosed her body in a seamless outfit from ankles to neck. Her hands hung, clasped together, in front of her.

"You didn't go!" He felt his face come alive, and somehow he crossed the distance between them without knowing how. Her eyes were the color of the grass. He wanted to pick her up and spin her around. Instead he just took both her hands in his. "You stayed!"

"No, Dominic. I didn't. I went through the gateway."

"You came back, then. You must have. Otherwise—" He stopped. Her hands held his in return, but a new distance opened up between them.

"I wasn't ready," she said, her gaze not leaving his face. "I needed to go back. I had to. I couldn't stay here with you, when I couldn't even be sure you *were* you. After what happened in Geodesica, between your facsimile and me, I felt angry and confused. I didn't know what I wanted. But I knew I wasn't happy.

"It took me a hundred years to realize that everything Humanity said was true. I had two choices: to look back into the past or to move forward into the future. I kept choosing the past—when I was on Bedlam; when I left here; when you left me. It was a decision I had to make, but the cost was great. The past is full of things that have passed and are better left that way. The uncertainty of the future is both its terror and its charm. I realize that now. But it took me a long time to come to that conclusion.

"Revenge was pointless—against the Archon and you. It solved nothing, and there was no way I could win. By the time I came to that conclusion, I knew I wasn't really *me* anymore. The old Melilah had smothered under the new. I forgot who she was. The sole person who remembered me was Isaac, and even he didn't recognize this strange, new me. I had lost myself in the past, in everything we'd left behind. There was only one way I could reclaim the person I had been, and try again."

Eogan felt age and grief radiating off her like steam. "My God. You lived it out, like Isaac. You waited until we came out of Geodesica, and then you took yourself back."

She shook her head lightly. "No. I didn't last the full distance. Not quite. Once I was absolutely certain of what I wanted, I dropped back into deep slow-time until the date of my return arrived. I don't have the stomach Isaac has for self-sacrifice." A sad smile crossed her features. "But apart from that detail, you're correct. My earlier self possessed everything I missed about who I was. It was a simple matter to copy her when she arrived and to integrate her back into myself. I feel whole again now. Angry; passionate; incomplete. And I can tell from your reaction that I look the same."

"Yes," he said. "Yes, you do."

"Well, that's a start." She smiled again. "But I'm not the same woman. Don't mistake me for her—the one who loved you the first time around, then tried to hate you when that failed. I've changed, just as you have changed. We're extensions of who we were when we first met, not continuations. In Bedlam, I tried to give up my memories; in the forests of Geodesica, I tried to give up the old you; in all the years since then, talking to Isaac, I railed and ranted about everything I'd lost: humanity; Bedlam; Geodesica. I'm on a different path now. It's time to stop thinking about the dead and concentrate on living. Our relationship isn't something I want to be a victim of; it's something I want to choose and work at. Just like Humanity, I have to let go of what I had in order to find out where what I *do* have might go. I don't know if we'll have a future together at the end of it, but I'm willing to explore the possibilities. Are you?"

For a long moment, he didn't know what to say. Her gaze seemed suddenly overwhelming, and he let go of her hands and looked out over the swaying grassy fields instead. Humanity was nowhere to be seen at all; the two of them were utterly alone. The endless blue sky pressed down upon him with the force of an entire planet's gravity. The whole universe seemed to be waiting for his response.

What exactly was Melilah offering him? He didn't know for certain—and he supposed that was the whole point. She patently wasn't who she had been, even though she had gone to so much trouble to rediscover herself. Behind that façade she possessed more experience than he could begin to comprehend. *Some age difference,* he thought, even as he took comfort from the fact that he recognized her still, knew without question who she was, despite everything. Some things never changed. But he knew it wouldn't be the same. It might not be anything at all. The attempt was the point. He had to try—and it seemed that, finally, she felt the same way.

He was certain of one thing. As nice as it had been to come to Earth, he yearned for vacuum and radiation and the enclosed spaces of a Cell. He needed space.

"I think we should take a trip," he said. "We talked about it once. Do you remember? Catching a trader to Friday and spending some time at the First Wave memorial? I don't think you were entirely serious about it."

"I wasn't. And Friday doesn't exist anymore. But there are a lot of other destinations open to us. You can still see the light of the original Milky Way from the Small Magellanic Cloud, you know. It's quite a sight."

"Is there anything you haven't already seen?"

"Plenty. I took the gate forward hundreds of thousands of years ago. We've got the universe to explore, and all the time we want."

He turned away from the view back to her. She seemed to be taking the idea seriously. "Are you sure it's what *you* want?"

"Positive," she said. "After everything we've been through, we deserve a holiday."

He laughed. "Indeed."

They walked together back to the tree on the low hill, where their hyperdimensional route to orbit waited.

+POSTLUDE

Bedlam: 1,224,527 CE

Isaac Deangelis, fresh out of the Onion and still feeling slightly vertiginous from the long, lonely journey, confronted an awe-inspiring sight. Millions of craft in a multitude of shapes orbited the system's primary star, all strung out along the orbit of the habitat that he had once called home. A babble of media connected the variegated throng. Barely had he arrived when a deluge of electromagnetic hails threatened to overwhelm him and his tiny ship.

"You're here!"

"Welcome!"

"Congratulations! You made it at last!"

He reeled, mentally, as he jockeyed into orbit with the others. The call had come through such a long time ago that he had assumed he would arrive much too late for whatever had been organized. His station was the farthest away from Bedlam, right on the very limit of Geodesica's reach. The message had taken months to arrive; he himself had been in transit for over two hundred years on the way back. He had expected to find nothing at all, just as he had left it.

Home, he thought.

And: *alone.* All through the system, entangled in the inhumanly complex skein of signals and data packets flashing from ship to ship, among the many versions of him who had been waiting for him, he tasted the absence of her. He knew that much from the recall message, too. Melilah had returned from Geodesica, then taken the long road back into the past before the temporal gate closed. She had subsequently visited him in Bedlam and at all the outposts scattered across the universe, including his, then disappeared. That he hadn't recognized her made him feel like an idiot. It was also, oddly, quite liberating. She had changed; she wasn't the Melilah he remembered. What, then, did he owe her?

And what did he owe the universe, if his last charge had released him from her service by going through the gateway and becoming a different person?

"It's good to be back here," he said to the gathering in general. His words were a rank understatement, but they summed up the simple, uncomplicated emotion he felt perfectly well. Bedlam was gone, along with Ah Kong and the primary's penchant for flares, but the system was still home. There was enough left for him to recognize. "I'm sorry it took me so long."

"There's no need to apologize," said a voice he recognized as his own, but with a depth of surety and presence he barely remembered possessing. He had been isolated and singular for so long, he had been accustomed to being that way. "I'm just glad you're here. You're the last. You complete us. You complete *me*."

Old, little-used pathways responded to handshakes they had never entirely forgotten. He leaned back into the embrace of his tiny ship and let his mind open to thoughts it couldn't contain, but of which he was an intimate part. His eyes closed in not ecstasy, but bliss.

So much became clear.

Melilah's journey was not his. Their fates had been linked for so long that it had been hard to disentangle them, but the time was overdue to do so. She had returned to the past with the intention of punishing the Archon for its deeds in Bedlam. He knew from the records of Coevality that this had not happened. What had she done instead, then? What other personal journey had she undergone?

The only way he could judge her was through their meetings. Grief; anger; bargaining; denial; resignation—he saw in them all the stages of grief psychologists had once believed in. Easy to believe, then, that mourning for Bedlam was all she had left; that, and humanity, and her complicated attachment to Dominic Eogan.

Such a journey: to see the Archon's actions vindicated; to watch the plan that was no plan unfold as humanity evolved and grew in directions unforeseen; to realize that the man who loved her lay a million years in the future! And everywhere the shadow of Geodesica, which had utterly changed her life through no ill intent of its own. Simply by existing.

She had been absolutely correct, the first time she came to him out of the gate from the future. Geodesica wasn't relevant in the larger scheme of things. People like Palmer Horsfall might confuse it with justice, just as Melilah herself had once believed it to be the solution to all her problems, but at the end of the day it was nothing more than itself. Its builders were dead and its purpose superseded. It was flotsam on the foam of the universe, like so much else.

Humanity was gone, but he remained. And he had seen so many things, inside the universe and out. What couldn't he accomplish now, given freedom and all the time left in the universe?

"I am Isaac Forge Deangelis," his higher self thought through all the versions of him gathered in Bedlam. "The time has come for me to do something for myself."

The entrance to Geodesica was free of obstruction. His first action on awakening in the system had been to clear it, with all due care and ceremony. The last remains of Palmer Horsfall and Jane Elderton, trapped on the horizon of a singularity, were now gone, as was the Archon and the notion of humanity. He too had been caught on the edge of things, watching passively as events turned around him, as the dolls played their games. Now it was time to stop being clay, to break out of his constraints, to make a different choice.

With the universe at his back—thinking of labyrinths, part of him left for dead, and the only alien humanity had ever known—he looked inward.

All the versions of him that had congregated in their ancient home smiled, as one.

GLOSSARY OF NAMES

PALMERS

Aesche
Bray
Christolphe (Negotiator Select)
Cobiac
Eogan (Chief Officer)
Flast
Horsfall (Chief Officer)
Sarian
Vermeulen (Science Officer)
Weightman (Chief Officer)

ARC CIRCUIT CITIZENS

Szilvia Animaz
Iona Attard (Doctor of Xenarcheology)
Athalia Awad
Melilah Awad
Angela Chen-Pushkaric
Yasu Emmell
Werner Gard
Gil Hurdowar
Bernard Krassay
James Pirelli
Luisa Pirelli
Kara Skirianos (ex-Speaker)
Ludelia Virgo (Professor of Humanist Science)

EXARCHS

Frederica Cazneaux (Mizar)
Lan Cochrane (Alioth)
Isaac Deangelis (Bedlam)
Jane Elderton (Sublime)
Lazarus Hails (Altitude)
Giorsal McGrath (Friday)

CELLS

Cirencester
Cowell
Inselmeer
Jaintiapur
Kwal Bahal
Nhulunbuy
Patrixbourne
Studenica
Umm-as-Shadid

PLACES IN BEDLAM

Albert Hall
Bacon Cathedral (Cultural)
Barabási Straight
ben-Avraham's
Bonabeau Fold (Residential)
Bornholdt Chasm
Faloutsos Junction
Granovetter
Havlin (Industrial)
Jeong Crescent
Milgram's Crossing (Basement)
Ormerod's
Pastor-Satorras (Scientific)

TABLE ONE
TIMELINE

2080–2150	First Wave of human colonization
2090	VOID field effect demonstrated
2100	First VOIDships in active service
2120	Bedlam First Wave colony founded
2121	True Singularity (Sol system)
2125	Bedlam First Wave colony destroyed by solar flare
2183	Melilah Awad born on Little Red
2192	Dominic Eogan born
2200–2250	Arc Systems recolonized; Great Bear Run and Arc Circuit established
2205	Bedlam recolonized
2239	Melilah Awad arrives at Bedlam
2257	Melilah Awad and Dominic Eogan meet
2276	Palmers guild formed
2287	Melilah Awad and Dominic Eogan part ways
2374	Isaac Forge Deangelis born
2395	Exarchate Expansion begins
2397	Exarchate Expansion complete
2407	Palmer Eogan joins the *Nhulunbuy*
2428	Sublime Catastrophe
2433	Palmer Eogan becomes chief officer of the *Nhulunbuy*
2437	The *Nhulunbuy* leaves Mizar for Bedlam
2438	Mizar Occlusion arrives at Bedlam

TABLE TWO NAMES OF ARC CIRCUIT SYSTEMS

SYSTEM NAME	ORIGINAL COLONY	EXARCHATE DESIGNATION
Phad	Phad 4	Phad-Simondson
Mizar	Mizar	Mizar-Cazneaux
Megrez	Megrez 8	Megrez-Mijolo
Asellus Primus	Prime One	Asellus Primus-Binard
Alioth	Alioth	Alioth-Cochrane
Alcor	Alcor 3a	Alcor-Magun
78 Ursa Major	Friday	Jamgotchian-McGrath
66781	Whitewater	Littlewood-Bohm
66704	Sublime	White-Elderton
65515	Schiller's End	Beall-Cammarano
64532	Eliza	Toma-Herczeg
62512	Bedlam	Lut-Deangelis
61946	New Eire	Michailogliou-Rawe
61100	Altitude	Kullervo-Hails
61053	Gabison's End	Ansell-Aad
59514	Little Red	Yugen-Palliaer
59432	Severance	Newbery-Vaas
59431	Scarecrow	Mei-Shun-Wah

MAP ONE
THE ARC CIRCUIT

Not to scale
(all measurements in light-years)
(systems listed according to
Hipparcos number or real name)

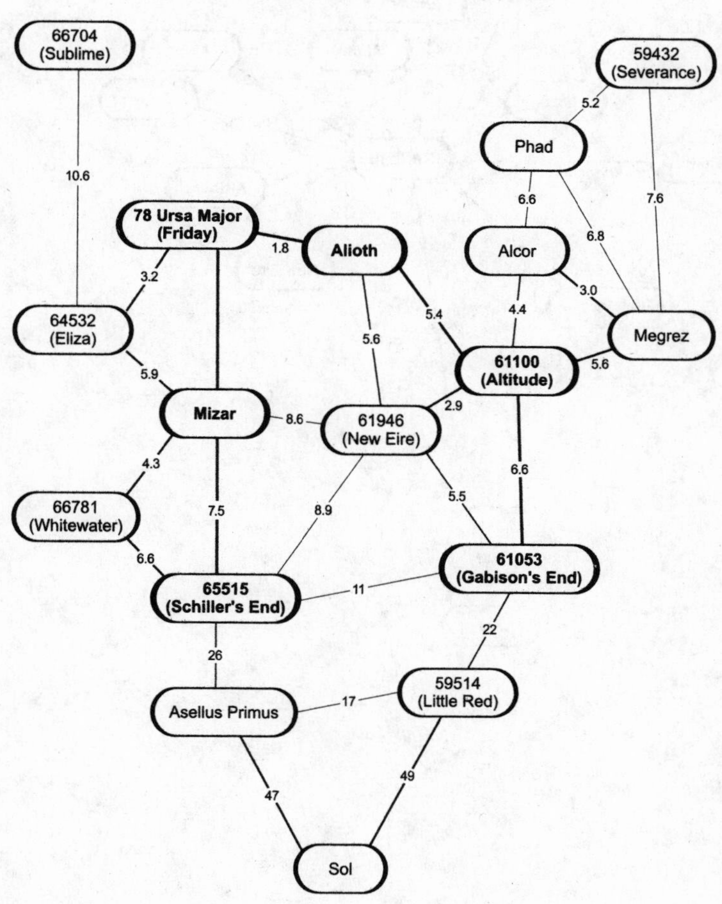

MAP TWO
BEDLAM ENVIRONS

Not to scale
(all measurements in light-years)

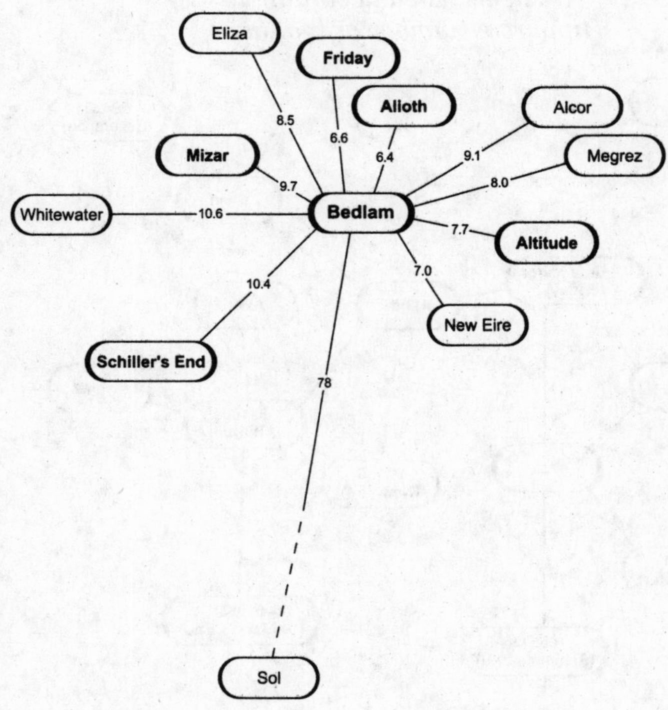

SEAN WILLIAMS has been writing full-time since 1990. He has won both of Australia's major SF awards, the Aurealis and the Ditmar.

SHANE DIX has been writing fiction since he was fifteen. In addition to science fiction, he has had published mainstream stories, poetry, and articles about the state of SF in film and television.

Together, they are also the *New York Times* bestselling authors of three Star Wars: Force Heretic books.